It takes a spec...
Outb...

The Australians' Brides

Three exciting, atmospheric romances set in Australia's Outback from favourite author Lilian Darcy

The Australians' Brides

LILIAN DARCY

All the characters in this book have no existence outside the imagination of the author, and have no relation whatsoever to anyone bearing the same name or names. They are not even distantly inspired by any individual known or unknown to the author, and all the incidents are pure invention.

First published in Great Britain 2012
by Mills & Boon, an imprint of Harlequin (UK) Limited,
Eton House, 18-24 Paradise Road, Richmond, Surrey TW9 1SR

THE AUSTRALIANS' BRIDES
© by Harlequin Enterprises II B.V./S.à.r.l 2012

The Runaway and the Cattleman, Princess in Disguise and *Outback Baby* were first published in Great Britain by Harlequin (UK) Limited in separate, single volumes.

The Runaway and the Cattleman © Lilian Darcy 2006
Princess in Disguise © Lilian Darcy 2006
Outback Baby © Lilian Darcy 2006

ISBN: 978 0 263 89679 4

05-0212

Printed and bound in Spain
by Blackprint CPI, Barcelona

THE RUNAWAY AND THE CATTLEMAN

BY
LILIAN DARCY

Bestselling romance author **Lilian Darcy** has written over seventy novels. She currently lives in Australia's capital city, Canberra, with her historian husband and their four children. When she is not writing or supporting her children's varied interests, Lilian likes to quilt, garden or cook. She also loves winter sports and travel.

Lilian's career highlights include numerous appearances on the Waldenbooks romance bestsellers list, three nominations in the Romance Writers of America's prestigious RITA® Award, and translation into twenty different languages. Find out more about Lilian and her books or contact her at www.liliandarcy.com

Chapter One

He looked like a cowboy, against the backdrop of rust-red outback dirt and endless blue sky.

Or to be more accurate, like every woman's fantasy of a cowboy.

An ancient, broad-brimmed hat tilted low over his forehead. It shaded his face so that the color of his eyes was impossible to read, but one look at his profile would tell a red-blooded woman all she needed to know. Strong jaw, firm mouth, an intensity in the way he watched the world...even when he looked as if he wasn't really seeing it.

His body was even stronger than his jaw, but he wasn't the type who needed to wear his T-shirts too tight to emphasize washboard abs and bulging biceps. The muscles were just there, hard and motionless beneath faded denim and stretch cotton. He'd learned to conserve his energy for when he really needed it—for a long day of boundary riding, cattle branding or herding his animals to fresh pasture. Right now, since he didn't need it, he leaned his tanned forearms on the wooden rail in front of him, the way he would have leaned them on a stockyard gate.

Yes, any woman who'd picked him as a cowboy would have been close. He was a cattleman, an Australian outback farmer, owner of his own huge spread of acreage. He was no one's wage slave, but answered only to his land, his animals and his family.

Nine out of ten women took a good look at him as they walked past. Eight out of ten were impressed with what they saw, and would have liked to find out more. Just what color were those eyes? Did he have tan lines around those solid upper arms? What did he have to say for himself? Did he like dressy blondes or down-to-earth brunettes? Was he available? Was he as good as he looked?

But if the cattleman noticed any of the female attention he was getting, it didn't show. You would have said that Callan Woods's thoughts were at least two hundred miles away, and you wouldn't have been wrong.

"Look at him, Brant! What are we going to do?"

Branton Smith felt helpless at his friend Dusty Tanner's question. Like Callan himself, they both lived most of their waking hours out of doors. They worked with their hands. When they struck trouble, it was something physical— drought or flood or fire or an injured beast—and the solution to it was physical, also.

They just worked harder. They climbed on a horse and herded cattle or sheep to higher ground. They got out of bed two hours earlier in the morning and fed their animals by hand, dropping feed bales off the back of a truck until their hands were callused like leather and every muscle burned. They were big, strong, capable men, and they had brains. They looked for active, assertive answers.

But what could they do about Callan?

"Just be there for him, I guess," Brant said in answer to Dusty's question.

He wasn't surprised at Dusty's bark of derisory laughter. "You sound like an advice column in a teenage magazine, mate!"

True.

Had to be cruddy advice, too, because they'd both "been there" for Callan since his wife Liz's death four years ago, and he only seemed to have folded in on himself even more this year.

He stood, as they did, with his forearms propped on the rail that kept spectators back from the racetrack, while around him swirled the color and noise of Australia's best-known outback racing carnival. Judging by Callan's thousand-yard stare, his slumped shoulders, his tight mouth and his silence, however, he barely knew that he was here.

The three men had been best mates for years, since attending Cliffside school in Sydney more than seventeen years ago. Then, they had been three strong, shy outback boys, boarding away from home for the first time, in the company of the sons of stockbrokers and car dealers and property tycoons.

Now they owned racehorses together, five sleek beautiful animals at the present time, of which two were racing at today's carnival. Three of their horses were trained at a place near Brant's extensive sheep-farming property west of the Snowy Mountains, while the two running today were with a trainer in Queensland, near Dusty.

As a hobby, the racing syndicate just about paid its way. As an exercise in mateship, it was solid gold.

Their spirited two-year-old mare Surprise Bouquet had put in a reasonable performance in her maiden event this morning. She'd placed fifth in a field of sixteen after a poor jump from the barrier, and she should do better next time around. Saltbush Bachelor was the horse they had real hopes for today.

Callan, Brant and Dusty couldn't meet face-to-face all that often, given the distance between their properties, but this race carnival was a tradition they kept to whenever they could. Callan had missed a couple of years when Liz had been ill. She'd died at around this time of year. A couple of weeks along in the calendar—end of September. Maybe that was part of Callan's problem. The Birdsville Races and September and Liz's death were all wrapped up together in his heart.

"He's thirty-three," Dusty muttered. "We can't let him go on thinking his life is over, Brant."

Standing beside his two mates, Callan wasn't thinking that.

Not exactly.

But yeah. He knew Brant and Dusty were concerned about him. They weren't all that subtle on the issue. Those frequent anxious looks, the muttered comments he didn't always hear but could guess the gist of, the over-hearty suggestions about going for a beer, the occasional comment about a woman— nothing too crude, just "nice legs" and that kind of thing— after which they'd both nudge him for an agreement, which he would dutifully give.

Yes, she had nice legs, the blonde or the brunette or the farmer's daughter with her hair hidden beneath her hat.

Brant and Dusty both thought it was time he moved on, found a new mother for his boys.

Callan had thought so, too, once.

Three years ago, to be exact, here at this same annual racing carnival.

To him, it felt like yesterday.

He could still remember the panic, the loneliness, the physical hunger, the ache for his own loss and the even harder ache for what his boys would miss without a mother, after that first endless year without Liz.

But, sheesh! What the hell had he been thinking that day? Had he really thought that a party-going, city-bred twenty-something with "nice legs," carrying a glass of champagne in one hand and in the other a race guide she wasn't interested in, could possess the slightest power to help him move on?

There had been a nightmarish wrongness about that woman's body. The freckles across her nose weren't Liz's freckles. Her hair wasn't Liz's shade of blonde. Her curves weren't right, or her voice. He'd been looking for all the wrong things, and he hadn't even found those.

"They're in the barrier," Brant reported, his voice rising to cut across Callan's thoughts. "He looked lively but not too wound up."

"And Garrett is hungry for this win," Dusty added. "He'll ride him just right."

Both men had binoculars pressed to their eyes, now. They didn't want to miss a second of the race, or of their horse's ride. They wanted Callan to care that Saltbush Bachelor was running with a good period of training and some successful starts behind him, and actually had a shot at a win.

The silk shirts of the jockeys shimmered with color in the bright sun, the way the desert air shimmered on the horizon. The nearby airfield had light planes lined up like minivans in a shopping mall's parking garage, and the population of the tiny outback town had temporarily swelled from a few hundred to several thousand. Callan could smell beer and barbecued sausages, sunscreen and horse feed and dust.

He roused himself enough to answer his two friends. "Yeah, Mick Garrett's a good jockey." But he didn't lift his own binoculars and barely noticed the anticipation that knotted their bodies and their voices as the race got underway.

Instead he thought about his boys back on Arakeela Creek

with their grandmother, thought about what he'd need to do with the cattle next week when he was home, thought again about three years ago here in Birdsville and that disaster of a nice-legged woman who could never in a million years have looked—or felt—or sounded—enough like Liz.

He thought about the other woman, too, a few months later—a blond and freckled Scandinavian backpacker whom he'd permitted to camp down by the Arakeela Gorge water hole, and who had been happy to make all the moves in what had soon turned out to be a limp disaster of a one-night stand.

Lord, he hated remembering! He'd been so crazed with grief and loneliness, but how could he have thought that hooking up with some stranger would do anything to heal him, let alone anything to provide him or his boys with a better future?

Watching Callan's mental distance and his thinned mouth, Brant and Dusty looked at each other again. Didn't need to speak about it, but spoke anyway.

"Does he even know it's started?" Dusty muttered.

"Knows," Brant theorized. "Doesn't care."

"If Salty wins—"

"Won't make a blind bit of difference to him. Hell, Dusty, what are we going to do? *Being there* is just bull. You're right. We both know it. He needs action."

"Action? We're doing everything we can. When he wanted to pull out of our racehorse syndicate, we basically told him he couldn't."

"And his mother talked him round on that, too."

The race wheeled around the far curve of the track and the jockeys' colors blurred. From this angle, it was impossible to see how Saltbush Bachelor was running. As long as he wasn't hemmed in at the rail. As long as Garrett didn't leave his run too late.

Beside Brant, two would-be Paris Hiltons were screaming for the horse they wrongly thought they'd bet on. Van Der

Kamp wasn't running until the next race, but neither Brant, Dusty nor Callan troubled to give the two overexcited young women this information.

"Kerry's worried," Brant went on, still talking about Callan's mother. "She phoned me last week and asked us to look out for him this weekend."

"Like we wouldn't anyway."

The momentum of the race picked up as the horses came around into the home straight. The Paris Hilton girls had realized their mistake over Van Der Kamp and were cheering for the correct horse, now—Salty himself.

"He's going to do it!" Brant yelled. "He's up there. It's going to be close. Can you see, Dusty? Callan?"

Callan didn't answer.

The horses thundered past, their legs a blur of pistonlike movements, their jockeys' colors once more tangled together. Just twenty meters to go, then ten.

"He's there, he's…no, he's not going to win, but second. He's—hell, he's losing ground, but he's going to get—" Brant stopped.

Second place? It was too close to call. They'd have to wait for the official result. Brant listened to the distorted sound of the PA system for several seconds and managed to catch winner and place-getters' names. Even allowing for the distortion, none of them sounded remotely like Saltbush Bachelor. Their horse had lost out for third place by a nose.

"So much for omens," said one of the Hilton types to the other.

"Guess we're not scoring ourselves an outback bachelor today," the other one replied.

Beside them, Callan didn't even react—despite their nice legs—and Brant and Dusty could only look at each other helplessly once again.

"Talk to your sister, Brant," Dusty suggested. A small, irritating bush fly buzzed near his lips. Like most outback-bred people, he'd learned not to open his mouth too wide when he spoke, which was an advantage in confidential conversation. "Maybe this needs a woman's touch. Nuala has a good head on her shoulders."

"A good head full of crazy ideas," Brant said.

"Maybe a crazy idea is just what we need."

"Yeah, because the plain, ordinary ones haven't worked, have they? Okay, I'll talk to her about it when I get back. But I'm warning you, it might not be an idea we want to hear."

Dusty got a stubborn look on his face. "If there's a chance of it helping Callan, mate, at this point I'll listen to anything."

Chapter Two

"So we're going to pay Nuala back *how*, for coming up with this dream scheme?" Dusty drawled to Brant, almost six months later.

The Birdsville Races had been held on the first weekend in September. This was a Friday night in late February. Their horses had had a couple of promising wins during the spring season. Brant's property had received higher than average rain, while Dusty's had sweltered in the intense Queensland summer heat. Kerry Woods had talked again to both men about how worried she was about Callan.

"You were the one who said you didn't care if it was crazy, as long as there was a chance it might help Callan, you'd do it," Brant reminded him, a little defensive on his sister's behalf, even though he'd had a few payback fantasies himself over the past couple of weeks, since the appearance of the February issue of *Today's Woman* magazine.

"And I'm here, aren't I?" Dusty retorted. "I did do it. I had my photo in that damned magazine. I had to list my hobbies and my background, and—" he hooked his fingers in the air to show the quote marks coming up "—*what I'm looking for in a woman and why I believe love can last.* And then the magazine didn't use a quarter of what I'd said."

"You did a better job with all those questions than I did," Brant said.

Dusty shrugged and grinned. "I was more honest."

"Yeah, mate, don't you have any self-protective instincts?"

"Plenty of 'em. I'm just not a very good liar. Does your sister really think Callan's going to find what he's looking for this way?"

Both men looked around the room. It was just after six in the evening, and the air-conditioning in this elegant waterfront venue battled against Sydney's lingering summer heat. The metropolitan beaches would be crowded with sleek, tanned bodies and sandy children. On the tangled city streets, traffic and exhaust fumes would still be thick, mingled with the blasts of restaurant smells evoking the cuisine of many nations. This was an attractive setting for a cocktail party, however, with its views over Darling Harbour, including a distant glimpse of the Harbour Bridge beyond the restored and remodeled shipping piers.

It was light-years away from the varied landscapes around Brant's, Dusty's and Callan's homes.

There had to be around fifty people in the room, Brant decided. They appeared to consist of twenty single outback men and twenty single urban women, as well as some journalists and photographers from the magazine and a handful of catering staff who were gliding around with drink trays and fiddly little morsels of fashionable food that looked way too scary to eat.

"Not *find* what he's looking for, find *out* what he's looking for, according to Nuala," he said to Dusty in clarification.

"Nuala, who has recently announced her engagement to a man she's known since she was, what, three?" Dusty pointed out. "Oh, yeah, she's a real expert on this relationship stuff."

"Getting Nuala's input on all this was your idea, I seem to recall. And she hasn't been going out with Chris since she was three," Brant said, in defense of his baby sister's credentials in the field. "She wouldn't look at him after she left school. She went to Europe for three years."

"She had boyfriends then?"

"Their names have been permanently blacked out of the Nuala Jane Smith archival records, she says, but, yeah, she had a few."

"So she really thinks—?"

"You want me to quote her?" Brant ticked his sister's arguments off on his fingers. "This will get Callan to focus on what he wants and what's missing from his life. It'll remind him that there are still some decent women in the world even without Liz in it. It'll show him he's not the only one whose heart is in—"

He stopped. *Pieces* he was going to say, but suddenly, they were no longer alone.

"Hi! Who do we have here? Dustin, right?" The overenthusiastic American woman discreetly consulted some notes on a clipboard, while a photographic flash went off in a man's hands, right next to her. Magazine people, both of them.

The flash made Dusty blink. If Dusty had been one of their own racehorses, Brant thought, the man would have shied and stepped a big hoof on the American's foot, including her spike heel. He would have broken several of her bones. "Call me Dusty," he said.

"Dusty…." The American beamed artificially. Her eyelids fluttered and she barely looked in his direction. She had sleek hair, a wide mouth and a distracted manner. Nice legs, too, Brant saw as he stepped back out of range. Owning racehorses gave a man a deep appreciation of good female legs.

Dusty gave them an interested glance, also. "Now, you're here to meet Mandy tonight, Dusty, and here she is!" the American said.

Ta-da!

Mandy stepped forward. She was around five foot four and her legs were pretty ordinary, but she had dark eyes and an eager smile. She was also totally thrilled with herself for correctly matching Dusty's personal details to his photograph and winning herself a place at the party tonight.

Dusty looked a little bewildered at her attitude, but when he answered the question she asked him and she listened with those big eyes fixed so intently on his face... Yeah, Brant thought he would probably have felt the ego stroke, too. It was nice when a woman was genuinely interested. He went in search of a drink, wondering with a faint stir of curiosity which of the as-yet-unpaired women in the room had been earmarked for him.

Passing Callan, he couldn't help but notice that his friend, the object of this whole outlandish exercise, was mentally miles away.

"Why am I here?" Jacinda Beale muttered to herself.

As always, she had reacted to this dressed-up, extravagant, city cocktail party like an animal caught in a searchlight. She didn't know a soul. She hadn't yet been introduced to the man she was supposed to meet.

The woman who was supposed to do the introducing—and who had introduced herself to Jacinda as Shay-from-the-magazine—flitted around looking almost as stressed out as most of the guests, many of whom were clearly too shy to mingle easily.

Why are you here, Jac?

Well, go ahead and pick an option, replied the cynical and panicky running commentary in Jacinda's brain. You're a scriptwriter, after all. Choosing between different character motivations is one of the skills of your trade.

There were several such options to choose from, some of which were more honest than others.

Because I gave in to an insane impulse and thought this might be fun...or, failing that, good for me.

Because Today's Woman *magazine is running a series of stories called "Wanted: Outback Wives," and I happened to a) guess correctly which Outback Wife-hunter's description of himself matched with which Outback Wife-hunter photo— it wasn't that hard!—and b) write a sufficiently appealing and correctly spelled letter outlining in three hundred words or less why I should get to meet him.*

Yes, believe it or not, an invitation to this cocktail party was meant to be a kind of prize.

Because I'm desperate, and I'll open any door that looks like it has a handle.

Because I'm a writer, so it's research.

That last one scared her, adding to the already powerful panicky feeling. Writers could claim that pretty much anything was research, and in the past for Jacinda, the claim had always been true. In the name of research, she'd tried on expensive jewellery, combed through a stranger's trash can, taken a ride on a seriously terrifying roller coaster, eaten in two or three of America's most famous restaurants... The list went on.

But was she really a writer anymore?

Heartbreak Hotel's head scriptwriter, Elaine Hutchison, still thought that she was.

"You're blocked, Jac," she'd said six weeks ago. "You have good reasons to be blocked, and you need a break. Take that gorgeous daughter of yours, cross an ocean, and don't come home for a month. By then, you'll be raring to go and I can give you Reece and Naomi's storyline because you are the *only* one I trust to make their dialogue remotely believable."

"Which ocean?" Jac had asked, because her initiative had also evaporated, along with her TV soap opera dialogue-writing skills.

"Any ocean, honey. Just make it a big one. Know what I'm saying? Know why I'm saying it?"

Elaine hadn't mentioned any names but, yes, Jac had known what she was saying, and why. She should put some distance between herself and Kurt until she was stronger, better equipped to move forward. She should recognize that despite Elaine's genuine friendship, she had divided loyal-ties because Kurt had the power to scuttle Elaine's own career as well as Jacinda's.

And the Pacific Ocean was the biggest ocean around—it conveniently washed ashore in California, too—so here she was on the far side of it, in Australia, at the bottom of the world, at the bottom of a glass, at a cocktail party she wasn't enjoying any better than she'd enjoyed all those dozens and dozens of cocktail parties with Kurt.

Even when she and Kurt had been in love.

Thud, went her heart.

Yes, she had been naive enough to love him once.

But their marriage had given her Carly, her precious daughter, so the news wasn't all bad.

"Jacinda?" said a woman's voice, in an American accent that matched Jac's own.

She turned to the energetic chestnut-haired magazine editor who'd greeted her on arrival. "Shay, hi…."

Introduction time.

There was a man hovering at Shay-from-the-magazine's elbow. Better looking than in his magazine photo, he appeared far less comfortable, however. The photo had shown him in his native element, with one long, jeans-clad leg

braced against a rust-red rock and his dusty felt hat silhouetted against a sky the color of tinted contact lenses. He'd had
his fingers laced in the fur of a big, tongue-lolling cattle
dog—also rust-red—and a smile that narrowed his brim-
shaded eyes so much you couldn't even see them.

Jac could see them now, however, and they were, oh, unbelievable. Blue and deep and smoky with a whole lot of emotions
that thirty seconds ago she might have thought would be too
complex for a down-to-earth South Australian cattle rancher.

Yes, *Today's Woman* hadn't confused the issue by laying
any false clues. The outback sky, the cattle dog and the fierce-
looking lizard on the rock, which Jac's Australian friend Lucy
had identified as a bearded dragon, had strongly suggested that
the man was Callan Woods, cattle rancher, not Brian Snow,
opal miner, or Damian Peterson, oil rigger, or any of the other
seventeen Outback Wife-hunters, whose photos and biograph-
ical details had appeared in the February issue of the
magazine.

There were a lot of lonely outback men in Australia,
Today's Woman claimed. It was a big country, where such
men ran free in their far-flung and sometimes lonely occupations, but had trouble finding the right woman.

Jac wasn't going to be that, she knew.

Not for this man.

But now wasn't the time to tell him so.

"Callan, meet Jacinda," Shay-from-the-magazine said
brightly.

"Hi. Yeah," was all he said.

He didn't look happy to be here…which gave them one
thing in common, at least.

"Would you believe how Jacinda matched you with your
photo, Callan?" Shay gushed. "She actually identified the
species of lizard sitting on the rock! Can you believe that?"

"Yeah? The bearded dragon?" A stirring of interest

appeared in those incredible eyes as he belatedly reached out to shake Jac's hand. He had a firm, dry grip, which he let go of a little too soon, as if he really, seriously, didn't want her to get the wrong idea.

"The lizard was the reason I chose you as the one I wanted to meet," Jac confessed. "My daughter thought he looked so cute."

Too late, she realized that it wasn't a very tactful line. Callan was supposed to be the cute one, not the reptilian wildlife on his land.

But Callan didn't seem to care about her gaffe. Seemed relieved about it, in fact. "Yeah, my son Lockie loves them," he said, his eyes getting brighter as he mentioned his boy. "He had one for a pet, but then he couldn't stand to see it caged."

"So you have kids, too?" Jac asked. She grabbed on to the subject immediately, since it might be the only conversational lifeline they could come up with together. "My daughter is four."

Then she listened as Callan Woods told her, "I have two boys. Lockie's ten. Josh is eight. We lost…" He stopped and took a breath. "That is, my wife died four years ago. I'm sorry. I should tell you that up front." He lowered his voice and glanced at Shay, who was already moving on to her next introduction, as if tonight's schedule was impossibly tight.

"It's okay," Jac told him.

He might not even have heard her reassurance. "I'm not really a…what was it…Wild Heart Looking For Love." He parodied the words from the magazine so that Jac could almost see them spelled with capitals. "Couple of my mates wanted to take part in this and they roped me in, too, for a bit of support."

He glanced over his shoulder and caught sight of two tall men. One of them was looking down at a short brunette who had her hand pinned to his arm. Callan gestured at the two men for Jac's benefit. They were his "mates." She knew the Australian expression by this time. "I'm doing it for them," he said. "For Brant and Dusty. I'm not seriously looking for anyone. I should be up front with you about that."

The mates were staring this way.

At Callan.

Jac was good at character motivation. She saw the anxious frowns on their faces and the way they assessed both their friend and Jac herself, and she recognized the truth at once, now that this man had told her about his loss.

Callan was doing it for them?

No, it was the other way around. Brant and Dusty were doing it for him.

She heard him swear under his breath and understood the painful way his own words must be echoing in his head. *My wife died four years ago.* She hated saying it, too. *Kurt and I are divorced now.* It felt as if you were ripping open your clothing to show total strangers your surgical scars.

"It's okay," she repeated quickly to Callan Woods. "This is a very artificial situation, isn't it? Anyone would be crazy to hold out serious hopes of meeting the right person, no matter how much they were looking for it. But I don't think that makes it a pointless exercise. You know, just to get a bit of practice…or…or validation, maybe. I'm divorced. And it was a horrible divorce." *See, I have scars, too.* "I actually can't think when I last talked to a man I don't know, purely for the pleasure of making some contact."

He nodded, but didn't make a direct reply. Maybe he was better at talking to his rust-colored dog. After a few seconds of silence, he said, "You're not Australian."

"No. The accent's a giveaway, isn't it?" She smiled, but he didn't smile back.

"But you're living here?" he said.

"No, again. On vacation. Staying with an Australian friend

I met in California a few years ago. Lucy. She's great. She's
babysitting my daughter tonight. She was the one who suggested I try that photo-matching thing in the magazine, just
for fun. Most of them were pretty easy."

"I guess it made sense, added more interest, having the
magazine turn it into a kind of contest."

"And, yes, it was fun," Jac agreed. "I'm not sorry I did it."
Oh.
Really?
Since when?

She'd spent the first twenty minutes of the cocktail party
feeling deeply sorry that she'd given in to such an insane
impulse at Lucy's prompting, but at some point very recently
that had changed. The blue eyes? The lizard? The fact that
Callan Woods wasn't serious about this, either?

"No," Callan agreed. "I wouldn't have done it, except for
my mates, but, yeah, so far it's turned out not to be as bad as
I thought."

Jac saw the expression in his eyes. Definitely relief. An
after-the-dentist kind of relief that she understood and shared,
and it felt nice to share the same emotion with a man again,
even if it was a man she didn't know.

"When do you fly home?" he asked.

"Tuesday. Three days from now. We've been here a month,
and I can't believe the time has flown so fast. I've loved all
of it, and so has Carly."

"Tuesday." He relaxed a little more. "So you're obviously
not serious about tonight, either."

"No."

"Thank heavens we got that established nice and early!"

They grinned at each other, grabbed a canapé each from
a passing tray and somehow kept talking for the next two
hours without quite noticing how quickly the party went by.

* * *

"Mine? A washout," Brant said over a state-of-the-art weekend urban café brunch the next morning, in answer to Dusty's question. "A total washout. She had a chip on her shoulder so big I'm surprised she could stand straight. When I told her that being single didn't bother me all that much, she acted as if I'd personally insulted her. She gave every one of my questions a one-syllable answer and couldn't come up with a single bit of small talk when it was her turn. Thank the Lord you didn't get her, Call."

"Why me?" Callan asked.

Brant frowned. "Why you, what?"

"Why is it good that I didn't get her? You think I'm particularly incapable of dealing with women with big shoulder chips and no small talk? Why?"

"Mine was great," Dusty cut in before Brant could answer, but not before he and Brant had exchanged a strange, uneasy, lightning-fast look. "A genuine, decent woman who knows what she wants and doesn't mind saying so. There's a good chance we'll stay in touch. I'm telling you, it was a heck of a lot better than I expected, the whole thing." He added quickly and awkwardly, "And, you know, I thought it was a promising idea from the start, so…"

Hang on a minute.

Dusty had a look on his face that Callan recognized. It spoke loudly of his awareness that he wasn't a very good liar, but what was he lying about?

Callan began slowly, putting the puzzle pieces in place as he spoke, "So *you* don't mind that you're single, Brant, and *you're* suddenly pretending you thought this was a promising way for an isolated outback cattleman to meet a future wife, Dusty, even though four seconds ago you pretty much stated the opposite…." He paused, watched the guilty expressions on his mates' faces. "Can one of you tell me the real reason we put ourselves through this?"

He wasn't stupid.

He didn't really need their answer.

Which was good, because they both stumbled through some garbled piece of bull dust and didn't actually give him one.

While the stumbling thing was still happening, he thought about whether he was angry with them—whether he wanted to be angry, whether he even had the energy.

Brant and Dusty had set him up in the worst way. They'd conspired behind his back. They'd conned him into putting his picture and his life story and his heartfelt feelings in a national women's magazine. Why? In the hope that he might meet someone? Or…or…start to believe in the possibility of someday meeting someone? Or…or…even just enjoy himself for a night and get a bit of an ego tickle from the bunch of eager women's letters the magazine had started sending him?

Angry about it?

To his own surprise he found himself grinning, after a moment. When all was said and done, they were his best friends. They meant well. They would never let him down. They were idiots, and he liked them.

"Serves you bloody right if yours was a washout, Branton Smith. Serves you right, Dustin Tanner, if you never hear from yours again. Me, like a prize con victim, thought I was helping you out, going along for the ride. Turns out I wasn't, and I'm not looking for anything beyond…yeah…keeping my boys happy, but I had a good time last night, talking to Jacinda."

He knew it couldn't go anywhere. He didn't want it to, and neither did she. That was probably the only reason they'd been able to talk to each other so freely in the first place—

because of the safety valve of her imminent departure and the glaring nature of his loss and her divorce.

She looked nothing like Liz, and that was a big plus, also. Where Liz had been compact and strong, Jacinda was long and willowy. She had big, luminous gray eyes, not twinkling, sensible green ones. She had wild dark hair, in contrast to Liz's neat, silky waterfall of medium blond, and an even, magnolia-olive skin tone, instead of fairness and freckles. Voices, accents, backgrounds, all of it was different and therefore much safer. Safe enough for him to feel as if Jacinda could be a friend, a new kind of friend, if he ever needed one.

This was how he saw her this morning—someone he might turn to, sometime in the future, for advice about his boys, or for a city woman's perspective.

He even had the address of Jacinda's friend Lucy in Sydney, and Jacinda's e-mail address back in America, and she had his, but he wasn't going to tell Brant and Dusty that. He just gave them another grin—a more teasing and evasive grin this time—and started talking about what they might do today, in each other's company, before heading out of Sydney and back to land and animals and family tomorrow.

And he felt better—easier in his heart—than he had in quite a while.

Jac honestly hadn't expected to see Callan again, even though they'd exchanged addresses.

His timing wasn't great. He showed up at seven in the evening, when she was in the middle of getting her daughter ready for bed. She and Carly had eaten, her friend Lucy was out tonight and now Carly was tired. She was tired enough to make a fuss about getting out of the bath even when her skin had gone wrinkly, so that Jac was wet all down her front when she encountered Callan at the apartment door. A minute or two later, Carly was suddenly *not* too tired to want to investigate the gift he'd brought for her immediately.

"It's just a little thing," Callan told Jac quietly, as Carly sat on the floor in her pink-stripes-and-teddy-bears pajamas and ripped at the bright paper. For Jac herself, Callan had brought flowers—a huge, gorgeous bunch of Australian things whose names she didn't know. "A paint-your-own-boomerang kit. Hope it's not more trouble than it's worth!"

"Could be, if she wants to sit down and paint it right now." She smiled to soften the statement. He had kids. He should understand. She added in a lower tone, "You didn't have to do this."

"I know, but I woke up this morning and—" He stopped and tried again. Came up with just three words. "I wanted to."

"You woke up this morning, but it's seven in the evening, now. Did it take you all day to make up your mind that you wanted to?" she teased. She'd decided last night that he had a sense of humor, but wanted to test this perception in a cooler light.

"Yep," he answered. "That's about right." His blue eyes glinted with amusement like sunshine on water. "Look, I guess it is getting late, but we could still eat somewhere, if you want."

So she had to tell him about Lucy being out, and Carly needing bed, and that she and her daughter had eaten already anyhow.

He nodded. "I should have called. You're right. I did leave it too late."

She thought about asking if he wanted coffee or a drink, but chickened out. Pick a character motivation. She didn't want to kiss him and discover she liked it—or discover she didn't. She didn't want to learn the hard way that they had nothing left to talk about, after those two easy hours last night. She definitely didn't want to send the wrong message about how lucky he might get by the end of this evening.

No!

"Thank you," she said instead. "The flowers are beautiful, and the gift for Carly. I really must get her into bed, now, or she'll be a mess tomorrow. She was up before six."

He looked at her wet front and her messy hair. She saw at once from his face that he'd read the situation correctly, and that he wasn't the kind of man to argue. Instead, he just gave her his courteous hope that she and Carly would have a good flight home, told her that if she ever needed anything—needed him, needed to write or phone—that she shouldn't hesitate.

"I mean that."

And Jac believed him. Didn't plan to put her trust in his words to the test, but found that the simple fact of believing him felt good—better, after Kurt, than she would have imagined possible.

Two days later, Jacinda and Carly's plane touched down at Los Angeles International Airport and reality kicked into their lives once more.

Jac had allowed herself and her daughter a day to get over the worst of their jet lag, but then Carly was back in full-day preschool, and Jac was back on the script-writing production line for her soap. The moment she walked into the writers' conferencing suite, a month on the opposite shore of the Pacific Ocean seemed to shrink to the size of a drop in that same ocean and she felt as if she'd never been away.

She didn't want to write.

She couldn't write.

Why the hell had she thought that she'd be able to write? She'd picked up the mail held for her at the post office on her way in, and among the bills and credit card solicitations were two birthday cards from Kurt, one for herself and one for Carly, since they'd both been February babies and had celebrated while they'd been away. His handwriting on the envelopes, alone, would have been enough to paralyze her, let alone what he'd written to her inside.

Jacinda, sweetheart, don't spend Carly's birthday out of the country next year, please. Trust me, you can't afford that kind of statement. Emotionally, financially. You just can't, and you should know that. I'm going to be pretty busy this spring, and I'll need Carly in my life to give me some balance. The network is rethinking its programming, and I'll be micromanaging certain areas.

Don't make the mistake of thinking I'm too busy to catch my own shows, even when they're no longer my day-to-day concern. Reece and Naomi have some great scenes coming up—taut, edgy dialogue written while you were away by a young male writer who's incredibly fresh. Elaine will be taking a good look at them with me. She's been wanting to juggle the team for a while now.

Happy thirty-second birthday. Hope you've used the break as an opportunity to clarify your priorities.
Deepest regards,
Kurt.

This was what blocked her so badly. This kind of communication from Kurt. All the time. Phone calls, e-mails, letters from his lawyer, and even innocent comments from Carly after she'd spent an afternoon with him and his new wife. The threats were always so carefully veiled that they almost sounded like reassurances.

He changed his mind about what he wanted, and then the threats changed, as if to suggest that Jacinda should have been two steps ahead of his thinking all along. The reminders of his power and control, and his ability to wreak both personal and professional consequences pricked at Jacinda like poisoned barbs.

She had custody of Carly now, yes, because so far it had suited Kurt to utter lines such as, "All I want is my daughter's best interests," but she knew that if he wanted the situation to change, he'd stop at nothing to achieve his goal. She also knew that even if he had no intention of ever suing for custody of their child, he'd hang the possibility over her head like a sword on a fraying thread purely because of the power it gave him.

She read the card over again, to convince herself that the sinister tone was all in her head, but it didn't work. She knew Kurt. She'd been married to him for seven years. He'd risen higher and higher in the universe of network television, and yet she knew he would never be too big or too important to let go of any of the dozens of chains of control that he loved to yank. Her own chain, Carly's, Elaine's...

Jacinda saw Elaine's concerned look in her direction, and quickly brought up the Reece and Naomi file on her computer. She had a summary of the scene she was supposed to write this morning. "Reece and Naomi meet at their favorite restaurant and argue over whether to continue their affair."

She centered REECE near the top of the page, pressed Enter, then Tab, then typed the word *Hi*. She managed to get NAOMI to say hi, also, but for an hour after that, the screen stayed blank, while the words *taut, edgy* and *fresh,* in Kurt's spiky handwriting, floated in front of her eyes. She felt ill to the pit of her stomach, and when Elaine took her for a pep talk over lunch, she couldn't eat a bite.

Elaine didn't do much better. "I have to be honest with you, Jac," she said, sounding tense. "I can't run this kind of interference for you much longer. You know Kurt."

"Yes, I do."

"He has me walking on quicksand, and he knows it. We have the mortgage, we have school fees…"

There was an awkward pause, and Jac knew what she had to say.

So she said it. "Elaine, don't ruin your own career trying to protect mine." And she saw the relief in the senior writer's eyes.

When she got back to her computer, she discovered that there was an e-mail from Callan Woods waiting for her. Until she caught sight of her daughter's smile of greeting at pre-school three hours later, it was the only pleasurable, decent, *safe* moment in her entire day.

Chapter Three

The mail flight would get here at any time now.

Beside the packed red dirt of the airstrip, Callan sat in the driver's seat of his four-wheel-drive. He had the door open and the windows down to catch the breeze. In mid-April, the dry daytime heat in the North Flinders Ranges could still be fierce, even though it was technically autumn.

Lockie and Josh were back at the Arakeela Creek homestead doing their morning schoolwork via the Internet and the School of the Air. Sometimes when there was a visitor coming, Callan would give them a morning off so that they could come and meet the plane, but this time he'd said no.

He heard the buzz of the plane in the distance. It came in low with the arid yet beautiful backdrop of the mountains behind it, and he felt an odd lurch in his stomach as it got closer.

Was he looking forward to this arrival?

Like so many of his emotions since Liz's death, this one shifted back and forth, giving him no consistent answer.

Callan didn't know why Jacinda and her daughter were coming to Arakeela Creek, nor how long they wanted to stay, but he did know that Jacinda was a mess, that she wouldn't have asked if she'd felt she had any other choice, and that he couldn't even have considered turning down her desperate plea.

They'd been e-mailing each other for six weeks. A couple of times he'd thought about calling her, but the idea had panicked him too much. The e-mail correspondence was good. Nice. Unthreatening. A phone call would have been a stretching of boundaries that he wasn't ready for and didn't see the point in, since their lives were so far apart, in so many ways.

He honestly hadn't expected anything to come out of the magazine thing, and yet something had—a small, new window into a different world, a friendship at a safe distance. He was also in e-mail contact with two of the Australian women who'd written to him, via the magazine, but in contrast to what he'd developed with Jacinda, those exchanges so far didn't feel nearly as honest or as easy, and he suspected that either he or the women themselves would soon let them dwindle away. Meanwhile, letters from more women continued to arrive.

Why had his e-mails to and from Jacinda felt so much better?

Because she was a writer by profession, and her natural fluency smoothed their exchanges in both directions?

Maybe.

Sometimes, she hadn't been fluent at all.

Meanwhile, Dusty seemed pretty happy with his own outcome to the magazine story and the cocktail party. He and that small brunette, Mandy, were still in touch. He was even talking about flying back down to Sydney to meet up with her again, and had written polite notes to the other women who'd contacted him to tell them thanks, but I'm not looking anymore. Dusty was the same with horses—only ever bet on one in each race, and always bet to win.

Brant was a lot less happy. He'd been receiving way more letters than he wanted. More than Callan, apparently, and Callan had already received quite a few. Since Brant's property was closer to Sydney and Melbourne, where most of the letters came from, he'd met and been out with a couple of the women who'd written.

So far he hadn't been impressed.

Or hadn't admitted to being impressed.

Possibly because at heart he was perfectly happy as he was. The whole magazine campaign had been Brant's sister's idea, Callan had learned.

The plane skimmed the ground at the far end of the airstrip, bounced up for a moment or two, then bumped down harder, keeping its wheels in contact with planet earth this time. It careened along at speed, its wings rocking a little, but gradually slowed to a sedate taxi, propellers still roaring.

Callan climbed out of his vehicle. He didn't bother to shut the door or take the keys. Six weeks seemed, simultaneously, like a long time and like no time at all. Would Jacinda look the way he remembered?

It hadn't been her physical attributes that had drawn him, and yet the memories were all good. Big eyes, sparkly smile, an emotional warmth that showed in her whole body. Rose-colored spectacles, maybe? At a closer acquaintance, would a living, breathing, three-dimensional Jacinda Beale have anything in common with the woman who'd e-mailed him almost every day since they'd met?

Her e-mails had been far briefer over the past couple of weeks, he remembered. Stilted, almost. Cryptic, definitely. Not fluent at all. She'd said she didn't want to talk about it, that she couldn't talk about it, but that she was having some problems.

Then there had been total silence for several days. He'd even sent her a "Jacinda, are you okay?" message, which he'd regretted a split second after hitting Send.

Next thing, her phone call.

From Sydney.

Shaky voice, tense attempts at humor, nothing but stark honesty when she came to the point. "Would Carly and I be able to come stay with you for a little while? I can't think of anywhere else to go. Everything's a mess."

"Sheesh, Jacinda! What's the problem?"

"I—I can't talk about it yet. But I promise it's *not* because I'm, like, wanted for homicide in eleven jurisdictions, if that helps."

"It sets a person's mind at rest, yeah."

"Callan, I'm sorry to be doing this. I can't stay with Lucy. And I can't— You are the only person I know who feels… your ranch is the only place that feels safe, so far away. Just until I catch my breath? Just until then, Callan. I—I do know it's a huge thing to ask."

How could he have said no?

Even if, right at this moment, he wished she hadn't asked.

The plane had come to a halt in its usual spot less than fifty meters from his four-wheel-drive. A private outback airstrip didn't need a terminal building, or even a sealed blacktop runway. The dust thrown up by the aircraft was still hanging in the air like a tea-and-milk-colored curtain. It drifted slowly to the east as the plane's door opened and its steps folded down.

Rob, the pilot, helped Jacinda out and then reached for Carly. The little girl took her mother's hand, while Rob went to get their bags from the back storage hatch where they were stowed. He brought out a mailbag, too, Callan noticed. It looked bulkier than usual. It had looked bulkier than usual for the past two months, so maybe "usual" was due for a new definition.

The bulky mailbag weighed on him. Rob was holding it up, grinning. He knew the story by now.

More letters to answer. More women Callan didn't really want to meet.

Something squeezed tight inside him as he watched the woman and the little girl walk toward him. Carly looked neat and pretty and a little overwhelmed at finding herself in a place like this, so totally different from Sydney and L.A. Her mother moved awkwardly, her body appearing stiff in contrast to the unruly dark hair that whipped and undulated like fast-flowing stream water in the breeze.

Callan lifted his hand in greeting, but Jacinda didn't even say hello, just, "I'm sorry," the moment she reached him. It could have been *I'm sorry, I think I'm about to get sick,* because her face was stark-white and she could hardly move her dry lips, but he knew she was apologizing for a whole lot more than that.

He had to struggle to get his priorities worked out. Her nausea came top of the list right now.

"Take some deep breaths. Walk around." He grabbed a plastic bottle of ice water from the four-wheel-drive and unscrewed the cap, wishing he'd brought a tin mug or something. Little Carly would probably like a drink, also, although she didn't look anywhere near as ill as her mother.

Jacinda took the bottle and managed a few sips, then nodded. Yes, the water helped.

"You don't have to apologize for anything," he told her. "And you definitely don't have to talk."

"Carly?" She gave the water bottle to her daughter, even though Callan could see how much she still needed it for herself.

While Carly drank, Jacinda sucked and blew some careful air. Her gray eyes began to look less panic-stricken and her color was coming back. Callan tried to remember his impression of her the night they'd met, and again the next day when he'd made that impulsive visit to her friend's place with flowers and a child's gift.

She'd lost weight, he thought. She looked thin, now, rather than willowy. She wasn't wearing makeup, but then she probably didn't need it when she wasn't pale green. Those eyes were so big and those lashes so dark, and her mouth was already the kind of shape that some women tried to paint in place without reference to their natural lip line.

He tried to decide whether she was beautiful...attractive...pretty. Each of those words meant something slightly different, but he couldn't make up his mind if any of them fit.

Striking, maybe. That was the word for how she looked.

He felt as if he'd been struck.

By lightning.

By a sideways wall of wind.

By a blow to the head.

He hadn't expected to feel so protective toward her, nor so helpless himself. Suddenly, he was more aware of his own masculinity than he had been in...hell...how long? Years?

He felt that if he were clumsy with her, in words or actions or assumptions, he might break her like a dried-out twig. He also sensed that she could just as easily break him, without her even knowing it, without her even understanding her power or his vulnerability.

Well, gee, that all made sense!

"Tell me when you're ready for the drive," he said, his voice too gruff in its pitch.

Rob had brought three suitcases, an overnight bag and that bulky mailbag over to the four-wheel-drive. "You want these...?" In the back, his gesture finished the question.

Callan nodded at him and he opened the vehicle's rear door and lifted them inside, exaggerating his effort with the mailbag to suggest that it was almost too heavy to lift, full of all those women's letters. Callan couldn't help grinning, even though he shook his head at the man's antics. They knew each other the way outback people often did: five minutes of contact a handful of times a month could feel like real friendship.

"The drive?" Jacinda said, meanwhile. "Where? How far?"

"To the homestead. It's about five clicks." She wouldn't understand the Australian slang, and she probably didn't measure her distances in kilometers, anyhow. "Three miles or so," he translated for her.

"Right." She looked relieved.

"But it's bumpy. We'll wait a bit."

"I want to see the lizard," Carly said, looking up at Callan as if she knew him.

"Got a few more hops, so I'll say no to that beer," Rob came in, leaning his hand on the top of the vehicle.

"Next time, mate," Callan answered, as if beer had indeed been mentioned.

The lines were almost scripted, the kind of running joke that sustained male relationships out here. Rob never had a beer when he was flying, but the unstated offer—like an offer of help in times of trouble—was always there.

The two men waved at each other and Rob headed back to the plane. Jacinda managed to call, "Thank you!" in his direction and he waved again.

"Pick you two up on your way back," he said, but was tactful enough not to ask when that might be.

"Can I see the lizard?" Carly repeated.

"She loved painting the boomerang. She's talked about you quite a lot," Jac murmured. To Carly she added, "I'm not sure if there are lizards here at the airstrip, honey. Maybe we'll have time to look for one tomorrow. Can Mommy have the water again now, please?"

This time, she could take it in gulps, and when she'd had a long drink, she gave a grin of relief. "Never tasted so good!"

But he saw that her hands were shaking.

Carly had started to look hot and sweaty in the sun. She didn't have a hat. Jacinda pushed the fine semiblond hair back from her wide little forehead and frowned. "Are you feeling sick from the plane, honey?"

"Not now. I was only a little, before, not as sick as you, Mommy."

"So Callan wants to drive us to his house. Are you ready?"

"Where's his house?"

Good question. You couldn't see the homestead from here. It was set above a loop of Arakeela Creek, just under a kilometer from the line of white-trunked eucalyptus trees that marked the creek bed, on the far side of a low rise. "You'll see it soon, Carly," he told her. "Let's get you strapped in."

"You use seat belts out here? When there are no other cars around for miles?" Jacinda asked.

"They keep your head from hitting the ceiling on the bumps."

She thought he was joking.

He had enough expertise at the wheel not to need to shatter her illusions on that point today, on the relatively well-made track between the airstrip and the homestead, but if she did any more extensive driving with him around the property, she'd soon find out the truth.

Once again, he wondered how long she would need to stay, what he could possibly do to make her feel welcome and entertained, and what would happen to such a new and untested kind of friendship in the isolation of the outback.

Most importantly, why had she fled her life in Los Angeles? What was she running from? And what was she hoping for, when she'd told him in such a desperate voice that she needed to catch her breath?

He couldn't ask.

Not yet.

* * *

Callan stayed silent for the first few minutes of the drive. Jacinda listened to the grind of the vehicle's engine and the squeak of its bodywork and springs on the unsealed track. The landscape they drove through was stark, yet she could already understand why some people would find it beautiful. She found it beautiful, herself. It was like looking at the very bones of the earth—bones that were colored clay red and ocher yellow and chalky white. In the distance, near an arc of eucalyptus trees, she saw a spreading herd of red-brown cattle grazing, their big bodies dwarfed by the sheer scale of ground and horizon and sky.

She knew she'd soon have to tell Callan why she was here, but not yet. She needed to wait until she was a little calmer and her blood sugar was a little higher, for a start. She wanted him to believe her. She needed him to understand how terrified she was and that her story wasn't the product of her bitter feelings toward Kurt and her writer's imagination— even if in some of her most paranoid, self-doubting moments, she had wondered if it was.

…Because if he didn't believe her, and if she and Carly weren't welcome here, she didn't know where else they could go.

"There's the homestead," Callan finally said.

His bare, brown forearm and hand came into Jac's body space, pointing strong and straight, across to the left of the vehicle. She'd forgotten what a powerful, sturdy build he had and, here in his natural element, the impression of strength was emphasized all the more. What would he look like on horseback, or wrestling with his cattle in a branding yard?

The mental images were too vivid and far too appealing. Kurt's strength had never been physical…or even emotional. Instead, it was based purely on money and influence. Callan's kind of strength would be so different, much simpler and more straightforward, and she needed that so much right now.

Right away she saw the cluster of buildings that he indicated, their forms and outlines growing clearer as the vehicle got closer. They had roofs painted a dark red that had faded to a dusty cherry color in the strong light and they were shaded by stands of willowy, small-leafed trees that she couldn't identify. Not eucalyptus. As a California resident, she knew those well. Some of the buildings were wooden, but the main house was made of sand-colored stone with a framing of reddish brick where walls met and windows opened.

She glimpsed something that looked like a vegetable garden. It contained a couple of short rows of orchard trees and was protected on two sides by walls made of some kind of dry brush, and on a third side by a screen of living shrubs. In a sparsely grassed field close to the house, several horses grazed or drank water from a metal trough, placed in the shade of some trees.

Several of the buildings had wide verandas, and all of them had metal water tanks hugging close on one side, to collect roof runoff when the rare rains came. Houses, storage sheds, barns, she didn't know what each building was for, but there was something very pretty and alluring about the grouping. It reminded her of circled wagons in an old-fashioned Western film, or a town in a desert oasis.

She had stretched a very new friendship by her desperate act of coming here, she knew, but at least she felt that she and Carly would be physically safe.

Far safer than she had felt they were in Los Angeles.

Safer than she'd felt at Lucy's after those phone calls had started coming at all hours—hang-ups, every one of them. They had to have been from Kurt.

"How big is your ranch?" she asked Callan.

"My station. We don't call them ranches here. It's around twenty-four hundred square kilometers."

"Wow!" It sounded like a satisfying number. "In acres, that would be…twice that? Four or five thousand?"

She was only guessing. Kurt had had a ranch around that size in eastern California. Six thousand acres. He used to spread his arms out and take a deep breath and tell everyone, "Man, this is a piece of land!"

But Callan laughed at her estimate. "Uh, a little bit bigger, actually. Nine hundred-odd square miles. In acres, six hundred thousand."

"Six *hundred* thousand? You're saying this is a *hundred* times bigger than my ex-husband's dude ranch?"

"It's a pretty small place compared to some in this country. Anna Creek, out west of Lake Eyre, is something like six million acres, the biggest pastoral lease in the world."

Jacinda didn't care about Anna Creek. "You own— heavens—*Rhode Island!*"

"Only I probably have a lot fewer cattle."

"How many? Don't tell me! More than the human population of the whole country?"

"Nowhere close. Again, around twenty-four hundred. One beast per square kilometer. It's arid, out here. The land just doesn't support more than that. Most of the time, they roam free, and they can be pretty hard to find when we want to round them up and send them to market."

She didn't care about the number of cattle, although she could well believe they were hard to locate in this vastness. Callan owned more land than the average European prince.

And a hundred times more land than Kurt.

Which probably shouldn't make her want to grin with pleasure, but it did.

"As far as the eye can see? It's all yours?"

"Yep." And though he said it quietly—lazily, almost—she could see the pride and satisfaction it gave him.

Soon they rumbled across a metal grid between two lines of fence, and a couple of hundred yards later, they'd reached the homestead. Callan parked the vehicle at a casual angle out front and switched off the engine. Two dogs raced around from the side of the house and greeted their human as if they hadn't seen him in a week. One was a black and white border collie and one was probably the red dog featured in Callan's magazine photo.

"Okay, Pippa," he said. "Okay, Flick. You like me. I get the message. But Jacinda and Carly don't need to get told the same thing, you hear? They're not used to wretches like you." He issued a couple of sharp commands and the dogs dashed over to sit in the shade of the house, pink tongues panting and lolling, attitudes repentant.

A screen door squeaked on its hinges and flapped back against the jamb, and three people materialized on the shaded veranda. They must have heard the vehicle's approach.

It wasn't hard to work out who they were—Callan's two boys and his mother, Kerry. All three of them had exactly his eyes—a glorious overload of piercing blue. He'd talked about them in his e-mails, and Jac knew that Kerry had been widowed by Callan's father's death eleven years ago and lived in a smaller cottage in this same grouping of buildings. That was probably it over there, about a minute's walk away. It was a smaller version of the main house, with the same faded red roof, the same brick-and-stone walls, and set beneath the same willowy trees.

"I can't get myself unstrapped, Mommy," came Carly's voice from the backseat.

Jacinda found that her own seat-belt catch was stiff, also. Thanks to its frequent exposure to dust, probably. She climbed out and opened the back door to help her daughter, aware that she was being stared at—in a welcoming way, but stared at all the same. Callan opened the four-wheel-drive's back door.

"Suitcases? I'll help," Kerry Woods said, coming down the stone steps that led from the veranda. "You're Jacinda and Carly, of course, and I'm Kerry." She patted Jac's shoulder and ruffled Carly's fine hair as Carly slid her little body down from the high vehicle to the ground. "Boys, don't just stand there, come and meet Carly. Someone to play with!"

"Does that mean we've finished school?"

"To play with *when* you've finished school, which is at lunchtime, as you well know, Lockie!"

It was now eleven-thirty, Jac saw when she looked at her watch. No, wait a minute, they were on central Australian time now, the pilot had said, which meant it was half an hour earlier here than it would be in Sydney.

"Did you have a good flight?" Kerry asked her.

"Yes, the view from the plane between Sydney and Broken Hill was fascinating. Um, I'm afraid between Broken Hill and here, though, I—"

"She looked pretty green when she landed," Callan cut in on a drawl.

Kerry made a sympathetic sound, and Carly asked her lizard question. The boys had gotten the dogs all excited again and they almost tripped Callan up as he reached the steps with the two heaviest suitcases. Josh ignored the lizard question and asked a jumbo-jet question of his own. Carly ignored that, but Lockie answered it in the derisive tone of an older brother. Kerry grabbed the third suitcase and mentioned tea and biscuits. The dogs said, *Yes, please!* Lockie and Josh protested about their schoolwork once more.

Chaos, all of it.

Fabulous, safe, friendly, normal, reassuring family chaos.

"I'd love some tea and biscuits," Jacinda said. She picked

up the bag that Rob-the-pilot had unloaded from the plane along with her luggage. "Should I bring this?"

"Uh, yeah, it's just the mail," Callan said.

"Wow! You get a lot of mail out here!"

"Not usually."

"More letters, Callan?" Kerry asked.

"I'm hoping most of it's other stuff."

"I think there are some books in here," Jacinda said and saw that he looked relieved.

She still felt shaky. The difficult flight, the remnants of jet lag following their trip from California four days ago, the fact that she hadn't been eating enough lately… Her blood sugar was down and she was stressed and emotionally stretched to the point where she thought she might snap like a perished elastic band.

Kerry must have seen at least a part of all this.

"Come inside," she said. "Boys, leave our visitors alone for a bit, until we get them settled. Callan, I made up both beds in the back corner room. It looks out on the garden, Jacinda, and there's a door opening to the back veranda. There's a bathroom just across the corridor, and I've forbidden the boys to use it while you're here. They can use Callan's. So if you want to freshen up, or if you want me to bring the tea to your room…"

Chaos.

Then peace.

Carly had already made friends with lizard-loving Lockie, if not yet with Josh, and wanted him to show her the garden. Inside the house, the air was pleasantly dim and cool in contrast to the bright light and heat outside. Along the corridor, Jac saw prize ribbons in different colors from various cattle shows tacked up on the wall. The three suitcases and the overnight bag sat in the middle of her new room, for when she felt ready to unpack. Callan's mailbag had disappeared somewhere, carried in his firm grip.

The guest room itself was spacious but modestly furnished—twin beds clothed in patchwork quilts, a ceiling fan, a freestanding varnished pine armoire, a matching chest of drawers with a mirror above, and a framed picture of a landscape that seemed to be made out of pieces of twig and leaf and bark.

Jacinda lay down on the bed and looked at the picture and at last felt truly safe. *At last.* She was far enough from Kurt, from his power and his contacts and his chains of influence and control. He wouldn't find Carly here, and even if he did, his power did not extend into this Rhode-Island-sized cattle kingdom.

She closed her eyes and her head still whirled, but at least her heart had stopped its skittering rhythm and had steadied to a regular beat. She couldn't stay here forever. Not more than a few weeks at most. Even in that time, she and Carly couldn't let themselves be a burden on Callan or his family. But for now, for now…

Twenty minutes later, as soon as she was sitting down with Kerry and Callan over their cookies and tea, she told them, "Please give me something to do. Anything. I mean that. I'd suggest something, only I don't know what you need. Dishwashing and cooking and vacuuming, obviously, but more than that. Don't treat me like a guest when I've dumped myself and my daughter on you like this."

She sounded sincere and almost pleading, Callan thought, and he knew it would be easier on all of them if he could find something for her to do. Mustering big, half-wild cattle on a dirty quad motorbike, maybe? Stretching wire on about four thousand meters of new fence? Harnessing herself to the faded red roofs and painting them?

Hmm. There was just a slight chance that in those areas, an ex–Los Angeles screenwriter wouldn't have the necessary skills.

Mum, help me on this….

His mother had brought out a set of blocks for Carly to play with and she was happy with them out on the veranda, visible through the screen door. The boys were back at their school desks, Josh working on math problems and Lockie struggling with a book report.

They did their lessons via Internet and mail through the South Australian School of the Air. Callan had done the same thing up until the age of twelve, back when the Internet hadn't existed and his teacher was just a scratchy, indistinct voice on the high-frequency radio. In general, the boys enjoyed their schooling and it gave them a vital contact with other kids and the outside world, but Lockie wasn't a keen reader or writer. They'd all been suffering through the book report this week.

"School?" his mother mouthed at Callan.

He was about to shake his head. He knew why she'd suggested it. If she didn't have to supervise the boys, she'd be free to get more done in the garden. She worked too hard already, though, and had done since Dad's death. Callan didn't want to give her a way to work even harder.

But Mum didn't give him time to nix the idea. "Lockie would love some help with his book report," she told Jacinda. "Callan said you were a writer…."

Jacinda gave a tight little nod. She looked as if she'd suddenly felt demon fingers on the back of her neck.

Callan jumped in. "Mum, I don't think—I think that's like asking a doctor for free medical advice at a party."

"No, it's fine," Jacinda said. "Really."

Callan could see it wasn't fine.

Worse, Jacinda thought that Mum had meant right this minute, and she'd already stood up and gone into the office-cum-schoolroom adjacent to where they were sitting. Or rather, where Josh was huddled over his math book and

Lockie was staring morosely at an almost-blank computer screen. "What's the book, Lockie?"

What'sthebookLockiewhat'sthebookLockiewhat'sthebookLockie…

The words echoed in Jacinda's head like a dinning bell for several seconds after she spoke them.

I can do this, she thought.

It would be insane if I couldn't do this.

But she'd had trouble even filling in the passenger arrival card coming in to Sydney's airport on the plane. She'd bought some postcards three days ago—twelve hours before her frantic call to Callan—and she'd left them behind at Lucy's, unable to face what they did to her well-being. She'd picked up a pen at one point, on the day she'd bought them, stared at the rectangle of card and teetered on the edge of a full-fledged panic attack.

It was just like the panic attack that was boiling up inside her now, like thunder clouds boiling on a humid summer horizon. Only this time, there was no teetering on the edge. The panic attack descended and she had no power to fight it off.

The computer screen was so familiar. That slightly shimmery white space with its edging of Microsoft Word icons and line numbers, the bright royal blue band across the top, not much darker than the awesome blue sky above Callan's land.

BOOK REPORT Lockie had typed, centered on the page like the words REECE and NAOMI. The heading vibrated and blurred and shouted at her.

She couldn't breathe. Words tangled in her head, a nightmarish mix of dialogue lines from *Heartbreak Hotel* scenes she'd written months ago and lines that Kurt had delivered to her in person—those velvety threats, and pseudocaring pieces of advice and upside-down accusations. A black, cold, reasonless pit of fear and dread opened in her stomach and flight was the only possible response.

Out of here, out of here, out of here.

Dimly aware that Lockie was talking to her, answering her question about the book, she fled the room, out through the screen door, past a startled Carly, down the steps, out across the wide, hard-baked piece of red ground to a stand of trees grouped around a shiny metal windmill and an open water tank. She came to a halt, gasping, blood thundering in her ears.

The black pit inside her slowly closed over, leaving a powerful memory of her fear, but not the fear itself. She grasped one of the trailing branches of the willowy tree and felt a trickle of tiny, dusky pink spheres fall into her hand. Fruits? They were dry and papery on the outside and, when she rubbed them between her fingertips, they smelled like pepper.

A breeze made the top of the windmill turn. It was shaped like a child's drawing of a flower, with a circle of metal petals like oars, and it turned with just enough force to pump an erratic stream of water up from the ground and into the tank, whose tarnished sides felt cool and clean in the sliver of midday shade.

Jac began to breathe again, but she was still shaking.

"What happened, Jacinda?" Callan said behind her. She'd heard the screen door and his footsteps, but hadn't really taken in the sounds of his approach. "He wasn't rude, was he?"

"No, no, nothing like that." She turned away from the tank's cool side. "It was me. My fault, completely."

"So what happened?" He stepped closer—close enough to see the tiny, convulsive shudders that vibrated her body. "Hey...."

He touched her arm, closing his fingers around the bones

just above her wrist. His hand felt heavy and strong and warm, and before she knew it, she'd pulled her own hand around to grab him in the same place—a kind of monkey grip.

They stayed that way, too close to each other. He could easily have rested his jutting chin on the top of her bent head, could have hugged her or breathed in her ear.

"Lately I've been having panic attacks," she said. "Please apologize to Lockie. He was in the middle of telling me about the book and I just…left."

"Bit more dramatic than that, Jacinda."

"I can't even remember how I got out of the room." Without planning to, she pushed her forehead into Callan's shoulder, somehow needing to be in contact with his rocklike steadiness. She smelled hot cotton, and the natural fragrance of male hair and skin.

He held her gently and made shushing sounds, the kind he'd have made to a frightened animal—which was exactly what she was, she thought. There had certainly been no human rationality in her flood of fear.

When he made a movement, she thought he was letting her go, and the cry of protest escaped her lips instinctively. She wasn't ready yet. He felt too good, too *right*. The air between them had caught fire with shared awareness, sucking the oxygen from her lungs. Again, it was animal, primal, physical. Her body craved the contact, needed it like warmth or food. You couldn't explain it, plot out the steps that had led up to it; it was just suddenly there.

She could feel his breathing, sense his response and his wariness. Grabbing on to his hands and kneading them with her own, she gabbled something that was part apology, part explanation, and didn't make much sense at all. Then she felt him push her away more firmly.

"Carly's worried about you," he murmured on a note of

warning. "She's coming down the steps now. And Mum's behind her."

"I'm sorry."

"No. Will you stop that? The apologizing?"

"You can let me go, now. I'm fine."

"Not sure if Mum's going to stop Carly from coming over here. This must look pretty, um, private."

He'd felt it, too. The awareness. She knew he had.

But he didn't like it any more than she did.

"Yes," she said. "Okay. Yes. Let me talk to them."

"Wait, though. Listen, I don't want to push, but I really can't afford...don't want...for my mother to get the wrong idea." He stepped back, making it clear what kind of wrong idea he meant. "Jacinda, when you can, as soon as you can, please, you have to give me some idea of why you're here."

Chapter Four

"Mum's giving the kids some lunch," Callan reported. "I've told her you and I needed to talk."

"Thanks. We do. I don't want to keep you in the dark about what's been going on."

"Sit on the bench. No hurry. Are you hungry? Thirsty?"

"I'm fine. I can wait."

He'd brought her out to the garden, and it was beautiful. She'd never realized herbs and vegetables could look so pretty. There were borders of rosemary and lavender and thyme, beds of young, fist-size lettuces set out in patterns of pale green alternating with dark greenish-red, orange-flowered marigolds like sentinels at the end of each row. Shade cloth stretched overhead protected some of the beds from the harshness of the midday sun, while brushwood screens kept out the dusty wind.

The soil looked rich and dark, nothing like the red- and ocher-hued earth of the surrounding country, so it must have been trucked in from elsewhere. Beyond the garden there was a chicken run, and she could see several rusty-brown and glossy black birds scratching happily, watched over by a magnificent rooster. Carly would love a newly-laid egg each morning.

Jac whooshed out a preparatory breath, knowing she couldn't spend the next hour admiring plants and hens. "Where to begin," she said.

"You had a bad divorce," Callan prompted. "But I thought that was over. Property settlement, custody, all set."

"So did I, but Kurt has other ideas. He wants Carly." Did he really? She still wasn't sure what game he was playing. "Or he wants to terrorize me with the idea that he wants Carly," she revised. "Which is working, by the way. I'm terrorized. His actions have gone beyond industry power games."

Kurt had always loved to play those, too.

"Yeah?" Callan studied her face for a moment with his piercing blue gaze, then seemed to realize it might be easier if they both looked away, that she wouldn't want her emotions under a microscope while she talked. He picked up some bits of gravel from under the bench and started tossing them lazily, as if they both had all the time in the world for this. Somewhere overhead, a crow cawed.

"Can I copy you with the rock-throwing thing?" Jac asked, and he grinned and deposited half his handful into her open palm. They threw gravel together for a minute in silence before she could work out how to begin. Decided in the end just to tell the story as straight as she could. "Last week, a woman that Carly didn't know, a complete stranger, tried to collect her from preschool. And she looked just like me."

The memory was still very fresh, and the words came tumbling out as she told Callan the full story. She'd seen the woman herself. Hadn't thought anything of it, had just idly registered that a slender female with long dark hair was getting into the same make, model and color of car as her own, fifty yards down the block from the preschool gate.

Maybe, yes, she'd had some idea in the back of her mind that Kurt himself might try to pick up Carly one day, even though he wasn't supposed to and the preschool staff knew it. She'd started coming ten minutes earlier than usual because of her suspicion, but she hadn't imagined a strategy as devious as this.

She had gone inside and found the head teacher, Helen Franz, sitting at her desk pale and shaking and unable to pick up the phone to call the police. The stranger had known Carly's name, her best friend's name, the teachers' names.

"This woman, this…this…*me* look-alike, comes past Helen toward Carly," Jac told Callan. "She says to Helen, 'Hi, Mrs. Franz, I'm a touch early, I signed her out on my way through,' and Helen says that's fine—because, you know, I have been coming early, the past few weeks—and that Carly is right here. 'Here's your mom, honey.' And she doesn't really look closely at this woman, but she has no suspicions at all and she's all set to let Carly go. That was what made Helen start shaking, afterward, when she realized what she'd almost done. I started shaking, too, as soon as she started telling me. So Helen's actually ready to let Carly go. 'That's fine, Jacinda,' she tells this woman. No suspicions.

"Except that Carly knows it's not me. She won't budge. Digs in her heels. Throws a tantrum, which isn't like her. The woman says, 'Sweetheart, you don't have time to finish your game.' And she has my mannerisms. My voice. Carly starts screaming. Helen comes closer to see what the problem is. Carly screams out, 'That's not my real mommy. It's an alien!' She's terrified. Completely terrified. Partly because the deception is so neat and close. It would have been less frightening for her, I think, if the woman hadn't looked anything like me at all."

"I can understand that," Callan muttered. He stretched his

arm along the garden bench. He'd finished with the gravel. He looked skeptical, but interested. "Yeah, that makes a lot of sense. It's…yeah…scary if someone looks right and wrong at the same time. It really gets to you."

"Meanwhile, Helen's still one step behind, at this stage. She looks up to find the woman heading out of there, just quietly slipping away. But fast. As if she's been given instructions to abort the mission the moment she's seriously challenged. She had my style of sunglasses, an outfit like one of mine, my hairstyle. She was really well rehearsed. *Coached,* Callan."

He looked at her, eyes narrowed in the bright light, and she saw the doubt still in place. Dropped her bits of gravel. Grabbed his arm with dusty fingers. "Yes, I know it sounds paranoid…crazy. But my ex-husband is a big-time TV producer. He has access to desperate actresses, expert makeup artists, wardrobe people, acting and movement coaches. He could pull it off like *that.*" She snapped her fingers. "I can put you in touch with Helen Franz if you want to hear it from her. We never called the police, in the end, because nothing actually happened, but she wrote up a full report. There were two other teachers in the room who witnessed the whole thing from a distance. It did happen, Callan!"

"I—I guess I'm not doubting it. But who would have gone along with something like that? It was a kidnapping attempt!"

"Kurt wouldn't have called it that when he hired the actress. He would have called it a reality TV show with hidden cameras, or a method-acting audition for a big movie role. He would have paid in five figures. And he's Kurt Beale. So people listen. Desperate actresses sure listen! They listen to anything! And they believe him. And they do what he says. He has the power, he has the control. He loves to use it. He's Kurt Beale," she repeated.

"Yeah?" Callan said. Then he gave a slow grin. "Well, I've never heard of him."

She closed her eyes. "I know. That's exactly why I'm here."

She told him about not being able to write anymore, about being scared the inspiration might never come back, about resigning from *Heartbreak Hotel* for Elaine's sake, about fleeing to Sydney and getting all those hang-up calls at Lucy's.

"And panicking," she added. "I know I'm panicking. I do know it. Overreacting, obsessing over worst-case scenarios. Do you know what a curse it can be, a writer's imagination? But there's no place I can draw the line, Callan. If you seriously asked me, is Kurt capable of taking Carly and hiding her somewhere so I'd never see her again? Is he capable of stalking me in the entertainment industry so that I'll never write again? Is he capable of murder, that kind of if-I-can't-have-her-then-no-one-can awful thing that some men do? There's no place I could draw the line and say, "No, I know Kurt, and I know he wouldn't do that." He *could* do it. Any of it. I know it."

"Hey…hey."

"Yeah, enough about me, right?" she tried to joke. "You look like you're thinking six hundred thousand acres isn't going to be big enough for both of us."

"No, no, the opposite. I wanted to tell you that six hundred thousand acres *is* big. We're isolated. You're safe here. For—well, for—"

He wanted the bottom line. How long did she want to stay?

"A month, okay?" she told him quickly. "Our return flight is in a month. I'll have something worked out by then."

I'll know if there's a chance I can ever go back to writing.

I'll decide on somewhere Carly and I can safely live. Texas, maybe. Vermont, or Maine. Somewhere like this, where there's space and air, and where Kurt has no power.

I'll have talked myself out of the panic attacks, and Carly won't sleepwalk anymore.

"Carly sleepwalks," she blurted out.

"Does she?"

"Yes, I should tell you, and the boys, and your mom. It started a couple of months ago, before we came to Sydney that first time. The doctor thought it might be the stress of the divorce and all the conflict, Kurt's games. She doesn't do it every night. Maybe once or twice a week."

"Is it dangerous?"

"No, but it's unpredictable, and she can get upset if she's woken up in the wrong place or the wrong way. I've been sleeping pretty lightly, though, so I always hear her getting up. If she's handled gently and not startled in any way, I can just lead her back to bed."

"I can't think how it would be a problem from our end. The boys are pretty sound sleepers. And Mum's in the other house."

"Yes, it's probably fine, but I thought you should know." They both sat silently for a moment, then she added, "You say *Mum,* not *Mom.*" She imitated the clipped sound of the word, compared to the longer American vowel.

"Yep. Short and sweet."

"I like it. What should I call her, by the way, your mom?"

"Just Kerry."

"And Carly?"

"I'd say keep on calling her Carly." He nodded thoughtfully. "Might confuse her if you changed it to Goldilocks, at this stage."

Jac laughed. "Well, Goldilocks is in fact her middle name, but I take your point." The moment of silly humor was nice. Unexpected. "No, I meant—"

"I know what you meant. What should Carly call Mum? Just Kerry. Or Gran, like the boys do. She won't mind either way."

"Thanks. Thank you from the bottom of my heart for this, Callan."

For seeming so relaxed about it.

For making her laugh when she wasn't expecting to.

For not being Kurt.

"Does she have any grandmothers of her own, your Carly?" he asked.

"No, she doesn't. Kurt's mother died just before he and I met. Mine, when I was twelve. My dad lives back east." She stood up, didn't want to talk about any of that, right now. "I love those chickens." She walked toward the wire mesh that separated them from the vegetable garden and called back, "I never realized their feathers would be so beautiful. The black ones are almost iridescent on their breasts."

"And they're good layers, too." His tone poked fun at her, just a little. Iridescent feathers? These birds weren't for decoration. They had a job to do!

"Is egg collecting something Carly and I could handle? She'd love it, I think."

"Sure." He stood up and came over, and they looked at the chickens side by side.

"Do they…like…bite? I'm good with horses. Kurt and I used to ride on his ranch."

If you could call six thousand acres a ranch.

She had, once.

But she'd seen Callan's place, now.

"But chickens…" She spread her hands. She didn't know anything about chickens. They hadn't fit with Kurt's image.

"They'll peck at anything that looks like it could be something to eat," Callan said. "Shoelaces, rings. But they'll stop when it doesn't taste good. And they're not aggressive. You can pet 'em and feed 'em out of your hand." He pulled some leafy sprigs of parsley from a garden bed and gave half of them to her, then bent down to hen level and stuck his parsley through the wire. A red-brown bird came peck-peck-pecking at once. "See? Try it."

She squatted. "Well, hi there, Little Red Hen."

"The boys have names for them. They can introduce you and Carly properly after lunch."

"Her ex-husband was stalking her," Callan told his mother. "Professionally and personally. She needed somewhere safe, and far."

"Well, Arakeela should be both," his mother said.

They stood on the veranda, watching the two female figures in the chook run—the adult and the little girl. Their clothing was bright in the midafternoon light and their hair glinted where the sun hit, one head dark and the other blond. Lockie and Josh had introduced Carly and her mum to the rooster, Darth Vader, and the hens, Furious, Gollum, Frodo, Shrek, Donkey, Princess and Hen.

Carly thought those names were great. Callan and Kerry could both hear her little voice saying, "Tell me which one's Frodo, again, Mommy?"

"Well, I know it was one of the black ones...."

The boys had gone, now, having shown Jacinda and Carly the chooks' favorite laying places. They were working on the quad-wheeled motorbikes in the shed, changing the oil. Most outback kids of their age got to ride quad bikes around the property when they helped with the cattle, but Callan was pretty strict about it. If Lockie and Josh were going to ride, they had to know how to take care of the bikes and they never rode one unless he was there.

"How long are they staying?" Kerry asked.

"Their return flight is a month from now, she said. I don't know how it's going to work out, Mum, to be honest, but I couldn't say no."

"Of course you couldn't! Do you think I'm suggesting it?"

"You seemed a bit doubtful."

"I could tell something was wrong, that's all. That she wasn't just a tourist friend wanting an outback stay."

"She's been having panic attacks. That was what happened with Lockie's book report before lunch. She doesn't know what she'll do for an income instead of writing, if the…you know…drive and hunger and inspiration never come back."

He knew nothing about writing. Couldn't imagine. How did you create a plot and action out of thin air? How did you dream up people who seemed so real that they jumped off the page or out of a TV screen like best friends? How did you string the words together, one by one, so that they added up to a story?

And yet he understood something about how she felt. He knew the same fear that the drive might never come back. He knew the huge sense of loss and failure, now that the hunger was gone. He had the same instinctive belief that without this certain special pool inside you, you were physically incomplete, even though the pool wasn't something tangible and solid like a limb.

"She probably just needs to rest her spirit," Kerry said. "Take the pressure off and forgive herself."

"I guess," he answered, not believing it could be that simple. Not in his own case.

Take the pressure off? Rest the spirit? Forgive yourself? Was that all it took?

His mother didn't know.

Hell, of course she didn't! And Callan would never tell her.

He hadn't breathed a word about the freckled blonde at the Birdsville Races three years ago. When he'd gone down to chat to the Scandinavian backpacker camping at the water hole a few months later, Mum had thought he was only protecting their land. He'd reported that he'd told the young woman about where it was safe to light a campfire and where best to photograph the wildlife that came to drink at the water hole at dusk.

Mum had no idea that he'd seen a phantom similarity to

Liz in both those women, and that the women themselves had picked up on the vibe. As Jacinda had said before lunch, however, when she'd told him about the woman at Carly's preschool, it was more terrifying to confront the differences when someone bore a passing resemblance to the person you loved.

They hadn't been Liz's freckles, her kind of blond, her skin, her body, her voice.

Why had he gone looking for something that he could never find?

No one, but no one—not Brant or Dusty, *no one*—had known about the Danish girl's open-eyed seduction attempt, or Callan's failure. No one ever would.

"We got eggs!" Carly shrieked out, coming out of the hen run. "Look, guys, we got eggs! Six! Mommy has four and I have two because my hands are too little. I have one brown one with white speckles and one brown one with brown speckles."

"Carly? Don't run so fast, honey," said her mum, coming up behind her, "because if you trip and fall, they'll break."

"But I want to show 'em to Callan and—" She slowed and looked back at her mother for guidance, asking in a stage whisper, "What's the lady's name?"

Jacinda looked at Callan and shrugged, asking a question with her face. Kerry or Gran? They'd discussed it—that joke about Goldilocks—but Jacinda clearly didn't know what to say. She had that vulnerable look about her again—the loss of grace, the slight slouch to her shoulders. It made her look thinner. And it made him want to give her promises about how he'd look after her that she would be bound to read the wrong way.

Before he could answer, Kerry stepped off the veranda.

"It's Gran, love," she said, in her usual plainspoken way. As she spoke, she leaned down to admire the eggs that had made Carly so excited. "You can call me Gran."

* * *

Jet lag crept up on Jacinda and Carly a short while after the evening meal. Jac tried to hide her yawns and droopiness, but Carly wasn't so polite. "Mommeee! I'm so tired! I wanna go to bed right now!" They were both fast asleep before eight o'clock.

At midnight, according to the clock on the table beside the bed, Jac woke up again. At first she couldn't work out why, then she saw the pale child-size shadow moving near the door. Carly was sleepwalking, and subconsciously she'd heard her daughter's familiar sounds.

She caught up to her in the corridor and tried to steer her back to bed. Carly wouldn't come. "Honey? This way… Come on, sweetheart."

"Butter banana on the machine in the morning." She talked in her sleep, too, and it never made any sense.

"Let's turn around and come back to bed," Jac repeated.

Carly's eyes were open, but she wasn't awake. She had a plan. She wanted something. And as always when sleep-walking, she was hard to dissuade. "I'm coming in the morning up," she said, pushing at Jac with firm little hands.

"Well, let's not, honey."

"No!" Carly said. "Up in the, in the out."

Maybe it was best to let her walk it off. The doctor had said that it wasn't dangerous to waken her, contrary to popular myth, but it did always end with Carly crying and talking about bad dreams that she would have forgotten by morning if Jac could get her back to bed while she was still asleep.

"Okay, Carly, want to show me?" She took her daughter's hand and let her lead the way.

They crept along the corridor, through the big, comfortable living room and out of the front door, first the solid wooden one and then the squeaky one with the insect-proof mesh. Oh, that squeak was loud! Would it wake Callan and the boys? Jac tried to close it quietly behind her.

Carly looked blindly around the yard, while Jacinda waited for her next move. An almost full moon shone high in the sky, a little flat on one side. It didn't look quite right, because it was upside-down in this country. Even with the moon so bright, the stars were incredible, thousands of pinpoints of light against a backdrop of solid ink. No city haze.

Carly went toward the steps leading down from the veranda, and Jac held her hand more tightly. She didn't stand as steady on her feet when she was asleep, even with her eyes open. She could easily trip and fall. At the last moment, she turned. Not going down the steps after all. There was a saggy old cane couch farther along the veranda, with a padded seat, recently recovered in a summery floral fabric with plenty of matching pillows, and she headed for that.

Jac thought, *Okay, honey, we can sit here for a while.* There was a mohair blanket draped over the back of it.

Carly nestled against her on the couch. "Yogurt, no yogurt," she said very distinctly. Then her face softened and she closed her eyes.

"No yogurt. I'll carry you back to bed in a minute," Jac whispered.

She unfolded the blanket and spread it over them both because the night had chilled considerably from the moment the sun had dropped out of sight. The blanket was hand-knitted in bright, alternating squares of pink and blue, and it was warm and soft. No hurry in getting back to bed. So nice to sit here with Carly and feel safe.

Callan found them there several minutes later. He'd heard that screen door, had guessed it was probably Jacinda, unable to sleep. They didn't lock doors around here at night. If anyone showed up with intentions good or bad, you'd hear their vehicle a mile off and the dogs would bark like crazy.

Still, after thinking about it and feeling himself grow more and more awake, something made him get up to check that everything was all right.

Yeah, it was fine. The two of them were dead to the world, snuggled together under the blanket. The fuzz of the fabric tickled Carly's nose and she pushed at it with her hand in her sleep. He moved to go back to bed himself, but the old board under his foot creaked and, coupled with Carly's movement, it disturbed Jacinda and she opened her eyes.

"Was she sleepwalking?" he asked.

"Yes, and we ended up here. I didn't mean to fall asleep myself. Did we waken you?" She looked down his body, then back up. He wore his usual white cotton T-shirt and navy blue pajama pants—respectable, Dad-type nightwear that couldn't possibly send the wrong message.

"I heard the screen door," he confessed.

She was wearing pink pajamas, herself, in kind of a plaid pattern on a cream background, and her dark hair fell over her shoulders like water falling over rock. Her skin looked shadowy inside the V of the pajama front, and even when she smiled, her lips stayed soft and full.

"Why does your mother sleep over at the little cottage?" she asked.

"Oh…uh…" He had no idea why her thoughts would have gone in that direction. "Just to give the two of us some space. She moved in there when I married Liz." Newlyweds…privacy…he didn't want to go there in his thoughts, and continued quickly, "She'll sleep in the main house if I'm away, of course, but she works pretty hard around here and sometimes she needs a break from the boys."

"Right. Of course."

"Why did you ask?"

She blinked. "I don't know. Gosh, I don't know!" She looked stricken and uncomfortable.

They stared at each other and she made a movement, shifting over for him, finding him a piece of the blanket. Without saying anything, he sat down and took the corner of the blanket. Its edges made two sides of a triangle, across his chest and back across his knees. A wave of warmth and sweetness hit him—clean hair and body heat and good laundering.

The old cane of the couch was a little saggy in the center, and his weight pushed Jacinda's thigh against his. Carly stretched in her sleep and began to encroach on his space, which stopped the contact between himself and her mom from becoming too intimate. This felt safe, even though it shouldn't have.

"Well, you know, ask anything you like," he told her. "I didn't mean you had to feel it wasn't your business."

Silence.

"It's so quiet," she murmured.

"Is it spooking you?"

"A little. I guess it's not quiet, really. The house creaks, and there are rustlings outside. Just now I heard…I think it was a frog. I'm hoping it was a frog."

"You mean as opposed to the notorious Greerson's death bat with its toxic venom and ability to chew through wire window screens to get to its human victims?"

"That one, yes."

"Well, their mating cries are very similar to a frog's, but Greerson's death bats don't usually come so close to the house except in summer."

She laughed. "You're terrible!"

"We do have some nice snakes, however, with a great line in nerve toxins."

"In the house?"

He sighed at this. "I really want to say no, Jacinda, but I'd be lying. Once in a while, in the really hot weather, snakes have been known to get into the house. And especially under the house."

She thought about this for a moment, and he waited for her to demand the next flight out of here, back to nice, safe Kurt and his power games in L.A. "So what should I tell Carly about snakes?" she finally asked.

"Not to go under the veranda. Not to play on the pile of fence posts by the big shed. If she sees one in the open, just stand still and let it get away, because it's more scared than she is. If she gets bitten—or thinks she might have been, because snake bites usually don't hurt—tell someone, stay calm and stay still."

"If she gets bitten, what happens?"

"She won't get bitten. I've lived on this land my whole life, apart from boarding school, and I never have."

"But if she does?"

"We put on a pressure bandage, keep her lying quiet and call the flying doctor."

"Which I'm hoping is not the same as the School of the Air, because I'm not sure what a doctor on a computer screen could do about snake bite."

"The flying doctor comes in an actual airplane, with a real nurse and real equipment and real snake antivenin."

"And takes her away to a real hospital, with me holding her hand the whole way, and she's fine."

"That's right. But the pressure bandage is pretty important. I'll show you where we keep them in the morning. And I'll show you how to put one on, just in case."

She nodded. "Got it. Thanks. So you've done some first-aid training?"

"A couple of different courses, yeah. So has Mum. Seems the sensible thing, out here."

"And is that how you run your land and your cattle, too? Sensibly?"

"Try to."

They kept talking. He was wide, wide awake and so was she. The moon drifted through its high arc toward the west, slowly shifting the deep blue shadows over the silver landscape. It was so warm under the blanket, against the chill of the desert night. Carly shifted occasionally, her body getting more and more relaxed, encroaching farther into his space.

Jacinda was a good listener, interested enough to ask the right questions, making him laugh, drawing out detail along with a few things he hadn't expected to say—like the way he still missed Dad, but thought his father would be proud of some of the changes he'd made at Arakeela, such as the land-care program and the low-stress stock-handling methods.

Callan thought he'd probably spooked Jacinda more than she'd admitted to regarding the snakes, but she hadn't panicked about it, she'd just asked for the practical detail. If it happened, what should she and Carly do?

And the fact that she hadn't panicked made Callan think more about her panic over Kurt. The last piece of his skepticism dried up like a mud puddle in the sun, replaced with trust. Whatever she was afraid of from her ex-husband, it had to be real or she would never have come this far, landed on him like this. She wasn't crazy or hysterical. She needed him, and even though he didn't know her that well yet, he wasn't going to let her down.

"Do you have any idea of the time?" she asked eventually. She hid a yawn behind her hand. "Has to be pretty late."

"By where the moon is, I'd say around three."

"Three? You mean we've been sitting here for three hours? Oh, Callan, I'm so sorry! You have work to do in the morning. I'm a guest with jet lag, I should never have kept you up like this."

"Have I been edging toward the door?"

"No, because Carly has both feet across your knees!"

"True, and who would think she'd have such bony heels?"

The little girl must have heard her name. Her eyelids flickered and her limbs twitched. Callan and Jacinda both held their breath. She seemed to settle, but then her chest started pumping up and down, her breathing shallow.

"I think she's having a bad dream," Jacinda murmured. Carly broke into crying and thrashing, and had to be woken up to chase the dream away. "It's okay, sweetheart, it wasn't real, it was a dream, just a bad dream. Open your eyes and look at me. Mommy's here, see? We're sitting on the porch. The moon is all bright. Callan is here. Everything's fine." In an aside to Callan, she added, "I'm going to take her to the bathroom and get her back to bed, but you go ahead."

She stood up, struggling to gather Carly into her arms at the same time.

"You're carrying her?"

"She'll get too wide awake if I let her walk."

"She looks heavy for you. Would she come to me?"

"It's fine." She smiled. "There's nothing builds upper-arm strength as effectively as having a child, right? Better than an expensive gym. Thanks for sitting up with me, Callan."

"No problem."

For some reason, they both looked back at the couch, where the mohair blanket had half-fallen to the veranda floor, then they looked at each other. And suddenly Callan knew why she'd asked that question about his mother sleeping in the cottage, three hours ago, even if Jacinda herself still didn't.

She'd unconsciously imagined how it would have looked to Mum if she'd happened to waken and find them sitting there together, under the same blanket, sharing the warm weight of Jacinda's sleeping child.

His mother had given him a particular kind of privacy

when he and Liz had been married, moving over to the cottage. When Liz had died, Mum hadn't moved back. Somewhere in her heart, although she never spoke about it, she must hope he'd someday need that kind of privacy again.

He should tell her gently not to hold her breath about it.

Chapter Five

"**S**aturdays and Sundays we don't have school," Lockie told Jac. He added, "It's the weekend," as if maybe Americans didn't know what weekends were.

His explanation covered the wilder-than-usual behavior of both boys this morning, which Carly had latched on to within minutes of waking at six. They kept early hours at Arakeela Downs. This was Jac's fourth awakening on the vast cattle station, and she had discovered that the dawns here were magical.

And chilly.

There was something satisfying about it. She would beat the predawn bite in the air by scrambling into layers of clothes, along with Carly, and head straight for the smell of coffee luring her toward the kitchen. Lockie, Josh and Callan would already be there, making a big, hot breakfast. Toast, bacon and fresh eggs with their lush orange yolks, or oatmeal and brown sugar, with hot apple or berry sauce.

They'd start eating just as the sun slid up over the horizon, and the colors of the rugged hills Jac could see from the kitchen windows would almost make her gasp. She and Carly would go out into the day as soon as they could. "To feed the chooks" was the excuse—Carly constantly referred to the hens as chooks, now; she'd be speaking a whole different language by the time they got back to the U.S.—but in reality, Jac just couldn't bear to miss the beauty of this part of the day.

The bare, ancient rock glowed like fire, slowly softening into browns and rusts and purples as the sun climbed higher. Dew drenched the yellow grass, the vegetable garden, the fruit trees, and made spiderwebs look like strings of diamonds. Flocks of birds in pastel pinks and whites and grays, or bright yellows, reds and greens, rose from the big eucalyptus trees in the wide creek bed and wheeled around calling their morning cries. The air was so fresh, she felt as if simply breathing it in would be enough to make her fly.

When Lockie had managed to sit down at the table, after teasing the dogs along with Carly and Josh at the back door, Jac asked him, "So what happens at weekends?"

"We get to go out with Dad. Riding boundary, checking the animals and the water."

Callan was listening. "Except today it's not work, it's a picnic," he said. "We're going to show Jacinda and Carly the water hole."

"Can we swim?" Lockie asked. "Can we get yabbies?"

"Yeah!" Josh's face lit up, too.

"Yabbies? What kind of a disease is that?" Jac asked the boys, grinning. It did sound like a disease, but from their eagerness she knew it couldn't be.

"A really nasty one!" Lockie grinned back. "Don't you have yabbies in America?"

"We're pretty advanced over there. Doctors have already found a cure."

"Yabbies you catch in the water hole and you cook them and eat them," Josh said. He was a little more serious than his big brother, a little more prickly and slower to warm to the American visitors, with their accents that belonged on TV and their ignorance regarding such obvious things as yabbies.

"Like big prawns," Callan said.

Setting silverware on the table, Jac looked up at him. "Shrimp?"

"Big freshwater ones." He poured the coffee into two big mugs and added a generous two inches of hot milk to each. The two of them liked their coffee the same way. It was one of the simple, reassuring things they had in common. Not important, you wouldn't think, but nice. "Yes, guys, we can swim and fish for yabbies," he said. "If you and Carly want to go on a picnic, Jacinda, that is."

He looked for her approval, courteous as always. They'd been over-the-top polite to each other since Tuesday night, and over-the-top careful about respecting each other's space. Which was dumb, really, because space hadn't been trespassed upon in any major way during those hours of moonlit talking on the veranda.

"If that's not interfering with your routine." Jac whacked the politeness ball right back over the net at him. She didn't know quite why they were both doing it. For safety, obviously, but she didn't really understand the source of the danger. "We'd love it."

Carly was nodding and clapping her hands.

"Doing something different on a Saturday *is* our routine," Callan said. "I like to check the water holes pretty often. Sometimes you get tourists leaving garbage, and you don't want that, or a dead animal fouling the water. Good drinking water's too important for the cattle and the wildlife out here."

"That makes sense." She found it interesting when he told

her this kind of stuff, but also suspected that when he slipped into the tour-guide routine, it was another safety valve.

"So we'll ride there, give the horses some serious exercise, take lunch, yabby nets, the whole kaboodle, light a fire, make a day of it. I'll see if Mum wants to come, but she'll probably stay at home."

"She's pretty amazing, your mom."

"Yeah, and I spend half my time trying to get her to be less amazing." He grinned, and relaxed. "Last flying doctor clinic we went to, that's what the doc told her. You need to cut down on the amazing, Mrs. Woods, it's pushing your blood pressure too high."

The kitchen timer beeped, which meant their boiled eggs were ready, and the five of them sat down to breakfast.

Like a family, Jacinda decided.

No, she *guessed* it, really.

She'd never been part of a family in that way.

Callan somehow read this information like a teleprompter, directly from her forehead, because as they ate he asked her, over a background of kid noise, "So where did you grow up? Where is your family from? Did you live your whole life in L.A.?"

"No, New Jersey, until I was twelve. Very different from L.A. but just as urban. I've never been in a place like this." She deliberately chose to focus on the geographical element of his questions, ignored the mention of family.

It didn't work.

"Why did you move?" Callan asked next.

Uhh… "When my mom died."

"Your dad didn't want the memories in New Jersey?"

"No, Dad stayed. I was the one who moved."

Okay, she was going to have to talk about it now, after giving him that revealing answer. It wasn't so terrible. She believed in honesty and didn't know why she was always so reluctant to unload this stuff. Because it made her sound too much like a stray mongrel puppy who'd never found the right home?

She hadn't thought of it quite like this before, but it made a connection.

Kurt had treated her like a stray puppy. He'd scooped her up, after they'd met at a script-writing seminar when she was still incredibly naive and raw. He'd had her professionally groomed, house-trained her himself, put a diamond collar round her neck, spoiled her rotten…. And then he'd lost interest when she still didn't perform like a pedigreed Best in Show.

Callan was waiting for her explanation.

"Dad didn't believe he could raise a teenage daughter on his own, you see," she said. "I have two brothers, but they're much older. They were eighteen and sixteen when I was born. Dad's seventy-eight now, and lives in a retirement home near my oldest brother, Andy."

She'd had a very solitary childhood. Her parents had both been in their forties when she was born, unprepared for their accidental return to diapers, night feeds, noisy play and bedtime stories. They'd expected her to entertain herself and she'd mostly eaten on her own, in front of a book. And then Mom had died….

"So Dad sent me to Mom's younger sister, because she had daughters and he thought she would know what to do." She pitched her voice quietly. Carly wasn't ready to hear about her mom's lonely childhood yet. Fortunately, she and the boys were keeping each other well entertained, vying for who could make the weirdest faces as they chewed.

Seated to Jac's left, around the corner of the table, Callan looked at her. He took a gulp of his coffee. She liked the way he held his mug, wrapping both hands around it in appreciation of the warmth. "But he was wrong about that? Your aunt didn't know what to do?"

"I was a bit different," Jac admitted. "I mean, don't go imagining Cinderella and her wicked stepmother, or anything. She tried very hard. And my cousins tried…only not quite so hard. They were three and five years older than me, beautiful, blonde and busy, both of them. They were into parties and dates and modeling assignments and dance classes. They had a whole…oh…family style that I had to slot into and mesh with. Frantic pace. Drive-through breakfasts and take-out dinners in front of TV, or on the run. Modeling portfolios and salon appointments and endless hours stuck in traffic on the way from one class to another. And I just didn't. Mesh with it, I mean. I'd grown up almost as an only child, with a very quiet life. I liked to read and think and imagine. I dreamed about horses and learning to ride. I was the polar opposite of cool. And even after the four years of ballet I took with my cousins, you would not want to see me dance!"

He nodded and stayed silent for a moment, then added with a tease in his voice, "But I'd like to see you ride."

She smiled at him, happy that he'd dropped the subject of family. "It'll be great to ride. But what will we do about Carly? She's been on a three-foot-tall Shetland pony a handful of times at Kurt's ranch, around and around on a flat piece of grass with someone holding the pony on a rope. She couldn't ride a horse of her own out here."

"We'll work something out."

"She can ride with me," Lockie said. "I'll show you how to gallop, Carlz. I'll show you Tammy's tricks. You wait!"

"Carlz" looked up at him, round-eyed and awestruck. "Yeah?" she breathed.

"Uh, Lockie, let's save the galloping and tricks for another time, okay?" Callan said. He got a glint in his eye when he saw how relieved Jac looked, then he dropped his voice and said to her, "Nice little friendship going between those two, though."

"Yes, and I think it's really good for her, Callan. I appreciate it."

Carly hadn't sleepwalked since that first night. Possibly because with all the activity generated by boys and dogs and chooks, horses to feed, gates to swing on, trees to climb and a million places to hide, by bedtime she was just too worn out to stir. This morning, as soon as she'd eaten her breakfast, she was off with the boys, who'd been dispatched to catch the horses, bring them to the feed shed where their tack was stored and get them ready.

"But Carly stays outside the paddock and outside the shed, okay?" Callan said, as all three kids fought to be the first one out the door. "She's too little, she doesn't know horses and they could kick if she spooks them."

"Will they remember?" Jac asked.

"Yep. They're good kids."

Jac liked his confidence, and after almost four days here, she trusted it. Given more responsibility and physical freedom than any child she'd ever met…let alone the child she'd once been, herself…the boys knew their boundaries and stayed within them. They understood the dangers in their world, and respected the rules Callan gave them to keep them safe. They'd keep Carly safe, also.

"…while we get the rest of the gear together," Callan said.

By the time they were ready to leave, the temperature had begun to climb, in tandem with the sun's climb through that heavenly, soaring sky. It would probably hit eighty or even ninety degrees by midafternoon, Jacinda knew. Everyone had swim gear under their clothes, and water bottles and towels in their saddlebags, as well as their share of picnic supplies. On a pair of medium-size, sturdy horses whose breed Jac didn't know, the boys also had yabby nets, bits of string and lumps of meat for bait.

Kerry was staying home, and Carly was riding right in

front of Callan on his big chestnut mare, Moss, her little pink backpack pressing against his stomach. She looked quite comfortable and happy up there. Her mommy was a little nervous about it, but Josh's old riding helmet and Callan's relaxed attitude helped a lot.

It was a wonderful ride. The dogs were wildly jealous, but Kerry wanted them at home with her for company. Their barks chased after the four horses and five humans for several minutes until the trail that followed the fence line cut down toward the dry creek bed and the hill between creek and homestead cut off the sound, at which point, "They can bark all they want but we don't have to hear," Callan said.

He let the boys lead the way and brought up the rear himself, with Jacinda in the middle. It felt good to know that he was behind her, that he would see right away if something went wrong and he'd know what to do about it.

Not that you could imagine anything going wrong on a day like today. A breeze tempered the sun's heat, and the stately river gums spread lacy patterns of shade over the rapidly warming earth. They startled a mob of red-coated kangaroos who'd been sleeping in some dry vegetation and the 'roos bounded away, over the smooth-worn rocks and deep sand of the creek bed. On the far side of the creek, there were cattle grazing on coarse yellow grass. Some of them looked up at the sound of the horses, but soon returned to browsing the ground.

"When does the creek actually flow?" Jacinda asked, craning around to Callan in her saddle. It was a different style from the ones on Kurt's ranch, not so high in front. "In winter?"

"Only when we've just had rain," Callan answered. He nudged Moss forward to close the distance between them a little. Carly sat there, so high. Her little body rocked with the motion of the horse's gait like she was born to it, and her helmet looked like a dusty white mushroom on top of her head. "It doesn't stay running for long. A couple of days. Enough to top up the water holes. Fortunately we have a string of good deep spring-fed ones in the gorge, and a couple more downstream."

"Does the creek water ever get to the sea?"

"Nope. It drains into Lake Frome, east of here."

"Which is dry, too, most of the time, right? A salt pan?" She'd been looking at a map and some books with Carly while the boys did schoolwork during the week.

"That's right. Salt and clay. Flat, as far as the eye can see. I like these mountains better."

"Well, yeah, because you own these mountains."

She couldn't keep the satisfaction out of her voice, and he picked up on it. "You really like that, don't you?"

Yes.

A lot.

The safety of it.

The strength.

"Almost as much as you do, Callan Woods."

He didn't answer, just did that lazy, open grin of his, which she could barely see beneath his brimmed stockman's hat. Correction—she could see the mouth, but not the eyes. Didn't matter. She already knew what the eyes looked like. Kept seeing them in her mind when she twisted back the right way in her saddle, bluer than this sky, brighter than sun on water.

It was midmorning when they reached the deep water hole lodged in the mouth of the red rock gorge. Callan and the boys led the horses down to drink, then tethered them in the shade on the creek bank, where they found tufts of coarse grass to chew on.

"Swim first?" he said.

"Is it really safe?"

"If you're sensible."

"So you mean it's not safe?" She imagined crocodiles.

"It's deep in parts, and it's cold."

"But no crocodiles?"

He laughed. "Not a one. But it's colder than you would think, especially once you go a few feet below the surface. Keep Carly in the shallows. See, it's like a beach. The sand's coarser than beach sand but it shelves down nice and easy."

"Mmm, okay." She could see for herself the way the water darkened from pale iced tea to syrupy cola. "Why is it that color?" she asked.

"It gets stained from the eucalyptus leaves. In some lights, it looks greener. The boys and I like to jump and dive in a couple of spots off the ledge on the far side, there, but we always check the places out first. I've been swimming in this water hole my whole life, but you can get tree branches wedged in the rocks that you can't see from the surface, and you don't want to get caught or hit your head."

"I'll stick with Carly in the shallows."

He was right. It was cold. Enough to make her gasp when she stepped into it from the warm sand. And it had a fresh, peaty kind of smell that she liked. Carly splashed and ducked and laughed, while Jac watched the boys and their dad swimming across an expanse of water that looked black from this angle, toward the rock ledge. They trod water back and forth, scoping out the depths for hidden dangers, then having determined that it was safe, no hidden snags, they hauled themselves out onto the rock, climbed to the high point, gave themselves a good long run-up and started to jump.

After fifteen minutes, Carly's teeth began to chatter. She lay on a towel in the sun for a short while, but soon warmed up again, put a T-shirt over her semidry swimsuit and was ready to make canal systems and miniature gardens in the sand. Lockie had had enough of the water, also. He swam back to the beach to get his towel, but Callan and Josh were still jumping and whooping, their voices echoing off the rock walls of the gorge behind them, the only human sound for miles around.

"Swim over and give it a go," Callan called out to Jacinda. He stood at the edge of the highest part of the ledge, a good twelve feet above the waterline.

Not in a million years, Jac thought.

"I'm watching Carly," she called back.

"Lockie's with her now. She's dressed. She'll be fine."

"No, really…"

"I'm going back to the sand, Dad," Josh said. He and Callan did one last whooping jump from the ledge together, with legs kicking wildly in the air and arms turning like windmills, then they swam toward the stretch of beach.

"She'll be fine with the boys," Callan repeated when he approached Jacinda, as if there'd been no break to the conversation. "She'd have to go in pretty far to get out of her depth here."

He touched bottom and stood waist-deep, then began to stride toward the beach, the water streaming from his body as he got closer and shallower. He reached Jacinda, his skin glistening and his dark, baggy swim shorts hanging low on his hips. He wasn't self-conscious about his body, just took it for granted.

Jac didn't. She saw hard bands and blocks of muscle, a shading from tan to pale halfway down his upper arm, a neat pattern of hair across his chest, and the way the cold and wet made every inch of his skin taut.

Standing calf-deep, he gestured behind him. "See, there's about six meters of sand all the way along this side, before it starts to shelve down. She's safe without you. And you'd be safe, too, if you came for a jump off the ledge. It's so much fun, Jac."

He used the same tone that some men might reserve for attempting to get a woman into bed, and it was the first

time he'd called her Jac, even though she'd asked him to
three days ago.

"Mmm…"

That's not an answer, she realized. *I can't believe I'm
even considering this.*

"Hey?" he cajoled. "Thinking about it? The rush as you
race forward and hit the air? It's so good. And you have to
yell, that's a requirement. Lockie first did it when he was five.
Promise you'll yell?"

Live a little, said his eyes. There was a contained eagerness
coming from him. He was like Carly about to give Mommy
a special piece of artwork from preschool. How could you not
respond just exactly the way those eyes begged you to?

"Callan, I'm not even promising to—"

"You need a reason to yell in life, sometimes, and this is
the best one I know."

"Yeah?"

I don't believe this.

I am considering it.

I'm seriously thinking about it.

The yelling idea is incredibly attractive.

Her heart started beating faster. She could smell horse on
her body, dust in the air, creek water in Carly's wet hair. She
was eight thousand miles from the place she called home, on
six hundred thousand acres of land.

And she was seriously wondering if she might be brave
enough to run and jump, while yelling, into a deep, creepy
water hole.

Just do it.

"Gotta earn those yabbies." Callan held out his hand,
ready to pull her up. Behind him, Lockie had started putting
lumps of meat inside old stocking feet and tying them with
string. Under his direction, Josh was searching for good long
sticks of eucalyptus to act as fishing poles.

"This is way outside of my comfort zone!" Jacinda warned as Callan's grip locked with hers.

A moment later, she reached a standing position and they came face-to-face, confronting Jac with something else that was way outside of her comfort zone. His hard, wet body, his slightly quickened breathing, his exhilarated grin. All of it was too close and too real when they stood just inches apart like this.

Feeling it, too, and clearly not liking it, he let her go and told her in an awkward way, "Strip, before you chicken out."

She was only wearing a T-shirt over her two-piece tank-style animal print swimsuit. She crossed her arms, peeled the T-shirt over her head and dropped it on a patch of dry sand safely distant from the kids' messy play. She discovered Callan looking over at the kids. His lean, strong neck looked too tight and twisted. It wasn't a natural angle. He'd been— what?—*averting his eyes* while she stripped?

In her animal print, she felt like Jane to his Tarzan. But had Tarzan been that much of a gentleman?

"I'm coming as far as the ledge, but I don't promise to jump," she said.

His head turned again, back to her, and a frown dropped away, replaced with a twinkle in the depths of those eyes. "We'll see," he drawled.

He grabbed her hand and galloped her into the water. Getting deeper in two seconds than she'd gone with Carly in fifteen minutes, she gasped again. He was right, the deeper you went, the colder it got. "Let me go!"

"Swim," he said, and struck off ahead of her with a powerful stroke.

She followed, terrified. The water felt so different to California pool water or salty ocean. So smooth. *Sooo* deep. How far down did it go? She had to fight away images of creatures lurking down there.

Before her imagination got out of control, they reached the

lower part of the ledge and she hauled herself up onto the warm rock, copying Callan's fluid movement with a more awkward one of her own. Her body tingled all over and she panted for breath.

"You did great," he told her. "You're a good fast swimmer."

"Only because things were chasing me."

"Bunyips?"

"Wha-a-at? There *is* something down there! I knew it! What the heck are bunyips? Oh sheesh, I'll never get back to the beach, now! I'll have to go the long way around, over the rocks."

Which didn't look easy.

"Don't panic. Bunyips are mythical. Kind of an Australian version of the Loch Ness monster."

"You know, Callan, there are people who don't think the Loch Ness monster is just mythical. I don't think these things should be dismissed. I've read articles about it, and there's also that in-some-ways-quite-credible urban myth about alligators in the New York—"

He wasn't listening. He'd somehow gotten hold of her hand again and they were climbing to the higher part of the ledge, over the rough shelves of rock that acted like steps. At the top, he turned away from the water and led her back into the shade of the gorge's overhanging sides. He had her in a kind of monkey grip now. He was holding her forearm in the circle of his fingers, and she held his forearm the same way. It was so strongly muscled that her fingers went barely halfway around.

"Repeat after me, Jac," he said. "Bunyips are mythical."

"Bunyips are mythical. But I have a very powerful imagination, I'm telling you."

"Okay, louder. Bunyips—are—mythical."

"Bunyips—are—mythical. And if they're not, you know how to scare them away, right?"

"Bunyips are mythical. And plus they're very friendly."

"Callan…"

"Right, now, let's go, but this time we'll yell it. Ready?" He didn't give her a chance to tell him she wasn't. Hand in hand, they sprinted forward, with Callan yelling at the top of his lungs. "Bunyips…are…"

Jac joined him on the last word, screaming it, whooping it, as they came to the end of the ledge and hit the air, legs still working wildly, arms flung high but still joined. *"Mythical!"* The word echoed off the gorge walls, bouncing like a ball, and she heard it come back to them while they were in midflight. Their voices seemed to claim this whole place.

She whooped again.

Felt a surge of utter exhilaration.

Hit the water.

Callan still had her hand. They went down, down into the icy darkness and she kicked frantically to bring herself back up, just as he was doing. She broke the surface gasping and laughing. "Get me out of here! I *know* there's a bunyip down there!"

"Wanna do it again?"

"Unnhh," she whimpered. "Unnhh!"

Do I?

Could I?

"Yes!"

They jumped together four more times, whooping and yelling and laughing, until Lockie complained, "Dad, you're scaring the yabbies! We haven't caught a single one."

"Try for them in that reach of water behind the rocks where it gets muddy," he called back to his son. "Are we done, Jacinda?"

"I think so," she said, breathless and starting to shiver.

The contrast between the cold water and the hot sun on the rocks felt wonderful with each jump and climb, but she'd had enough, and Carly must be getting hungry. They were cooking sausages and lamb chops for a midday barbecue, and Callan still had to light the fire. They swam back, side by side, no bunyips in sight, nothing nipping at her toes.

Walking through the shallows, she confessed, "I was so scared, Callan, you have no idea!"

"It's a healthy kind of scared, though, isn't it? You push the fear back with yelling, and then you feel great."

"How would you know? You said you'd been doing it your whole life. You can't ever have been scared here."

"I haven't been scared *of* here—of the water hole."

"Or bunyips."

"Or bunyips." He paused. "But I've been here, scared." Paused again. "I've come here a few times to try and yell it away, and it's always worked."

"Scared of what, then, if not the water hole?" She said it before she thought, shouldn't have needed to ask.

"After Liz died." His voice went quiet and his body went still, reluctant and stiff. "Scared of—"

"I'm sorry, I'm sorry. You don't need to spell it out. I understand."

He gave a short nod. "Yeah, there was nothing unique about it."

"I'm sorry," she said again, but she didn't show that he'd heard.

"I got given some, you know, brochures at the hospital in Port Augusta," he said. "Information leaflets. About bereavement. And they had lists of things I might be feeling, and I was. Feeling those things. All of them. It's stupid. I hated having my whole gutful of emotions put onto a bloody list. There were lists of things you could do about the emotions, too. Ways of getting help, ways to help get yourself through it."

"But those lists didn't have yelling and jumping into the water hole?"

"Nope."

And that was good, Jac understood, so Callan had jumped into the water hole a lot.

She felt privileged, sincerely privileged, that he'd wanted to push her to do it, and very glad that she had. She was pretty sure he didn't offer the same opportunity for terror and yelling to just anyone. She was very sure he was right to think that she needed it.

Bunyips were mythical.

And Kurt's power games were a long way away.

"Got one! Got one! Got one!" Josh shrieked out.

About twenty seconds later, Carly screamed, "Mommy, I got one, too!"

"Let Lockie put it in the bucket for you, Carlz," Callan warned her quickly. "It might nip you with its claw if you touch it. Lockie—?"

"I'm helping her, Dad, it's okay."

"Let's get that fire going."

He grabbed his towel and dried himself with the vigor of a dog shaking its wet coat, then dragged his T-shirt and jeans over his still-damp body, hauled on his sturdy riding boots and went to work unpacking backpacks and saddlebags, while Jac was slower to cover her damp swimsuit with her clothes. She couldn't help watching Callan as she dressed.

There was a circle of big river stones in the shade near the creek bank. The remnants of charcoal within it, as well as the blackened sides of the stones themselves, told Jac that the circle was another detail to this place that Callan had known his whole life.

"Want to find some bark and sticks?" he said.

She gathered what he'd asked for, while he broke thicker wood into short lengths with a downward jerk of his foot. He had a fire going within minutes, with water heating in a tin pot that he called a billycan. Out here in the middle of the day, the light was so bright you could barely see the flames, but you could feel the heat and the water was soon steaming.

Jac checked on the yabby tally. The kids had twelve in their red plastic bucket, but the yield seemed to be slowing and interest had waned. "The bait meat's losing its flavor," Josh said.

"And yabbies aren't stupid. They're on to us," Lockie decided. "Twelve'll have to be enough." He stood up, leaving the bucket behind, and wandered in the direction of the horses.

"They're our appetizer," Jac said, without thinking.

"We're going to eat them?" Carly wailed. "We can't *eat* them!"

They were kind of cute, in a large, shrimpy sort of way, Jac conceded, with blue and black and green markings that would turn red and pink when they were cooked. Too cute to eat?

"Nah, it's okay. They won't know it's even happening," Josh told Carly in a matter-of-fact voice.

"How come they won't know?" she asked.

Over by the fire, Callan called out, "Lockie, can you grab the tea bags while you're there?" Lockie was still with the horses, looking for something in a saddlebag.

"Dad drops them into the boiling water and they don't even have time to feel it. If I was a yabby, I'd way, *way* rather be eaten by a human than anything else."

"Why, Josh?" Carly asked seriously.

"Because anything else would be eating me alive."

"Eww! Yeah! Alive! Are you listening, yabbies?" Carly spoke seriously to the scrabbling contents of the red bucket. "We're nice, kind humans. We're not going to eat you alive."

Which seemed to deal with the whole *too cute* issue, thank goodness.

Ten minutes later, Carly was eating a hot yabby sandwich, with butter, pepper and salt.

Jac ate one, too, and it sure tasted good. "This is one of those moments when I blink and shake my head and can't believe I'm here," she told Callan, hard on the heels of the last mouthful, her lips still tasting of butter and salt.

"Yeah?" Callan waved pungent blue smoke away from his face.

He had a blackened and very rickety wire grill balanced on the stones over a heap of coals. It looked as if someone had fashioned it out of old fencing wire, but it held the lamb chops and sausages just fine, and they smelled even better than the yabby sandwich had tasted.

In a little pan, also blackened, he had onions frying in the froth from half a can of beer. The other half of the can he drank in occasional satisfied gulps, while Jacinda sipped on a mug of hot tea.

"I've just eaten something that a week ago I'd never even heard of," she said. "I've swum in terrifying water, chock-full of bunyips. I've let you tell me about snakes in the house without screaming."

"I noticed you didn't scream." He gave her his usual grin. "I was impressed."

"Thank you. Meanwhile, there's a road faintly visible over there that you claim leads eventually to Adelaide, but there hasn't been a car on it since we got here, what, an hour ago? In fact, have I seen or heard a car since Tuesday? I don't think so."

"There have been cars."

"I haven't noticed them. I've been too busy. It's incredible here. Carly is—Carly will—I hope Carly never forgets this. It's going to change who she is."

And "Carly" is code for "Carly and me."

It's going to change who I am, even more, but there are limits to my new yelling-and-jumping-induced bravery, and I'm not prepared to say that out loud.

"Wouldn't be surprised if it changes the boys, too," Callan answered.

He flipped a couple of lamb chops with a pair of tarnished tongs, drained the last of the beer and looked at her with those steady blue eyes, and she suspected…decided…hoped…that "the boys" was code, also.

Chapter Six

"Dad?" Through a fog of steam, the bathroom door clicked shut behind the new arrival.

"What's up, Lockie?"

"Can I talk to you for a sec?" The tone was reluctant, yet confiding.

"Can't it wait until I'm done in the shower?" Callan had been caught this way by Lockie before.

His evening shower was one of the few intervals in his day that were both relaxing and private, and maybe that was why Lockie came looking for him here. He knew the two of them wouldn't be disturbed by Josh or Gran or the dogs or, tonight, Carly or her mother.

The shower ran on bore water from deep in the ground, which meant it was as hard as nails but hot and steamy and in plentiful supply. Conserving water was deeply bred into anyone who lived beyond Australia's coastal fringe, but four minutes of steamy peace per day was, surely, not too much to ask.

Apparently, yes.

"Well, you see, the thing is…" Lockie trailed off. The reluctance had increased.

Callan sighed and surrendered his peace, realizing he wasn't dealing with a mere request for homework intervention or a new computer game, here. "Go ahead, spit it out."

"You know when we were at the water hole today?"

"I have a faint memory of something like that, yes, even though it's been a whole four hours since we left the place."

Out it came in a sudden rush. "I left my Game Boy behind on a rock."

"You what?" Callan shut off the water and reached around the edge of the shower curtain for his towel. "You brought your Game Boy down there? Why?"

"In case I got bored."

"But you didn't get bored. I didn't even see you with it."

"I got it out after we stopped yabbying, but then we had lunch and I forgot about it and I left it and I only remembered it now."

"Right."

"Sorry, Dad."

"What do you think we should do about it?" He wrapped the towel around his waist and slid the shower curtain aside, confronting his son.

He was strict about this kind of thing, and Lockie knew it. The boys were good, usually. Callan had trained them that way. They always left a gate the way they found it. They did a job, then put their tools away. They didn't leave feed bags open to attract vermin, or riding gear lying around to get its leather cracked in the sun.

"I think I should go back first thing in the morning and get it," Lockie said. "Like, very, very first thing."

"I think you're right," Callan said. "And I think you know I'm not happy about this. How long did you have to save up your pocket money to buy that thing? A year?"

"I'm not happy about it, either."

It was almost fully dark out, now, and they were just about to eat. Mum had cooked something special, the way she often did on a Saturday or Sunday. Smelled like lasagna and garlic bread, and the kids had already discovered and reported that there would be hot peach cake and ice cream for dessert.

Callan was hungry. He'd been up since five-thirty this morning. He didn't want to have to stir from the house again tonight.

"Is it going to be safe on a rock all night?" Lockie asked him.

"Yeah, that's what I'm wondering. What do you think?"

"If dew gets in it, or a 'roo knocks it off, or a cow steps on it, it could get destroyed."

"All those things are possible."

"So maybe I should go now," Lockie said.

"No, Lockie." Callan sighed. He wasn't going to send a ten-year-old out alone on horseback or a quad bike after dark, on the tail of a long day. "We'll eat, and then I'll go."

"I can come with you."

"Nope." Lockie looked yawning and droopy-eyed already. He'd helped with the horses, done various yard chores. He didn't need to come. "You can watch some TV, then read in bed for a bit and go to sleep."

"I can pay you my pocket money for the next couple of months, like, for your time."

Callan laughed. "No, you can just not do it ever again."

"Thanks, Dad."

He told Mum about the problem as he helped her serve out the meal, which was indeed lasagna, and he felt hungry enough to eat a whole trayful.

"Take Jacinda with you," she said at once. "You won't ride, will you? You'll take the four-wheel-drive?"

"Seems best. Although it's rough, getting to that spot in a vehicle, especially in the dark."

"You can walk the last few hundred meters. But you must take Jacinda. Two pairs of eyes. Even if Lockie thinks he can describe to you exactly which rock it's on."

Which Lockie couldn't.

"If Jacinda wants to come," Callan said.

"Of course I'll come," Jac told him.

They'd just eaten Kerry's fabulous meal, all appetites sharp after the day spent outdoors. She felt deliciously sated, and she felt exhausted. It was very tempting to pick up on the various outs he'd offered her and let him go alone. If she was too tired, if she didn't think Carly would settle to sleep without her, if a rough ride in a four-wheel-drive held no appeal…

But she'd vowed earlier in the week to jump at any chance to help around here. Searching a creek bed with a flashlight in the dark was definitely something she could do.

"So Gran will put me to bed?" Carly wanted to know.

"That's right, ducks," Kerry said cheerfully.

"Yes," Jac agreed, wondering how many new nicknames her daughter would have at the end of four weeks. She already answered quite happily to Carlz and ducks. "And I'll creep in and kiss you as soon as I get back, beautiful."

"Kiss me now, too."

"Of course."

A few minutes later, Jac had a not-very-suitable pink angora sweater over her T-shirt, and two flashlights in her lap, and she was seated next to Callan in the four-wheel-drive, ready to leave.

He hadn't exaggerated about the rough ride. "Problem is,"

he half yelled above the engine noise, as they bounced and lurched along, "there's a track, but you tend to lose it in the dark."

"Because it's not much of a track, if it's what we rode along today."

"You have a point."

"Ow! And I'm going to have some bruises!" Her shoulder bumped the door.

"Sorry, I should have insisted that this would be way too much fun for you in one day."

"After the fun of the bunyip jumping?"

"But you did like the horse riding and the barbecue, right?"

"I liked the bunyip jumping, too, Callan."

Instinctively, they turned to look at each other at the same moment. His face was shadowed and indistinct in the darkness, but she could see that grin. And she could feel the awareness, the way she'd been feeling it at certain moments for the past four days.

They were both so cautious about it, so full of doubt. It was still only a hint in the air, like the smell of approaching rain or the sound of a church bell across city rooftops. Distant. You had to strain to catch it. The rain might pass over different terrain and never fall. The wind might carry the sound of the bells away.

And they might very easily never act on this…this little zing, this recognition. They might let it go. Smile and move on. It might fade as they got to know each other better, if what they saw on the surface wasn't reflected deeper within.

Or they might get too scared, because things like this rarely stayed simple for long.

For now, it made Jacinda's heart beat faster sometimes, it made her stomach go wobbly, and she watched these things happening in her body and didn't know what to think.

The vehicle lurched again, throwing her in his direction, this time. They jarred against each other, one solid, the other soft. He reached and clamped an arm around her shoulder, working the wheel with one hand. "Going to stop under that tree, and we'll walk the rest."

The awareness hit again, stronger in her because she'd felt his body against hers, harder to resist. It made her breathing go shallow. It started her wondering.

The tree he'd mentioned loomed in the headlights, its trunk the same grayish white as the horse Jac had ridden today. After a couple more lurches and the screech of pro-testing suspension, Callan braked beneath it, switched off the engine and jumped out.

Jacinda followed him, handing him a flashlight.

"See that moon?" he said. "We hardly need these." He tossed it up in his hand and caught it. "We can leave them switched off until we're searching the rocks." Lockie's de-scription of the Game Boy's location had been vague.

They tramped along in the dark, surrounded by the same magical blue and silver shadows and shapes that Jacinda had noticed the other night. They didn't talk. Callan had said as they drove that there might still be wildlife at the water hole at this hour. They always came down at dawn and dusk to drink. "And if we're quiet, we can take a look."

It was good not to talk. Good just to walk along, listening to the sound of their feet on rock and sand, listening to the way Callan's boots creaked, aware of the way he moved with such sure-footed balance and such economy.

In Los Angeles, everyone seemed to talk all the time. They were chained to their cell phones, locked in meetings, constantly updating arrangements, passing messages through secretaries. There was a whole, ever-shifting hierarchy re-garding who Kurt would speak to directly, who he'd call back right away, who he'd fob off on an assistant and who he wouldn't call back at all.

There was a standard repertoire of lies and evasions. *I love the script. This is so fresh. We're in contract negotiations right now. Our marriage is rock solid.* Jacinda had believed way too many of those statements for way too long—believed them when she'd heard them from Kurt, from his staff, from his so-called friends.

She'd had a solitary childhood. Too much silence. First, her parents' quiet, immaculate home, and then her own protective silences, withdrawing to the inner kingdom of her imagination, as she sat squashed into the corner seat in the back of the car while Aunt Peggy drove her cousins around.

When Kurt had brought her into his world, fresh from taking her college degree in English and creative writing, she'd loved the opening of new horizons; she'd loved all the talk, meeting other writers, traveling to Europe, adventures on yachts and ski slopes and horseback. She'd wanted to talk and hadn't needed silence, at first.

But then she'd hit overload, and had discovered that her distant, reluctant parents had given her a positive legacy, after all. Silence could be good sometimes. It could be necessary. It didn't mean that communication disappeared. Sometimes you could understand more about a person when you left some space between all the words.

"We should start looking for the wretched thing," Callan finally said. His voice sounded a little rusty, as if he hadn't wanted to break into the rhythm of their walking. "Here's the water hole just ahead."

"Can we check for kangaroos first?" she asked him on a whisper.

"They're much less scary than bunyips, I promise."

"No, I want to see them drinking. You said we might."

He looked at her, gave a quick nod, grabbed her hand and they crept toward the water hole. It looked still and beautiful, but they crouched behind a rock, waiting and watching for several minutes, and there were no animals there.

Only the two of them.

Jac didn't feel quite human tonight, alone with Callan in the desert. Watching the water hole for signs of movement, she heard his breathing, felt his body like a flannel-and-denim-covered magnet just inches away. A man like this gave masculinity a whole new meaning, reminded a woman that human beings were animals, too.

"We were a bit late for them, I guess," he said, as they walked back toward the ring of barbecue stones in the creek bed. "It's better when there's still some daylight. We'll make a special trip one day. You can bring your camera."

She'd forgotten it on their picnic, today. "That would be great. Could we get up extra early and come at dawn? I just love the light and the air then."

"We can climb Mount Hindley, watch the sunrise, make breakfast over the fire in the creek. Would that be good?"

"Oh, it would be wonderful!"

He gave her a look. They still hadn't switched their flash-lights on. "You sure you're from L.A.?"

"Last time I checked."

"You're supposed to like shopping malls better than water holes, aren't you?"

"I like new things." She thought about it for a moment. "No, that's not right. That sounds like I am talking shopping malls." She tried again. "I like being made to see things in a new way. Like dawn."

"Dawn is new?"

"It's new for me. In L.A. dawn means you stayed out late at a party, or you had to set the alarm early for a flight. If you do see the sunrise, you only see it through glass. You don't smell it, or feel the dew falling on your skin. Here, dawn is…yes, new. It notches my senses up higher, makes me aware. And writers need that. Writers—" She stopped.

There was an old, fallen eucalyptus tree lying on the creek

bed at this point. Its trunk was as big as a concrete culvert pipe, as hard and smooth as iron. Without taking his eyes from her face, Callan leaned his lower back against the curved wood as if the two of them had all the time in the world. He put his flashlight down on the tree trunk beside him, tested its balance for a moment, then let it go.

"Tell me about writers," he prompted.

But Jacinda shook her head and closed her eyes against the idea. "Doesn't matter."

"No, it was important," Callan insisted. "I was interested. Say it."

She faced him, ignoring the invitation in his body language that told her to lean against the horizontal trunk, too. Those bells of awareness weren't so distant or so faint, now. The breeze had carried the sound this way and it was clearer, much closer. But she still had the freedom to ignore the bells, if she wanted.

"I don't know if I'm a writer anymore, that's all," she said. "I think it's gone. Was it ever really there, I wonder?"

"Hey, you made a living at it."

"I had an ear for dialogue, and I could make those crazy soap-opera plot twists semibelievable when I put the right words into the characters' mouths. Was it ever more than that? If it was, I can't remember." She laughed, moved a little closer to him, although she was barely aware of it, and reached her hand out to the tree trunk. It wasn't white or gray, it was silver, and scoured to satin by years of sun and wind. "I have this novel somewhere," she confessed. "Not finished. Miles from finished. A few early chapters and some notes, and snatches of dialogue from a couple of big scenes later on."

"Was it any good?"

"Listen to you, asking me something like that!" She laughed and leaned her hip against the wood. They were like two strangers propped at a bar, trading life stories with loosened tongues.

"It's a really naive question, isn't it?" he said. "Sorry."

"No, no, it's not naive. Well, I guess it is. But it's good naive. No one in L.A. would ever ask that question because of course I'm going to say it's good. I'm trying to sell it, aren't I? I'm going to put the right spin on it, package it into a sound bite. Do you know there are people in the industry there who can talk up a project so well that they get development money for script after script even when they've never actually written a word?"

"They're the ones who sound like they're not writers."

"Truth is, Callan, I have no idea if my novel is any good. I have no idea if it's important. Finishable. Remotely saleable. I just have no idea."

"But you must have known, once."

"I think it's been dying inside me for a long time."

"But you think dawn in the North Flinders Ranges might bring it back."

She shook her head again.

"Yes." He rolled his body ninety degrees so that they faced each other. "Because that's where this started. You were telling me why you loved our dawn, and why you needed to see new things. Because you're a writer."

"Let's find Lockie's Game Boy."

"You hope you can get it back. Being a writer, I mean." He put his hand on her arm. "You really want to get it back. It's important to you."

"It's not your problem, Callan."

"No, but I can understand—" He stopped suddenly. "No, you're right, it's not my problem."

She knew there was more he wanted to say. Or didn't want to say, but could have said. The words stayed locked inside him, powerful and important in some way.

Stuck.

Too scary.

Her thigh was pushing lightly against his. They weren't pretending anymore. He held her softly, weighing their options as he weighed her in his arms. *Let each other go, or pull tighter? Hey, Jac? What do you want? The same as me? Yes, I know what you want....*

She looked up into his face.

New.

She hadn't known him at all two months ago, and even after the magazine article and the cocktail party, this face had only existed in her memory like a few snapshots and video clips. E-mailing him, she had remembered the first smile of relief he'd given her when he'd realized she wasn't serious about the Outback Wives thing, either, and his quiet good manners the following evening when he'd brought her and Carly the gift and the flowers.

She'd kept his picture from the magazine and, to be honest, she'd looked at it a couple of times. Learned it by heart, along with all the things the picture said about him.

New, but fascinating.

He wasn't smiling. His mouth was flat and closed and smooth. She liked its shape. She loved his eyes, and the lines of his brows and jaw. Above his mouth, she found a small stretch of skin that he'd missed this morning when he'd shaved. She brushed it with the ball of her thumb, the way she'd have brushed a streak of dirt from Carly's face, and it felt rough.

She waited for him to make the next move—it sounded too clinical and cold, putting it like that—but he didn't. He didn't let her go, either, just kept that light hold, and watched her watching him. She could still feel the roughness of the beard stubble on her thumb, long after she'd taken her hand away. The tension built and became unbearable. He bent his head, suddenly, and pushed his forehead against her neck, whooshing out a breath into the soft angora of her sweater.

"Oh, Lord, Jacinda!"

"I want to kiss you," she blurted out, because *someone* had to say it, someone had to take some action.

"I want to kiss you, too."

"So do it. Please?"

He was so tense, she could feel it, every muscle knotted tight enough to hurt. He breathed against her neck this time, then touched his mouth to her skin there, the movement dry and soft. He made a sound deep in his chest, imprinted his lips on her skin once again. They were so warm.

She waited.

For more.

Oh, Lord, this was unbearable.

Wonderful and unbearable.

Why didn't he move?

You might have thought he was holding a grenade with the pin already pulled. They both stood turned to stone…except that stone was never as warm and alive as his body. She couldn't hold on to this any longer; she wanted to force that mouth to move on her neck, to come and find her.

Tilting her jaw, she rubbed her face against him like a cat. She tightened the press of her body, rocked her hips a little. He was aroused. She could feel it. Finally—*finally!*—he moved to find her lips, only brushing them at first, then softening his mouth, tasting her.

"Yes," she said. The word was part of the kiss. "Like this."

It was such a relief to get there at last, such a release. She wrapped her arms around his neck, parted her lips, felt the pleasure spinning through her, tasted the faint notes of peach and vanilla in his mouth. He wanted this, so she didn't disguise her own need, deepened the contact until they were drinking each other and tangling their tongues. She gave him everything with her kiss—thanks and hunger and happiness and hope.

That was what you had to do, at some point. You just had to give yourself to it and wait until afterward to see how it felt, what you wanted next, what the repercussions might be.

Yes, she and Carly were leaving in three and a half weeks, going back to Sydney. Two days after that, they'd fly out of the country, to a future she hadn't begun to work out yet. But none of that was enough of a reason never to kiss this man, never to give or to explore.

She gave some more, slid her hands around and ran them down his back, over the tight curve of his denim-clad backside. She pulled him closer. Mmm. Their legs pressed harder together, and she knew he would feel her breasts, too, not Hollywood huge but neat and nice and female.

Mmm, Callan.

She let the hot mound at the top of her thighs squash against his hardness, the denim of two pairs of jeans diluting the intimacy. Oh, but she wished the denim wasn't there! She wanted his fingers dragging aside the lace edge of her underwear, wanted everything he could do to her, wanted the words he would say, and the convulsive tensing of his whole body.

It was like jumping into the water hole. You started, you ran, you yelled, and you didn't want to stop. She just hadn't expected the idea of stopping to feel so impossible and wrong. She didn't care that the air had started to chill, that the sand would be hard and scratchy and cold, that they might get spied on by mythical bunyips, she just *wanted*.

Him.

The escape.

The heat.

The newness.

How long did it take her to understand that he hadn't traveled toward the same place?

Too long.

He had to drag his mouth and his legs away before she realized, before she sensed the change in him—she could practically hear the squeal of the brakes—and then she felt foolish…and a little too naked…because the zing in the air was more like a force field now. It pushed her away, didn't draw her closer, and he'd already started to apologize before she had a chance to draw her first breath of non-Callan-tasting air.

"I'm sorry. I'm sorry," he said. "I'm so sorry!"

"For what?" She blinked.

"This… I shouldn't have done this." He'd half turned back to the fallen log in a gesture of self-protection, and every angle in his body screamed regret. What didn't he want her to see or know? She already knew he was aroused. So was she. Her body throbbed, her mouth tingled, and she was hot and moist and swollen. It shouldn't be a source of shame for either of them. It was human…normal…wonderful.

"Why, Callan?" She felt too bewildered to keep it from showing. "It was—it was good, wasn't it? Real nice."

Real nice? Sheesh, no wonder she didn't dare call herself a writer anymore! *Real nice* bore as much connection to what she'd felt in his arms as cheap hamburger meat bore to sirloin steak.

"It—it— Yes, it was nice. But it sets up—I shouldn't have done it." He circled around, his actions restless, erratic and unpredictable, like a freshly filled balloon escaping from somebody's grip before they'd knotted the opening. Whoosh. All over the place.

"Kissed me?" she said. "What does it set up? It doesn't set up anything."

In her confusion, she came across as indignant to the point of anger, and way too aggressive. The whole atmosphere between them jarred her spirit. How could the physical connection have simply…evaporated?

"Not anything bad, anyhow," she went on, trying to speak more reasonably. "Please don't think I'm expecting—" She made some vague circles with her hand, not wanting to put her expectations or lack of them into concrete phrasing. She was only here for a few weeks. She hadn't been thinking ahead, nailing down a prescribed pathway.

"I'm sorry," he said again. "I'm not saying you're responsible for any of this."

Any of what?

"I don't know what the problem is, Callan." She said it gently because he looked so troubled.

"Yeah, neither do I." The words came out on a growl. "But whatever it is, it's mine, not yours. Okay?"

"Okay," she echoed obediently. "Um, in that case, thanks for a fabulous kiss. Shall we leave it at that?"

He nodded, but didn't look grateful that she'd let him off the hook. "Best to." His circles around the creek bed grew wider. "We have to find that damned Game Boy," he muttered. "They're going to wonder what's happened to us, up at the house."

I'm wondering what's happened to us, too, Jacinda thought. *And I'm not up at the house. I'm right here. I'm looking right at you, Callan, and I have no idea.*

She didn't join in his search. Or not wholeheartedly, anyway. She was still too confused, didn't know whether she should be burning with mortification, angry with him, or whether all of that would have been an overreaction. He looked as if he felt all of those same emotions on her behalf anyhow. He didn't look happy with himself. Didn't look happy with the entire universe.

He muttered something about Lockie's carelessness…stupid electronic toys…shouldn't ever have let him buy the thing in the first place…kids got spoiled with that stuff.

Then he found it, sitting in what was probably the first

place they should have tried, on a rock near where the horses had stood in the shade. He expressed his relief in a profanity and headed directly for the four-wheel-drive, his strong shoulders hunched as if to keep Jacinda safely away.

They drove back to the homestead, the jolting of the vehicle echoing her jarred confidence. He'd said it wasn't her fault, but that was such a classic line. *It's not you, it's me.* Did anyone ever mean it when they said that?

Wheeling around in the front yard, he eyed the lit-up house with a bull-like glowering stare. "Looks like Mum's still getting the kids to bed."

"Carly gets overtired sometimes, after a long day, and it's hard to settle her down. I hope Kerry's not having trouble with her."

"We're all tired. So please, just forget this ever happened. All of it." He sounded angry, and she didn't understand.

"Do you want us to leave, Callan?"

"What?" His eyes narrowed. "No! Heck, no! That would be even worse." He struggled with himself and she decided that if he was angry, he wasn't angry with her, which made her shaky with relief because the memories of Kurt's veiled, terrorizing anger were still too strong. "Please stay," he said. "If you can. If you can forget tonight."

"I'll try." Then something made her add, touching him on the arm, "But no, Callan, I don't want to forget it. It was—"

"But I do," he cut in.

She didn't have time to cut off her final words. "—so good."

He didn't say anything. Didn't look at her. Just opened the creaky door and climbed out of the vehicle.

Chapter Seven

That night, Jacinda couldn't sleep for thinking about it... thinking about him. The way he'd kissed her. The way he'd turned his back.

It must have been after one in the morning by the time the memories released her body from its prison of sensual awareness, and her mind from circular questions. Even then, she had a restless night and was shocked to see how bright the morning light had grown when she woke up.

Eight-thirty, already?

Carly was long gone. Jac could hear her outside with the boys. Dressing, she heard a car, also, its engine missing some beats as the sound dropped to idling level in the front yard. She could make out an adult male voice that didn't sound like Callan's.

"Oh, that's Pete," Kerry told her a few minutes later, in the kitchen. She stood at the sink, washing fresh eggs and vegetables. "He's one of our local North Flinders people, the

Adnyamathanha. He used to be a stockman here, but he lives at the settlement at Nepabunna, now. He still drops over pretty often to help Callan out."

"Drops over?" Jacinda repeated. "How far is Nepabunna from here?" Callan had mentioned the place, she thought, but she'd gotten the impression it wasn't very near.

Kerry grinned, the same open, wicked grin that genetics had also given to her son. "Just a hop. Around a hundred and fifty kays. Ninety miles to you."

"It's okay. I'm learning to translate distances. And a hundred and fifty kilometers is just a hop?"

"It's practically next door."

"Well, so I've learned a new definition for *next door*, too."

"And it's handy for us that he is that close, because some things are a bit much for me, these days. We take on a couple of seasonals when we're doing a big muster, but when they're not around, it's just Callan and Pete. They're driving out to Springer's Well today, working on a new mustering yard Callan's been wanting to put up, and doing some tagging. Lockie's going with them, I think."

"Oh. Right. Carly will miss him."

Carly and *him* being code for *I* and *Callan*.

He's avoiding me, she decided, *because of last night at the water hole.*

Or else I'm kidding myself to think our kiss was that important to him, even in a negative, let's-forget-it-ever-happened way, and he's just building a mustering yard.

Whatever that was.

Going outside to find Carly several minutes later, she saw that Lockie and the two men were ready to leave. They were taking the chunky four-wheel-drive truck that Jac had seen garaged in a shed, and its rear tray was filled with the pile of heavy fence posts that Callan had warned Jac and Carly away from last week because of the snakes that might be living underneath.

Callan stood on top of the posts, tanned legs braced and broad shoulders working loosely as he casually caught the tools that Pete tossed up to him. He wore sturdy work gloves— possibly as a concession to the snakes—khaki shorts that came halfway down his thighs, heavy boots and the ever-present hat.

He looked so gorgeous like that—so physical, so strong, so much in his element—it made her ache.

Last night made her ache.

He waved at her and she waved back, starting to smile.

Then he turned away.

She stood like a marble statue, rocked by the strength of her response to the sight of him, stomach dropping at the brevity of that wave, hoping none of it showed. He was saying something to Pete, whose full head of white hair contrasted in the sunlight with skin that looked like hot chocolate fudge, dark and shiny.

Callan was definitely avoiding her.

Leaping down from the rear tray, he went around to the driver's side of the vehicle and climbed in, calling Lockie at the same time. "We need to get going, mate." Lockie scrambled into the middle of the front seat, Pete climbed in after him and Callan revved up the engine.

The truck circled out of the yard in the usual boiling mass of dust, bouncing its cargo of fence posts noisily up and down. Pippa and Flick stood in the back like sentinels and barked at the rush of air that increased as the vehicle picked up speed. Carly and Josh ran from the dust, shrieking as if pretending it was chasing them like a monster, up the veranda and into the house.

Callan waved at Jacinda again through the dry, choking curtain. Lockie and Pete did the same, and then they disappeared from sight heading down the track that headed toward the alleged road to Adelaide.

Jacinda's breathing went sharp in her chest and she was shocked at how vulnerable she felt. Because of one kiss? Because it hadn't ended with the promise of more? Because Callan's wave and turn told her he'd meant what he'd said, last night, and the fact that he hadn't stopped to introduce her to Pete only served to emphasize his state of mind?

Or just because she wasn't going to see him all day?

"I'm too emotional. It's just stupid," she muttered, moving aimlessly around the yard as she listened to the ebbing sound of the engine.

But she'd always been this way. She knew it. Could manage to pep talk herself out of it sometimes, if she was really careful about it. Today it might be tough, because there was so much going on inside her. Yesterday, she'd felt so alive. Exhilarated. Proud of herself. She'd jumped into that water hole. She'd heard the echo of her voice thrown back from the rocks like a battle cry.

All of that was still there in this potent mix of feelings, but she didn't know what to do with it, how to match it against Callan and his apparent rejection.

There was more to his reaction than met the eye. She felt sure of it. With time, she would understand and it would be all right.

Give it time, just give it time.

Turning to go back inside the house, the sudden certainty calmed her spirit, gave her direction, but then she hit the shade of the veranda and the certainty ebbed just as suddenly as it had come, the emotional transition as sharp as the physical one between heat and shade.

Callan wasn't Kurt.

Kurt was the king of complex, incomprehensible reactions, shifting layers that you had to peel back and pick apart. Callan was probably as simple and uncomplicated as he seemed. He'd kissed her. He'd defeated that initial impulse of curiosity and chemistry between them. He'd decided that any kind of involvement was a mistake. He'd stopped. He didn't want it to happen again, and he'd told her so.

Get a grip, Jacinda.

In the kitchen, Kerry was kneading bread dough, while Carly and Josh bickered over LEGO in the next room. Josh still acted more protective of his territory than Lockie did. He wasn't quite convinced that Carly's presence at Arakeela Creek was a plus. "I need all the curved bits for my tower," Jac heard him say.

"But I'm making a tower, too."

"I started making my tower, first. You're not old enough for LEGO. Your fingers aren't good enough."

"Yes, they are."

"They're not, and anyway, I started my tower, first."

Kerry and Jac looked at each other, wondering about intervention. "Give it another minute?" Kerry suggested.

"Can you teach me what to do with the bread, while we listen and hold our breath?"

Kerry laughed. "That's about right, isn't it, holding our breath?"

"I wonder why Carly and Lockie do so much better together. He's that much older, I guess, and she's less of a threat to his space."

"More than that." Kerry paused for thought and thumped away at the elastic ball of dough, flinging it with some violence onto a floured wooden board. The nearest store was several hours away, so if you wanted fresh bread out here, you made it yourself. When Jac smelled it baking, every second day, she practically drooled.

"Josh is like Callan, I think," Kerry said after a moment. "He works hard to get his life just the way he wants it, and then he doesn't like it to change."

"That's Callan?"

"It's a part of Callan." Kerry paused in her thumping and

began to knead, pushing the dough away from herself so that it stretched into an oval, then folding it toward herself again and rotating it ninety degrees. The fluid efficiency of the movement said that she'd done this thousands of times before. "Which makes him sound too rigid, doesn't it?" she added, shooting a sharp look at Jac.

"I wouldn't say he was rigid, from what I've seen of him," she answered carefully.

"No, he's not. I'm glad you can see that. He just…needs time with some things."

They were both silent for a moment, and the air felt a little too heavy, too full of meaning. Kerry seemed extra alert to nuances today, watchful somehow.

Watchful of me. Watchful of Callan and me, and the way I react to his name.

Jac didn't know if that was a good thing, or not. What had Kerry thought about the two of them taking so long to retrieve Lockie's Game Boy last night? What had she sensed in the air between them?

"Want to have a go at this, then?" the older woman said eventually.

"Can I? Will I ruin it? I've never made bread before. Should I thump, or knead?"

"I've done enough thumping. It releases the gluten in the flour, makes the bread lighter and more elastic. And it's good for working out your aggression."

On cue, they heard Carly's voice rise in an angry scream. "You did that on purpose!"

"Somebody else is working out some aggression, I think," Kerry drawled. She strode out to the children, the firm rhythm of her feet signaling a no-nonsense approach. "Joshie, we need to work this out," Jacinda heard.

She began tentatively kneading, thinking that Kerry was probably the best equipped to handle the situation, in this instance. Kneading bread dough was tougher than it looked, however.

Push, fold, quarter turn. Push, fold, quarter turn. Tougher than it looked, but it felt good. The dough was like a baby's skin, satiny smooth and warm from its first rising. The dusting of flour slipped across it like talcum powder on that same baby's tush. Push, fold, quarter turn. Physical, creative, satisfying. Human beings had been doing it for thousands of years.

Kerry and Josh discussed LEGO towers in the next room—the possibility of two towers, of coordinated efforts to make a whole village of towers, square ones as well as curved, of Carly being the assistant and Josh helping her with bits that were too fiddly for her fingers. Eventually hurt feelings were soothed and territorial impulses reined in.

"We'll see how long it lasts," Kerry drawled again when she returned.

"And that's what Callan was like?" She couldn't help talking about him, despite what Kerry might think.

"Actually, no, he was pretty good at sharing," the older woman answered. "They're close in age, him and his sister. Nicky's only fifteen months younger, so he never had to adjust to her as something new. As far as he was concerned, she was always there."

"And she lives in Adelaide, now? Is that right?"

"A couple of hours north of there, the Clare Valley. She studied agriculture and married a farmer, but he has vineyards, not cattle."

"You must have found it hard when she moved so far away."

"To be honest, Clare was better than I'd hoped. I was afraid she might end up in Sydney or Perth!"

"Still, is it hard to keep in close touch?"

"Not with a bit of effort. We e-mail a lot, and take turns

to phone each other every week. Sundays usually. Tonight it's my turn. I send her drawings from the boys and she sends me magazine articles and newspaper clippings and we gossip about those. Silly things like celebrity marriages. We're big fans of Prince Frederik and Princess Mary! But I'd communicate with Nicky by carrier pigeon if I had to. I don't think it really matters what you talk about, either, if it helps you stay close. And I'm getting my first grand-daughter in two months! I'll be going down to stay with them, then."

"That's wonderful."

Except that Jacinda was a little regretful that she'd nudged the conversation away from Callan. She had an itchy, secret urge to talk about him that she couldn't remember feeling since her teens, when telling her friends, "I don't even *like* Matt Walker," had given her the delectable excuse to say a certain male classmate's name out loud.

"If Callan doesn't like change, we're probably imposing on you even more than I'd realized, with our visit," she said after another moment of silence.

"I shouldn't have said it. I'm not putting it the right way." Another pause. "I'm thinking about Liz, not about you and Carly." The words came out in a rush, as if Kerry might regret anything she said too slowly.

"Oh, okay."

Kerry divided the ball of dough in two and began shaping each piece into a log, ready for the greased loaf tins she had waiting on the countertop. "You see, thinking about the future, about the boys, about how lonely Callan must some-times feel—how lonely I *know* he feels—I worry that any woman who's not Liz is going to scare him too much. He's never been any good at asking for help. Which means he's going to have to get past the fear on his own, and I'm not sure how he'll do it. Or if he can."

She opened the oven door and it squeaked. After putting the tins on a lower shelf, she spread a damp dish towel on the top shelf. Jacinda knew that in the moist, tepid space of the oven, the loaves would rise to a high dome shape over the next hour. Squeak went the oven door as Kerry closed it again. Neither she nor Jacinda had spoken.

It's my turn, though.

Talking like this, in the middle of routine household chores, made it easier to tackle tough subjects, she decided. When you were silent as you gathered the right words, other activity was still going on and the silence didn't seem so difficult.

"I think…I wonder if…" she tried after a moment. "I think he's stronger than that, Kerry." She thought about what he'd said yesterday about yelling and jumping to get rid of the fear. He had his own strategies. They might not be the ones suggested in the hospital leaflets—he didn't *want* them to be the ones in the hospital leaflets—but they were strategies, all the same.

Kerry looked eager, as if she itched to talk about Callan, too. "Has he said something to you? Has he talked much about Liz?"

"Not much. A little. He's said—"

"No, please!" She warded off Jac's words with her hands. "Don't tell me what he said. I'm not asking for that. But I do worry."

"Of course you do." Jacinda was a mother, just as Kerry was. She knew. "But I think Callan at least does know what he's fighting in himself." He'd talked about the *fear,* and this made more sense now. The fear of change. The fear, if Kerry was right, of there being no one in the whole world to match Liz. "And you know, Kerry, when you understand the enemy, that's always an advantage."

"True. He is a fighter. In his own way. *Always* in his own way!" She laughed, and ran water into the electric jug, which she then placed on the countertop and plugged in.

"Yeah, I've noticed that, too."

"The boys do him a lot of good. Lockie, now that he's getting older."

"It's funny," Jac said. "Before I had Carly, I always assumed I'd be the big influence on her. That I'd make her who she was. And of course I am doing that. But I think she's changed me more than I've changed her. I never realized that would happen, that kids had such, oh, *influence*. Kerry, does that make sense?"

"It does."

They talked about it a little more—kids and change, Callan and Liz. Nothing earth-shattering. Some of it a little tentative, still. But nice.

"Are you having coffee?" Kerry asked. "It'll only be instant." The electric jug was about to boil.

"Instant is fine. I'd love a cup." Jac got the coffee down from the shelf while Kerry found two mugs and poured the boiling water in, leaving plenty of room for Jacinda's big dollop of milk. Kerry had filled the jug just an inch or two higher than she needed, and rather than waste the precious water, she poured it in to soak the mixing bowl she'd used for the bread dough. Jac made a mental note to take more care with saving water from now on. Her shower, this morning, for example...

"Is it a pain in the butt, doing that?" she asked suddenly.

Kerry looked surprised. "Doing what?"

"Thinking about saving water all the time. Every drop. Pouring the dregs from the electric jug into the dough bowl. Piping the shower and laundry water out to the garden so it gets used twice."

"I guess I don't think about it, it's such second nature. It's part of living here, and I love living here."

"Teach me, won't you? Don't let me do the wrong thing, here, without thinking. Make sure you teach me." All at once, for some reason, the words meant more. She wasn't just talking about saving water. She was talking about Callan.

Teach me about Callan.
Don't let me do the wrong thing with Callan.

If Kerry understood, she didn't refer to the fact directly. Instead, she poured milk into the two mugs, gave Jacinda's the extra zap in the microwave that she liked. Handing Jac the hot mug, she took a big breath.

"Callan and Liz were too alike," she said, at the faster pace she seemed to use when she wasn't quite comfortable with what she was saying. Her voice had dropped, too, in case there was any chance of Josh listening in the other room. "I don't want to say that, because it sounds critical. I loved Liz. I was so happy that Callan had found someone like her, someone who belonged here and belonged in his life. If I could have, I would have gone in her place. People say that. But I really would have gone in her place."

"I know you would."

"They were the kind of couple that grows together. Like two trees, the way trees shape each other sometimes. They would even have looked alike, after fifty years. She was the kind of wife a man should have for fifty years. She was so safe for him, though. It made it even harder when she died." She looked across the top of her coffee mug, her expression appealing for Jac to understand. "Does that make any sense at all?"

"You mean, if their marriage had been more of a challenge…?"

"Yes. Callan would have been equal to a more challenging marriage. And it might have left him…" She slowed and stopped, stuck for the right words. "Better prepared." She shook her head impatiently. "It still sounds wrong. I can't put it right. I can't say it without it sounding like I'm criticizing him, or her, or their marriage."

"No, but I understand."

And I wonder what it is that you're not saying. I'm not

*used to this, Kerry. I haven't had a woman like you in my life
before, to talk to. I lost my mother too soon, and I was never
close enough to my aunt, so, no, I'm not used to this.*

*Are you telling me that I could be good for Callan, even
if I'm nothing like Liz? Because I'm nothing like Liz? Do you
want me to be a part of his awakening from grief, Kerry? Or
are you warning me away because I could never truly
belong? I'm only here a few more weeks....*

Despite her best hopes, despite the creative act of helping
with the bread, despite playing with Carly and Josh, and
working in the garden, Jac stayed restless and uncertain and
churned up inside all day.

At four, she needed more air and space than the homestead
and its garden could provide. "I thought I'd go for a walk
down to the creek, Kerry, if that's all right with you," she told
Callan's mother. "I'll take Carly with me."

"Leave her if you'd rather," Kerry answered. "She's
quite happy with her drawing, and I'm making them a
snack in a minute."

"Thanks. All right, then. I will leave her."

Not knowing how long it would take her to walk this restlessness away, Jac was happy that Kerry had suggested leaving Carly behind. She really wanted to stride, breathe, think
uninterrupted thoughts. She drank a big glass of water, found
her hat and sunglasses and set out, following the fence line
down to the wide swathe of dry creek bed, the same way they
had gone yesterday on horseback.

When she reached the creek, however, she turned north
along it instead of south, wanting to explore some new
ground. Keeping to the creek bed itself, she covered the
distance slowly because the sand was deep in some places,
uneven in others, and there were stretches of rock and
smoothly worn river stones as well.

The late afternoon was pleasantly still—cool in the shade

and hot in the sun. She heard birds overhead, and disturbed a couple of lizards. If there were snakes, they had sensed the vibration of her footfalls and disappeared before she caught sight of them, as Callan had said they would.

She didn't want to think about Callan.

"Five days down, twenty-three to go," she said aloud to the eucalyptus trees. She had to make some decisions about the future. At least examine the possibilities.

It was frightening how little pull she felt toward home. Pull? More like dread. Running through a mental list of California friends as she'd done many times before, she couldn't think of a single one who would risk alienating Kurt by taking her side, or by helping her in any way. They'd support her with lip service as they'd done since her separation from Carly's father, but nothing more.

Lip service wasn't enough.

And who did she have farther afield?

She thought about her two brothers, and her father, back east, and knew she'd let those relationships slide more than she should have done. She could have phoned or e-mailed more often, over the past few years. She should have made more of an effort to see her brothers for holidays.

It wasn't enough of an excuse to say that they hadn't met her halfway, even though it was true. If she'd worked harder at it, kept pushing, giving something to the relationship, they surely would have seen some value in getting closer to their little sister after a while. Their kids were almost grown, but teenagers might have loved a cute baby cousin.

She thought about the way Callan and Kerry had stayed so close yet still managed to give each other space, thought about the love in Kerry's voice when she'd talked about Nicky hundreds of miles away, her coming baby, all the ways they found to communicate, and the determination when Kerry had said that she would contact Nicky by carrier pigeon if there was no other way. Families didn't just chug along like magic, maintenance-free engines. They had to be worked at like anything else.

Jacinda had never made a conscious decision that working on her relationship with her brothers was important to her but she could make that decision now.

Was it too late?

If she'd had a pen and some postcards in her pocket, she would have scribbled greetings to her brothers on the spot. If she'd had a car, she would have jumped into it and zipped to the nearest—

Store.

What "nearest store"?

It was well over a hundred miles away.

Still, the idea of making contact, even with such a trivial, tentative first step as an e-mail or a postcard from outback Australia, stayed with her and felt important. She'd have to ask Callan. Maybe he or Kerry had some cards. Or maybe they were planning a trip into Leigh Creek soon—they did that fairly often, she thought—so she could buy some, to replace the ones she'd left in Sydney in a panic. She felt more confident about being able to write postcards, now.

But how did the mail plane work? Where did you get the postage stamps? Definitely, she needed to talk to Callan.

And it was probably about time to turn around and start heading back.

The journey back along the creek bed seemed farther than she would have thought, and she realized that she'd lost track of time while she'd been thinking about her future and her family. The color of the sky had begun to change. If she didn't soon reach the line of fence marching at right angles into and across the creek, she might miss it in the fading light.

No, here it was, at last, just visible. In the distance, as she climbed through it and up out of the creek bed, she saw one of those familiar trails of dust. It marked the track that led from the main road to the homestead, which meant it had to be Callan, Lockie and Pete returning from their long day's work just in time for a good wash before the evening meal.

Her heart lifted and lurched at the same time.

Callan.

Who'd kissed her last night and then turned away.

Callan, who got his life the way he wanted, and then resisted change, which was pretty much the opposite of what Jac needed to do. Her life wasn't the way she wanted it, right now, but changing it was easier said than done.

Thinking about this and not about where she was going— it was getting hard to see the detail of the terrain, despite the huge yellow full moon rising—she tripped on a loose rock and instinctively grabbed the top line of fence wire for support.

It was barbed.

In the front seat of the truck, Lockie slept, his head lolling onto Pete's shoulder. At some point, Pete had lifted the head gently and placed his own felt bushman's hat there for a makeshift pillow. Callan himself was tired enough to consider that the squashed hat looked darned comfortable. The dogs were flung out on the now-empty rear tray sleeping, too, and when Pete lowered Lockie's head back down, he didn't even stir. He'd worked well today, and he'd learned some new skills.

At the wheel, Callan blinked several times to keep himself alert. His eyes felt gritty from the dust and his head ached from squinting in the bright light for hours, even though he'd worn sunglasses. They'd made some good progress on the new mustering yard, but they'd need several more days yet. Pete wasn't as strong or quick as he used to be. And they might run out of supplies before they were done. He had a new shipment to pick up sometime this week in Leigh Creek.

Turning in front of the homestead, he felt a surge of well-being at the sight of the lights, and his aching muscles began to relax. There would be dinner waiting. He might have a beer with the meal. Jacinda could cook, he'd discovered. Maybe she would have convinced Mum to let her do so today and they'd get to taste some new California creation or an Asian stir-fry. His stomach growled in anticipation, and he knew a shower would feel pretty good, too.

Even better than the meal and hot, clean water, there would be people. Mum, Josh, Carly…and Jac. His treacherous heart jumped sideways as he thought about her, but he couldn't dwell on the reaction right now. Pete was pushing his big hand against Lockie's slumped shoulder.

"Wake up, little mate," Pete said. "Dinner's up."

"You staying for it, Pete?" Callan asked him, as Lockie opened bleary eyes.

The older man shook his head. "Headin' home."

"Come in for a bit."

"Do that, I won't get goin' again. Have to stay all night."

"I already told you to do that."

Pete shook his head again. "Gettin' home. Got some things to check up on."

"Well, bring your gear tomorrow and stay tomorrow night."

"Maybe." He was already heading for his car, with around two hours of nighttime driving still ahead of him, and the return trip first thing in the morning. He was a tough one.

Lockie had woken up. "I'm starving!"

"Let's see what's cooking."

Pippa and Flick followed them onto the veranda and found the fresh food and water Callan's mother had already put out for them.

Inside the house, there was a fabulous aroma coming from the kitchen, but no sign of food on the table, which surprised Callan a little. Mum would have heard the truck. She would have known how ready they'd be for the meal. Josh and Carly had had baths and were prowling around in their nightwear, looking almost as hungry as Callan felt. His mother appeared with bathwater damp on her shirt and he asked, "Should I set the table?"

"I'm getting worried, Callan. Jacinda's not back."

"Not back?" His heart did another of those weird lurches that risked becoming a habit. "Where did she go?"

"For a walk, two and a half hours ago. Longer."

"What did she take? How long was she planning to be gone? It's almost dark out there!"

"I know. I thought she'd be gone half an hour. I'm not even sure she had water with her."

"Feed the kids," he said, energy surging back into him and hunger forgotten. "I'll get the dogs, and we'll head to the creek on foot to look for her. I'm not going to treat this as a crisis just yet."

"I'll do that for you!" his mother answered. "I like Jacinda a lot, and she's no fool…." She touched his arm, as if it was important that he know how she felt about Jacinda.

"No, she's not," he agreed.

And I've lived here all my life. I'm not going to panic because a grown woman is an hour late back to the house.

"But, Callan, she has no idea what this country can do to people who make mistakes."

"I know. Listen, if I'm not back in half an hour, get Moss saddled for me."

In the space of two minutes, he'd packed water and a couple of snacks into a backpack, as well as the jacket he'd found hanging in her room. He'd also packed the first-aid kit and a long roll of bandage.

Watching as he dropped it into the backpack, little pajama-clad Carly got a stricken look on her face. On top of hunger, fatigue and his own lurking fear, her frightened reaction didn't help.

"Where is Mommy? Why isn't she back?" she said.

Chapter Eight

The barbed wire had pierced and torn the skin on Jacinda's palm in four places. It stung and throbbed, and the remaining half mile to the homestead felt like ten times that distance as she thought about taking each cautious step in the dark. She didn't want to trip again. She needed better shoes. Proper hiking boots or something. And she shouldn't have stayed out so long, even though she'd needed all that time to think.

I'll try e-mailing Andy and Tom tonight, on Callan's computer, she decided as she started walking again. She then spent the next five minutes of carefully trod distance trying to work out when she'd last done so. Could it really be more than two years?

The dogs started barking when she still had two hundred yards of fence to follow. They sounded overexcited and ready for action, but surely they didn't think she was a stranger?

Someone must have let them through the gate because they came at her out of the darkness with a speed that frightened her, still letting out high, urgent sounds. She saw a circle of light behind them, bouncing in time to someone's stride, then heard Callan's voice.

"Jac, is that you?" He raised the flashlight in her direction.

"Yes, and please tell Pippa and Flick that I'm friendly!"

He whistled at the dogs as he came closer and they ran to heel beside him, panting and turning their faces up to him as if they expected a reward. "Yes, guys, well done, you found her," he told them.

"Found me?" Jac reached them, while Callan was still bending down to the dogs.

"Please don't scare us like that again, okay?" He pointed the flashlight beam away from her and toward the ground, but it had already shone into her face and dazzled her vision and she had spots before her eyes.

"Scare you?" She blinked, covered her closed eyes with her hand for a moment, but her vision was slow to clear and, when she opened them again, she could still barely see him. She could sense him, though. That big body, that aura of dust and hard work. "Callan, I wasn't lost or anything." She peered at him. It was the first time they'd talked all day. "Were you worried?"

Stupid question. He didn't look worried, she saw at last as the spots faded. He looked angry, slapping the flashlight in a slow rhythm against his hard, denim-clad thigh and narrowing his eyes. "How much water did you have with you?" he demanded.

"I had a big drink before I left."

"And did you take a jacket? Even a cotton sweater?"

"I only went for a quick breath of fresh air." She began to guess that these weren't adequate answers.

"And you were gone nearly three hours."

"I know. I was thinking about a few things. Time got away from me a bit, and I didn't turn back along the creek as soon as

I should have. I was a bit shocked to see that the light was going." Instinctively, she touched the sunglasses on top of her head, useless now. She had her baseball cap folded and stuffed into the back pocket of her jeans, equally useless once the sun went.

"Sunglasses aren't a survival kit."

He poked at them with a rigid finger, pushing them farther back into her hair—a gesture that could have been tender in other circumstances, but wasn't this time. It brought him closer, though, and she remembered with every sense and every nerve ending how she'd felt in his arms last night.

"If you'd twisted your ankle on a tree root and had to sit there all night until we found you," he went on, "you would have been happy in short sleeves without a drop to drink or a morsel of food, with the temperature dropping into the forties, is that right?"

"Well…"

"People who get lost or hurt out here…people who don't have the right gear…people whose engines break down and they go looking for help instead of staying with their vehicle…they die, Jacinda, and it doesn't take that long, either." His voice rasped and dropped deeper. "This country doesn't forgive mistakes."

"Shoot, I didn't think, did I?" she realized aloud.

He whooshed out a sigh, bent down once again to Pippa and gave her a rough pat, his strong hand splayed out in her thick fur. The way he marshaled his emotions was almost palpable. His shoulder muscles moved under his shirt. "I guess I never spelled it out to you," he said, after a moment. "Too busy giving you a crash course in snake behavior."

"Which I very much appreciated!" She took a breath. "You're right, I should have taken water and a jacket. Shouldn't have needed a crash course in that kind of basic common sense. And I did grab on to the barbed wire, just now, so common sense has definitely deserted me this evening."

"We've both been a bit…yeah…off beam today," he growled, and she knew he was thinking about last night.

"See, I've spiked my hand." She blurted out, then grabbed the flashlight from him, pointed the beam at her palm and showed him.

"We'll need to take care of that as soon as we get back to the house. Are you up to date on your tetanus shot?"

"Lord, I have no idea! No, wait a minute." She remembered that she'd had one when Carly was a baby, as part of a routine health check with her doctor. "Yes, I would be." Thank goodness, one area in which she could impress him as faintly sensible. "Have I upset Kerry, too?" she added, thinking about her earlier conversation with Callan's mother.

Liz would never have let something like this happen. Gone off without water, food or clothing? Never!

She had belonged here, body and soul.

And yet Kerry considered this to have been a mixed blessing.

"She was pretty concerned when Pete and Lockie and I got back before you did," Callan said. "She couldn't tell me what you'd taken with you." He was silent for a moment. "Sorry I was angry. We didn't know where to start looking, didn't want to worry Carly."

"Is she worried?"

"Mum's with her," he hedged. "Dinner's on the table."

"She *is* worried. Oh, hell!" She began to stride back to the house, and Callan and the dogs went with her.

"Best way for you to learn, I guess," Callan said.

"You're right. I'll know next time."

"Forget it. Forget that I was angry, please. It didn't help."

"We're both tired."

And what's the bet that Carly has a sleepwalking episode tonight? Jac added to herself inwardly.

Carly rushed into her arms back at the homestead, as soon as they saw each other. "Mommy, I thought a snake bit you. I thought you were lost."

"It was my fault, sweetheart. I was fine, but I should have let Kerry know exactly where I'd be, and I should have turned back sooner. I won't make that mistake again."

"Gran was worried about you."

"I know she was."

Pressed against Carly's warm little back, Jac's injured palm throbbed. The decision to contact Andy and Tom felt like less of a positive step than it had seemed a short while ago, and when she asked after dinner if she could use Callan's computer to send some e-mails, she sat in front of a blank screen for too long before anything would come.

Finally, with her left hand crisscrossed in fresh Band-Aids and still smarting after the run-in with the barbed-wire fence, she typed, Hi, Andy! Guess what? I'm in Australia! Visiting a friend at a place called Arakeela Creek. With Carly, of course. Don't run to get a map. It won't be marked. Even though it's the size of Rhode Island. How are the kids? How's Dad? You can reach me at this e-mail address until May 13. Let me know how you're doing. Your sister, Jacinda.

Just in case he'd forgotten her name?

She looked at the words on the screen. She thought about all the other things she could have said. Talked about Kurt? Apologized for not keeping in better contact? At least re-drafted it into some slightly more complex and grammatical sentences? *With Carly, of course* had no verb.

A familiar feeling of panic and dread began to flutter inside her, making Kerry's fabulous chicken casserole sit uneasily in her stomach, and she knew that for now, these few stilted phrases would have to be enough. She hit Send and Receive, then copied the sent message and pasted it into a new one addressed to Tom, cut the *How's Dad?* sentence and replaced it with Any special news?

"And I used to call myself a writer," she muttered.

When she hit Send and Receive again, she got a system message telling her that the message to Andy had bounced. Checking again after a wait of less than a minute, she was told that Tom's had bounced, also. In the long interval since she'd last made contact this way, both her brothers' e-mail addresses had changed.

Coming in to his office to see if she needed any help with his computer and e-mail system, Callan could see her disappointment, she knew, even though she tried to hide it.

"Do you want to try calling them instead?" he asked. He looked to be fresh out of the shower. The ends of his hair were still wet against his neck and his tanned skin looked smooth. He smelled of soap and steam.

She thought about the time difference, and said, "Too early in the morning there." It was eight in the evening here and Carly was already asleep, which meant six-thirty in the morning on the U.S. east coast. Then she added more honestly, "And anyway, over the phone I don't think I'd know what to say."

"That's too bad." He looked sincerely disappointed.

In her?

For her?

In her brothers?

Either way, it made her determined not to give up so easily. "But would you have any postcards, or something?" she asked. "I'd like Andy and Tom to at least know where I am, in case…well, they don't often get in touch, but you never know."

"I have to head into Leigh Creek later in the week to pick up some supplies. You can get postcards there, and anything else you need. Have a think about it. Your own brand of

shampoo, or any food that Carly likes that we don't have.
We'll bring her with us. It's a bit of a drive, but we can have
some stops along the way."

"Thanks," she said. "That'd be great."

And if Carly was with them, Jac surely wouldn't spend
the whole drive remembering how it felt to kiss him, the way
she was doing now….

They didn't quite know what to do or say next, how to end
the conversation. Callan picked up some unopened letters
from a big pile on the corner of the desk and let them drop
back down. Was he planning to apologize again for getting
angry at her about her poorly planned walk? She didn't want
that. Nor did she want any more awkward references to last
night.

It was gone, finished, done with.

She had to keep telling herself that.

"You've got quite a pile of mail there," she said quickly,
to deflect the subject onto something…anything…safer.

"Forwarded from the magazine," he answered, and only
then did she realize what the letters were.

From women.

Hoping Callan was "sincerely looking for an Outback
Wife."

Looking closer, she saw that all of them were still sealed.
"You haven't opened them?"

"I've opened a ton of 'em. And I've replied. I was
e-mailing a couple of them for a while, but that's tailed off.
These are just the letters from the past two mail flights, which
I…uh…haven't gotten to, yet."

"My goodness! You need a secretary!"

He grinned, and some of that easy, familiar humor between
them came creeping back. "Are you applying for the position?"

So they looked at the letters together, and she helped him
with his replies. Kerry brought them each a mug of tea and

offered her opinion of a woman who stressed the importance of Callan being "visually literate."

"Whatever that means! Give her a discouraging answer!"

"Want to draft some replies, Mum?" Callan offered.

"Oh, no, thank you! I'll leave you to it!" She quickly disappeared.

In the next letter they opened, a woman announced that if she and Callan became involved, she was "prepared to live in the wilderness for up to two years before we renegotiate a move to a more urban environment."

This one received one of the polite "Thanks for your interest, but I'm not looking for anything right now" replies that Callan had become impressively fluent with by now.

A few letters later, a girl called Tracey "hadn't had much luck with men, because I'm shy, which I know is my fault. I have a good family—two brothers and a sister, my mum and dad—and we're close, but I'd move away from Ballarat for the right man. I'd want to take things slow, though. I think marriage, or any relationship, is too important to get wrong because you haven't thought it through."

"She sounds nice," Jacinda said. "You should write her a good letter."

"She looks nice, too," answered Callan, showing her a simple snapshot of a slightly chunky woman of around twenty-five or so, with a tomboy smile and light brown hair.

Jac leaned closer to see the picture better, and her arm brushed Callan's. Turning instinctively, she found him looking at her and could read his face like a book.

She looks nice, but right now you're the woman I want. It's too complicated so I'm not going to give in to it, but you're definitely the woman I want.

"Maybe we've done enough secretarial work for tonight," he said on an uncomfortable growl. "I'll write something back to her tomorrow."

Jac nodded. "This is more words than I've strung together in—well, a while."

Frustrated, she knew she needed something more, something other than drafting polite lines to people that neither she nor Callan really knew—and, yes, she included her brothers in that. A need was building inside her, demanding release and expression. It made her scared and it made her twitchy, and she'd only ever known one way to get the feeling under control.

She needed to…really, genuinely, seriously…write.

"I'm going to check on Carly," she told him, even though she knew Carly was asleep. She wanted to see if by some faint chance she had writing materials in a forgotten outer sleeve of one of her suitcases.

"Callan, would you have a legal pad or a notebook I could use?" Jacinda looked a little tense about asking the question.

A lot tense, in fact. Meeting in front of the waistband of her jeans, her fingers zipped back and forth as she rubbed her nails together, making a buzzing, clicking sort of sound that gave out way too much of a clue as to her state of mind. She didn't seem to notice that she was doing it.

"Even just some scrap paper?" she added, as if she only had a shopping list to write.

"One of the boys' old school notebooks?" Callan suggested. He pretended he hadn't noticed the tension, or the sound and movement of the fingernails, even though his gaze kept pulling in that direction. "They get a new set every year and some of the ones from last year still have a lot of blank pages. Would that work?"

"It'd be great."

She looked relieved that she'd managed to ask the question, that he hadn't asked too many questions of his own in response, and that she'd gotten an easy answer. Her hands

dropped to her sides, but the thick denim waistband of the
jeans stood out a little from her tightly drawn in stomach,
showing the weight she must have lost in recent months, and
Callan kept looking there, at the place where the clicking fingernails had been, for just a second or two too long.

"Let me dig one out," he said, dragging his eyes upward,
trying to forget how clearly he'd pictured himself seated in
a squashy armchair. He would have grabbed her as she went
by. He would have wrapped his arms around that willowy
waist of hers, and hugged the tension out of those drawn-in
stomach muscles.

He wanted to tell her to put the weight back on so that she
filled out the lean lines of the jeans. He wanted to apologize
again about coming down too hard on her tonight about going
for a walk with no water. He hadn't exaggerated the potential danger in this country, but he could have skipped the
anger, because the anger was far more about…something
else.

He wanted to thank her for helping him with the letters.
He knew it must have been hard at first, despite the way she'd
relaxed into it. Yes, and he wanted to tell her exactly how he
came to understand so much regarding her tension and fear
about the whole writing thing, even though he'd hadn't tried
to write a poem or a story since high school.

"I'm sorry, if it's too much trouble at this hour it can wait
until morning," she said quickly, ready to backtrack on the
whole writing idea at the slightest excuse.

"It's fine."

True, he was about to head off for bed. It already felt
overdue after the long day working on the new mustering
yard with Lockie and Pete, and the heart-pumping but mercifully short-lived interval when he'd feared that Jacinda
might be lost. But he was still racked with guilt and regret
about what had happened down at the water hole last night.

They should have simply been tracking down Lockie's Game Boy and getting the hell out of there, instead of watching for wildlife and exchanging life stories and—

Yeah.

Guilt and regret and awareness rushed through him, none of it helped by having sat with her in his office writing polite rejection letters to other women for almost an hour.

It wasn't Jacinda's fault.

It was totally, utterly him.

Had he managed to get that across to her? Could finding an old schoolbook of Lockie's for her, without asking her what she wanted to use it for, in any way make up for the way he'd turned away from her down at the creek, and then again back at the house? Make up for the way he'd barely been able to look at her this morning, hadn't introduced her to Pete, and was almost sinfully grateful that she'd slept in so that they hadn't needed to confront each other over breakfast? For the way he'd been angry at her tonight, the moment that first flood of relief at her safety had ebbed away?

Why the heck had he let last night's kiss happen at all? He'd known it would end that way.

Only maybe he hadn't known.

Maybe he'd been kidding himself all along.

In his office, he dug out the cardboard file box where he kept the boys' old schoolbooks. He didn't know why he hung on to them. Because it was easier than throwing them out? He wouldn't have said he was the nostalgic type, and yet he did have a problem with change, didn't he?

Mum had talked about it a couple of times since Liz's death. Mum's attitude had been helpful rather than accusing, but there'd been the hint of criticism all the same. He'd never wanted to go away to school, as a twelve-year-old, and it had taken him months—had taken hooking up with Dusty and Brant—for him to settle into Cliffside.

And now here were these stupid schoolbooks he put away every year like a pack rat, because something inside him wouldn't allow them to get thrown away.

He took out a stack of them and flipped through, finding worksheets about the ocean and weather, and words with *sh* in them that gave him a little twist inside because of the fact that Liz, who would have been so proud and so interested, had never seen them.

Was that why he kept them? Some stupid, illogical, subconscious, impossible belief that if he kept them long enough, her benign spirit would pay a visit and take a look?

Brrr, shake it off, Callan.

How much working space did Jacinda need? He didn't want to slight her writing ability with just three pages, or scare her with a whole blank book. He thought he understood too much about her fears.

Jacinda looked nothing like Liz. He'd told himself lately that he'd been looking too hard for Liz in those other two women, three years ago, and maybe he'd seriously believed last night, down at the creek, that with her long dark hair and olive skin, Jacinda looked different enough to cure the problem.

The Problem.

A cure?

Maybe it was only getting worse. A man hit his sexual peak by twenty. At thirty-four, things could easily have started to slide. The level of need. The frequency. Had losing Liz pushed him so far away from his natural potency that he'd never claw back the lost ground?

Everything had been fine…fantastic…powerful…intense…while he and Jacinda had kissed last night. The chemistry between them was huge, not something you could explain or trace to its source but something animal and instinctive. Water on a thirsty day. A completion. She had tasted so good.

He loved the way she moved. Loved how at first she'd been happy just to wait and feel those motionless, paralyzed lips of his against her neck while he gathered his courage and gloried in his unexpected and almost shocking need.

Oh hell, he'd wanted her so badly and it had felt so good to rediscover how that felt. A little later, he'd loved her moments of hunger and impatience, too. How could a man's ego not be gratified by that? She wanted him, and she hadn't kept it a secret.

But then the pressure of her needs and her expectations had hit. He'd felt her heat against him, telling him she wanted more, insisting it with warm, full pressure, and he'd panicked and…oh, hell…deflated and pulled away—*hopefully* before she could have noticed.

He hadn't compared her to Liz. He hadn't—was this wrong?—even thought about Liz while he was kissing Jacinda. Not for a second. And when he'd panicked, it had been about the other women, the two very different blondes, and the excruciating awkwardness that had played out both times when his performance had fizzled.

He could still remember it in painful detail. The girl at the races, with her disinterested *Whatever…* when he'd stumbled through an apology and hinted at an explanation. *After my wife…* If the girl had noticed his raspy throat and horrible struggle for words, she hadn't reacted. She'd already been putting on her clothes, miffed at her disappointing night.

The other woman, the backpacker, had soothed him like a baby at first. He'd felt foolish, so uncomfortable at her sickly reassurance. It was the way you talked to a three-year-old who couldn't get his pants on the right way around.

Never mind, sweetheart, we'll keep working on it and you'll do better next time.

She'd turned the whole thing into a personal challenge. Dr. Birgit, Scandinavian Erotic Therapist, to the rescue. He'd felt as if they were writing a new chapter in a sex manual, full of strenuous gymnastic positions and clinical efforts at stimulation.

None of which had worked.

Oh, jeez!

Stop thinking about it!

Here. How about this book? He flipped through Joshie's "Journal Writing" notebook from three years ago and saw several pages of painstaking numbers showing the date, and labored sentences summarizing his day. "We wnt to the crek. I rod Sam. His sadel sliped. I staid on. Dad fixded it up tite agen."

The book had about twenty spare pages left at the end of it. If Jacinda could fill those, she might not feel so tense and uncomfortable about asking him for more.

He hoped she did fill them, because he could tell it was important to her.

He put the file box away, closed his office door and took the notebook along the corridor to where she waited for him in the kitchen. Her hands still didn't seem to know what to do with themselves. She hugged herself, finger-combed her hair, picked up a cleaning sponge and wiped down the countertop even though it was clean already.

"Oh, you found something?" she said, when she saw the book in his grip. She smiled eagerly, but dropped the smile too soon, as if she didn't want him to guess that this remotely mattered to her.

Too late for that.

Handing it over, he hid the depth of his understanding and told her, "Just let me know when you need another one."

"Thanks," was all she said.

After asking Callan so impatiently for paper to write on, Jacinda left Josh's old notebook blank that night. She looked at it for a while, standing alone in the kitchen after Callan had gone, fingers and brain tingling to begin, but then fatigue overtook her.

And doubt.

What would she write in it, anyhow?

What was the point?

The simple act of having to ask Callan for it seemed to have doubled the pressure. Even though she'd tried to play it down, he wasn't stupid. He was a practical man. He'd expect results. He had no idea about writing. He'd want to see six new chapters of her long-gone novel by tomorrow night.

Why had she brought the subject up? She could probably write down all the words left inside her on the inside of her wrist or the palm of her hand. She should have asked for a Post-it note.

Carly did sleepwalk at midnight that night, after her earlier fear about Mommy's safety out in the dark. Or was it because she'd picked up on Jac's own tension over—well, various things? Carly's emotional radar was scary, sometimes, and Jac wondered how much Kurt's behavior during the separation and divorce had affected her daughter deep inside where it might never clearly show.

During her nighttime escapade, Carly had a drink of water in the kitchen, went to the bathroom and checked on the dogs sleeping on the veranda, all of it in her sleep. Then, fortunately, she seemed happy to be led back to bed. Jacinda slid gratefully between her own sheets and didn't lie awake for another hour as she'd feared she might.

And when she awoke the next morning to the sound of Darth Vader crowing in the chook run, heralding first light, the second thing that came into her head after looking across at her beautiful and safely sleeping daughter was the notebook Callan had given her, and its blank pages.

She wanted to fill them.

She did.

It was a hunger that postcards could never satisfy.

Even though every scrap of the doubt was still there, the need was stronger, and wouldn't go away. She craved the physical act of holding a pen in her hand and moving it across the paper. She *needed* to think about words, much better words than just, "How're you doing?" and "Thank you for your letter." Dressing quickly, she grabbed the book, found the pen she'd taken last night from a jar on the kitchen benchtop and went out to the veranda.

No one else was up. No sounds of movement came from Callan's room farther along. No light was visible in Kerry's little cottage across the dusty front yard. It was the coldest hour of the day. Jacinda sat on the cane couch, spread the mohair blanket over her legs and pulled it up over her shoulders. She thought about coffee but decided to wait, not wanting to risk disturbing Callan if he was having a rare lie-in.

She opened the notebook and found the first empty page. The lines on one side were widely spaced, suitable for a child's first efforts at literacy, and on the opposite side, the paper was completely blank, ready to be filled by a stick figure and a clumsy tree.

Five minutes went by, but nothing happened. She was tempted to doodle. Her fingers tended to make all these elaborate curly patterns and shapes without her even thinking about it on the rare occasions when she wrote by hand. But she resisted the doodling. She wanted to wait for words.

And finally they came.

"I'm sitting here," she wrote, "watching light seep upward into the sky like the curtain rising on a Broadway show."

It didn't rank with classical literature's great opening sentences, but she told herself not to care. *It doesn't matter,*

Jacinda. Just keep going. There doesn't have to be a story, or a direction, or a logical sequence. Not yet. Not ever. You're not selling this. You're not showing it to a soul. No, not to Callan, if he asks. So just keep writing.

Her hand had begun to ache and she'd penned four pages when Callan found her. The light was on over at Kerry's, and she could hear the boys in the kitchen. She must have been sitting here almost an hour.

"Want coffee?" Callan offered.

He stood beside the wicker couch, looking too tall, and she had to fight the need to cover her page because he had a bird's-eye view and could have read it if he'd wanted to. As it happened, he wasn't looking at the page, he was looking at her face.

"I'll come inside in a minute," she told him, twisting toward him and leaning her elbow over the paper as if it were just a casual, accidental movement.

"No, I can bring it out for you," he said. "You're busy."

"No, I'm— That rooster of yours doesn't like visitors to sleep in, does he?" she joked lamely. "I'm only filling in time till Carly wakes up."

"Well, she has."

So you're not buying my excuses, Callan?

Could you pretend, at least?

"Oh, does she want me?" She shifted, started to close the book.

"She's with the boys. She's fine." He leaned down and flipped the pages open again, and their fingers touched. He pulled his hand away. "Keep going, and I'll bring the coffee."

"No, no, I'm finished. I'm done. It's okay."

"You looked like you were still working on it."

"It's not work. It's nothing."

"Still, keep going and I'll bring your coffee out," he repeated stubbornly, for the third time.

"Okay. Thanks." She didn't want to argue anymore, because if she argued, he'd have questions about what she'd written, and she didn't want questions.

He didn't seem in a hurry to get the coffee he'd offered, however. He just stood there, leaning against the open doorway, making her skin itch and ripple with awareness. His body was magnetic. She wanted to grab his hip or push her face into his chest and smell his shirt.

Finally, mercifully—after probably a whole six seconds had elapsed—he asked, "Did I give you enough? I mean, are there enough pages left in the notebook? Because there are a couple more I can give you. And I have printer paper, too. Or if you want to use the computer again…"

"For the moment, I'm fine with this." She laid her hand across the half-filled page.

It was, seriously, years since she'd written this much by hand, and yet she hadn't even considered Callan's computer, she realized. Somehow, this was the method that felt right for now, this filling of white paper with blue scrawl. She liked the physical act of scribbling out a wrong word, or jetting an arrow across the page toward a sentence added in after further thought.

Callan still hadn't left.

"I'm guessing you don't plan to show me right this minute." He smiled, but she wasn't in the mood to get teased on this.

"No."

"No?"

She covered the page protectively with her arm once more. "It's nothing. It's terrible. It's just— It's not a story, or anything. It's just little snatches. Impressions."

"Like a poem."

"Not even that. Sort of like a poem." *Unnh!* "I might turn some of it into a poem later."

"And then you can show me." He gave her a sly look, and there was the promise of a grin hovering on his face.

"No! Please don't… *Please* don't treat this like a joke, Callan, or like tasting a batch of cookies I've made. It's not like that. I couldn't—I'm sorry, I don't have a sense of humor about it, and I can't explain that, I can't explain why it's important, I just—"

"Hey…hey."

Oh crud, now he'd sat down, frowning and concerned. Now she'd really turned this into something. She should have fobbed him off, just agreed that, yes, it was a poem and that, sure, yes, she'd show it to him when it was done, and hope that the whole thing would drop from his mind because surely he had better things to think about.

"I'm not treating it like a joke, Jac," he said.

His blue eyes were fixed on her, as motionless as the surface of the water hole at night, as deep and bright as the midday outback sky. The old, sagging couch pushed them closer together, the way it had on her first night here, as shameless as a professional matchmaker. *Go on,* it said, *feel his thigh pressed against yours. Don't fight it. You like it.*

"I'm not laughing at you about this." His voice had a husky note in it. "I wouldn't. I know it's important."

"It's not important." She pushed her hand against his upper arm and tried to shimmy her butt sideways so the matchmaking couch didn't get its wicked way. Callan leaned back, respecting her need for space, still watching her. "It's stupid," she said. "Writing really doesn't matter. If I never wrote another word in my life, the universe would not be a poorer place."

"You don't believe that."

She laughed. "No, I don't, but I should! Because it doesn't make sense that it's so important. I'm not expecting you to understand any of this."

"Give me some credit."

"No, I didn't mean that you're not smart or— You're not a writer, that's all."

"Do I have to be? Isn't there only one thing I need to understand? Without it, you're incomplete," he said simply.

She nodded silently, stunned at the words.

Yes.

She'd never heard it put so plainly.

Without it she was incomplete.

"You just said it," she stammered. "Y-you're so right. How—?"

"Everyone has things like that. Their kids, their work, their land. Their gardening, their guitar playing, their sport." His tone had changed, sounded more distant and defensive, like a lecture. But then he couldn't sustain it, and seemed to give up the attempt. His voice dropped again, the pitch low and personal. "You don't need to ask yourself or anyone else why writing is important, Jacinda. You just need to know— I have to have this in my life to feel complete. That's okay. That's no big deal. The bad, impossible part is that if something takes it away, it kills you, doesn't it? It cripples you, torments you, until you find a way to get it back."

"How did you know that?" It was almost a whisper. Barely aware of her action, she grabbed his hand, let the couch lean her in closer to him. "Just hearing you say it is…great, such a relief…thank you. For taking it seriously. For saying it. But how did you know about the torment?"

His body sagged. His eye contact dropped as if the thread of communication between them had been sliced through. He looked as if he was talking to the floorboards or to his shoes, not to her.

"Hell, Jacinda! D'you honestly think you're the only one it's ever happened to?" he muttered.

Chapter Nine

Callan wouldn't follow through.

Jacinda didn't push or demand, but she wanted to understand what he meant. How had it happened to him? Where was he incomplete? He couldn't be talking about the loss of Liz, because there was grief in that, yes, but no shame and she was certain that she'd seen shame in him when he'd said those words.

D'you honestly think you're the only one it's ever happened to?

Shame? Why?

They had common ground, it wasn't a source of shame, and she thought they should grab at it and make use of it, but he clammed up and wouldn't talk about it, said it wasn't important, he couldn't explain, she should just forget it. Carly's arrival on the veranda a moment or two later gave him an easy way out that he snatched up as shamelessly as a serial dater might claim, "I lost your phone number."

"Woo-hoo, Carlz!" he said. "Ready for another big day?"

Knowing how much she didn't want to feel pressured about her writing and therefore not wanting to pressure Callan in return, Jac let it go for the time being. Instead, she hugged Carly, closed Lockie's old notebook and took it into the house. Four pages was enough for now. Four pages was good. Even a sentence would have been good, so four pages was actually great.

Three days later, she'd written fifteen.

They still weren't a part of anything. Too disjointed and personal for a story. Too poetic for a diary. Not jazzy and chatty enough for a blog on the Net.

She wrote about the colors of her favorite hen's feathers in the sun, about the feel of bread dough in her hands, and the words that Kerry had used when she'd taught the recipe and the technique. She wrote two pages of stuff she imagined herself yelling at Kurt, not in his huge executive office or out front of Carly's preschool, but the things she would have yelled if she'd been standing on the rock ledge at the water hole about to jump in, while Kurt was down on the sand— and okay, admittedly, since this was a fantasy, *cowering* there.

She wrote out the words *six hundred thousand acres* and they looked really good on the page, much better than just the numbers. They looked so good that she found out some other numbers from Callan—the distance around the perimeter of Lake Frome, the length of all the fences on his land, the height above sea level of Mount Hindley and Mount Fitton and Mount Neil—and wrote those down in words, also.

She wrote about all the new things Carly did, and the new discoveries she made.

Including a snake.

Yep, bit of a shock, that. She and Carly had gone out to collect eggs before lunch on Tuesday and hadn't even seen the huge, silent thing coiled against the shade cloth at the side of the chook house until they were close enough to touch.

Oh…dear…Lord.

Her heart had felt like it had stopped, but Carly's scream was more one of surprise than fear. Kerry had come running from her vegetable garden and had quickly been able to tell them it was only a carpet python.

Right.

Only.

Harmless, Kerry had said. Really. Wouldn't even squeeze you to death, which had been Jac's second theory, once she'd abandoned the toxic venom idea.

"Take a look at it, Carly," Kerry had invited, and Carly had looked.

From a little farther away, so had Jac.

They'd seen the markings and Kerry had told Carly her version of an Australian aboriginal myth about a lizard and a snake who had taken turns to paint markings on each other's backs, which had kept both Carly and Jacinda looking at the python long enough to really see its beauty.

Because it was beautiful. The markings were like the neat stitches in a knitting pattern, with subtle variations of creams and yellows on a background of brownish gray—gorgeous and neat and intricate. Jacinda was discovering so much that was beautiful on Callan's land, and Callan watched her doing it, knew she was writing about it, and seemed to be happy with that, even though he didn't say very much.

On Thursday, they drove for three hours with Carly to Leigh Creek in the truck, and picked up fence posts and post-cards, among other supplies. The town was modern and neat and pretty, with young, white-trunked eucalyptus trees and drought-tolerant shrubs flowering pink, yellow and red. For lunch they stopped in a tiny and much older railway town called Copley just a few miles to the north of Leigh Creek

and ate at Tulloch's Bush Bakery and Quandong Café—
well-known in the area, apparently, as well as a popular
tourist stop.

"You have to taste a quandong pie for dessert," Callan
decreed, so the three of them ate the wild peach treats, which
tasted deliciously tangy and tart, something like rhubarb,
inside a shortcrust pastry with crumbly German-style streusel
on top.

Jac sat in the café for a little longer and wrote her postcards, while Callan entertained Carly by taking her for a
wander around the quiet little town. The postcards were
tough, and there were lots of places where her pen hovered
over an uncompleted line while she searched for words. But
she managed to fill the space in the end, and included
Callan's e-mail address. "I'd love to hear from you, if you
get a chance," she told both her brothers, hoping they would
realize that she meant it, hoping they'd care enough to
respond.

On the long journey home, Carly fell asleep in the seat
between them, and with her sweet-scented little head on Jac's
shoulder, Jac got sleepy as well. They'd left pretty early this
morning, and Callan had even let her drive for part of the
journey. In a truck of this size, on outback roads, it had been
a challenge but she couldn't have chickened out. It seemed
important, right now, to push herself in new ways, to prove
her own strength—to herself, more than to anyone else.

Proving yourself did definitely leave you sleepy, though.

The smooth gravel of the road hummed and hissed
beneath the wheels, and even the sight of a group of kangaroos bounding away across the red ground didn't do more
than make her eyes widen again for a few moments.

Callan teased her when she woke up again. "You had a
good nap, there, judging by the size of the wet patch on
your shirt."

"Oh! Was I—?"

Drooling? True, Carly sometimes did, in her sleep.

Without speaking, he handed Jac a tissue, but there was no wet patch that she could find. She wadded the tissue up and pelted him with it. "I was not!"

"Snoring, muttering, reciting Shakespeare and your bank account number. Kept me awake, so thanks."

"I was not! Pass me another tissue!" Even though it wasn't a very effective weapon.

"Okay, I won't mention any of the other things you do in your sleep."

"I snoozed lightly. For about ten minutes."

"Forty-five, actually."

"You mean we're nearly back?" Taking a better look at the surrounding country, she recognized Mount Hindley approaching to the right. She knew its distinctive silhouette, now. "Oh, we are! I really did sleep!"

"Yeah, my conversation was that interesting."

"You didn't say a word!"

They grinned at each other over Carly's head and it just felt good.

On Friday evening, he asked her, "Do you still want to see the animals drinking, down at the water?"

"I'd love to."

"Because we could do it tomorrow, if you want."

Apart from Thursday's trip into town, he'd been working hard since Sunday to get the new mustering yard completed, going out to Springer's Well with Pete first thing every morning and not returning until late in the afternoon, leaving Lockie behind after that first day because of School of the Air. The mustering yard was almost completed now, Jacinda knew, ready for the next roundup of cattle for trucking to the sales down south.

Pete had had enough of the twice-daily drive between

Arakeela Downs and Nepabunna by Monday afternoon, on top of the even rougher trip out to Springer's Well, so he'd stayed at the homestead overnight on Monday and Tuesday nights to give them longer working days.

He had slept on the front veranda, wrapped in a sleeping bag laid on top of the ancient canvas of an army camp stretcher. He'd been an easy guest. Didn't talk too much. Didn't make a mess. Ate whatever was put in front of him.

And he'd told Carly stories about the mythical Akurra serpent, whose activities explained the existence of the water holes and gorges all over this region, as well as the existence of Lake Frome. "Big rocks in the creek, Akurra's eggs. Belly rumbles 'cos he drank too much saltwater, and you can feel it under your feet. You feel one day, Carly, if the earth ever shakes a bit, that's Akurra."

Mythical serpents, real carpet pythons, yabby sandwiches…Carly took it all in stride. But her little legs probably weren't yet equal to a dawn climb up Mount Hindley, so Callan suggested that this time they leave all the kids and Kerry behind. He packed breakfast and hiking supplies that evening, and suggested that Jac bring a day pack, too.

"For water and sunscreen, your towel, your camera, and somewhere to put your sweatshirt once the sun gets higher."

Packing these items, Jac thought about the second schoolwork notebook that Callan had given her today—"In case you're in danger of filling up the first one," he'd said, and she dropped that in, also, along with a pen. She thought she was probably just giving herself unnecessary extra weight.

If he hadn't made that rash promise about a dawn hike to Jacinda down at the water hole last Saturday night, he wouldn't be doing this, Callan knew. He set the alarm for five-thirty because they wanted to get to the top of Mount Hindley to see the sun's first rays, but he didn't need its jangling sound to rouse him. He'd already been lying awake since four forty-five, locked in a whole slew of illogical feelings.

The thought of several glorious early morning hours alone with Jac made him heat up way too much.

He just liked her.

A lot.

Her company. Her outlook. Her smile.

And he was a man, so liking channeled itself into predictable pathways.

Physical ones.

He knew that his mood changed when he walked into the house and she was there. His spirits lifted, floating his energy levels up along with them the way empty fuel cans used to float the scrappy wooden rafts he and Nicky had hammered together to ferry around the water hole as kids.

Who noticed?

Someone had to.

Mum wasn't blind, and her hearing was pretty sharp, too. Could she hear the way his voice changed? He got more talkative, louder. He laughed more. He threw Carly up in the air, wrestled with Josh, told bad jokes to Lockie, got all three kids overexcited before bedtime just because he was too keyed up himself and couldn't keep it dammed back.

And Jacinda reacted the same way.

He could see it and hear it and feel it because all of it echoed exactly what was happening inside him.

Their eyes met too often. They found too many reasons to share a smile. The smallest scraps of conversation took on a richer meaning. Shared coffee in the mornings was cozier. Jokes were funnier. It took him longer to wind down enough to sleep at night.

Sometimes he felt so exhilarated by it, as if he were suddenly equipped to rule the world. Or his corner of it, anyhow—those six hundred thousand acres that impressed her so much.

The new mustering yard was great, structured to minimize stress and injury to the cattle. His yield and his prices were definitely going to improve. The long-range weather forecast held the hope of rain, and he'd put in some new dams just last year—Jacinda called them ponds—to conserve as much of the runoff as he could.

He'd talked to her about all this and she'd listened and nodded and told him, "I had no idea so much research and thought had to go into running cattle in this kind of country." And he'd thought, yes, he had skills and knowledge and strength that he took for granted, things that could impress a woman that he'd never seen in that light before.

Not even with Liz, because Liz had grown up with cattlemen and had taken it all for granted, too, just the way he did.

What did Mum see?

What did Pete see?

Pete had irritated the heck out of him, earlier in the week, with the ancient-tribal-wisdom routine that he liked to pull on unsuspecting victims from time to time.

No, it wasn't really a con, because Pete was pretty wise in a lot of ways, but Callan had felt conned, all the same. He'd felt naked and exposed.

What *did* Pete see?

What was all that biblical-style stuff about seasons turning and everything having its place and its time? He liked Pete's conversation better when it was about fence posts and calving. On Wednesday afternoon, they'd had a big, pointless argument about wildflowers.

"Desert pea? It's too soon, Pete. We had those freak thunderstorms a month or two ago, I know, but the flowers won't be out for a few weeks yet, I'd say. Maybe not until spring."

"Yeah, but happens that way, sometimes. So busy saying

it's too soon, and that's right when you see 'em, red flowers dripping on the ground like blood, right where the rainwater soaked into the ground."

"I still say it's too soon."

"You want your friend to see 'em before she goes," Pete had said. It was a statement, not a question. "You're not happy, because you think she won't."

And he was right.

Callan liked Jacinda so much, he wanted to show her dawn from Mount Hindley, and Pete's ancestors' rock carvings farther up in the gorge, and the bloodred, black-eyed Sturt's desert pea flowers blooming on his land.

"Got your camera?" he asked her, as they walked out to the four-wheel-drive parked in its usual crooked spot in front of the house.

They moved and spoke quietly because the kids were still asleep. Mum's light was on. She'd have made her early morning cup of tea and would be drinking it in bed, in her quilted dressing gown. She'd be dressed and over at the main house before Carly and the boys had finished wiping the sleep from their eyes.

"Yep," Jacinda answered, holding up her day pack. "Remembered it this time." She shivered a little.

"Cold?" he asked. It wasn't an award-winning question. Of course she was cold. So was he. They'd need to get moving before they would warm up.

"A bit, but I'm fine."

He liked that about her, too. She didn't complain. Being cold or hungry or scared or wet…or confronted by a carpet python…or teased about drooling…was never enough on its own to spoil her mood. She took things in stride, just like her daughter did.

Yeah, but there were limits.

Monday morning, five days ago, on the veranda.

Sheesh, what had he said?

You think you're the only one it's ever happened to?

Callan, idiot, you can't say things like that in a naked moment and then drop it and refuse to talk.

It was still sitting there, the conversational elephant that they both pretended they didn't see. Jac didn't know what he'd meant, and he wasn't going to tell her, so they would both just have to ride it out until the memory of Monday morning wasn't so fresh and didn't matter anymore.

Maybe papering it over with fresh memories of things like going into Leigh Creek with Carly, eating quandong pies, climbing Mount Hindley at dawn and watching yellow-footed rock wallabies come down to drink would help.

He warmed the engine and took his usual semicircular route around and out of the yard. They parked beside the dry creek bed under the same tree as last Saturday night, which was a mistake because it reminded him of…all sorts of things. But if he'd parked somewhere different, it might have looked as if he was avoiding that spot, which would just be crazy.

The sky had begun to soften in the east, but the air was still cold and the dew heavy.

"I love being awake and out of the house this early," Jac said, but she shivered again as she spoke.

Which made him want to put his arms around her to keep her warm.

He hiked faster, instead, moving his feet over the rocks the way he'd been doing all his life, forgetting that her stride wouldn't be as sure-footed or as wide. She didn't ask him to slow down until they were almost at the top of the mountain, and then her request came just a few seconds too late.

"Callan, could you—? Yikes! Ouch!"

She'd stepped onto an unsteady rock and it had tipped. She stumbled several steps and grazed her calf on another rock before almost falling to her knees.

"I'm sorry." Oh, damn! She'd already hurt herself once this week, on that strand of barbed-wire fence while he'd feared she was lost. She'd only removed the Band-Aids Thursday morning. "I was going too fast. Wanted to warm us up."

He doubled back to her, not reaching her as fast as he wanted to. He definitely shouldn't have let himself get so far ahead. She bent down and started picking dirt from the graze, wincing and frowning.

"Let me," he said.

"It's nothing. The skin is barely broken."

"What about this?" He took her arm and turned it over so she could see. She had a graze there, too, which she hadn't even noticed yet, a scrape between her elbow and wrist where blood was beginning to well up.

She made a sound of frustration and impatience. "I shouldn't have tried to go so fast."

"It was my fault. You were only trying to keep up, and I have better boots than you."

She smiled, tucking in the corner of her mouth. "That's right. Blame it on the boots, not the hopeless city-bred American."

"Don't. It really was my fault."

Together, they washed the grazes, dried them with the towel and put a couple of Band-Aids on the deepest scrapes, both of them finding too many reasons to apologize. Any awkwardness wasn't in their first-aid techniques, it was in their emotions. He felt as if he shouldn't be touching her, but that would have been impractical.

Oh, crikey!

Would he ever learn to act naturally around her?

He didn't hold out a lot of hope.

"We must be almost at the top," she said when they were ready to start moving again.

"Just about." It felt good to find something safe to talk about! "See that cairn of rocks up ahead? That marks the official summit."

"Did your family build it?"

It was a good-sized pile of stones, grading from larger at the base to smaller at the top, a couple of meters high.

"No, it's been here way longer than we have, over a hundred and fifty years. A couple of brothers, the Haymans, built it when they first ran sheep here in the 1850s."

"Do you know the whole history of your land, then, Callan?"

"Pretty much."

"And the aboriginal myths?"

"And the geology. You're standing on some pretty nice quartzite."

She laughed, intrigued and pleased for some reason. "Am I?"

"Yep, although down in the gorge itself it's granite. I can show you some maps. And I have satellite pictures, too. Those are fascinating, when you look at—" He stopped.

Or not.

Because she couldn't be that interested, could she? She was just being polite.

"Finish," she said.

"The way the land folds," he summarized quickly, "but, no, I'm done on geology. Let me know if you ever do want to see pictures. Speaking of which, get your camera out or you'll miss the sunrise."

She nodded, swung her day pack off her shoulders and found the natty little piece of digital technology. He watched her switch it on, position herself on a rock, line up her shot. There was a moment of stillness and expectation. The whole earth waited, and Jac waited with it.

Callan's body felt warm and loose from the walk, a little

dusty around his bare lower legs. He was thirsty, but didn't even want to breathe right now, let alone fiddle around in search of his water bottle. He just wanted to watch Jac watching the dawn.

She wore stretchy black shorts that finished snugly halfway down her lean, smooth thighs, and her legs were bare until they disappeared inside a pair of chunky white tennis socks just above her ankles. She had her backside parked on a rock and her knees bent up to provide a steady resting point for her elbows.

The sleeves of her navy sweatshirt were pushed up. Beyond gracefully bent wrists, her hands looked delicate yet sure as they held the camera, and she'd turned her baseball cap around the wrong way like a kid, so that the peak wouldn't get in the way of her view.

"Oh, it's fabulous...fabulous," she whispered.

The horizon began to burn and the first rays shot across the landscape, setting it alight with molten gold. She clicked her camera, got impatient with her position and stood up, circling the whole three hundred and sixty degrees twice, clicked and clicking, as the light changed and flared and shifted around her. It settled on a herd of cattle, turning them from dark blobs into distinctive red-brown silhouettes, etched with a glow. Finally, she lowered the camera and smiled.

And he came so close to grabbing that back-to-front baseball cap off her head, throwing it on the ground and kissing her, except...except...all the terrifying reasons from the other night were still there, and he didn't see how they were ever going to let him alone.

"I want to see the satellite pictures and hear about the history, Callan," she told him. "Don't think that you're ever boring about this place, because you're not."

"Yeah, it had occurred to me as a possibility," he managed to say.

"No. Not a possibility. Okay?"

He just nodded, relieved but still wondering if she was simply being polite.

"Mmm, I need some water," she said.

They both drank, then she put her camera away and asked, "Will we miss the kangaroos again?"

"We should get down into the gorge, before the sun climbs too high, yes."

He stayed behind her, this time. The sun at this height was already warm on their bare legs, but when they got lower, the gorge was still in shade. It was magical. They saw several kangaroos and a pair of yellow-footed rock wallabies, impossibly nimble and sure-footed as they bounded back up the rugged sides of the gorge after their morning drink. A family of emus showed up, too, their big curved backs heaped with the usual pile of untidy gray-brown feathers that bounced as they got startled by the human presence and ran.

Jacinda took more photos, then went to put her camera away.

"I brought breakfast, if you want it," Callan told her. "We can light the fire. Or we can head back."

She twisted to look back at him, trying to read what he really wanted, not wanting to be a time-waster or a nuisance. "Can we stay? Is there work you have to do?"

"We can stay. I'm getting pretty hungry."

And I don't want to end this, because it's too good.

She helped him with the fire. He'd brought an old pan, eggs and bacon, bread to make toast, a couple of garden tomatoes to grill, long-life milk, instant coffee and the billycan to boil the water in. They got everything ready, but the flames were still too high to start cooking. Their hungry stomachs would have to wait for glowing coals.

Jacinda looked at her day pack a couple of times in an uneasy kind of way and he almost teased her about it. Was she checking no snakes were lurking, eager to crawl inside?

Finally, she blurted out, "I brought my…Lockie's…notebook. Would you mind if I scribbled in it for a little while?"

Of course he didn't mind.

And he tried not to watch, because he knew that somehow it was private. She didn't like to feel herself under the spotlight of someone else's observation when she stared at the blank page or scratched the ballpoint pen impatiently back and forth over a wrong word—or even when she was writing smoothly and unconsciously smiling at the fact that it was going well.

Okay, so that meant he *was* watching. Sneaking glances, anyhow.

Even though the flames had still not died back quite right, he started cooking to distract himself, putting strips of bacon and halves of tomato into the pan and poking at them with a barbecue fork more than he needed to. He knew he shouldn't keep spying on Jac's tentative new relationship with written words.

He was so busy not noticing her write that he didn't notice when she stopped. Her question sneaked up and leaped at him like an enemy ambush. "Callan, tell me what you meant the other day, that I'm not the only one it's ever happened to."

He whipped around, bringing the sizzling pan with him and almost losing the freshly cooked eggs over the rim. She had the notebook open in her lap and the pen still in her hand. What was she going to do? Record his answer?

She looked startled at his sudden movement. Her gaze dropped to the pan. "Careful…."

"Sheesh, Jacinda!" he said on a hiss.

The ambush metaphor still held. He felt like a soldier, taken by surprise but on such a hair trigger that he was ready for the attack anyhow, weapon fully loaded. He bristled all over, prepared to lie under oath, stay silent under torture, neutralize the onslaught in any way he could.

He wasn't going to talk about this!

* * *

Wrong, wrong, wrong, Jacinda realized at once, watching Callan set the pan of eggs down on a rock without looking at it.

They'd each gotten to different places during the past ten minutes of silence, she saw. She had felt increasingly peaceful, close to Callan, at home….

And braver, because some nice snatches of language were happening on her page, and writing well always made her brave. Out of nowhere, she'd had an insight into one of the half-forgotten but very real characters in her old, unfinished novel, and suddenly that character wasn't half-forgotten anymore, but was right here, as if sitting beside Jac, her story clamoring to be told.

When she'd looked up from her writing, she'd seen Callan crouched by the fire, his muscles pulling under his shirt as he reached to poke the coals or flip the toast on the old wire rack. He wasn't saying anything, wasn't looking her way, and she thought he must be feeling peaceful, too, happy about being together like this, enjoying each other's uninterrupted company, sharing the same appreciation of nature's gifts at this fresh hour.

The question hadn't felt abrupt to her. It had felt right.

But it wasn't right.

She could see it instantly in the way he turned, the way his face changed, the sharpness in his voice, the appalled expression in his eyes.

Sheesh, Jacinda! In her head, she echoed his own exclamation.

You could have led up to it better, couldn't you, Jac? Given him some warning?

She let her notebook slide to the ground and stood up, covering the few yards of physical distance between them—

and hopefully some of the miles of emotional distance—in one breath…in four heartbeats.

"Callan." She put her hand on his arm and he flinched. "I didn't intend for it to be such a tough question."

"Okay…"

"I'm sorry, I'm too self-absorbed over this. You seemed to understand so much the other day. About the whole thing with my writing. The problem. The block. The incompleteness. And today it was flowing so well. I have to thank you, because I never imagined finding a place where I'd feel so safe, after what was happening with Kurt at home. And I just wanted to understand about you, in return, that's all. I wanted to hear from you about the incompleteness that happened to you, and what you did about it. What worked for you, when you solved it."

He froze.

Wrong again, Jac.

Hell, how could her intentions have been so good and still have led to such a mess?

He closed his eyes, gritted his teeth. When he answered, she could hardly hear. "I haven't solved it."

He broke roughly away from her, turning his back to her just the way he had on Saturday night.

Guarding himself.

Guarding against some power she had over him, or some threat she was unconsciously making. Either way, she didn't understand.

But her bravery was still in place—that sizzling sense of capability and strength that good writing could give her. And that meant she wasn't prepared to let the issue go.

"Please don't turn your back, Callan," she said and stepped toward him.

He didn't move, apart from thrusting his hands down into the pockets of his shorts. He didn't speak, either.

"You turned your back the other night, too, when we were here," she pressed on. "You know when I mean. Looking for Lockie's Game Boy, when we—"

"Yes, I know when you mean."

She reached him, but his body language practically screamed at her not to touch. It created physical pain because she wanted to touch him so much.

"I would really like to talk about this, Callan. To understand it."

He laughed, as if she was being completely naive.

Maybe she was, because the bravery was still there inside her, only she was kidding herself that it came from her good writing.

It didn't.

It came from something else.

Desire.

She wanted Callan so much, and at some level she *trusted* the wanting—*had* to trust it because it was that powerful, and she knew, despite everything he said—and did—and didn't do—that it reflected back at her from him with equal force. He wanted her, too.

"Okay, then we won't talk," she said, standing behind him and wrapping her arms around his rigid body. "For the moment, we'll just do this…."

His torso was as hard as a board, vibrating with tension, and her touch didn't soften him at all. If she'd been feeling even a fraction less brave, less sure, she would have let him go, her face flaming with embarrassment at his rejection.

But if it was the desire, after all, that had made her brave, it was the writing that had made her see clearly and she knew…just *knew*…that he wasn't rejecting her. There was something way more complex going on here.

She slid her hands up to his shoulders and began to caress him, running from his warm, solid neck and out to his upper arms, over and over again. Soon, she let her fingers trespass farther, touching his jaw, brushing the lobes of his ears, feathering into his hair. Still, he didn't soften or move.

"Prebreakfast massage," she murmured. "The sun's on my back, so I'm getting a massage, too. Whatever's happening, Callan, don't be angry. Don't push me away."

He didn't answer, but his breath came out in a shuddering sigh.

"If you're going to tell me to stop, then you have to tell me why," she said.

Silence. She kept touching him.

"I'm not going to tell you to stop," he finally answered.

She didn't jump on his words, she just let them hang. Then she leaned her cheek against his back, slid her hands between his rigid upper arms and his sides and began to stroke them down his chest. To begin with, she stopped at his ribs, which moved up and down with his breathing. His back moved with his breathing, also, pushing against her breasts. Her nipples were hard against his body. Could he feel?

She let her caress drop lower, reaching the waistband of his shorts, and then his hips, drifting in toward the center, and she forgot about anything more she might want from these moments because they were so precious and delicious all on their own.

He moved.

At last.

His body snaked around and he held her. She wanted to kiss him, take his face in her hands and press her mouth over his, imprint her taste onto him, drink him, make him respond. More than that, however, she wanted him to talk, which meant she couldn't capture his mouth. Not yet.

"You said you were incomplete, and you didn't mean incomplete because you'd lost Liz," she whispered. "We haven't known each other very long, but you're important to me,

Callan. You're good to me. Good for me. And I trust you. I wish you'd trust me, because we can help each other better then."

"I trust you. I don't need help." She thought he was going to push her away at that point, but he didn't. After a moment, like an afterthought, he added, "But I want you. Oh, I *want* you."

"Yes…"

"But that's where I'm incomplete, Jacinda. God, can I say it? Am I saying it?" He was talking more to himself than to her. His whole body was shuddering, shaking.

"I don't understand."

"I couldn't satisfy you, that's the problem. I couldn't satisfy either of us. I haven't been able to in four years, since—" He broke off and swore beneath his breath, then looked her full in the face with his blue eyes burning. "You see, I'm impotent," he said, and she knew for him these had to be the ugliest two words in the world.

Chapter Ten

One wrong word.

All she would need to do would be to say one wrong word at this point and everything between them—the trust, the chemistry—would be shattered, Jacinda knew.

And yet silence was wrong, too, which meant she had to think fast. She held on to him, understanding the tight, rigid state of his body much better now, and she wondered how arrogant she must be to even hope that her touch could soften him, after what he'd just said.

"Thank you for telling me," she said quietly, just before the silence grew too heavy.

"Well, you pretty much gave me no choice."

"No. Okay."

"So there you have it."

She waited for him to move, to disengage physically and emotionally from their close body contact, but he stayed where he was, and so did she. "Who have you talked to about it?" she asked.

Letting her head fall lightly against his chest, she felt the strong beat of his heart. There was nothing wrong with his circulation, for sure, and absolutely nothing wrong with his ability to arouse a woman.

"You," he answered her. "Just now." His voice was barely human, more like a growl.

"Not a doctor?" She was moved—and scared—that she was the one who'd heard his confession, when no one else had.

"No, not a doctor."

"Shouldn't you?"

"Hey, do people need doctors anymore? All that trouble and expense? We can scare ourselves for free on the Internet."

"So you've looked it up there?"

"I couldn't find anything that seemed…relevant. It was all too much about side effects from illness. Prostate cancer. Diabetes. Physical things."

"So you think this is emo—?"

"I don't want to talk about it, Jacinda."

No hesitation. No doubt. The same tone he'd used when he'd said *I don't need help*.

She didn't have the right to push any further, and he'd pulled out of her arms so she couldn't even touch him anymore.

"We should eat then," she answered carefully. "You rescued the fried eggs, we shouldn't let them get cold. But first can I say again, thank you for telling me?"

"That means you're going to bring the subject up again, right?" He moved farther away, picked up the panful of eggs. Every nuance of his body language screamed at her to keep her distance.

"I'm remembering how this started, you see. Because you understood about my writer's block. We have common ground, Callan. You were the one to work that out first. If we can help each other, I don't want to let this go."

"Don't—just *don't*—talk about helping me."

"Okay." She took a breath. "Boy, that bacon smells good!"

They ate, sitting on adjacent rocks, and every bite tasted fabulous after the early morning climb and all the fresh air.

Well, she's still here, Callan thought, dragging in a long, hot mouthful of smoky coffee.

Which put her in the same category as Birgit. The blonde at the races would have been long gone by now. Jacinda would go the sex-therapist route, take his admission of sexual inadequacy as a personal challenge. He hadn't told Birgit that his failure with her wasn't his first, so she'd used phrases like *getting you back in the mood* and *scary the first time, with someone new.*

He felt defensive. Didn't want to hear any of those kinds of lines from Jacinda, the way he hadn't wanted to read the pamphlets on bereavement from the hospital. He would prefer that they spent the remaining two and a half weeks of her visit in total, monklike silence. From beneath the concealing brim of his hat, he watched her, waiting for her to pounce. It took him a while to understand that she wasn't planning to.

She ate with a mixture of fastidiousness and greed that no one could have faked. It wasn't intended to seduce, but, Lord, he found it sexy! Something deep in his body began to stir again. Putting egg, bacon and tomato inside a sandwich of two bits of toast, she opened her mouth wide and bit down on it hard and slow, closing her eyes. The liquid egg yolk burst, leaked from her lips and ran down her chin, and she opened her eyes and laughed.

Running her index finger up to push the yolk back into her mouth, she said, "I wish this could be breakfast every day.

Salt? Cholesterol? Who cares! The sun evaporates that stuff, right?" She swallowed, grinned, and then apologized for talking with her mouth full.

A small, irritating black bush fly buzzed around her face and she waved it away, her hand soft. Callan remembered how her fingers had felt on his body just now, pushing for his response. He took another gulp of coffee, to disguise the fact that his breathing wasn't quite steady.

A fantasy flashed into his mind, as complete as an edited piece of film. He would spread out a blanket on the sand—never mind that he hadn't brought one with him—and he'd fall asleep. Jacinda would seduce him without waking him. He would believe the whole thing to be a dream. She'd take off his clothes with whisper-soft movements. He would feel her breath, the brush of her hair on his skin.

The sun would climb and the air would heat up. Her naked body would almost burn him as she slid over him, wrapping him in her long limbs. He'd thrust into her, hard as a rock, engulfed by her silky heat and, because it was a dream, he wouldn't think any of those panicky, mood-destroying thoughts for a second and they'd surge over the crest of the wave together. Success, before the concept of failure had even entered his head.

Failure.

The stirring, swelling, expectant feeling sank away like water down a plug hole.

Callan, just finish your breakfast.

"Do we have time to swim?" Jacinda asked, as he drained the last mouthful of coffee.

"It would be pretty cold," he said, dampening the idea down the way his body had just dampened down its own need. "The sun isn't on the water, yet."

"The water's cold even with the sun on it. I don't mind. I think a swim would be good."

For both of us, the words implied.

Therapy.

Or a cure.

Yeah, and she was probably right. The outback version of a cold shower. Not that he needed one right at this moment, but maybe she did. He knew she wanted him, and he'd left her hanging.

"We'd better put the fire out, first," he said.

She remembered the way they'd done it last week and shoveled on scoops of creek sand with the billycan, smothering the dying coals. "Is that enough?"

"It's fine. You'd have to be unlucky to start a bushfire in these conditions, even if you left it in flames."

"But you like to play it safe."

"A few minutes of work versus hundred-and-fifty-year-old creek bed trees? You bet!"

They packed up the egg carton, the jar of coffee and the rest of the breakfast things, and then she started rummaging in her day pack for her swimming costume. Callan had another fantasy. She'd forgotten it back at the house. She'd have to swim naked. They'd both—

"Why are things always in the last place you look?" she said, dragging the two pieces of animal-print fabric from the side pocket.

"Because once you've found them, you stop looking," he told her.

She stared at him, blank faced, and then she laughed. "Cattleman's logic?"

"There's an impressive intellect at work under this hat, I'm telling you."

She laughed again, and he felt better. No more fantasies invaded his brain. His muscles weren't knotted quite so tightly. The empty, angry feeling had gone. First and foremost, they were friends. He had to remind himself of that, hang on to it, trust it.

Trust her.

And not look at her while she changed.

She helped by disappearing behind the pale trunk of a huge tree overhanging the creek and he took off his shorts, boots and shirt while she was out of sight, to reveal the dark gray swim trunks he'd put on this morning just in case.

Wearing her neat, figure-hugging costume, having left her clothes in a tidy pile beside her day pack, Jacinda screamed all the way along the sand, like a jet coming down a runway. "If I take this fast, I won't notice the temperature," she yelled, then disappeared in a flurry of splashed-up water. Twisting, she launched onto her back with her arms spread out, still yelling. "Hey, are you coming, Callan? It's *freezing!*"

"After that sales pitch…" He launched toward her and ended up deeper, wetter and probably colder, competitive the way he'd been with Nicky as a child. Couldn't let any female get too far ahead of him, but appreciated the ones who gave him a good run for his money.

Like Liz.

He felt a twist of regret and loss and impatience. Why had he thought about Liz now? Why did he have to make everything so hard for himself? Liz would have been the last person to approve of the way he tied himself in knots.

Go for it, Callan.

He could almost hear Liz's voice, saying the words.

But go for what?

"Are we jumping and yelling and bunyipping today?" Jac asked.

"What, we're not cold enough already? We need to get colder?"

"We need to keep moving. The rocks up on the ledge are starting to get into the sun. They'll warm us up. I didn't yell loud enough, the first time. I want to do it again."

"Race you to the ledge," he said, and won.

Just.

"You let me get that close to a win." She was breathing hard, making her chest rise and fall in the water. He wanted to look down, ogle her breasts. He was tense and prickly and awkward and aware, and knew she felt pretty much the same. "You were going easy on me. Weren't you?"

"You'll never know, will you?"

She flicked water in his face, and then they both climbed onto the ledge.

The way they'd done last Saturday, they ran and jumped and yelled, swam and climbed and ran to jump again. "Why *is* this so good?" Jac said. The highest parts of the rock ledge were in full sun, now, and the smooth granite warmed rapidly. They sat on it, stretching their legs out and making wet imprints that shrank to a vanishing point as the moisture dried. "This should go in a self-help book."

"You ever think of writing one of those?" Callan suggested. "They sell pretty well, don't they?"

"Never, no matter how well they sell. I don't think I have enough answers for myself, let alone for anyone else!"

"I can't imagine self-help books give people real answers. I've looked at some. They always make it sound too easy. And if they do give answers… What about your novel? Doesn't a novel need answers?"

"Yes, but they're messy ones. Nice and human and flawed. Not definitive."

"But basically, with a novel, you control the universe. You can make it all work out just the way you want. That must be pretty nice."

"Not always. I mean, it is nice, but you can't always do it. You'd be surprised. Characters sometimes refuse to behave."

"Make them."

"You can't. They have minds of their own. If they don't,

then they're made of cardboard and readers can tell. I mean, I've never finished my novel so I don't know why I'm sounding like such an authority on the strength of thirty thousand words. All I know is, there have definitely been times when my characters didn't behave, and the right thing seemed to be to let them take control."

"When you talk about your writing, when you're really involved in it, your face changes." He'd noticed it before, but the change was more marked, today.

"Does it?" She pressed her hands to her cheeks, embarrassed, laughing a little. "Hope the wind doesn't shift direction, then."

"No, it's a good kind of change. Your eyes get a spark in them. You smile more. You move more. Are you working on your novel, in Lockie's notebook?"

"No." She shook her head vigorously. "No, I'm not." She paused. "At least…"

"So you are?"

"Oh…no…I had a couple of thoughts about my main character, that's all. I'm sure it doesn't mean anything. I haven't written a word."

"Are you going to try? You should. You shouldn't give up on something like that. You shouldn't let it defeat you."

She moved abruptly on the rock, shoulders squaring and bent arm snapping straight. "You are so unfair, do you know that?" she almost yelled.

Startled, he realized she was angry, not kidding around. She jumped up, headed toward the water, then circled back.

"So unfair!" she repeated even louder, and she was blinking back tears.

Before he could respond, she'd slipped into the water and started heading for the beach, her crawl messy and furious, lots of splash and not much speed. He followed and caught up easily, grabbed her wet shoulder and turned her around

just at the place where they could both stand without difficulty, chest deep.

"Don't say something like that and walk away," he told
her.

"Why the hell not? You do it to me! How many times now
have you said something important about what's going on
inside you and then just walked away?"

Oh.

She meant *that*.

Of course.

"That's different," he growled.

"Why? Your manhood is of universal, earth-shattering importance, but the disappearance of my creativity…my livelihood…is a minor irritation? We can chat about one in a light,
friendly way, lots of helpful hints from you about how to get
it right, while the other is this doom-laden, forbidden, terrifying, ghastly topic that has me beating myself up because I've
accidentally—despite a burning, huge need to…oh…just be
your friend about it, Callan—said and done a couple of
slightly, and totally unintended, sensitive things? Is that how
it is?"

"You're telling me the two things are related? Not being
able to write, and not being able to—?" He stopped. "You're
telling me that they're parallel? Equal?"

"Yes! Damn it! Isn't that part of what lets us understand
each other? Care about each other, even? Care, probably,
way more than is sensible, in my case." She blinked again.

Creek water or tears?

He wasn't sure.

He *was* sure that she was still angry.

And, so help him, it turned him on. He felt his heart rate
speeding up, and his breathing, and the air in his nostrils and
deep in his lungs was suddenly full of some indefinable aura
of wanting and need that he and Jacinda had manufactured

together like a powerful scent. This time, after all the false starts, he couldn't imagine it ebbing away. This time, he was sure he could get it right, because she was so different, so much more important in his life than those other women had been.

She looked like a sleek wet leopard in her animal print, with her shoulders getting tanned from the sun and her hair streaming down her back. The water came level with her breasts, floating them higher so that they swelled smooth and neat and round above the curved and normally modest neckline of her suit.

Her black lashes were spiky and thick with water, and her gray eyes seemed huge. They flashed at him. The tension in her whole body was electric.

"Jacinda…" he said.

"I'm trying *so hard* to find a way to get my writing back. I've told you how important it is. You almost… I've even thought you understood. More than I would have expected. Because of— Yes, your own problem. I've told you how it's helping me, being here. I've been…really naked to you about it, a couple of times."

"You don't think I've been naked?"

"You have. Which is why you should understand how hard it is, and not *push* me about my novel." She paused. "But I probably overreacted."

"And I didn't think," he said.

"Let's forget it."

She bobbed down into the water, letting herself float on her back with her arms spread wide, trying to relax. Her hair floated away from her like water weed and she stretched out her neck. Moisture gleamed on her fine-pored skin. The water lapped at the hip-level gap between the two halves of her swimsuit, showing her flat, olive-skinned stomach.

He didn't take his eyes off her for a second, and she must

have known he was watching her, she must have felt it like an electric current zapping between them in the water. His whole body crawled with aching desire like some dizzying illness, only the feeling was too good to be a disease.

When she stood up again, one swimsuit strap had drifted down off her shoulder, peeling the animal-print fabric half-way down her breast. Her thumb came to hook it back up, but he closed his hand over hers and said, "Don't. Please don't. Leave it down. Please."

She looked at him, and didn't need to ask why.

Which was good, because he couldn't have given her an answer. If he thought about anything…*anything*…except the immediacy of this moment, then he feared the moment would go.

In the water, they drifted against each other. The cold was unimportant. He felt her thighs, tight and cool and as slippery as satin, wrapping around him while her arms wrapped around his neck. Her eyes were wide and clear, their gaze fixed on his face. He cupped her backside in his hands and pulled her tighter against him, slid his fingers down and along to her inner thighs, where he stroked her.

She kissed him, her mouth wet and flavored with creek water, cool at her lips but warm within. He kissed her back, deeper than the other night, harder and stronger and longer. The sun dried their faces and heated their skin, contrasting with the cool water that moved around their legs.

He bent his knees and dipped her deep in the water again, kept kissing her with their faces submerged then pulled up to break the surface again and let their contact break. He still didn't speak. Couldn't. But wanted more. He found the second strap on her swimsuit, the one that was still in place, and lowered that, as well.

She didn't protest.

Not a word.

But she watched him and her eyes said, "Keep going."

He slid the tank-style swimsuit top down to her waist and her bared breasts moved lightly in the water, her nipples the color of cinnamon and strawberry mixed together. The swimsuit top bunched awkwardly so she raised her arms and he pulled it over her head, flung it toward the beach, didn't look to see if it had safely gotten that far.

She stepped back a couple of paces, to where the water only came just above her waist, and stood up, letting her body stream with dazzling wetness. She had her spine straight and her shoulders softly square. She knew he couldn't take his eyes from her jutting breasts and she didn't want him to.

The sun steamed the water from her skin and caught in her hair and she lifted her face higher into the bright light and closed her eyes. He could see just how much she loved the freedom of this place, the air and the space for miles around, no one to see them, nothing to get in the way of the sun on their skin and their primal awareness of each other.

He closed the distance, kissed her mouth, her jaw, her neck, and her tight, beautiful nipples, one and then the other. Her breathing sped up and she closed her eyes, pressed his mouth harder against her breast and arched her spine. He took her deeper into his mouth, sucking hard, lifting her higher. Each breast fitted just right, swelled just a little bit beyond the size of his cupped hands.

He was hard, throbbing, in pain.

And she knew.

Easing him into the shallows, she stroked his back, slipped her thumbs inside the waistband of his swim shorts and dragged them down. Then she lay back in the water and pulled his arms toward her so that he slid up her body, his hardness brushing the one remaining barrier of fabric between them at her groin. He heard her breath hiss in at the contact, felt her pushing her hips up so that he'd feel her again.

Oh, God.

He reached between them, cupped his hand over the warm mound between her legs. She pushed harder, and beneath the water his finger slid the fabric aside and slipped inside the two sweet folds. She gasped and writhed, her body trembling with its need for more, and he gave it to her.

But then he felt a change. She began to hold herself back, pressed her hand over his, and opened her eyes. The hesitation lasted only a few seconds, and he could see so clearly what she was thinking, the questions in her head.

Tease or keep going? What's going to make him stay aroused? What's going to keep the momentum? If I think about my own pleasure is that going to ruin everything for him?

Half a dozen other doubts and concerns, too, for all he knew.

Her hand slid awkwardly up his arm, and she whispered, "Not yet."

And despite how sure and confident he'd been just a short while earlier, that was all it took for everything to go wrong. It was like snatching at a piece of thistledown in the wind. You grabbed, and the thistledown floated farther away. You chased it and grabbed again, crushing its delicate fibers in your palm, forgetting why you'd reached for it in the first place.

"Callan?"

"I'm sor—"

"Don't apologize," she begged. "Please don't. It was my fault."

He laughed.

"It *was!* I stopped. I didn't know—"

"What to do next, because I'm such a delicate flower, one wrong move—"

"And I made it. I made the wrong move."

"It shouldn't be such a knife edge. Hell, it feels so strong between us sometimes—I like you, Jac, I want you—you'd think I could withstand twenty wrong moves and still get there."

He slid out of the water and onto the warm sand, hugging his arms around his knees, hiding the evidence of his failure. The sun beat onto his back, a slap more than a caress by this time. They should have headed back to the homestead way before this.

She followed him and knelt in front of him, her posture caving in the way he'd noticed it did when she lost confidence. Was his self-doubt contagious? She crossed her arms in front of her, covering her breasts. He didn't think it was deliberate. "What could I do to bring it back, Callan?" she asked him softly.

With no answers, thankful at least that she'd managed to avoid the phrase *help you* he just shook his head and closed his eyes.

It must only have been about thirty seconds later that Jac heard a vehicle. At first she thought it was something else. Wind in the eucalyptus trees, or one of the airplanes that occasionally flew overhead. But it got louder and she recognized the grind of an engine making its way slowly over the rough track in their direction. Kerry surely wouldn't have come looking for them yet, would she? They'd probably been gone longer than planned, but not by that much.

Oh, shoot, and where was the top of her swimsuit?

Scrambling to her feet, she went looking for it, hearing the vehicle get closer and closer. Make that vehicles, plural. There were two more driving in convoy behind the first one, she saw, as she picked up her sand-encrusted top from the hot ground. Still bare and dripping, Callan found his swim trunks and pulled them on, then crossed the creek bed to meet the vehicles, which gave her time to soak the sand off her top and pull it awkwardly down over her body.

Her throbbing body.

Her breasts still felt swollen, with hardened nipples at their crests, and she had an aching fullness where he'd touched her, and tingling skin that baked where the sun hit her shoulders and back but still felt cool along her arms and around her sides.

If they'd kept going, if Callan had been able to make love to her, they would have been discovered or at the very least interrupted. She'd never been a sexual exhibitionist, but right now in a heartbeat she'd have exchanged flagrant, shameless discovery for this feeling of failure and mess.

She felt stupid for having thought that a block as deep and real as Callan's could be overcome by a few sexy moves on her part, or even by the real and deep-rooted strength of her own desire. And she felt stupid for having believed that they'd established enough trust, enough depth, enough commitment.

Good grief, commitment?

The word fit nowhere.

She and Carly were leaving this place in two and a half weeks, in quest of a place to belong on the far side of the world. Those postcards she'd written to her brothers on Thursday at the café might have reached Adelaide by now. They were such a tiny step in creating a future for herself, but it was the only step that made any sense—the start of a plan, at least.

Move east, close enough to Andy and Dad in New Jersey or Tom in upstate New York so that they could get together every week if they wanted.

Work on her relationship with Andy, Dad, Tom and her nieces and nephews so that they *did* want to spend time with her and Carly, because Kerry had shown her it was possible and worthwhile.

Live on her savings and Kurt's ungenerous alimony for a year while she wrote…tried to write…worked out if there was a chance she'd be able to write and sell…her novel. If she couldn't, then at least Carly would be in school by that time, and Jac could get office work or possibly teach.

The plan didn't—couldn't—include Callan, his family, his land or his problems.

She found the rest of her clothing and struggled into it, her wet swimsuit dragging against the dry fabric of T-shirt and stretchy Lycra shorts. The sand didn't help, either. Her feet were covered in it, and it ended up gritty and uncomfortable inside her socks and shoes.

She could see Callan still talking to the new arrivals, nodding and gesturing, pointing to places on a map they'd unfolded and spread on the hood of one vehicle. She thought about going over there but before she could decide if it was the right thing he'd left the group and returned across the creek bed to the water hole.

"They're going to camp here," he said, and she could see how glad he was to have such an obvious and impersonal subject to talk about.

He wasn't planning to launch into a rehash of sensitive issues any time soon, and he was probably right. She wondered if they'd ever rediscover the same peace and intimacy that they'd found this morning, and that still hadn't been enough.

"They've picked a good spot!" she said, meeting him halfway.

He nodded, brushing dry sand from his forearms and calves, which gave him a good excuse not to look at her. The air almost crackled with the distance he'd put in place. How long would it last? Would she dare try to break it? Was there any point?

"They're part of a four-wheel-drive touring club," he said.

"Seem pretty responsible, and well-equipped. They're planning on staying three nights, and hiking up the gorge tomorrow. I'm glad we did our dawn climb this morning, or we'd have had company."

"Do you charge them for camping here?" She held out the towel she hadn't taken the time to use, but he shook his head and she could see he'd dried off almost completely in the sun and didn't need it. "It's your land, after all."

"We've thought about it, but it'd be more trouble than it was worth. We'd have to put up signs and garbage facilities, even a pit toilet, and that would only encourage more people to use the place."

"The water hole's a pretty sensitive ecosystem, isn't it? It wouldn't take much tourism for it to be ruined."

"We don't get too much tourist traffic out here. We're not on the main road to Leigh Creek, and our side road ends just a few clicks from the homestead, at Wiltana Bore. A generation ago, that made Arakeela a pretty lonely place, sometimes, but there're so many more tourists coming up here now, you're right, it's become a good thing."

"So you never get to know any of them? They don't invite you down to their campfire for a beer?"

"Sometimes," he said, and he sounded awkward about it, as if sharing campfire tales wasn't something he liked doing even when he did get an invitation. "We should head back."

"Yes." Pick up on his cues and leave everything unsaid? Or speak? Suddenly, that felt wrong. "Callan—"

"Can you grab the breakfast things and put them in the vehicle?" he cut in quickly. "I'd better get my shirt on or I'll start to burn."

So we're not even going to acknowledge that we're not talking about it, Callan? That's it? We're left hanging?

And yet, when she thought about it, she didn't know what else they could do.

Chapter Eleven

"Callan!" said Brant's voice on the phone a week and a half later.

"Hey…" Callan answered, glad to hear his friend and yet cautious at the same time—a stunning display of inconsistency in his attitude that was becoming far too familiar.

Beyond the closed door of his office, where he'd been working on some financial spreadsheets, he heard a background of typical evening sounds. Kerry called Lockie to help her with the dinner dishes. Water ran in a pipe. Josh accidentally turned the CD player up too loud, then turned it down again.

"We had two winners today," Brant said, and Callan could hear background noise at his end, also. It sounded like Brant's sister's voice. "I thought you'd like to know. Gypsy Caravan romped home in Albury, and Rae gave Lucite a try in a maiden event at Rose Hill." Rae Middleton was one of their trainers, based near Brant. "We weren't sure she was ready for a metropolitan race yet. Rae had talked about giving her more country starts, but she did us proud and got home by a nose. It was a small field, but it's still a good win."

"That's great." For once, Callan was able to sound as if he meant it. The racehorses took his mind off things he didn't want to dwell on, questions for which he had no answers. "I thought Lucite had some good stuff in her."

The water stopped running. He heard footsteps coming along the corridor.

Jac's.

He could recognize them easily, now.

"Mmm, you're half-asleep already, aren't you, sweetheart?" she said, just outside the office door, and he knew she must have Carly in her arms, taking her along to bed.

"Rae's got plans, now," Brant said. "She's thinking Group races in her next prep, maybe even the Melbourne Cup in a couple of years. The mare's a stayer."

"Not that Rae's aiming too high, or anything," Callan drawled, because horse racing in Australia didn't get any bigger than the Melbourne Cup. The whole state of Victoria took a public holiday on the first Tuesday in November for the big race day, and the prize purse was huge.

"Speaking of aiming high," Brant said, "I'm here to tell you that I have to be smashing you in the letters tally, at this point."

"Letters? Oh, from the Outback Wives women."

Change the subject, Branton, please.

Brant didn't. "Dusty reckons he's had about a hundred and fifty, and he's written back a nice fat *no* to all of them, because of Mandy. Me, I'm up over two hundred, and they're still coming."

"Yeah, and I'd be somewhere in between," Callan admitted. He had given a bundle of replies to Rob this morning, and had mailed several more two weeks ago in Leigh Creek, along with Jacinda's postcards to her brothers.

He heard her come back along the corridor, and then her

voice again in the kitchen, muffled by distance and the closed office door. "She couldn't even stay awake for a story. Anything I can help with, Kerry?"

"No, love, Lockie and I are doing fine, here."

"I'll be on the veranda, then."

Writing, Callan guessed.

"And Dusty and I are going to have to crawl over broken glass as punishment, at some point, for putting you through this whole *Today's Woman* deal?" Brant said into his ear. "Is that the message I'm getting?"

"Something like that."

There was a silence at the far end of the phone, then Brant asked cautiously, "So you're not going to meet any of them?"

Brant didn't know that Jacinda—who had to count as one of "them"—was staying here, and had been for three weeks. Now would be the obvious moment to tell him.

The words stuck in his chest and wouldn't come.

Brant didn't have to know, Callan decided. Because right at this moment, he just wasn't up to putting the necessary positive-yet-casual spin on the whole thing. He would end up saying too much, giving away more than he wanted to. Letting Brant and Dusty see how much of a mess he still was after four years without Liz was what had gotten him into this situation in the first place. He should learn to hide his damned feelings better.

But if it hadn't been for the magazine and its Wanted: Outback Wives, he never would have met Jac....

He tried that idea on for size and it felt so weird that he couldn't contemplate it.

He didn't want Jac and Carly to go...but he was counting the seven remaining days. He'd dragged those swim shorts of his onto his body seconds after he'd first heard the campers down at the water hole ten days ago, but he still felt naked whenever Jac was around.

Her presence in his house was so warm, it enriched all of

them…but when he found himself pricking up his ears for the sound of her voice, he felt ill and attempted to avoid her for hours afterward. He wished they'd never met…but he couldn't picture the universe without her, now.

He didn't know how to handle any of this.

Friendship was such an unsatisfying word, sometimes, but anything else held more pitfalls than the worst track on his property held ruts. He'd been sending out some pretty strong signals, since his failure with Jac down at the water hole, that she should keep her distance, that if she was ever tempted to try some more of Birgit's helpful sexual therapy then for heck's sake just damn well *don't,* and over the past week and a half she'd been scrupulous about it.

They hadn't so much as touched.

"What about you? Who have you met?" he asked Brant, since he considered attack to be the best form of defense, and a crucial strategy in male friendship. "I bet they've all looked like the back end of a bus, because who else would look at a sheep farmer like you?" Gratuitous, jokey insults usually worked pretty well, too. Anything to get this onto a safer level.

"I have met many female bus ends in my time, Callan, mate, for sure, and recent samplings have lowered bus-end technology to new depths," Brant said. "Now Nuala's got some wretched European friend arriving tomorrow in a state of crisis, and the words *on your best behavior* have been heard beneath our roof. I wish she'd hurry up and get married!"

"The European friend?"

"No, Nuala! Because then she'll be Chris's problem and I'll get some peace. Bloody wedding's not until September."

"You'll live," Callan drawled.

"Not if the European friend decides to stay until then."

They talked a bit more about their horses, and he ended up being glad that Brant had called, which he hadn't been at all sure about at some points during their conversation.

After he'd put down the phone, he went into the living room and stepped over to the window that looked out on the section of veranda where Jac had taken to sitting, in that rickety cane couch that needed either repairing or throwing out.

Yes, she had one of Lockie's notebooks in her lap and a pen in her hand.

He wouldn't disturb her.

But he envied her.

She'd been writing like crazy two hours every night for days, and a couple of times during the day he'd caught her snatching a moment to jot down some phrases in a folded up bit of paper she apparently kept in her front jeans pocket. She kept a pencil in there, too, a tiny stub of a thing that fit snugly there and didn't poke into her when she sat down.

He could see the fresh creativity flowering inside her, could see the miraculous, glowing effect it had on her, and she kept bloody well *thanking* him for it. *Thank you for making this possible, Callan. Thank you for showing me your beautiful land. Thank you for giving me peace and safety when I needed it most. Just for everything.*

And her gray eyes shone when she said it, and her cheeks went pink, and energy and satisfaction sang in her whole body, and dear God how he envied her!

The only consolation was that he didn't think the envy showed.

He managed to keep himself tightly enough bound inside that nothing showed, and he worked as hard as he'd ever worked in his life, overhauling the engine in the truck, doing the final work on the mustering yard with Pete, riding out to tag cattle, checking lines of fence and fixing broken strands of wire or putting new posts in places where the fence itself probably didn't need to exist at all.

"Take Jacinda for some company," his mother had suggested a couple of times.

"No, she might want to write."

"She's only writing in the evenings."

"She probably feels she can't write in the day, because there's too much to do. You know she likes to help out wherever she can."

"She doesn't need to do that every day. Take her with you, and she can sit under a tree and write while you work," Mum had persisted.

She knew nothing about what had happened two Saturdays ago down at the water hole, but she'd probably started guessing all the wrong things.

"But if she needs the computer—" he'd said.

And he hadn't been surprised when Mum still wouldn't let the subject go. "She seems to like writing by hand."

Still watching Jacinda through the window, Callan saw her pick up her pen and scribble several lines, before looking into the distance with a searching expression, then writing another few words. It was dark out, but the evening was still mild. She'd kicked off her shoes and curled her bare feet up onto the couch, and she was in short sleeves. A pool of light fell over her page, and half of her body, from a clip-on lamp he'd set up there for her last week.

On an impulse, he went out to her. "I'm driving out to Wiltana Bore tomorrow," he said, "to do some maintenance on the windmill. Do you want to come? See a different part of the property? You can sit in the shade and sip cool drinks and write, while you watch me work. See how the other half lives."

She nodded slowly. "I'd like that." Then she gave a sudden grin. "I mean, you head out of here every morning in a truck or on a horse and you claim it's working. It'd be good to get some proof."

"I'll put on a star performance." Humor was one of the things working best between them right now.

"Ooh, in that case, I'll take photos!"

"We'll leave right after breakfast," he told her, and felt a little less tense.

When Callan had gone back inside a moment later, Jacinda wondered about the invitation. Kerry had probably suggested it. The two women had good-humored tussles with each other about how much Jac should help around the place, and how much her writing time should be protected.

Jac wasn't yet convinced that she had anything worth protecting, while Kerry had begun to treat the subject with reverence, pronouncing the words *your writing* as if they were spelled with capitals. Jac appreciated the fact that her creative endeavors weren't considered a frivolous hobby, but she still felt like a fraud.

And she felt like a fraud climbing into the four-wheel-drive beside Callan the next morning, with her notebook and pen in the small backpack that had become known as hers. They were bringing morning tea but not lunch because he'd said the job should only take a couple of hours.

How much writing would she really get done?

Why had he asked her, when for the past week and a half he'd avoided any time alone in her company?

He was back to playing the Flinders Ranges tour guide, it turned out, with the unstated subtext that these were things she should see before she left.

Which was getting to be soon.

Six days from now, they'd probably be out at the airstrip, waiting for Rob and the mail plane to arrive.

"It's harsher country out this way," Callan told her as they drove. "You might not like it."

It's the tour-guide routine I don't like, she wanted to tell him, *even though you're getting pretty good at it.*

The country *was* harsh, and somewhat farther from the homestead than the "few clicks" he'd claimed one day recently. Fifteen kilometers slid by on the four-wheel-drive's odometer before Jac saw the tank and windmill, with a large group of glossy, red-brown Santa Gertrudis cattle gathered around it, drinking from the metal trough that the tank fed into. The rocky ranges looked distant from this point, as the parched land flattened in the east toward Lake Frome.

Callan got out his tools and his oil for greasing the wind-mill's moving parts, while Jac unpacked the flask of iced coffee they'd brought, found some shade beneath a scrubby tree, set up her camp stool, her drinking mug and her shady hat…and couldn't write a word.

She wasn't blocked; she was just restless—distracted by Callan's familiar body at work, full of questions, almost ready to take flight in the light breeze along with a hawk she could see soaring overhead in the usual yawning blue. After five minutes in her folding canvas chair, she got up again, put down her notebook and pen, poured mugs of cold, ice-cream-thickened coffee for herself and Callan and wandered over to him. He stood at the base of the windmill, whose daisy-petal iron blades creaked as they turned in the breeze.

"Anything I can do?" she asked.

"Nothing's coming with the writing?"

"Not right now. I might, oh, describe the cattle, or some-thing, in a minute."

"Go and say hi to 'em, they won't bite. Actually, they'll probably run."

"I wish they were on the other side of that fence, to be honest."

"I don't, since that's not my land!"

She laughed. "No? You mean your land does end? There is life beyond Arakeela Creek?"

He clicked his tongue. "So I'm told."

Skirting the cattle, who were far more interested in water than in her, Jac went closer to the fence. It was impressive, over six feet high, a fitting border to Callan's kingdom, she thought. Coming back to him, sipping the icy coffee as she walked, she said, "No wonder you're always fixing fences." She gestured back at the line of netting and posts. "I didn't know Santa Gertrudis could jump that high." She smiled.

Straight-faced, he answered, "They've been taking lessons from the 'roos. You don't often see it, but you'll be impressed if you do, a whole flock of Big Red Santas going boiing-boiing-boiing." He bounced his hand up and down, giving her a strong and cartoonlike mental image of the "flock" of leaping cows.

She laughed again. "You are such a nut!"

He grinned back at her and their eyes met, but that didn't feel comfortable—friendly kidding around felt fine, but not eye contact—so they both looked at the fence once more.

"Seriously, though, this fence isn't my job," Callan told her. "It's the Dog Fence."

"The what?"

"Over five and a half thousand kilometers. Longest fence in the world, dividing the north from the south and keeping the dogs on the other side."

"Because people in the south of this country don't like poodles and cocker spaniels?"

"Well, poodles, they're pretty deadly, yeah, but worse are the dingoes—the wild dogs the aborigines brought with them twenty thousand or so years ago. Dingoes and sheep don't mix. Settlers built the fence originally to keep the rabbits out of the north, but the rabbits just laughed because they were already there. So then the fence switched to keeping the dingoes out of the south, out of sheep-grazing country, and that works pretty well. It's patrolled for breaks, or drifted sand."

"Patrolled. Half of your boundary fence is actually pa-trolled." The fact made this place seem even more like his own personal kingdom. "But you don't graze sheep here at Arakeela," she remembered.

"Some properties in the Flinders still do, and of course farther south."

"I can't believe it, a three-thousand-mile fence."

"Write about it," he suggested.

So she did.

And she wrote about the sound the windmill made, and the sulfurous, salty tang of the water, and the rich, almost cherry red color of Santa Gertrudis cowhide in the sun. Then she looked at Callan perched on the top of the windmill with a big metal tool in his hand and wrote about him, and realized that one of the male characters in her novel had changed, over the past week or so.

Her broad-shouldered Chicago lawyer, Russ, moved and looked and laughed like Callan now, and...oh drat, she had to face this because Russ himself had been trying to tell her so for days, only she hadn't wanted to listen...Russ didn't want to be a lawyer anymore. He'd thrown down his brief-case in an act of rebellion and picked up a wide-brimmed cat-tleman's hat instead.

What the heck was she going to do with him?

When they got back to the house, she asked Kerry, "How are you managing? Is Carly being a nuisance while the boys are doing school?"

"No, she's fine. She's always fine!"

"W-would it be all right if I kept writing this afternoon?"

"Isn't that what I've been telling you to do?"

"And do you think Callan would be okay with me creating some new files on his computer? I know the boys will want to use the school one."

"He's offered you his computer whenever you want, Jac." Kerry patted her shoulder.

"Well, I might start right now, then."

Callan had already gone off on his next task, after making some sandwiches the size of doorstops to take with him for

his lunch. His office was quiet. Jacinda closed the door to encourage Carly not to disturb her, and was immediately surrounded by the vivid and complex aura of Callan's
personality.

The space was simple, practical, unpretentious. The computer was almost new, but the battered desk it sat upon could
have counted as a colonial-era antique. Beside the mouse pad
sat a brightly painted plaster drink coaster that one of the kids
had made for Callan's coffee mug, and on the wall in a long
line above the window, he'd tacked up paintings, also done
by Lockie and Josh.

Most of the bookshelves were filled with cattle-breeding
journals, horse-racing manuals, tomes on *Tax for Primary
Producers* and the like, but there were three or four shelves
that looked more like exhibits in a natural-history museum,
set out with neat displays of aboriginal stone axes and spear-
heads, or interesting rock samples, or snake skins and bird
nests and feathers.

There was also a picture of a medium-blond young woman
cradling a newborn baby in her arms, and Jac knew, because
she'd seen other pictures of the same woman in several places
around the house, that this was Lockie with Liz.

Russ.

I'm supposed to be making decisions about Russ.

Who really, absolutely, seriously refused to be a lawyer
anymore.

She found Callan's word-processing program, set up a
folder called Jacinda—Novel, and created a new file. The
words flowed fast, and soon she didn't even hear the sound
of the kids or Kerry.

First, she typed in some of the handwritten scenes she'd
worked on over the past few days, and when she came to the
end of those, she just kept going, starting a new file for plot
and character notes and one for the lines of dialogue that kept

coming out of Russ's mouth even though she didn't yet know where they'd fit in the book.

She ended up switching back and forth between all three files as new ideas came to her, sending each file to the bottom of the screen when it wasn't immediately required, and putting things in the wrong file occasionally when she got really absorbed. A couple of times she searched the Internet for research, and left some of the most useful sites at the bottom of the screen, also, so she could access them quickly if she needed them again a page or two further on.

At one point, her concentration broke for a moment and she thought about Callan and Wiltana Bore and that nutty image of the Santa Gertrudis herd leaping like cartoon kangaroos. She grinned to herself. A warm, giddy, happy feeling flooded into her.

Callan, you are such a nut....

Russ needed a sense of humor, too.

Yes! Something else she should have seen in him before.

Her fingers moved again on the computer keys.

At one point, Kerry tiptoed in and whispered, "Tea," then tiptoed out again, leaving a steaming mug and a piece of lemon cake on a plate near her elbow. At another point, Callan must have arrived back, because she was dimly aware of his heavy footfalls coming along the corridor and passing by. She forgot about him and kept writing, and suddenly it was six o'clock and Kerry was calling her for the evening meal, which they usually ate at this hour.

Remorseful that she'd left Kerry with the household chores and all three kids for so long, she quickly closed her files and the Internet sites and went to make sure that Carly washed her hands.

Despite the remorse, she knew it was the best day of writing she'd done in years.

* * *

Jac hadn't closed her files properly, Callan discovered when he went into his office after dinner and his shower, to check some Web site information on cattle vaccination.

Mum had told him Jac had been writing on the computer all afternoon, and then he'd seen for himself how she had hurried to the dinner table with a guilty look on her face, saying, "I'm sorry, I should have stopped an hour ago."

He wondered if she'd remembered to back up. Probably not. This computer had one of those key-fob-sized removable drives and he kept it in a bird's nest on the bookshelf, which wasn't the most obvious location. He took it out of the bird's nest, leaned past the swivel chair and plugged it in, then copied in the files. At the bottom of the screen, she'd left one named Bits, which made him smile because that had been the name of one of their dogs here at Arakeela, long ago.

He opened it, and that was indeed what it contained. Bits. Snatches of notes and writing that she hadn't found a place for yet, some of it in paragraphs, some of it just single lines. Not thinking that it could be private—after all, she'd said this was a novel, intended for a whole audience of readers—he took a closer look.

And found himself.

C's silhouette against this improbable sky belongs like a puzzle piece snapped in place, Callan read, leaning his hand on the desk as he scrolled the mouse down. *His muscles work, his body moves, his eyes fix on what he's doing and I watch all of it, thinking about all the ways this body is different from the pumped-up ones I've seen in L.A. gyms.*

The breeze shifts and the windmill turns its metal daisy face. Southern Cross *reads the windmill company's name on the rudder blade, as it swings more clearly into view.* Don't fall, C, *I silently beg. And I know he won't. There's a trust I*

*have in his body—its skills, its strength, its utter compe-
tence—that I've never felt before. I would let this man's body
take me anywhere. I would lean on it as far as the ends of the
earth. I would cradle it and protect it, believing it would
break in a thousand pieces while protecting me, if breaking
was required.*

*This is what a woman wants. Or (let's not generalize!) it's
what Megan wants from Russ, anyway. Not just the physical
hunger, but the physical trust. It was never enough for her
that Russ knew contracts and civil statutes and partnership
deals. She needed a body as well as a mind. Maybe she's
more like an animal (I'm more like an animal) than I thought.
That's why Russ being a lawyer just* didn't work!

Behind him, the door opened, and he turned to see Jacinda
herself, her hair pulled back in a ponytail, the sleeves of her
cotton top pushed to the elbows and splashes of dish-washing
water on her front. Her cheeks were pink from standing over
the steaming sink, and she had the aura of energy he was
starting to realize meant she was still riding high on the good
writing she'd done today.

"Callan, I'm sorry to bother you," she began, "but I
couldn't find the removable drive before dinner, so I
didn't—" She stopped, and her voice changed. "Is that one
of my files?"

He ignored the question. "You wrote about me."

This crystallized her attention even more than the open
file. "You've *read* it?"

Still he ignored her. "C. That's me. That's today. Up on
the windmill at Wiltana Bore. You put me in your book."

"You read my work without asking."

They weren't listening to each other—or only enough to
make both of them angrier. Callan stood with his hand resting
on the mouse, and Jac might have thought he was threatening to delete the whole file, the way her gaze zeroed in on

his finger then flicked angrily back to the screen. Right now he didn't care if the file did disappear. "I'm your research material, and you never said."

"This is draft stuff." She was indignant, impatient. She pushed her sleeves up higher and propped her hands on her hips. "Not even that. Character notes. You're not in the book, Callan. And you *read* it!"

"You'd left the file onscreen and I was backing up for you, that's all. I read it because…" Hell, this sounded stupid! "We had a dog called Bits, once. You've said it's a novel. How can that be private, when you hope someday people will pay to read it?" Any hint of defensiveness disappeared as he realized again what this would mean. "Pay to read about me, Callan Woods. Me, stripped raw."

"It's not you," she repeated through gritted teeth, her patience exaggerated. "It's notes. And *it is private*. This is how writers work, Callan. We take all these little strands and mix them up and mull over them and in the process they change and lose that personal quality, but to start with, in this form… Do you know how naked it feels to have *anyone* read that raw stuff?"

"Do you know how naked it feels to read about 'C' up on the windmill, with his trustworthy body!"

They glared at each other again. Jac's eyes flashed darker than usual, her cheeks got even pinker, and the little gold dangly earrings she wore flashed, too, as she jutted out an angry jaw, and he thought, *This is sexual frustration. This is irrational. We are both irrational, and over the top, and crazy. We are making a big sexually frustrated mountain out of a tiny privacy-issue molehill and I don't know how to stop, because I want her so much it feels like an illness.*

And I don't want her to leave in six days and take a part of me with her in her damned book, because what's she going to leave behind for me, in return? What am I ever going to get out of this, since the one thing we both want, I can't deliver?

He closed his eyes and hunched his shoulders, still gripping the mouse and feeling overwhelmed.

"So it's bad that I trust your body that much?" Jacinda said. She didn't sound quite so angry now.

"I don't know why you would." He let go of the mouse, leaned on the desk, whooshed out a breath. "How many times has it let you down, now?"

"Not many," she said softly, stepping closer. "I'd be up for more. It's you who's running for the hills, Callan. That's what this is really about, isn't it?"

"Yeah, for you, too, and I wonder why." He added harshly, "Maybe I just don't want the ego-orientated sexual-therapy approach you're prepared to offer. The Jacinda Beale patented cure."

"That is a really awful thing to say!"

"And I don't want my body in your book, Jacinda. I don't want any part of me in your book."

"Well, that's your problem, not mine!" she snapped back at him, and in an instant they were bristling and snarling at each other again, like two angry dogs. "Because I've told you, Russ is *not you!*"

He turned away from her, tired of the stalemate they'd reached.

"I'm checking the e-mail," he muttered. "Your files are backed up. I keep the removable drive in the bird's nest, next time you need it."

Chapter Twelve

Jacinda didn't stay to watch Callan's list of new e-mail messages cascade onto the screen. She was too angry, too hurt and too confused.

Deep down, she knew that they were both right to be angry…privacy had been invaded on both sides…but not this angry. She would have said that they trusted each other—that him reading her work shouldn't have felt like such an invasion, and that her using him as a key into Russ's character shouldn't have felt like such a piece of theft.

Carly was already asleep. Restless, hugely keyed up and on edge, Jac went into their room and checked on her anyhow, in an attempt to get her emotional compass pointing back in the right direction, but it didn't help.

Even bending down and inhaling the sweet, familiar scent of her daughter's hair and whispering, "You and me together, sweetheart," didn't help, because she knew she needed Callan in her life, as well, the way Megan was starting to need Russ.

She prowled out of the bedroom again and went onto the veranda—the place where she'd first put real words down on paper again, the place where she and Callan had shared that first really strong connection, beneath the moonlight on her first night here.

All those "firsts." Any day now, she and Carly would be starting the "lasts." Their last visit to the water hole, their last egg-collecting expedition in the chook pen, Carly's last morning as an honorary student at the School of the Air. The more personal "lasts," Jac's last things with Callan—last cup of coffee, last hug. Those, she didn't even want to think about.

But she couldn't help it.

Last joke, last shared grin.

She remembered those kangaroo-jumping cattle again, and got that same silly grin on her face.

Oh, hell, she couldn't stay angry with him!

She was in love with him.

He found her still standing there several minutes later, and he didn't seem angry anymore, either. The guts had gone out of the emotion, the same as they had for her, but whether he'd come to the same realization as she had about what this meant, she didn't know.

"There's an e-mail for you," he said. "A-dot-Dugan, at one of those big American addresses. I didn't open it. Is it just junk?"

"No," she said blankly. "A. Dugan? That's Andy. Andy Dugan. My brother."

Omigosh, Andy had replied! He'd actually replied, within a couple of days of receiving her postcard!

She felt a ridiculous surge of feeling and the prick of tears. "Can I take a look right now? Are you busy on there?"

"No, I'm done. Of course you can look."

She stepped toward the doorway into the house where he stood holding it open, and it was probably the closest they'd gotten to each other in days. She saw him draw in a breath and lift his hand as if to touch her, but then he thought better of it and turned away.

"Just switch off the monitor when you're finished, can you?" was all he said.

"Sure."

He half turned back again. "And can we forget about yelling at each other just now?"

"Oh, please, yes! Both apologize, maybe?" she suggested.

"I overreacted. I'm sorry."

"So did I, and I'm sorry, too."

Apologies, however, were sometimes the easy way out. Sitting down at Callan's desk, Jac opened the e-mail.

Hey, Jacinda, it was nice to hear from you! she read.

Andy told her some items of news—his wife, Debbie, had bought an art-framing business, their second boy would be starting college in the fall—and asked her some questions about her life. What was she doing so far away? Debbie had noticed recently that her name wasn't listed on the credits of *Heartbreak Hotel* anymore. How come?

It touched Jac that he and Debbie even remembered which soap she'd written for, and she e-mailed right back, answering his questions as best she could without dumping too much on him. She also told him, I'm thinking Carly and I may relocate to the tristate area soon, and it would be great to see you when we do.

"So your brother got your postcard," Callan said to her when she emerged from his office a little later and met up with him in the kitchen.

"Yes, and it was a nice e-mail in reply. I wonder if I'll hear from Tom. Upstate where he is, he may still not have gotten the card."

Andy's e-mail gave a healthy lift to her spirits, which was a pity, in hindsight, because this only meant they had further to fall the next day, and by ten in the morning they'd come crashing down like an airplane in a tailspin, hard on the heels of Lucy's phone call from Sydney.

"I haven't wanted to worry you," she said, "but Kurt's been calling."

"The hang-ups?"

"He's not hanging up anymore, he's staying on the line. I—I had to let you know. I know it's not what you want to hear. He's got to the point where he's threatening and abusive, now, and he's convinced that I know where you are."

"Did you tell him? Oh, Lord, did you?"

"Jacinda, mate, I don't know! You're on some farm in outback south Australia that's civilized enough to have e-mail and a phone."

"Have you told him that? Have you told him anything? What kind of threats?"

"That he'll track you down. That Carly will disappear and you'll never find her, because you're no good for her and he's the best father who ever lived." Lucy's voice came through jittery and thready with fear. "Jac, he's sounding weird and scary—drugs, maybe?—and just now he told me he had plane tickets to Sydney and he touches down in two days."

"Tickets, plural?"

"For him and…I can't remember the term he used. Body-guards. Entourage. His paid muscle, anyhow."

"That'd fit," Jac had to admit. Kurt loved having black-shirted, eye-shaded security people walking three paces behind him most of the time. In the past, she used to joke about it, but he'd never been able to laugh about things like that.

"He knows where I live, doesn't he?" Lucy said. "You gave him my street address when you stayed here before."

"Yes, I did. Oh my God, Lucy, I did." He was Carly's father, after all, and at that point he hadn't seemed anywhere near this out of control. "I'm so sorry!"

"And he says he's coming," Lucy said. "Can you find out if it's true? He probably thinks you're still here, and when he finds out you're not… I want to call the police, but I won't yet. Not until you've talked to someone in California, because maybe none of what he's saying is true."

Kurt had never been prone to empty threats. Feeling sick to her stomach, Jac didn't tell Lucy this yet. "I'll call you back," she told her friend, "after I've talked to Elaine."

It was five in the evening in L.A. and calling from the phone in Callan's office, she got her former boss on her cell phone, in the middle of bumper-to-bumper traffic on the freeway. The connection kept threatening to cut out, which made the conversation even tougher than it needed to be.

"I can't talk detail on that, right now," Elaine said in a guarded tone.

"Because you have someone there?"

"That's right."

"Not Kurt?"

"No, honey, but you know that particular bank has a lot of branches in this area."

"Right. But you can listen."

"And I am."

She summarized Lucy's phone call. "Does it fit with what's happening at your end, Elaine?"

"This traffic. It's a mess."

"Elaine, I'm losing you."

"Connection's fine here, at the moment."

"Not the connection. What you meant. A mess? Kurt's a mess? I just want to know if Lucy should contact the Sydney police. And I want to know if Carly is in danger." Her voice cracked, she sucked up a sob, and at that moment Callan's office door opened and there was her daughter, blond and big-eyed and the most precious, important thing in the world. "Everything's fine, honey," she said brightly.

"Does that mean we should finish now and I should call you back?" Elaine asked.

"No, I meant— You should definitely call me back, but I was talking to Carly. Carly knows everything is fine," she added for her daughter's benefit.

"But you don't?"

"No, not at all."

"I am going to call you back, okay? I promise."

"When?"

Elaine said guardedly, "When I have more information."

But she didn't call back all day, and when Jacinda tried her cell phone, her landline and her work phone, she got machines and messages every time.

Just before dinner, figuring that it was around one in the morning in L.A. and Elaine wasn't going to call back tonight, she called Lucy again and said, "If you want to talk to the police in Sydney, go ahead, but we don't know what flight he's on, or even what airline, and there's no guarantee he'll travel under his own name. I'm sorry. I'm so sorry to have involved you in all this, Lucy. And I wish there was more I could tell you."

"This is her ex-husband?" Kerry asked Callan, while Jacinda was putting Carly to bed.

"Yes."

"What's going on?"

"Apparently he's making threats. He told her friend he's coming out here."

"Here to Arakeela Creek?"

"He doesn't know that this is where she and Carly are, but Jac's afraid he'll do something to Lucy to get her to tell him." Callan shook his head, knowing it sounded bizarre. "Jac is very jittery about it. I don't know if she's right to be."

"She wouldn't say anything to me. Not really. A problem at home, that was all, and she was waiting for an important call. I want to hug her and tell her everything's going to be all right, but you're right, we just don't know. Carly has picked up on Jac being so tense. She's a perceptive little thing. They're leaving in less than five days, Callan."

His mother spoke the words tentatively, then left them hanging in the air. He wanted to yell at her, "You think I don't know that?" but he didn't. She meant well. She was asking something from him—an idea of where Jacinda and Carly might fit in his future, if anywhere—but he couldn't give her that because he didn't know.

Mum left the house to cross to her little cottage a few minutes later, after saying good-night to the boys. She liked a quiet hour or two on her own before she went to bed, but Callan couldn't help wondering if there was more to her prompt departure this evening. Was she tactfully leaving the other two adults alone? What did she expect to happen?

Nothing did. Only this ache of tension and uncertainty and failure deep in his bones.

What could he do for Jacinda?

Nothing.

Hadn't he already proved that more than once to them both?

By eight, Lockie and Josh had conked out for the night. They had the sound, steady sleep habits of active kids, and weren't as aware of Jacinda's tension as her daughter was. Jac had spent longer in the bedroom putting Carly to bed tonight.

When she came into the kitchen at last, as Callan was making tea, he asked her, "Asleep?"

"Finally. I read two stories and sang three songs, and she was still restless, but finally when I patted her back she drifted off."

"What are you going to do?"

"Read, maybe. I'll have some tea, if there's enough in the pot."

"I meant about your ex-husband's threats."

"I need to hear from Elaine."

"He can't kidnap Carly off my land, Jac. He can't hurt you here." It was true. He believed that. But it sounded lame.

"You wouldn't think so, would you?" she said. "But something's not right. Why is he making these impossible threats? I'm upset for Lucy. I need to be able to tell her if she could conceivably be in danger. It's like an episode from a bad spy show on TV. I don't understand what he's trying to do, or why. I'm going to keep trying Elaine in the morning. She promised she'd call back!"

"Are you going to be able to sleep?"

She shrugged. "Eventually."

Eventually, Jac did sleep.

She must have fallen off at about midnight, and by then she was so tired that she slept deeply for a solid two hours. Then something woke her when the electric clock radio beside the bed read 2:09. She didn't know what had roused her, at first, and lay there with her heart pounding in blank fear, her emotions immediately locking back into the state of nervous tension they'd been in all day.

Creak…thump.

That noise.

I know that noise.

It was the flap of the screen door leading to the veranda, she realized, and there it was again. Creak…thump. Creak…thump. It was swinging wide open on its hinges and hitting the wall. Carly tended to forget to close it sometimes, so Jacinda knew the sound well.

Carly.

Twisting, Jac looked over to Carly's bed, but there was no moon tonight and the room was pitch-black. She had to feel her way across the space, her tired eyes questing for the dim shape of a humped quilt and a head on the pillow.

The bed was empty.

And it was stupid to panic about it because Carly hadn't been…couldn't have been…kidnapped by Kurt in the middle of the night…although Kurt was still to blame. After sensing her mother's stress all day, Carly was sleepwalking.

Creak…thump. The screen door flapped again. She had probably gone out to pat the dogs on the veranda.

Jac switched on the light in their room so that she could see her way down the corridor without waking Callan or the boys in their nearby rooms with too much sudden brightness. She passed through the living room and, yes, the front door was open and the screen door was flapping, just as she'd thought.

But Carly wasn't with the dogs. They snoozed on their old blankets, opening their eyes long enough to say a doggy version of "Hi, Jac, what are you doing here in the middle of the night?" before losing interest and snoozing again. The blankets were crooked along one edge, as if they might have been scuffed out of place by a little girl's knees, so maybe she had been here at some point.

Jac checked the cane couch, but Carly wasn't there, either. She walked all the way around the veranda, hampered by the lack of moonlight, then she found the flashlight that Callan kept on the windowsill beside the front door and went out to the chicken coop, in case Carly had gone on a midnight egg hunt. But the chooks were fast asleep, lined up on their perches, and the gates to their run and coop and the vegetable garden were all shut.

Back in the house, with her heart and breathing beginning to get faster, she checked Carly's bed again in case she'd just…what…*imagined* its emptiness and that flapping screen door?

She hadn't.

The bed was still empty.

She woke up Callan, shaking his shoulder and speaking before he'd even moved.

"Carly went sleepwalking, Callan, and I didn't hear her until the screen door woke me up, and now I can't find her. Anywhere."

He sat up, dragged his fingers across his creased eyes. "Sorry, say that again." His voice was deep and creaky with sleep, and he smelled warm, and like almond-scented soap. The white T-shirt he usually wore to bed stretched across his chest, twisted from the way he'd rolled in the bed.

"Carly went sleepwalking outside. The screen door woke me up, flapping."

Creak…thump. It did it again as she spoke, moved by the night breeze, and only then did she realize what this implied.

"Carly must have left it open," she said. "But that doesn't mean she only went through it fifteen minutes ago, does it? I—I got to sleep around midnight and now it's two thirty. She could have been wandering out there for two hours."

Callan threw back the bedcovers and stood, his bare feet slapping onto the wooden floor. "She's not with the dogs?"

"That was the first place I looked. I went all around the house, and out to the garden and the chicken run."

He nodded, but didn't speak, then crossed the room and flicked on the switch beside the door. They both blinked in the sudden light. He grabbed a windproof jacket and shrugged into it over the T-shirt, dropped his pajama pants, hauled jeans over his long legs and naked hips, and slid his sockless feet into his old elastic-sided riding boots. He was ready in less than a minute.

"She can't have gone far," he said. "And it's not a cold night, thank goodness."

"But it's supposed to be hot again tomorrow, isn't it?"

"Low thirties," he confirmed, using the centigrade scale that temperature was measured in here. She knew that meant at least ninety degrees, and Carly would have no water with her. "But Jac, those temperatures are hours away. Don't think that far ahead."

"How can I help it?"

"Get dressed. I'll grab another flashlight. We won't wake Mum and the boys yet."

But Kerry heard them calling Carly's name around the out-buildings within a few minutes, and appeared at the front door of her cottage in her dressing gown. "She's sleepwalking?"

"She must be," Jac said. She hugged her arms across her body. As Callan had said, it wasn't a very cold night but, in her haste, she'd only slipped into a thin angora sweater, a colorless dark gray in the dimness, as well as panties, jeans, socks and running shoes. "But I didn't hear her go."

"She can't have gone far," Kerry promised, just as Callan had.

Jacinda didn't believe them. Carly could be tenacious when she walked in her sleep. What kind of an idea did she have in her head? There could easily be no logic to what she had done. Could she have gone to the water hole? She'd never been down there on foot, only on horseback and by vehicle. She probably had no idea of the distance at night, on her small legs, even if she did know the right direction to set off in.

Or would she have gone to visit the horses? She'd been getting more interested in them over the past week or so, and less scared of their size and unpredictable behavior. A few days ago, Jac had let Lockie lead Carly around on the quietest of them, a ten-year-old gelding, which was the one

Josh usually rode, and all three children had been so cute about it.

"That's great, Carlz!" Lockie had kept saying to her, while Carly had worn a huge grin on her face.

Josh had half walked, half skipped—backward—about ten yards in front of them, watching their every move and giving frequent cautions.

"Isn't he a great little horse? If you fall off, don't scream and scare him, Carlz."

Jacinda smiled at the memory, but then the smile turned into a half sob, because if Carly's tame little ride the other day had encouraged her to go looking for the horses in the middle of the night...

The animals weren't stabled but left free in their paddock, which had to be at least ten acres in size. Callan nodded at her suggestion that Carly might have gone in that direction and together they walked past the outbuildings toward the fence and gate. Jac's left foot hurt with every step. She'd pulled on her sock so carelessly that it had bunched into a crease that would give her a blister if they did much more walking tonight.

A blister wasn't important, but if they did walk as far as the water hole and it slowed her down... The issue crystallized into a small, self-contained agony that was a subset of the vast agony of Carly's disappearance, which itself came on top of Kurt's bizarre, threatening phone calls to Sydney that she still didn't understand.

Should she stop and fix the sock?

Which would waste more time? Fix it? Leave it?

The bite of pain and the torment of indecision remained with her.

When they reached the paddock fence, Callan played his powerful flashlight over the dry ground until he found the horses in one corner, asleep.

"I can't see her," he said needlessly, because Jac had been watching the moving pool of light along the ground as intently as he had. "But I didn't sweep the whole paddock. Could she have fallen asleep on the ground somewhere?"

"I— She could have. She's so unpredictable."

Jac couldn't go on speaking, but her thoughts just wouldn't stop.

As Callan painstakingly swept the flashlight beam back and forth through the huge field, Jac remembered everything he had said to her the night she hadn't returned from her walk before dark, all that stuff about survival in this country without food or water and how a human being didn't last long.

She remembered his warnings about snakes, thought about the cold depth of the water hole beyond the first shallow slope of sand if Carly did somehow get that far. She couldn't swim.

She pictured the cattle grids where fences and tracks met, and imagined Carly trying to cross one in the dark and slipping between the thick metal bars. Would her leg get jammed or broken?

She remembered the pitiless terrain stretching beyond Wiltana Bore, the stories of doomed explorers in the nineteenth century, and the name of a mountain she'd seen on the map not far north of here—Mount Hopeless.

"I can't see her," Callan said at last. "But there was something over in the northwest corner—a shadow—a shape. About her size. It's worth taking a look."

He unhooked the chain that kept the gate shut and let Jacinda through, then followed her, and they tramped through the paddock. Callan kept his flashlight beam trained on the place where he thought he'd seen a shadow, while Jacinda pointed hers toward the ground ahead of them.

The circle of light should have been comforting, but somehow it wasn't. It created a barrier between them and the darkness, turning the vast nightscape into an alien universe.

Trying to go faster, Jac tripped more than once. "Is it too soon to call?" she said. "If it is her, shouldn't we call her?"

"Yes, go ahead. If it is her, she hasn't moved, though, so she might be asleep."

"She'll wake up if she hears my voice." She called her daughter's name over and over, but there was no sound or movement in reply.

After a couple of hundred yards, Callan slowed and stopped. "It's nothing," he said heavily. "Just a dip in the terrain. It flattened out as we got closer, and now it's disappeared. It's not her."

Jac's legs felt as if they wouldn't carry her any farther, and the blister on her foot must have burst. It stung insistently, a final piece of meaningless cruelty that somehow reminded her of Kurt and his meaningless cruelty, reminded her of Elaine failing to call her back yesterday, of Lucy feeling threatened in Sydney, and the possibility of Kurt himself finding his way out here by chartered helicopter, so that even if they found Carly tonight and she was safe…

Her knees shook so hard that she began to lower herself to the ground in the middle of the paddock, gasping for air, no strength left. Callan caught her and gathered her up into his arms. He didn't speak, but his body was warm and hard and strong and she needed it more than she'd ever needed a man's touch in her life.

"Help me, Callan," she gasped. "Help me."

"Anything, Jac." He pressed hard, urgent kisses into her hair. "God, you must know that by now. *Anything.*"

"You told me how easy it is for someone to die out here, if they get lost."

"I should never have said that." His voice dipped and rasped. "I should never have scared you like that."

"No. I needed to hear it. Because it's true. I can work that out for myself. The way the day heats up, even in the middle of what's supposed to be fall. The way the laundry dries so fast." Her voice cracked. Such a stupid thing, laundry drying in half an hour, but it reminded her of how soon a human being would dry out and crave for water. "But now Carly's lost. If we don't find her…"

"We will. Don't even say it."

"How do you know we will?"

"Because I'll die trying."

For several heartbeats, they just held each other, but Jacinda felt precious time trickling away and soon pulled back. "We have to keep looking, but I don't know where. Where do we try next? How do we do this?"

"Listen, it must be three, by now, or later." He ran his hands down her arms over and over as he spoke, in firm strokes that he might have used on a frightened horse. That was how she felt—like an animal in terror, beyond rationality. "If there's no sign of her by first light—that's only a couple of hours away—we'll call the emergency services and they'll start a full-scale search. She can't have got far."

"Stop saying that. When we don't know what direction she went in, even a couple of miles is too far. She'll be terrified if she wakes up in the dark with no idea of where she is and how she got there. Oh, Callan!"

He kept stroking her arms, wouldn't allow her panic to overwhelm him, or respond to her impatience. It helped just a little. "First, let's go back to the house," he said. "We should check through it again, and then we'll have to wake the boys."

And finally something clicked in Jacinda's mind that she'd been too panicky to realize before.

"Check through it again?" she echoed blankly. "Oh dear Lord, I didn't look in the house!"

"You what?"

"I didn't check to see if she'd come back in the house."

His hands stilled on her shoulders. "You said you did. You said you went all around the house."

"I meant the outside of the house, on the veranda."

He squeezed her waist, the movement shaky along with his voice. "You didn't say that, Jac, sweetheart."

She pressed her fingers to her head, heart pounding even harder. "You're right. Oh dear God, you're right. I heard the screen door and I was sure she'd gone outside. Both times before when she's walked in her sleep, here, she's gone out to the veranda. And even when I realized it was the wind making the door flap, I didn't make the connection. I didn't think it might mean she'd come back into the house."

"Let's check."

"Yes. Oh, yes!"

They both broke into a run, stumbling back through the horse paddock to the gate. As they reached the track that led between the outbuildings, Kerry came around the corner of the feed shed. "She's nowhere here. I've checked behind every hay bale and every bag of grain. Oh, Jacinda..."

Not stopping, Callan called back to her, "We're checking the house more thoroughly. She definitely came out through the front door, but she might have gone back in. She may still be there, asleep somewhere that Jac didn't see her before."

Kerry muttered a fervent prayer that Callan was right and followed them slowly, still wearing her dressing gown and slippers, while Jacinda felt ill with this new hope mingling with the cold pit of fear still inside her.

Carly might be in the house.

But she might not.

It had been so quiet before. If she was anywhere inside, then she must be sleeping peacefully again or Jac would have heard her movements. Passing through the living room earlier, she hadn't noticed Carly then.

Please let her be there, please let her be there, please let her be there...

Ahead of Callan, she sprinted up the veranda steps, clattered across the old floorboards and swung open the door, not caring how much noise she made. The living room was empty, the dining room, the kitchen. Along the corridor, she passed Callan's office on one side and his bedroom on the other. She switched on the lights.

No Carly.

"She's not in the bathroom or the laundry," Callan said behind her.

And then Jac got to Lockie's room and there she was.

Carly.

Her precious, innocent daughter.

Fast asleep, like an angel.

Snuggled next to Lockie in his single bed.

Safe.

Jacinda moaned with relief. The strength simply drained away from her legs the way it had done out in the paddock, and just as before, if Callan hadn't been standing behind her to take her weight, she would have fallen.

"She's here," she whispered. "There with Lockie. Look! Oh, thank God, thank God!"

In comparison with Jac's immediate, concrete fears about heat and thirst and lack of shelter, she couldn't consider that Kurt's bizarre threats still presented a danger. Carly was here. She was safe.

And Callan would keep them all that way, or die trying.

He'd said so, and she believed him.

She began to cry, with sobs that shook her whole body but managed to stay silent because she didn't want to wake the sleeping children and let them see how scared she'd been. Callan held her from behind, his arms wrapped hard and tight around her waist, beneath the soft weight of her breasts, his chin resting on her shoulder and his head tilted toward hers.

"It's okay," he soothed her. "Everything's all right now." He brushed his cheek against her hair, but didn't touch her with his mouth. Even in her sweeping flood of relief, she noticed it.

"I know," she answered him jerkily between her sobs. "That's why I'm crying. Because everything is all right, and I've just spent half an hour imagining all the worst ways it might not have been. Oh, and Callan, there were so *many* disasters I could think of!"

He laughed softly, squeezed her tighter. "Makes life interesting, out here."

"I'm not looking for that kind of interesting!" She leaned back against him, wanting so badly to turn into his arms but not sensing the right signals from him. Even now, with feelings running so high, he had that wall in place.

"And nothing happened," he said, "so you can go back to being bored tomorrow."

"Don't tease me."

"I'm not," he whispered. "Not really. I just want you to stop shaking."

"Then keep holding me, please." His arms and his body heat felt very, very good.

They watched the two sleeping children in silence for a few moments. Lockie was curled on his side, facing away from the window and into the room. Carly had wedged herself between him and the wall, and was lying on her back with her hair tangled around her on the pillow and one leg kicked free of the sheet and light cotton blanket. Her face was as soft and relaxed as a sleeping kitten's, and if Jac listened very carefully, she could hear both children breathing.

Carly feels so safe here, she realized. *She feels as if she belongs.* Otherwise, she never would have come to Lockie

in the night. *I feel as if I belong, too, but in just over four days,
we're going away.*

She almost said it.

Callan, I want to stay.

But then they heard Kerry's footsteps, and the creak of
the screen door once again. "Is it safe to let you go now?"
Callan asked.

"Only if you get me an enormous mug of medicinal
brandy once you've told your mom everything's all right."

"I'll check the pantry and see if there's enough for both of
us." He opened his arms and let her go, and she leaned against
the doorjamb instead and watched him as he walked away.

"Hot chocolate will do," she said to his retreating back.

"Mum?" Jac heard Callan say a moment later, in the living
room. "Carly's fine. She was in the house all along, cuddled
up with Lockie."

Kerry came out with all the heartfelt thanks and relief that
Jacinda hadn't been able to express out loud. She made her
way slowly down the corridor, still leaning her hand against
the wall as she went because she felt so shaky.

"We're having some hot chocolate, Mum, do you want
any?" Callan asked as Jac reached the living room.

"No, thanks. I'm going to head straight back to bed." She
hugged Jacinda. "Callan can lock the doors at night from now
on. We don't worry too much about people breaking in,
around here. I never thought we'd have to take precautions
against someone breaking out! She's such a sweetheart, Jac.
I was so worried!"

Jac hugged her back. "You're a sweetheart, too, Kerry. Oh,
I'm still weak at the knees!"

"Are you going to put her back in her own bed?"

"I'd better. Lockie would probably thank me for it,
because sometimes she kicks!"

Chapter Thirteen

"Want to sit on the veranda?" Callan asked, appearing from the kitchen with two mugs of hot chocolate in his hands.

"That would be great." Jac had become very fond of that old cane couch.

She'd transferred Carly back into her own bed with no trouble, just now. Lockie had woken briefly as she leaned across him to attempt the awkward maneuver of gathering a sleeping four-year-old into her arms.

"Are you taking her back to her bed?" he'd asked sleepily.

"Yes, did she wake you when she climbed in?"

"It's okay. I think she had a bad dream. I made up a story for her and she went back to sleep, and then I did, too."

"Thanks for taking care of her so well." She'd hugged Lockie, once again close to tears.

For all sorts of reasons.

Out on the veranda, with only a little light spilling through the living-room window from the lamp Callan had left on, the hot chocolate smelled…different.

"What did you put in this?" Jac asked him, catching the aroma as they both sat down on the couch. Callan had taken off his jacket and kicked off his boots.

"Baileys Irish Cream."

"Ah."

"I was serious about the medicinal brandy, even if you weren't."

"I can easily be persuaded to be serious about it." She took a cautious sip. It tasted fabulous, made her forget about the broken blister still smarting on her foot and soothed the adrenaline still pumping in her system. "How much did you put in?"

"Just a thimbleful."

"Good…I think."

"You've seen the kind I mean, a thimble for a seamstress with this huge, enormous thumb." He outlined its shape in the air, the size of an eggplant.

She laughed, and he grinned back at her. He knew she liked it when he made her laugh. "You know what I keep thinking about?" she said.

"What?"

"Those cows you were teasing me about at Wiltana Bore, jumping like kangaroos, boiing-boiing-boiing."

"They'll recognize it as a separate breed, soon. The Jumping Santa Gertrudis."

"It's such a silly picture in my head. I can see it like a movie scene. They've got these serious expressions on their long faces, you know, with those flared, supercilious nostrils, and their tails—like fancy curtain cords with a big tassel on the end, nothing like kangaroo tails!—their tails are swinging up and down, and their knees are bending like folding chair legs, and for some reason it's just…funny. Every time it comes into my head."

He was still grinning, pleased. "Yeah?" Complacent, also.

He definitely knew that she liked it when he made her laugh.

So how come he didn't know everything else she liked about him? How come he wouldn't let her get closer, or even consider letting her work with him through his terrible emotional and physical block? She'd fallen in love with him, she didn't want to leave this place, and there was this impossible thing standing in the way.

Callan, I want you, but I know if I told you that, you'd feel the pressure and shut down again. Do you realize how little time we have left? Four days! Is there no way we can get past this?

She didn't even know how to ask.

They sat in silence for several minutes, letting the hot chocolate make them sleepy and the Bailey's Irish Cream infuse their limbs with its relaxing slow burn.

Carly was safe.

In her relief, Jacinda wasn't frightened of Kurt's threats right now. For Lucy's sake, and possibly Elaine's, she had to deal with them as soon as she could, but they seemed like shadowboxing, completely impotent compared to the genuine danger she'd glimpsed tonight when she'd thought that her daughter might be seriously lost.

Impotent.

Hmm, there was a word, and it didn't—shouldn't—couldn't—apply to a man like Callan.

He had said tonight that he would find her daughter or die trying, and she had believed him utterly. She knew his strength and capability would never let her down, and would never turn into the kind of meaningless show of force that Kurt resorted to so much.

This had to count for something. It had to give her some hope.

She finished her hot chocolate and put the empty mug

down on the veranda floor beside the couch, then slipped off her shoes and those troublesome, blister-making socks. Callan was still drinking, his mug only half-drained. She stopped fighting the sag of the couch and let it ease her closer to him, then leaned her head against his shoulder.

"Thank you for staying calm enough to realize my mistake about checking in the house," she said.

"No worries."

Which meant "you're welcome" and was just as much of a formula as the American phrase, she now knew.

After a moment, she tried again. "Lockie woke up when I reached for Carly. He told me she'd had a bad dream and he'd made up a story to get her back to sleep. He's so good with her, Callan, and she obviously feels so safe with him. I love watching them together."

"He's a good kid. All three of them are. I know Josh can be a bit prickly and territorial, sometimes."

"He's fine. It's natural. We're new in his world, and he's not convinced that we belong."

Do we belong, Callan?

If he'd understood her unstated question, he didn't answer it.

Silence fell once more, and she didn't know if the electricity in the air was the good kind, or not.

"Cold?" Callan asked, when the pause in the conversation had stretched halfway to the starlit horizon. He sounded awkward.

"Yes, getting to be." She was still only wearing that single layer of fine angora and her jeans.

The hand-knit mohair blanket was folded and draped over the back of the couch as usual. Callan hadn't waited for her response, but had put down his now-empty mug, reached around and was sliding the blanket across their legs before Jac understood his intent. At which point she practically stopped breathing, because a man only did something like that if he was looking for an excuse.

Didn't he?

She waited, not daring to speak or move.

She waited for a long time.

Nothing.

Nothing but a tension that you could have cut into slices, it was so thick. She could feel the warm pressure of Callan's thigh against hers. She could feel his breathing, the only movement he made. When she dared to look at him, she saw so many details that she loved—the fine lines around his eyes because he'd spent so much time squinting in the sun, the determined angle of his jaw, the smooth curve of his lower lip.

Would they sit here physically warm but emotionally frozen until morning? It could only be an hour or so away by this time.

"Help me."

For a moment she thought she'd heard him wrong, the words were muttered so low and with such intensity. "Callan?" she whispered.

He said it again, pressing a hot hand over hers, resting on her thigh, and squeezing it until it almost hurt. "Help me, Jacinda," in just the same, desperate, last-ditch, heartrending way that she'd said these exact words to him out in the horse paddock more than an hour ago.

Help me, or I'm lost to hope forever.

Help me, or I don't know how I can survive.

Help me, because you're the only person in the world who can, and I've never asked anyone for something this important before.

Understanding all these things that he didn't say, she turned to him, freed herself from his grip and took his face between her hands, hope and responsibility choking her throat. "Will you really let me?" she whispered.

He closed his eyes and nodded, and Jac knew there was no room for any more doubt or any more questions, let alone any mistakes. This was it. The last chance he'd ever allow either of them.

The pressure felt intense, and for at least a minute she didn't have the slightest idea how to begin. She simply sat there holding his face softly between her palms, listening to the breaths he couldn't manage to keep steady, and watching his motionless, expectant mouth and flickering lids.

"Oh, Callan…" she breathed.

It felt like the first time she'd held his hand and jumped into the water hole. It felt like the first time she'd ever been kissed, years ago. She knew she was running out of time. Another moment and he'd lose faith that she wanted this at all.

Frightened about the impending significance of every touch, she brushed her mouth lightly across his. At first, his lips stayed motionless, and she wondered automatically, after just a few seconds, is this not working?

Well, it won't work, you foolish woman, if you're going to think like this every step of the way.

Get it right, Jac.

The first step is your own attitude.

His mouth was so beautiful, perfect to tease. There was no hurry, she reminded herself, and no hardship in taking this slowly, letting the tension build. With one hand still cupping his face and one resting lightly against his shoulder and bare neck, she took her time with every soft, slow kiss and let go of the pressure, the urgency, and even the possibility of failure. When she felt this way about him, when she loved him this much, surely there was no such word.

His eyes stayed closed, which allowed her to get greedy.

She could watch his face between every kiss, study the shape of his cheekbones and his chin, see the moment when her mouth trailed away from his once more and made his lower lip drop open on a sudden in-breath of hungry need.

He wanted her back.

The press of her mouth. The taste of her.

Yes. Good.

She pulled her head back a few inches more, anticipating that he'd try to push forward to her in his impatience.

Oh, no, Callan, not yet. Feel what you're missing, first. When he leaned toward her, she touched her fingertips to his mouth, warding him back. "No, not yet," she whispered and brushed her fingers slowly across to his jaw and away.

This time, she made him wait longer for her kiss, letting her lips hover just a fraction of an inch from his so that he could feel her warmth but couldn't find the contact.

Not yet, not yet.

Feel me, and wait.

Ah, he'd opened his eyes. "What are you doing to me, woman?" he muttered.

"Nothing," she whispered back. "Just loving you. In my own sweet time. In my own lazy, lazy way."

He groaned.

Then he took control. His mouth closed over hers, the kiss deep and full, his tongue sweeping against hers, with the taste of chocolate and sweet, alcohol-laced cream still strong. Jac was already aching and swollen, her nipples tingling against the soft, clingy caress of her sweater, but she could wait. Oh, when kisses were this good, she could wait for a very long time.

He began to touch her, brushing his knuckles across the swell of her breasts, through the knit fabric's inadequate barrier. "You cut a few corners getting dressed just now," he said softly.

"Is that against the dress code around here?"

"Not at this hour. It…uh…might be a requirement, from now on. It's great." He cupped her through the fuzzy angora, and it tickled. Well, there should be a sexier word than *tickled* for this. It felt so soft and she was so achingly sensitive. "Are my hands cold?" he asked.

"I can't tell."

He slipped them inside the lower band of the sweater. "Can you tell now?"

"They're…mmm…they're fine."

"Good. So far, so good."

"Good all the way, Callan, no matter what bumps we hit and how long it takes."

"I like the bumps I'm hitting now."

"Mmm, yeah, I'm pretty fond of those ones, too."

They laughed and he kissed her again, his cattleman's hands deliciously rough on her skin despite the tender way he touched her. She touched him in return, running her hands over the muscles that spoke of meaningful strength and vast physical experience, and dwelling in places where her touch made him shudder with need.

"You know what?" she whispered eventually.

"What?"

"I'm still having a problem with the dress code. It's too formal."

"You could be right."

"Can I make some suggestions?"

"I'm in your hands."

"If I can follow through on my suggestions, there'll be quite a bit more of you in my hands." She plucked at the waistband of his jeans, showing her impatience at the barrier.

"In that case, suggest away," he whispered.

"The T-shirt could go."

"That only leaves me with the jeans."

"Those must go, too. I'll keep you warm, I promise."

"If I comply with this new dress code, do I get a wish list of my own?"

"A dress-code wish list?"

"I think the dress code is already established. To achieve compliance with current standards, you'll need to lose the sweater and the jeans and what's beneath them." He slipped a hand across her breast again. "If anything," he added with scrupulous attention to probability.

"So what's your wish list?" She sat up, crossed her arms obediently and pulled the sweater over her head, knowing he was watching every move. When she'd tossed the sweater aside, he wrapped his arms around her and buried his face in the valley between her breasts, a low sound coming from deep in his throat.

"That we stay out here," he said. He began a trail of slow kisses up toward her throat. "That we…maybe…make each other laugh a little bit instead of staying all earnest about this."

It was a plea for emotional protection, Jac understood. "We seem to be pretty good at making each other laugh," she agreed.

"It's nice, Jac. I love it."

And I love you, she thought.

She didn't dare to say it yet.

"It's very nice," she agreed instead.

"Mmm." He kissed her neck. "What were we talking about?"

"Nothing. We'd finished. Dress code, wish list. We're done with the planning stage…." Jac replayed those last words in her head and decided they sounded a little scary, a little too heavy on the expectations. She didn't give herself or Callan time to freeze up over it. "Now we're into im-ple-men-tation," she whispered, her breath caressing his ear.

"Good grief, I had no idea that was such a sexy word," he mumbled. "Can you say it for me again?"

She drew out the word even longer this time, her tongue caressing the *l* and her lips pouting on the *tion*. Then she added, "Hold still, Callan, I'm taking off your T-shirt...."

Oh, and when she did, he was so beautiful. He pulled her against him and his chest was a wall of warmth and hard strength. Her breasts squashed between them, the contact intimate and tender, male against female, so right and perfect, meant to be.

She reached down for the fastening of his jeans, but the fabric had pulled tight there because of the male awakening beneath, and she fumbled and couldn't slip the hard piece of metal through. "Need an expert?" he said, shifting back.

"Yes."

She watched. He pushed his hips forward and twisted his hand on the fastening. She'd never before experienced this shameless need to see a man, to see him hard and straining against the faded blue denim, then freeing himself and springing outward as he unzipped the jeans and worked them down.

She touched him and he shuddered at the light sensation on the taut satin skin. She lay back along the couch and pulled him on top of her, and he slid his hands inside the back of her jeans and cupped her, pressing her closer even though she arched her hips upward, as desperate as he was for full contact.

"Jac... We have to lose the jeans."

They fought over the task, fingers getting in each other's way. He rolled to kneel on the floorboards, and dragged the denim and the slip of underlying lace down her legs in a single movement, while she lifted and shimmied her hips. Then he trailed his mouth the whole way up her body, lingering in all the places she wanted him to.

By the time he reached her mouth and they were lying length to length along the couch, she was in a white heat of wanting.

And he was ready for her.

The old cane creaked beneath them, its sagging center holding their entwined bodies like a giant cupped hand. She wrapped her legs around his body and arched back, aching for his first thrust. It was clumsy. The couch sagged too much. They couldn't find each other.

It doesn't matter, she coached herself inwardly. *It doesn't matter. We'll get there.*

Then, out in the chicken run, Darth Vader crowed.

Hell, it was almost morning. Opening her eyes, Jac could see that the sky at the horizon had just begun to grow pale. She feverishly attempted to calculate how much time they had left. Forty minutes? Half an hour? Then she felt Callan's slackening impatience and heard his shuddering sigh. "Oh hell, Jacinda, I'm sor—"

"Don't say it! Don't you dare say it!" she told him fiercely. She gripped him so hard with her legs that the muscles of her inner thighs hurt. "Don't you dare pull away!"

"The kids'll be awake soon."

"Not this early! It's still almost pitch dark. Shut up, you bloody rooster!" she hissed at the creature, over her shoulder, in the direction of the chicken run. "Callan, I have to tell you, your alarm-clock system here needs some adjustment."

"Jacinda—"

"*No!* You wanted to laugh, we're going to laugh. You didn't want to get too earnest about this. Well, we're not! This is funny. Ridiculous, and typical, and funny. We have a conspiracy going on between a puritanical couch with a hole in the bottom of it and a spoilsport of a rooster, and we're not giving in to it! I don't know what kind of agenda those two have got going, whether it's a work-ethic thing, or the idea that bed is the only acceptable place for this kind of behavior, but Callan, damn it…damn it…"

She stopped gabbling, stopped the doomed attempt to

make him laugh, and just started kissing him because that had been so good, that had gotten them both so, so close.

Close to the edge.

Close to each other.

He lay on top of her, and even though he kissed her back, with a warm, soft mouth, she could tell he wasn't feeling the magic, the way they both had been before. So she stopped kissing him, threaded her fingers through his scented, slippery hair and pulled his head down to her chest. "Talk to me," she said. "Tell him about those other women, the ones who were so wrong for you that this could happen."

He swore.

"Tell me, so I can hunt them down and kill them with my bare hands."

At last he laughed. "Oh Lord, Jac…!"

"I want names, ages, occupations, distinguishing marks."

He laughed again, then he rasped out a sigh. Then with his head still pillowed on her chest, he told her about the blonde at the races and the Danish girl camped down at the creek, and when he had finished, he almost broke her heart when he said, "And I don't know why I expected this time to be any different."

She had a choice.

Nurse the broken heart, or fight to fix it.

She chose to fight, because she knew his heart had to be broken, too, for him to say something like that. She echoed his statement. "Why did you expect it to be different, Callan? Don't you know the answer to that by now? Because—"

She wanted so badly to say, "Because I love you," but that was still just a little bit too hard, when it brought with it so many decisions about a radically different future, so she bit it back and said something almost as important. "Because this is me!"

"Hmm?" He lifted his head for a moment.

"This is me. Just me. No one else. Not a blonde. Not a backpacker. Definitely not a sexual therapist. Me." She gripped his shoulders and spoke so fiercely that she was almost yelling. "I went bunyip-jumping with you when I was terrified about it. I laughed at your kangaroo cows. I drink my coffee the same way you do. Don't—*don't* put me in a basket with anyone else, when I'm nothing like those other women and by now you have to know it. That hurts. It really hurts, Callan," she finished on a whisper, and buried her face in his hair.

Jacinda was right.

Callan lay on her, protecting her from his weight by resting one side of his body against the back of the couch. Beneath the softness of her breasts, he could feel the rhythm of her breathing against his cheek, and she was right. She was nothing like those other women.

And yet he'd still failed with her.

That was the point where logic had stopped and emotion—blind fear—had kicked in. But she was right. Something was different, because he was still here, feeling the way she held him and kissed him, any bit of him she could reach. Hair and ear and temple and eyelid. He hadn't shut down and turned away, and neither had she.

She still had more to give. She wanted to keep trying.

She was right. It was different. They knew each other, and she cared about him, and they were both still here.

Something hard and painful in his heart began to let go and break away. He felt renewed and ready to go forward, no longer stuck in the same sad, pessimistic place he'd locked himself into.

Jacinda.

Because of Jac, he could do this.

Without speaking, he shifted and slid along the couch until

he could share the pillow where her head rested, then he held her breast, feeling its warm, rounded weight and the nipple that was still peaked with desire. He began to caress her, forgetting about dawn, the past, the kids, the sag in the couch. Her skin was so fine and soft. She smelled so familiar and sweet.

"Jacinda…" he said, and she understood what he wanted and what he was telling her, just with the whispered sound of her name.

She turned toward him and they half rolled until he lay beneath her. She bent to kiss him, her mouth hot and moist. Her nipples brushed against his chest while her thighs parted and pinned him down. He couldn't believe how fast his need accelerated. Zero to sixty in five seconds. Sixty to a hundred in ten more. His body remembered exactly where it had been twenty minutes ago and exactly what it wanted.

She was ready, and this time there was no clumsiness. He lifted his hips and slid into her, his breath catching halfway to his lungs. Ahh. He held her soft, satiny cheeks and pulled her even closer, so that the sweet sensation of the way she enclosed him grew even more intense.

Unbearably intense.

And when she moved against him like this, opening wider, pressing harder, matching his rhythm, sliding her body on his, raggedly breathing out his name, the whole universe seemed to zero in to this single place, this one segment of time and they surged over the crest of their wave together and clung to each other for sheer survival.

He was still lying with his eyes closed, motionless and breathless and lost, when he felt her fingertips press gently against his mouth. What was this about?

"In case you're planning to say something I don't want to hear," she whispered in explanation, when he opened his eyes and frowned at her.

He laid his hand over hers and slid it away. "Like what?"

"Etiquette-book stuff." She kissed the corner of his mouth.

"You mean th—"

"Yes. I don't want to hear it. You can tell me that the earth moved, if you want, but nothing beginning with *th*. That's banned."

"Did the earth move for you?"

"Like the San Andreas fault." She grinned. "Oh, damn, now I want to say it to you. Thank you, Callan."

"You said it was banned."

"I'm inconsistent."

"Jac—"

"I'm still inconsistent. You are not saying it. You are beautiful, and wonderful, and complete, and you are not saying it."

She sat up and stretched, giving him a slow, creamy smile like a satisfied cat. Then she reached for her sweater, untangled the sleeves and dropped it over her head.

Darth Vader crowed again. Callan had the vague idea he'd been hearing that sound at intervals for quite a while, now, and when he looked at the sky it was on fire at the horizon and pale blue everywhere else. Over at the cottage, his mother's kitchen light was on, and inside the house he heard a couple of thumps. The kids were up.

He found his jeans and dragged them on. Jacinda was watching him, the lower half of her body wrapped in the mohair blanket. They smiled at each other, tired and replete and very content.

"It's going to be a beautiful day," he said.

"I dreamed I was in Lockie's bed," Carly said to Jac, finding her on the way to the bathroom and reaching up for a morning hug.

Wearing the jeans she'd only just managed to climb into in time out on the veranda a minute ago, Jac crouched down to small-daughter level. "You *were* in his bed, honey, for a couple of hours. You must have been sleepwalking, because you went outside to the veranda."

"Did I?"

"I think you might have gone to pat the dogs. But then you came back in and went to see Lockie, and you had a bad dream. He told you a story and you went back to sleep, right beside him, but later on I came and carried you back to your own bed. Do you remember any of that?"

Carly shook her head and laughed. "No! I did all those things?"

She'd been told about her nighttime wanderings before, and always found it very silly and funny that she could do all those things in her sleep and not remember the next morning.

Jac thought about telling her that they'd thought she was lost out in the open, but that would involve admitting how terrified she'd been, and Carly was already too closely attuned to Mommy's emotional barometer. It was almost certainly why she'd begun to sleepwalk in the first place.

Because Jac had been so overwrought about Kurt.

Still holding Carly lightly around her little waist, she felt her stomach lurch. She'd shower and change, and then she'd try calling Elaine once more, because whether she panicked about it or not, whether Kurt's threats were real or simply games, she had to find out what was going on.

When she came into the kitchen after her shower, she found Callan there with Carly and the boys, making breakfast. It was only a few minutes after seven, but this still made it a slightly later morning than usual. Pouring two mugs of coffee, Callan smiled at her across the room and she smiled back, and got a warm, goofy sort of happy feeling inside, that she could see in him, also, glowing like ripe fruit in the sun.

Yeah, aren't we great?

Wasn't it good?

Isn't this a beautiful morning?

Mmm.

"Want—?" he began, but the rest of his sentence was cut across by the sound of the wall phone ringing.

Elaine.

Jac knew it would be Elaine.

She was the first one to reach the telephone, and when she snatched it up, she heard her former boss's voice. Callan poured milk into the coffee mugs and put them in the microwave, then dropped bread into the toaster.

"Honey, I'm so sorry I didn't get back to you yesterday!" Elaine said. "Things were so crazy, and then I worked out the time and it was going to be the middle of the night down there so I had to wait. It's around eight-thirty by you now, right?"

"Seven."

"So I still got it wrong. That's weird."

"Never mind about working out the time difference, Elaine." She was already sweating and newly on edge, her hands clammy and cold. "Just tell me what's been going on."

"Well, it's all over now."

"All over?" Dear Lord, what did she mean?

"I couldn't talk yesterday because I was with Lauren," Elaine said.

Lauren was Kurt's new wife, a blond twentysomething, with ambitions even larger than her surgically—

Yeah, well.

That was water under the bridge, now.

A year ago, Jac had wasted quite a lot of precious emotional energy on hating the woman, but the bad feelings had gone when she'd realized that Lauren could have been any one of a hundred near-identical variations on the same theme…and when Jac had discovered that she actually felt sorry for her.

Kurt was the problem, not the trophy babe he happened to choose.

"But you can talk now?" Jac prompted Elaine. "So please don't make it cryptic!"

"Honey, Kurt's ill."

"Ill?"

"Mentally ill. He's been diagnosed with bipolar disorder."

Jac came out with an incoherent sound of shock and saw Callan's concerned look, across the room.

Elaine went on quickly, "Manic depression, they used to call it, and it's very treatable. It's been building over several months, but he's in the hospital now, medicated and resting."

"That sounds—" Her mouth would barely move.

"Yes, it's the best thing for him," Elaine agreed, brisk and sympathetic, as if Jacinda had come out with a coherent line. "He was completely exhausted. He was barely sleeping, supposedly putting all these fabulous projects together, but most of them don't exist. And Lauren found out he was having her followed."

"Poor girl! They've been married less than a year!"

"She called me, we were in the car, yesterday, going to their house. He wouldn't listen to us, we had to get professional help. It was a crazy day, in more ways than one. He's been getting increasingly delusional over the past month or two, talking about the president directing a movie he'd written that would bring about world peace, and calling people on the Fortune 500 list to ask them to invest in it. *And* sending Jacinda Beale look-alikes to your daughter's preschool, and threatening to fly to Sydney and take her."

"Those bits I knew," Jac said weakly. "I'll call Lucy right away and tell her she doesn't have to worry now."

"Those are the bits that scared you, but trust me, things were scarier at this end, for a while yesterday, when he wouldn't accept that he had a problem."

"So—So— None of what happened…all his power games…even the divorce…?"

"Honey, listen to me, you and I both know that Kurt is and always has been a power-hungry control freak, so don't go thinking that you divorced your husband when he was ill and needed you. This has developed since then. And when his medication has been balanced right—which may take time— he'll still be a power-hungry control freak, except not a de-lusional one who's going to threaten your friends and try and kidnap your daughter. Okay?"

"That's—that's—"

"It's good news," Elaine announced, since Jac couldn't work out what it was, right now. "It means you can come home and get on with your life and be safe with Carly." After a tiny pause, she added, "And we can even talk about you coming back to the show."

"I don't want to come back to the show." The words fell out of her mouth before she even knew she was going to say them, but then she heard them echoing in the air and knew that she wouldn't take them back.

Kurt or no Kurt, writing block or no writing block, she didn't want to go back to writing dialogue for *Heartbreak Hotel*.

"You see, I've started working on a—"

"Don't say a screenplay," Elaine cut in. "Please, please, if you care about me at all, do not say a screenplay. I had the drinks waiter from the studio catering team give me his screenplay yesterday, while I was on the phone listening to Lauren sobbing in terror about Kurt at the other end, and it was the twentieth unsolicited and previously undiscovered gem of movie-making brilliance I've been privileged to receive this week."

"It's not a screenplay, Elaine, it's a novel."

"Thank God! Someone else's problem!"

"And—and I think Carly and I might be moving back east, to be nearer to my brothers and my dad. You know, and for a change."

There was a silence at the far end of the line. Then Elaine said blankly, "Leave L.A.?"

"I think so."

"Wow."

"I think it's the right thing." Jac caught Callan's expression as he pulled the mugs of coffee from the microwave. She couldn't read it, but she knew he was following everything she said.

"Wow!" Elaine said again.

"Yeah, it's been an interesting few weeks."

"And on that note, I should go. Back to my interesting life, interesting work and tedious, tedious amateur screenplays. I'll see you when you get back, though? You'll have to pack up your life here, first?"

"And I'd like to visit Kurt. Of course you'll see me, Elaine."

"We can talk detail, then, okay?"

"Sounds great." A few moments later, she put down the phone.

The kitchen was suddenly much quieter. Carly, Lockie and Josh shoveled in their eggs and bacon and gulped their hot chocolate. Pippa had somehow wangled her way inside and was thumping her tail against the table leg, her eyes trained hopefully on the food. Kerry would probably be over any minute now.

And Callan was watching Jac, his face as intent as Pippa's but his agenda much less clear. "Here's your coffee, Jac," he said quietly. "I was going to ask if you wanted toast."

"Everything's fine now," she told him. "Well…it's more complicated than just *fine,* I guess, but I'll explain later on, once the kids are doing their school."

"It's safe for you to go back."

"Yes."

She waited for him to say, "Don't! Stay!" but he didn't, he just repeated his question about toast and she accepted some, knowing she would barely manage three bites.

Chapter Fourteen

"That's everything?" Kerry asked.

She stood back and looked at the suitcases lined up on the dusty ground beside the four-wheel-drive. Her shoulders slumped a little and a helpless expression flitted across her face.

"I've checked pretty thoroughly through the house," Jacinda said.

"Yes, so did I," Kerry agreed. "Is Callan…?" She turned toward the veranda steps.

"Looking for his hat, I think."

Kerry nodded. "Well…" She looked around again. Sighed. Straightened her shoulders. "Where's Josh?"

Callan had appeared, hat on his head. It was tipped too low over his eyes, Jac thought. "Josh is in the feed shed and won't come out," he said. "Jac and Carly, he says to tell you goodbye."

"Should you make him—?" Kerry began.

He shook his head. "I'm not going to force the issue."

He began to load Carly and Jacinda's suitcases into the back of the vehicle.

They were leaving today.

Since Friday, time seemed to have sped up, and never before had Jacinda been so aware of a human being's powerlessness in its grip. She'd hung onto every moment, savored it, made memories like photographs, telling herself, *I have to remember this. I have to lock this in, so when I think back on it, I'll be able to feel it again and know how strong and how important it was. Even if I never have a reason to come back.*

She'd told herself this while feeding the hens, picking lemons in the garden and helping the kids with their School of the Air. She'd said it to herself on Saturday when they'd all gone on horseback down to the water hole once more, this time with Kerry and the dogs as well. She'd said it as she'd kneaded bread dough, and when she'd watched Callan ride on horseback into the yard with Pete after an overnight boundary ride yesterday afternoon.

Most of all, she'd thought it…felt it…when she and Callan had made love together, on the old cane couch at night and on a blanket spread over a shady curve of the creek bed on Sunday just before noon.

Never in his bed.

She'd noticed that.

It had frozen inside her like a splinter of ice in her heart, and it meant that, deep down, she wasn't so surprised that he was letting her go today. Why would he try to keep her here when, after all the emotional distance they'd traveled together over the past four weeks, all the ways they'd healed and changed and been good for each other, he still wouldn't let her fully into his life?

"Lockie, say goodbye to Carly," Callan growled at his elder son now.

"G'bye, Carly." Lockie lifted his little friend off her feet and gave her a hard squeeze. She could barely breathe, but she was laughing when he put her down again.

"Bye, Lockie," she said.

He turned to his dad. "But when are they coming back?"

"Now's not the time to talk about that, okay?"

Lockie knew that tone in his father's voice. He didn't argue, just gave Jac a quick goodbye hug as well.

"Aren't you guys coming out to the airstrip, Kerry?" Jacinda said. The suitcases were in. The rear door was shut.

"Best not," the older woman answered. Her smile was wide and stiff. "I'm rotten with goodbyes. I hate them. If I was eight years old, I'd be with Joshie, hiding in the feed shed. Let me give you a hug, love."

I'm going to cry, Jacinda knew. *I don't want this. And I don't think Kerry wants it, either. She doesn't understand why Callan is letting us go. Why is it happening?*

She had waited since Friday for Callan to talk about the future, about how he felt. It was *obvious* how he felt, she often thought, but then he said nothing, he kept her out of his bed, and she began to doubt, and the words she wanted to blurt to him stayed shut away inside her.

I love you.

I want to stay.

Sometimes, like Kerry, she felt as if she were eight years old. She was a kid who desperately wanted to be asked for a sleepover at her best friend's house and couldn't believe the best friend hadn't suggested it. Just how sinfully rude would it have been to bring up the idea herself?

Callan, I love you and I'm sleeping over. For the rest of my life.

She couldn't do it.

Not when he hadn't made love to her in his own bed.

Not when he and Pete had disappeared off to the far horizon for twenty of the last precious hours of her stay.

"Bye, Kerry," she said against a shoulder covered in sun-heated cotton, fighting the tightness in her throat and the sting of tears. "I can't tell you how much this has meant to me, these past four weeks."

"It's flown by. We've loved having you. Carly is precious."

"I don't to go." But the words came out muffled against Kerry's shirt, and no one heard.

"Jump in, Carly," Callan said.

He opened the rear door and, as always, it creaked because of the red desert dust that had worked its way into the hinges. Jac wondered if she'd ever again hear a creaking car door or the flap of a screen door against a porch wall without thinking of this place, and of him.

Lockie threw a stick to Flick and Pippa, then ran after them as they chased it, calling, "Come on, Pippa, come on, Flick, race you to the shed." Jac thought he was probably scared he might cry. She climbed into the front passenger seat, didn't even make her usual frequent mistake of going around to the wrong side. She'd gotten used to the fact that the driver sat on the right in this country.

By late this afternoon, she and Carly would be in Sydney. On Thursday, they'd fly home, and it would still be Thursday when they got there, with a list no doubt several pages long to prepare—all the things they'd need to do before they moved east.

Jac had had an e-mail from Tom last night, and a second one from Andy this morning, saying that he and Debbie would love to see her if she came east. Dad was getting pretty vague, but he talked about her from time to time. He'd asked Andy recently if Andy thought it was the right thing to have sent Jacinda to live with her aunt, all those years ago.

I told him it was the best thing he could do at the time, Andy had written. I'm not going to hurt him by encouraging regrets at this point in his life, Jacinda, but it would be great if we could make more of an effort to stay in touch, wouldn't it, even if it's just through e-mail?

Callan started the engine. Kerry waved and smiled madly for a moment, then turned abruptly and hurried up the steps, across the veranda and into the house. Carly kept waving, even though—if you left out Lockie, Pippa and Flick, just about to disappear around a corner of the feed shed—there wasn't anyone to wave to, anymore.

Carly was sad about leaving, but too little to really understand just how hard it would be for them ever to come here again, let alone how much Jac felt she and Carly were losing as they made these awkward goodbyes.

They drove out to the airstrip, and Jac could already see Rob's mail plane approaching over the dry, rugged mountains to the south. The plane's wheels hit the earth just as Callan brought the four-wheel-drive to a halt. He switched off the engine, but then he didn't move.

Waiting for Rob.

Waiting for Rob with his whole body in a knot of tension and not saying a word.

Jac couldn't take it anymore.

"I'm going to stretch my legs," she said, opening the door and sliding out. "Carly, wait here, honey, till we're ready to walk to the plane."

Carly nodded, her gaze dropped down at something in her lap, and Jac leaned back into the vehicle and looked more closely to see what she was doing. She had a tissue spread like a napkin across her thighs, and she was painstakingly pulling apart some lavender flowers she must have picked from the garden shortly before they'd left, and dropping the bits of lavender onto the tissue.

Jac could smell them now. "So you're busy and happy with the flowers?" she said.

"Uh-huh. I'm making aloe-vera tissues."

"Are you, sweetheart? Good girl. They'll be lovely." She shut the door carefully and circled away from the vehicle.

But Callan followed her, which meant they had to stand together, watching the mail plane coming toward them with its wake of rust-red dust like the train of a regal robe. Callan watched with particular intensity, it seemed to Jacinda, as if his focus on the plane and Rob gave him an excuse not to focus on her.

It really was unbearable.

"Don't wait," she told him. "Rob's here. He's waving at us, giving us the thumbs-up. There's obviously no problem with the aircraft, which means we'll be taking off again in a couple of minutes. There's no need for you to wait. I'm the same as your mom. I hate goodbyes."

I hate this *goodbye.*

But then she saw that Rob had one of those damned mailbags he brought every week, so of course Callan needed to wait. He saw the mailbag, nodded at Rob and gave a thumbs-up back to him, and then he kept looking at the bag, tense and intent, as Rob began walking toward them.

Jac gathered her courage and turned to him for that last hug she'd been dreading for half her stay. "Callan—" she began, not having the slightest idea of what she could say as an exit line without crying.

"Do you think you could come back?" he said.

"I'm sorry?" she answered weakly, while thinking, *No, this is wrong. This isn't what I wanted.*

If she'd hoped for anything, it would have been *Don't go.* Not this. *Come back* wasn't necessarily even something people meant when they said it. It was the kind of thing flight attendants said on airplanes.

We look forward to seeing you again next time you choose to fly with us.

Next time you're passing by Arakeela Creek, do stop in for tea.

She looked up at Callan and found a tight face with eyes still half-hidden beneath the brim of his hat. They had their arms around each other, but it felt clumsy and uncomfortable and not right. "I know you have to leave," he said. "But I want you to come back."

"Callan—"

"Come back and—"

"G'day, Callan, hello Jacinda." Rob had almost reached them, his strides confident and long, his expression cheerful. "I've got it, mate. It's right here in the bag. Are you ready for it?"

"Ready for it?" Callan echoed in a strange tone, letting go of Jacinda and almost pushing her away. "I am stuffing this up so totally, Rob, it's not funny. She thinks I have a good sense of humor, she didn't know I could be the butt of my own joke, but yes, I am ready for it. Can you give it to me, then give us a minute or so?"

"No worries." Rob tossed him the mailbag. "I'll give you as long as you want."

Jacinda had no idea what was happening, but she didn't like it. Callan was eager about some package delivery, while her heart slowly burned to ash inside her?

With the mailbag in his hands, Callan didn't seem to know what to do with it. He held it, pleating it up in his hands the way women pleated the open top of a stocking, then he rummaged inside.

Rob had gone off to pull bits of bark off one of the few pieces of decent vegetation beside the airstrip. His body language said that he was being as tactful as a simple man knew how, but Jac couldn't see the need. Meanwhile, was Carly still making her "aloe-vera tissues" in the backseat of the vehicle?

She craned to look. Yes. Good.

"Jacinda, will you marry me?" Callan said in a desperate tone, and her head whirled around.

He had a blue velvet box in his hands. It was open, and inside was a ring. She saw the bright wink and dazzle of diamond and gold in the sunlight, and couldn't speak. He pinched it awkwardly between his fingers and pulled it out.

"I know you have to leave now," he went on. "I know you have to wind up your life in L.A., but after that, don't move east to your brothers. I've seen you building on that plan the whole time you've been here and now I'm telling you to just give it up. Maybe that's too selfish. I don't care. Come back here with Carly, and be my wife."

He flipped the ring over and over in his fingers. Jacinda couldn't speak, could barely breathe.

"I had to get this over the Internet," Callan said, stumbling over his words. "I don't know if it'll fit, if you'll like it."

She did. It was simple and finely made, and right now a ring made from braided horse hair would have been more than good enough.

"I didn't even know if Rob would have it with him this trip, but if you say yes…if you think you might manage to say yes…I didn't want you to leave without something like this, you see. I want you to carry it with you, because… This has probably been the worst proposal in the world…."

"It's getting better by the second," she said shakily.

"But…you're carrying my heart, too, and if there's any danger of you forgetting that, when you'll be so far away…" He stopped, then tried again, slipped the ring onto her finger—it was a couple of sizes too big—and laced their hands together. His voice was so husky it was barely there. "I just wanted you to have this so you'd know, every moment of every day, that I love you, and you're carrying my heart."

It had definitely not been the worst proposal in the world.

"Yes, oh, yes!" Jacinda gasped out.

"Yes? You'll come back? You'll marry me?"

"Yes, because I love you and you're carrying my heart, too, but, Callan…" Jac started to cry, because it was the best proposal in the world but the timing was still terrible. "*Now* you say this? When Rob's waiting to take us away? The propellers are still spinning." She stroked his face. "Couldn't you have picked a time a tiny, tiny bit less like the absolute last minute?"

Was she laughing or crying? She didn't know anymore.

"But I didn't know what you'd say." Callan held her close, his head bent and his forehead pressed against hers. "I thought maybe for you this was just…an interval. You gave me everything on Friday morning, more than I'd imagined or dared to hope for, but then you seemed to hold back, little by little. You had your plans for moving east. You were so happy this morning when that second e-mail from Andy came."

"You never had me in your bed. We never slept together, Callan. We only made love. In other places. *You* held back, and then you disappeared with Pete. I didn't know what to think."

"I'm a one-woman man, Jacinda, that's all."

Something cold stabbed in her stomach. "But you want to marry me…" Her mouth felt numb. "Even though I'm not the woman?"

"Oh, hell! No! No! One woman at a time! That's what I mean. And this time it's you. The woman is one hundred percent you." He kissed her, fast and sure. "But I had to say my last goodbye to Liz before I could ask you to marry me and share my bed and my life and my future. That's where I went with Pete, to a couple of the places I used to ride to with Liz that I haven't shown you yet. Pete knew. To say goodbye. Now the only woman in my life is you. If you want to be."

"Oh, I want to be! And I don't want to go. I'd lost any hope that you'd wanted something like this, and now I have to go. Rob's waiting. The airstrip, Callan? Not the water hole on Saturday. Not even the chicken run this morning. The airstrip? Now? With the propellers going?" She was still laughing and crying at the same time, with the ring slipping too loose on her finger.

"If it had all gone pear-shaped, you see, if you'd said no, you couldn't exactly have called a cab to pick you up and take you and Carly to a nearby motel. I didn't want to make everything awkward if I had it all wrong." He kissed her lightly once more. "Gotta think of things like that, out here."

"Oh, trust me, I'm going to be thinking of things like that all eight thousand miles of the journey home!"

Rob detached himself from the scraggly tree he'd just stripped half-bare and wandered across to them. "I have a bit of a schedule today, Callan," he said apologetically. "My boss might think I should be getting on with it."

Callan got a hunted look on his face and Jacinda held him harder. "Another five minutes?" he said.

Rob grinned. "From the look of the two of you, I don't think five minutes is going to be anywhere near enough. Jacinda, how about you change your flights out of Broken Hill and Sydney over the phone, and I come back for you next week?"

Jacinda and Callan looked at each other. "Yes!" they both said, and laughed because they'd been too desperate and emotional to think of it themselves.

Five minutes later, when they pulled up in front of the house, Pippa and Flick came racing around the corner of the feed shed and greeted the vehicle as if they hadn't seen Callan, Jac and Carly in a week. The screen door squeaked on its hinges and flapped back against the veranda wall, and three people appeared, each of them with eyes exactly like

Callan's—a glorious overload of piercing blue. They must have heard the four-wheel-drive, and two of them—the smaller ones—were grinning.

"Jac, you came back," Kerry said in a shaky voice, too emotional to smile.

Lockie and Josh had questions. Carly couldn't get herself unstrapped from the backseat. When she showed Lockie her "aloe-vera tissues" a cascade of tiny bits of lavender rained all the way down the front of her little dress. Jacinda told Kerry about the ring and the proposal and the short trip she and Carly would be making back to the U.S.—the west coast to deal with arrangements, and then the east coast to visit family.

Kerry wondered why they were talking about it out here, when they could be inside discussing the details over a cup of tea. The boys asked if they could maybe have the rest of the morning off school. Callan said yes, knowing he'd just been conned, and Pippa and Flick barked as joyously as if they'd been given the same reprieve.

Chaos, all of it, like the day four weeks ago when Jacinda and Carly had arrived.

Fabulous, safe, friendly, normal, reassuring family chaos.

My chaos, Jac thought. She sighed and smiled and leaned back against Callan's sun-warmed shoulder as he wrapped his arms around her from behind and nuzzled her neck.

"Welcome home," he said.

* * * * *

PRINCESS IN DISGUISE

BY
LILIAN DARCY

Chapter One

Sox was a terrific dog.

She was born to work with sheep, the kind of dog you thanked your lucky stars for over and over again. Brant could send her up the hill and she would muster the mob down to him all on her own. She would tear back and forth, ever alert for breakaways, pushing them toward the yard with scarcely a bark, and working on a level of instinct that training could never fully replicate.

She jumped fences like a kangaroo, and sometimes her eyes begged him with an almost Shakespearean eloquence for more work to do. Ple-e-ease, are we mustering sheep today?

She loved it.

Brant relied on her, and right now hers was the only ear he could confide in.

"Tell me those three lame ewes don't mean anything, Soxie," he said to her.

They were both riding the four-wheeler down the hill at

a considerable clip. It was a beautiful afternoon, unseason-
ably warm for mid-May. Fluffy white clouds floated in a blue
sky, birds sang and in the distance on the road from Holbrook
Brant glimpsed the red flash of a fast-moving car heading in
this direction. The bright color toned with a pair of crimson
rosellas who flew past, weaving an intricate flight pattern in
the air and twittering as they went, then the car disappeared
behind a stand of breeze-tossed, sunlit trees.

It wasn't the kind of day for bad news about his sheep.

Brant straddled the four-wheeler's wide seat, his hands
and feet working the controls, and Sox sat crosswise on the
back, craning around the side of his body, panting at him,
waiting to find out what sheep-related adventure the two of
them were going to have next.

Unfortunately, she couldn't reassure him about the lame
ewes.

"It's not foot rot," he told her. He'd taken a good look at
the hooves in question, had cleaned them out and pared them
back, taking care not to draw blood or expose soft tissue.
There had definitely been some inflammation and underrun-
ning. "Don't tell me it's foot rot, okay, because I don't want
to hear it. I am not contacting the Pastures Protection Board
yet."

It could be foot rot.

After a long, crippling drought, there'd been a warm
autumn with good rains, the right conditions to activate and
spread the bacteria, and if any of those four thousand pregnant ewes he'd just paid top dollar for had been infected
when they'd arrived here recently, then his entire acreage
could soon harbour the disease.

The implications were too expensive to bear thinking
about, and the worst-case scenarios could play out for almost
a year.

Sox nudged her compact black-and-tan body closer to
Brant, as if she could tell he was worried. He felt her warmth

and her panting motion against his back. They swooped down the green, rolling terrain, over a well-worn metal grid and along the fence line toward the house.

Brant kept thinking about sheep feet, thinking about the ghastly prospect of disease, of a third of his stock's value and his year's income getting slashed down at a single stroke—six figures' worth of loss—thinking of all those months of extra work and expense and concern…

…None of which he wanted to share with his sister, because Nuala and Chris were getting married in a few months, Chris had his own stock and acreage to think about and Brant didn't want to rain on their parade.

And then he saw the bright red car again, just inside his main gate and definitely heading this way. It was a zippy little machine, gleaming and well maintained.

Not a farmer's car.

His spirits sank even further. He knew what kind of a visitor this would be.

Female.

A stranger.

A city girl.

Over the past few months he'd met enough women like this to last him a lifetime, and even the nicest of them hadn't struck any meaningful sparks. Recently, one of them—not the nicest—had spread his address around to some of her friends and now he had new ones dropping in unannounced at the most impossible times.

Such as when he'd just discovered that at least three of his new ewes had gone lame.

The red car dipped down into the creek and temporarily disappeared once more. Brant and Sox had almost reached the house. He parked the four-wheeler in the carport, chained the dog and went inside, kicking off his boots in the mudroom on the way. He found a note from his sister on the kitchen countertop.

"Don't forget Misha…"

Misha. Nuala's friend from Europe.

The red car.

He'd completely forgotten.

"She'll be here around three-thirty or four," Nuala's note continued. "I should be back, but if I'm not, be nice to her."

Be nice to the strange woman in the zippy red car.

Great.

Just what he felt like.

Since a self-invited international guest should start off in the right spirit of proving herself useful, Misha had stopped her little red rental car at Inverlochie's roadside mailbox on her way to her friend Nuala's Australian sheep farm and collected the mail.

There was quite a large sheaf of it, bundled together with a brown rubber band. Branton Smith, Inverlochie, Hill Road via Holbrook, NSW 2644, read the address on the topmost letter, in loopy purple handwriting. Misha had stashed the bundle neatly on her front passenger seat, along with the flowers she'd bought in Albury for Nuala. Both items sat on top of the case of wine she'd bought at a drive-through liquor store for Nuala's brother Brant, whom she'd never met.

But when she arrived at Nuala's and found Brant there to greet her, he didn't seem very pleased at what she'd done.

"You have to be Misha," he said to her through the open driver's-side window when she'd stopped the car in front of the low, sprawling house. His broad shoulders hunched with tension, his gray eyes looked smoky and hard, and his expression could only be labelled a scowl.

"I do have to be," she agreed, spreading her hands in mock resignation, "even when I don't want to."

Expecting a smile from him, she didn't get so much as a flicker.

"And I've brought your mail," she said, in case that helped.

It didn't.

He glanced down at the bundle of letters and groaned. Unless he was groaning at the wine and the flowers. "Nuala's not here," he told her. "You're a bit earlier than we thought."

"I probably drove too fast."

"You shouldn't, around here. We don't have those massive autobahn things you're used to in Europe."

"We don't have those massive autobahn things much, either, in Langemark. I'm pretty experienced on rural roads."

He didn't seem impressed.

Although he was impress*ive*, she had to admit—a taller, darker, stronger and way more masculine version of Nuala, who'd never had any trouble attracting the opposite sex. Brant wouldn't, either. He had wind-rumpled dark hair, strong cheekbones and chin, sinful lashes, muscles like braids of thick rope below the rolled sleeves of a gray-green, mud-stained sweatshirt, and that aura of basic maleness that aftershave could never disguise…or imitate.

There was something built in to the genes in this family that couldn't be explained purely by their hard-working farm background, their intelligence or their good looks. For a long time, Misha had thought that Nuala—loyal whirlwind, sexy tomboy—would end up with some European billionaire or aristocrat, but although she'd introduced her friend to plenty such men during Nuala's month-long stay in Langemark three years ago, Nuala had never been seriously interested.

"They're too civilized," she'd said. "They're tame."

Now she was home in Australia again, and happily engaged to Chris, the Farmer Next Door. Misha looked forward to meeting the man who was uncivilized enough for her friend.

…But back to Brant, who had just opened the car door for her.

Used to such attention, Misha dipped her head in acknowledgment, smiled at him from beneath her lashes and began to climb out—knees together, pivot, leg slide, step—only to catch him rolling his eyes and sighing between his nice white teeth. Just in case she hadn't picked up on the subtle body language, he looked at his watch and frowned at the time.

He might be good-looking, but he displayed as much charm as a paparazzo snapping a drunken heiress outside a nightclub bathroom door, which wasn't much charm at all, Misha knew, because she'd witnessed such incidents herself.

"Thank you so much for having me to stay, Brant," she said, keeping her own well-practiced guard of charm firmly in place. "It's so good of you, and it's wonderful to meet you at last."

Reaching a standing position, she held out her hand but he didn't take it. "You wouldn't want to," he said, showing her a dirt-stained palm.

"Hey, I can wash afterward, can't I?"

Misha kept her hand where it was, and finally he responded by stretching out his own. She wished she hadn't pushed the issue. His grip was brief and bone crushing, as if to demonstrate that he was both busier and very much stronger than she was. She knew those things already.

"The wine is for you," she said. "Just a small token of my appreciation that you're able to have me here."

"No problem," he drawled. His mouth barely moved, which allowed her to see its exact shape, and to realize that it was perfect, not too fleshy, not too thin. With a mouth like that, he should have a far better idea about smiling.

"And of course the flowers are for Nu. Will she be long?" she asked, feeling fatigue begin to overtake her like the cold winter mists that rolled over Langemark on dark December days.

Determined to keep the press at bay, she'd flown anonymously in coach class from Europe to Melbourne. She'd had a wait of several hours for her connecting flight to Albury, followed by forty-five minutes of driving on the wrong side of the car, on the wrong side of the road, to reach Inverlochie.

Her cinnamon-and-cream Mette Janssen skirt and top were limp, and her feet had swollen inside her matching Furlanetto pumps. She should have thought the travelling-coach-class-incognito thing through a little better and worn flats.

It was three in the afternoon here, which meant it was six in the morning in Langemark, and goodness knew what time in whichever time zone Gian-Marco was in today. Spain, still? The Spanish Grand Prix had only just finished.

Nuala's brother looked at his watch again. "Not long. Maybe half an hour," he said.

"Right." At this point, half an hour was twenty-nine minutes too long, and any thought that involved Gian-Marco Ponti was a mistake.

To hide the sudden tears in her eyes, Misha leaned back into the car and snapped the release on the trunk, then walked around to the rear of the vehicle. Brant got there first, lifted the trunk lid and surveyed her Van Limbeck suitcases, her matching carry-on bag and her purse. He held out his dirt-stained hands again.

"Point taken," Misha told him, feigning a cheerful attitude. "I'll bring them in myself."

She'd already heaved the first one onto the ground before he answered. "Sorry, I meant I'd wash these hands, and then I'd do it."

"Well, if you can show me my room, wash your hands, and still beat me back out here, I'll very kindly let you bring the second suitcase, the wine, the flowers and the carry-on bag," she said, counting the seconds until she could be alone.

I'm a surly yob today, I should apologize, Brant thought, giving his hands a rough scrub with even rougher soap. He dried them on a towel he hoped was cleaner than the hands had been, and headed quickly back out to Nuala's friend's car.

Good.

He'd arrived first.

No dazzling sheaf of silky blond hair, no Scandinavian blue eyes, no hundred-watt smile, no smooth pancake-hued tan or willowy, well-engineered, designer-fashion-clad limbs in sight.

Now he could at least do the decent thing and bring in the gifts she'd brought, along with the rest of her luggage. He took the wine and the flowers first, then went back for a second trip. The heavy, expensive suitcase bulged and so did the carry-on bag, and he wondered what this Misha person had seen fit to bring with her. Twenty pairs of shoes?

What did she expect? Why was she here?

Nuala had been cagey about it. "Personal problems. She just needs to get away for a while. She needs some space and some anonymity."

Nuala was not her usual self, these days. The wedding was scheduled for the first weekend in September and it had gone to her head, the way forthcoming weddings apparently could even for the most down-to-earth of women. She spent hours on the phone to Mum in Sydney every week, and she was planning a visit up there soon, because Mum warned that she'd already slipped direly behind schedule in her quest for the perfect dress.

Brant was skeptical.

Behind schedule?

September was still more than three months away.

But he appreciated the wedding as a way to bring Mum and Nuala closer.

For a long time, the two of them hadn't seemed to have much in common. At heart, Nuala was such a country girl, while Mum had never been totally happy here. Less than a year after Dad's death six years ago, she'd remarried a friend of theirs from racing circles—a wealthy Sydney business-man. She'd signed over the ownership of Inverlochie to her two children and settled to a life of socializing, race-going, charity work and renovating Frank McLaren's Double Bay mansion.

Brant and Nuala had both realized she would be happier in the city, but it hadn't given them many points of contact. Then Nuala had spent two and a half years seeing the world in a way that Mum considered far too menial—camp coun-sellor in the USA, chalet-girl cook in France, volunteer aid worker in India. Now, with the wedding coming up, Mum and Nuala had points of contact in spades. Although it irri-tated the heck out of him to hear this endless angsting over guest lists and venues and color schemes, he didn't make any attempt to get Nuala to tone down.

"I can't break her confidence, Brant," Nuala had said about Misha. "But you should know before she gets here that things are *very* difficult for her at the moment, and she needs our absolute discretion and support."

Yeah.

Very difficult.

With top-quality European luggage and clothes that even he could see must have serious designer labels.

He felt deeply, deeply sorry for her.

Forget the apology.

He was back to surly.

And for the first time in his adult life, he had overdosed on women, especially well-groomed women who were mak-ing a big effort. He'd been out with at least a dozen differ-ent women this year and he'd had his fill of flirtatious games, transparent agendas, the sound of ticking biological clocks, misguided expectations, too much makeup, pushy seduction attempts, attitudes of entitlement, airhead questions about his farm, the whole gamut.

He had so much on his plate. Prices for his nineteen-

a puddle, as if the driver expected to lurch into a ten-foot-deep ditch at any moment and never get out alive.

"This is going to be one of your women," Nuala predicted.

Unfairly.

"*My* women?" Brant was really not in the mood for this.

"Well, they haven't been coming to see me!"

"No, they wouldn't be here if it wasn't for you! They wouldn't ever have heard of me. And they definitely would not have seen my photo on the front page of a national magazine. Do *not* call them my women, okay?"

"Sorry…" She shrugged and made a face and had the grace to admit, "It has been getting a bit out of hand lately, hasn't it?"

The white car made a final cautious curve around a final puddle and came to a halt, at which point Brant recognized the driver, with her sleek, plum-colored hair and not-so-sleek pear-shaped build. What was her name? Hell, his mind had gone blank! Lauren, he remembered, just in time.

They'd had a lunch date in Albury some weeks ago, after she'd written to him in care of the magazine. They'd spoken a couple of times by phone since. She'd seemed okay, but he'd made the mistake of giving her his address, since she'd seemed so interested in the farm. She'd passed it around, so that even though *Today's Woman* magazine's Wanted: Outback Wives campaign had officially closed now, he was still getting letters and drop-ins.

This time, she'd brought three of her friends.

They all grinned as they climbed out of the car. One of them tossed her hair, and another whispered something to Lauren that made her nod and twist her features into a raunchy look.

"Hi, Brant," Lauren said. "We have a proposition for you that's going to be great fun for all of us. Did you get my letter about it yet, or are we a bit ahead of ourselves?"

"Uh, I don't think I got your letter."

"Well, good, because it'll be much better to tell you about it in person."

A short distance away, the sliding door on the front veranda opened and Misha stepped out of the house, wearing sunglasses and a borrowed gray-brown felt farmer's hat pulled low over her forehead. "Nuala!" she said, her voice cracking, and the two women rushed up to each other and hugged hard then started talking in low, intense tones.

"This isn't a good time, Lauren," Brant told his latest visitor bluntly.

"Well, you know, we don't have to get going on it this minute," Lauren said, sparing a fleeting glance at Misha.

"Get going on what?"

Lauren dimpled. "We had this great idea, you see, kind of a reality-TV-show thing. Well, you know, not real TV, obviously, but the same way they do it on a lot of those shows. A process of elimination."

"A what?"

"You know, you're looking, the four of us are looking… Why don't we be, you know, upfront about that? We could all go out, for dinner tonight or whatever, and at the end of the evening, you eliminate one of us, and after we've been on, you know, four or five dates, there's only one of us left and that's obviously the one you like best." She paused expectantly.

Brant couldn't come out with a word, not even a strangled exclamation.

Lauren took note of his reaction and launched into selling the idea a little harder. "We just thought it would be fun. You know, you're stuck out here in the middle of nowhere, with nothing to do, we thought you'd appreciate a creative way to find the right woman. I mean, you must already have a creative outlook about it, and, you know, an open attitude, or you wouldn't have entered the Outback Wives campaign in the first place."

Her friends were making her awkward and nervous, Brant could see. All those awkward *you knows*. She hadn't been this silly—or else he hadn't been in such a disgusting mood—when they'd met for lunch. Hell, how could he deal with this? He didn't want to hurt her, but it was ludicrous to find himself in this situation.

As for his part in the Outback Wives campaign…

Nuala's idea.

Of course.

Brant and his other best mate Dusty had been seriously concerned about their friend Callan for quite some time. Callan had lost his wife to cancer four years ago, and he was still hurting about it, didn't have the slightest idea how to find someone new to share his life and help him with his two boys.

He had a huge piece of acreage in the Flinders Ranges in South Australia, and ran cattle there. It was beautiful country on a grand scale—the real outback in every sense—but it was arid and unpopulated and at their past few get-togethers Callan had seemed so lonely and lost, not meeting anyone new and not even thinking that someone new might be good for him.

Nuala had read about the magazine's quest to bring interested women together with single men in far-flung parts of the country. She'd suggested that Dusty and Brant take part and rope Callan in with them. As the classic line went, it had seemed like a good idea at the time.

Maybe it still was a good idea. Callan had been e-mailing a couple of the women who'd contacted him through the magazine, and Brant had an inkling that it had done him some good. They'd spoken by phone yesterday and Callan had sounded better—stronger and more upbeat. That flat, wooden tone had gone from his voice, and, Brant hoped, the thousand-yard stare from his eyes, also.

But Brant hadn't wanted his own face advertising the

whole Wanted: Outback Wives thing on the front cover of the magazine, he wasn't wild about the follow-up story he'd semi-committed himself to, and he definitely didn't want silly women showing up here with their reality-TV-style elimination games. Nor did he intend to tell Lauren or her friends that he'd only taken part in the whole thing for the sake of a friend.

He just wanted to get rid of her.

"I'm sorry," he said bluntly, in the end. "I don't think it would be fun."

He saw Nuala edging Misha closer, so that they could both hear what was going on…and, he hoped, help him get rid of the visitors. Nuala had begun to make covert can-you-please-wind-this-up signals with her finger. Misha had pulled her hat even lower. If she was that bothered by the relatively mild autumn sunshine, it was lucky she hadn't come in summer.

He added, "And I'd like to offer you a cup of tea, or something, Lauren, but I really can't today."

"Rain check?" Lauren brought out the dimples again.

"Uh, no."

"Oh, come on, Brant!" she wailed. "Where's your sense of humor?"

Not joking, he told her, "I left it in a sheep paddock about half an hour ago."

Then he shot a glance at Nuala, saw her eyes widen in alarm and cursed himself for letting the bitter line slip out. If he wasn't careful, she'd quickly guess that something was wrong. She knew as well as he did how quickly disaster could overtake a farmer's life. He was going to have to get his act down better than this.

"No, seriously," he said. "I'll have to call you, because nothing's going to work for this weekend."

"The weekend's not for another two days, Brant."

"For the next two days *and* the weekend," he corrected himself.

It took another ten minutes to fob Lauren off with the promise of coffee in Albury next week, get rid of the four women, apologize to Misha, agree with Nuala that they'd need to put a lock on the gate, and convince her—lying about it for all he was worth—that the comment about leaving his sense of humor behind in the paddock had been nothing more than a joke.

Chapter Two

Heading back into the house, watching Brant carry her heavy suitcase with no visible muscular effort about four paces in front, Misha said quietly to Nuala, "Would I be able to call, um, Thingy?" She couldn't even say his name, today, without getting the familiar tight, tearful feeling, along with a sense of confusion and disappointment and being totally alone.

"Of course." Nuala lowered her voice, but her brother could probably still hear both of them. "Use Brant's office, it's nice and private."

"Thanks. I so appreciate all of this, Nu." She hugged her friend again, knowing that Nuala would feel through their body contact that she'd lost weight.

"Oh, stop! Do you want to call him right now?"

"Get it over with, I think."

"So things are pretty bad?"

"We had a big fight, and I still have no idea if he was right about what he said or if I'm being an idiot even to consider believing him." She spoke faster, needing to get the basic story out and over with. "I mean, we're supposedly engaged. Although, are we? I don't feel I even know. Officially, we are. Officially, the wedding's at the end of September. Officially, I've been told that even if the whole relationship goes down the tube—and I don't know if it has—I'm not allowed to break it off publicly until some time in June."

"Why? Told by your parents?"

"By the whole country, practically. Well, you know, various advisers and government types. Christian and Graziella are having another baby."

"Oh, lovely!"

"It hasn't been announced yet. They're waiting another few weeks, until the end of the first trimester, and when they do announce it, they don't want the news clouded by anything negative from me. As well, there are these new laws in the pipeline, and a broken engagement could send the wrong message, influence the vote." She flapped her hands, dismissing the details until she and Nuala had more of a chance to talk.

Nu seemed to understand without the detail. "That's terrible! Even your parents are telling you that?"

"Mom and Dad understand that it's hard, but you know, duty comes first. Except duty just makes it harder to work out what's going on purely between the two of us. If we love each other, I should be able to believe him, and that's what he says."

"So he says those other women—"

"—are just Formula One groupies he has to fight off with a barge pole and if I really loved him, then I'd trust him when he says he hasn't slept with any of them."

"So he's turning it into your problem."

Misha's throat tightened again, and she felt a senseless need to defend her fiancé. "But maybe he's right and it is my problem…"

"Call him. See how you feel after that. Where is he?"

"I don't know. Spain? Monaco? I'll try him on his cell."

"I'm going to feed animals." Nuala squeezed Misha's arm. "We'll talk soon, okay?"

But when Nuala had shown her into Brant's very neat, business-like office, the phone rang before she could key in Gian-Marco's number. Hearing the shower running in the adjacent bathroom and guessing that no one else was available to take the call, she picked up. Took a message. Someone called Shay-from-the-magazine, saying that the photo shoot and story interview were scheduled for next week, and could they confirm a day and time? Could Brant please call Shay back?

Without giving her own name, and trying to make her light European-American accent anonymous, Misha scribbled down the details dutifully, like an executive assistant. But her heart was sinking. What was this about?

Surely—*surely*—Nuala wouldn't have done anything so crass as to organize a magazine story about her presence in Australia! Nuala knew how Misha felt about that kind of thing. It had to be something else, but anything to do with the press made her miserable and stressed at the moment.

She took a couple of minutes to coach herself into a more rational attitude. Those magazine photos of her fiancé and the dark-haired French actress could easily have been faked. If she loved Gian-Marco, she should believe him.

His proposal seven months ago had been so romantic, and perfectly staged in every detail. He'd taken her on a hot-air balloon ride over the vineyards and lavender fields of Provence, and asked her to marry him three hundred feet off the ground. They'd toasted each other with champagne and he'd given her an enormous solitaire diamond ring. He'd said he loved her so many times. But that was before the fight...

Knowing her stomach wasn't going to settle until she'd done the deed, she called him.

"Checking up on me?" was almost the first thing he said.

It was a short, tense conversation, and it didn't dampen a single one of her doubts. Had she heard a woman's voice in the background? Did Gian-Marco *want* to make her feel like a jealous, irrational hag? He'd succeeded.

And he'd made her cry.

Determined not to have either Brant or Nuala—particularly Brant—see reddened eyes and a swollen nose, Misha remained in the office for several minutes after she'd put down the phone, imprisoned by her tears, imprisoned by family expectations and relentlessly unfolding wedding plans that made it so hard to know her own heart.

She finally had her hand on the door handle ready to open it and make an urgent dash for the bathroom to tidy up the final smears of emotional evidence when she heard Nuala and Brant talking out in the open-plan living room.

She froze.

"By the way, who's Thingy?" Brant said. "The one she wanted to call."

"Her fiancé," answered Nu.

"Whose name she's apparently forgotten."

Nuala sighed like a teacher with a slow, stubborn pupil. "Brant, when a woman doesn't want outsiders to know who she's talking about, or when she's uncertain or upset about the relationship in any way, she prefers not to use the man's name, okay?"

"If you say so."

"Sometimes, in fact, in really dire situations, she is *unable* to use the man's name without crying."

Yep, thought Misha.

"So the use of the term *Thingy...*?"

"Indicates caution and doubt and problems."

Yep, again.

"If the relationship actually breaks up," Nuala continued, "the woman may look for a more distancing term such as *The Creep*."

The Creep.

Good one.

Must remember that, in case I need it.

"Right. But Misha isn't at that point with Thingy yet, right? So maybe I should know his actual name." Brant's patient tone was heavy and exaggerated.

"Um, it's Gian-Marco Ponti," Nuala said.

Misha held her breath, waiting for a reaction that didn't take long to come. Her parents had reacted the same way last year when they'd first found out she was going out with him.

"Gian-Marco—*that* Gian-Marco Ponti? The racing driver? Formula One? The Mercer-Fernandez team? In contention with Ferrari and Renault and—?"

"That's the one," Nuala agreed on a drawl. "And I should also mention—and I really don't want you to make a big deal out of this, Brant, because she'd hate it—but the thing is, she's a princess."

"Yeah, well, I'd already worked that out for myself," Misha heard. The tone was sour.

"You had?" Nuala said.

Damn, thought Misha.

If she couldn't even pull off the incognito thing for half an afternoon…

She used to be so good at it.

But her relationship with Gian-Marco had put her picture in more magazines over the past year than she'd featured in during the entire previous twenty-six years of her life. Her mother had always insisted on as much privacy as possible for her royal offspring, and even though Mom's own laid-back Colorado upbringing had been impossible to replicate for her children, she'd done her very best.

And then I had to go fall in love with a Formula One driver…

Way more people recognized her now than had recognized her during her chalet-girl ski season with Nuala three years ago.

"Expensive luggage, designer clothes," Brant listed in the other room. "She thinks a barrage of charm and a gorgeous smile can get her anything she wants…"

"Misha's not like that, but I actually meant—"

"…and she magnifies the kind of personal problem that everybody has to deal with from time to time into a piece of major tragedy and hysteria that requires everyone around her to drop everything and rush to her immediate assistance."

"She's not like that, either. She really isn't, Brant. It's other people who magnify her personal problems. Because the thing is—"

"Of course I could tell she was a princess," Brant continued, ignoring his sister completely. "Do you think she's the only one I've ever met? You've been a bit of a princess yourself lately, Nu, with this wedding in the works."

"Uh, yeah, point taken, but you see that's not the kind of princess I meant."

Approximately forty-five seconds later, Misha heard the explosion of disbelieving profanity that she'd been expecting for some time.

Out in the living room, Nuala lowered her voice to a hiss of warning and locked an iron grip onto her brother's arm. "Don't overreact, Brant, she hates that. Had you heard of her?"

"Of course I'd heard of her," Brant said, ready to overreact ten times more strongly, if he perceived the slightest need. "You've talked about her a lot since you got back from your trip."

"No, I mean, of course, yes, you've heard of Misha. But had you heard of Princess Artemisia Helena de Marinceski-Sauverin?"

And he had.

He wasn't proud about it, but thanks to a lengthy spell in a doctor's waiting room a couple of months ago after he'd gotten an infected barbed-wire gash on his hand, he was up to date on his celebrity-magazine reading, and he had indeed heard of the European princess who was about to take up temporary residence beneath his roof.

He'd heard of her elder brother Prince Christian, heir to the centuries-old throne of Langemark, and of his charming Italian wife Princess Graziella and their two young sons. He'd seen pictures of the two royal residences, the Gunnarsborg Palace and Rostvald Castle, with their stunning artwork, furnishings and decor. And he'd read about Princess Artemisia Helena and her American-born mother's alleged heartbreak at her allegedly wild ways.

Would the adrenaline junkie junior royal ever settle down? the magazines wondered. Close friends claimed that the princess's engagement and upcoming wedding to Gian-Marco Ponti was no more than a stopgap measure to keep Queen Rose from laying down the law about her daughter's wilful behavior. What did hip, sexy Artemisia Helena really feel?

Et cetera.

Shoot, it was embarrassing that he remembered it all in this much detail.

It was probably even more embarrassing that he hadn't had an inkling until now—hadn't recognized her when he first saw her this afternoon, hadn't ever thought to ask Nu about "my friend Misha's" background. Nuala had been deliberately cagey about it, he realized.

"I've read a bit about her," he confessed.

"But the magazines always get it wrong, you see. She hates the labels and the scandal and these supposed 'close friends' who are always ready to dish the dirt on her innermost feelings. She's really down-to-earth, she's—"

"Hang on a sec. Can I debate that last point? Down-to-earth in four-inch heels?"

"She has a public image to maintain, of course. But when she's in a situation where she can just be herself—*please* let her be herself while she's here, Brant, and don't go all weird with her."

"All weird?"

"You have to treat her like she's one of us. Take her riding, and skiing if she's still here when the season starts, do all that stuff with her, but she'll want to help out on the farm, too. She won't mind getting dirty."

"That I don't believe. Do you know how much I don't need something like this right now, Nu? A bleeping princess?"

"You're overreacting. Please just—" Nuala stopped. They'd both heard the click of the office door, and half a minute later, Misha appeared, signalling the end of the current opportunity to talk about her in heated whispers behind her back.

She smiled at them brightly. "Thanks for that. I got onto him. He's in Paris. I won't be making international calls every day, I promise. And I called my parents to tell them I got here safely. Now, once I've unpacked and changed, what do you want me to do? Cook? Clean? Brand? Shear?"

"Could you handling some mulesing?" Brant suggested unkindly.

It didn't faze her.

"Well, I'll give it a shot," she said energetically at once, then added in a somewhat less confident tone, "if you tell me what it is."

This was why it didn't faze her. Ignorance was bliss.

Nuala frowned at him, and he knew he was being a surly yob again, and that any minute Nu would want to know why. He didn't want to tell her about the lame ewes.

Okay, sis, I'll stop.

He mirrored the princess's smile, instead, feeling as if the stretch of his face muscles must look more like a grimace of pain.

"How about I just show you around the place?" he said. On the third-to-last word, his voice cracked like a fourteen-year-old's. He clenched his teeth harder and his jaw began to ache.

Chapter Three

"So, have you ever ridden a four-wheeler before?" Brant asked. He expected, and received, a negative answer.

"But I'd love to try," the princess added.

She appeared to be sincere. She'd changed out of the designer skirt and top and killer heels into running shoes, a Wedgwood-blue cotton sweater and jeans. All of these items might be designer, too, but at least they didn't look brand-new. The outfit hugged her whip-thin figure, but showed its strength, too. She had real legs, not feeble sticks. She had a couple of very definitely curvy bits, and a way of moving that said she wasn't afraid of using her body.

He unchained the dogs then handed her the helmet.

"Why do you keep them chained up?" she asked as Sox and Mon began to circle around the place, frantic with excitement.

"They're working dogs. If they're left to run where they like, they get all sorts of bad habits and they're useless."

"It doesn't seem very kind, to work them then keep them tied in one place."

He just grinned at her. "You watch them for a week, then tell me if they're not the luckiest dogs in the world."

"They look pretty happy right now," she admitted. "What breed are they?"

"Kelpies. Australian sheepdogs."

"And what are their names?"

"Sox and Mon."

"Short and sweet."

"Sheepdogs usually have short names. Yelling 'Marmaduke' across a paddock doesn't seem like fun after the first few hundred times, most farmers find."

She laughed. "Okay, Sox and Mon. Hi, girl. Hi, you. I love your tan eyebrows." She gave each of them a sturdy pat across their shoulders.

He showed her the accelerator on the four-wheeler's right handlebar, the hand brakes, the foot brake and how to work the gears with her left foot. She nodded, mentioned that she had a motorcycle license and had had a couple of rides in the past on a Ducati and a "Kwaka" 750, both impressive bikes. She seemed keen to get started.

And, wow, she wasn't like any other female city visitor he'd ever had here. She took a couple of experimental circuits around the grass and along the track at a sedate speed to get familiar with how the gears and brake responded, and then she gunned the thing. With the iffy starter on the two-wheel trail bike holding him back for a couple of minutes, he had trouble catching up to her, and he only did so because she stopped when she got to the first choice of route so she could ask which way they were going.

The magazines in the doctor's waiting room had been right about one thing, at least.

The princess was an adrenaline junkie.

"Over the grid and into the paddock," he told her. He had Sox on the back of the trail bike and Mon panting on the ground beside him. "From the saddle between those two hills you can see most of Inverlochie."

They pretty much raced each other up toward the saddle, peeling away from the track that led down to the shearing shed and careening across the grass. He would have won, except that he kept slowing to look sideways and make sure she wasn't doing anything stupid. Four-wheeler farm bikes had the dubious distinction of being the number-one cause of vehicular fatalities in this country, and it probably wouldn't be a popular move from an international diplomacy perspective if he killed the princess on her very first day here.

But, no, she had good instincts, picked the clearest trajectory, didn't crash over every bit of fallen timber or tip the four-wheeler at too steep an angle on the side of the slope. The sheep at the foot of the hill milled around and headed for higher ground and the dogs were so keen to round them up that he had to feel sorry for them.

"We're not working right now," he told them. "This is just for fun."

He heard the princess whoop and laugh and yell a couple of times, and when they stopped at the saddle she was breathless. Her cheeks glowed inside the confines of the helmet, and her hair soon recovered its bounce when she took the helmet off and tossed her head. "That was fantastic!" She climbed off the bike and spun slowly around, looking at the sky, the green paddocks, the distant mountains.

"You can get an even better view from the top of the hill," he told her, gesturing to the right where the slope grew much steeper, "but it's pretty tricky taking a four-wheeler up there."

"This is good enough," she said, and followed his arm as he showed her the fences that marked the edge of the property, the shearing shed at the bottom of the hill and the old fibro-cement cottage beside it that no one lived in anymore. "How many acres is it, all told?"

"Around three thousand."

"Does that give you a full-time living?"

"In this part of the country it does. It wouldn't further west. Out in the desert, my mate Callan needs six hundred thousand acres to run a viable herd of cattle, and our friend Dusty's station is even bigger."

"Wow! But I bet their land isn't so pretty as this."

"Callan's is rugged, Dusty's is flat and flood-prone. I like my land, and these rolling hills. Here, most years we can run around six thousand ewes, plus twenty-five hundred wethers, and right now we have sixty-five rams. I've never had to work off-farm, and Nuala and I can manage with contractors in busy periods, instead of having to employ another person full-time."

She asked several more questions, about the work that was coming up at this time of year, about his long-term plans, about the issue of humane farming practices, and he reached a conclusion that hadn't been covered in the magazines.

The princess was very bright.

He knew that Nuala, and Misha herself, would hate that he kept thinking of her as "the princess" but it was just so weird. His face didn't feel as though it fit him anymore. He couldn't find the right expression for it. Smile insanely? Hold his cheek muscles in deferential stillness, with tight, pruny lips and a sort of butler-like refusal to show inappropriate emotion?

Nu just treats her like a person, so do that, he kept coaching himself. But today wasn't a good day in that area. Even without the princess stuff, he was hiding his real thoughts, and his real self. He'd taken a gamble, temporarily overstocking his land so that he could buy in the new ewes he wanted before actually getting rid of the old ones.

The sale of those was already contracted, but the buyer hadn't wanted to take delivery for another three weeks, and, yes, it was risky to have so much stock here at once, but he'd done it because he'd thought the payoff was worth it and the risk was low. He was a good farmer, and he knew it. He could supplement the stock's grazing with feed grain if he thought they needed it.

If the new ewes had foot rot, however…

Smile, Brant.

Just keep smiling at Nu, smiling at the pretty princess, the way you smiled at all those women who liked your picture in a magazine, because you're keeping this foot-rot problem to yourself, smiling all the while, until you've had a better chance to check it out and you're sure.

No wonder he couldn't get a handle on how to behave.

He looked at the sheep on the hill, couldn't spot any obvious signs of lameness in the ones who were moving. It was getting late in the day and the sun had begun to dip toward the horizon. There was a broken bank of cloud in the west, and sun and shadow came and went across the ground, making the light change from soft purple to green and gold, and back again. To the east, the layered hills became higher and steeper and more thickly clothed in dark blue forest as they rose toward the Snowy Mountains, which didn't have any snow on them yet because it was only autumn.

"It's so beautiful. It's stunning, Brant," Misha said. "Absolutely stunning."

He blinked and looked, just as the sun broke from beneath the pile of western clouds once more.

Shafts of golden light radiated outward and washed between the eucalpytus trees, making them glow with rich, warm bronze and rust and tan. The new lambs in one of the lower paddocks looked as white, next to their dust-stained mothers, as the sulphur-crested cockatoos that squabbled in a nearby treetop. The water in the dams that had been filled by the recent rains looked like sheets of molten metal, and the grass was green, green, green.

It *was* beautiful.

How long since he'd really looked at it?

Too long.

Oh, hell, and this was why it was all worth it, all the worry over wool prices and the health of his livestock, the early-morning starts and long days, the frustrations with contractors, the filthy fingernails, all of it.

Because sometimes he got to zoom up to the green saddle of ground halfway up the hill, look at his very own land bathed in unearthly late-afternoon light, and take in deep, enormous breaths of his very own clean, beautiful air.

Today, as it happened, he was breathing clean air with a princess.

Princess or no princess, he knew he wouldn't want any other way of life.

"We should head back," he said, after several minutes of silence during which he forgot all about the princess thing. "It'll be getting dark soon."

Back at the house, Misha disappeared for a shower, Nuala was on the phone to Mum in Sydney, and Brant could smell Irish stew in a big pot on the stove. He set the table in front of the living-room fire that Nuala had lit, found some wet laundry in the machine and chucked it in the dryer, then came back into the kitchen to discover Nuala still arguing with Mum.

"Well, it can't be this week," she was saying, "Because I have my friend Misha here. I know that means putting it off until—" She stopped and listened for a moment. "And that's too late? Why is it too late?" More listening. "But what if I don't want a specially made gown? Can't I buy one off the rack?"

Apparently she couldn't.

"And you're right about the venue," she agreed. "If it's going to be in Sydney, then, yes, a decision's getting pretty urgent. I guess you're right about the wedding dress, too. Look, I'll have to see what Brant and Misha say. Chris will be okay with this week, and he won't mind that he can't come. He says I'm to organize it how I want. But it really can't be—?" She listened. "No, you have to pack and all that stuff. I know. Okay."

"What's up?" Brant asked when she'd put down the phone and made a resigned face in his direction.

"Mum says I have to come to Sydney *this week* to finalize the dress and the venue, because next Wednesday, a week from today, she and Frank are heading off on their cruise, which means Monday and Tuesday she has to pack and finish off her to-do list."

"So go to Sydney," he told her. Nuala had a tendency to complicate the most simple decisions lately.

"Well, I was supposed to help Chris with lamb-marking. He won't mind that, but—"

"You were supposed to help me with lamb-marking, too." It was only the mildest reproach. Brant knew Nuala's loyalties were in transition, between the farm she'd grown up on and the one fifteen minutes drive away where she'd be spending her future.

"I was going to split between you," she said.

"Go to Sydney," he repeated stoically. "Chris and I'll take turns helping each other. It's a twenty-five-day cruise, isn't it?"

"That was Mum's point. If we leave it much longer, she says I'll end up getting married in a thirty-dollar nylon dress at ten o'clock on a Thursday morning in the local Scout hall. I thought she was exaggerating a bit, there, but I don't want to arrange it all without her, and—"

"Get up at five, leave at five-thirty, you can be there by late morning. Stay until Wednesday and see Mum and Frank off on the cruise."

"And leave Misha alone with you?"

Oh.

Right.

The princess.

Who turned out to be listening in the doorway, with the

wet ends of her blond hair still curling around her swan-like neck. "It's fine," she said. "I can help with lamb-marking."

Brant and Nuala stayed respectfully silent.

"I *can!*" She went from zero to indignant in three seconds. "Gosh, Nu, you of all people, I thought, would *not* assume that I'd be too prissy for something like that! Forget the fingernails. Forget the engagement ring. I didn't even wear it on the plane. What does it involve? Getting a bit of wool grease on my hands?"

She was impressive.

"Um, not quite," Nuala said. "Bit, uh, messier than that."

"Well! Still! When have you known me to back down from a challenge? How many times in France did we climb the Aiguille Bleue together and ski the *couloirs* when no one else had made tracks there? How many times did I manage to cover cooking at your chalet as well as mine on the same night, without the guests ever knowing, so we could buy each other extra time off?"

"Half the season, Mish. We took turns."

"Exactly! How many drunken package tourists did I fend off with my psychotic-aromatherapist routine? Look at me, Nu!" She bracketed her hands on each side of her jaw. "This is more than just a princessy face, you know!" She batted her eyelids at ninety beats a minute and gave a toothy but still helplessly gorgeous grin.

Nuala was laughing by this time, while Brant was thinking, psychotic aromatherapist? Something stirred inside him, a giddy feeling he hadn't experienced in quite a while.

"Fine," Nu said. "Go ahead. Help with lamb-marking. But don't say we didn't warn you, Mish."

The princess put her hands on her hips. "Have I *ever* said that you didn't warn me? Have I *ever* acted unwarned?"

"I want to see the psychotic-aromatherapist routine," Brant blurted out.

"No chance!" Her blue eyes were sparkling.

Brant could see that she must have been great as a fellow chalet girl. He presumed she'd worked under a fake name, because she couldn't have had people knowing who she was. It must have been one of the most liberating periods of her life. He began to understand why she and his sister were friends.

But, thanks to his own insistence, he would be stuck entertaining her on his own for the next few days while Nuala went to Sydney, and somehow, despite everything she'd said, he didn't think lamb-marking would quite cut it as a way of spending ten or twelve hours every day.

He'd have to take her places. Dinner in that swish restaurant that had opened in what used to be the Bilbandra pub. A tour along the banks of the Murray River. Riding horses, if she knew how, which being a princess she probably did. They didn't keep horses at Inverlochie but he had friends who ran trail rides on their property.

There'd have to be some whole pretence to everyone about who Misha was. He remembered how she'd worn sunglasses and pulled one of Nuala's old hats down so low over her forehead this afternoon, when Lauren and her friends were here. It made sense now. He'd have to watch everything he said, put on a performance the way he had for at least seventy percent of the would-be Outback Wives who'd contacted him through the magazine since February. He could do it, all of it, but it was an extra effort he didn't need right now.

Great.

Just great.

His brief interlude of appreciating her humor and her evident gutsiness cut out and left him tense and sour again.

"Oh," Misha suddenly said. "There was a phone message for you earlier, Brant, I wrote it down but forgot to tell you. Shay-from-the-magazine? About a story and shooting some photos."

Nuala had heard something in her tone. "Not photos of

you, Mish, you know I wouldn't do something like that," she said quickly, and explained about *Today's Woman* and the Wanted: Outback Wives campaign. "They're doing a follow-up story about Brant, because he was their—"

"Don't say it," Brant warned.

"—number one—"

"Nuala…!"

"—and he got the most—"

"Stop!"

"Okay, okay." She was silent for a whole five seconds, then burst out, "No, I have to say it! He got the most letters! Women think my big brother is hot. That is such a hoot, Mish, but cute, too, do you know what I mean?"

At this point Brant just gritted his teeth and went to return the call from Shay Russell at *Today's Woman* magazine.

"Something's up with him," Nuala told Misha.

They were now sitting at the kitchen table drinking the first hot sips from big mugs of coffee while Nuala's fabulous Irish stew simmered on the stove and a long loaf of garlic bread got toasted in the oven. Outside the landscape had darkened. Dogs and chickens had been fed, Nuala had opened a bottle of red wine to let it breathe, and at some point she'd lit the fire in the slow combustion stove in the living room. From where she sat, Misha could see the flames leaping behind the glass and could feel the spreading warmth.

"But I don't know what it is," Nuala went on. "I'm sorry. I know I'm bugging him with the wedding details, it's probably that. The thing is, Mish, you've been a princess your whole life, you're used to it and it's a chore for you, but September is going to be my one shot at it, princess for a day, and I want to embrace it with my whole soul, because after that it's going to be pretty much muddy boots and sheep-smelling hands for the rest of my life—which, as a long-term thing, is far more the real me."

She gave a vague gesture that took in the high-ceilinged old house with its eccentric additions, as well as the fenced paddocks and rolling hills outside. A satisfied smile hovered on her lips, and Misha understood the reason for her happiness. She was where she belonged, and it wasn't hard to imagine how good it would feel to belong in a place like this.

"But Mum is ecstatic that I'm finally acting like a girl. She almost cancelled the cruise. Brant is being—" She shook her head. "I'm sorry."

"Hey," Misha soothed her. "I'll deal with it. I won't act like a girl for a second."

"He actually likes girls."

"I can see he has a strong personality, pretty intense in his reactions."

"He's one of the best men in the world to have on your side when you need him. But, honestly, there have been some really idiotic girls around since the totally-my-idea magazine thing." She thought for a moment. "I guess it's that as much as the wedding. I guess there's nothing else going on."

She frowned.

Brant came back from the office, poured coffee for himself and sat down at the table with them. "Story's set up for Monday," he said. "Misha, you'd better hide in the shearing shed."

"Hide in the—?"

"While the magazine people are here. If you don't want to get discovered and get your cover blown, that is. I can see the headlines now. Princess Incognito In Australia."

"I can see them, too," Misha agreed. "Although your sub-editing needs work. You have to get *Sex Scandal* or *Out of Control* in there, somehow. *Diet Danger* is a good one, too, if you're really stuck."

For the first time in four hours, he laughed—a surprised and almost grateful jolt of sound, accompanied by an electric flash of appreciation in his gray eyes and a lift of his strong jaw. Misha had never seen a man's face change so fast, with such a radical effect. She wondered what he'd look like when he wasn't stressed and in a bad mood.

Magazine-cover material, of course.

As Nu had let slip, it was official.

And then the phone rang and he lunged toward the office again with a frustrated, impatient growl. What had she been wondering just a second ago? What he was like when he wasn't in a bad mood? It didn't look as if she'd ever get to find out.

"Let the machine pick up, Brant," Nuala told him. "I'll grab it if it's Chris or Mum. Anyone else can go jump."

He slowed and the tightly wound energy drained out of him. He took his coffee and flopped onto the couch that sat in the corner of the big farm kitchen. All three of them listened to his to-the-point recorded announcement. "You've reached the Smiths at Inverlochie. Please leave a message after the tone."

Then they heard Lauren. "Brant, I'm so-o-o sorry about today. It was a dumb idea. My friends talked me into it. They're heading back to Melbourne on Friday, but I'm in the area over the weekend. You know, just sightseeing, doing some food and wine, and looking around. If you want to get together, here are the numbers where you can reach me."

She gave them—hotel and cell phone—then repeated them slowly.

"I hope you've written those down! Plus I'll drop in, shall I? See what you're up to? It would be great to hang out with you. I could, like, shear, or something. Or we could hit the pub for a beer. Whatever you want. Talk to you soon. Pick up if you're there…"

"She doesn't give up, does she?" Brant muttered, hauling himself up from the couch again, as if something was hunting him and he couldn't find a safe place to rest. The muscles in his forearms looked like rope about to reach its breaking strain. "Can we eat, do you think?"

"It's ready whenever you want," Nuala said, and Brant pulled the garlic bread from the oven with his bare hands, opened the foil and tossed the bread into a dish. It smelled like heaven.

"Guess you're not there," the voice continued on the answering machine. "So… You'll get back to me, and—"

Mercifully, the message timer that cut off the caller after thirty seconds spared them from any more of Lauren's perky desperation. Hauling the heavy cooking pot to the other table—the one in front of the fire that he had set earlier, ready for their meal, Brant uttered a single, blunt word. "Why?"

"Because the magazine people put you on the cover," Nuala said. She picked up the open wine bottle and they all moved to the other table to eat.

Brant had left his coffee barely drunk. "That doesn't make sense."

"But some people are like that," Misha said. "They zero in on the person they think everyone else is going to want the most."

"Usually that's you, Mish," Nuala pointed out.

Unnecessarily.

"I know." She controlled a sigh. "I've been thinking about that a bit, lately."

She'd wondered if this had been the attraction for Gian-Marco—that in a room full of interesting, attractive, pedigreed women, she was very often the one that men wanted the most.

Gian-Marco was a professional driver on the most high-profile racing circuit in the world. He hungered to win. But she'd thought until recently that it was the hunger they had in common, the love of a good healthy adrenaline rush, not the fact that he was an instinctive winner and she was just another prize.

Which was it, really?

The answer was important.

Answers to recent questions raised about his faithfulness by some pretty flagrant—if conceivably faked—photos in the press were important, too. If he was the kind of man who went all out with a woman and then stopped wanting her as soon as she was safely his, then the man she thought she had fallen in love with before their engagement didn't really exist.

This was why she'd fled Europe—to work out the truth about Gian-Marco and her own feelings in peace, without the pressure of publicity or wedding arrangements, and without the word *duty* ever getting mentioned. It had been a desperate action, and she wished she hadn't needed to do it.

Basically, she was a mess. She would seize on any distractions, any kind of healing that she could find, while she was here.

"You're lucky, Nu," she told her friend. "You and Chris want each other…love each other…for all the right reasons—for what you can share, not what you can get from each other."

"You see, you *get* that, Mish!" Nuala said, spreading her arms like an opera singer. "You understand. So many people don't. You see why I'm friends with this woman, Brant?"

"I'm certainly seeing a few things in common," he drawled. Misha wasn't convinced it was a compliment.

They settled down to eat. Nuala told Misha more about the whole magazine thing, about Brant's friend Callan who'd needed help learning to live again. "But I'm sorry I ever came up with the idea now," she said.

"Don't be," Brant answered. "Callan's sounded pretty good the last couple of times I've talked to him. I'm not sure if he's serious about anyone, but I think it's helped him to get over Liz. Even with all the crud I've been getting lately from people like Lauren, it was worth it. And Dusty's practically engaged."

"To that Mandy woman?"

"Why is she that Mandy woman? You've never met her. She could be wonderful."

Nuala shook her head and made some concerned clucking sounds. "I don't like the vibe."

"What vibe?"

"You told me about the magazine cocktail party. I could pick up the vibe from that."

"What vibe, Nu?" Brant said patiently.

"Well, as we've discussed, there are women who'll go right for the man they think every other woman in the room will want, and then there are women who'll grab the first one that's put in front of them. Mandy fell squarely into the second group, from what you said. See Dusty, grab Dusty."

"Dusty's pretty down-to-earth. Maybe that's what he wants."

Nuala looked at Misha and opened her hands. Can you believe anyone could come up with such a bizarre theory, and is there a chance you could possibly agree with him, her body language said.

Misha shook her head, slow and exaggerated. Not in a million years.

No, I didn't think so, said Nu's face.

Brant laughed again. "You two!"

"People sometimes thought we were sisters, in France," Nuala confessed.

"You look nothing alike."

"Some sisters don't. But thanks to Misha's total lack of imagination when coming up with a fake name, we were both Smith, we cooked in chalets next door to each other and we finished each other's sentences."

"Or, as just now," Brant suggested, "you didn't bother with verbal communication at all."

"That, too," Misha agreed.

It was so nice.

For at least twenty minutes.

Misha had a glass and a half of wine, which was about

twice as much as she usually drank. She had four pieces of garlic bread, and a large second helping of stew, and they talked about all sorts of things. Mostly she and Nuala did the actual talking, admittedly, but Brant's listening wasn't as morose and hostile as she might have expected. They didn't get anywhere near the subject of Formula One racing drivers or the ethics of the press.

And then the phone rang again.

The machine picked up. "Hi-i!" said Lauren brightly after Brant's announcement. "Look, I've just had a thought. How about a weekend in Melbourne? It doesn't have to be this weekend if you're not free, but we could arrange something for next weekend, or the one after. I know I'm being a bit pushy here, but I really, you know…this sounds stupid, I hate saying it into a machine, if you're there, do you want to pick up?" Several seconds of silent waiting. "I guess you're not. I guess you'll get this later. Well, anyhow, I really intuitively felt something between us. There, I said it. Doesn't it sound stupid?"

"Yes, love," Nuala commented to the answering machine in the other room. "It does."

"But didn't you?" Lauren plowed on. "Feel it? I felt that you did. I'm going to stop now before I really embarrass myself. I'm not used to being this pushy, but what's that ancient Chinese curse? May you live in interesting times? And I think we do live in interesting times. Different times. No one knows the rules anymore, and I think it's tough for women to—" The machine cut out again.

Brant had one hand over his face, his head bent forward, and the other hand gripping his wineglass so hard Misha expected to see the stem snap. She thought about teasing him, but then she might be the thing that got snapped instead. Even Nuala wasn't smiling.

"I'm sorry, sorry, sorry," she mouthed to Misha.

"Apologize to your brother, not me," Misha mouthed back.

"Do you know what we have to do?" Nuala announced aloud.

Brant groaned.

"No, this is the answer. I'm serious. This'll get rid of her, get rid of the other women, and get Shay-from-the-magazine off your back."

"What, Nuala?" growled Brant, from within the depths of his despair. Misha couldn't see his face at all, just some dark hair flopping over his hand, and his chin dropped toward his empty plate.

"Look, the only people you'll be fooling will be people who don't count, people you don't even know. I can tell you're stressed, Brant. I don't know if it's the fallout from the whole *Today's Woman* thing or what, but—"

"Of course it's not *or what*, of course it's the magazine," he cut in quickly. Misha noticed the uncomfortable way he shifted in his seat. "Just get to the point. If you have one."

"I always have a point. And it's this." Nuala paused, then announced as if she'd just invented sliced bread, "The two of you should pretend to be engaged."

Chapter Four

"I apologize on my friend's behalf, Brant," Misha said. "Her mind has been poisoned by reading too many bridal magazines."

Brant glanced at his sister, feeling sour. "She's leaving for Sydney first thing tomorrow, thank goodness."

"Although I don't think that's going to act as a detox, given the purpose of the trip."

Nuala clapped her hands. "You're ganging up on me! I love it!"

"Five-thirty in the morning, aren't you, Nuala." he said. It was an order, not a question.

He'd had enough.

And he didn't want to tell her about the lame ewes.

"Yes. Or maybe even five. Mum really wants to get in a solid day. She's putting together a schedule."

"Fortunately, it's not fatal," Misha promised him, eyes twinkling and inviting Brant to laugh.

She'd made him do so a couple of times tonight. The action had felt rusty but welcome, like when you oiled an old hinge and it finally began to work smoothly. Even though this latest business of the lame ewes had only started today, he'd had a background level of higher-than-usual stress for… hell…years. Wool prices, drought…

He'd craved a bold strategy that would pay off in one huge, giddy burst, but now he was back balanced on the knife edge of doubt and worry. He hadn't realized, until Misha had made him laugh, how little he'd been laughing lately, how tight he'd been.

"There'll be a long convalescence after the honeymoon, and then she'll be okay again," Misha was saying.

"If the rest of us live that long," he pointed out.

"And there may be a relapse when she starts shopping for baby clothes."

"I'll warn Chris," he drawled.

Misha looked at him, and the promise of a smile on her face was sexier than the actual smile would have been. She was pretty nice, pretty funny, pretty down-to-earth. She was also…pretty. Beautiful, actually. Those blue eyes were huge, and for a blonde—even a slightly salon-highlighted blonde—she had incredible lashes, thick and long and dark. That mouth, too, so full and lushly curved…

He took a breath that wasn't quite steady, and then he remembered.

She was a bloody princess.

A princess, and he had to entertain her without Nuala's help for the next six or seven days.

He woke at five-thirty the next morning—an early start, because usually he slept in until around six. Nuala was already up and dressed and packing a snack to eat en route.

She kissed him on the cheek. "Thanks for this, Brant."

"You should thank Misha," he answered. "You're skipping out on her more than you're skipping out on me."

"She understands. She's great."

He avoided the trap of agreeing with her, and headed out to the four-wheeler, unchaining Mon so that she could ride on the back. Breakfast could wait. He wanted to take a better look at those ewes.

They were sluggish at this hour, a little indignant at being disturbed so early. It was only just beginning to get light. Mon roused them into action and they milled down toward the mustering yard, where he could set up portable sections of gate and fence as well as making use of the permanent rectangle of enclosed grass.

His fences weren't in great shape. Merinos had such a strong herd instinct and such a docile temperament that they stayed put, but the crossbreeds he was getting into now tended to push against sagging sections of mesh and barge their way through, especially the lambs. He was going to have to repair or replace quite a number of stretches soon.

Between the two of them, he and Mon got a couple of hundred ewes into the yard and closed the gate. The light had grown stronger, and the sky pale at the horizon. He could watch the animals as they milled around and see if any of them seemed lame, have a good look at some more feet, clean them out and settle his doubts.

These ewes had come with a written guarantee as to their condition, but a lot of farmers were doing it much tougher than he was right now, and sometimes a seller conveniently overlooked a problem. Guarantees weren't always accurate. Nor were they always enforceable. He'd had these ewes for over two weeks. The seller would have a good case, at this point, for claiming that they'd left his land disease free, and that the problem must lie in Inverlochie's soil.

As far as he could tell, only one out of this batch of ewes looked lame. After checking some healthy feet and some that had more dirt packed into them than they should have, he got hold of the lame ewe and took a look at hers, with their two surprisingly dainty sections, like the chunky heel of a fashionable shoe.

Her front right foot didn't look good. It showed separation of the hoof from the horn, reddening in between the two sections of hoof and a soreness that looked like abscesses. As he'd done yesterday, he cleaned it and pared it carefully, then imagined having to do the same to his entire stock.

One ewe in two hundred, and only one of her feet. Did it mean anything?

He told himself it didn't, that foot rot wasn't the only reason for red, sore feet, especially when only one of the four was affected, and decided he'd monitor the situation for a bit longer. He wouldn't rope the Pastures Protection Board in yet, because then the whole thing would be out of his control. He let the sheep out of the yard and back into the paddock. Typically, having not wanted to be yarded in the first place, they now didn't realize that they were supposed to leave and Mon had to race around convincing them.

She didn't have the same razor-sharp instincts for the work that Sox did, but she was a good dog if she was given the right instructions. He whistled and yelled, "Wa-ay back, back around, back around," and off the sheep started, and just as they really began to push along up toward the saddle he saw…thought he saw…a couple more of them limping.

Feeling as if he had a rock in his stomach, he went back to the house for breakfast.

Having a diploma from a very prestigious French gourmet cooking school under her belt, as well as four months' experience cooking three meals a day plus afternoon tea for a chaletful of hungry skiers, Misha could whip up a good breakfast. She could also interpret the state of a kitchen sink, dishwasher and draining basket to determine how many people had already eaten that morning, and Brant hadn't.

Still dozing at the time, she'd heard the two vehicles before dawn—Nuala heading for Sydney and Brant on the four-wheeler going off to do something important with sheep. By the time she heard the four-wheeler coming back again, she had apricot-oatmeal muffins fresh from the oven, coffee grounds sitting in the plunger waiting for their boiling water, and grilled tomatoes, mushrooms and bacon ready to serve on whole-wheat toast.

She could have done a pretty amazing cheese omelette with herbed scones, also, but had decided to save her really star-quality cooking ammunition for another day. Somehow, it had become important to her overnight, while she slept, that Branton Smith should not have any reason to conclude she was a lazy ditz with an overdeveloped sense of entitlement.

She wasn't any of those things, and she would have thought the fact was obvious, but he wouldn't be the first man to make all the wrong assumptions about her, despite the evidence.

Gian-Marco…did he have her all wrong, too? Should she give him back his ring? How much would that hurt? She wasn't wearing it at the moment—the stone was just so huge, it got in the way—but maybe she should put it back on.

She heard Brant out in the mudroom, kicking off his boots and washing his hands, and then he appeared with his bare, brown feet scuffing the floor below his jeans. The jeans hung low on his hips, showing off the lean length of his body.

Timing it perfectly, Misha put bread in the toaster and boiling water in the coffee plunger, then went to meet him wearing Nuala's old, oversize blue-and-white-striped chalet-girl apron. "Ready for breakfast?"

If she'd hoped for hungry, lit-up eyes or an appreciative

sniff of the fabulous aromas she'd created…well, bad luck. "You didn't have to do this," he growled.

"No, I know that, but I wanted to."

"What is it?"

She told him.

"You really didn't have to. I'm okay with toast and coffee."

"There are those things, too. It's all ready."

He followed her into the kitchen, where she had everything set up at the old table, instead of at the more formal one in the living room where they'd eaten last night. Sitting down and reaching at once for the coffee, he said, "I was thinking you might like to go riding today. We don't keep horses, but I can tee it up with some friends. They have a beautiful property with river frontage and sections of rolling, wooded country that are great for trail riding."

"I thought we were marking lambs today."

"*We* are not marking lambs any day. Chris and I can mark lambs tomorrow."

"He called. He says he'll be here by nine."

"I'll call him back and cancel."

She sighed. "I know why you're doing this, Brant, and you don't have to. I won't let you. You have to get those lambs marked…" For some reason she kept picturing hot-pink felt-tip pens being involved in the process. "…and I'm a fast learner. I got the impression it's messy…" She'd probably get completely encrusted with pink ink. "…so just lend me some old clothes."

He looked at her in total silence for at least thirty seconds, and his body language shouted, *You're really asking for it, aren't you?* so clearly that she almost laughed. "Chris is coming at nine?" he finally said.

"Yep."

"Meeting us up at the yard?"

"So he says."

Another beat of silence, then, "I'll lend you a shirt."

* * *

Ten hours later, Misha no longer had any illusion that pink ink was involved in the lamb-marking process. She was encrusted, yes, but the substance was much darker in color and consisted of bodily fluids she didn't want to examine too closely. Standing under a flood of hot shower water, she understood the reason for having a nail brush right there in the soap dish, and she used it energetically on her fingers. She also treated her hair with conditioner and three lots of shampoo.

Any princess in her right mind would be back in Albury by this time, totally traumatized and waiting with hysterical impatience for the next flight—especially since they were lamb-marking again tomorrow, at Chris's—but Misha actually felt…good.

Tired.

Satisfied.

With a sense of freedom she hadn't felt in months.

And *clean,* thanks to this heavenly steaming water.

She now knew how to pick up a bleating, woolly bundle, lay it in the worn old cradle and hook its hind legs into the two spiral-shaped curls of metal that kept the bleating bundle in place. She knew where to stick the needle that vaccinated the little guys against about six different diseases at once.

She knew how to rotate the cradle around to Brant and Chris who tackled the next much messier stages in the process, and she knew how to unhook the hind legs of the docked, marked and—where applicable—castrated lambs and swing them back down to the freedom of the grassy yard where their mothers would join them as soon as each batch was done.

She had helped to muster each successive paddock full of sheep into the yard. She'd wrestled with "wet" and "dry" ewes who didn't want to be sorted into the right group and tried to go through the wrong race into the wrong yard. She'd yelled at the mothers and talked baby talk to the lambs and combed her fingers through the incredibly long, fine, soft crimp of their wool. Shearers had the softest hands, she'd learned, because of the lanolin.

Brant and Chris, she thought, had been grudgingly impressed. Chris seemed like a great guy, the steady, physically adept, rough-hewn and slightly uncivilized kind that Nu had always wanted. He had very sexy eyes. And Brant had looked a little more relaxed today. If he'd frowned a bit at some of the sheep and wrestled a few of them into a position where he could examine their sheepy feet, it couldn't mean anything bad or serious, because he'd told Chris cheerfully, "Just checking. They're fine."

For the icing on the cake, after the long day, she might just manage to get her aching body dried and dressed and drag herself into the kitchen to knock together one of her chalet-girl dinners, if she could find some decent ingredients. She had already assured Brant confidently, out in the sheep paddock half an ago, that she would do so. "It'll take twenty minutes."

"Yeah? I don't think so, Misha, after you've been standing in this sheep yard or riding a four-wheeler for nine hours."

"You wait."

"Let me get on the phone when I'm back at the house and get something else fixed up for us."

It had sounded like an empty threat and she'd ignored it.

Filo-pastry parcels filled with herbed chicken, maybe, she decided as she turned off the shower water. With steamed vegetables and a soup. She remembered how she and Nu used to cut the timing too fine sometimes on a really good skiing day, zooming back down the powder-covered slopes on their last run, yelling to each other about garnishing tricks or side dishes to jazz up a meal.

Twenty minutes would be a stretch, but she could do it in

forty. Brant would soon learn that it was never safe to set her any kind of a challenge.

There was a knock at the bathroom door.

"I'm almost done," she called out, wrapping herself in a purple towel as big and thick and fluffy as a sheep's fleece.

"No, it's fine, I'll use the laundry," Brant called back. "I just wanted to tell you to put on a dress for tonight."

She opened the door. "*What?*"

"Suggest that you put on a dress. Might want to. I mean, it's up to you." He seemed disturbed by something. Her reaction. Or maybe the towel. "I thought…but if you don't have dresses…if a dress is too princessy…"

"Look, I said I was happy to cook for you—and Chris, if he's still here."

"He's gone home."

"But, I'm sorry, that doesn't mean you can dictate what I wear while I'm doing it."

"No. No!" He shook his head, as if irritated at her misunderstanding. "I thought we'd eat out. Didn't I say that? I made us a reservation at Tarragon."

"At what?"

"The best restaurant in the area. It used to be just the Bilbandra pub, down the road, but some corporate types in Sydney bought it before the Olympics—that's not important. There are new owners now, who've opened a restaurant. Called it Tarragon. You worked hard today and I was never seriously going to let you cook. Sheesh, of course not! I thought you realized."

They looked at each other, a little taken aback by how quickly they'd both misunderstood.

A little disappointed, too, in Misha's case, about how it felt.

She'd been so relaxed with him today. She'd had that sense of marvelling disbelief that always came when she was doing something different, rising to a challenge. Hey, I'm working on a farm with sheep, and I'm doing a pretty good job. Nuala had had it the time she'd come to stay in Lange-mark. Hey, I'm in a palace with eighteen-foot-high ceilings, eating my banana with a gold-filigreed knife and fork.

It didn't matter what kind of circumstance gave you the feeling, it was the feeling that counted—that you were really alive, stretching yourself, receptive and sizzling and on fire, making memories that made you believe in yourself and that would never go away.

"Sorry," Brant said gruffly.

"My fault. I jumped to the wrong conclusion."

"No problem."

In her initial anger, Misha had opened the bathroom door too wide. Now, after yelling through it about wanting her to wear a dress, Brant was standing too close. He hadn't show-ered yet, but he'd washed as far as his elbows and stripped off his outer clothing. He wore only stained jeans and an ancient white T-shirt, so threadbare it was almost transpar-ent. She could see the strong shape of his chest and stomach muscles, and the curved line where his tan ended at his collarbone.

She saw his gaze flick to her shoulder. Droplets of water still clung there, because she hadn't really had a chance to dry off yet, she'd only flung the towel around herself—thank goodness it was big—and tucked a corner in at the top.

She took in a breath of air that suddenly felt overheated and too rich, and backed away from the feeling, away from their shared realization that she was dressed in a towel and he was wearing a see-through shirt. They were alone in the house, and she had a strong inkling that he was thinking about this, too. Thinking about what could happen, if either of them wanted it to.

Her body crawled, and parts of it suddenly ached. It con-fused her, made her think about Gian-Marco and what he might be doing right now. Was he with the actress? Did he miss her and think about her at all? Did he still value his prize princess, now that he'd won her?

"Maybe not a dress," she said.

But I'll wear Gian-Marco's ring. See how that feels.

"Whatever you want. It's a nice place. They have open fires. And tablecloths."

"Wow! Tablecloths! I don't think I've ever seen one of those!"

Brant's teeth threatened to grit together. "As opposed to throwaway place mats, I meant."

Again. Missing his point. What was wrong with her?

And why was she so disappointed about it?

"I'm sorry," she said, closing her eyes. Which helped more than it should. "I'll be ready in five minutes."

"You're really into these impossible promises about timing, aren't you?"

Her eyes flew open again.

He was grinning.

She grinned back. "You just wait and see!"

Misha really was ready to leave by the time Brant had finished his shower and dressed.

Okay, so those activities took more than five minutes, but she hadn't been through the hour and a half of obsessive grooming he'd envisaged, nor did she look overdressed. Her makeup was so subtle he decided she might not even be wearing any, and she had her hair in a little knot at the back of her head, with some wispy bits hanging down. She wore plain black trousers, a soft, silky pale blouse-type thing and a neat, shimmery, darker jacket-type thing on top of that, sewn with some beady bits.

Or something.

Oh, and earrings. Gold. Little.

It was possibly fortunate that he had not gone into the field of fashion journalism.

Their thoughts had travelled in a similar direction. "These are made of wool," she said, running her hands down the side seams of her trousers. "Is there any chance it could have come from Inverlochie sheep? They were designed and made in Italy."

"It's possible," he said. "Inverlochie wool is fine enough for that high end of the market."

"They feel fabulous. Some wool is too prickly and thick, but these are so soft and light." She ran her hands over the fabric again, making a swishy sound against her thighs.

Brant wished she would stop doing it. He kept thinking about her wrapped in that purple towel, earlier—the way it draped her body but left her shoulders bare, the contrast between the dark, plummy color of the fabric and the shimmery blond of her hair, the suggestion of her nakedness beneath.

"That's one of the goals with superfine wool," he managed to say. "The softness, the way it can be spun and woven very fine. It was tough for us when the bottom fell out of the market. I was proud of our beautiful wool, but no one will pay us what it's worth anymore."

"Competition from synthetic fibers?"

"Basically, yes."

It was ten minutes to seven. They needed to get going. He grabbed a bottle of the wine Misha had brought yesterday, and they went out to the car. As usual, he didn't bother to lock the house.

"I suppose that seems strange to you," he said, because it always seemed strange to city visitors and they always commented.

"Um, no, well, we never lock up at home, either," she answered.

"Oh, you don't?"

"Because there are always palace guards."

"Oh. Right. Of course."

She laughed. "I know. It's bizarre. You don't have to say it."

You're a princess.

How could I forget?

I wish you hadn't reminded me, because I can feel this getting weird again.

"What do we do tonight if you're recognized?" he asked.

"It won't happen," she predicted confidently. "I mean, I know people are always spotting Elvis in their local supermarket—"

"Yeah, all the time, around here, and you should see what he buys!"

She laughed again. "But with celebrities in living form, it tends to be different. I am so-o-o *not* where anyone would expect me to be, in a place like this. No one will make the connection. I'm not that well-known. Sometimes I'll get accused of looking like someone famous, but it's usually an actress. And I always do my hair and makeup differently when I'm being just Misha, and I have a couple of other strategies. Seems to work."

She flicked a blond strand behind her ear.

She looked like a pixie on a hot date.

Except that this was as far from being a hot date as Misha was from her family palace, he reminded himself quickly. He'd been on at least a dozen dates like this over the past few months, thanks to the Wanted: Outback Wives campaign—evenings spent entertaining women with whom he had nothing in common.

It was a Thursday night and Tarragon was half-empty. The two fires in the open grates were lit because of the evening chill, and two or three couples sat at the tables, as well as a party of four on the far side of the room. Misha took off her jackety thing....

Brant, he coached himself, it's a jacket, okay? Not a *jackety thing*. Just because it seems too clingy and shimmery and beady and soft for a jacket, and it probably cost about five thousand dollars, that doesn't mean it's not a jacket. Get over it.

…and then she looked around. As always, she seemed interested in what she saw, ready to find it new and fascinating, ready to ask questions.

Oddly, this suddenly left him feeling flat.

She's eaten fancy meals like the ones they serve here a million times. Her main goal for the evening is not to be recognized.

Oh, yes, and to stay awake.

He saw her hiding a yawn behind her hand. Maybe she'd have liked it better if he'd run into town for pizza to eat in front of TV. He found himself hoping for something different, to keep her entertained…and to keep her eyes open. Irish folk musicians. A knockdown marital argument at the adjacent table. An oil fire in the kitchen.

"I liked Europe," he said, abrupt and desperate.

"Oh, good," she murmured politely in reply. "When were you there? Which places did you see?"

He told her about the agricultural exchange in Holland eight years ago, and the travel he'd done, how he'd liked the sense of history and the subtle shadings of culture. "Australia must seem so brash and young to you."

"I like that," she answered. "I love the space. It gives you a freedom to be yourself. I think Australians carry the freedom with them when they travel. And I loved the smell of the air when I was driving here yesterday, so tangy and fresh."

They continued this polite and overcareful complimenting of each other's heritage for a bit too long, then took refuge in the menus that had arrived. They ordered, and about a minute afterward, the "something different" that Brant had hoped for actually happened, and he remembered the old saying, "Be careful what you wish for."

Lauren Whatshername arrived with her three friends.

Brant saw them as soon as they came in, but was able to watch them being shown to a table and set up with menus and big, paper-parasol-decorated drinks before they saw him. He didn't mention it to Misha, who had her back to them, but that turned out to be a mistake because when two of the friends came over in a posse, leaving Lauren and the third friend hiding and whispering intensely behind their menus, Misha was unprepared.

"I don't know how you can do this to a wonderful girl like Lauren," the first friend hissed in Brant's face, leaning toward him over the table.

Misha jumped.

"She is the best, sweetest, nicest person," said the second friend, nipping past Brant's far elbow in a flanking pincer movement worthy of Napoleon in battle against the Russians. "She has the worst luck with men, time after time, and *this* is why. Because there are people like you, who just trample on her good intentions, hurt her, betray her, lie to her—"

She shot a narrow-eyed look in Misha's direction, and Brant discovered that Misha had picked up the wine list and positioned it so that it shadowed the guarded expression on her face.

"I can't believe you can sit here like this with someone else, ignoring her," the friend continued, "when all she wanted was to make a connection, develop a friendship. She trusted you enough to be open with you about how she felt, and you couldn't even return her call."

Which was true.

He'd gone to bed early last night, he'd woken at five-thirty, and he'd been marking lambs all day. He'd forgotten all about it.

"Couldn't even come over to our table and say hello," said the second friend.

"He's reserved, sometimes," Misha murmured suddenly, from behind the wine list. "It can take a while for people to see past that."

The older couple at the next table had heard the indignant

voices and were looking in Brant's direction. The woman muttered something to her husband and he raised his thick gray brows.

"You *put* yourself in that magazine, Branton Smith!" said Friend One. "You sent a message. Lauren, like a whole lot of other women, took that message in good faith—"

Misha put down the wine list. She was now wearing a pair of large reading glasses with pearlescent red rims. They didn't suit her at all. "The thing is, he met me," she said to Lauren's friends. "And as of last night, we're engaged. So I'm afraid for Lauren it's hands off." She smiled sweetly. "Can you tell her? Sorry to be blunt."

She took Brant's hand across the table and squeezed it with the grip of a woman strong enough to wrestle lambs in and out of lamb-marking cradles for hours at a time. Lauren's friends looked shocked. They turned open-mouthed, wide-eyed faces to Brant, who hadn't a clue what to say.

"I hope she'll be happy for us, and understand about Brant not calling her back," Misha went on. "This is very new, and we're very excited about it. See my ring, isn't it gorgeous?"

She held out her left hand, showing what had to be Gian-Marco Ponti's engagement gift. Brant hadn't even noticed she was wearing it tonight, even though the solitaire rock in the middle of it was huge. Had she spoken to her fiancé again? Or was she simply celebrating the fact that she had clean hands?

She frowned at the ring for a moment, and he saw her eyes cloud with a distant expression that she quickly schooled away. He guessed she had to be well trained in hiding her feelings in public. Maybe she could give him a few lessons.

"And…well…I guess we're just not thinking straight, either of us," she finished prettily. Not for the first time, he noticed how perfect her English was. "We apologize."

She beamed at Brant, beamed at Lauren's overemotional friends, beamed at the couple at the next table, beamed at her ring and wiggled her hand to make it twinkle in the firelight.

None of it worked.

"You *two-timed* her?" Friend One said to Brant.

"You wrote to him?" Friend Two asked Misha.

Misha nodded, still smiling widely in the ugly red glasses. Nobody would have recognized Elvis in those glasses, let alone a privacy-loving European princess. Brant guessed that this was the whole point.

"Isn't that romantic?" she said to Lauren's friends. "I wasn't hoping for anything as special as this. We've been so lucky."

"When did you write?" said Friend Two.

"The day I bought the magazine with his picture on the cover."

"So you must have written to him before Lauren even got to see the magazine?" She made it sound like a flagrant case of insider trading.

"Yes, but it's taken us a while. He was cautious about it."

"So Lauren never had a chance," said Friend One to Brant, "And you couldn't *tell* her that?"

"It's been hard…" Misha murmured.

Lauren's friends were not sympathetic to how hard it had been. They huffed indignantly back to their table. A word that might have been *witch* floated back to Brant's ears, and he could see them delivering a full report to Lauren and Friend Three seconds later. Four pairs of cold, resentful eyes lanced dagger-like looks across the restaurant.

"Well, I tried…" Misha muttered. "It's a good strategy, but when people have that kind of a martyr complex, and have friends with a full-blown case of Martyr by Proxy Syndrome, what can you do? Or should I ask, do you and this woman have a large slice of shared past that I don't know about?"

"Just coffee."

"How much coffee?"

"One cup each." Brant realized he needed to seize control of the conversation. "What," he asked her, without moving his lips, "was that stuff with the ring all about?"

"You have to trust me," Misha replied in an undertone.

She was still gripping his hand, and she looked into his eyes as if they were pools of liquid mist. It was an impressive performance.

"Here's the thing, though," he said. "I don't."

"Really, Brant, because this is my best area. I lost my virginity to the tabloid press a long time ago and this is the best strategy, the best we can do with the material available. Nuala was right last night. Fake romance. Used all the time."

"Yeah?"

"Generates publicity for bad movies. Douses scandal about unsavory sexual practices. Or in our case, gets rid of pushy women with martyr complexes and overinvolved female friends, and explains presence on sheep farm of strange and suspiciously royal-looking European visitor."

"Royal-looking? Not in those glasses."

"I know. Hideous. Don't you love them? I keep them specifically for when I suspect I'm in the presence of serious celebrity magazine junkies."

"You're as crazy as my sister, do you know that?" Brant told her.

And she also somehow managed to make the strategy of a pretend engagement sound like good, clean fun, which was a whole concept he'd sort of forgotten about just lately.

"Shared craziness has been the basis for a beautiful friendship," she said. "We can keep up the engagement idea for the magazine interview on Monday if you want, so that you don't get inundated with more visits and letters, or we can drop it in an hour when we leave here. Up to you."

"Can I get back to you on that?"

"Sure. As long as we make it convincing while we're doing it. Because I like a challenge."

He caught the twinkle in her eye and couldn't help laughing. "So do I, Mish. Always have."

"There you go. We can improvise."

She made the last word sound astonishingly sexual, although he didn't think she had any idea that she'd done so.

"Let's improvise," he agreed.

"Right now?"

"Um, sure." What did she mean by that?

He found out seconds later when she leaned forward and kissed him on the mouth across the table.

Chapter Five

Brant's lips tasted sweet and warm and shocking. They made Misha tingle. They were like a mouthful of champagne when you expected plain water. The soft, intimate contact sent a jet of sensation pulsing through her body.

She sat back at once, startled by what she'd done. It was over so fast. You could hardly count it as a kiss. She'd intended it as a bit of silly pretense, and it was. In which case, why did it feel so significant? Why had his eyes darkened? Why was all this heat flooding into her cheeks?

"Oops," she murmured, staring down at her gleaming white plate. "We can just rewind that moment, if you want."

He didn't answer, and she felt worse. She'd expected him to meet her halfway and agree that the moment hadn't even happened. Trivial impulse. Rational adults. Business as usual. That kind of thing.

Or, even better, laugh it off altogether.

"Say something, Brant," she blurted out.

"I'm trying to think of something funny about frogs, but nothing's leaping out at me."

She laughed. "Frogs? Leaping out?"

"You know. Kissing them. But I'm not a prince and you're already a—" He stopped. "And you have probably heard dumb jokes about frogs and fairy tales your whole life from every mortal you've ever met."

"Mortal? Um, Brant, I hate to break it to you but I'm actually not a fairy princess, just the regular kind."

"Sorry. I do know that. But what's the opposite of royal? I'm sorry." He dropped his voice to an anguished murmur. "Granted, we'll go with pretending to be engaged, tonight and then on Monday with the people from the magazine, but do you mind not kissing me again unless you really have to?"

"Sure," she said brightly. "No problem. You know, it was only for authenticity."

And it's still burning on my mouth. It lasted a quarter of a second. He's begging me not to repeat it. I'm obsessing about it. What's going on?

"But we can get authenticity…um, somewhere else," she finished.

"It's not that I didn't like it, as such."

"Oh, *as such?*"

"It's just that Nu told me you were engaged to Whatshis-name…"

Misha let out a helpless sigh the moment she heard her fiancé's name, even though Brant hadn't actually said it. He noticed the sigh, and she was angry with herself for not managing to hold it back. She needed to get a grip, or the first thing that would happen when she flew back to Europe would be a front-page photo of Princess Artemisia Helena In Tears After Mystery Trip.

"…and I wanted to make sure you know that I'm well aware of the boundaries," Brant finished.

"The real question for me at the moment is, is Whatshisname aware of the boundaries?" she said, almost as if she were talking to Nu.

The fact that she trusted her friend so completely gave her an instant passport to trusting her friend's brother, also. This was probably a mistake.

"Yeah, my sister mentioned that issue, too," he said.

"Oh, she did?"

"No detail." He raised his hands, fending off any suggestion that Nuala might have been indiscreet. "Just enough to fill me in."

Their appetizers appeared, and they both began to eat. Misha had already forgotten what she'd ordered, and hardly noticed what she put in her mouth.

"Did you see any of the pictures?" she asked. "Of Whatshisname and the actress, I mean."

"No, I didn't."

"Lucky you. There were two of them, actually. A brunette and a blonde."

She had a sheaf of the pictures in an envelope in her suitcase. They had been taken from several different European tabloids and magazines, and helpfully cut out and mounted on sheets of pristine ivory card stock by the press office at the palace—although admittedly she'd had to lean on the staff pretty hard to get them actually to give her the pictures. They'd fobbed her off about it for days, probably under orders from the queen.

"You could argue that two women are better than one," Brant suggested. "Because it means he's not seriously involved with either of them."

"I thought of that."

She hadn't had a chance to show the pictures to Nuala yet, and suddenly, she wondered what it would be like to get a man's opinion, instead. A whole lot blunter and less supportive, probably. The trouble with having a friend you trusted and who really cared about you was that she tended to tell you only the things you wanted to hear.

"But you're not convinced," Brant said.

"Ask me in the morning, and again in the afternoon and you'll get two different answers. For a start, I have to work out my definition of *not seriously*."

And when you didn't know what things you wanted to hear, it could get messy. With the wedding only just over four months away, was she seriously considering breaking off her engagement, once the palace had decreed that she could? Would she only pretend to end it, as a piece of strategy, to try and get an emotional reaction from Gian-Marco? What did it say about her feelings, and about him, if she could even consider playing such games? Why was honesty such a rare commodity in her life?

And, forget all this complex analysis, how did she *feel*?

"How's your meal?" Brant asked, as if he knew she had too many questions running in her head and wanted to help her shut them down.

She looked down at it vaguely. "Oh, fine."

It was…oh, right, mushroom risotto.

Perfect princess food.

She ordered it at restaurants all the time, or requested it to appear on formal banquet menus. Not too much chewing, neat and easy to sneak into your mouth during breaks in the conversation, and no sloppy sauce to splash on your outfit. Sometimes, if the food was wrong at official functions, or if someone kept her talking too long, she didn't manage to eat at all.

One memorable time, when she'd had nine official lunches and dinners in four different countries in one week, she'd eaten mushroom risotto eight times. She thought this probably didn't happen to the British royal family. They probably had their menus coordinated at an international strategic level to avoid repetition. But Langemark was a pretty small country, and she wasn't the heir to the throne.

Thank goodness!

For that blessing, a lifetime supply of mushroom risotto was a small price to pay.

Brant did one of his silences, and she belatedly realized she'd said something wrong. It took her the rest of her appetizer to backtrack through the past few minutes and work out the problem, at which point she sounded too fake and forced when she told him, "Really, it's delicious. This is a lovely place. Thanks for thinking to bring me here."

"The next time we're not cooking, we'll have takeaway pizza by the fire," he told her.

"Can I tell you something?"

"Go ahead."

"Pizza by the fire would be a huge treat."

The tension drained out of him, and she knew she'd gotten the problem right. He had wanted to treat a princess in the manner to which she was accustomed. This princess would prefer anything but, and it had taken her too long to get the point across.

Misha had forgotten to take the red glasses off.

Brant had forgotten about them, too, while they sat talking over their meal. At first, he would look up from his plate and get startled by the unexpected sight of such large, ugly frames in such an impossible pearlescent red color, but once they'd become absorbed in what they were saying, he didn't notice the glasses anymore.

At some point, Lauren and her friends must have left, because when he and Misha finally stood up to go, their table was empty and already set with new silverware and crockery. At some point, also, time had speeded up, because it couldn't possibly be almost eleven o'clock as he stopped the car in front of the darkened house.

He intended to open the door for Misha, but she darted out of the vehicle before he could even get to the door handle on his own side. She waited for him, leaning a hand on the engined-warmed metal of the car, and she wore that little smile he was beginning to recognize and understand. She'd jumped out of the car so fast precisely because she didn't want the fuss of someone standing there doing all the work for her.

"Thanks for a great evening," he told her, meaning it. He hadn't thought about the farm, his finances or his ewes' feet in hours. "I know it would have been nothing special for you, getting dressed up and eating fancy food. In fact, I'm sorry I put you through it, but if it's any consolation, it was special for me. Time out. I don't get enough of that."

"You're welcome, Brant," she said. "And if I seemed too blasé about the food, I'm just a spoiled brat who doesn't know when she's well off."

"You're not a spoiled brat."

"You wait." She grinned at him. "I can be when I want."

"How often is that?"

She spread her hands and shrugged. "When the palace says I'm allowed to."

"The big, bad palace. Can I tell you something? Don't get upset about it."

"What?"

"Did you know you were still wearing those glasses?"

Her mouth dropped open and a hand flew up to her face. She burst out laughing. "And you couldn't tell me until now because they make me look so unbearably sexy, right? You thought the entire restaurant needed such a vision of loveliness to gaze at all through their meal."

She snatched them away from her face, and folded them. "Next time, I'm going to wear the wig."

"You don't have a wig."

"Trust me, I have a wig. Gorgeous synthetic chocolate-brown curls. It's for emergencies only, but a princess has to be prepared."

"Wear it on Monday," he told her. "I want a pretend engagement to a woman with pretend hair."

She laughed. Possibly she was even blushing a little. "But, as previously discussed, no pretend kisses?"

"Uh, no. If that's okay." They walked toward the house in silence, feet crunching softly on the mix of damp earth and gravel. "I mean, I wouldn't want you to think—"

"That you hadn't enjoyed it *as such*," she mimicked, and he groaned.

"Is that what I said?"

"Yep."

"Is there a way I can save us both from embarrassment on this subject, by explaining better what I actually meant? That I actually did enjoy—"

"Don't think so. Better stop before the hole gets even deeper."

"Right." He thought it already had.

They went into the house and he told her goodnight, hoping they'd both have forgotten about that sweet, unexpected and far too pleasant press of her lips on his by the morning.

The horses broke from the barrier on the far side of the course and belted around the rail, their initial tight grouping soon strung out so that individual horses and their jockeys' colors were easier to see. Brant nudged Misha, his gaze fixed on the distant movement. "Can you see him, pale blue and white, about a length and a half behind the front runner?"

"Yes, but he's closing in, I think."

She willed Trans Pacific to reach the front, willed those powerful, elegant legs to drum even faster, to lengthen their stride. She had her hands clenched into fists, and her neck craning to see better. She'd been to racing carnivals before. The most glamorous such events in the racing world—Royal Ascot in England, the Kentucky Derby—but this was so much better.

It was the first time she'd dressed like this, for a start.

Baseball cap, running shoes and a borrowed windproof jacket of Nuala's, instead of the usual heels, floaty fabric and pretty hat. The fashion photographers would have dropped her from their roster of targets after a single glance.

If they'd been here.

They weren't, of course.

At a country race meeting on an ordinary Saturday in late autumn, there was no one to photograph, and the only press coverage of the event would consist of dry listings of results in the sports pages of a few newspapers tomorrow.

For the first time, Misha could actually watch the races, read about the horses and their form, watch them warming up or giving their jockeys trouble on the way into the barrier, as they got ready for the start. It was so much more interesting than tottering around in the wrong shoes in the most exclusive enclave of the members' section, getting fawned over by dignitaries she didn't know, and very often with goose bumps all over her. Today, she was actually comfortable.

And there was plenty to look at. Several old-fashioned wooden bookies' stands had been set up in the no-frills pavilion between the public grandstand and the members' area, while the bookies kept their cash in cavernous bags made of cracked leather so old that she wondered how many generations had used them before.

Some of the bookies covered race meetings in the capital cities, while others took bets on this track's events. The bags and stands were complemented by nifty little computerized ticket printers, and there was a confusing selection of race-viewing on TV screens, also, to bring the atmosphere into the twenty-first century.

A rather red-faced groom-to-be was having a bucks' party before his upcoming wedding, and there were families treating the day as a picnic. The racing club had provided a free jumping castle for the children, but many of them were more interested in rolling down a short but steep section of grass, which had a great view of the winning post. They had red cheeks and grass marks on their arms and legs, and didn't seem the least bit interested in the thunder of hooves galloping in their direction, louder by the second.

Four young women had set up a gourmet meal for themselves on a picnic blanket, and were wearing adorable hats that they must have made themselves—pinned and folded confections of tulle, feathers, beading and silk flowers. Misha couldn't imagine what the bucks' party guests were thinking of. The girls looked pretty and sweet, but not one of the men paid them any attention.

The horses galloped into the straight on their way to the winning post. From this angle, their wildly working hooves seemed to tangle together and it was impossible to see who was in front. Not Trans Pacific. At least two other horses challenged him and each other for the lead.

But as the field came closer Misha could see that the jockey was really making Trans Pacific run, standing high and forward in the saddle and urging him on. He passed one horse, then another, and as the thoroughbreds swept past her she yelled out, "Go, Trans Pacific! Go!" and saw the horse overtake the leader fifty yards short of the winning post. He came home a comfortable two lengths ahead.

The other thing she'd never done at the races before was to bet.

"How much did we win?" she gasped out to Brant. She grabbed his arm and bounced up and down.

"Seventeen dollars and fifty cents."

"Is that *all?*" But she was still grinning.

He grinned back, under his farmer's felt hat. "We only put on five dollars, and he was running at three and a half to one."

"So we've made twelve whole dollars and fifty cents profit. When we've split it between us, I can just about buy a cheap bottle of wine. This is incredible!"

"Careful, or you'll get seriously rich this afternoon. It'll go to your head and you won't know what to do with yourself."

"Why didn't we put more on? A thousand, or something."

"Because Trans Pacific might have lost. You said you wanted to have fun. I wasn't going to let you lose a bundle on a horse I thought might not live up to its promise."

"Even though you own it."

"Part of it."

"Which part?"

"Well, the legs obviously. The money drains right down through them and into the ground with a hobby like this."

"Seriously?"

"Seriously? I own twenty-five percent and so does Callan. Dusty owns forty, and our trainers usually take out a ten percent ownership, also."

"No, but I meant seriously there's no money in racing? Because I can see how much fun it could be."

"There's a lot of money in racing, but you can never guarantee that you're going to get any of it. The costs are enormous and the results are uncertain. You can have a slew of poor runs, but your costs are just as high when you lose. You can have wins, but if they're not the right ones you don't make much. They reckon only about ten percent of race horses turn a profit during their career. When you do win, your jockey gets a percentage, so does your trainer. The prize for first in this race was $3,500. Which makes my share around $750."

"So why do you do it?"

"Because it's fun, and because it's a good way to make sure I don't lose touch with my mates."

"Callan and Dusty. Nuala has mentioned them."

"Between us we own seven horses now. Bought a couple of new ones a few months ago, but those aren't in serious work yet. Four of them are trained here—the stable's on the far side of the course—the other three in Queensland, not too far from Dusty."

"Do I get to meet your trainer?"

"She'll be in the mounting yard. Let's head over."

They clomped along through the lush grass to where jockeys had dismounted, flimsy racing saddles had been removed and weights were about to be checked. "Rae!" Brant called to a wiry woman in her forties. "Someone wants to meet you."

"Oh, don't say that." Misha pulled the dark blue baseball cap down her forehead and pushed her sunglasses further up her nose. "Michelle Smith, okay?" She squeezed his arm.

He ignored her. "Mish, this is our trainer, Rae Middleton. Rae, Misha wants to know how she can make a lot of money out of racing without doing any work."

Rae let out a warm laugh and her eyes crinkled up. Nice eyes, in a lively, no-nonsense face. She looked as if she spent a lot of time squinting at horses on the far side of a training track. She also looked as if she really enjoyed what she did.

"I think they had the technique down perfect in that *Back to the Future* movie," she said. "All you need is a thoroughbred racing website with a good archive of past results…and a time machine. But where's the adventure in that?"

"None," Misha said. "Which is why Brant actually got it the wrong way around. I'm interested in what it's like making a tiny bit of money out of racing by doing a lot of work."

"Aha!" Rae's eyes lit up. "Now you're talking!"

The three of them talked together for about ten minutes. Mostly this meant that Brant asked Rae questions about things like nominations and acceptances, starts and wins, gear changes and barrier trials, and Rae answered him. Misha struggled to understand most of it, but found it interesting all the same, and when she managed to slip in a question and they explained something, she understood a little more. Then Rae had to go and talk to a jockey before the next race.

"You never introduced me properly," Misha said to Brant when she'd gone.

"And did she mind?"

"She didn't seem to. She just talked to us. It was great."

"I'm learning, you see. Soon I'll be able to write the book. The care and feeding of a princess in disguise."

"You've improved markedly with the feeding since Thursday night, I have to say."

Today, they'd had steak sandwiches for lunch, eaten standing up on the grass beside the track, with slatherings of tomato ketchup, mustard and fried onions. Last night, dinner had been a reheated quiche that Nu had left in the freezer, along with bread and cheese and olives and salami, laid out on the coffee table and eaten while watching TV.

"Anything that liberates you from silverware and small talk, right?" Brant said.

"Pretty much. You have no idea what a great change it is to have my mouth really, really full!"

"Let's go and look at the next starters in the mounting yard. We have to make a considered decision on the best option for our five dollars."

"Five dollars again? We're going all out!"

They stayed until the last race, losing their five dollars on every one, and then he took her to the local pub for a drink on the way home. For dinner they zipped around the kitchen together with rock music playing, and made spaghetti Bolognese and salad.

Brant's recipe.

Misha had never learned to cook anything that simple.

"I know it involves eating with silverware," he said, "But I thought a single fork was a pretty good compromise."

Misha called home again that night and told her mother, "I'm glad I came."

"Have you made a decision, sweetheart?"

"Not yet. I'm still clearing my head. And you know, they're on the bottom of the world down here. Upside down. All the locals walk around with their feet on the ground and strangely enough it doesn't look as if they're going to fall off, but that's only because they're used to it. I think I'm going to need a little more practice before I can steer myself in the right direction without the blood rushing to my head."

"That's my crazy girl."

She lowered her voice to a more serious pitch. "But do you see what I'm saying, Mom?"

"I see what you're saying." Her mother the queen sighed at the far end of the line. "I do. Believe me, I would never choose to put this pressure on you, to make you wait for Christian and Graziella's pregnancy announcement, or make your private life into something so political, but the fact is, leaving aside any gossip and scandal, your actions influence the whole country, and—"

"I know. It's time the outdated divorce laws in Langemark were changed, but if I'm seen to behave in a shallow and fickle way by cancelling my engagement four months before a massive royal wedding, there could be a backlash against the morals of the younger generation and parliament will vote the other way. I got a letter about it from Dad's senior adviser, just in case I forgot our riveting conversation on the subject."

"And he sent a copy to me. And I'm aching for you, honey, but I agree with him. Right now, duty to Langemark comes first, your heart comes second."

"Have you seen it, by the way? My heart? I think I might have forgotten to bring it with me."

"I'll check your room," her mother drawled, and they ended the conversation soon after.

On Sunday, Brant took Misha horseback riding. Anticipating the possibility and hoping for it, Misha had brought her riding gear with her. Two-tone jodhpurs in cinnamon and sand that fit her like a second skin, almost-new custom-fitted riding boots in polished black leather with classic brown tops, a cheeky little stretch top that matched the jods, a jacket that matched the top, and a crash helmet covered in black velvet.

Brant looked appalled at the sight of her.

She glared at him. "It's what I have, okay? I meet with a consultant about my wardrobe. She calls me Your Highness, rules me with a rod of iron and doesn't offer me the combat pants option. I can put on jeans if you promise you have cream for chafed thigh skin."

"The jods are fine. But maybe the boots could get swapped for an old pair of Nu's? Those ones could get wet, or scratched or—"

"And here I thought we were spending the morning in a dressage arena."

He looked sideways at her. "You're telling me that's the kind of riding you want, today?"

"Please! No!"

She emerged from her room ten minutes later wearing Nuala's elastic-sided boots, Nuala's wind jacket and a hot-pink T-shirt of her own. "Better?"

"I really do like the jods."

They were out of the house and on the road by seven, driving for about twenty minutes toward the mountains, where he had friends with a farm that took vacation visitors in a set of cute little cabins on the property. Since schools were in session at this time of year, the place was quiet and they had their pick of the trail-riding horses, all of them looking glossy-coated and well fed.

They each chose one of the largest and most spirited animals, then took a grassy, forested route that led to a stretch of tumbling mountain river. In the shade, the air was crisp and cool, but the sun's heat still packed some power, even in late autumn, and the contrast between cool shadows and open glades felt delicious in Misha's lungs and on her skin.

They'd packed picnic supplies for a morning snack, but

nothing fancy, just a flask of hot coffee, some cheese and biscuits, apples and slices of chocolate cake. They tethered the horses by the river, spread their rain jackets out on the grass to sit on, and ate to the sound of water gurgling over smooth-worn river pebbles, and birds calling in the thicker, wilder forest on the far side. The air smelled of eucalyptus and warm stone.

After they'd eaten, Misha took off her socks and Nu's riding boots, scraped her stretchy jodhpurs up to her knees and paddled calf deep in the water until her feet no longer felt the cold. The sun pressed with satisfying warmth on her back and the horses looked just as content as she felt. So did Brant. He'd stayed on the grass, and when she saw him lying on his back with his felt farmer's hat over his eyes, she thought he was probably asleep.

It was so peaceful here. No flashes of sunlight bouncing off a camera lens hidden in the bushes. No curious crowds watching her reaction to Gian-Marco's Grand Prix race when they should be watching the race itself. No palace protocol or palace staff, or even the discreet security guards who hovered in the background when she and Gian-Marco went clubbing or skiing or visiting friends.

Dad had wanted her to bring a couple of people. She'd had to fight hard to be allowed to travel on her own, and Mom had needed to step in and convince the king that she could be safe this way.

She felt incredibly safe, and incredibly free.

Giddy about it.

Ready to let it go totally to her head.

She didn't even mind that Nuala was in Sydney. She and Nu talked too much, sometimes. Women often did. They analyzed their feelings to death. This was what she needed. Simply the peace, simply the space. No pressure to make any decisions until she wanted to. No insistence from anyone that she had to present a clear and consistent picture of how she felt. For a little longer, she could simply *be*.

She trailed a stick in the water and watched the braided surface patterns making intricate shadows on the pebbled riverbed below. She saw a school of tiny, semitranslucent fish darting in miraculous unison, zipping out of her way then darting off in another direction when something else startled them. The cold water ruffled like lace around her calves. Past and future vanished for a blessed interval, and all she thought about was this: the sun, the river, the space and the peace.

Suddenly, Brant appeared beside her. Over the rush and gurgle of the water, she hadn't heard him.

"You're awake?" she said.

"Didn't mean to fall asleep."

"This is so beautiful."

"We should have brought a camera."

"No. No cameras," she said quickly. "Photos are so flat. Even videos. I want my whole body to remember this. My mouth and my ears and the soles of my feet. It's perfect."

"But we have to get back." She could see how reluctantly he said it. "I have the last paddock of sheep to muster into the yard for lamb-marking today, and Chris still has more he needs help with. We won't get anything done tomorrow morning, because of the people coming from the magazine."

She nodded, hiding what she felt. "Let's go, then."

Peace and space and breathing air into your lungs until your head went dizzy…those things never lasted for her. It was all right for Brant. He would come here dozens more times in his life, while Misha wondered if she'd ever have a perfect morning like this one again. They paddled back to the river bank, getting their wet feet encrusted with coarse sand and bits of grass.

"Did we bring a towel?" she asked.

"Forgot. We can sun-dry them, then use my jacket to get off the sand. I won't need to wear it. It's not going to rain."

So they lay in the sun for a few precious minutes longer, letting their feet dry. Misha wiggled her sandy toes in the sun, saw that her pink polish had gotten chipped in a couple of places by the river pebbles, and didn't care. Brant came over and offered her the jacket, but she shook her head. Please could she have just one minute more?

He misunderstood.

Leaning back on her hands in the grass, she watched it happening like a car-crash test in slow motion. He thought she wanted him to use the jacket on her feet. He bent down and folded the jacket so that the plaid flannel lining faced outward and started to brush the sand and slivers of grass away. It was soft and warm and tickly, like the feeling inside her on Thursday night when she'd discovered she was still wearing her horrible red glasses an hour and a half after she'd put them on and Brant hadn't said a word.

She laughed and wriggled, and he stopped. "Is that okay now?"

"There's a bit more sand on the side of my other foot, but it's okay. My socks won't mind."

"Let me get it. You don't want to have blisters when you're riding."

"Shall I do yours?" she said a little later, when she'd put on her socks and boots.

He just handed her the jacket without a word. She'd begun to work on his second foot before either of them spoke.

Brant said, "Tomorrow." Then he stopped.

She sat back on her heels and looked at him.

"Nuala's pretend engagement idea. Do you still want to go with that? We haven't talked about it since Thursday night."

"Do you want to go with it?"

"I hope it'll stop the phone from ringing so much. And it's probably not fair of me to tell you all this female attention is driving me nuts. I know you have your own problems…."

"Mmm."

"But, ah hell, Misha, it's driving me nuts. If the Outback

Wives thing would just go away after this article, I'd breathe a sigh of relief, and I think if we did a convincing engagement story I'd get left alone. But that's to my advantage, not yours. I wouldn't want to push you into it."

He flicked a quick look in her direction and somehow she knew he was thinking about the way she'd kissed him on Thursday night—that small, silly, innocent touch of her mouth that he'd begged her not to repeat. The moment felt awkward, so she quickly told him, "I'm okay. It's just for a few hours. How hard could it be?"

"That's what you thought about lamb-marking."

"And I did great at lamb-marking."

"You're right," he agreed. "How hard could it be."

They smiled at each other, then they had a fabulous long, easy canter back to the stables. It turned into a racing gallop two hundred yards from the end, and Brant and his horse won by a nose.

Chapter Six

"Are you really going to wear the wig?" Brant asked.

He'd had a call from Shay-from-the-magazine a short while ago, saying that she and her photographer should be at Inverlochie's front gate within half an hour. He planned to meet them there, to show them the way down to the house. He'd given Shay directions, but she was apparently convinced she would get lost in such a vast, impenetrable wilderness without personal guidance. About to jump in the four-wheel drive, he'd discovered Misha on her way to the bathroom armed with her hairy disguise.

"You said you wanted me to," she reminded him.

"I was only half serious."

"But I'm a hundred-percent serious about not getting recognized, Brant, especially by journalists whose job it is to keep up on Adrenaline Junkie Princesses who are Out of Control, so I'm going for major wig insurance. You're heading down to the gate?"

"I should. I got the impression Shay has never been out of Sydney."

"I'm thinking, don't mention me, okay? Just let me appear on the scene in all my glory. You won't recognize me. So don't gasp!"

Dimples popped into her cheeks when she smiled this kind of teasing half smile, Brant noticed. They were adorable, and they terrified him.

"Gasp? Oh, because supposedly you always look that way?" he suggested after a moment, a little too slow in grasping her meaning. What was wrong with him?

"Exactly!" she said, and dimpled again.

"I'm scared, now." Too true!

"As you should be."

They laughed.

Getting to be a habit.

And it was a habit he liked too much.

"You almost look as if you're expecting to enjoy this," he said to Misha, and she shrugged like a little boy whose mischievous intentions are written all over his face.

"Think it might be a bit of an adventure," she said lightly, and then disappeared into the bathroom before he could react. When the reaction came, as he went outside, it was that same lifting of his spirits that he kept feeling when she was around. On the one hand, he liked it. It was a breath of fresh air. On the other…

Yeah.

As before.

He was terrified.

As he climbed into the vehicle, he thought about everything that had been on his mind when Misha had first arrived five days ago and his gut lurched. The lame sheep, the gamble of overstocking his land, the never-ending quest to compensate for the plunge in wool prices, the possibility of having to drop out of the racing syndicate with Callan and Dusty.

This was by far the most obvious way to cut his expenses and yet he didn't want to consider it, didn't want to take the sensible approach. Their beautiful horses bound them together across Australia's huge distances. If Brant sold his share, he knew he could end up losing his friends as well. He'd almost prefer to lose Inverlochie itself.

Entertaining the princess had made him forget his problems for hours at a time, but when they came back, they flooded in with a vengeance.

"I'm not going to lose this place," he muttered to himself, guiding the vehicle around a muddy patch on the track.

He knew his stepfather wouldn't let it happen, for a start. One word to Mum, and there could be an injection of clean, healthy capital in Inverlochie's bank account within a few days. In a way, this made his situation worse. He simply couldn't see himself going cap in hand to anyone, let alone the man who'd married his mother just a year after a lifetime of hard work on this place had worn out his father's heart.

He wanted to solve his own problems, not look for handouts, even from family. In fact, he thought he'd probably sell rather than ask for help from Frank, Chris, the bank or anyone else.

He didn't blame Mum for marrying the man. He liked Frank. He didn't even blame her for never quite adjusting to the reality of being a farmer's wife. In the beginning, she'd had these rose-tinted, optimistic ideas about pottering around in a vegetable garden and making hot breakfasts at dawn. It hadn't worked out that way very often. She'd been needed too much for the heavier work.

Sometimes, during shearing, she would have to go down to the shed and work as the roustabout, sweeping the wool and dags from the lanolin-stained wooden floor, or lifting the light, greasy fleeces to the sorting table and picking out the matted or discolored pieces. She'd get yelled at all day.

"Wool away!"

"Wool *away*, dammit, Helen!"

Paid by the number of sheep shorn, not by the hour, shearers wanted their shearing space swept the instant a freshly shorn sheep scrabbled down the chute to the yard, so that they could get to work on the next animal on a clean piece of floor. They wore special soft shoes made of carpet to give flexibility to their feet as they twisted and bent to maneuver the animals around, and they could get half-crippled by bruised soles if pebble-hard, dag-encrusted bits of wool were left beneath them too often. It was like hiking with a stone in your shoe.

"Wool *away!*" while sheep bawled and shearing blades buzzed and the odors of lanolin and sweat and fermented grass filled the air.

Mum hated the yelling, the impatience, the swearing, the mess and the smell. After a few hours of it, her face would start to grow tighter and tighter. She would flinch at every raised voice and she would eventually, inevitably, flee the shed in tears before the end of the day.

Dad would always go after her, abject about having to put her through this kind of work in seasons when an extra man hired for the job was a luxury they couldn't afford. Mum herself had wanted to save the money so that Brant could go to boarding school in Sydney.

Hanging around the shed as a kid, Brant had seen the tension and the unhappiness, despite the love. From the age of eight, he'd begged to be allowed to do the work himself, but Mum and Dad had united on that issue. Not until he was older and stronger. They had let him start when he was fourteen, when he was home on breaks from school, and he'd dealt with the tongue-lashing and teasing from the shearers instead of his mother.

As for helping with lamb-marking, Mum hated the sight of such mess, and she'd never even tried. She'd loved Dad sincerely, but she was so much happier with Frank.

Brant couldn't switch allegiance in the same way. He

wouldn't tarnish his father's memory by failing with the farm while there was breath in his body, but he was on his own, dealing with Inverlochie's problems. He knew it, and he had better not kid himself about anything different.

He reached the gate, but there was no sign of the magazine people yet. He climbed out of the vehicle and let his eyes roam over the sheep he could see from this spot. Lambs lolloped through the green grass after their mothers on their woolly white legs, their recent experience in the marking cradle completely forgotten.

A couple of the mothers lolloped, too, and he tried to assess their gait from this impossible distance. Stepping over a rock? Compensating for uneven ground? He didn't think so. It was more than that. At least a dozen of this particular mob looked lame today.

He thought about his father again. Dad had always been such a responsible farmer. He'd planted tracts of his land with native vegetation years before environmental issues had become a priority for most farmers. He'd always studied the latest edicts on disease prevention. He'd cooperated with the authorities whenever he could.

In Brant's situation, Dad would contact the Pastures Protection Board. He wouldn't knowingly hobble another farmer with tainted stock. And the contracted sale ewes would indeed be tainted, if the new ones were. All a healthy sheep had to do was cross a path walked by a foot-rot-infected animal, and the bacteria could get passed on.

If this was foot rot.

Brant still didn't believe it could be, and that was the only thing holding him back, now, but the time had come to make sure. His inspection of those muddy hooves had been too governed by emotion and self-interest. He desperately wanted to see something less serious like dermatitis or shelly hoof, so of course he interpreted the signs to fit. The time had come for tests.

Tomorrow, he decided. He'd phone the Pastures Protec-tion Board tomorrow. They'd send someone out to take a sample, probably on Wednesday, the day that Nuala was due back. Maybe he could get rid of the P.P.B. guy before she arrived and she still wouldn't need to know. As for Misha, she wouldn't even realize who the guy was.

He saw a white station wagon slowing as it approached the gate. Male driver, female passenger. It had to be Shay Russell and her photographer. He went over, opened the gate, introduced himself and welcomed them to his land.

He shook hands with Shay and the photographer, Mark, and promised Shay that she wouldn't see any snakes, while secretly hoping that the snakes chose to cooperate with this statement and stayed hidden or asleep. If Shay screamed, fainted and hit her head on the ground, his insurance situa-tion might be unclear.

When they reached the house, he somehow expected to find Misha waiting for them, artistically posed in her fake hair and some designer farm clothes. Fringed white silk shirt and cowboy hat, maybe, above those glove-tight stretchy designer jodhpurs from yesterday. As Misha had suggested, he hadn't mentioned her yet, and now she was nowhere in sight.

"Can we use your dogs?" the photographer asked, and this was when Brant heard the four-wheeler roaring down the hill.

He looked in that direction, and Shay and Mark followed his gaze. Misha had left the helmet behind. She wore a wide-brimmed hat jammed down over the fake brunette curls, and sunglasses with silver lenses. A dark-brown, thigh-length oilskin flapped open in the breeze, above scuffed riding boots and jeans. She even had Sox perched on the back of the bike for that final authentic touch.

Mostly, sheep farmers hated to have their dog answering orders from anyone else, but this time Brant just grinned. It would be hard to imagine a more convincing performance as a farmer's fiancée, and Misha hadn't yet even opened her mouth.

Catching sight of them, as she approached at what seemed like sixty miles an hour, she lifted a hand and waved. The four-wheeler bounced over the rough ground without the slightest slackening of speed. Then she yelled at him, at the top of her lungs. "The mob from the creek paddock's mustered up to the hill, Brant, but there's a poddy lamb we'll have to go after later on, and a couple of them are scouring."

She'd made up this information completely, of course, but she and Brant were the only ones who knew that. Zooming in a wide arc around the rough dirt driveway in front of the house, she screeched the four-wheeler to a halt on the grass, cut the engine and clacked the gearing into Neutral with her left foot.

"Hi," she said breathlessly to Shay and Mark, swinging her leg over the top of the four-wheeler as if dismounting a horse. She smiled widely and stuck out her hand, giving each visitor a hearty shake. "You must be from the magazine. I'm Mish. Has Brant…?" She trailed off artfully, with her head tilted to one side.

"Mentioned you?" he came in, recognizing his cue. "No, I haven't had a chance…uh…sweetheart. Shay and Mark, this is Mish."

"Short for Michelle," Misha supplied. "But please keep it to Mish."

"My fiancée," Brant explained. The word sounded strange in his mouth. Coy and formal, yet intimate, too.

"Wha-a-at?" Shay wailed at once. "Your fiancée, Brant? But you're supposed to be our—" She stopped.

Bachelor-farmer poster boy, Brant finished for her in his head.

He felt a sudden rush of gratitude to Misha for getting him off the hook with her sparkly ring and brown wig, and to his sister for coming up with such a crazy piece of pretense in the first place. It was going to work, and he was going to need it.

"I mean, that's great." Shay pressed her fingers to her temples and squeezed her eyes tightly shut, adjusting her thinking the way an orthodontist adjusted a kid's braces. Then she widened her eyes and clasped her hands against her heart. "But please, please tell me you met through the magazine, or I'm not sure we'll still have a sto-o-ory." The wail returned to her tone.

Misha and Brant exchanged a quick glance.

"Isn't there always a story behind two people falling in love?" Misha said.

She pulled off her hat—rather carefully, Brant noticed, so that there was no danger of the wig coming with it—and did her dimpliest smile as she cast a glowing look in his direction. She came up to him and slipped her arm through his.

"Actually, that's sweet," Shay said. "It's darling. It is." She let out a whimper and flapped her hands. "Completely darling. And it's true. There always is a story. But this was supposed to be about how many le-e-etters you've had, Brant."

With a visible effort, she managed to contain and repress the wail once more.

"It was supposed to be about how impressed you've been by the wonderful city women eager to abandon everything they've ever known for the adventure of an outback romance," she went on. "And to be honest, how hot all these women seem to think—" She stopped. "Well, that was the angle I'd planned, anyhow, and not that I wanted to treat you as a sex object or anything."

She still looked very stressed.

"No, I'm sure you didn't," Brant told her kindly.

He didn't want to ruin her day by scuttling her story. But then, he didn't want to ruin the next six months of his own life with an overdose of the wrong women, either.

Shay commanded brightly, "Tell me how it all happened."

She had a very attractive smile. "You're right. We can work with this. Our readers really love the heartwarming stuff. It's heartwarming, right? Let me adjust my thinking a little—" She pressed her fingers to her temples again. "We'll have a great story. Maybe if we could feature two or three developing romances, over the next few issues, or even wedding bells and a baby on the way…"

She whipped out an electronic organizer and began keying in notes about the change in plan before Mish and Brant managed to answer any of her questions.

"Well, I am a city woman, originally," Misha said. She held out her arm so that Brant would come and hug her, and he did. She felt good—pliant and strong and warm. "So you still have that angle."

"A wonderful city woman," Brant corrected her. Hell, had he ever given a woman a look this dewy-eyed before? If so, had it ever been this easy? It felt like looking over the edge of a cliff and discovering that the sheer vertical drop went a lot farther down than you'd thought.

Misha added, "From Denver, Colorado." Which was where Queen Rose had been born and raised, Brant knew.

He approved that the princess had stuck as close to the truth as possible. Not that he was particularly familiar with the strategies involved in out-and-out royal lying, but a base level of reality had to make the fantasy easier, surely.

"Wow!" said Shay. "And you're going to make a life out here, now, Michelle? In the outback."

Misha laughed. The brown curls swung around her face. She made a great blonde, but she'd be pretty impressive as a brunette as well. "My fiancé doesn't consider this to be the outback. He thinks it's incredibly civilized. I mean, there's green grass and take-out pizza less than a hundred miles away."

Mark-the-photographer suddenly spoke, after he'd been standing in the background watching the conversation with eyes narrowed against the bright light like watching some kind of three-way tennis match. "I'm hearing an accent," he said, his own voice bluntly Australian.

"Oh, and you don't mean from Colorado?" Misha answered brightly. "Yes, my father's company sent us to the Netherlands for several years when I was in my early teens. I picked up the language, and an accent along with it, and I've never quite gotten rid of it. A few years ago, my father's company sent him here, to Melbourne, which is how I ended up in Australia."

"So the accent's Dutch?" Mark said. "*Houdt u van Australië?*"

Brant still remembered the Dutch he'd learned during his farming exchange, understood the simple question about liking this country, and detected an Australian accent thick enough to spread on toast.

Misha replied without batting an eyelid, "*Ja, natuurlijk, zeer.*" Her Dutch accent was perfect. In Langemark, he knew, they spoke a closely related language. And naturally, yes, she liked it here.

The photographer nodded. "Just wondered. I've spent a bit of time there." Then he turned to Shay. "So we'll have both of them in the shots? And the dog?"

Sox had jumped down from the four-wheeler and was racing around as usual, begging for some work to do. Round up the visitors? Put them in a sheep yard? Bark at them and stop them from jumping through a fence?

"You want to do the photos first and then the story, or the other way around?" Mark continued.

"Photos," Shay said. "We need a couple of action shots first, then somewhere that looks pretty."

She eyed the house, but seemed unimpressed. Misha and Brant exchanged a look that said, what, she thinks the house isn't pretty enough?

Brant felt himself flood with a sudden, ridiculous desire for all of this to be true. For Mish to be his fiancée, originally from Colorado, totally at home on the farm, not in any way, shape or form a princess, and completely in agreement with his own opinion that the higgledy-piggledy old house, with the wisteria twisting up the veranda posts and the galvanized iron roof needing a fresh coat of dark green paint, was very pretty indeed.

"How about by the citrus trees?" Misha suggested.

"I think we need sheep," Shay answered. "You know. Snow-white flocks gambolling in the meadows, or whatever it is that sheep do."

"Paddocks," Misha said, as if she'd been using the word her whole life. "And I don't know if you've noticed, but these sheep aren't all that snow-white. They won't be until they've been shorn in the spring, and then they'll be naked and a lot skinnier."

"Right," Shay nodded, while Brant thought, wow.

This princess was seriously good at faking her identity. She sounded as if she knew all about sheep. He remembered all the questions she'd asked while they were marking lambs on Thursday and Friday. Clearly she'd filed every bit of it away for future use. He'd started to like this about her a lot—that she was genuinely interested in all sorts of things, even if she might never need to think about them again.

While Mark got out his camera equipment and stalked around looking for somewhere prettier and more sheep-farm-like than the house, Shay asked questions, all of which made Brant realize that neither he nor Misha had done their home-work on this.

Had they met through the magazine?

In the blink of an eye, Misha decided yes, which con-formed with what she'd told Lauren the other night. "I don't even buy *Today's Woman* normally," she confided to Shay.

Probably true. Brant didn't think it sold in Langemark. And definitely not the Australian edition.

"But that month," she went on, "when Brant's picture

was on the cover, some strange intuition made me walk past the magazine rack and reach out for it. I wrote to him that same evening."

Lies, lies, lies.

"I don't remember your letter," Shay said.

"But I'm sure you didn't read them all," Misha answered without a flicker of hesitation.

"No, I'm afraid not. But I do wish I'd read yours."

Misha cast Brant a lingering glance. "It wasn't anything special," she said. "I'm not sure that it really matters how two people meet. The point is, we did, and from that moment things moved very quickly. I felt so at home the day Brant first brought me here. Some aspects of this life are a challenge, but I know it's going to work out for us."

All of which had to be lies, too, but she said it so convincingly that again Brant had this odd, wishful ache low in his stomach. He wondered how his life might have been different if Mum had felt this way about Inverlochie, or if his long-ago Dutch girlfriend Beatrix had.

"Could you get back on that quad bike thing?" the photographer asked, his equipment unpacked and ready. "Could the two of you fit on it together? Could we have you rounding up some sheep, or something? I mean, you could look as if you are. No need to do it for real."

"Well, as long as we don't have to do it for real," Brant said, and Misha rewarded him with a quick glance, her princess-blue eyes glinting like a naughty child's.

Mark directed them as if this were a Hollywood movie costing a hundred million dollars. He wanted Brant on the front of the bike, working the controls, with Misha squashed in right behind him, her arms wrapped around his body and her head resting on this back. No hats, please, or their eyes would be shaded too much. Sunglasses? Pushed up against their hair if they wanted.

Misha obediently and carefully lifted hers.

Mark wanted them in the middle of a mob of sheep, which meant they all had to head over to the gate leading to the creek paddock, Mark and Shay lugging the camera equipment while Brant and Misha puttered along in first gear. Then Sox and Mon had to corral some animals with their barking and running so that the reluctant sheep would stay in the frame.

"There! Stop right there!" Mark said. The sheep didn't listen, and the dogs were confused. A big woolly mass of ewe almost knocked the camera tripod over.

The photographer swore and Misha began to giggle. Brant could feel her body shaking against his back, and her laugh sounded like a mix of music, bubbling water and kookaburras sitting in an old gum tree. "Maybe I should get down with the sheep and Mark should put a pregnant ewe on the bike with you," she muttered.

"Stay put," he growled back at her, trying not to laugh himself. Also trying not to think that what he could feel most clearly against his back was her breasts. "He's an artist. Give him his creative space. And let's get this over with, because I'm marking lambs with Chris over at his place again this afternoon."

"Want me?"

She doesn't mean it that way.

"We'll manage," he said out loud.

"If I promise to be useful?"

"If you're crazy enough to want to be useful around here, you're always welcome, Misha, you know that." Brant heard himself putting too much meaning and importance into the words and had a fresh inkling of the trouble he was in.

Serious.

Painful.

"Closer!" Mark said. "Can you, Michelle?"

"Just call me Mish," she answered, and obediently slid her thighs right against Brant's on the four-wheeler's broad seat.

Oh, yes, he was in trouble, all right! He hoped he

wouldn't have to get off this bike too quickly because then it would show.

The camera clicked away.

"And you, Brant?" Shay said. "You trust this city girl?"

"From the bottom of my heart." His voice came out husky, and he had to cough to clear his throat. The whole performance came way too easily.

"That should be enough," the photographer said eventually. "Can we head back to the house for some static shots?"

Thanks to Brant's determined focus on thoughts of cold showers, they could.

The dogs pushed the sheep out of the fenced corner of the paddock and everyone came back through the gate.

Some minutes later, Mark was ready with his camera again. He'd chosen the citrus trees for one set of shots, and as a backup, the cane chairs on the veranda, angled to face a different way. "That way, we get the backdrop of this vine-thing and the paddock, but we don't have to see the peeling roof."

"I told you it needed painting," Misha murmured to Brant, as if she really had.

Mark posed them like dolls. Brant's arm around Misha's warm body, slightly stiff and rustly in his oilskin. Sox sitting in front of them on a convenient stump, tongue hanging out as Brant used his free hand to give her the muscular patting she liked.

Sunglasses back up, please, Mark requested.

Misha raised her sunglasses again and her wig slipped. Just a tiny bit. Brant was sure he was the only person who'd noticed. "Careful," he muttered, squeezing her.

"I know," she muttered back. "I don't like this guy, much. Sometimes I don't know which is worse, formal photo shoots or candid ones."

"Yeah? I'd have thought it would be no contest," Brant said. He kept his voice low. "At least today we have some control over how we look."

"But sometimes, especially if it's a formal portrait with…" She looked uncomfortable. "…you know…with the jewels…"

Oh, right. Of course. The jewels.

"…it just takes so long!"

"You'd rather be lamb-marking."

"Seriously, I think I would."

He couldn't manage to believe her.

Too much of him wanted to.

Mark clicked off his camera about a thousand times—maybe a slight exaggeration, but not much. Turn this way. Smile more. Smile less. Move your hand to her upper arm. Look down at Mish. Look up at Brant.

"You're right," Brant said in the end. "This gets boring very fast."

His arms felt wooden and stiff, even against Misha's pliant warmth. He tried to soften the pose, to make this look more genuine, but as soon as he did so, it felt *too* genuine and he wanted to take it further, into territory that was uncharted and forbidden.

She was a princess.

She was engaged.

She could never belong here, never truly fit into his life. He'd seen it with his own parents.

If he hadn't been pinned in place by the camera lens, he never would have touched her, because all this brought him was a strange regret that he didn't fully understand.

"I'd rather there was a whole rugby scrum of paparazzi hiding in the bushes so we could just get on with our lives," he told her, "and good luck to them if they caught us doing anything more scandalous than feeding the dogs."

Next they moved to the veranda and he had to stand behind Misha with his hand on her shoulder, which if anything was worse. He could see the side of her neck, its fine column tickled by strands of that ridiculous hair. He wanted to sweep the hair back. Or, no, even better, pull it right off, pick apart whatever pins or nets were holding her real hair in place and bury his face in the blond strands.

Fifteen different women he'd been out with since his face had appeared on the cover of the magazine, and not one of them had affected him like this.

"Now, shall we have coffee while we talk?" Shay suggested brightly. "We're running out of time." She looked at her watch after she said it. Brant suspected she tended to run out of time before she even got up in the mornings. She was an attractive women, intelligent and with a sensitive mouth, but she had an edge, and he could tell she was fairly driven. "But I really want to get to the heart of your romance, so our readers get that feel-good sense that true love really happens."

"Wow! And that comes with coffee included?" Misha teased.

Brant hid a snort of laughter behind his hand.

Mark commandeered coffee for himself but didn't stay in the room while they talked on the veranda. "Bathroom?" he asked, then put his coffee down after a couple of sips, disappeared in that direction and stayed away for quite some time.

"Tell me what it is you love the most about each other," Shay said, after she'd covered some more obvious questions such as what Misha did for a living. She was a gourmet caterer, it turned out, with a diploma from a French cooking school. "Brant? You first?" She added in a token fashion, "I know it's hard."

But it wasn't.

It was surprisingly easy.

"She's gutsy, she's hardworking, she's funny, she has more life in her heart and her mind than anyone I've ever met," he said, all of it true.

"And you, Misha?"

"He's loyal and funny and honest and honorable. He

works hard and loves his land and his animals, but it's not the only thing he thinks about. He knows there's a whole world out there, and he's a part of it, even when he's so far from what we'd think of as its center."

"You mean somewhere like New York?"

"Yes, or Paris, or Rome."

"And when's the wedding?"

They looked at each other.

"No date set yet," Brant began.

"September," said Misha at exactly the same time.

"Uh-huh," agreed Shay. "No date, but roughly September." She made a note in her organizer. "That's great. Maybe we could come back then and do a—"

"No!" Brant and Misha told her in one voice, just as Mark came onto the veranda again. "No wedding story!"

"Fascinating place," he said. "There's been more than one addition over the years, I'm guessing."

"That's right," Brant answered. "The original place was little more than a hut, but they built things to last in those days."

"Are you living here, Misha, or are you still based in Melbourne?"

"Melbourne," she answered. "I have things to wind up before I move."

Mark nodded and didn't ask any further questions. He seemed to have lost interest. Misha excused herself and slipped into the house for a moment, not returning until Brant had convinced Shay that she and her photographer could find their way back out to the gate without his personal escort.

"I'll be in touch if I have any more questions," Shay said, scribbling down some final notes. "Our readers are going to love the story, especially if I can track down a couple of other serious relationships. If we do another 'Wanted: Outback Wives' article later in the year, we'll get a whole lot more participants because of your own romance." She darted forward and gave Misha a quick hug. "Seriously, I admire you, being prepared to sacrifice so much."

I admire you, but I don't understand you at all, said her face.

"It's not a sacrifice," Misha told her, smiling. "I feel incredibly lucky."

When the car had driven away, she said to Brant, "I think the photographer was snooping in my bedroom."

"Snooping? You think he recognized you?"

"If he did, he didn't let it show. And Nu put my suitcase and my passport in that big closet in the laundry, so I don't think there was anything too princessy for him to find."

"That's good. Nu's not stupid."

"Now, thank heavens, I can take off this wig, because it's so hot!"

"And anyhow, you're better as a blonde."

"I'll take that as a compliment."

She pulled the wig from her head and shook out her hair. They grinned at each other, with the wig still dangling in Misha's hand, just as, in the distance several hundred metres away, Shay and Mark's car curved around the hill on its way out to the gate. The side windows caught the sun and flashed a sudden sparkle of light back toward the house.

Chapter Seven

"We'll make it to Chris's by one," Brant said, looking at his watch as he warmed up the engine of the tray-backed four-wheel drive.

Sox was back there, along with some equipment and a pile of old hessian sacks for her to lie on. She trotted back and forth impatiently with her tongue hanging out, ignoring the sacks, excited about going for a drive and hoping it had something to do with sheep.

"Is that what you told him?" Misha asked.

"I said I didn't know, because it depended on Shay and Mark, and when they left. Tried to phone him just now but he must be still in the paddock."

"Should we have brought him some lunch?"

"You mean those exciting peanut butter sandwiches I made? He's probably done his own." Brant circled up to the track.

Misha felt almost as happy as Sox.

Nobody would have believed it, but it was true.

She had a healthy appreciation for city life, high fashion, extreme sport, motor racing, fine food, politics, charity work and the arts, but still there was something about bouncing along in an old truck, hearing its bodywork squeaking, knowing you were about to spend the afternoon out in the fresh air and sunshine, working hard and getting dirty.

No. Definitely, nobody would have believed she would enjoy this.

Mom, maybe.

Langemark's beloved Queen Rose had had ranchers for grandparents on her father's side. She'd spent her teenage vacations branding cattle and riding fence. When Mish was a child, Mom had sat on her bed sometimes, just before heading out to a state dinner or a palace banquet all dressed in her tiara, her sparkling sapphire-and-diamond necklace and some long, glamorous gown, and she'd told Misha stories about her own childhood.

Mom had turned her back on her heritage when she'd married a European king because she'd fallen in love with him. She barely even returned to the United States for visits, because she didn't want to draw the huge, uncontrollable and intrusive machinery of the American press into her royal life.

She'd been so discreet about it that America almost hadn't noticed it had raised its own queen, but she'd paid the price. Those early stories were just about all Misha knew of her mother's family.

But maybe some of it had stayed in her blood, all the same.

The sun twinkled between the trunks of the trees as they drove. Misha lowered the window several inches and breathed in the air. The eucalyptus gave it a tang she'd never smelled anywhere else. They took the side road that led toward Chris's farm, and she saw horses grazing and a litter of rusty old machinery parts on a neighboring property. They had somehow acquired an odd beauty as they decayed.

Up ahead, the owner of the old machinery was moving

some of his stock across the road. He had gates open on both sides and dogs working the ewes and lambs, who bleated and milled around and threatened to go the wrong way. One of the dogs jumped up and ran across the sheeps' woolly backs like running across a piece of carpet, and the animals didn't even seem to feel it.

"Is it dangerous, moving stock?" Misha asked, thinking of cars coming too fast down this road.

"Can be," Brant answered, slowing the truck. "And it can muck up the ground. Mostly it's fine and there are a lot of reasons for needing to move them, but you don't do it for fun. It can spread disease."

"Really? Is that rare?"

"This guy here had a foot-rot outbreak a couple of years ago." He made a jerky, grinding gear change, slowing the truck a little more. "It meant Chris couldn't shift some of his animals where he wanted, because his property kind of encircles this one and there's a right of way that was contaminated."

He braked.

And slewed.

"What the—? Damn, do we have a flat?" he muttered.

Twisting the wheel steadily back the other way, he brought the vehicle to a controlled halt on the grassy verge fifty metres from the mob, and the farmer on his noisy trail bike raised a hand as if to say, "Thanks, mate, we'll be across in a minute, and out of your way." If they did have a flat, the farmer hadn't seen it.

Brant jumped out of the car and Misha followed. "Do we?" she asked.

But she could see it for herself—the rubber of the right front wheel squashed against the road like a strange kind of black fruit with all the pulp sucked out.

"Don't worry," Brant said. "There's a spare."

"Does Sox get to run around while it's changed?"

Brant looked at her. "She's going to be busy this afternoon, so she should really stay on the truck, but that bothers you, doesn't it?"

"Sometimes," she admitted. "Dogs are people, too."

He laughed, shook his head and clicked his tongue at such odd ideas, then whistled to Sox and she jumped down and began to nose around in the grass on either side of the road. "Happy now?" he said.

"Sox is."

What the dog's sense of smell told her appeared to be as fascinating as a fast-paced novel, and she did some digging, as well. Brant got out the hydraulic jack, the tools and the spare, and Misha felt useless.

Her least favorite feeling.

"Can I help?"

"Have you ever changed a tire before?"

"Um, no, not as such." Changing Lego wheels for her nephews didn't count. "But I'd never marked lambs before, either, this time last week."

He loosened a couple of nuts by banging on the handle of the whatever-it-was-called, then sat back on his heels and gave her the same look as before—guarded, cynical, half-amused. "Would you like to learn, in case the chauffeur ever has an off day?"

She flinched a little, because he'd sounded impatient about it, and as if he still thought she was very spoiled. But she told him cheerfully, "He might. And then he'd be really grateful that I knew how to hitch up my ball gown, put my tiara on the backseat of the Rolls and get down and do it."

He raised an eyebrow at this, but said, "Here, it's pretty easy," as he handed her the metal tool.

And it was easy, but it took a while—longer than if Misha hadn't made a point about learning to do it, and had just let Brant change the tire on his own. The sheep had all been moved into their new paddock and the farmer and his dogs were nowhere in sight by the time the truck got moving again.

Sox settled into her position in the back, chewing on something. She'd already had a fabulous afternoon. You just wouldn't believe who had passed this way over the past couple of weeks, and what they'd smelled like. Now she could take a rest until the next fun thing happened.

Arriving at Chris's, they found him just shutting the last piece of portable yard behind a sizeable mob of ewes and autumn lambs, and got directly to work helping him. For several hours, everything went smoothly. Just the usual mess, and sheep who didn't know what they were meant to do next.

"*This* way you great galoot!" Misha yelled, bracing herself against a piece of fence and pushing on a thick, woolly rump.

She'd discovered that she liked the feel of the deep fleece, and that she even liked the stubborn way the animals moved. Their inches-thick coats protected them and you could handle them quite hard without them feeling anything more than a friendly shove.

"Yes! There you go! See? Was it so hard to get with your friends?"

This lot of ewes and lambs seemed extra skittish, and the dogs were having trouble, particularly Sox, even though Misha had seen how good she usually was at this, and how much she loved it.

"Push 'em up, Sox!" Brant yelled. "Push 'em up."

The ewes bawled, some of their cries pitched high and others low, while the lambs gave their little bleats, and Sox seemed unable to handle them at all. Her running back and forth grew rapidly more frantic, and instead of barking she began to howl.

"Sheesh, what's wrong with you, Soxie?" Brant yelled again, charging across the yard to prevent a ewe from breaking away and tangling herself in a floppy section of fence.

The dog began to flinch and shake, and could no longer control her bodily functions. It was horrible to watch. Chris had stopped working. Brant had frozen for a moment, but now he raced up to Sox and grabbed hold of her, not yelling anymore but dropping his voice to a whisper.

"Oh, hell, Soxie, oh, hell. What's wrong with you?" he repeated. His gray eyes burned as he watched the dog writhe and heave and howl and squat on the ground. "Chris…" He swore a couple of times, almost on a sob. "I think she must have taken a bait." He patted the little kelpie, but even his touch and the sound of his voice seemed to trigger her flinching.

Chris strode over, not wasting any time. Misha knew exactly why her friend wanted to spend her life with this man. He was straight as an arrow and worked incredibly hard. He really knew what he was doing. "Have you baited your place lately?" he asked Brant.

"Before lambing, but I picked up all the ones that hadn't been taken after two weeks, I'd swear I did. I marked them all." He wiped a strand of hair out of his eyes, leaving a smudge of dirt on his forehead.

"Same here. Doesn't matter where she picked it up, anyhow. The point is to get it out of her. Do you have salt in your truck?" He put his hand on Brant's shoulder.

"Yes. Yes, I do. Misha, in the glove box there's a bag of it. Can you get it? We have to make her vomit."

"Not the vet…?" Misha said. "An antidote?"

"This is Ten-Eighty, it's bait for feral animals who'll take the lambs. There's no antidote." His whole face was screwed up and his lips looked dry and white. "We have to get it out of her stomach before she absorbs any more and just pray it wasn't a lethal dose."

Misha went to the truck feeling ill. Sox was a mess. She looked as if she was trying to bring up her stomach on her own but it wasn't happening. In between her convulsive heaves, she kept on howling.

Brant's expression got even grimmer. His jaw jutted and he had grooves of stress around his pale mouth. Misha knew Sox was his favorite dog—the best he'd had in years, he'd told her. "You couldn't put a dollar value on her."

She found the bag of salt in the glove compartment, searching there with shaking hands. She brought it to him, but couldn't watch as he struggled and struggled to get a dose of it down the writhing dog's throat.

"Sox, come on, girl," he begged her, still with that wrenching note in his voice that made Misha want to go close to him and just hold him like a little boy. "Come on and just let me do this. Sorry, sorry, I know you don't like it, but I have to do it, girl."

He pinned her hard against his body, forcing her to be still, and Misha could see the amount of strength he had to use.

"Come on, Soxie, you know I wouldn't hurt you." His muscles were like knots.

"Where can she have picked it up?" Chris said. He tried to get near enough to help, but Brant waved him away.

"I've got her now. Come on, Soxie."

"Brant, I'd swear I've got no baits on this place now."

"It can take hours to show symptoms. It doesn't have to have come from your place. But where's she been?"

"Beside the road," Misha said. Oh, dear lord! Her throat constricted and she felt even sicker than before. This was *her* fault. "Brant, when I persuaded you to let her off the truck when we had the flat, she was nosing around beside the road and she was chewing on something."

"Barry Andrews," Brant said.

He'd gotten the salt into the dog, at last, and the reaction wasn't long in coming. Sox was miserable and all he could do was croon to her in between trying to work out how this had happened and whether the dog had a chance at life. "Okay, Soxie, there you go. Okay, girl."

None of them thought about the sheep, who milled around

or stood and stared, bleating. "It has to have been one of Barry's baits," Brant finished.

"Barry? Yes, he never picks them up, he forgets where he's put them," Chris said, pacing in the damp green grass. "He would have baited before lambing, too."

"When, I wonder. That's the critical thing. Was he slack with that, too, so it's only just been done… Soxie, girl, it's okay. This is good, you're getting it up. Come on, girl, hang in there." Brant's voice cracked. "If he's only just done it a week or two ago, then the poison's fresh and it could be lethal. If she's showing symptoms like this… We'll know pretty soon, won't we?"

"Doesn't take long," Chris agreed. His mouth barely moved, but Misha knew he felt as bad as Brant. He was pacing back and forth, eyes narrowed and jaw set, looking at his own dogs as if fearing the onset of the painful symptoms in them, as well.

"Come on, Soxie," Brant begged. "Don't let any of it stay in."

"The vet," Misha said again. "Couldn't the vet do more?"

In her world, you had people for this stuff. Experts to turn to. The royal palace veterinarian. A royal purveyor of emetics for dogs. This was her fault for getting Brant to let Sox off the truck, and there just had to be a better and more certain answer than a dose of plain old salt. She wanted to cry. She wanted someone else to step in and solve this.

"This is all he'd do," Brant told her. "He might use something different to bring up her stomach, might have gotten it down her gullet a little more gently and quickly than I managed to, but the effect would be the same. We just have to wait now." His voice cracked again. "See if she makes it through."

"Take her down to the house," Chris said. Once again he put a hand on Brant's shoulder, trusting action more than words. "The sheep are bothering her. The noise. They get hypersensitive to light and noise when the poison starts to act, it's one of the symptoms."

"I know. I know. She's miserable."

"So let her have some peace and quiet, mate. Take her down."

Brant looked both vague and stubborn. "We have about sixty lambs still to do."

Chris turned to Misha with a question in his eyes.

"Chris and I can finish the lambs," she said at once, and was rewarded by the relief that flooded Brant's face.

"Thanks," he told her. "And this wasn't your fault. This happens. This is farming."

"She's getting quieter, now, don't you think?" Chris said.

The little black-and-tan stomach had stopped heaving, and the dog's trembling had eased. Brant took off his dirt-stained sweatshirt, laid it on the hessian sacks in the back of the truck and settled Sox tenderly on top, then drove slowly and carefully through the paddock to Chris's house, avoiding every pothole and every bump.

Misha's heart went with the man and the dog all the way.

Chapter Eight

Sox survived.

They didn't leave Chris's until well after dark, and this time Misha had the little kelpie on some old towels on her lap in the front passenger seat. The dog seemed limp and exhausted, laying her head down and not moving at all, but Brant promised the princess that it would be okay, now.

The poisoning had stopped its progression. It hadn't moved on to convulsions and coma as it would have done by now if Soxie was going to die.

In fact, she would have died already, he knew, because he wouldn't have let her go on suffering.

Misha was gentle with her, stroking her furry forehead and rubbing her softly between the shoulder blades. "Good girl," she crooned. "Good dog. Good little Soxie." Sox rewarded her with a faint lift of her tail.

"You got the lambs finished, did you?" Brant asked. He felt as washed out as Sox looked.

"Yes. That's why we were so late getting back to the house. It took awhile."

"I guess it is late," he said vaguely. "I lost track."

"It's after seven."

"So you've been working in the dark?"

"It was all right. Chris angled his truck so the headlights shone at us and we could see what we were doing."

"You're a star, Mish, do you know that?"

"I know I nearly killed your best dog today, wanting you to let her off the truck. What's so starry about that?"

"You didn't nearly kill her. You have to stop thinking that way, okay? Barry Andrews is not a particularly efficient farmer, but even if he was, it's pretty easy to overlook a bait, and impossible to make sure a dog doesn't get one. It's just one of the risks that has to be faced for the sake of protecting the lambs. Why do you think I keep salt in my glove box? Because it's a recommendation from the Department of Agriculture, since it's so easy for farm dogs to get hold of bait that's not meant for them."

"Have you ever had to use the salt before?"

"Not with Sox or Mon. Once, years ago, when Dad was still working the farm."

"Did it work that time?"

"No," he remembered, and could still feel the frustration and the hurt. "It was a fresh bait, on our place. A lethal dose. Baz died." He cleared his throat. "How 'bout we get pizza tonight?"

"Please!" she said, and they didn't talk about poisoned bait anymore.

"May I show you these?" Misha asked Brant. "Would you mind?" She had slipped along to her room a moment ago, and returned with a big white envelope.

"No problem. What are they?" Brant reached for the second-to-last slice of the ham-and-pineapple pizza.

They'd been so hungry after the difficult day and spartan lunch, they'd ordered a napolitana as well. That one was all gone, after a satisfying interval of munching in front of the television without the need for polite conversation. The princess had a healthy appetite, and when she'd finished eating, there was a shiny spot of pizza grease in the middle of her top lip.

"I mentioned them the other day," she reminded him. "I've been meaning to get them out, but…well, I just hadn't found the right moment, before this. The photos of Whatshisname and two women, remember? One's the French actress."

"Right. Okay."

"I'd…um…be interested in a man's opinion." She lifted her chin a little. "Your opinion."

This had him sitting up straighter, and banished the feeling of sleepy relaxation created by pizza, beer and a hot fire, on top of all the stress over Sox. He had shut the little kelpie in the laundry tonight instead of leaving her out in her kennel, and he kept checking on her at regular intervals. She still seemed listless but not in any of that awful pain and distress that had overtaken her out in Chris's paddock. She'd lapped at some water, but hadn't eaten yet.

Waiting for his answer, Misha held the envelope full of photographs in front of her like a piece of medieval armor. She stood several feet from the fire, looking like a small island of princess surrounded by a large sea of Brant's day-to-day life.

Her blond hair stood out against a backdrop of farming books piled on a shelf. Gold earrings glinted, while in a corner of the ceiling above her head there stretched a dusty cobweb no one had had a chance to vacuum away. A pretty European-American accent swamped the sounds of bleating sheep and howling dog that still echoed in his ears.

She'd scrubbed herself in the shower at Chris's after the

last of the lamb-marking, having gotten too filthy even for a fifteen-minute homeward drive in a dusty old truck with a sick dog on her lap.

After the shower, she'd borrowed some of the clothes that Nu kept at Chris's, but while Brant drove to town to pick up the pizzas they'd ordered by phone, she'd changed again, this time into Princess Casual: designer jeans, a cream silk top, a pink cashmere sweater and a pair of glittery pink, beaded, thongy, sandal-like things that were more air than shoe.

Until now, she'd looked very relaxed and impossibly pampered, sipping on her beer, wiggling her bare pink toes at the luxurious heat of the fire, licking a bit of melted cheese from her thumb, as delicate as a kitten having a bath. The way she held those photos, however, told Brant that he'd better be careful. He'd better be quite clear on what she was asking for. He wished Nu were here, because then Misha would be showing *her* the paparazzi pics instead.

"I don't want to get pizza grease on them," he said. "Maybe I should go and wash."

"Oh, please do get pizza grease on them! I have! That's all they're worth. They should have great big splodges of rancid pizza grease all over them." This didn't explain why she clung on to them so hard.

"Are you sure?"

"Plus, the palace has duplicates."

Of course.

"It's not my idea that all this stuff gets collected and filed," she protested hotly, even though he hadn't spoken. "Don't make me apologize for it."

"I won't."

She shook her head slowly, clicking her tongue. She almost smiled, but didn't quite get there. "Your face says everything, you know."

"Sometimes, that's a good thing. I'm honest. What do you want me to do with them, Mish?"

She looked at him with her big blue eyes, as if willing him to come up with his own answer, but he really didn't want to get this wrong, so he waited and made her say it straight out. Eventually, she did, telling him in a strained voice, "I want to know, from a man's perspective, if you think he's sleeping with them. And… and if he is, if it's important, and what I should do about it."

Her face begged him to take her seriously, to realize that this was important in her world, the way saving Sox's life had been important to him.

"You think I can tell you all that from a few photos and some shallow press stories?" he asked her slowly.

"I think you'll seriously try."

Misha slid the pictures out of the envelope, her movements neat and efficient. They were matted onto pieces of thin card. She moved the two pizza boxes out of the way, then fanned the pictures out over the table and stepped back, awaiting his opinion. There were about ten or twelve of them, complete with loud headlines, extravagant captions and paragraphs of text.

He leaned on the table, studied the left-most photo in the fan she'd laid out and read the first headline and part of the first caption, wondering what it would be like to see his own name written there.

Playboy Formula One Star Branton Smith.

Nah. Not for him.

He could have been a Playboy Sheep Farmer if he'd given Shay Russell what she wanted this morning with the magazine story, but this didn't appeal, either.

He stopped reading, remembering that he'd never yet seen a newspaper article on the wool industry written by a city journalist that had managed to get all its facts straight. And he was sure Shay wouldn't have all her facts straight today, either. He should ignore the text of all these tabloid articles and just look at the pictures instead.

"So?" Misha asked, way before he was ready to make a comment.

He slid a covert look in her direction. She'd taken a step closer to the table, and had her hands clasped near her mouth with her thumbs sticking up. She bit on them nervously, her eyelids lowered a little so that her lashes screened the blue. The shiny spot of grease had gone from her lip because she nibbled at it when she wasn't nibbling on the thumbs.

What did she want? She was a princess. She had staff who sifted through every newspaper in Europe for any reference to her family, her friends or herself. She had professional people to deliver lines like:

"Tell them, No comment," or "Cancel your commitments for the next month," or "Break off the engagement," or even "It doesn't matter if he's sleeping with them or not, it's what these photos do to the public image of the royal family, and to your reputation. The palace will issue a statement."

So why was she asking him? Being Nuala's brother hardly qualified him for anything in this kind of area. What could he give her?

"Be honest," she suddenly commanded him. It answered his unspoken question. Honesty was the thing he could give her, when there were probably a lot of people in her life who never gave her that. "You have to be honest," she repeated, "or I'll be sorry I asked."

Commands, and now blackmail.

The blackmail worked.

For some reason, he didn't want her to be sorry she'd asked.

"Well, for a start," he said, straightening to face her. "I wouldn't take the slightest notice of what the captions say, or the stories themselves."

She nodded and shut her eyes for a moment, dismissing the point as obvious. She'd no doubt spent a good ten or fifteen years taking no notice of what was written about her.

"So we're down to the photos," he said. "The body language."

Did he know anything about body language? He pivoted back to the table and looked more closely, feeling Misha's arm brush his as she came beside him to watch his expression, her body still tight with tension.

Concentrate, Brant.

Seven pictures of Gian-Marco Ponti with a blonde. Five pictures of Gian-Marco Ponti with a brunette. In most of the pictures, the figures were grainy and unclear, but two of them—the ones in the French magazine—had been taken in daylight instead of at night. Both of these featured the blonde and Whatshisname at a pavement café table. They had coffee cups sitting in front of them, the blonde was leaning close, and Whatshisname was smiling.

The blonde's face didn't show, but her eagerness did. She had her wrist turned upward, and Gian-Marco was stroking it lightly with one finger. She wore a dark top, off the shoulder. It had to be cut pretty low, and the way she was leaning forward said very frankly, "Take a look. It's all yours."

Anybody would have said that these two people were having an affair.

Brant looked at the clearest picture featuring the brunette, taken outside a nightclub. The brunette draped herself over the racing driver like a fur coat. She rested her open hand against his chest, and her head on his shoulder, twisting her neck a little so she could look up at him. She looked quite drunk, and some of her makeup had smudged.

Gian-Marco had his upper body half turned away from her, and he pointed at something, out of the picture. His mouth dropped open, not in a smile but as if he was speaking. At first Brant thought that the racing driver appeared totally uninterested in the brunette, but then he ignored the turned face, the open mouth and the gesturing arm and focused on other things instead.

.

Gian-Marco was holding up the sagging woman, supporting her with the whole length of his body. He had his spare arm wrapped tightly around her waist, and he was frowning. He seemed angry, but not at the woman in his arms. When you looked closely, it was an incredibly protective pose.

Brant looked back at the pictures of the racing driver and the blonde.

"He doesn't care two hoots about her," he said, pointing. "This one, he cares about." He tapped the brunette on her grainy shoulder. Too late, he thought to ask, "Which one's the actress?"

"The brunette."

"She's the one featured in most of the rumors?"

"Yes."

"Ah."

Her breath hissed into her lungs. "Okay. That's what I thought. That's what the pictures said to me, too."

Standing beside him she looked smaller, suddenly—not the same woman as the one who'd done most of a seasoned farmer's work this afternoon with Chris's lambs, nor the accomplished spin doctor who'd answered all of Shay Russell's questions so smoothly in her curly brown wig this morning.

She said in a small voice, "He's having an affair with her, and you're saying it's more than just a one-night stand."

"But we could both be wrong."

Forget honesty.

Misha looked as if he'd hit her, and Brant didn't want to strip any more layers from her courageous heart.

"Yeah?" she said. "Could we?"

"I mean, of course the press are going to pick the most compromising pictures, aren't they?" he argued, with a good deal of energy. "They're going to go for the ones that most make it look as if something's happening. Even if it's not."

"That's true, too."

Brant felt foolishly rewarded by her approval until she added, with a brittle smile, "You see? Isn't this fun, fun, fun? Trying to work out who's lying, who's manipulating who, trying to hide your own feelings from public scrutiny before you even know what your feelings are."

"Woo-hoo, yes, it's great fun. I want to go on the roller coaster, next."

There was a beat of silence, then she drew in another of those hissing, unhappy breaths. "You thought I was spoiled, on Wednesday, when I arrived."

"Well, I— Did you hear me talking to Nu?" He wanted to tell her he'd already changed his mind quite thoroughly on this point, but she didn't give him time.

"And I am spoiled," she went on heatedly. "When I have needs, people rush to meet them. When I have whims, they're fulfilled. Physically, I never have to clean up my own mess. At home, I would never have tried to give that emetic to Sox today, I would have reached straight for the phone and the best veterinarian in Langemark would have gotten a high-speed police escort to the palace."

"That's not your fault."

She ignored him. "But emotionally, no one can help. Emotionally, I'm on my own. And when you don't know what to think or feel…" She'd switched pronouns—*you* instead of *I*—but Brant wasn't tricked into thinking she'd distanced herself. "…it's not useful to have people telling you what's in the best interests of your public image, or the best interests of the king and queen, or even the best interests of the Langemark economy."

"No, I'm sure it isn't."

"And if you are going to break off your engagement, Your Highness—" She adopted a deferential court adviser's tone. "—please don't do it yet, because of your sister-in-law's pregnancy announcement that won't be made for a few more weeks, and because of the effect your decision may have on the proposed changes to Langemarkian divorce and family law that are due for debate and voting before the summer recess in June."

"You've had that?"

"Said to me. In those words. Last week. *After* I'd cried on my mother's shoulder, but *before* the photos were matted onto the card. Sometimes the press office gets a little behind."

She was trying to make him laugh, but she had tears in her eyes.

"Really, though, Mish?"

"Yep, I was officially asked to maintain the public perception that Gian-Marco Ponti and I are engaged and that the wedding is going ahead in late September, no matter what my private feelings might turn out to be, because my ridiculous little personal life could affect the future of hundreds of other Langemarkian marriages, as well as public reaction to a new royal baby on the way. In that kind of hothouse, how can I know what to think? How can I know what to feel?"

"Oh hell, Misha." He hugged her without even thinking about it, wrapping his arms all the way around her warm body and pulling her close. Resting his cheek against her blond hair, he could smell the floral fragrance of shampoo.

"Not hell," she said into the shoulder of his shirt. "I'm one of the luckiest people in the world. But it's not always perfect."

Right now this part of it felt perfect to him. She felt perfect, in his arms, needing him. It was hopeless. He couldn't afford to feel so protective toward her. And when the protectiveness was tinged with…something else…he could afford it even less. On Thursday night he'd asked her not to repeat that lush pink strawberry of a kiss, and now, just four days later, he'd grabbed hold of her and didn't want to let her go.

Nice contradiction, Brant, but you know the underlying reasons are the same. You want her, the way Gian-Marco Ponti wants the blonde who's offering herself. But you would protect her the way he's protecting the brunette.

She swept into your life like a royal tornado and you already care about her too much.

You've gone all Sheep Farmer in Shining Armor, and it's lucky Nu isn't here or she'd guess.

And laugh.

And tell you very kindly not to be an idiot, because Princess Artemisia Helena de Marinceski-Sauverin is way out of your league and if you think she's going to hock a tiara or two to help you through the rocky stretch on the farm, then you're crazy.

Except that Nuala knew full well he'd never take that kind of help from anybody, let alone this woman.

"Sorry," she whispered.

He felt her arms snaking against his body, her hands coming to rest lightly against his back. He also felt the tremulous hold she had on herself, and sensed the questions zinging in her head. He could feel every delicate fingertip, feel the tickle of every strand of her hair.

"What for?" he asked.

He hadn't let go.

He couldn't.

"You said not to kiss you." Her breath made a puff of warm air on his neck, then she rested her lips in the same spot.

She wasn't kissing him. Kissing required movement, and at this point she wasn't moving at all. Neither was he. He didn't dare. His whole universe might explode if he moved a muscle.

"You're not kissing me," he said.

"A hug is pretty much the same." She barely lifted her mouth from his skin.

He could feel her breasts, neat and squishy. He thought they'd be exactly the size to fill his cupped hands, and desperately wanted to see if he was right, wanted to slip her body out of some pale, lacy wisp of a bra and touch her with nothing getting in the way. He wanted to know what her nipples looked like, and how her breathing sounded when she was aroused.

He'd only met her five days ago. How could he want her this much, with everything he knew about all the distances and differences between them?

"No…Mish…a hug is not the same." He struggled to speak without betraying his own uneven breathing. "A hug is completely different."

For a while, neither of them spoke and still neither of them moved. Brant felt the heat of the fire flooding through the room. He was light-headed, with the giddy optimism that Sox's heroic survival and two beers had given him, on top of hours of work outdoors.

Of course there was nothing wrong with his sheep. Of course it was okay to kiss a princess, even when she lived on the other side of the world and her monthly clothing allowance probably matched the size of his bank loan.

No need to let her go.

No need to think.

Just be.

"But it doesn't have to be different," she said, then slid her hand around his waist to the front and lifted it, running it up his chest to cradle his jaw. "It can be quite important and good. It can go places."

Her touch was so light. His skin tingled at the roots of his hair, and his whole body began to throb. She kissed his cheek, her lips soft and tentative as if she didn't know how she might react to the texture of his skin.

"All sorts of places, it can go," she whispered.

She was testing herself.

And him?

Her mouth moved closer to his, advancing just a tiny bit closer with each kiss, one soft, questing press after another.

He wanted *so much* to turn his head and meet her. Just an inch of movement would do it. He wanted to close his lips over hers and fill her mouth, take her whole mouth, kissing her until she gasped for air, clawed at his back and moaned. He was on fire.

Another few seconds and she would arrive where he wanted her. Their lips would meet, hers would part and he'd crush her with the strength of his kiss, taste her and drink her in and give them both a memory that would stay inside them forever.

He wouldn't be able to stop.

Another few seconds and he seriously wouldn't be able to stop, so any rational thinking needed to be done right now.

"Misha, what are you doing?" Her lips moved another fraction of an inch closer. His voice sounded like a rusty gate. He really didn't want to say the words. "Come on. What the hell are you doing? What do you want, with something like this? What would we really be doing here?"

She stopped. Dropped her head so that it was her forehead that pressed into his cheek, not her lips. They both stood stock-still. He could still feel her breasts. Her breathing went in and out like an air pump, fast and shaky. He could feel her hips, and the hardness of his own arousal pressing against her. He had his hands on the tight curve of her backside, and didn't even remember moving them down, but, oh, it felt good to have them there, locking her against his body.

"Trying to find out what it feels like to be Gian-Marco," she said. "I think that's what I'm doing. I—I'm not sure."

He should have guessed. He should have overcome the effect of pizza and beer on his mood. He should have sensed the hidden motivation just in her breathing, in her fingers, in her silence.

It kicked at him, painful and unexpected.

He was her little emotional petri dish, where she could cook up a couple of experiments about the kind of relationship she wanted with her European fiancé. Would she take lovers, after they married? What kind of men would she choose?

He, Brant, was only a struggling sheep farmer, safely distant from paparazzi and royal protocol.

Safely unimportant, like Gian-Marco's blonde.

Safe to test herself with.

Safe to kiss.

Safe to leave.

"And?" he managed to ask.

"I—I don't know." She pulled away, and wrapped her arms around her own body instead of Brant's. Her eyes glittered and swam. "Don't make me answer that question. Not tonight."

"I don't think we should try to answer it any night," he decided out loud, bluntly. "It's not my business what kind of a relationship you choose to have, or what you decide you want about faithfulness and trust."

She nodded, her cheeks stained with color. "No. Okay. You're right, I guess it isn't."

He dragged in another breath and spoke even more harshly, this time. "It's not my business, Misha, and I won't be used."

Her eyes narrowed. "Is that what you think I was doing?"

"Well, isn't it? What else could it be?"

"I—I don't know. And I'm sorry." She stepped back to the table and gathered up the forgotten photos like a pack of oversize playing cards, stacked them neatly and slid them back into the envelope. "Thank you for helping me with this." Her tone had changed. "With working out what was really going on in the photos."

"If we're right about it."

"Oh, I think we're right."

She gave Brant a polite little smile that didn't reach her eyes, and he could almost see the protective emotional shutters coming down. He realized just how much of herself she'd given away tonight, and knew without a doubt just how much she'd regret it later on.

He wished his sister were here.

Chapter Nine

Brant was over at Chris's when Nuala got back from Sydney at two o'clock on Wednesday afternoon.

He'd had someone out here inspecting some aspect of the property this morning, but he hadn't told Misha why. He'd been pretty vague about it. Farm admin. Routine. She hadn't questioned him more closely on the subject because, basically, they weren't really speaking to each other.

This was less awkward than it sounded. You really didn't need to speak to someone that much when you managed to avoid being in the same room with them whenever possible. Brant showered, Misha made coffee. Misha read by the fire, Brant stared at the computer in the farm office.

Easy.

She was dying to see Nuala—someone to *vent* to. When she saw the familiar car coming down the track, her heart went fluttery and light, but a part of this was awkwardness, she knew, rather than anticipation. What on earth was she going to tell Nu? The strange atmosphere between herself and Brant stuck out like a sore thumb and surely her friend would ask.

What's up with you two, anyhow?

Um, I sort of tried to seduce your brother. But it didn't work. He's angry with me—he has to be—and I'm angry with myself. What was I trying to prove? Why did I risk my friendship with you in such a stupid way, Nu? And my friendship with him. This hurt and confusion about Gian-Marco and the engagement is no excuse.

Nuala arrived like a whirlwind. She hugged Misha and started talking about the wedding before she'd even shut the car door.

"We've booked the venue—Randwick—lucky to get the date, apparently. It's gorgeous. I can show you on the Internet. Chris is going to be speechless. And I have the dress. Which of course he is *not* going to see until the day. Mum and I are looking at the different menus. They have such an incredible choice, I get hungry just reading the descriptions and it's so hard to decide."

"Will people really mind what they eat, though?" Misha asked gently. "I won't. We're all going to be there for you and Chris, not for the free food."

Nuala looked a little shocked. "I want to create memories people will treasure. Your jaded palate is in a different league from most people's, Mish, don't forget."

"Too true! Hey, though, you look gorgeous! The hair, the eyebrows. Did you have a facial?"

"All of that. Manicure. Clothes." She posed and beamed. "But meanwhile I've still only narrowed the choice of florist down to three. One of them does all this really sleek Japanese-style design but I'm not sure if that fits the rest of the mood. And invitations are still up in the air. Which is not so good because we're running out of time. The plain silver on white looks really good, but I don't think it goes with the cream and sage, but when I looked at sage for the invitations it looked hard to read and just not the right shade."

"Nu, you're forgetting to breathe," Misha said.

"Am I?" She slapped the flat of her hand against her chest and frowned. "Hmm, maybe I am." She gasped in a lungful of air, then asked, "Is Brant around?"

"No, he's at Chris's."

"Lamb-marking, still?"

"No, that's finished. Something else today. Crutching?"

"He's so good, helping Chris out. Has he been good?" She grabbed Misha's arm suddenly, and studied her face. "Has he looked after you?"

"Yes, he's been great." She had trouble with Nuala's searching stare, and tried to deflect her attention onto something different. "We had a scare with Soxie," she said quickly. "She took a Ten-Eighty wild dog bait. We think it was one Barry Andrews had put beside the road and forgotten about."

"Oh, poor Sox!"

"But Brant got her to bring most of it up and she's fine, now."

"Oh, poor, poor dog, I'll give her a hug. Gosh, and you're sounding like a farmer's daughter. I'm sorry, I haven't even called since Sunday, but Mum and I were just exhausted, you have no idea."

"I do, a bit."

"Oh, of course you do!" Nuala squeezed the air out of Misha's lungs in a fierce hug. "Sorry! How are you?" She pulled back, narrowed her eyes and studied Misha's face. "You look great. A lot better. Tell me how you are."

I sort of tried to seduce your brother, but it didn't work and I don't know what I was thinking. I actually looked better than this three days ago. Can you tell me why I'm so confused?

The words stayed inside her.

"Can we go into the house and have coffee?" she asked instead, thinking maybe they could talk then—around the safer edges of the subject, anyway. The coffee suggestion came out way too needy.

Try not to sound as if you're begging, Mish.

"Umm, not yet?" Nuala gave an apologetic wince. "I'm going to dump my bag and head straight to Chris's. Mum says he has to come up to Sydney as soon as possible and see the venue, see what we're planning—they got away on their cruise with no problems, it looks like a gorgeous ship—and I have an idea he's going to dig in his heels and refuse, but it's important, I want his involvement, so…"

"Breathe, Nu."

"I am. I promise." Nuala rushed into the house, dumped her bag of Sydney clothes on her bed, grabbed a glass of water at the kitchen sink and rushed back out to the car. "Talk later?" she suggested, through the driver's-side window.

Misha saw a huge pale-blue-and-gold ring binder on the backseat, and glimpsed the words *My Wedding Planner* in an elegant script. Chris wouldn't know what had hit him.

Nuala roared up the track, leaving Misha staring after her, with frustration throbbing at her temples and uncertainty turning the bones in her legs to mush.

Nu was back seventy-five minutes later, in just as much of a rush but a whole lot less bubbly.

Well, unless sobs counted as bubbles.

With the polite avoidance thing that was going on between herself and Brant, Misha had pleaded a headache—genuine, but mild—and hadn't gone with him to Chris's today. Instead, she'd spent much of her time sitting in the swing-seat on the veranda, drinking fizzy lemon squash and pretending to read a classic murder mystery.

The sun shone and the temperature had to be at least seventy degrees, unseasonable for late autumn and just gorgeous. Birds sang, sheep mothers called to sheep babies, and very occasionally came the sound of an airplane high overhead, or a vehicle somewhere in the distance.

So much peace and space, just as there had been three days ago, on Sunday, when Misha and Brant had gone riding by the river. Except that she'd stupidly spoiled it all by trying to get inside Gian-Marco's skin, get inside the skin of her planned marriage with him to see if she could live that way, each of them with casual lovers on the side.

I couldn't.

Five minutes of misunderstanding and layered motivations and chemistry like nuclear fission with Brant on Monday night, and she knew it as categorically as she knew her own name. It would tear her apart, having a husband and a lover at the same time. It would wreck her life.

But how unfair had it been for her to conduct such an experiment with another human being? Especially with someone like Brant?

He was probably right to be angry.

Was he angry? She didn't actually know, because he'd withdrawn so much—and so had she—that his attitude remained a mystery. Mutual courtesy could be a very effective shield.

And here was Nu back from Chris's in tears.

She barged into Misha's arms the same way Christian's little boys at home barged at their mother when they were having a tantrum. Her face was swollen and red and wet, and she probably hadn't been very safe behind the wheel. For several minutes, all she could say was, "C-C-Chris s-s-says... C-C-Chris s-s-says..."

"What's up?" Misha crooned. "What does he say, honey?"

Nuala gave one last gasping hiccup of a sob and grew suddenly calm. "The wedding's off," she said.

Brant approached the house not knowing what to expect.

He hadn't heard a single word of the argument between Nuala and Chris, but then he hadn't needed to. Slammed car doors, intense whispering over by the temporary yard full of bawling ewes, Nuala's storming stride across an open pad-dock with Chris storming just as hard as he pursued her, an ominous silence after they both disappeared behind some rocks and trees, Nu's final departure with jets of damp grass and mud flying from her back wheels as she gunned the four-wheel drive over to the gate.

It told its own story.

He'd kept to his post beside the crutching trailer belong-ing to the hired team who'd come in to tackle Chris's preg-nant ewes. Chris didn't want his animals to have a lot of dirty, dragging wool around their back ends when they lambed in the spring, so like most farmers, he got rid of it in a quick, localized shearing before the pregnancies became too far advanced. Brant and Chris had been rounding up mobs of sheep and getting them yarded ready for the crutchers all day.

One of the hired men had been "feeling crook." Hungover, Brant suspected. The man wasn't pulling his weight and there was tension between him and the others. Equipment had broken, ewes hadn't cooperated, even Chris's best dog wasn't his usual self today. They'd both thought about Sox and the bait, but Shep wasn't ill, just distracted for mysteri-ous doggy reasons of his own.

Then Nuala had entered the mix, still dressed in an outfit Mum must have bought her in Sydney, including shoes that were probably now ruined by the mud and grass in the paddock. She'd had her hair cut and somehow…erm…lightened, he vaguely thought. Her nails were manicured and various uniden-tifiable things had possibly been done to her face.

She glowed, basically, but she wanted Chris to stop muster-ing sheep now, this minute, and go back to the house with her so she could talk him through her wedding planner page by page and get his opinion on tiny little decisions that he wasn't remotely interested in, during a long day of crutching sheep.

Should the rosebuds be apricot or peach?

Chris hadn't realized there was a difference.

And what did he think of her new look?

Chris confessed that he hadn't specifically noticed it was new. Although she looked great, of course.

How many choices of main course? Two, or three? And did enough people like pork? Or would fish be better?

"Do we really have to bloody do this bloody now?" Chris had said in frustration after several minutes.

Cue the slammed car door, after Nu had dumped the wedding planner onto the backseat.

When she had stormed off home, Chris came back to the crutching trailer without a word and they got on with the job. By the time they'd finished, the light had almost disappeared. The trailer and the hired crutchers jolted back toward town, planning a stop at the pub. Chris asked Brant if he wanted to clean up a bit and have a beer before he went home. Brant picked up on the signals and said thanks but no.

"Shall I get her to call you?" he asked.

"Up to her," Chris growled. "She knows the number."

Right.

Now, Brant parked the car beneath the carport and cautiously entered the house. Apparently Nuala and Misha hadn't heard him. There was music playing and a cooking pot lid jumping up and down on top of boiling water on the stove, and the sounds muffled his arrival.

The evening had already chilled down after the day's spring-like warmth, and the fire flamed in the slow-combustion stove, with its fan making a low hum. He stopped in the darkened corridor long enough to catch his breath, and watched the backs of the two women's heads as they talked.

"But there are two kinds of fights, Nu, don't you think?" Misha said.

She had her feet up on the coffee table, and was painting her toenails as she talked. There were cotton balls wedged between each toe, and it made Brant ticklish just to look at them. He had a deeply scary moment of remembering that she had really sexy toes, and wondering what color polish she'd chosen this time. Same pink as before? It was like an out-of-body experience, and he was glad when it ebbed away. He'd never thought about nail polish before in his life.

"What kinds?" Nuala asked her.

"Well, there's the kind that…oh…strips the whole relationship back to bits of crumbled bone, and there's the kind that's…well…cushioned by this sense of trust, even when you're yelling at each other."

"Mmm?"

"Don't you think this one with Chris might be the cushion kind, not the bone kind?" Misha capped the nail polish and sat back on the couch.

"You're talking about trust? I *trusted* that he understood that this wedding was important to me!"

"He does understand. But maybe you didn't pick your moment."

"We both said some horrible things. How do we backtrack from that?"

"Hot horrible things, or cold horrible things?"

Nu laughed. Sounded pretty creaky and tired. "Stop giving me these weird choices, Misha. Cushions and bones, hot and cold. Just make it simple and tell me what you mean."

"Well, my fight with Gian-Marco—"

Okay, I can't stand here listening, Brant realized. He entered the room and flung them a greeting. They turned toward him in surprise. He said, "I'm filthy," and went straight to the bathroom to shower.

"Tell me about your fight with Gian-Marco," Nuala said to Misha, when Brant was safely out of earshot and she'd jumped up briefly to add pasta to the wildly boiling water in the kitchen.

Brant had startled both of them with his sudden appearance. They'd been talking too intently to hear his car outside.

"Cold horrible," Misha said. "Definitely." She was thinking all of this stuff through as she went, none of it was related to any conclusions she'd reached earlier. "Just…cold."

She thought about it some more.

"No care, you know? I can remember in my teens when I used to fight a lot with my mother, I'd really yell at her sometimes. I'd fling all this hot, passionate stuff at her, but she knew—we both knew—that I didn't really mean it because it was all fiery and…I don't know if this is making any sense."

"Maybe," Nu agreed carefully. "Hot horrible can be good, you're saying."

"Yes, extravagant, wild stuff that gets vented out of your system. The next day, you won't even remember why you felt it so strongly, because the love will be back again. And the love is strong enough."

"Chris was busy. My timing wasn't great," Nu conceded. "I was so excited. You know, you noticed my eyebrow shaping and hair right away, and my hands, and my outfit, but Chris didn't at all. And I've ruined the shoes. But I guess…"

"Who do women dress for?" Misha leaned forward and began to take the cotton balls out from between her toes. "Who, really? Other women! Men don't notice details but they notice the result."

Which was pretty, in the case of her toenails. It almost made up for the fact that turning into a farm princess instead of the palace kind had temporarily wrecked her hands.

"If Chris thinks you're beautiful," she continued, "in a slimy oilskin with rain-drenched rat-tailed hair and a red nose—and he does, right?—then he might think you're twice as beautiful in a new outfit with a fresh eyebrow wax, but he won't have a clue what the difference is."

"So this was a hot fight, not a cold fight, and cold fights are the nasty ones. The deal breakers. That's what you're saying?"

"The theory is still evolving, but yes. That's what I'm say-ing."

Nuala slumped her head against the back of the couch. "It's exhausting, being in love and planning a wedding at the same time. People should do those two things separately." She blew a blast of air from her lips as she thought about this. "Boy, that didn't make sense, did it?" she concluded.

"So is the wedding back on?"

"If Chris wants it to be. If my apologizing is enough."

"It will be. He wants to marry you, Nu."

"Do you think so?"

"Are you kidding? The way he looks at you? You don't know how much I envy you, because I realize now that Gian-Marco has never looked at me that way." She managed to joke, "Or not when I've been wearing a slimy oilskin in the rain, anyhow."

Nuala closed her eyes for a moment.

"Mish, I've been a bad friend since you got here, flying off to Sydney and obsessing so much about my own stuff," she said. "Tell me more about the cold horrible fight you had with Gian-Marco. Tell me where you're up to in how you feel."

So Misha did.

She talked about understanding that she'd get torn in half if she tried to have a lover on the side, but not how she'd managed to discover this about herself. She talked about shattered trust and public pretense and the pressure of expec-tations. She talked about not knowing the exact moment when her feelings for Gian-Marco had begun to die, but re-alizing now that they *had* died, and she couldn't bring them back. Her words went all over the place, and her voice fogged up several times, but when she'd said it all, she felt better and clearer.

"Do you know what you're going to do?" Nuala asked in the end.

She felt a sudden icy certainty. "Yes. I know."

Showing Nuala the ring finger on her left hand, she slowly drew off the sparkling solitaire diamond set in its pink-gold band. "This is what I'm going to do. It's what has happened in my heart, already. Keep it safe somewhere for me while I'm here? I don't want to look at it. Or think about it. Or think about what this is all going to mean."

"Mean?"

"Princess stuff, Nu. Don't you remember what it was like when you stayed with me? St. Margrethe's Cathedral has its calendar blacked out for a week and a half before the wedding and three days after it. No other weddings during that time, no church services. The Langemark National Orchestra changed its summer touring schedule so we could have some of their musicians playing at the reception. When I flew out here, in my silly little emotional crisis, all these letters had to get sent from the palace, regretting that Her Royal Highness would be unable to attend this or that function, even though some events had been in my official diary for months. I've already disappointed people. There are rumors at home that the princess has had a breakdown."

"Oh, Mish!"

"The nation is worried about me. Meanwhile, I have a designer almost finished with my dress, thinking it's going to make her career in international fashion. Mette Janssen. She's lovely. I love her clothes. You've seen them. I wear them to pieces, but she's not really known outside of Langemark, and my wedding would have brought her name to the whole of Europe, and probably North America, too."

"You can't go ahead with a wedding so as not to disappoint the dress designer."

"I know. I know! But I am not supposed to do something like this. I am not supposed to set a whole royal wedding juggernaut in motion and then bring it to a screeching halt, just because the tiny issue of my fiancé's infidelity has put a slight dampener on the proceedings."

"Misha...!"

"And you can't tell anyone about it, okay? Not anyone. Not your brother. Not Chris. I don't think I can even tell Gian-Marco himself, yet, from what my parents were telling me about duty and secrecy before I left."

"That's hard!"

"It'll be all right. I'm not going back to Europe until Graziella's pregnancy has been announced, which should be pretty soon. I don't want to exist in that kind of dishonest limbo. And I don't want to see all the stories about Gian-Marco and that actress in the press while the palace is still pretending things are fine. I just..." She blinked back tears. "...need a bit more time here, where it's easier. If you'll have me."

Nuala hugged her. "If we'll have you? Mish, I'm telling you! We may refuse to ever let you go!"

Brant emerged from the shower, wrapped in a towel from the waist down and wishing he'd thought to bring his clean clothes along to the bathroom with him. It was a real nuisance only having one shower when you had a princess in the house. He found himself thinking about putting in a second bathroom, which was crazy.

He should be looking forward to getting rid of the princess, instead.

She and Nuala were still sitting on the couch in front of the fire as he passed behind them on the way to his room. They'd opened a bottle of red wine and got out cheese, crackers and olives, and they seemed to be talking about fashion.

Nuala looked much happier, he discovered when he'd dressed and returned to the warmth. She hopped up to drain her pasta and announced over her shoulder that they could eat whenever he wanted.

Her disappearance into the kitchen left Brant alone with Misha for the first time since Monday night.

He hesitated.

They'd been doing really well with keeping their distance from each other.

Why rock the boat?

He'd had the Pastures Protection Board take their sample from one of his lame ewe's hooves this morning. He'd seen the inflammation for himself, and so had the P.P.B. guy, but it could be shelly hoof or ovine interdigital dermatitis. Over the next week, he should just get on with his work, wait for their verdict, keep on staying safely away from the princess and eventually life should…might…get back to normal.

On the other hand…

He stepped several paces closer and asked, "Did you get her sorted out?" Probably not the best way of putting it, but he felt so awkward. His tongue had knotted itself, and so had his brain.

Misha nodded and said quietly, "I think they're going to be all right. It was just one of those pre-wedding emotional blips. She's going to phone him after dinner, when she's given him a bit more space, and I expect she'll go over there. They love each other. They both want to fix this, not make it worse."

"I heard you talking. Some of it," he added hastily. "Thanks. She wouldn't have been as honest with me, and I wouldn't have known what to say. I'm glad you were here."

Ah, hell, look at her, she was blushing!

It started him off, too. He could feel the color creeping all the way up his neck and into his cheeks, burning him like a fever until a sweat broke out around his temples.

"Um, that's fine, Brant," she said. "She's my best friend. I'm glad I'm here, too."

They both kept watching each other, poised in odd positions like wary animals pricking their ears as they sensed danger. Misha sat up too straight, her hands curved over her knees. Brant hovered halfway between the couch and the fire, blocking her heat.

He should apologize about Monday night, he knew that. He'd been considering it ever since, but avoiding her had seemed easier than working out whether he'd overreacted with his accusation that he was only her experiment.

Tonight it seemed much clearer.

He'd been emotionally wrung out on Monday night, after thinking for almost two gut-wrenching hours that he could lose Sox. Misha had acted like a trouper the whole day, with Shay, with Chris, with Sox herself. One tiny misstep, not even a real kiss, and he'd jumped down her throat. His over-sensitivity was far more his own fault than hers.

"Sorry about Monday," he said. "About what I said. You know, there are worse things than being someone's…um… experiment."

But were there worse ways to apologize? Doubtful. Oh, *shoot!*

She tucked in the corner of her mouth. "Lots of worse things, Brant. Still, you deserved better."

"No, no, hang on, I'm not angling for you to apologize, too."

"But how about if I do?" she suggested brightly. "Then we can forget the whole thing and not have to keep sidling out of the room like nervous little crabs when we see the other one coming?"

He laughed, washed with a major flood of relief at her down-to-earth attitude. "You know what? That's a really good idea!"

Chapter Ten

"**W**hat do you mean you can't find the sample?" Brant said into the phone, to a disembodied male voice at the Pastures Protection Board. "Your guy took it a week ago. He labelled it and dated it and filled in all the right blanks on the form." He listened to the voice at the other end of the line. "But you can't find it." He managed to keep his voice below a yell. "And that's why you haven't contacted me with a result. I see."

He resisted the temptation to throw the phone at the wall, and arranged to have someone come back out as soon as possible and take a second sample for analysis. He was told it couldn't be today, probably tomorrow, and this left him in a state of further restlessness and frustration. He'd called the P.P.B. lab expecting a result, which, whether negative or positive, would have triggered more phone calls and a lot of work.

Now he'd be in a limbo of uncertainty for at least another week, and he had nothing else prepared to do today. It was just after eight-thirty in the morning. He'd already checked the sheep before breakfast and they were all fine.

Fine, but lame, in that same slowly growing number of cases, mostly on the front feet. They'd had more rain over the past few days, and the weather was still warm, which would keep the infection brewing whether it was foot rot or something less serious. He hadn't cleaned out or pared any individual hooves this morning. At that point, he'd believed he'd be hearing a definitive verdict today, which would make cleaning a few hooves an academic exercise.

But no, thanks to a bureaucratic stuff-up, he'd have to wait. He hated the powerlessness of the feeling.

The house was quiet. A clock ticked on the kitchen wall and the smell of breakfast coffee lingered in the air. Nuala had already gone to Chris's. She'd spent most of her days and several of her nights there since getting back from Sydney just over a week ago, and Brant knew that she and Chris were both working hard. Chris had promised that he'd go to Sydney with her for a couple of nights very soon, once he was on top of various jobs he had to do on his property.

Here at Inverlochie, Misha had convinced Brant that she could help muster his spring-lambing ewes for the hired crutching team just as effectively as she'd helped with lamb-marking—"You've seen me on that four-wheeler, Brant. It's such a buzz, I love it!"—so they'd been working hard, also. Misha zoomed around the grassy paddocks with almost as much energy and enthusiasm as Sox, whooping when she went over a bump, and he smiled whenever he thought about it.

Crutching had finished now, however.

Brant had a long list of repair jobs to do, and somehow that out-of-the-blue second bathroom idea hadn't gone away. He wanted to look at the potential cost, and where best to put in an extension, but all of it could wait today. He was too restless to put his mind to some new project—especially when he didn't know why it had suddenly struck him as such a good idea.

And the princess was overdue for a royal tour.

He found her picking a bucketful of lemons and grape-fruit in the stand of citrus trees. "Smell them, Brant!" she commanded him eagerly. "I never realized fresh-picked lemons smelled so much better than the ones you get in a wedge on the side of your plate. They're like lemon to the power of ten."

She held one out and he sniffed obediently and of course she was right. It was like inhaling the color yellow, and you could almost feel the sweet, tangy fragrance bursting in your nose.

"Are you busy today?" he asked her.

"You tell me! I had plans for a lemon chiffon pie, and lemon chicken, and grapefruit sorbet—you may detect a citrus theme, there—but you know that, like any normal red-blooded royal, I'd far rather be covered in lanolin and dog hair and unmentionable sheep by-products, so…"

"Do you ever just sit down?"

"Nope." She grinned. "Not often. It's more fun to do stuff."

"Okay, in that case, would you like to climb Australia's highest mountain?"

Not what Misha had been expecting. In fact, she almost dropped her bucket of citrus on the ground. She thought about the suggestion for a moment, envisaging ice picks and belaying pins, ropes and harnesses, swirling mist and sheer, giddy drops.

"Sure," she answered. "It sounds great."

Then she envisaged her body roped against Brant's, his arms reaching across to help her find the right handholds, his weight supporting her and his muscles moving just beyond her reach, and liked this second set of mental pictures far too much.

"Be ready to leave in half an hour?"

"Fifteen minutes, if you want." She looked down at her jeans, peacock-blue knit top and once-white running shoes. "Do I need to change?"

"You're fine."

"I'm going to sack the palace wardrobe consultant and hire you."

They loaded day packs, water, hats, snacks and warm jackets, but Misha noted the lack of serious climbing gear in the back of the truck. "Do we hire the equipment?" she asked. "You know, the ropes and stuff."

Brant laughed. "No. We go up in the chairlift."

Inside the house, the phone rang and he raced for it before Misha could assimilate the chairlift idea. She noted that he hadn't been moving toward the telephone with such an air of dread over the past few days. Lauren hadn't called again after the awkward encounter at Tarragon almost two weeks ago, and the June issue of *Today's Woman* had appeared in stores on Monday.

Publicly, Brant was no longer on the market.

The fact seemed to have taken a certain weight off his mind.

And the chairlift was probably a good thing. Much better than being roped together.

Blinking in the bright light, she realized she'd left her sunglasses on the kitchen bench and went in to retrieve them.

"You are kidding me!" she heard Brant say. "For heaven's sake, if you want any private life left, don't tell Shay Russell about it because she'll want to do a story. Not planning to? Good." He listened for a moment. "Hey, don't thank me. I seem to remember you were ready to kill Dusty and me for this at one stage." He listened again. "But that was before Jacinda? Mate, if I was there I'd punch you on the arm until you had bruises. It's great news. Now, if we could just get some of our horses over the line in a big win or two, I'd start to think there was some point in the three of us being friends."

Misha found her sunglasses and saw Brant's camera sitting at the end of the bench. She picked it up, wondering about it. So often, she avoided going anywhere near photographic equipment. Cameras caused her enough trouble and irritation in her public life, why let them impinge on her private existence as well?

He put down the phone, after a bit more talk about racehorses, and saw what she was doing. "Want to?" he asked. "We can easily fit it in one of the day packs."

"Let's take it," she said, surprising herself. "If we don't end up using it, that's okay, too."

But it might be nice to have a picture of Brant to take home with her to Langemark…

"My friend Callan is getting married," he told her. "That was him on the phone just now, with the news. He sounded…" Brant paused, grappling with a typical male's total lack of vocabulary for occasions like this. "…pretty good," he came up with. "And guess how they met?"

"Can I go out on a limb, in the light of recent events and a couple of discussions with Nu, and suggest…*Today's Woman* and 'Wanted: Outback Wives'?"

"Do you think I should go back through all my letters and see who I missed?"

"No, I think you should be happy for your friend, because it's great for him, and while you're feeling happy, take me up Australia's highest mountain. In a chairlift? Seriously?"

"Well, not all the way."

"So, after the chairlift there's some kind of hired roller-skate arrangement for the last six miles?"

"Hired kangaroo pouches, so you were close."

"Okay, now I've stopped believing in the chairlift, too."

"Hmm, and maybe there's a little talk we need to have about Santa Claus."

"You are in a nutty mood today, Brant."

And your eyes are different. They're not smoking and suffering today. What's been on your mind, Brant? And what's changed?

"Yeah, I'm actually pretty happy about Callan," he said. "Gets a few things in perspective."

What "things" he didn't specify…and Misha still didn't know what to believe about how they'd get to the top of the mountain.

To begin with, they drove.

"Got to have a royal tour, Your Highness, while you're here," Brant said.

The country they passed through became wilder and more beautiful as they left the farming country near the banks of the Murray River and went higher into the mountains. This was part of a huge national park, and the ruggedly folded terrain was clothed in thick eucalyptus forest, some of it still showing the ravages of major bushfires several years earlier.

The air had its usual fresh tang, and they crossed over little mountain creeks that hurtled their way down the narrow ravine-like valleys. Beside one of them, they stopped to drink hot tea from a flask and eat the oatmeal and coconut cookies that Nuala had made this week.

They took photos—idiotic ones of Brant hanging from a tree and Misha gesturing at the landscape like a TV quiz show hostess presenting the major prize—and she couldn't remember if she'd ever had such fun being on either end of a camera lens. They even set the camera on a tree stump and posed on a rock with cheesy, frozen grins.

"How long did you set the timer for, Brant?"

"Fifteen seconds."

"This has got to be longer than—"

Click. Just when she had her tongue stuck between her teeth as she talked.

"Want to take another one?" Brant suggested, holding the camera between them so they could both see the tiny picture on the digital display. Their arms brushed together.

"Keep this one," she said. "It's more the real me than tiaras and smiles."

"I wonder if that's really true…" he said softly, but she let the comment go.

After winding upward through stands of huge trees and litters of moss-covered boulders they reached a gap in the terrain, and soon after that, an alpine ski village appeared, its pretty chalets perched on one steep side of the valley, while on the other the ski lifts marched toward the treeless peaks, across slopes still bare of snow.

"So we really are going up in a chairlift?"

"You didn't believe me." Brant sighed loudly. "There's just no trust anymore…"

She laughed at him and pelted him with a strikingly patterned piece of bark she'd collected earlier. He deserved it!

The chairlift rose almost two thousand feet above the village, a slow, spectacular, and near-silent drift skyward, which landed them above the tree line in a terrain of round granite rocks and low, gnarled bushes. Next, a metal walkway guided them to the top of Australia, at just under seven and a half thousand feet. They ate a distinctly chilly, windy, late picnic lunch right on the top.

Mount Koshuzko, the mountain was called. Kozushko. Kosziosko. Something like that. As they ate, Brant attempted to spell it for her but failed, and even though Misha knew five different European languages, Polish wasn't one of them, so she did no better when she tried. Eventually, they found a sign and read the correct spelling on that.

Kosciuszko.

"Why does your number-one mountain get a Polish name?"

"Because a Polish explorer was the first person to officially reach the summit, and that's what he picked."

"If you ever had the chance to name a mountain, what would you call it?" The wind whipped Misha's hair out of its ponytail strand by strand as they stood looking at the sign.

"Not something that hard to spell," Brant said. Misha couldn't see his eyes behind the sunglasses, but she had found herself helplessly watching the back pockets of his jeans every time he walked ahead of her on the way up.

Well, not watching the pockets, exactly…

"But what?" she asked him. Which was scarier? Wanting to see a man's eyes, or watching his… ahem… back pockets?

"Would depend what kind of a mountain it was."

"So you'd go for the literal. Mount Snow, or Mount Granite."

"Something like that. Mount Eruption. Mount Bloody Steep."

"Mount Blisters on My Heels."

"Have you? Got blisters?" He looked concerned and glanced down the mountain to where the walkway wound its way for three or four miles back to the top of the chairlift.

"No, I'm fine. Just kidding."

"We should be heading back if we want to take a break in the village and still get home before dark."

They'd already had such a good day. Coming down in the chairlift, Misha felt as if she could have jumped off it and soared right down to Thredbo village in the valley. In the distance to the east she could see the layers of blue-tinted hills getting lower, turning into farmland and disappearing toward a hazy horizon. They stopped in the village and had tall drinks of soda and lime on an outdoor deck in the three o'clock sunshine. They talked about skiing, and tried to imagine these slopes covered in snow.

"I bet you're good at it," Brant said.

"I'm fast. But I'm untidy. And sometimes I whoop and yell all the way down."

"Not very royal of you. I've heard your whoop."

"Not very courtly of you to point that out. Thanks for my royal tour, Brant. Can I tell you the best thing about it?"

"The ride in the kangaroo pouch?"

"Okay, I can pelt you with this piece of wet lemon from my drink, if you insist."

"Tell me the best thing about it."

"You didn't make me cut any ceremonial ribbons or open those little curtains they put in front of commemorative plaques. Those things are so fiddly! They get stuck!"

"There's a bottle of champagne in the fridge at home. You can smash it against my truck and launch it into the creek for its maiden voyage, if you ever feel the need."

"You're too good to me!"

"I'm just a beautiful person, Mish, what can I say?"

They smiled at each other and it lasted a few seconds too long. Got sort of tangly and warm, and Misha's breathing caught in her chest. She didn't know what to do next, and hoped that Brant would do it for her, without giving her another second to think. Something unexpected and dramatic and sexy and—

He was the first one to break their eye contact. Misha almost heard the snap. He looked down with a frown, dragged his keys out of his pocket and muttered something about getting back before dark.

"You must be tired." He stood without waiting for her answer, and maybe he was right about the tired thing, because her energy level suddenly went dead flat.

On the long, winding drive back to Inverlochie, she dozed off in the passenger seat and stayed asleep until Brant stopped to open the farm gate. Even then, she kept her eyes shut for some seconds longer. It was just too hard to rouse herself, but she knew that soon she'd have to. It was the passenger's job to open the gate, and Brant was waiting for her.

"Sorry," she mumbled to him. "I'm going to get out and do it, I really am. Just let me wake up a bit, first."

"It's okay. I'll do it." His voice sounded gravelly and reluctant.

"No."

Silence. Except for the engine ticking.

After an interval she opened her eyes and found him leaning his head and arms on the wheel, making no move to get out of the truck. "Are you asleep, too?"

He twisted his head and looked at her, his eyes their usual smoky hue. "No." She looked back at him, and neither of them moved. "I'm awake." He sighed between his teeth. "I'm just not in any hurry to open the gate."

They kept sitting. The shadows had grown long by this time, and the light had done the gorgeous green-and-gold thing that it did most evenings. Any minute, the sun would dip behind a tree or a hill in the west and the shadows would pool together and grow blue and cold.

"Why, Brant?"

"Don't want to be a sheep farmer today," he said.

"No?"

"Nope, I'd rather be royal. Or maybe just a duke. Something easy, with no pressure."

"You wouldn't. And I'm not even going to get into the issue of pressure. But why?"

He sighed again, and started to get out of the car. She leaned across and put a hand on his shoulder, flattened her mouth stubbornly and frowned at him, demanding an answer. "Why?"

He sat slowly back, leaving one leg on the ground and the truck door half open. A puff of breeze tossed the top branches of the big eucalyptus tree that overhung the gate, and a flock of sulphur-crested cockatoos squabbled in another tree near the creek. A car went past with its headlights on against the fading light, and in the truck's side mirror Mish saw the driver lift his hand in one of those Australian country greetings that people gave whether they knew each other or not. Instinctively, she gave him a royal wave in reply.

Silence.

"I think my new ewes have got foot rot," Brant said.

Foot rot.

New to her personal universe.

"Haven't they been wearing their pool shoes in the hot tub change room?" she teased him gently. "I'm sorry, Brant, I don't know what foot rot means."

She took her hand away, but her body stayed where it was, a little closer to him than it had been before.

"It's caused by a kind of bacteria."

He pulled his leg back into the vehicle, let the door swing shut and twisted to face her. The truck cab felt as if it had shrunk to half the size. Because the sun had gone, now, and the light was fading?

"It spreads really easily in warm, damp soil," he went on, "and we've had such a warm autumn and such good rain. It ruins their feet and makes them lame. It can get really serious, and there are strict regulations about reporting it. When I bought them, they came certified against disease."

"So shouldn't they—?"

"But I see some of them limping. I've checked a few feet and they don't look right. Reddened and inflamed, with the horn separating from the hoof. Which can be foot rot, or it can be a couple of other things. And the new ones have crossed tracks with the ones I'm selling, which means those could be infected, too. I had someone in from the Pastures Protection Board to take a sample last week, and thought I'd hear the verdict today. Thought I'd know one way or the other if I'm going to be slashing six figures off my cash flow this year, because if the stock are infected I can't follow through on the contracted sale. Phoned the P.P.B. first thing this morning, as soon as their office opened. But they've lost the sample and they have to take another one, which means another week of doubt. And waiting. And if it is foot rot, then the effort and expense of getting rid of it is massive. And today I'm sick of it, Misha. Just sick of it. On top of the wool prices, and the drought we had. I had to get out of the house. We had a great day. But now we're back. I'm back to this. And I'm sick of it."

He sounded that way—heartsick and tired to the bone. Misha was amazed at how well he'd managed to keep it to himself, amazed at all the times he'd still managed to be funny with her, or patient when she did something wrong with the sheep, or generous in entertaining her.

"Nu hasn't said anything," she blurted out, wanting to say all sorts of other stuff as well. That he mustn't worry. That she'd help.

Which was naive and idiotic, because she'd flown in as a brief visitor, and she would fly out again soon, back to her own life, immune to his problems.

They both knew it.

Knew it despite this strange, shrinking truck cab that kept pushing them closer together.

"I haven't told her," Brant said. "She'll think it's her problem, and it's not. I'm buying out her share in the farm—hoping to—if I can afford it—after the wedding. Chris has a big bank loan. There's a chunk of his land, beautiful pasture, that he'll have to sell off if he can't pay the loan down. If I can give Nu her capital share from Inverlochie by the end of September, they'll be well set up, but if this foot-rot thing is confirmed…"

"Is it fatal? Isn't there a cure?"

"There is, but it's a heck of a lot of work, and it's expensive. You can't spray sheep like fruit trees. Every animal will need individual treatment, every hoof will need to be cleaned out. Footbaths, hoof-paring, culling of the ones that are slow to respond to treatment. I'll probably end up selling hundreds of otherwise fine animals straight to slaughter at rock-bottom price." He shifted suddenly. "This isn't your business. Let me open that gate."

He leaned on the door, but again she held him back. This time, her hand hit the bare flesh on his forearm, instead of the shirt wrapping his shoulder. She left it there a little too long, and he had time to look down at the now-ragged manicure on her fingers before she snatched them away.

"You've been carrying this on your own for how long?" she asked.

"Since the day you got here."

"Ah. I guess that explains a couple of things from that afternoon."

"Yes. Sorry. I was a bit of a yob."

"That's boy spelled backwards, have you noticed?"

"Is it? Should probably be something else spelled backwards. D-a-e-h-k-c-i—" He stopped. "I'm going to open the gate. We can't sit here forever just because I don't want to get home and start thinking about my limping sheep."

"What can I do, Brant?" She slid her hand up his arm, feeling the chemistry and knowing that he did, too.

"Well, you could open the gate…"

"All right. Okay. You're right. It's not my problem. But I wish you'd at least talk to Nu."

"No. Don't tell her, okay? And don't *hint*." He mimicked her accent and raised the pitch of his voice. "Nuala, I don't want to betray your brother's confidence but I should tell you there's something you really need to talk to him about, relating to sheep feet."

"Is that what you think I'd do?"

"You might."

"When you've asked me straight out to say nothing? Of course I'll respect that, Brant!"

He whooshed out a breath, then took another one. "I know you will. I'm sorry."

"It hurts me when you think badly of me. It hurts me quite a lot." Somehow, her hand had landed on his knee, now.

When had she put it there? And the truck cab had gotten so small she was amazed that either of them could still breathe.

"Does it?"

"Yes."

"Open the gate." He closed his eyes. His hand came down on top of hers. It felt so warm. "Please?"

"Open your eyes."

He did, and they looked at each other. She turned her palm up and curled her fingers, and their grips locked together. His eyes fell to her mouth, and she could feel his gaze like the touch of warm fingers.

"I don't know how it feels to have lame sheep, Brant, but I know how it feels when you can't talk about what's going on inside you or about what you're afraid of. I know how it feels when you have to hide it and lie about it and pretend everything's fine."

He answered harshly, "It would be more useful if you knew how it felt to have lame sheep."

"Oh, shoot! No, it wouldn't!" She blinked back sudden tears. "It wouldn't, Brant! You've told me all this, and it's important. Now don't push me away, just because I haven't been studying the sheep-disease manual since I was six. Just don't push me away!"

He heaved out a huge sigh. "Yeah? What am I supposed to do, then?"

They both knew. Misha was the one to say it.

"Pull me closer," she whispered.

Silence

"Open the gate," he told her.

"You don't want me to."

"No, but what I want doesn't count. How can it?" Except that he'd already settled her shoulder into the crook of his arm and reached to touch her. His whole body eased against hers in all the places where they could touch, and it felt magic and right and so important. "How can it?" he repeated.

"It counts for me," Misha said.

"For now, it does."

"Yes, for now." She cupped his jaw, her nose only an inch or two from his. His mouth was like a magnet. "I thought the whole point of this, of us sitting here, was that you didn't want to think beyond now."

He groaned and began to kiss her.

No games. Just the hunger.

For a moment, she simply accepted his mouth over hers, cajoling and imperious and single-minded. She gave in to its demands and let her lips fall apart, let his tongue find hers. She felt paralyzed by the strength of her body's reaction.

When she responded, it was like a leaf getting swept away in a current of water. No choice, no other way. She tasted him, letting her tongue sweep the inside of his mouth in an almost desperate level of intimacy, letting her body press hard against his, as if no kiss could ever go deep enough to satisfy her need for him, or his for her.

Time stopped, and the rest of the world went away. This was so unspeakably precious. Worth everything. Worth more than anything she'd ever had or known or felt in her life. It had to be a kind of magic. Nothing else explained how she could have gotten this far in her charmed existence and never felt so right in a man's arms before.

Gian-Marco hovered at the edge of her mind, as insubstantial and unreal as a shadow. She'd never felt this way when he had kissed her. There was no logic to a feeling like this. The feeling just *was*. This kiss felt like nothing else in her life. She would cross oceans for this. She would fight battles. The earth's magnetic field might shift for the sake of this kiss.

It went on forever, until they were breathless, until Misha couldn't tell where her body ended and his began.

She wrapped her arms around his neck and whispered, "Do you have any idea what this is doing to me?"

"Some. To me, too." He kissed her neck, his face warm and slightly rough against her skin. "Misha…"

"I'm only talking because…because otherwise we might sit here all night."

"Would that be bad? I don't care."

"There are better places."

He drew back a little and looked at her, and she realized just how long they must have been here locked together because she could barely see his face, it was so dark outside. "Is that what you want?"

"Yes."

He looked at her some more, and she wasn't quite sure what he could see in her face, or what he wanted. Finally he said, "Open the gate." It sounded more like a prayer than a request.

She climbed out of the car, her whole body throbbing and shaky and dizzy and dazed, her legs moving like rubber. She unhooked the tarnished metal chain and swung the gate open, then stood leaning on it as Brant drove through. He lifted his hand from the wheel and waved and smiled at her, and the smile almost melted her into the ground. She swung the gate back, hooked the chain, climbed in the cab, and Brant said, "I don't think I can drive."

"No?"

He stopped the engine, put on the brake, leaned against her once more, not even kissing her, just holding her with his face pressed into her neck again and his arms almost trembling. "Can you feel my heart?" he said. He took her hand and laid it against his chest. "You must be able to feel it."

"I can only feel mine."

"The same? Just pounding?"

"Yes. Who knew? We both need a coronary care unit."

"We need a bed," he said bluntly.

"That brings us back to the driving problem."

"I'd better try harder this time."

Misha helped, by resting the whole of one forearm along his thigh, and her head on his shoulder. It seemed to work. He got the car going, remembered to turn on the headlights this time, stalled the engine going up the hill after they'd crossed the creek, swore beneath his breath.

"We could walk," she suggested.

"No…"

When they came around the bend and first glimpsed the house through the trees, it looked dark. "Nu must still be at Chris's," Misha said.

"I forgot about Nu. Yeah, she's not here, is she?" He screeched to a halt beside the house and couldn't find the light switch inside the mudroom door. Misha had to grab on to the waistband of his jeans while she waited, because she couldn't bear to lose the contact and he forgot about the light and kissed her again.

For a long time.

Finally, they made it as far as the kitchen and found a note on the bench. They read it together, with their bodies pressed against each other like two trees growing in the same place.

Gone to Sydney with Chris. Back Monday. He has Tom Andrews checking the place so no need to go over. Have fun. Love, Nu.

"Shall we have fun?" Brant asked.

"No, let's be miserable." Misha pillowed her head on his shoulder, within kissing distance of his jaw. "So much more unusual and interesting."

"Okay, but miserable together."

"Definitely together."

"Are you hungry?" He rested his chin on her hair, and it felt like a kind of shelter, the place where she belonged, the place that would keep her safe.

"No," she told him.

"Good." He didn't move, and at first that was okay.

She stayed, feeling the safety and the bliss. But then she realized that he was struggling. His body had stiffened and he wasn't giving as much.

"Are you going to carry me to your bed?" she prompted him, pressing her hips against him.

"Where's Gian-Marco in this, Mish?" he said abruptly.

She sighed. "He's in Europe."

"That's not an answer."

"Yes, it is," she insisted, fierce about it. "He's in Europe and I'm on the other side of the world. I don't know what he's doing, but no doubt it's something involving a woman. He doesn't know what I'm doing, but he probably thinks I'm doing something, too, involving a man. So I will. And then we're even."

"Is that what this is about?"

"No. Of course it isn't."

"So what's it really about?"

"Boy, you want me to have all the answers tonight!"

"Yeah, because I sure as hell don't have any."

Silence.

Time for her to say to Brant, actually, we're not engaged anymore. Nuala's minding the ring for me. I haven't told Gian-Marco yet, and it can't be publicly announced until I get the go-ahead from the palace. But I can tell you, because I know you won't say a word.

There would be a kind of protection in staying silent, though, wouldn't there? She could fly out of here in another week or two and Brant wouldn't need to know how big a piece of her heart she was leaving behind. Which might be handy if she didn't know that, either.

Protection versus honesty.

Safety versus risk.

She thought about it, listening to Brant's strong, thudding heartbeat against her ear. He didn't move. Finally, she heard herself say in a thin voice, "Brant, if you're thinking this is the same as what happened ten days ago, after we looked at those photos—"

He cut her off. "I don't care if it is, or it isn't." She felt his arms tighten until the breath squeezed out of her lungs. "Don't tell me, okay, because I just don't care. If you want to do this, if you're still engaged to him but you want to do this anyway, then it's your business. I don't care." His teeth gritted over the words. "This is here and now. I'll take whatever you're offering."

"Bed. Take me to bed."

He lifted her up without a word and carried her toward his room, pressing hot, hard kisses against her hair and temple and cheek with every step.

Chapter Eleven

He shouldn't be shaking this hard, Brant knew.

What would Misha think? She'd feel it, because he had her whole body pressed against his chest as he carried her to his room, not even feeling her weight.

And what would she think tomorrow, when she was rational again, about his admission that he didn't care about Gian-Marco, that all his scruples had flown to the four winds in the face of his need, and he'd take anything he could get?

Brant thought of himself as a strong man. He knew he was strong. Physically. Emotionally. All the ways a man could be strong. He worked hard. He honored the people he cared about, looked after his stock and his land. He did the right thing, and he usually knew pretty fast what the right thing was. He was generous when people needed him, and tough if anyone tried to run him around.

He had choked on tears last week when he'd thought he might lose his beloved dog, but he would have put a gun to

Sox's head and shot her to relieve her suffering if he'd thought she had taken a lethal, irreversible dose of that bait. He knew he wouldn't have flinched. He'd had to shoot animals before.

This meant strength, in his world—knowing when to be tender, knowing when to be tough.

None of this fitted with what he was feeling now, and with what he had just said to Misha about her relationship with Gian-Marco Ponti. He was the kind of man who took everything on his own terms, not someone else's. He'd never needed to beg in his life.

"Put me down, Brant," Misha whispered when they reached the doorway to his bedroom.

There. She'd come to her senses.

Or she was pushing him to come to his.

He still didn't care. He wanted this too much.

"No. I won't put you down." He bundled her tighter, feeling the curve of her rear end against his arm, and the squash of her breast against his body.

"But I can't kiss you properly like this." She leaned her head against his shoulder, and he felt the caress of her breath against his neck as she whispered to him, "I can't…take off my clothes. Or feel enough of you against me."

Oh, geez.

She meant *that?*

This was still *yes?*

He put her down in a half a second and they folded against each other, breathing hard. He stroked the silk of her hair and buried his face in it, inhaling her soft scents. She splayed her hands against his backside and pulled him close, showing how much she wanted him. He had to fight not to crush her with the strength of his arms, because it felt as if he could only get enough of her if he wrapped her tighter and tighter. He was still shaking.

He'd never wanted a woman like this, or felt so out of his

depth. He'd never made love to someone with such a total bedrock of awareness that it couldn't last, that it was only a fling. He just wasn't that type. He didn't look for endings until they happened. He only slept with a woman if he cared enough about her to think that there might be more.

Liking and desire went together in his heart, but in this case they also went nowhere.

She lived in Europe.

She was—probably—engaged to another man.

She was a bloody princess.

He should have way more pride.

And he didn't care. What he felt about her was so powerful that it overrode everything else.

He kissed her the way he'd kissed her in the car by the gate, engulfing her mouth with his, drinking the taste of her yet still hungry for more. She made some sounds in her throat, little protests that seemed to say this was too much, but that she wanted more of it anyway.

Oh, she wanted more? So did he! He wanted her sweet, swollen heat against him, wanted to push into her, hear the sounds she made, claim her with the invasive intimacy of everything he did to her body.

Misha wanted it, too.

She told him so in the way she moved, snaking against him, letting him feel her body, and told him so again in her shallow, unsteady breathing. She crossed her arms and lifted her blue top over her head, making her breasts pull upward in her cream lace bra. They looked so beautiful, high and neat and round. He cupped her, feeling the peaked nipples and aching to kiss them, stroking them with his thumb, outlining the swelling curves with feverish fingers.

She smiled at him, unsnapped the bra, dropped it from her shoulders in a single cat-like whip of movement that made her bounce. Then she tossed the bra aside, showing off the essence of her female shape with a mixture of sauciness and delicacy that made him laugh even as he bent and touched his lips to the tender, darkened skin. "Misha, you're so beautiful," he whispered.

"So are you. I want to see you." She let her eyes travel from his mouth and down to his neck and chest. "And I want to touch. Everything."

He heard his T-shirt rip as he pulled it over his head, then she stepped toward him and helped him with his jeans, freeing him to the teasing, silken caress of her fingers. He didn't think this whole thing was going to last for very long. He doubted he'd be able to summon the patience or the restraint.

"Your jeans now," he said.

"Just the jeans?"

"And what's underneath." He could hardly get out the words.

And she could hardly breathe. He watched her shimmy her jeans down over her hips, leaving a semitransparent piece of net and lace that matched the forgotten bra. It outlined the shape of her—that peachy rear end and the swollen triangle between her thighs.

Outlined it so beautifully that he added quickly, "No, leave those on," and stepped close to her again and touched her through the lace and felt her quiver.

He was right to guess that it wouldn't last long.

Neither of them could wait.

They fell onto the bed, panting out their impatience like animals with four pairs of hands each. He touched her everywhere, used his mouth on her, tasting heat and musky sweetness. She would have marks on her neck in the morning, but neither of them cared. He found a contraceptive in the drawer beside the bed and stumbled over an apology for his slowness in getting the packet open.

"Don't apologize," she said. She rolled toward him. Her hair tumbled over her eyes and she brushed it back, watching his face. "You're taking responsibility. That's enough."

When he was ready, she reached for him and lifted her

hips toward him and still he didn't tell her to get rid of the lace, he just moved it aside and pushed into her, powerful and slow. He heard her gasp out his name, but he couldn't say a word, and for a timeless interval of heat and pulsing and darkness and climbing, climbing urgency, they both had everything they wanted in the whole world.

"Now I'm hungry," Misha said, because she could think of a few other things to say that seemed too scary, and that she might regret.

"Thank you," Brant drawled. "The earth moved for me, too."

Misha slid up, propped herself on her elbow and ran a finger down his nose. "Hey, are you saying my bedroom manners need work?" She kissed him, and rested her hand on his chest. "Weren't the non-verbal signals extravagant enough? This mattress will never be the same again. The earth did move. It shook."

"Good." It came out like a growl.

"Are we spoiling it now?"

"No." He pulled her head down to his chest and wrapped his arm around her. He whispered, "But don't get hungry yet. Please? Let's just stay here awhile."

This felt so different.

She had an uncomfortable, unhappy flashback to Gian-Marco. Some men rolled over and fell asleep after they'd made love, she knew. Others jumped up and charged into the shower, as if the deed was something you needed to wash off before contamination set in. Gian-Marco fell into the second group.

Brant was in a group of his own. He stayed. He held her. Pulled the quilt around her shoulders to keep them both warm. Squeezed her a little bit. Kissed the first place his lips found. Cupped a hand gently against her breast. Traced the outline of her mouth with the tip of his finger. Told her a story about Sox getting so excited one day when he called her to the truck that she misjudged her enormous flying leap into the back of it and landed on the ground on the far side. "If you ever want to see a visibly embarrassed dog, that'll do it."

"This is what you're thinking about? Flying dogs?" she teased him lazily. "I'm scared about your subtext. What can possibly be the association here?"

"Well, I think that's what would probably happen to me if I tried to jump into the back of a truck right now. I'd overshoot."

"This is a way of saying…?"

"It feels very good, that's all."

"It does," she agreed. "Okay, I promise not to be hungry for another half hour."

"Make it an hour, and…you know…there might be time for something else."

"Ooh."

An hour and a quarter, actually.

Or an hour and a half, if you counted the shower they eventually…and very lazily…shared.

"Now I'm hungry," Brant said, so they had a silly, giggly time in the kitchen scrounging emergency rations that Misha had never tasted before, like instant cups of soup and freezer sausage rolls and packet macaroni and cheese. Postbed junk food had a lot going for it, she discovered.

Later, she slept in his bed.

Because he asked.

She loved that.

He captured her outside the bathroom just as she was about to go to her room, wrapped his arms around her and nuzzled her ear. "Will you stay with me all night? Is that… against the rules, or anything?"

"There are no rules," she whispered back, loving the clean smell of him and the reined-in strength as he held her, as if he was afraid she might break if he squeezed her too tight…or as if he was afraid she might say no. "I'd love to stay with you."

* * *

On Monday, just before dark, Nuala came back from Sydney and Brant's perfect interlude in a fool's paradise came to an end.

Chris dropped his fiancée at the house but didn't come in for more than a quick greeting to Brant and Misha because he wanted to get home and check his animals. Nu was so tired he refused to let her go with him. "I know what you're going to be like tonight."

Nu was indignant. "Not that bad!" But she never slept well in the city, because of the traffic noise, and, of course, her mind had been buzzing as usual with the details of the wedding. Chris no doubt had the right idea.

"Come over tomorrow, first thing," he told her. "You know I'll be up."

They kissed quickly, and he climbed back in the car. Visible through the kitchen window, Nu stood watching him until the vehicle disappeared into the trees. You'd never guess that they'd known each other most of their lives.

"It was so good that we went," she told Brant and Misha a few minutes later.

The two of them were making a real dinner together tonight, because somehow over the past five days they'd been too busy to cook and had eaten all the emergency rations. They'd been riding again. They'd hired a canoe and gone paddling on the Murray River, getting very wet and slightly sunburned, and bringing spicy Thai food home to eat as night fell.

They'd done the essential work around the property, but very little more than that. To be honest, Brant had neglected a few things, and he still didn't care. The Pastures Protection Board guy had come back to take a second sample from a ewe's foot, blaming the lost sample on someone else. He was blunt about what he saw. "There's definitely some infection in this one."

"But it's not spreading as fast as I would expect if it was foot rot."

"Yeah, well, it would be if this was November or February. You're bloody lucky the weather's much cooler."

Brant had felt stressed and sick to his stomach for the next hour, and then Misha had brought an afternoon picnic up to the mustering yard on the back of the four-wheeler and they'd zoomed up to the top of the hill together. She'd spread a blanket on the ground in the sunny lee of the round granite boulders and they'd peeled off each other's clothes right there in the open air and climbed halfway to heaven.

He'd tried to get a few things done. A couple of repair projects had fizzled out because Misha apparently found Brant particularly appealing in an old flannel shirt with a hammer hooked into the back pocket of his jeans. This, he didn't get. "I do actually own a suit, Mish," he'd said to her. "I'm not a total Neanderthal, and I really feel I should prove it to you sometime."

"One suit?"

"Well…yeah. I only need it a couple of times a year."

"And it's personally tailored by Giorgio Armani?"

"Mish—"

"Don't answer! I'm teasing! I like you in the shirts and jeans, Brant. They're…real."

Real.

He, too, valued things that were real. And everything about the past five days had felt real to him. Real kisses, real laughter, real conversations, real heat…

But now Nuala was back and he remembered that reality could show more than one face.

"He understands now," she was saying, still talking about Chris and the wedding. "And he likes everything I decided on. He still thinks it's going to cost too much, but he knows how much Mum and Frank want to, and that Frank can afford it, so he's letting it go."

She yawned and covered her mouth. Her skin looked

slightly papery with fatigue. Apparently they'd only stopped for petrol on the drive home, and she hadn't succeeded in dozing off when Chris was driving.

"And have you calmed down yet?" Brant couldn't help asking.

"I'm slightly less crazy about the whole thing. And we've settled on a florist and on the design and wording of the invitations, which were the last two really important things that had to be done at this point—"

"So for the invitations did you go with sage?" Misha cut in. Either she cared, or she was a good actress.

A good actress, Brant decided half a second later when she put her hand softly on his backside behind the open refrigerator door where Nuala couldn't see. She kept the hand there until the last possible moment, then closed the fridge door and shot him a sly, smiling glance.

"Sage and gold on cream," Nuala said, scrabbling in her bag for some lip cream. "I love it. I mean you'd have to see the shade of sage to picture how it's going to work."

"You are joking!" Brant had to say. "There are *shades* of sage?" Misha brushed past him on her way to the sink and he felt the nudge of her breast and the tickle of her fingers at his waist.

As always, he wanted more of her than this.

Now.

He wished there were a hundred shades of sage, and that Nu and Chris had had to ponder each and every one. They should have stayed in Sydney another week.

"No, no, it's really called something else." Nu waved her hand impatiently, then put the lip cream away. "But as far as I'm concerned, it's a shade of sage. I'm not obsessing about this, you know, the way some brides do! Gosh, but my lips had better not be this dry in September!"

"No," Brant said with heavy irony. "You're not obsessing at all. Heaven forbid anyone should think that."

His sister stuck out her tongue, and he hoped she hadn't seen the moment just before that where he'd returned Misha's earlier gesture from behind the fridge door, with embellishment and with no camouflaging white goods in the way. He really wished Nu had gone to Chris's tonight.

He wished it more thoroughly when the three of them sat down to eat and he kept wanting to look at Misha or touch her under the table but couldn't because he knew Nuala would see. He didn't want any of this to be a secret, but somehow, without even asking, he knew that it was. He knew this was what Misha herself would want.

Lifelong love a princess publicized.

Brief illicit flings she kept to herself.

If Brant had consulted only his own feelings, he would have shouted this whole thing from the rooftops.

And, yeah, did he know how much trouble he was in?

Down to the very last drop.

"So what have you two been up to while I've been away?" Nu asked brightly. "Brant, I hope you've kept her entertained and haven't just made her work!"

"He's kept me thoroughly entertained, don't worry," Misha said, and Brant could hear the mischief in her voice—nothing too obvious, just meant for him.

Oh, hell, he wanted to look at her! It was as if a puppeteer had a string attached to his head and was pulling it sideways. He looked. He just couldn't stop himself, and found Misha looking at him, her lips softly parted, her blue eyes shining and her fingers brushing her neck just the way he wanted to do. They smiled and looked quickly away.

Nuala frowned.

"We went riding and canoeing, and we climbed the big Polish mountain," Misha said quickly, as if she thought there could have been something significant in Nuala's frown. "The one we can't spell. He was awful, Nu, he wouldn't tell me beforehand how you get to the top and I had this mental picture of ice picks and harnesses and the works, and when he found out that's what I was picturing, he tried to tell me, no, they have kangaroo pouches to rent."

"That's my brother," Nuala said lightly. "Awful." An odd expression screwed up her face, then her look grew more guarded. "You must have been dreading the kangaroo pouches, Mish," she teased, with a slight edge. "You obviously believe every word he says, which you absolutely shouldn't. Seriously. I'm warning you."

"Dreading them," Misha agreed. "And thanks for the warning. But we had a great day. Didn't we, Brant?"

"Just about perfect."

"I'll wash up," Nuala announced at the end of the meal. "Brant, could you dry? Then I'm going straight to bed!"

"I think I will, too," said Misha, and her tone was so innocent that Brant had no idea if it was a secret invitation or not.

She disappeared, which gave Nuala just the opportunity she turned out to have been angling for.

"What is going on around here, Brant?" she hissed, as she jetted hot water into the sink, wetting the front of her shirt. She made a sound of irritation at the mess, then squirted in an overdose of lime-flavored detergent that smelled artificial and unpleasant. "What happened while Chris and I were gone? What the hell do you think you're doing?"

A week ago, Brant would have thought she'd somehow guessed about the problem with the sheep. Tonight he knew better, but hedged anyway.

"Well, I'm thinking of putting in a second bathroom," he said. "And getting a dishwasher."

"Oh, stop! Do you think I didn't notice? Over dinner? The way you and Misha looked at each other? From the moment I got back, I could tell there was some kind of atmosphere, but I didn't put it all together until that look. Which was unmistakable."

Brant could find no words.

Which was fine, because Nu was still in full spate.

"If you hurt her, I'm warning you, I will *not* forgive you for it! I cannot believe it! She is so vulnerable at the moment, because of Gian-Marco's infidelity, and you must know that. If she's somehow trying to pay him back by getting involved with you, then it's going to backfire on her big-time, because she's just not the kind of person who can do that."

"No?" he croaked out.

"She'd be a mess. She was already a mess when she got here. If you make everything worse…! If you take advantage of her doubts…! You had all those opportunities with the women who wrote to the magazine, and you couldn't be bothered, could you? It wasn't enough of a challenge, or something. But Misha, who deserves way better—and who is, let me tell you, Brant, *so* far out of your league it's almost a joke—Misha, of all people, is the one you pick."

Brant picked up a clean wet glass to dry, his whole body operating on automatic. He couldn't even feel it move. "Why…" He stopped and cleared his throat. "Why do you assume I'm only in it for the challenge? Or that I'm taking an unfair advantage?"

"Well, aren't you? Come on, get out a clean tea towel, that one's already half-wet. You've had your chances with women, Brant. You're thirty-four and you're not married and Mum and I—"

"Oh, hell, you and Mum have been talking?"

"She asked me a couple of weeks ago why I thought you still weren't married."

"And what did you say?"

"That I assumed you didn't want to be. Because you easily could, if you did. Gaby Fry, Alison Carter, Mary-Theresa Gordon." She ticked off a couple more names of local girls he'd been out with over the years—girls he'd liked but had still somehow known weren't right for him as a long-term thing. "You have a lot to offer, you're stable and you are a good-looking man, Brant."

"Oh, shoot, this again? Magazine-cover material. I know. You don't think I like it, do you? And if you really think I'd play it up and use it with someone like Misha, even if I had the power…" He shook his head, his stomach knotted and sour.

She ignored him. "You're funny, you work hard and you know how to play, too. And right now, yes, you're playing. That's all I can conclude. You know she's only here for a few weeks. You're taking advantage of her when she's vulnerable and I'm not going to let you do it."

"Why do you assume I'd hurt her? Why do you think that's the way it would work?"

"I said. Because she's vulnerable. Just because she's a princess… She still has a heart."

"Yes, she does." He didn't really know what was going on in that heart regarding Gian-Marco, but he knew the heart was there. He'd felt it, beating hard and warm and true against his own skin. "But you're right about one thing. She's out of my league. And don't worry. I know it."

"The only thing in your favor."

"You are being incredibly unfair." The words strained in his throat. He'd been unprepared for this attack, and his defenses were all over the place. "Can you stop? Please? Now? I am not in the mood."

Nuala turned off the water too suddenly and the pipes thumped. She pivoted and stared at him, her mouth dropped open. "How am I being unfair? What are you saying?"

Her eyes glittered with suspicion and fatigue. Her cheeks were too pink.

"Nothing. I'd just prefer to talk about something else, that's all."

"No, you have to tell me what you mean." She stamped her foot like a spoiled five-year-old.

"Why? So you can ride roughshod over that, too?" He threw the wet dishtowel down. "Leave the washing-up till the morning and go to bed. Chris was right to avoid you tonight. You get very, very ratty when you're tired, Nuala. Let's both hope we've forgotten all of this in the morning."

But he saw how wide her eyes were, and he knew she'd guessed how deep his feelings ran. Let her stew on it. Let her feel guilty or horrified or sorry for him or whatever she wanted to feel. He wasn't going to talk about it. Couldn't stand the idea of admitting to any of it in words. He was going to bed.

Chapter Twelve

Misha must have heard him coming along the corridor past her room, after the blowup with Nuala.

His bedrooom door opened quietly as he stood there in the old black martial arts pants he wore as pajamas, and he heard the whisper of bare feet on the wooden floor. He'd stripped off his undershirt and was on the point of climbing into bed, his gut sour after Nuala's illogical attack. Turning to the door, he froze at the sight of Misha, the shirt still balled in his hands.

"Hi," she said. "Is this okay?"

She had on a drifty, ankle-length white nightgown that he hadn't seen before. It was made of some fine fabric that was almost transparent apart from panels of almost equally transparent lacy stuff in various places. Across her breasts, for example.

He nodded in answer to her question, but couldn't speak.

"I mean, Nu looked so tired she'll be out cold in three minutes." She hesitated and almost stammered. "B-but if it's not okay, just say."

"Of course it's okay," he said softly. He dropped the shirt on the floor. "If it's okay for you. You're the one who—" He stopped.

"Finish," she commanded, her slight smile totally assured and her voice taking on a cooing note. She did that, sometimes—spoke as if she was so used to being obeyed that she didn't even think about another possibility and could word her orders with perfect sweetness.

He finished, as ordered, gritting his teeth. "The one who has the most to lose."

She frowned. "I guess. I'm not thinking that way right now."

He could have done without those last two words.

Right now.

All of this was only about right now for her. A royal holiday romance that would come to an end the day she left here, if not before. She probably didn't have a clue that he'd begun to envisage more than that.

She closed the door silently behind her, then wrapped her arms across her body. The nightgown floated around her legs in the brief draft made by the door, and settled again. Its sleeves came down to her wrists and the neck was high. If it hadn't been for the open working of the lace and the semi-transparency of the fabric it would have been a very chaste garment indeed.

She came toward him.

"I hadn't picked you for a Victorian maiden in your night wear," he said, to keep her back until he decided if he could really do this tonight.

Or ever again.

She dismissed the maiden idea. "It was a gift from the Langemark Lacemakers Guild on my twenty-first birthday. I love how floaty and soft it is." She gave her sexiest smile. "But sometimes I wear gold silk with tiny little straps and a hemline that barely gets to my thighs."

"Do you?"

Okay. He could do this tonight.

And as many times again as she wanted.

He'd face the future when it happened.

She came closer and he reached out for her, discovering fabric so thin it was like soft tissue paper. He brushed it lightly against her skin as he ran his hands down her back, stopping at the creases of her thighs. He was already aroused, and she would feel it.

"Mmm…" She sighed against him and he could hardly breathe.

He brushed his mouth against her neck and felt her shiver with expectation and need. After only five days of this, he knew so much about her body and her responses, the way they matched his own and the way they surprised him. She loved it when he kissed her neck. And when he touched her breasts so softly. She loved it when he breathed heat against her swollen nipple through the delicate holes in the lace. And when he whispered his intentions in her ear.

"Now?" she whispered back.

"You can strip first, if you want."

"That's good, too." The nightgown disappeared in a saucy flash.

Her body whipped as she removed it, her breasts jiggled and he groaned. They fell on the bed. He lay on top of her and she began to touch him lazily, as if they had all night. He could handle all night. Mmm, and he could handle her fingers running down his back, and her thighs parting to accommodate his burgeoning size.

"What was Nuala talking to you about in the kitchen?" she asked lazily.

"She was a real pain. Grumpy as a bear with a sore head." He rolled to the side as he spoke. He couldn't touch her properly like this, squashing her into the mattress.

"And?"

"Nothing. I'll be glad when she's bloody married."

"You think that's what's going on with her? The wedding?"

"I think it had better be, or the marriage isn't going to last. I didn't have her down as the type who'd think she had the answer to everyone's major life questions purely by virtue of the ring on her finger, but there it is."

Misha didn't press him for more detail, which was good because he would have said too much. And all of it wrong and impossible. "We can forget Nu," she whispered.

"Who?"

She laughed. "Exactly!" He felt a ridiculous spurt of pleasure at having entertained her, even in such a minor way. "You…" She ran her finger down his nose. And down. And down. "Oh, you."

"Me, what?"

"Just you. You make me feel happy."

As if this was all that mattered.

Brant decided to pretend it was, just for tonight.

Again.

His sixth night in a row of "just tonight." He wondered how long he'd be able to maintain that delusion, how many more nights of this they would have, and then she reached up and held his face between her hands and kissed him, and for the thousandth time he didn't care, just gave himself to her sweetness, her eagerness and her heat.

"Are you asleep, Brant?"

Misha knew he wasn't. She could feel it in his body, hear it in his breathing. The clock beside the bed said it was four in the morning, and both of them were lying awake in the dark. She couldn't see his eyes, but somehow knew that he'd been staring blindly at the ceiling for a while.

"Sorry," he said.

"No, it's okay, you didn't wake me." She eased against his

body. "Well… Maybe you did. But in a good way." He felt resistant to her slyly sensual movement. She wondered what Nuala had really said to him last night in the kitchen. Nu could be overprotective sometimes.

And sometimes she was right.

Had she guessed just how much had happened while she was in Sydney?

Would Misha tell her?

Telling her felt too hard. The instinct to put the right spin on it ran deep. A princess wasn't supposed to make mistakes in love, and she already had a huge one of those, zooming his way around the Formula One circuit in Europe at this very moment, with blondes and brunettes dangling from his arm like charms on a bracelet. How much of what she was doing with Brant was simply running away from all of that?

Oh, but running away felt good!

His body had softened into her curves, now. She slid her thigh over his and stroked his chest. It felt familiar and good. If the communication between their bodies was all that counted, then she might just keep running in this direction and never go back.

"Come here, woman," he growled at her and she moved on top of him, letting her nipples brush his chest and running her fingers into his hair.

"Yeah?" she whispered. "What do you want from me?"

"Show me what's on offer."

And she did.

Misha fell into a doze again afterward, and didn't waken until she heard Brant moving around the still-darkened room and felt the cold space in the bed beside her. The clock read five-thirty.

"What's up?" she asked him creakily.

"I am. Couldn't sleep any more. It's almost morning."

"Spoken like a farmer."

"That's what I am." There was an odd note in his voice, and she immediately thought about his stock, and the concerns he'd shared with her last week.

"Are you going out on the four-wheeler to do a check?"

"No. Thought I'd head to the track and watch the horses being worked. There's a race meeting next Saturday, and Trans Pacific and Santari are both running. I want to know what Rae thinks about their form."

Misha scrambled quickly to her feet. "I'll come with you."

For a moment, she almost thought he was going to tell her no, but then he nodded. "Eat breakfast when we get back?" he suggested.

"My stomach won't wake up until nine."

He nodded again, and she knew something wasn't right. What was he thinking about? His sheep?

Out at the track, he relaxed, which meant that Misha could, too. Her moods had become so attuned to his now that she knew more than Nuala did about what was on his mind. She leaned on the white-painted wooden rail beside him and watched as a thoroughbred and rider galloped toward them. Once again she was astonished as she had been so often over the past couple of weeks at finding herself here, now, in a moment like this.

The rail was slick with dew, and the wet grass at her feet had already soaked the toes of her running shoes. The morning sun had only just floated above the horizon, and the air was cold enough to make the sweat rise as steam from each horse's back, but there was something exhilarating about being here, something about the sheer beauty of such highly trained yet spirited beasts perfecting what they were born and bred to do.

It was like being on a film set or behind the stage of a theater. This was a part of horse racing that only a few people got to see. She could watch it over and over again and never lose interest, she thought.

At a full gallop, the horse came past. The jockey stood high in the short stirrups and leaned close over Santari's neck, his knees knocked together. He slowed and dropped into the saddle, then wheeled around and came back at a trot toward where Rae stood watching.

"There," she said, turning to Brant. "Nice?"

"Beautiful," Brant agreed.

The jockey called out something to Rae about the horse's run, and she nodded. "Give him a good cooldown, Joe, before you bring him in."

"You think he can keep it up over the full sixteen hundred?" Brant asked.

"I'm sure he can. But we'll see on Saturday. I've got him in the Class Four."

"Stacking it against him, there."

"He has the potential, Brant, and word is getting out. He's going to be running as the favorite. We should race him a couple more times this prep, then spell him so he's ready to be back in full work by spring, and then we should enter him in some bigger races. Why hold him back?"

"What do you think, Mish?" Brant asked her.

She spread her hands and laughed. "I think this is the best fun. But if you're asking whether Santari's a good racehorse, you have a trainer for questions like that. Or else you could find a pair of dice. They'd be bound to give you a more accurate forecast than I could. I thought he looked beautiful, that's all."

They followed Rae into the stables and her apprentice jockey led the next horse out for its morning trackwork, while Misha walked up and down the stalls looking at the others. They were such fabulous animals. Trans Pacific had just been taken for a swim in the round and luridly green concrete equine swimming pool, and Rae's stablehand dried him down with the efficient pull of a long, bendy metal sweat scraper. Its serrated edge groomed away old hair and left the horse as sleek as polished mahogany.

"Why are racehorses always groomed so perfectly?" Misha asked.

"Because a lot of people bet on the prettiest." Rae grinned. She now stood in a horse stall that passed as an office-cum-coatroom, making handwritten notes about feeds on a computer printout. "And don't you perform better when your body feels good? Brushing them is like a massage."

"Do they know they've done something good when they win?"

"Some of 'em do." She gestured at a big bay in the opposite stall. "This lovely boy over here does. The day after a win, he holds his head up, he's so proud of himself. When he loses, he's hanging his neck down to his knees, doesn't want to look at anyone. Some of 'em you don't know what's going on in their heads, what they think about it all."

"Who else have you got running next Saturday?" Brant asked.

"Just my Extra Fresh in the thousand-meter Class Two. He practically rolls over and cries for his mother if he's tried over sixteen hundred, but on a sprint he's going to be hard to beat at the weekend, and he doesn't mind a slow track if we get more rain."

"And how many people know that?"

Rae looked at him and paused, the pen still in her hand. "Not that many, now that you ask."

"Yeah?"

"He looked like such a stayer when I first put him in work last year, and he won a couple of times at the longer distances—small fields, nothing too impressive—but I've never raced him at this distance. He got an injury and he's had a big holiday and this will be his first run since we've brought him back up, but every day in trackwork he's been telling us, 'I'm a sprinter!' so this time I'm going to listen to him and let him prove himself. But I don't think the bookies or the punters have caught on to his potential, yet."

"Any idea what odds he'll get?"

"He's up against a couple of promising Canberra horses, as well as one of Len Radic's mares who rocketed home at Albury at this distance a couple of weeks ago. I'll be surprised if he's shorter than ten to one. Looking for a home for your five dollars?"

"Might be. At that kind of a return." Brant added slyly, "As long as he's a sure bet."

Rae laughed. "If you believe any horse is ever a sure bet, I've got a nice little opera house up in Sydney I could sell you at rock-bottom price. Great location, right on the Harbour. The roof looks like white sails, you might have seen pictures."

Brant laughed, too. "See you on the weekend, Rae."

On the drive back to Inverlochie, Misha asked him, "What was all that about Extra Fresh? You're going to put your five dollars on him, not on your own horses?"

"They're running in different races. I can put money on all three."

"Five dollars at ten to one, I like the profit margin."

"It does have a certain appeal," Brant agreed.

He reached a straight piece of road and floored the pedal, bringing the four-wheel drive up to over a hundred kilometers per hour. There was a bend coming up and he knew he'd have to slow, maybe even brake, but right now he wanted the speed.

This morning, watching the apprentice taking Santari through his paces, he'd felt envious of the man. He needed something like that—a thundering gallop around a wide, deserted loop of lush grass, blowing the cobwebs out of his brain, along with the stress over his stock, the annoyance at Nu, and his gut knowledge that she was one hundred percent right, in the important half of what she'd said.

The princess was out of his league.

He shouldn't have let Misha into his bed last night. He should have remembered his pride. He'd awoken with this knowledge at four, and she'd still been lying beside him, her body soft and deliciously warm. That was when he should have fled the room and drowned this frustration in some early-morning work. He shouldn't have made love to her again. He shouldn't have let her come with him to the track.

And the visit to the horses and their trainer hadn't helped, anyway. He felt even more restless, brooding and stubborn, and craved something that would burn up some adrenaline, some extravagant, risky action on his part that would make a difference *now,* to his future prospects and his current mood.

Waiting for bad news always tortured him.

Waiting for rain. Waiting for the market to improve. Waiting for the verdict on the hoof infection. Waiting for Misha to leave. Too much waiting. Too little he could do about it, except blow out his frustration in some pointless extravagance of speed.

"Woo-hoo, Brant, did you want to jump up on Santari the way I did?" Misha teased him. "I've never seen you go this fast."

"Yeah, I could see you on a racehorse," he teased back. "And you're about the right size. Ever consider a career as a jockey?"

She laughed. "I almost asked Rae this morning if I could give Santari a try, but she looked like a woman who knows how to say no."

"She's pretty protective when it comes to her horses."

He approached the bend and slowed as required, accepting his responsibility to play things safe when it came to the crunch. Beside him, Misha sighed and settled back into her seat, and they didn't talk for the rest of the journey home.

Chapter Thirteen

"Sorry I was so ratty last night," Nuala said to Brant.

She had waited until Misha was settled with coffee and a newspaper, following their dawn visit to the track, and had dragged Brant into her bedroom and closed the door.

"That's fine," he told her quickly, because he didn't want to talk about it. He reached for the door, but with one small sidestep Nu got there first and blocked it off.

She fixed him with an earnest gaze. "I stand by what I said, but my delivery could have been better."

"Apology accepted. Now can I have the door?"

She still didn't move. "I mean it, Brant. Either you're going to hurt her because this is just a fling for you, or even worse…what you sort of didn't say last night…"

"What I *didn't* say?"

"What was written all over your face."

"Can we leave my face out of it?"

"She *is* out of your league. That was the wrong way to put

it. Too harsh. But it's realistic. My friendship with her…it's like a vacation for both of us. We get a taste of each other's worlds. But I can't see how those worlds could ever connect permanently. I mean, wouldn't it turn Inverlochie into a hobby farm? You're so proud of this place." She shook her head, then added on a desperate rush, as if she knew how much he would hate hearing the words, "I really, really don't want you to get hurt, either."

"You're too good to me," he drawled.

"Don't take it the wrong way."

"Do I have to pick you up and lift you sideways, Nu? I've got things to do this morning."

"Just…be careful."

"I promise not to drop you, is that good enough?"

"You really don't want to have this conversation, do you?"

"You are so perceptive."

Nuala sighed and opened the door with exaggerated courtesy. "Okay, big brother." She looked at him with a less exhausted version of that wide-eyed, searching expression she'd given him last night and he felt like a complete fool, and a naked one at that.

He escaped out of her room and into the fresh air, breathing it like a prisoner released after a twenty-year sentence. He spent the whole morning cleaning and paring sheep feet, and with the help of Sox and Mon separating any animals with suspect hooves so that he could muster them down to the shearing shed and give them a night on the dry wooden floor.

If this wasn't foot rot, then a spell of relief from his wet, green paddocks might help. He should probably have tried it days ago, and he should definitely have worked harder at cleaning out their hooves, particularly after the latest bout of rain and unseasonable warmth.

He'd been…yeah…distracted.

There were at least sixty ewes and their lambs milling

around the big wooden shed by the time he'd finished, and there were two more big paddocks of sheep he hadn't had time for, yet.

The really stupid, incomprehensible problem about the entire morning was that the foot-rot scare had begun to seem like the least of his troubles.

"Honey?" said Queen Rose over the phone on Friday morning. On the far side of the world, she sounded as if she were in the next room.

"Mom?"

"Can you talk? Are there people around?"

"No, I'm all by myself."

Misha took the cordless phone and walked to the window. The four-wheel drive was absent from its usual crooked parking spot, and she couldn't see the other farm vehicles from here. She knew she was alone in the house, however.

Nuala was over at Chris's, as usual—she'd stayed the night there—and Brant was already out with his sheep. Since Nuala and Chris's return from Sydney on Monday, Brant had told Misha in no uncertain terms, "You're not here to work yourself into the ground, but this is my livelihood and I need to get a few things done. Don't sit around bored. Take that rental car of yours and go into town for coffee, or down to Albury to shop."

Today, she planned to do just that, but it was still only seven in the morning. Thinking about the time difference between here and Langemark, she realized out loud, "Mom, you must be up late over there."

"We've just had the summer closing of parliament." Which always entailed a huge formal banquet, Misha knew. It could run well past midnight.

Her heart jumped as she understood what this meant. "So the new divorce laws had their vote?"

"They only just squeaked into the schedule. It was the

final item before the formal closing, and the debate went on a lot longer than expected. Another half hour and I don't know what they would have done. Held it over until fall, or convened an extra session after the formal closing."

"And did the new laws pass?"

"Yes, but it was close. It could easily have gone the wrong way. And tonight at the banquet Christian and Graziella announced her pregnancy. She's not quite at the three-month mark yet, but she had an ultrasound and she says the baby's turning somersaults in there. Her doctor thinks she's doing great."

"In other words…"

Her mother took a deep breath. "Yes. Honey, if you've made a decision and you want the palace to issue a statement, it can go ahead."

Misha's stomach dropped to her knees. She hadn't expected this to be such a big moment, but suddenly it was. Her hand shook slightly as she slid open the French door that led to the veranda, and stepped out into the fresh morning air. The sun still hung in the trees to the east, and it was chilly. She shivered and began to pace as she and her mother talked.

On the grass, a pair of crimson rosella parrots searched for seeds. Nuala had told her a few days ago that crimson rosellas mated for life, and since then she'd realized how often she saw the pretty birds in pairs, feeding or flying together. It seemed like an omen somehow.

"Artemisia Helena? Are you there? Are you all right, sweetheart?" her mother said, her voice sharpened by a concern which was also reflected in her use of Misha's full name. "Have you decided yet what you're going to do?"

She struggled to speak. "I need to talk to Gian-Marco face-to-face. I can't do it by phone."

"But you do want to call it off?"

She reached the end of the veranda and turned, took a deep breath. "Mom, has Dad ever cheated on you?"

"Oh, honey, that's not a question I ever wanted you to need to ask!"

"I'm not suggesting—"

"I know you're not. You're asking me if all men are like Gian-Marco and I hate that you'd even think that. Your father and I have been each other's one and only since the day we met—and I think the fact that he'd played the field a little before that day only helped him to realize how special we were together, so I've never held it against him or asked for details! You're worth more than this, Misha, you deserve better than a man you can't trust."

"This is what you've thought all along, isn't it?"

"I've thought you could do better. I know you can. But I understood the attraction, and I wasn't going to stand in your way if it was what you really wanted. Sweetheart, I think you're always going to need a little speed and action in your life, a little excitement, and that's not wrong, but you have to be so careful about where you go looking for it. You have to see below the surface."

"This has been such a mess. I need to fly back now, don't I? It can't go dragging on. There's too much riding on it. I need to talk to Gian-Marco, then to people like Mette Janssen and the bishop at St. Margrethe's."

"The palace can take care of all that."

"No," she told her mother firmly. "Not all of it. Some people deserve to hear from me directly. Don't say anything to anyone until I get back, will you? Except Dad, of course."

"Not even to Christian and Graziella?"

"Not yet. I'd rather tell them myself. I'll book my ticket this afternoon, for the first flight I can get."

"Tomorrow," her mother assumed.

"You're cute, Mrs. Queen. I'm on my unescorted Michelle Smith passport, remember? You've forgotten all about that lowly level of existence. Doors don't just fall open, nor do seats on international flights instantly free up."

Mrs. Queen ignored her teasing and urged seriously, "Soon, though."

"Soon," Misha agreed.

She added a visit to a travel agent to her list of things to do in Albury, and then thought about Brant and everything she'd be losing and letting go of when she told him goodbye. They'd known each other for just over three weeks.

None of it seemed real, and she wanted her mother's arms.

"As soon as I can," she said, her voice fogging up, and she paced up and down the veranda for a long time after she'd pressed the End Call button on the phone.

"Sunday," the travel agent in Albury told her later that morning. "Unless you want the stop over in Tokyo, or the flight changes in Singapore and Athens, in which case Saturday. No? You'd rather the direct Melbourne-Bahrain-Langemark, on Langemark Air? It's a small carrier, but they have a great reputation, don't they? Much better food!"

"Their mushroom risotto is pretty good," Misha agreed, not really thinking about it.

The travel agent confirmed the reservation and Misha paid with her unlimited funds credit card. Then she went and bought Snowy Mountains souvenir T-shirts for her little nephews, bottles of local award-winning wine for her father and brother, a range of Australian-grown teas and coffees for Graziella, and a silver souvenir teaspoon for Mom.

Mom had begun collecting spoons as a child, and still did. Forty years ago, the spoons had rattled around in an old cookie tin in Mom's Colorado bedroom. Now they had their own display room at the palace, lined with gleaming chrome and glass cases featuring interior track lighting and midnight-blue velvet shelves. Recent acquisitions tended to have been bestowed by visiting heads of state and were made of solid gold.

And yet, Misha realized, Mom's pleasure in her collection hadn't changed. There was some essence to the experience that had stayed exactly the same. Fingering the little silver spoon in its flimsy box, Misha somehow felt there was a message for her in Her Majesty's Spoon Collection, but she wasn't quite sure what it was.

She ate lunch at a café—pumpkin soup, a bread roll, hot tea and a piece of chocolate-caramel slice—with her head buried in a crime novel she'd just purchased at the nearby bookstore. Driving back to Inverlochie, she thought about telling Brant that she was leaving in less than two days and almost had to stop the car because her legs suddenly didn't work right.

"This is crazy!" she said aloud to the car and the road, and managed to keep going safely.

Brant wasn't at the house. Hardly a surprise, since it was midafternoon. The dogs weren't around, either, which meant the three of them were probably out in a paddock somewhere, so she hitched her floaty skirt up to her knees by tucking in handfuls of fabric at her waist, took the little two-wheeler motorcycle that he often rode himself and went looking for him.

The weather was exactly as it had been the day she'd first arrived here twenty-three days ago. Sun shone in a blue sky. A breeze teased at her clothing, sometimes dying back, sometimes rising in innocuous gusts. Huge fluffy white clouds surfed the heavens. As she roared up the track, one of them crossed the sun, darkening the grass and chilling the air, but it was soon gone. You never would have known that this was early June, and officially winter now.

Misha bounced over the grass on the noisy machine and got some exhilarating air as she went over a stock grid too fast and momentarily took off. Whee-ee! She didn't see Brant or the dogs in the mustering yard, but finally found him in the shearing shed, down beside the creek where the original farmhouse had once stood, along with an abandoned cottage now almost covered by renegade roses. She left the motorcycle parked beside the four-wheeler, with the helmet dangling on the handlebars.

This was the first time she'd been inside the shearing shed. It was a funny old building, classic in its design, due for renovation. She'd passed several of them on other properties in the area and appreciated their odd charm, now. Climbing the rough concrete ramp on the outside, she heard the clatter of hooves on the slatted wooden floor and then Brant's impatient voice cursing the animals.

"You bloody stubborn moron!" Somehow, he still managed to sound kind of *fond* of his sheep as he said it. It was very cute.

Inside, he didn't see her immediately and she took advantage of the fact to pause and watch him. Light spilled into the musty interior through various holes and openings, making the space look like a theater, atmospherically lit. There was a strong smell of damp wool and lanolin that Misha had gotten used to now, and actually liked.

Brant wore an old, collarless blue cotton business shirt with the sleeves taken off at the shoulder seams and the top two buttons missing, and he'd been working hard enough to oil his skin in a sheen of sweat which glistened in the dusty shafts of light, etching the clean lines of his muscles.

He saw her and pushed a ewe quickly down the ramp that led to the ground-level yard. They waved to each other without a word. He picked up a water bottle and tipped his head back to pour a long stream of cold liquid down his throat. He let it splash over his shirt-clad chest and shoulders, then grabbed a towel from a table and buried his face in the thick fabric. He moved it roughly over his bare arms to buff away the smears of sweat and water-dampened dirt.

Misha couldn't drag her gaze away. He emerged from the towel with the ends of his hair curling still slightly damp against his neck, threw the rectangle of fabric aside, crossed the lanolin-stained floor and came up to her.

"Hi," she said at last.

"Hi." He looked at her outfit of peasant skirt and blouse in various ocean colors, accessorized with beaded peacock-blue slides and a little turquoise jewelry. The whole thing pretty much said exactly what it was—incognito princess dresses down for a day out in a country town. "So you went to Albury?"

She nodded. "I got—" She stopped.

Some souvenirs for my family.

She couldn't say it, because she knew where it would lead—to the fact that she'd booked her flight home for Sunday, and she couldn't...didn't feel ready to...just *couldn't*... tell him this yet.

"—a few things," she finished. "A crime novel. But it's too gory and dark. I should have paid more attention to the blood dripping down the cover. How are things here?"

"I'm looking at a few hooves, cleaning them out and paring them back, trying to work out if keeping the lame ones in here on the dry floor overnight is doing any good."

"But you thought you'd get a result from the P.P.B. on their test today, and know for sure."

"I phoned them first thing this morning. Monday, they're saying now."

Monday.

"So you have to wait the whole weekend?"

And I'll be gone before you have an answer.

"It isn't foot rot," he said. "I really don't think it is. And I don't think it's O.I.D."

"Tell me what that stands for," she commanded.

"Ovine interdigital dermatitis. Forget it right now. You're never going to need to say it."

"Ovine interdigital dermatitis," she repeated at him, and stuck out her tongue.

"I think it's shelly hoof. See? If you'd waited you could have said that one, instead. Much easier."

She laughed. "I like that disease best, so far. You're right. It has the prettiest name. The sheep grow cute little seashells on their feet. Let's definitely go for that one."

"Okay, agreed. We'll tell the P.P.B. guys to forget the sample, we've made our own decision. Hey, or we could invent a completely new disease."

"Inverlochie limp."

"Rain-dance fever."

"I think we have a great future as official disease namers, and we're really onto something with this."

The word *future* echoed in Misha's head after she'd said it, spoiling the light moment. It carried too much weight. It acted like an invisible force field, keeping her out of Brant's body space so that there was no danger they'd kiss. He seemed to sense the force field, also. He rocked back on his heels a little, and leaned a hand on one of the wooden columns that supported the roof.

They looked at each other.

"So…I'm about done here. Is there anything you—" he cleared his throat "—want to do?" A chorus of sound came from the sheep and he turned to look at them, frowning and glaze-eyed.

"I booked my flight home," she blurted out. "For the day after tomorrow."

The beat of silence that followed her words stretched out for too long. They both understood the importance of her announcement, and there didn't seem to be any easy words to say. She'd intended to skirt around the subject for a little longer, and then to bring it up more carefully, with some prefacing remarks about how much she appreciated and valued—

Oh, forget it, it was done now.

And prefacing remarks would not have made it any easier.

"Let's go outside," Brant said finally.

Misha followed him, noting the deep thrust of his hands into his pockets, and the tight lift of his shoulders. He headed for the creek, which looped lazy and slow toward its confluence with the Murray River some miles downstream.

There was a fallen eucalyptus tree lying at an angle to the

creek bank, its leaves and lesser branches long gone and only its trunk remaining, now polished by the weather to a smooth, hard silver-gray. The trunk had the girth of a racehorse and the same quality of silkiness and sheen. They both hauled themselves up on it and sat side by side.

Misha kicked off her shoes and let them fall onto the narrow band of grass between the log and the water. She felt fluttery and churned up in her stomach, scared of what they might say to each other. And what they might hold back.

"So that's good news," Brant guessed at last.

"Yes."

He was right.

Of course he was.

Of course it had to count as good news.

"But you'll have to tell me why." His voice held a rusty note. His usual directness had gone. "I know it was complicated. You haven't told me—"

"I'm not going to marry Gian-Marco. I should be telling him that before I tell you, but… It still is complicated. He hasn't called. Neither have I. I—I don't even know where he is. I'm going home to Langemark, then I'll take it from there."

"You can't announce it yet, right? Or the palace can't? You told me all this, but I haven't—I've tried not—Well, I just haven't thought about it."

Misha knew why. They'd both put considerable energy into pretending that Gian-Marco Ponti, and in fact her whole life in Europe, just didn't exist, and that only Inverlochie was real…which hadn't been that hard, because Inverlochie felt like the realest place she'd ever been.

"Parliament voted on the new laws last night and they passed," she told Brant. "Christian and Graziella announced her pregnancy. I'll talk to Gian-Marco and find out if he has a preference for how the broken engagement is handled publicly. I probably shouldn't have hidden out here for so long."

"So long? Three weeks?"

"I needed it."

"Three weeks isn't long."

"No. But sometimes it doesn't take a long time to make this kind of journey. If that makes sense."

"The journey toward knowing what you have to do."

"That's right."

It took longer to separate all the tangled strands of feeling, however. Misha knew she would only begin to do that once she returned home. And even then she knew that Inverlochie was a place she never wanted her heart to lose for as long as she lived.

And she wouldn't lose it, she remembered. Nuala was still her best friend, and Nu planned to spend her life on Chris's farm just a few miles away.

She imagined herself visiting occasionally, down the years. Seeing Nu's kids. "Gosh, you've grown!" Briefly shaking off the suffocating formality of her public life in Europe and snatching some precious private days. Nu and Chris would organize a barbecue and Brant would come over. "Misha, this is my wife. Fifibelle, my sweetheart, let me introduce you to Princess Artemisia and her husband Count Ladislaw of Stetzenberg."

Or something.

Her imagination really didn't stretch as far as naming or picturing a future wife of Brant's or a future husband of her own.

It didn't even stretch as far as returning her rental car on Sunday and taking the first flight from Albury to Melbourne.

"But is it okay if I still come to the races with you tomorrow?" she asked Brant, as if he'd banned her from all his activities now that she was about to leave.

"Sheesh, of course it is, Mish! Why wouldn't it be?"

Ah. Why?

Because she suddenly understood what she'd really been asking.

Is it okay if I still kiss you?

Was it okay?

It had to be.

She let her body ease toward his just a little. Not enough to touch. Possibly not even enough for him to notice. Then she froze, her shoulders hunched and her fingers resting on their tips on the gray eucalyptus trunk.

Maybe it *wasn't* okay for her to still kiss him.

It was crazy for her to still want to, she realized, now that real life was timetabled to start again at exactly nine-fifteen on Sunday morning, which was when she'd have to steer her little red rental car around the puddles on the track to Inverlochie's gate for the last time.

Change the subject, Mish, and change it fast.

She opened her mouth and took a breath, ready to launch into some inane question about what they should do for dinner, the two of them, because Nu had already said she and Chris were going out. Before she could frame the first word, Brant twisted around and pulled her into his arms.

Why am I doing this?

Brant knew it was crazy and self-destructive. But then a proud and stressed-out sheep farmer getting involved with a European princess had been both of those things from the very beginning and the knowledge hadn't stopped him.

He had this bizarre, wrongheaded sensation that, yes, he was working against the clock but that, like a horse coming from behind in a big race with several hundred meters to run, this was still somehow *winnable*—that if he kissed Misha just right, made love to her just right, said and did all the right things between now and Sunday morning, then she'd stay and everything would fall into place.

Logic told him it wouldn't happen, but he refused to listen and kissed her harder, deeper, sweeter, with his heart totally on the line.

How much did she know about how he felt?

Her lips had parted with the first touch of his mouth and she'd sighed against him as if she'd been waiting for him to take the lead. She touched his neck, her fingers delicate and soft, not teasing but exploring. He leaned his cheek against her hand and kept kissing her, letting her hair brush his face, wondering if that dousing of ice-cold drinking water back in the shed had done enough to freshen him.

It hadn't.

"Mmm," she said, pulling away. "I'm kissing a sheep."

He heard the laugh in her voice.

Oh, *hell!*

Seconds later, she'd tipped them both off the log, down the short grassy slope of the bank and into the cold, clear water. They both gasped and he let out a yell as they came to rest half-sitting and half-lying on the coarsely sanded bed. It was shallow, up to Misha's breasts in her sitting position.

"I shouldn't have done that!" She took in a gasping, laughing breath and fell back to soak herself up to the neck, then came forward on all fours to push Brant farther under.

The water wasn't really that cold—nowhere near enough to make him forget what he wanted. He'd already grown used to it and it felt great to wash off the rest of the grime from the shearing shed. He dunked his head and let the water comb through his hair, then sat up, scrubbed his hands with the rough sand, rinsed them off and used them to clean his face.

"Fresh as a daisy," Misha said.

"So I can kiss you again now?"

"Please kiss me," she said softly. "I might die if you don't."

They almost crawled toward each other, pushing against the smooth braiding of the current. Misha's gypsyish clothing was plastered against her body, and her hair streamed with water.

She was still laughing and it made her clumsy. Gracefully

clumsy, if that was possible. Her backside swung, taut and neat beneath the sodden skirt, as she pushed against the water. One hand gave way beneath her for a moment in a patch of soft sand, and she had hair dripping in her eyes. None of it seemed to trouble her one bit. She had the spirit of someone with ancestors as gutsy and determined as Brant's own.

Maybe he *could* still win this, he thought hazily, watching her teasing mouth.

Maybe he really could. As long as this kiss was perfect.

She twisted to kneel in the current and he eased her onto his angled thighs, holding her close. His lips met hers, cool and wet, and she tasted of creek water, earthy and clean at the same time. He pushed the wet hair back from her forehead then closed his hand over her breast. It was taut from the cold water, and the soaking fabric of her top and bra clung like a second skin.

He barely even felt the water, was only aware of it because of the way it changed her body. She felt like pure marble, like a mermaid, as supple as the current itself. He touched her everywhere he could reach and his tongue swam in her mouth. Minutes passed, and he lost all sense of time. He felt her pull him to his feet, and on the way up he wrapped his arms close around her hips and kissed her through her wet clothes from her lower belly to her throat before reaching her mouth once more.

She was shaking. So was he, probably, although he couldn't feel it. He had wild thoughts about taking her right here. Pushing her skirt out of the way and just taking her. On the fallen eucalyptus trunk. In the water itself. In that patch of mud on the bank. Could he? Would that make this kiss into the perfect thing he wanted?

She pressed harder against him and he tightened his own arms, deepening the hungry exploration of his mouth, sliding his thigh between her legs. She pulled back from the kiss, holding his face between her hands and showering more kisses—short, feverish ones—on his jaw and temples and nose.

"B-Brant," she said, "I'm s-sorry but I'm s-so cold. I d-don't think I can do this."

Oh, hell.

"Cold?" he echoed stupidly, then stepped back and looked at her.

This was why her body trembled. Despite the warmth of his mouth, her lips were blue, and goose bumps stuck out all over her skin. When he took his arms away, she immediately wrapped her own around her, but it didn't help. She looked stiff and miserably uncomfortable.

"Let me get you out of here," he mumbled. "I'm so sorry!" He began to help her toward the bank.

"It was my f-fault. I p-pulled us off the log. Was okay at f-first, but not now." She could hardly get the words out, her mouth was so numb.

The sun had gone behind a cloud. There was a bank of them building in the west, which would probably mean more rain overnight. What time was it? After four? And it was June. It would be dark in just over an hour. He felt the chill now himself. The breeze freshened and she couldn't control her shaking.

On the dry ground, they both felt colder. The wind was sharper up here, beyond the shelter of the creek's banks, and it cut through their wet clothing, ripping their body warmth from their skin and blowing it away. His brain felt as numb as his fingers, and it took him too long to realize that the only sensible thing to do was to go directly back to the house. There was nothing here to warm them, and no way to get dry.

"We'll take the four-wheeler," he said. "Never mind about the other bike. It can stay here. You ride behind me and that way at least you won't get the headwind as we ride."

"I'll be f-fine once we're back at the house."

They huddled together and ran shivering to the four-wheeler, which he had trouble starting because his fingers had stiffened so much. Why hadn't he felt the cold before?

Easy—because he'd been too busy delivering the perfect kiss.

Ironic.

Sad.

It was probably the worst kiss of her life.

On the rough journey back to the house, he saw that the bank of clouds had already built thicker in the west. The sun had well and truly disappeared behind them, gone for the day. The wind cut through his wet shirt like a knife, and he doubted that his body would give Misha much shelter.

She'd had to drag her wet, clinging skirt up to her thighs in order to straddle the bike, which meant that her legs were bare, and they'd put her shoes in the storage hatch at the back because she couldn't grip them with her numb hands or slide them onto her soaking feet.

He had to help her off the wide seat when they reached the house.

"I'm s-sorry, my legs are so stiff. They just won't move. This was my fault, B-Brant."

"No," he told her tersely as he lifted her to the ground. "It was mine."

Nuala agreed with him. He saw Chris's car parked out front, and found the two of them in the house, having coffee and talking about seeing a movie tonight. Nu took one look at Misha's purple, shivering body and said, "Brant? What have you done to her now? Has she been helping again? Mish, you mustn't. *What* can have made you this wet?"

Brant held back the information that he was as wet and cold as she was. "We fell in the creek."

"Fell?"

"It was my f-fault," Misha said again. "I pushed him."

He started toward his bedroom, knowing he couldn't afford to get sick. He needed to get warm as much as Misha did. "Run her a bath, Nu, can you? Fill it. Hot. And make her some tea."

"Yes, your lordship, and what are you going to do?"

"Get into some dry clothes." He squeezed the hem of his shirt and water dripped onto the floor. "See this? It's not sweat."

Nuala looked at them both as if she were a harried mother, dealing with a pair of very naughty children.

Chapter Fourteen

It rained heavily overnight.

The track was graded Heavy for this afternoon's race meeting, and by the look of the sky it could get worse as the day progressed. There were patches of blue, but the clouds were low and the wind was cold. Winter had arrived with a vengeance, several days after its official start date.

The gray, unpredictable weather suited Brant's mood down to the ground. It had taken him two hours to really warm up last night. He'd been stubborn about it. Nuala had lit the fire, but he made Misha sit close to it, and since he didn't trust himself to sit close to *her*, this meant he had to retreat beyond the reach of its radiance.

"Make yourself some packet soup," Nuala had suggested. "Or let me do it."

She'd relented in her intial assumption that Misha's frigid state was his fault, but her offer of soup came to nothing because Brant and Misha had eaten all the packet soups last week, and hadn't yet bought more.

Chris had identified the best movie option, and he and Nuala announced their intention to go into Albury early and eat Chinese beforehand. "Who's coming with us?" Nu had asked. "Misha?" Pause. "Brant?"

"I won't," he'd said quickly, so that if Misha wanted to go but *didn't* want to spend time with a country-bred man whom she might never see again after Sunday and who had effectively attempted to, let's face it, *kiss her to death* that afternoon, she was free to do so. "But Misha…?"

"Yes, Mish, please come," Nu had said.

And Misha had gone.

Brant had spent a wakeful night assuming she wouldn't come to the race meeting and telling himself this was a good thing, but when their paths crossed over lunch, she asked him, "So when's the first race? What time do we have to leave?" and, so help him, he just didn't have it in him to turn her off.

They arrived at the track at one.

Misha wrapped her dusty pink Mette Janssen coat more closely around her and jammed her matching Arne Norte velour hat lower over her ears, being careful not to pull on the suede rosebuds and assorted bits of trim. She'd dressed up a little today, not to conform to high fashion or her royal role, but because the coat and hat were the warmest garments she'd brought with her and she'd had her quota of almost freezing to death for this month, thanks.

Brant's immediate interpretation of her action with the coat and hat was to tell her, "You shouldn't have come."

"It's going to be fun," she answered firmly, but inside she wasn't so sure.

Yesterday's life-threatening kiss in the creek still hung between them like an icy mist. Brant had been distant and different ever since. At first she'd thought it was simply the bone-chilling cold. He'd insisted on her taking that bath, and

Nu had filled it so enthusiastically that by the time she was done there was no hot water left.

Brant had kept saying that he was fine. He'd put on dry clothes and was standing by the fire when she emerged from the bathroom, but then he'd made way for her so she could have the heat, and…oh…just hadn't been in the mood to talk, or something. He'd sat as far from her as he could.

He'd still been moving his hands stiffly, at that point. She knew he must have almost frozen on the four-wheeler, coming back to the house. He'd been up early that morning, as usual. He was probably just tired and needed some time to himself.

So she'd said yes to Nuala's suggestion of Chinese food and the movie, hadn't gone to Brant's room last night when she returned home, and planned for today to count as a fresh start.

A final fresh start, since she was leaving tomorrow. She'd spent most of the morning packing.

But a fresh start required a shared commitment to the issue, and Brant wasn't playing ball. Something was seriously wrong.

"Made a decision on our five dollars for the first race?" she asked him. They were running out of time. The horses were already parading beside their strappers in the mounting yard.

"I'm not betting," Brant said. "Not on this one."

Misha stayed upbeat. "Well, I am. And I'm going to be a total girl and go for the prettiest horse, which is number five. American Prairie. Look at her, she's a supermodel, with that dark mane and sassy gait."

American Prairie romped home, and Misha was wealthier by fifteen Australian dollars. She was as happy about it as if it had been a thousand times that much. Santari ran in the second race, and Brant didn't place a bet on him, either. Misha put on another five dollars, and he won easily by about eight lengths, but he'd been the clear favorite so she only pocketed a gain of three dollars. Once again, she was thrilled.

"What was that horse Rae was telling you about the other day?" she prompted Brant, still foolishly looking for a way to lift his mood and bridge the distance.

Being brutally honest with herself, she wanted to spend tonight in his bed. It felt so wrong that they'd barely touched each other today. She wanted the bittersweet delight of a final night together, and knew that a part of her seriously hoped tomorrow might never come.

"Extra Fresh?" she went on. "Oh, I see he's in Race Three, coming up. Aha, I've guessed your strategy now. You're saving all your five-dollar bills for today and sinking them on him." She tried a grin and waited for his reaction.

"I'm thinking of backing him for eighty thousand," Brant said.

"What?" She felt a sudden chill. "I heard that wrong."

"You didn't," he said casually. "He's at ten to one for the win, and Rae seemed pretty confident about him."

"She offered to sell you the Sydney Opera House at the same time, remember?"

"I could make a tax-free profit of $720,000 in one afternoon, and stop worrying about the farm. I wouldn't owe anyone a cent. I'd be my own man."

"You could lose. You would be very *likely* to lose. Brant, you don't make bets like that."

She'd met people who did—oil and technology billionaires who sank a million on a single race and shrugged when they lost, and decaying European aristocrats with a serious gambling problem who traded on their family name and made doomed, desperate attempts to restore their fortunes with flashes of mystical intuition.

But Brant was different.

She felt cold.

He must not do this.

She couldn't understand why he'd even consider it. She knew there was an element of the risk taker in him. It was something they shared. But the risks they both loved weren't of this type.

She looked up at him, feeling every inch of the distance between them, trying to work out what was going on. He stared out at the track, where the horses from the second race were still cantering back toward the stands after their run. There was a grim calm to his expression, and she felt as welcome beside him as a buzzing fly.

"Brant?" she said. "Don't."

"Why not? Because I might lose? That's a bit pathetic, isn't it?"

"Because you know as well as I do that it's not a courageous act. Some people think it is, but it isn't. It's deluded and desperate and not right. Five dollars…pocket change… a reason to cheer for a pretty horse, yes, but—"

"Stop, can you? It's not a decision that needs your involvement." He looked at her—glared at her, really—and she wanted to cry the way she would have cried if he'd slapped her in the face.

She felt as if he had slapped her.

No. As if he'd closed the door on her when she was begging for him to let her inside.

"I *want* to be involved!" she insisted. "You brought me here for a fun afternoon."

"I've tried to provide a fair bit of entertainment for you over the past three weeks, Misha, but you're leaving tomorrow and this is my life, not yours."

"Are you doing this…because I'm leaving?" she dared to guess, and immediately felt like a foolish, pampered princess who thought the whole world revolved around her, because he just laughed.

"It could have a little more to do with bank loans and diseased sheep, don't you think? You talk about desperation.

Well, I am desperate. I don't want to borrow money from my stepfather or from anyone else—"

Me, she realized bleakly.

"—and Rae is confident that Extra Fresh can win."

She should let it go, at this point. A part of her—the princess part—was convinced that she should. The princess should smile politely at Brant the way she'd smiled at oil billionaires at Ascot in the past and say, "Good luck, then. If you win, will there be champagne?"

Uninvolved.

No reason to care.

But the woman who existed totally without reference to the princess part of her just couldn't do it.

"But you think it's shelly hoof!" she said instead. "And you'll know for sure on Monday. Why pick now to act like some Regency rake in a historical novel?" She took a shaky breath. "Why are you so *angry* with me?"

"I'm not," he said sharply. "I'm angry with myself."

"Why?"

"Because of yesterday."

"Because we got wet and cold, kissing in the creek like a pair of teenagers? That's something to laugh about."

"Because—" He stopped, shook his head and turned away, and she thought she heard him mutter the word *perfect* under his breath.

Perfect afternoon.

Perfect emotional mess.

"I'm not letting this go!" she told him.

"Do you have a choice? I'll say it again. This is not your decision. It is not even your business. If I want to place the bet, then I will."

"Well, I don't have to stay and watch you do it!"

"You have my permission to leave, Misha."

"I don't need your permission. And I am."

She turned on her heel and pushed through a group of

people heading toward the mounting yard before he could see that she was about to cry. She knew he wouldn't follow her. That was the whole point. His bet wasn't her business, Inverlochie and his entire life weren't her business, and her emotional response wasn't his.

She was leaving tomorrow, she'd never belonged here, and he'd decided to cut short the whole messy, awkward process of saying, "Thank-you and good-bye" by disengaging half a day ahead of time. She'd be sleeping in her own bed tonight.

Circling through the pavilion, she found the side exit and pushed through the open gate, then realized she'd have to call a taxi if she wanted to get back to Inverlochie. She found a helpful race club official who gallantly did it for her, then stood in the cold wind waiting for it to arrive. It took a long time, and she heard the voice of the race caller announcing that the last horse had gone into the gate for Race Three just as the driver pulled up beside her and enquired, "Smith?"

"That's me."

As the taxi drove away, she couldn't help craning to try and watch the race. The horses had come into the turn, but she didn't have a clear view. Trees and a shed got in the way. What colors was Extra Fresh wearing? Was he leading the field?

It was no good. The taxi turned a corner and she couldn't see.

"You're a long way out of town," the driver told her when they reached the road that led to Inverlochie.

"Yes, another ten kilometers, roughly, and another kilometer of track to the house. But I'll just get you to drop me off at the gate."

"Save a couple of dollars?"

"That's right." She thought the driver would probably take one look at the mud on the track after last night's rain and refuse to go farther, anyhow.

She ruined her shoes and blistered her feet walking it.

The house was empty. It was just after three o'clock. She went to Brant's computer and tried checking the results of the race on the Internet but they weren't yet posted on the website she found, not even the ones for the first race. Maybe nothing would appear until the whole meeting was over.

The wait seemed unbearable. She'd always hated waiting. If there was going to be bad news, just let it happen, please, so she could take whatever action she could to deal with it and then get on with her life.

Had Brant placed the bet?

Had Extra Fresh won?

She couldn't stand the uncertainty, and, princess-like, identified the service she needed and went directly to it—she called the local branch of the national betting agency and got an answer to one of her questions.

Extra Fresh had run second.

She felt ill, wanted to draw down eighty thousand Australian dollars from her unlimited credit account to give to Brant today, but she knew this would be the worst thing in the world she could possibly do, for him or for herself.

Instead, she changed into farm clothes—mostly Nuala's—unchained Sox and took her for a fast, bumpy, aimless ride on the four-wheeler, across the muddy paddocks. Nuala must have taken Mon over to Chris's because she wasn't in her kennel.

"Why is he doing this, Soxie?" she asked the dog, as Sox stood sentinel behind her on the seat of the bike. "It's to push me away, isn't it? It's his way of telling me, just in case I was in any doubt, that I'm not a part of his life, and he can stuff it up any damn way he wants to, no matter how much I might want to help. Well, great. Okay. Message received."

Message *not* received.

She zipped into a paddock she hadn't been in before, at the far reach of Inverlochie's acreage, and saw some sheep trying to get to a mud-verged, brimming pond for a drink.

They were Brant's valuable rams. She recognized the fact even at a distance because of their curling horns.

One of them was in trouble. The others had found the tiny stream which fed the pond and were drinking from that, but this independent fellow had tried to go across the mud and he was stuck on a steep, sticky, eroded section that led down to the water. Coming closer, she saw that one whole side of his woolly body was slicked with mud and he was lying sideways, bawling his frustration as he repeatedly tried and failed to haul himself to his feet.

"This is not my business, Sox," Misha told the dog.

Sox had a different opinion. She jumped down from the four-wheeler and said with every movement of her athletic kelpie's body, "Tell me what we're doing to rescue the ram, Captain Princess."

"We're going back to the house. You're getting chained up, I'm leaving a note for Brant about the ram, because it's his problem, then I'm going to Chris's to see Nu and we're having a girls' night. I don't care where. The local male strip club, maybe. A biker bar in Melbourne. It's only, what, three or four hours' drive? Maybe we can get tattooed."

"Nope," Sox said. "Not going back to the house."

"Yeah, I'm just making that up," Misha agreed. "You can read my mind. But I've never hauled a ram out of mud before. Any ideas?"

Sox panted.

"Panting is limited as a mode of communication, do you realize?" She switched off the four-wheeler's engine and climbed off it.

The other rams barged away at her approach, and the stuck one tried to do the same, then sank back into his sticky prison. He was getting tired. How long had he been here? She knew that Brant usually checked all his paddocks every morning, but the animal could have got stuck since. How long could a sheep survive in this position?

She went closer, and this time the ram stayed quiet, too exhausted to struggle. Assessing his position, she doubted she could pull him free just using her own strength, even if Sox somehow understood how to help her. But if she used the four-wheeler?

She checked the rear hatch and found rope. Tie it to the ram's front feet, maybe—the ones he again tried to haul himself onto, while his back legs were thoroughly stuck. But would that damage his quite slender legs?

"Am I insane, Soxie?"

Sox panted her total approval of Misha's existence, which suddenly made her want to cry. "You have no idea I'm leaving, do you? No idea how much I totally and utterly do not belong here."

She was going to free the ram. She felt as stubborn about it as Brant had been this afternoon at the track. She was going to prove to him that she could belong here if she wanted to, that she understood Inverlochie's place in his life and would never want to change that. And she wasn't going to do it in some stupid, ineffectual, ill-thought way, either. She was going to think it through and get it right.

Nu's jacket.

She pulled it off, assessing its potential as a sling, and decided, yes, if she could get it around the ram's back and armpits—leg pits?—she could attach the sleeves to the rope and…

Then what?

The four-wheeler. Attach the rope to that, and if she could position the four-wheeler in the right spot, she'd have enough traction, Sox could bark up a storm at the ram and then the silly thing would do some of the work himself. She actually thought that between the three of them, they could do this.

And it seemed important. Eighty thousand dollars' worth of proof that when she and Brant said goodbye to each other tomorrow morning, it shouldn't be said with bitterness and failure but with care.

She cared about this place.

She cared about his life.

She cared about *him!*

She looked at the terrain, the four-wheeler and the ram's position, and then moved the vehicle. It was a little hairy, getting it into the right spot on such steep, slippery ground. Getting Nuala's jacket around the ram was a struggle, too, and she hoped it would hold. She knotted the sleeves to the rope and the rope to the four-wheeler, and this was easier, even if the knots themselves would have earned her a failing grade on a camp-craft test.

"Okay, now, Soxie, do you know what we're doing? What's all that stuff Brant says to you? Wa-ay back, back around. All that sheepdog stuff. Do you know what I'm talking about? Could you just stand there behind him and bark so he gets the idea?"

She straddled the four-wheeler and started the engine, then took a deep breath. "Here goes, guys."

It worked. At first.

Sox barked, the ram bawled and began to slither, the four-wheeler moved slowly forward, skidding in the mud. And then it tipped and fell. The engine stalled on the way down. Misha landed in the mud, her torso on the downward side of the slope and her leg pinned beneath the four-wheeler.

Behind her, the ram bawled and struggled, tangled itself briefly in Nuala's jacket and then the jacket slipped over his back and he lolloped away, indignant and skittish and heavy with mud but free.

"We did it, Soxie!" Misha said. "Uh, not sure if I can get the bike standing up again, though."

She couldn't even get herself standing up. It was just ridiculous, she thought at first. Silly. All she had to do, surely, was slide her leg out, or maybe dig it down into the mud a bit deeper and then slide it out.

She looked at her mud-smeared, diamond-encrusted

watch, and it read three forty-five. Later than she would have thought. She must have spent a good twenty minutes working over the ram already.

Sox barked at her. "It's not as easy as it looks, girl," she told the dog.

She pulled, and something hurt. She pulled harder and it hurt more, so she stopped. She tried the digging-down idea, but the rest of her body had no traction in the mud, especially tilted downhill as it was, and after a further fifteen minutes of theorizing and struggling and swearing and catching her breath, she had to accept what had happened.

"Sox, I'm trapped. Can you go get help?"

Chapter Fifteen

When Brant got home from the track at four-fifteen, a taxi had pulled up at Inverlochie's gate, and a man stood beside it, along with a small wheeled suitcase. He was arguing with the driver in fluent but exotically accented English.

"How am I supposed to get to the house?" he yelled. "I can't even see it. And it is about to rain." He saw Brant pull over beside the taxi in his four-wheel drive. "Is it you who lives here?" he demanded.

At this point, Brant recognized him. "Yes, this is my place," he said.

"So he's your problem now, mate?" the driver asked tersely.

"Yep. No worries." He turned to the newcomer. "Gian-Marco, isn't it?"

The man nodded, his dark eyes flashing and his lips pouted like a child's. He looked like a Formula One version of the young Elvis. "If I had known it was this difficult to get around in outback Australia, I would have hired one of those battery-operated toy cars they offered me at the car rental."

"This isn't the outback, mate," the taxi driver drawled, saving Brant the trouble.

"I'll put your luggage in the back," he said to the racing driver. "Mind opening the gate?"

"Sure." Gian-Marco walked toward it, and the taxi drove off.

Brant loaded the suitcase and went through the opened gate. Gian-Marco shut it behind him and climbed into the front. "Let's just confirm. Am I in the right place?"

"If you're looking for Misha, yes."

"This is the house of her friend Nu."

"That's right. I'm her brother. Nu's brother," he added stupidly, as if Gian-Marco might otherwise have thought he was Prince Christian of Langemark. "I'm Brant."

"And where is Misha?"

"Did you tell her you were coming? Did she call you?"

"No. I wanted to surprise her. To be honest, I felt a little threatened by some…" He stopped, took out a folded piece of paper from his jacket pocket and thrust it into Brant's field of vision as he drove. "Is this you?"

Brant glanced at the piece of paper, then batted it away. "Wait till we get to the house. I can't look at it now. Is what me?"

"Hot new Aussie man."

This wasn't making any sense.

Well, nothing much would make sense to him at the moment, Brant recognized, after the horrible afternoon at the track—his stubbornness, his need to stir up a fight and prove to Misha that she didn't belong. His heartbeat quickened. They would reach the house in another two minutes and he'd have to face her.

With Gian-Marco Ponti in tow.

"Hot new Aussie man?" he echoed blankly.

"Only one magazine picked up the story, because, really, you can't know it's her, the picture is so blurred. It could be anyone. But the magazine says it is Misha. Princess Incognito Heals Her Broken Heart Down Under With Hot New Aussie Man," he quoted on a drawl. "Even if it's true, it's still trash, as always. But I thought it was time she and I ended the hostility, since we are getting married in three and a half months and most of the population of Langemark is involved in organizing the wedding."

Brant stopped the car, five hundred meters from the house. "Show me that."

He snatched it from Gian-Marco's obliging hand, his whole gut in a tangle of painful knots. The picture was less blurred to his eye than the racing driver had suggested. He knew at once when it must have been taken, and from where.

It showed himself and Misha standing in the front yard here at Inverlochie. Her blond hair was tossed loosely around her shoulders and they were grinning at each other. She had something in her hand that was hard to identify, unless you already knew what it was.

Brant did.

It was her brown curly wig.

The photo had been taken from almost exactly this spot, from the passenger-side window of a car travelling in the opposite direction, the day Shay and the photographer had done the story on him for *Today's Woman* magazine.

"Why are you here?" he asked Gian-Marco.

He shrugged. "To see if it's true. To tell her I've finished with Ariane. To get her back."

She doesn't want you back.

"So you do know that you've lost her, then?" he asked.

Gian-Marco laughed. "There's a very short distance, my friend, between losing a woman and having her crawling on the floor with her arms wrapped around your knees begging that you'll take her back."

"Is there? I wouldn't know. I don't treat women like that."

"Maybe you should," Gian-Marco said.

They didn't like each other.

Surprise, surprise.

Brant wrenched the four-wheel drive back into gear and gunned the remaining distance to the house.

"Where is Misha?" the racing driver asked again, the moment Brant had switched off the engine.

"I don't know," he answered, through gritted teeth.

It was the truth. He had no idea if she'd come directly home after their argument at the track. She might be halfway to Melbourne by now. The thought gave him a bitter, self-destructive kind of satisfaction. They both knew she had to leave. It might be easiest if she'd already gone, without a messy goodbye.

"She must be here!" Gian-Marco said.

"Oh, because you've shown up wanting her?"

"No, because the taxi driver said this was the second trip he'd made to this place this afternoon, and his first passenger, a very attractive blonde, had been happy to walk from the gate."

That sounded like Misha.

"Right," Brant agreed. "Then I guess she's here."

Except that she wasn't. Her rental car was parked out front, but the house was empty and silent, and when he called out, there was no reply. He abandoned Gian-Marco and checked the dogs, but their kennels were empty, too.

Drops of rain began to fall. He took his phone out of his pocket and called Nuala to find out if she'd taken the dogs, but she must have gone out in a paddock with Chris, because her phone was out of range and Chris's landline didn't pick up, either. Walking around to the carport at the side of the house, he discovered that the four-wheeler was gone.

"Is there a chance of coffee?" Gian-Marco asked, back inside. He seemed impatient and dissatisfied, but not the least bit concerned at Misha's absence.

Brant made the coffee quickly, because around here you acted hospitably toward guests, even ones that you didn't want. He poured a mug for himself, but after one sip he couldn't drink it.

"Misha must have gone for a run on the four-wheeler," he told his visitor. "Because it should be in the carport, and it isn't. Why the hell didn't you tell her you were coming? At least call from Melbourne, or something."

"I like the element of surprise. Take my advice, if you're ever in a situation like this. When you surprise a woman, you learn how she really feels. Besides, I wasn't sure when I'd fit the trip into my schedule."

"Well, she's leaving tomorrow. If you'd left it another couple of days your two planes would have passed each other in flight."

"She's leaving? What has she said?" He looked more alert and tense, suddenly. "She's gotten over her stupid attitude to the attention I get from other women, then? And the business of Ariane? It meant something for a while, yes, but it's over, now. A man is entitled to one last piece of freedom before he marries a princess, I think!"

"Look, this is between the two of you. I'm not going to get involved."

He *wasn't* involved. He'd signalled the fact pretty strongly to Misha herself, this afternoon, and he didn't regret it. Felt icy cold when he thought back on it, but didn't regret it, all the same.

Outside, he saw the rain coming down more heavily, and listened for the sound of the four-wheeler coming back. It was after four-thirty now, and the light had begun to go.

"Where is she?" Gian-Marco asked, showing his first sign of concern.

"I'm beginning to wonder the same thing." Brant frowned and looked out the window, then found himself saying, "She wasn't in a great mood when I last saw her," which earned him a sharp look from the Formula One driver.

"So she's punishing you? Giving you a scare? Just what she did to me by flying out here in the first place!"

"It's not." Brant knew Misha's reasons for coming here, and he trusted them.

"Listen, I don't care what's been going on with the two of you," Gian-Marco said, "if this is her attempt to pay me back for Ariane, if there is any truth to the story in the magazine. I want her back, but I'm not going to stand here waiting for her. I have a reservation at a motel." He checked a printed travel itinerary and read out the name of the place, pronouncing it uncertainly. "Could you run me there?"

With pleasure.

It was located in Holbrook. Not far.

But then Brant thought about Misha, the missing four-wheeler and the fact that she still wasn't back, and felt his spine begin to crawl. "Just let me make a couple of phone calls, first."

He tried Chris's house, and this time Nuala picked up. "I took Mon, but I didn't take Sox," she said, in answer to his question. "What do you mean Misha isn't back?"

He explained, avoiding any detail concerning their argument over that massive, crazy, self-punishing bet. "And Gian-Marco's here," he added.

"*What?* Listen, I'm leaving here right now and coming home. If you go looking for her, leave me a note saying which paddocks you're checking first, and I'll check the rest."

Brant put down the phone and Gian-Marco picked up his suitcase. "So? You know the name of the motel to tell Misha, when she deigns to return?"

"I'm going out to look for her." He felt his anger rising, along with his alarm. "Don't you want to help? Or at least wait to see if she's all right?"

Gian-Marco made an impatient sound. "Of course she's all right! She's like a little cat, that one. Nine lives." He grinned suddenly, his olive-skinned face lighting up with wicked appreciation. "And she tries to live all of them at once."

It was the first thing he'd said about Misha that Brant actually agreed with, and the first moment he'd been able to understand a part of why she might have once fallen for this man.

"She does a pretty good job of it, too," he said to Gian-Marco. "But if she's a cat... Cats don't like the rain."

It had grown even heavier, like a silver-gray curtain where it overflowed the gutters on the roof of the house and poured down to the ground. He remembered how quickly she'd started to shiver yesterday in the creek. Why would she stay out in this? Not to punish him. Gian-Marco was wrong. She never behaved that way.

His pulses quickened and an urgent energy flooded him. "I'm going to look for her. Something might have happened. You can wait here, or come with me."

Gian-Marco unleashed a rapid flood of Italian, half under his breath, and began an impatient pacing through the room, drawing in long mouthfuls of coffee at frequent intervals. "I'll wait," he said. "What use would I be?"

"There's more coffee in the plunger," Brant told him, then grabbed a rain jacket and a helmet from the mudroom and left the house.

The two-wheeler motorcycle was still down at the shearing shed, he remembered. Jumping into the four-wheel drive, he drove down there, his wheels slithering in the mud as he took the bends too fast and tried to scan the paddocks as he went. At the shearing shed, the iffy starter motor on the bike gave him its usual trouble and he cursed it until it finally started.

It was a difficult little machine to ride in these conditions, but it offered the best way of reaching the rougher parts of the farm. He stuck to the grass whenever he could, circling through this lowest paddock first and sending up jets of water when he wheeled through the sheets of rainwater spreading wider on the ground. No sign of Misha, the four-wheeler or Sox.

Now that he was right out in the weather, his sense of urgency soared and his stomach began to jump. Gian-Marco was an egocentric idiot to put this down to female games-playing. Something must have happened to her.

Something *had* happened to her.

He knew it deep in his gut, suddenly, and the knowledge went beyond his awareness of the accident rate of four-wheelers on farms and the increased danger in these conditions. He knew with every cell in his body that something was wrong, and could almost feel her need for him. She was out here somewhere, waiting for him to come, and he had to find her.

Oh, dear God!

He gunned the motorbike faster, until his own safety was in question, and had to fight to slow himself down, act rationally, think about where he should look and how the sight of her and the four-wheeler might be distorted by the fading light and thickening rain. He combed the creek paddock, the hill paddock, the front paddock, and then he went around the hill, over two more grids and across toward his far boundary fence. That was when he saw Sox come charging toward him.

"Oh, hell, where is she, Soxie? Have you been with her? Show me, girl, come on!" He felt newly energized by finding the dog, but ill at the fact that Sox was alone.

She wagged her tail and jumped up on the back of the bike. Feeling the continued thumping of her tail, he knew he must be heading in the right direction, and rode farther into the paddock until he saw Misha and the four-wheeler at last—both on their sides, sodden wet and muddy, on the steep slope of bare earth leading down to the dam he'd had bulldozed last spring.

Was she moving?

Was she conscious?

Was she...don't even think about it...alive?

"Misha!" he called out to her through a bone-dry mouth.

He couldn't hear a reply over the sound of the bike's raucous engine, and his level of fear climbed still higher.

Oh, dear God, if I lose her...I can't lose her...I might only see her a handful of times in my life after tomorrow, but as long as she's all right... That's all that matters. She just has to be somewhere in the world, *safe*, for the rest of my life.

He skidded to a halt on the grass and almost lost control of the machine. It fell over, and he didn't care. He ripped off the helmet and dropped it on the ground, struggled to say her name, and at last, just as the sound left his mouth, he saw her move.

"Mish! Oh, hell, Misha!"

"Tell me the truth, Brant," she called weakly. "Your dog has never seen any old episodes of *Lassie* on cable TV, has she?"

"*What?*" He lunged clumsily toward her, slipping again on the grass.

"She stayed right by me." Sox rushed up to her again, panting, and she patted the dog in a series of weak, shaky caresses. "She was a sweetheart. She kept me company. I think she would have stayed with me all night. But I wanted her to go and find you...like Lassie always did...and she wouldn't...and I started thinking...that you'd never come."

She was crying now, gasping, jerky sobs that shook her shoulders and stopped her from breathing. He gathered her into his arms, his heart light with relief and his head dizzy, and began to kiss her wet, muddy, ice-cold face, but then she hissed and told him, "Don't. It hurts if you pull on me. That's why I couldn't get free. As soon as I try to pull on my leg, it just hurts worse and worse." Her voice cracked again on the last word.

"Oh, lord, I have to get this thing off you!" He knew it

would be too heavy for him to lift on his own, especially in these conditions and especially in the controlled way that would make sure he didn't hurt her any further. He cursed himself for not insisting that Gian-Marco come with him, and knew he'd only avoided pushing the issue out of his own distaste for the other man's company.

Having done some first aid, he also knew that if her leg was seriously crushed, then it could be dangerous to remove the weight without medical help, but for the life of him he couldn't remember the detail on that. How long would it take to get an ambulance out here, anyway? What was the safest thing?

His relief, a minute ago, had been premature.

"Can you move your toes?" he asked. "Do you have feeling down there?"

"Feeling? My whole leg is half-frozen! I might never get the nerve endings back the way they were."

"But you can feel sensations? Cold? Mud? Pain? Move your toes for me, Mish."

She understood the implication behind the questions and nodded slowly. Seconds later she announced, "I can move it fine. I can feel mud oozing on it, and it only hurts when I try to pull it. I—I really don't think it's crushed. Just… pinned."

He reached down and squeezed her hand, but couldn't speak.

Searching the darkening landscape through the rain, willing himself to stay calm and rational, he found a thick, iron-hard eucalyptus branch torn from a big tree in some long-gone storm and now lying on the ground. He rolled a football-sized, lichen-covered granite rock down the slope and positioned it on the mud, then balanced the branch on top of it and slid the end of the branch under the side of the four-wheeler.

Would it hold? Would the mud be too soft? What if he had to leave her on her own again and go back to the house?

"I'm going to lever it up," he told Misha, hiding his doubts. "But I won't be able to move it completely. When the pressure's gone, slide out."

Fast, he wanted to add, but didn't.

If the branch gave way, or his own strength did…

He couldn't think about it.

With branch, rock and Misha in the right positions and ready, he pushed and the four-wheeler moved. She clenched her teeth and let out a high-pitched groan of intense effort as she dragged her body down the slope.

"Free?" he grunted. His whole body was shaking with the strain. He heard a crack as the branch began to break.

"Yes! Free!"

"Keep going!"

She rolled through the mud just as the wood cracked and splintered, dropping the four-wheeler back onto the ground. They were both shaking, while Sox ran anxiously back and forth between them.

"Can you stand? Oh, hell, Misha!"

"I'm okay. I'm okay," she sobbed. "Oh, thank God you came! Thank God you could get it off!" She stood awkwardly, the half-numb leg unable to bear her weight as yet. He checked it for bleeding, saw the hard dent in her flesh where the four-wheeler had pinned her, but the skin wasn't broken and neither was the bone. "Don't let me go…"

"As if I would." He held her hard, supporting her and making a vain attempt to warm her with the press of his body. "Why were you under that four-wheeler?"

"There was a ram stuck."

"Where?"

"There in the mud. You can see the marks where he was struggling. I got him out. I rigged up a sling with Nu's jacket, and moved him enough so he could free himself, but the slope was too steep and the four-wheeler tipped. I think the ram's okay. He went off with the others. I don't know where they are, now." Her knees began to buckle as she tried to survey the darkening slopes in search of him.

The rain poured down on them both, and he could feel how cold she was, and how precarious on her feet. It was almost dark. "Shh," he soothed her. "Forget about the ram. If he went off with the others, he must be in pretty good shape. I'll check them in the morning. Let's get back to the house."

Where Gian-Marco was waiting.

He didn't know how to tell her.

"First, Brant…"

"Yes?"

"Did you place that bet?" She stroked his face and looked at him, her eyes narrowed.

He didn't want to talk about it now. "Extra Fresh ran second."

"I know. I checked with the betting agency. Did you place the bet?"

"It's not—" he began.

"Don't *tell* me it's not my business!" She fought her way out of his arms and staggered two lopsided paces, rubbing at her leg. She gave a sob, part anger, part frustration, part pain.

He grabbed her back again and pulled her close. "Misha… You can't walk properly yet. Don't let's—"

"I've just spent an hour and a half stuck in the freezing mud proving that your life *is* my business," she yelled, gripping his arms and shaking him. "So damn well *tell* me if you placed a bet that would have left you eighty thousand dollars in the hole!"

He sighed. "No. I didn't. Okay? Happy?"

He felt the relief flood through her body as he held her, and knew he couldn't hold back the news about Gian-Marco any longer.

"I put a hundred dollars, win or place, on another one of Rae's horses in the next race," he said. "It's the biggest punt

I've ever made in my life and it didn't made a dent in how I felt, didn't help at all, but she came in third, so I made a profit of twenty-five dollars. Which is…so irrelevant I can't believe I'm wasting the words." He took a breath. "Then I got home, Mish, and there was a taxi standing at the front gate…"

"*Madre del dio!* Look at you!"

"If you'll excuse me, Gian-Marco, I'll just freshen up a little before we talk."

He burst out laughing at this, cutting right through Misha's attempt to erect a force field of royal manners. "Can I tell you that you still look beautiful?"

"Be my guest."

She walked steadily to the bathroom, concealing her utter lack of preparation for any of this. Brant hadn't placed that huge, horrible bet at the track, which counted as one check in the plus column, but he'd said nothing in response to what she'd told him about rescuing the ram—about proving to him that this place was her business. She'd given away so much, and he'd stubbornly and deliberately ignored it all.

And now Gian-Marco was here in Brant's living room, with a newly arrived Nuala keeping a suspicious watch over him and ready to say something one hundred percent supportive but massively tactless at the first opportunity.

My worlds have collided, and one of them is going to get destroyed….

The shower helped a tiny bit. She actually warmed up faster than she had done yesterday, because at least she'd been dressed appropriately in the first place this time, and even without Nu's jacket, the wool sweater she had on beneath it had helped her retain body warmth.

Wool was like that, she'd learned since coming here. It was one of the few fibers that remained an effective form of insulation when wet.

Under the streaming hot water, she laughed at herself.

Feeling proud and possessive about the favorable properties of wool fiber?

Oh, shoot, she was in deep here!

Nuala brought her the clothes she'd asked for and she
dressed in the bathroom. A princess didn't dart along the corridor to her bedroom wrapped in a towel when she had the
male representatives of the two radically conflicting halves
of her life waiting for her in an adjacent room.

"Are you okay?" Nu asked, through three inches of open
bathroom door.

"I'm fine, thanks."

"I'm not asking Princess Artemisia Helena of Langemark,
I'm asking Mish."

"In that case, no, I'm a total mess. But at least my leg's
stopped tingling. I think it's going to have a pretty big
bruise."

There was a beat of silence. "If you need to stay at
Chris's tonight…"

"I—I have no idea, Nu."

"You wanted your ring?"

"Yes. To give back to him."

Nuala handed it through the steamy opening in the doorway. "I'll let you get dressed."

When Misha emerged ten minutes later, she saw only
Gian-Marco. "Where are Brant and Nuala?"

He shrugged. "She has driven him in some vehicle to
pick up some other vehicle from beside some kind of shed.
Being tactful."

"Nu is rarely tactful. That's why I like her. I get tired of
tact. So we'll just cut to the heart of this, shall we?"

Gian-Marco laughed and came toward her, his hand ready
to caress her face. He had a good line in caresses—little
strokings on the inside of a woman's wrist, gentle pinches
of a cheek or chin, the ball of a thumb run along a lower lip.
They'd always worked, somehow, even when Misha had

known from the beginning how well practiced and frequently repeated they were.

She'd appreciated his expertise.

She liked people who were good at what they did.

Today, she cut him off, circling her own fingers around his wrist and then taking his hand. "I'm breaking off the engagement."

"Ba-by, don't get hysterical…"

She smiled. "Don't try that stuff, okay? It's stopped working. I'm not building up to a fight or a scene, here. I'm not playing games. I'm just giving you back your ring." She took it out of her pocket and gave it to him, depositing it in the palm of his hand and curling his fingers over it with a kindly pat.

I'm immune, she thought. I'm free of him. His charisma and selfishness and glamor, and all those little moments when he makes an effort and creates a connection, makes a woman feel as if she's the only one in the world. It's all gone. Coming here was the right thing, no matter what happens next.

Because she never would have had the freedom and space to make this emotional journey under the public eye at home.

His eyes glinted and challenged her, as he spread his hands. "Misha-a-a, no…"

"It's not a game."

"No?"

"I know you love to think it is." She looked into his face for signs of hurt or panic, but couldn't find any, confirming her instinct that this was more about ego for him. "I know you want me to appreciate that you've flown all this way out here to…whatever. Sweep me off my feet. But the engagement's off. I'm flying home tomorrow. I'll arrange everything with the palace. If you want to make a statement of your own, can you run it by the press office first?"

He got angry. "This is stupid, Misha! It has gone on long

enough, hasn't it?" He wrapped an arm around her waist and pulled her hard against his groin, letting his eyes sweep down her body so that she could see the thick curve of his black lashes. "You and I, we understand each other. You like a bit of excitement as much as I do. Are you really going to tell me that a few stupid photos in the press—which you've been a victim of yourself, now, you saw the cutting I brought—is going to ruin what we have? We're getting married in September and I can't wait. Don't you remember how I proposed to you? Don't you remember how good it was? We can live our whole lives like that."

He gave her his gorgeous, heart-stopping grin.

She pulled away. "Brant said you needed someone to run you to your motel in town. I'll get my keys."

"I won't stay there. There's no point now I've seen you. Drive me back to Melbourne, and we can have a luxurious night in the best hotel. We can go to dinner, drink champagne, go clubbing and fly out together tomorrow. Which airline are you on?"

"No, Gian-Marco."

"Okay, okay, the motel, then, since you are being stubborn tonight." He'd backed down so quickly that she knew he planned to seduce her into a different arrangement once they were alone in the car.

She gritted her teeth. "I'll get my keys."

Nuala dropped Brant at the four-wheel drive parked beside the shearing shed and wheeled around at once to head back to the house. "I don't trust that man alone with her," she explained, yelling the words through the driver's-side window of her own vehicle.

"But you trust Misha, don't you?" Brant said. "Leave them on their own a little longer to work it out, Nu."

She hadn't heard.

He followed her along the muddy track, holding back his

speed. Nu could play the fifth wheel if she wanted, but he was staying out of the way. It was a contradictory decision. Every cell in his body wanted to charge in there like a wounded bull, boot the Formula One driver out of his house, take Misha in his arms and tell her, "Stay. Don't go tomorrow. Don't go, *ever.* Just stay."

But he wasn't going to do it.

No matter what happened with Gian-Marco, Misha needed to go home to Langemark and he needed to prove to himself that Inverlochie was still a profitable concern without taking help from anyone else.

Back at the house, the rain had temporarily stopped, although the trees still dripped in the darkness. Must be time to eat, but no one had even thought about it. He climbed out of the vehicle and met Misha coming out of the house.

"I'm driving Gian-Marco to his motel," she announced in a brittle voice that was far too bright and upbeat. "Want me to pick up pizza on the way back?"

"Misha, you have to go with him," Brant heard himself say.

In the light spilling from the house, her eyes widened. "*Go* with him? You…you want me to? You can't!"

"You have more to talk about, don't you? You have to work out a press statement for the palace. You're supposed to be getting married in three and a half months. There must be…protocol. Don't turn it into a mess by not communicating with him properly, because you know it'll all go public."

"Brant—"

"You'll regret it. Do this right. You're leaving tomorrow anyway, first thing in the morning. You're packed. What's the sense in staying any longer?"

Misha heard Brant's relentless logic in disbelief. Nuala had come into the house a few minutes ago with the air of a suspicious dog face-to-face with the mailman. Now she was standing guard while Gian-Marco went to the bathroom.

He'd be out any minute. Misha intended to deliver him to his motel, pick up pizza—she really wanted pizza—then come right back here and...

"A whole night's not worth anything to you, Brant?" she whispered. "Our last night?"

"I think you should leave," he repeated. "I think it would be easiest...for both of us...if you leave tonight."

His stubbornness goaded her, and stripped everything down to its starkest level of truth.

"I don't want to leave at all," she blurted out. "I want to stay."

"No." His jaw looked as if it had turned to stone. "That's only postponing the inevitable. And you're braver than that, Mish."

"Am I?"

"Yes. You have to go. You have to talk to Gian-Marco to-night and fly back to Langemark tomorrow. That's your life. You have to live it, work it out."

"I'll talk to Gian-Marco, then I'll come back here. With pizza."

"You have to leave, and start living your life. You're already packed. So go with Gian-Marco now. Forget the damn pizza."

He meant it.

She could see it in the way he held his body, the way he didn't look at her, and she could hear it in the way he kept repeating the same thing over and over. He'd made up his mind. He was ending it right now, and the last night she'd wanted so badly because...because even another hour with him would be precious and worthwhile...it would never happen.

She heard Gian-Marco behind her. "Ready?"

"Gian-Marco—"

"I am dead on my feet. We'll talk in the car."

"I'll get your bags," Brant said.

"There are still things I haven't packed. Last-minute things."

"Pack them. We'll wait." He said *we* as if he was some kind of prison overseer, standing by to make sure that the execution went ahead. "Do you need Nuala to help?"

"No, it's just a few things to go in my carry-on bag." She couldn't even think, and knew she was bound to leave something behind.

Her hairbrush in front of the mirror.

A discarded sweater on the arm of a chair.

Her heart, bleeding.

"Put your suitcases out in the corridor and I'll load them in," Brant said steadily. "Go, because it's already getting late."

She couldn't speak, just nodded and fled on shaky legs toward the house.

Chapter Sixteen

"Oh, sweetheart, it's so wonderful to see you!"

"You, too, Mom. It's—it's such a long flight!"

Queen Rose enfolded Misha in a mother's warm, familiar hug, in the morning room at Rostvald Castle, traditionally the summer residence of the Marinceski-Sauverin family for over three hundred years. The aroma of rich coffee filled the air, and two members of the royal staff waited for the resumption of their planning meeting with the queen, who was dressed impeccably as usual, in a cream angora cardigan and pearls over a silk blouse and linen skirt. Outside, the early-summer sunshine shone brightly on the gravel walks and beds of formal flowers, and the air felt steamy and mild.

"I'm sorry I didn't come to the airport," Queen Rose said. "But you know how it is."

Misha knew how it was. If ever the king and queen met a flight at Rendhagen's international airport, the runway was closed to all traffic for at least an hour, and every incoming or outgoing passenger experienced major disruption and delays.

"You've put on some weight, I think," her mother said.

"I've been eating well and working hard."

"Working?"

"Around the farm."

"Nuala expected that from you?"

"No, of course she didn't expect it, but you know me. I get bored. It was different. Great, actually."

"But you're on edge. You're tired…" She looked at Misha, then turned to her staff. "We'll pick up after lunch, I think," she said. "I'd like some time with the princess."

The two women nodded and told Misha cordially that they were happy that her break had been a success, then left the room.

"Gian-Marco showed up," Misha said as soon as the heavy gold-and-cream-painted door had closed behind them. "The day before I left. He'd seen an article in the press."

"Oh, I know the one. Only one magazine picked up the story, thank goodness. The others must have thought the picture of you was too blurred, which it was. The palace issued a statement saying there was no truth to the report. It really could have been anyone."

"You didn't tell me about seeing it."

"I didn't see the point."

"So you didn't believe it either."

"Hot New Aussie Man?" Mom quirked her mouth. "Should I have?"

"It was, um, Nu's brother. That's all." Misha managed to make her voice sound casual, even though she couldn't say Brant's name.

Her mother accepted the statement. "You were telling me about Gian-Marco," she said.

"I told him the engagement's off. He had…uh…a little

trouble coming to grips with the idea, but he's got a handle on it now."

She knew her mother would recognize a certain amount of understatement.

And she hated to think back on her drive into Holbrook that rainy, horrible night. Just two nights ago, she registered in disbelief. Here in Langemark, it was still only Monday morning. Gian-Marco had laughed at her as they drove. He'd ridiculed her, tried to seduce her, made promises to her, sworn that once they were married he would be utterly faithful, insisted that if she went through with cancelling their wedding she would break his heart.

She'd stayed firm.

He'd moved on to insulting her—*frigid, naive*, and *neurotic* were the words she remembered—and had slammed the car door when they reached the motel. Gritting her teeth, she'd stayed long enough to make sure he was successfully checked in, and then she'd left. She hadn't told him where she was going.

Melbourne.

Three and a half hours through the increasing rain, farther from Inverlochie…and Nu's brother…with every swish of the windscreen wipers.

She'd checked into an airport hotel, thankful that she'd learned from Gian-Marco that he would be flying on a different airline when he went back, with London his final destination in readiness for the British Grand Prix. Right now, she didn't know where he was. Midair, possibly.

"Can we draft a formal announcement right now, Mom?" she said quickly. "While it's being vetted, I'll call Mette Janssen and the bishop at St. Margrethe's." She thought of a few more people who deserved to hear the news personally. The director of the Langemark National Orchestra. Some of the younger and livelier members of Europe's various royal families, with whom she was friendly. "I want to get it public and over with as quickly as possible, and when the dust has settled I want to—"

She stopped. She had no idea what she was going to do next. Ahead of her, the summer dragged. Her schedule had been filled with planning meetings about the wedding—all of Nuala's concerns about menu and decor and guest list, magnified tenfold in the case of a princess.

Those cancelled meetings would leave a gap, as would her scheduled trips to the US in July and Hungary in August to watch Gian-Marco race, also to be cancelled now. She had her charity work, various public appearances, the usual wardrobe and scheduling meetings, twice-weekly riding sessions.

All of it seemed pointless.

The only thing that held any appeal was the time she always spent with Christian and Graziella's two boys in summer. Graziella was a slightly overprotective parent, and Misha liked to tease her sister-in-law a little, just occasionally, by getting the boys wet and muddy in Rostvald Lake, or hyping them up with chasing games right before bedtime.

"Graziella's still feeling pretty queasy," her mother said, as if she'd read Misha's mind. "Maybe we could have the boys here for an extra couple of weeks and leave her in Rendhagen to rest."

For a moment her spirits lifted. "That would be great!" But then she frowned. "And after that, Mom, I have to find something real to do, something that has a direction and a goal. I can't live my life like this, or I'm eventually going to meet someone else like Gian-Marco who's wrong for me, and repeat the pattern all over again. I—I couldn't bear that. I don't want to."

She couldn't picture such a man right now. She could only see Brant, who felt so right—him and his world—but who'd sent her away without even a final night together. He'd shaken her hand before she climbed into her rental car on Saturday night, in the same distant, smoldering way he'd shaken it the afternoon they'd first met.

"You're flying back to Australia at the end of August for Nuala's wedding…" Mom said.

Misha was all too aware of this. She said with desperation creeping into her voice, "By then, I have to know what I'm doing next."

For the first time, she began to have the tiniest inkling that Brant might have done the right thing in sending her away.

Brant gave himself three weeks and three days—the amount of time that Misha had spent at Inverlochie. He hadn't heard from her, and hadn't expected to.

He knew that Nuala had had an e-mail, though, because on Tuesday morning she confronted him at breakfast, flourishing a sheet of paper printed out from the computer, demanding to know, "What the heck is Misha asking me about, here? Do I know if you've had a result on the test sample from the P.P.B? What test sample from the P.P.B., Brant? What does she mean?"

"I had them come out and test the new ewes for foot rot."

"*What?* We have infected sheep? And you didn't tell me?"

"We don't have infected sheep. It's shelly hoof. I got the result yesterday. It has delayed the contracted sale on the other ewes, but their feet are still in good condition so it hasn't affected the price. They'll be going this week. The new ones will need a bit more work. I was getting pretty sure it was shelly hoof even before the P.P.B. got back to me, so I've been doing some cleaning and paring, but there's more still to do. Time lost, but not money, apart from a couple of days' worth of contract labor."

"And you didn't tell me?"

"You can help with the hooves if you want."

"You didn't *tell* me!"

"Boy, I will be so glad when this wedding is done with!"

"This has nothing to do with the wedding, Brant."

"But it has to do with your future, and Chris's. What would you have done if it had been foot rot?"

"Told you that you couldn't buy out my share of Inverlochie at the price we agreed."

"Exactly."

"You're horrible!"

"Because I want to safeguard your future with Chris?"

"Because you keep me so totally out of the loop!"

"Yes, because when I tell you things, you start yelling."

"What else aren't you telling me?" Nuala demanded. "Misha sounds a bit strange in her e-mail. What did you two talk about on Saturday night, while I was babysitting Gian-Marco? What is going on?"

It was a long three weeks and three days.

At the end of it, Brant bought a plane ticket to Europe, and this time, since Nuala didn't want to be kept out of the loop, he told her what he was doing.

Her reaction was terrifying—she barely said a word.

Delivering him to the airport in Albury, having promised that Sox, Mon, the chickens and several thousand sheep would be fine under her care in his absence, she gave him a huge hug. "You're a good person, Brant."

"Not horrible, after all?"

She hissed in a breath through her teeth. "I just hope you have a chance at what you want, that's all."

"You don't think I have the ghost of a one, do you?"

Nuala pressed her lips together and shrugged. He fought her pessimism in his heart halfway around the world.

Two little boys needed a garden hose jetted over them before they even went onto the pristine sandstone-paved castle terrace, let alone inside. Misha took them around through the castle's kitchen garden, where tender green lettuces and spinach plants sat in military rows almost ready for picking, and the frond-like leaves of carrots grew taller every day.

The royal trio startled the head gardener. This was his domain, not theirs. He hurried toward them, frantically wiping his dirt-stained hands on the back of his pants. "Your Highness…"

"We got a bit wet," Misha announced. "We need a hose."

"A hose?"

"To wash off."

"The water is cold."

"So was the water in the lake. We'll live."

"Your Highness…" He picked up the length of green plastic, but couldn't bring himself to hose down a toddler prince, a princess and the four-year-old who was second in line to the Langemarkian throne.

Sensing his scruples, Misha kindly took it from him and squirted her nephews, raising a series of happy, hysterical shrieks and ending up half-drenched herself as they splashed her.

"Your Highness…" the head gardener said for the third time.

She turned. "Seriously, we're fine, we're—" She stopped.

"Hello, Misha."

Brant.

Not possible. Simply not possible. She'd had three e-mails from Nuala since she'd left. Nu had said nothing about this! Nu would have warned her. Someone on the castle staff would have warned her. All of Nuala's family and contact details were on file for security so it was no surprise that Brant had been allowed in, but… how could he be here?

Then she saw Mom's principal private secretary rounding a turreted corner of the castle, wringing her hands nervously, and realized that this was the warning. Miss Heiningen had been looking for her, but it was Brant who had immediately known to follow the sound of the shrieks.

"Um, we're a little wet," she told him.

"I know," he said. "I've seen you this way before."

He was grinning.

And at the same time frowning.

Misha wasn't thrilled with the frown.

"Take…" she said to Miss Heiningen. "Take…"

Oh, shoot, she'd started shaking. He'd come. He'd just shown up. And she was thrilled and scared and all over the place.

"You want me to take the boys." Miss Heiningen looked slightly appalled at the request, because they still weren't very clean. Her training gained the upper hand, however. "Come along, darlings," she said to them, polite and bright. "A little more under the hose and then we can go inside via the—the—"

"Scullery," Misha suggested. The stone-floored space offered further washing possibilities, and was her own favorite entrance to Rostvald Castle. She suspected that Miss Heiningen may never have used it.

When the secretary and the two sodden princes disappeared in that direction, and the head gardener took himself discreetly to a distant toolshed, she discovered how hard her heart was beating, and that she hadn't taken a decent breath in quite a while. Her denim shorts had patches of moisture all across the front, and so did her pale pink T-shirt.

She looked down.

Yep. Semitransparent in several places.

But Brant had seen her looking worse.

"You didn't tell me you were coming. I didn't…miss a message, or—I—I know I didn't."

"Somebody told me recently that surprising a woman can sometimes be a good idea, when you want to find out how she really feels."

"How she feels?" Misha echoed shakily. "Oh, lord, can't you tell? I can't believe it." She pressed damp hands to her burning cheeks, and then a fist to her beating heart.

"Wh-what are you doing here?" she asked him, still aware of the frown on his face.

"Feeling slightly encouraged by the fact that you still get messy even when you're living in a castle." He came closer.

"That is not an answer."

"Make this easier for me, Mish, please?" he muttered, taking her hands. She stepped back about two inches and shook her head, panicking totally. "I've come all this way. I left you alone for nearly four weeks, but now I need to know. What were they for you, those nights we spent together? And the days? A holiday fling? Or something real? You have to tell me if I have this all wrong."

"You were the one who sent me away," she whispered back. She gripped his hands harder, and his familiar warmth and scent surrounded her. "I said I didn't want to leave, that I wanted to stay, and you refused to listen. I so much wanted one last precious night together, and you said no. You kept telling me over and over, you have to go, you have to go. As if you didn't want me at all."

"No, sweetheart…"

"I drove all the way to Melbourne that night, wondering how it had happened, how I could have made it different. Miserable about it. And still worrying about those damn sheep!" She gave a shaky laugh.

"How could I let you stay, when you'd only come to Inverlochie because of another man, and because you needed the space? Your real life is here, and my real life is on the farm. You had to come back…"

It sounded too much like another rejection, and yet he'd flown halfway round the world to deliver it. Had she gotten it wrong again?

"…even if only to sort out your future so you could leave again," he finished.

"Leave again?"

"Yes." He dropped his voice so she could barely hear. They

were still gripping each other's hands, their arms twisted together and their thighs touching. "To be with me. To live in my world."

"You want me with you?"

He swore under his breath. "Misha, I've wanted you since about the second day after we met, but I know it's crazy. It's impossible. You know how I live. I'm not rich or powerful or famous. Nu said something... she said that even if something could happen between us, it would turn Inverlochie into a hobby farm and I don't want that. I'm successful in my own terms, but not in the eyes of the world."

"You're successful in mine."

"Yes? I'm just a farmer with land and family and animals and friends that I care about."

"You think that's not the best kind of success? It's where my own mother came from."

"I hoped...I didn't know. But I had to give it a chance. If there was a hope in hell that you felt the same, that my priorities were important to you, that my life...my way of life...meant something to you, I had to give it the best shot I possibly could. But I had to give you a chance to say no, too, to get your feet back on the ground."

"And that meant sending me away..." She'd begun to understand this herself—that she had more to prove to both of them than rescuing one ram in a muddy paddock could achieve. She'd done so much difficult thinking since she'd been back in Langemark.

"Yes, and then coming after you." He parted his lips and brushed them across hers. Her whole body began to tingle, and to remember. "To see if three weeks could count for something, to see if they were still important, and if you wanted to try to make this work."

"I do." Because she knew now that it was real. "Oh, Brant, I do!"

They held each other. With the beautiful castle rising behind Misha, and the lake sparkling through the trees, Brant's arms were what felt like home—her place of safety, her place of belonging, her future. He kissed her more deeply, his mouth so perfect and right in the way it moved on hers, but their kiss was only the beginning. After a moment he pulled away and looked into her eyes.

"Don't promise too much yet. We have a lot to work out. I'm not going to let you rush it, or rush it myself. We can't mess this up."

"We're not going to mess it up." She touched his face, tracing the lines of his lips, cupping his jaw. "Oh, Brant, I will do anything not to mess this up!"

"Me, too," he muttered, his mouth warm against her hair. "Whatever it takes. With my whole heart, and every breath in my body."

And she knew he meant every word.

The bride looked so beautiful. She swept onto the dance floor with her new husband, calm and confident and smiling. They squeezed each other's hands in a gesture of commitment and reassurance which said more than words, and then they began their first dance as man and wife.

At the bridal table beside Brant, Misha's vision grew blurred.

Nuala had almost gotten through her wedding day at last. It had gone without a hitch, every bit of it beautiful, and incredibly the universe had not come tumbling down around her.

"Our turn," Brant whispered to Misha as she watched Nuala's gorgeous silk dress floating and swirling through the room.

He pulled her lightly to her feet and they joined Nu and Chris, Frank and Helen McLaren, and Chris's parents on the dance floor. "Do you think there's a chance Nu will get back to normal after tonight?" he whispered to her.

"Do you want her to?" she whispered back.

He looked at her in astonishment for a moment, because indeed Nuala had been pretty emotional—translation, unbearable—over the past few months, but after some thought, he said slowly, "You know what, I guess in a way I don't. When she isn't hysterical over the wedding, she looks pretty happy."

"She does," Misha agreed. She whispered a kiss against his jaw and added, "But not as happy as me."

"No? Got some more detail on that statement for me?"

But she only smiled at him.

He knew how happy she was. And he knew why.

He'd stayed at Rostvald Castle for six weeks over the summer—six weeks of sun and sailing on the lake, hiking and horseback riding in the woods, picnic meals and formal functions, playing with the little princes and taking anonymous minibreaks in picturesque little hotels dotted around Langemark, or in nearby Denmark and Sweden.

Eventually, of course, he'd had to fly home, but this time they had both known that their separation was only a temporary thing. Misha had her ticket to fly out for Nuala's wedding, and when she had shown up at Inverlochie this week as planned, several days ahead of time, Brant had seen the mountain of luggage she'd brought with her and his eyes had lit up.

"Planning a long stay?" he'd drawled.

"I've cleared my calendar until November. I hear there's some shearing to do."

Nuala and Chris would be flying to an island in the Pacific tomorrow morning for a two-week stay, but Misha felt as if she and Brant were already on their honeymoon. Only one thing remained to complete her certainty about the future— the fateful words from Brant himself.

She knew him pretty well by this time, and when he bent his head even closer toward her as they danced, she knew what he was going to say. Other people had joined in the bridal couple's first dance, now. Chris's two sisters and their husbands, relatives and friends all circled on the floor.

Misha's heart felt as light as Nu's swirling dress, and she didn't need hot-air balloons, champagne and a huge diamond ring this time around. She needed exactly what she had—people she cared about nearby, and a private moment in the middle of a crowd, with the man she loved.

"Is it our turn, Misha?" he whispered, just as he had before they started to dance. "Our turn for this next? You know how much I want it. Will you marry me?"

"Yes, oh, yes!" she said, and they danced until they were laughing and dizzy.

Later, when Nuala threw her bouquet, Misha leaped into the air like a basketball player and caught it in one hand.

Epilogue

They were married the following June.

The sun shone that afternoon, making the king's hair gleam with distinguished shadings of silver beside Misha in the royal horse-drawn coach on the way to St. Margrethe's Cathedral. "So, sweetheart?" he said gently, the rhythmic clip-clop of hooves forming a backdrop of sound that kept his words private despite the two footmen and the coach driver, for her ears alone.

"So, I'll be glad when it's over," she answered.

"But it's what the people wanted. We had to do it this way, so the whole country could celebrate."

Thousands of people lined the streets, waving the flags of Langemark and Australia, cheering and calling out their good wishes. Misha knew that Brant would be able to hear them from where he waited in the cathedral, and she felt a flutter of nerves, knowing how much it had cost him to put himself through all of this—the preparations, the protocol, the publicity, the television cameras in the cathedral and the foreign dignitaries at the bridal banquet.

"And it's your farewell," her father added quietly.

Because she and Brant were not returning to Langemark after their honeymoon in Hawaii. It had been announced to the people of Langemark that Princess Misha would be making her home in Australia and giving up her public duties. She and her husband would visit, of course, but her role as a princess would be very much a part-time one now.

"Is that really okay, Papa?" she asked, with a sudden pang. "I know you and Mom love him, but would you have preferred to find a role for him here?"

The king was silent for a moment, then he began slowly, "When your mother married me, she married a kingdom as much as a man. When she and I talked about you and Brant, we realized that you were doing the same. The challenge will be just as great as the one your mother faced, and the rewards will be just as rich. We had no doubt, when we thought about it, that you would rise to such a challenge, and that it was the right thing." He squeezed her silk-clad shoulders. "But we will miss you so much."

He pressed his lips together and couldn't speak. Waving an absent hand at the cheering crowd, he took a moment to gather himself and finally put on a smile. "This reminds me... I commissioned your groom to buy a gift, and I wanted to give it to you before we reached the cathedral, so we are running out of time."

They had rounded a corner and there was St. Margrethe's, the guard of honor, the crimson carpet and the coach containing Misha's attendants just pulling up in front.

"A gift...now?" Misha said.

"This may be the only time in the whole day when you and I are alone." At a moment like this, the well-wishing crowds didn't count. "You are wearing the St. Sebastian diamond tiara for your wedding, but when you take it off, you'll need to replace it with something very different. Think of me when you wear it, sweetheart, and think of your mother, and know how much we love you and wish you well."

He placed the gift in her lap. It was light, a round box wrapped in white and gold paper. She pulled the end of the ornate bow and slipped her freshly manicured nails beneath the seam in the paper, reached for the box lid, lifted it aside… then laughed.

Her father the king had commissioned her groom the sheep farmer to buy her a brand-new Australian sheep farmer's broad-brimmed felt hat. She lifted it up and the crowd saw it and cheered. "What do you think?" she asked the king. "This? Or the tiara?"

"They both suit you admirably, my dear," her father said.

Then the royal coach pulled up beside the sweep of pristine carpet and Misha alighted and went to meet Brant, to pledge her life and her heart to him. He was waiting for her, with a smile on his face and a light in his eyes that she vowed would keep burning forever.

* * * * *

OUTBACK BABY

BY
LILIAN DARCY

Chapter One

The best way to get work done on an airplane was not to look out the window.

As always, Shay Russell had a ton of work to do, so she didn't look out the window once in three flights. Taking off from Sydney airport, she opened her laptop the moment the flight attendants announced that it was permitted, and barely took her eyes from the screen long enough to ask for coffee.

It came lukewarm, and was accompanied by the cookies she'd by this time learned to call *biscuits* when talking to Australians.

She was from New York.

She was busy.

She wished she didn't have to adapt her vocabulary to Australian conditions, even though she'd been here for a year. Half the TV here came direct from the U.S. Australians knew what the word *cookie* meant. Culturally, her

New York–based boss at *Today's Woman* magazine considered Australia to be the fifty-first state. He was wrong, as it happened, but she wished Australia would listen to him. It would make her job a lot easier.

Between Brisbane and a dot on the map called Charleville, she stayed focused on laptop, electronic organizer and handwritten notes. And on the mail plane's final hop to Roscommon Downs, she thought solely about her magazine's circulation figures until she felt the final dip of the descent.

The wheels had just touched down when she finally looked up to see the sun glinting on a wide stretch of silvery lake lapping almost to the edge of the airstrip.

Pretty.

Birds wheeled in a blue sky. Other birds splashed lacy arcs of water into the air as they landed on the lake and folded their wings. Some dark reddish brown cattle grazed on the thin stretch of grass between the airstrip and the water.

Very pretty.

She would take some photos of it, with the hopefully photogenic Dustin Tanner and his new fiancée, Mandy, smiling in the foreground. It might even make a good enough cover shot for the magazine. She was pushing the "Wanted: Outback Wives" campaign as hard as she could, but the shot would need to be pretty special.

As soon as the plane came to a halt, she hopped up out of her seat, impatient for the pilot to open the door and let her out. She was the only passenger, and hers was the only suitcase he had to unload. It was the small, efficient, wheeled kind, and she grabbed it from him saying a quick, "Thank you," and began to trundle it along the hard, damp clay of the airstrip toward the four-wheel-drive vehicle awaiting her.

"No worries, love," the pilot said in reply, apparently in as much of a hurry as she was.

Looking at the pretty lake—the pretty *big* lake—he pulled a couple of boxes from the bowels of the aircraft. He put them on the ground, waved at the man standing beside the vehicle, wrenched the cargo hatch closed and leaped straight back into his tiny cockpit.

While walking toward the waiting vehicle, Shay remembered a research detail she needed from her assistant for next week, and flipped her electronic organizer out of her jacket pocket to note it down in cryptic shorthand, keyed in with one hand. She'd gotten very good at that. Her stride stayed exactly the same.

Somebody passed her. A woman, heading for the plane. "Have fun," the short brunette said, but didn't stop.

"You, too," answered Shay, equally brief. She was still looking at the tiny screen in her hand.

Behind her, the airplane engines began to rise to a screaming state of readiness for takeoff. Ahead, a man in sunglasses, a gray polo shirt and jeans waited beside the four-wheel drive, as motionless as the trunk of a tree. It might be Dustin Tanner, but she wasn't sure because they'd only met once, months ago. She vaguely thought he'd had a couple of friends who'd also submitted their details for the "Wanted: Outback Wives" campaign. A guy with blue eyes, from South Australia? Callum? No, Callan. Or was she confusing both men with other people?

They'd had such a huge response from single farmers all over Australia, it was hardly surprising that she couldn't keep track. Even though Dustin had been pictured in the magazine at the beginning of the year, she'd retained no visual memory of him at all.

Reaching the solitary figure, she hedged her bets and simply stuck out her hand. "Shay Russell."

"Shay…" He muttered something under his breath. Then he swore. "The magazine!"

"That's right." She smiled. "We—"

"Met in Sydney, at the magazine cocktail party," he finished, to her relief. He flipped his sunglasses up and wiped his fingers across his eyes before dropping the dark lenses back into place. "That's a while ago."

"Yes. Yes, it is," she agreed.

So this tall, dark, strongly built stranger was indeed Dustin. Good. There need be no more fear of awkward misunderstandings if he had turned out to be a ranch hand, or whatever they called them out here.

Shay switched at once into professional-gush mode, at the same time remembering with the unused portion of her brain that there was something else she needed Sonya to research for her in Sydney. Would she be able to e-mail or phone from here?

"Thanks so much for agreeing to a follow-up story, Dustin."

"Call me Dusty, but the thing is—"

"Dusty. We are so excited about the whole thing. An engagement, with the wedding date already set! It's wonderful. It will thrill our readers, to find out that our campaign has had some success stories so quickly." She hated gushing. He didn't seem too impressed by it, either, so she stopped and switched tack. "Um, can I put my bag in the back or something?"

Fifty yards away, she heard the plane begin to taxi along the red dirt runway. The engine speed seemed particularly high and the noise made talking difficult.

"I'm sorry?" His strongly drawn face wore a blank expression.

"Put—my—bag—in—the—back," she yelled.

"But…didn't you see her?" He still looked blank. His not-too-full, not-too-thin bottom lip dropped open, showing even white teeth.

"No, I said—" she began, even louder.

He cut her off. "I'm talking about the engagement. It's off. It's only just happened." He wiped his eyes with his fingers again, this time barely troubling to push the sunglasses out of the way. "That's her. You spoke. Didn't she say?" He pointed over her shoulder.

Shay turned, followed his gesturing arm and saw the plane's wheels just leaving the ground. The airstrip shimmered with what looked like a desert mirage. Dusty swore again.

"Her?" she echoed. "Mandy? Your fiancée? In the plane? As in…leaving?"

"Right. Ex-fiancée. It's over. She's not coming back."

Shay looked helplessly at her surroundings—at the damp airstrip, at the flat horizon, at that really quite enormous lake. It appeared to spread around to the opposite side of the airstrip as well, which made the airstrip's location an odd choice. It was more like an island than an airfield.

"The engagement is over?" she clarified to Dusty, just in case she'd still gotten it wrong, because—because—

Oh, hell!

"Yes," he said, and walked past her to pick up the boxes that the pilot had left on the ground.

As he came back in her direction a few moments later, carrying the boxes, she looked at him more closely.

Hmm.

She wasn't surprised that Mandy had gone.

Or maybe he only looked like this *because* Mandy had gone. He was rigid with suppressed emotion, and there were lines of stress folded into deep grooves at the corners of his nicely shaped mouth.

He had an ancient felt hat wadded into one hand, and hair that could do with a good brush. His polo shirt was untucked on one side, but he'd pushed it too tight into the waistband of his jeans on the other. She had an out-of-character maternal impulse to fix his clothing.

Was it maternal? There was a sudden kick of awareness inside her that in better circumstances he might actually be a very good-looking man, the kind to appeal to a very different set of female instincts. He had a great facial bone structure, an impressively tight, hard stomach and not an ounce of fat on his entire frame, but, maternal impulse or not, she'd have to tactfully persuade him to tidy up a little before—

Before the photos for the magazine story?

Shoot!

Triple shoot!

The realization ambushed her again. Her story was dead.

She had personally introduced this couple, Dustin and Mandy, at the cocktail party in February that had launched phase two of *Today's Woman* magazine's "Wanted: Outback Wives" campaign. They had apparently hit it off at once. They'd spent most of the evening together, and had started e-mailing and calling each other as soon as Dustin had returned to Roscommon Downs.

He had come down to Sydney to see Mandy and she had come up here to see him. They had fallen in love with satisfying speed. Dustin had proposed. Mandy had accepted and had called Shay, all tearful and excited, to announce the news and ask if Shay wanted to do a follow-up story. The woman had displayed a naked hunger for the publicity, but Shay wanted the story anyhow.

And now Mandy had called off the whole thing.

It hit Shay like a blow to the stomach.

She'd come all this way…time out of her schedule… forcible separation from her office space…extra expenses to justify…for nothing. Her hair was already turning to frizz in the lake-induced humidity. And for some incomprehensible reason, neither Dusty nor Mandy had managed to tell her not to come before she'd gotten here.

She opened her mouth and took a big breath, ready to cut her losses and launch into some rapid-fire questions about getting away again—ASAP. The plane with Mandy in it had already taken off, which was an incredible nuisance. When was the next mail flight? Shay had been scheduled to leave tomorrow afternoon, but if she could go very first thing in the morning instead, she wouldn't have wasted a totally timetable-crippling, career-scuttling, nervous breakdown–inducing amount of time on this fiasco of a romance.

But then something stopped her from speaking—a sudden rush of intuition and understanding that was the equivalent of someone clapping their hand across her mouth to prevent her foot from shoving itself in.

Dusty is feeling really bad about this, she realized.

Gutted, as Australians said. That was why he had failed to clarify the situation in time.

Shay would have to possess the hide of a rhino and the tact of a flea to pester him about flight schedules right now.

"I'm sorry, this is bad timing, isn't it?" she said. He'd put the boxes in the back of the four-wheel drive and pushed his sunglasses up again. He had incredible eyes, the color of deep pools of warm brandy, and his eyes were suffering. His mouth said he was trying not to let it show, but the eyes were winning. "To have me show up like this? I'm sure you'd rather be alone."

"Uh, yeah. It's okay." His mouth barely moved as he spoke. His square jaw looked as if someone had wired it shut.

"Well, no. It's not okay. I've been there. I know." It was the same for everyone, wasn't it? "You want to lick your wounds and eat junk food."

"Junk food?"

"Yeah, fat, salt and chocolate. A broken heart is *the* best flavor enhancer."

He didn't smile. They were strangers, and he wasn't ready. She thought she could see a chink of vulnerability inside him like hot lava behind the cracking seam in a rock. He was deeply uncomfortable about it, too. He wore the vulnerability like boots that didn't fit.

Meanwhile, she'd triggered too many of her own bad memories.

She remembered the weight she'd put on two years ago, and only just managed to lose again, after her most recent, should-have-been-perfect-for-her art museum curator boyfriend Adam had intellectualized his way out of their relationship. He'd fed her all this stuff about "meetings of the mind" and "fractured perceptions" that she'd tried so hard to understand, but no longer bought for a second.

Her discovery two weeks later that he had already been sleeping with someone else had something to do with her change in attitude. She'd been so hurt, and then so angry. She'd buried herself in work even more than usual because success was definitely the best path to recovery. She hadn't been out with anyone since, and that was just fine.

Once bitten, twice shy.

Or in her case, three times bitten, shy until further notice.

"Don't worry about the story for a minute," she said to him. "I'm really sorry. You said it only just happened?"

She wanted to touch him, give a sympathetic pat to his shoulder or arm—both body parts were so sturdy and well muscled—but managed not to. His body language screamed at her not to get that close, not to break down his rock-hard defenses with too much feminine understanding.

What did outback cattlemen do in this situation? They

couldn't stay up half the night crying over chocolate with their women friends, and wondering out loud and in great detail what they'd done wrong. They had to suffer in silence.

"She came out of the bedroom with her bags packed twenty minutes ago," he said. "I thought she was happy. I thought we both wanted the same things."

"So you haven't even been able to talk to each other about it?"

"There was nothing to say. This place *wasn't what she'd been expecting*, apparently." His tone placed bitter quotation marks around the words. "Once she'd said that, there was really nothing left to talk about." And he didn't look as if he wanted to talk about it now. His voice was rough and every word abrupt. It occurred to her that maybe he was always like this. "Look, we'd better head back to the house. And don't worry, I'll live."

He picked up her suitcase, heaved it in beside the boxes, closed the rear door, then came round to her side. He held the passenger door at a courteous angle, inviting her to slide into the high seat. She did so and, as she passed him, she became aware once again of what an impressive physique he had. The way he held himself, his whole body looked like carved sandstone.

"I won't trespass on your privacy any longer than I have to," she said.

She understood that she must be the last person Dustin Tanner wanted to be with because she could only remind him of Mandy and the way the two of them had met. And she was no less anxious to get out of here than he was to get rid of her. It gave them one thing in common, at least.

He came around to the driver's side, climbed in and started the engine.

"When's the next flight?" she asked.

"That's an interesting question," he growled. The vehicle idled as he looked sideways at her. There was an extra light of suffering emotion in the brandy-brown eyes. Impatience stretched to breaking point, she realized. "Notice the floodwater?"

The question brought her up short and she forgot about his broken heart. "The—? You mean the lake? Is it higher than—?"

He barked out a laugh. "This?" He gestured at the silvery expanse. "It's not a lake! It's Cooper's Creek, flooded nearly a hundred miles wide, and it's still rising. We've been pretty dry here, but they had several inches of rain in the headwaters of the Thomson River and the Barcoo. There've been flood warnings on the weather report for the Channel Country for days."

"Uh, right, but I tend to focus on the weather a little closer to where I live."

Like, the small amount of weather she could see from her apartment's bedroom window in Sydney. Even then she usually found it irrelevant. She spent most of her time in a high-rise office. There, the air was dry and the temperature stayed at around seventy degrees Fahrenheit all year round.

"And Grant didn't tell you?"

"Grant?"

"The pilot."

"We didn't talk much." Certainly not about weather. "I was working on my laptop."

"You must have seen how much of a hurry he was in to get out of here?"

"Well, yes, but…" She trailed off, feeling dumb and out of touch. For a journalist, she had failed to ask any of the right questions. "So—so the next flight might not be until…" She hazarded a guess. "…The day after tomorrow?"

The vehicle started moving. Dusty looped it in an arc so he could head back the way he'd come. He pointed across Shay's line of sight, to the far end of the airstrip, above which the airplane taking Mandy away was still visible, hanging like a baby's crib mobile in the yawning blue sky. "See that?" He wasn't pointing at the plane.

"Oh—my—lord," she whispered. What she'd seen in the distance as the plane had taken off had not been a desert mirage. She could see it much more clearly now. The lake had invaded a third of the airstrip in a silent silver tide, visibly higher than it had been when the plane had first landed.

"The flood peak is still to come. The water's rising fast. The airstrip could be out of action for as long as three weeks."

"Three *weeks?*"

"Even when the water goes down, it's hard to take off if your wheels are stuck in thirty centimeters of mud. It'll need regrading before it's any use."

"So—so I'd have to take a bus?" Surely the public roads would be better maintained and more sensibly located than this ill-thought private airstrip.

"You think there's a bus out here?" A smile flickered and died on his face.

She knew he was feeling bad, that he had a broken heart and needed kid-glove treatment, but this time the words came anyway. "Okay. There's no plane. There's no bus. I get that. And I don't suppose there's a boat." Her voice rose to a frustrated yell. "So will you just damn well stop making me feel like an idiot and tell me how I am going to get out of here?"

She wasn't.

Unbelievable.

Short of chartering a helicopter, which Dusty mentioned but she knew would run to, probably, a thousand dollars an hour, it appeared she was stuck. Roads were awash, low bridges were under two meters of water, cattle were being moved urgently to higher ground.

According to Dusty—his name should have been Muddy—people were stranded in way less comfortable circumstances than they were here at Roscommon Downs, so she had no right to complain. Even though she was only here thanks to him and Mandy in the first place, he seemed to feel that she should count herself lucky, and grateful.

"We have plenty of food and water, and plenty of room," he told her. "There's enough high ground for the stock, most have been moved already, and we have enough manpower on the ground to move the rest, so we've got no choppers coming in. No emergency service is going to make you a priority, I'm sorry, so if you want a flight out of here, yes, you'll have to hire a private one and pay for it yourself. If there's one available."

"You could have told me this before I got here! You could have told me before the damned plane left!"

"I would have thought you might see news reports on the flooding, realize it was risky and not show up. To be honest, I'd totally forgotten you were coming until you got here, and even then it didn't click until you said your name."

"But Sonya confirmed—"

"Sonya spoke to Mandy," he cut in.

"Mandy—"

"Wanted the story and her picture in the magazine, even if she didn't want the engagement. I had no idea she'd confirmed your visit. I've been pretty busy."

"Sounds like you weren't talking to each other much."

"Apparently. I didn't notice."

"You didn't *notice?*"

"I hate those kinds of games. If she had problems, she should have said something straight out, not tried to manipulate me into asking what was wrong."

Silence.

Shay didn't know what to say.

Finally, she ventured, "So it'll probably be for…?"

"A couple of weeks. It depends on whether there's any more rain. If we had a medical emergency, you might be able to hitch a ride out on a rescue helicopter. Our boreman's wife has a baby due in four weeks."

So what was he suggesting? That she give the woman curry and strong drink to bring the birth on early?

Maybe I could find a hunting gun and shoot myself in the foot….

For a moment, Shay almost considered the idea.

You know, it could work….

Just a flesh wound. Something that would require evacuation and qualified medical intervention but wouldn't threaten her life. Something that would allow her to use her laptop in the hospital and would leave her free of scars.

Perfect. I'm contemplating a bullet to protect my career.

Her boss would probably expect no less.

She gave a half-hysterical hiccup and tried to think about what being stuck here for two weeks would actually mean. For a start, would her boss in New York believe her, or would he think it was merely a thin cover story for a personal crisis of some kind? Tom Radcliff was notoriously unsympathetic to any senior personnel with time-consuming private lives.

The Australian edition of *Today's Woman* had launched ten months ago, and Shay had been promoted to editor-in-chief, flown to Sydney ahead of the launch and put in charge—partly because she showed no evidence of having a private life at all. So far, the promotion was not an enhancement to her résumé. Circulation figures had been disappointing. Shay had her theories about why, but Tom didn't want to hear them.

Recently, the series of articles centered around their campaign to match lonely farmers with willing women had shown the promise of paying off. The story Shay herself had tracked down and written for the June issue was particularly strong, she thought. City-bred European-American girl falls in love with good-looking Aussie sheep farmer. Brant and Michelle—"But please call me Mish"—made a gorgeous yet down-to-earth couple.

Was this kind of story strong enough? Her boss only ever revealed the hard numbers on his own timetable—one that was designed to keep his staff under maximum stress—so she couldn't know for sure.

She had pushed hard for the whole "Wanted: Outback Wives" idea, and she needed it to pay off, and soon, or Tom would pull her back to the U.S. He would put her on *Boring Hobbies Monthly* or *Make Your Own Plumbing Fixtures* or one of the other dry yet solidly successful special-interest magazines that were part of the Shieldpress Corporation's publishing stable, and her climb up the ladder would effectively end.

She'd fought hard for her career and she wanted it.

Really wanted it.

Didn't want that horrible realization she'd seen happen to other people that somehow you'd missed the boat, taken a wrong turn, been sidelined or overtaken or promoted sideways and everyone else had seen the writing on the wall before you had.

Absolutely did not want to run into Adam—or Jason, or Todd—in the lobby of Carnegie Hall and have to say to them, "Me? My career? Oh, I'm editing the women's pages of *Gun Dealer News* now."

Her hunger to feel like a success snapped at her heels like a wild dog. It woke her every morning at dawn with a sick feeling in her stomach and chased her late into the night. It had her eating take-out meals in front of her computer and yelling at dumb ideas in meetings, and only getting as much work as she did out of her staff because she herself so clearly put in way more than they did.

To sell *Today's Woman* to the Australian market, she needed top international celebrity gossip, a good astrologist for Your Stars, some lifestyle and cooking, a couple of thought-provoking articles, and heartwarming *local* human interest, and she had to get it right, which was why she'd chased this romantic outback-engagement story herself instead of leaving it in the hands of more junior staff.

Now, as well as wasting her time, she was stuck.

Through the front window, she saw water spreading across the track ahead, and asked Dusty Tanner, "Where are we headed?"

"To the main homestead."

"Will we make it? Or would we be better off in a submarine?"

"This is the last stretch of low-lying ground."

"The whole place seems like low-lying ground, to me. Why have a cattle ranch—I mean, station—" she corrected herself. *Biscuit* versus *cookie, station* versus *ranch*; why did Australians have to invent new, non-American words for everything? "On flood-prone land?"

"Because it's just about the best natural fattening country on the planet."

"When it's not flooded," she pointed out.

"You've struck it lucky. It doesn't flood this bad every season. This is the first time we've had the airstrip under water in four years."

"Well, aren't I just so fortunate?"

They didn't like each other.

The fact was suddenly apparent to both of them and magnified by the close confines of the vehicle. Something coalesced in the air like perfumed smoke and made Shay's stomach jump. She stabbed her finger on the window button and it lowered with a hum, bringing the scent of grass, mud and rain, but doing nothing for her sudden claustrophobia.

Dusty's strong arms worked the steering wheel back and forth as he avoided more water on the road. The movement brought his elbow too far into her body space. He had one of those big, manly arms that Shay had seen in gyms, and she'd never liked men who made too much of their physical strength. She liked her males civilized, intellectual and good-mannered.

Maybe Dusty would be good-mannered enough to pick up on her desire for silence and respect it.

Nope.

"You'll be okay," he said. "We'll make the best of it."

"Thanks. Do you have any evidence for those claims?"

"Maybe if I told you a bit about the place," he said.

"Sure. If you think it will help." She could see a large cluster of buildings and greenery near the top of a low rise. Behind the buildings, probably a couple of miles away, rocky cliffs rose above the flood plain, looking hardly more substantial than a garden wall.

"Well, for a start, it's big, almost half a million hectares."

"I'd like to be impressed, but you'll have to translate."

"One point two-five million acres."

"Now I'm impressed." She knew she sounded insincere. Over a million acres? Huge, but just a number, and the only number she wanted to hear right now was an accurate estimate on how many hours before she could get out of here.

"Many of these places are owned by international agribusiness," Dusty said. "They have a whole slew of properties scattered all over the country, and put in a manager on each one. But we've managed to keep Roscommon Downs in the family since my great grandfather's time. My dad's health has failed a bit, so my parents have moved to Longreach, which is our nearest decent-size town."

Shay pricked up her ears. "Oh, yes?"

Walking distance? Or better make that *wading* distance.

He must have read her mind. "Three hundred and sixty kilometers from here, a lot of it under water."

She did a quick conversion in her head. Over two hundred and twenty miles. She'd die before she got there. Literally.

"We have a good staff, eleven people not counting me," he went on, as if he hadn't just completely broken her spirit with the news about Longreach.

"That many?" This surprised her.

"We're almost a village. Twenty-five people. We have married couples, and kids, a governess running a school. She has six students this year."

A few of the shattered pieces of her spirit glued themselves back together. Kids. A school. Other women. Small mercies, maybe, but a heck of a lot better than the kind of Robinson Crusoe scenario she'd begun to picture—herself stranded on a shrinking island in the floodwaters with what was very possibly the least civilized man she'd ever met, and one who seemed totally uninterested in helping her to get out of here.

"I'll look forward to getting to know them," she said weakly, wondering if any of them had a dinghy and knew how to row.

"Mandy didn't—" He stopped. "Uh, didn't."

Was this a recommendation that Shay shouldn't get to

know the station residents either? They reached the build-ings. Nobody seemed to be around, which meant that she could focus on infrastructure instead of greetings. Climb-ing out, she assessed everything she could see.

There were several large sheds and a cluster of neat cot-tages. One larger dwelling looked more like a motel, with several doors opening onto a veranda and a couple of larger rooms at one end.

Dusty had parked in front of the main house—the homestead. Shay had been in Australia long enough to recognize the architectural style, even when it was sur-rounded by thick green shrubbery like this place. "This is the house," he said, stating the obvious as if it hurt him to get the words out.

It was a Queenslander—a single, sprawling level of living space, made of wood painted in soft pastel shades, surrounded by shady verandas, and built high on wooden stilts. The empty space beneath the house had been en-closed by pretty wooden lattice, but the stilts would allow cool breezes to circulate beneath.

And floodwaters? Would it keep them out, too?

Looking around, she decided they were on high enough ground to stay safe, even if the immense spread of water rose several meters higher.

Dusty grabbed her compact little suitcase, snapped the pull-along handle shut, ignored the option of wheeling it, and picked it up as if it weighed less than a bag of grocer-ies. Possibly it did. She'd packed light. One complete change of clothing and an extra set of underwear for an emergency—which this officially now was. The underwear would have been more useful if it had had jet packs at-tached.

Most of the contents of her luggage consisted of short-story manuscripts submitted for the magazine's Good Read section. They'd had a contest recently: "Could You Be a Writer?" Unfortunately, about three hundred of the submissions had come from people who absolutely and utterly *couldn't*, but the stories in her suitcase belonged to the short list of thirty, which she and two junior editors would cull to five finalists before the winner was judged by a panel of professionals.

On the plus side, with all that reading she'd have something to do while she was here. On the minus side, she'd need to alternate her two outfits and wash one of them every night, and she'd left her styling wand and blow-dryer at home. By bedtime, she was going to look like Shirley Temple with her finger in a lightbulb socket.

"I could put you in the single men's quarters," Dusty told her with no hint of sarcasm, "but you'd probably be happier here."

They went up the half flight of wooden steps together, and Shay held her breath.

To her surprise, the place was beautiful. More latticework enclosed the veranda almost to waist height, making it feel like an airy extension of the house itself. The old wooden floorboards were stained a dark teak color and gleamed with varnish. The furnishings, both on the veranda and inside the house, had an Asian feel with big blue-and-white planter pots, and a couple of exquisite inlaid wooden cabinets, as well as regency-striped couches in dusty blue and cream that somehow matched the cool, clean atmosphere while almost begging Shay to sit down.

Following Dusty, she resisted the temptation. She'd have plenty of time to turn catatonic later on.

Passing the dining room, she saw a breakfront filled with Asian china and Italian glass, and on the walls there was a mixture of framed art that ranged from kids' drawings dedicated in wobbly print *To Grandma* through to what looked like original modern landscapes in oils.

Strangely enough, the effect was very appealing, and she realized how cleverly the colors and themes of each picture had been balanced. Whoever had decorated this place—*Grandma* maybe?—had a great eye.

"But this is just lovely!" she exclaimed, sounding way too surprised about it.

"Yeah, even though my mother took the best stuff with her and Dad to Longreach," Dusty drawled, throwing Shay a look that said he knew exactly what she'd pictured instead—corrugated iron walls flapping in the breeze, and six-week-old dishes in the sink.

He led her to a bedroom that opened via French doors onto the veranda and had a similar atmosphere of dark wood and blue-and-white coloring. It was cool and quiet and restful; it had a bathroom just across the corridor; it had books, a ceiling fan and a rocking chair, and Shay knew that as soon as Dusty told her where to plug in her phone recharger and her laptop, she would feel about sixty percent more fine about this whole thing than she'd believed possible ten minutes ago.

Except that she didn't.

She felt four hundred percent worse.

Because when she had her overnight bag on the bed and her portable office up and running and Dusty had left her alone, she discovered an urgent e-mail from Sonya, sent about half an hour ago, just seconds after the final time she'd checked her system on the plane.

Crisis, Shay! Abort outback engagement story mission, stat! Tom wants you in New York tomorrow!

Chapter Two

Dusty's unwanted guest stayed in her room for much longer than he'd expected.

He wasn't sure what to do about it.

It was a nuisance.

He had expected her to appear again, and he would have offered her tea or coffee and something to eat. He would have given her a towel and explained that the shower water would be hard to keep at the right temperature today because Wayne needed to bleed the air out of the pump. He would have said to make herself at home, and told her what time to show up in the dining room of the single men's quarters for the evening meal.

It was largely his fault that she hadn't gone straight back on the plane and saved them both this unwanted complication, but that didn't make him feel any more warmly toward her.

Now, thinking that she could appear at any moment, he

hung around, on edge. There were a hundred other things he could be doing, but he couldn't just leave the house. She was a guest, and around here you looked after your guests. Should he knock on her door? Write her a note?

He didn't want her here, didn't want to have to consider an impatient city-bred workaholic stranger's needs. The breakup with Mandy had been a gut-wrenching mess, and Shay-from-the-magazine's presence only reminded him about all the mistakes he'd made in the relationship from the very beginning. His whole system felt sour whenever he thought about it.

Hell, he was usually so sensible, so down-to-earth, but could he pick the right woman? Clearly not.

How could he have been so blinded by Mandy's apparent eagerness?

It wasn't even as if the chemistry between them had been that hot. This was one of the things he'd told himself in the moments when he'd allowed himself to have doubts. "I'm not rushing into this. I can tell, because it's not about lust." He knew a thing or two about lust. "And that's so often what makes people jump in too fast. This is solid. It's friendship and partnership and shared goals, and it's going to work."

He felt like an idiot. He knew that he had earned the respect of everyone who worked here for reasons that ran deeper than his degree of success with women, but all the same he didn't want Dave and Jane, or Prim and Letty, or Luke and Andy and Wayne talking about him and Mandy behind his back.

He wasn't hurt. He'd already discovered that, with a sort of numb surprise. But he felt empty, increasingly angry with himself, and deeply disappointed.

Putting the electric jug on to boil for a cup of coffee he didn't really want, he ran through the past four months again, and the mistakes remained on display in just the same unflattering light. He'd heard too much of what he'd wanted to hear from Mandy's lips. He'd seen too much of what he'd wanted to see in the way she'd behaved. He'd missed so many clues. Would he ever find a woman who played things straight?

"I *have* to get out of here!" said an American voice behind him. He hadn't heard her arrive in the kitchen doorway because of the rising noise of the water for his coffee coming to the boil.

He turned around, surprised at the intensity in her tone, to discover that her lips had gone white and she looked as if she might collapse onto the floor. "Are you okay?" he asked.

"I'm fine. Totally fine. I just have to get out of here," she repeated. "Tonight. I have to be on a flight out of Brisbane in the morning. I have to get to a critical meeting in New York."

"I thought we talked this through on the way here."

"Yes, but the situation's changed." She clenched her fists. Somehow, she must have found time to do something to her hair. It fluffed out around her face in bouncy corkscrews, and suited her better than the sleek dark chestnut curtain that he'd seen blowing in the breeze out at the airstrip.

"The floodwaters haven't," he pointed out to her. "Except that they're probably higher." The electric jug reached a final crescendo of bubbling and clicked off, adding emphasis to his statement.

"You said I could charter a helicopter."

"I said if there's one available. And do you know how much it would cost?"

"Yes. The earth. I'll just have to wear it."

She closed her eyes, as if embarking on a minute's silence in memory of her deceased bank account. Then she opened them again and he noticed their color for the first time—an electric jade that was too intense for his taste, even though it went very nicely with her creamy skin and that hair—almost the same color as his cattle. She was the kind of woman who didn't know when to stop, never looked back to see who she'd trampled on, and had no idea of the way life worked in a place like this.

"Tell me who to call," she commanded him.

"It's four in the afternoon," he pointed out.

"I know. That's why I'm giving out this slight sense of urgency, Dusty." The sarcasm cut like a blunt bread knife. They didn't like each other much. She thought he was an insensitive brute, and he *knew* she was a power-hungry careerist with tunnel vision and no life. "You said you use helicopters for mustering."

"The company we use is based two hours' flying time away."

"But they'd take on private charters, surely. Where would they fly me to?" She took an agitated step toward him, glaring her impatience for his answers. She was pretty tall. Had to be around five-ten, which meant that even though he was over six feet on the old scale, she could look him almost straight in the eye.

"Depends where your flight to Brisbane leaves from. Longreach or Charleville," he said.

"I haven't made a reservation, yet. Longreach or Charleville? I'll get on the phone now." She'd already begun to move.

"There won't be any flights leaving late enough for you to get to Brisbane today." He shouldn't be enjoying this, but a part of him was—the same part of him that was still angry about Mandy, and the part of him that suddenly felt very sorry for anyone who had to work for Shay Russell.

She was so melodramatic, so clueless, so alien to the pace of life out here. Her eyes had narrowed, reducing the bright jade color to two thin chips, and if, out at the airstrip, she had seemed to have at least some idea of what a tough day this had been for him, she'd clearly forgotten about it now. "I *have* to—"

"Look," he told her patiently, "even if you can get a hired chopper to leave the ground at its home base in the next half hour, which is unlikely, you can't possibly get to Longreach or Charleville before nine tonight, and there are no flights at that hour."

"The chopper can take me all the way to Brisbane."

"Yeah? It's over eight hundred miles. At least eight hours, even in a fast machine like a Robinson R22, plus refueling. And it leaves out the issue of night flying, and the fact that every available pilot's going to be booked solid, locating herds and pushing them to higher ground. What time's your flight out of Brisbane tomorrow?"

"I haven't booked that yet, either."

"O-kay." It was like talking to a spoiled child. Any minute she'd start stomping her feet.

In the back of his mind niggled the thought that he might have a better chance of getting her out of here in a chopper than she would if she simply called charter companies cold. He had favors he could call in, and everyone knew the Tanner family.

He weighed his options. It was no contest, really. Getting thousands of cattle to safety, versus getting a workaholic American magazine journalist to some meeting in New York. In the past he'd seen the bloated carcasses of cattle who'd died in floods. The cattle had to come first.

"That flying doctor service you talked about…" she began, her desperation like a magnetic field.

This time, he just looked at her.

"So I'm going to lose my job," she muttered, her shoulders sagging and her lips numb as well as white.

"If your job requires meeting impossible expectations like getting from here to New York in twenty-four hours, personally, I'd have ditched it long ago."

At this point, she lost it. Color flooded into her face in two bright pink blobs. Her eyes darkened. She was shaking.

"What qualifies you to say that?" Her voice rose, tight and strident. "You have no right to make judgments about my life. I shouldn't be here at all! If you didn't know this time a week ago that your relationship with Mandy was in trouble, then what the hell is wrong with you?"

He flinched. "You're right. I should have known about Mandy. Believe me, though, if I could get rid of you, I would."

"Do you have any idea how much trouble you'd have saved me if you'd had an atom of perception about how your supposed fiancée was feeling—"

Yes. He did. He'd have saved himself just a bit of it, also.

"—before she had to spell it out in words of one syllable?"

He flinched again. She'd made him feel like a fool, despite the good brain he knew he possessed. "Look, do we have to talk about it?"

"We have to work out how I'm going to get out of this place!" she yelled. "It is absolutely critical that I am not stuck here for two weeks! Or even for two *days!* And I really do not think it is too much to ask for a little help from you, a local, in working out how I'm going to achieve that! Do you understand, or do I have to say it all over again?"

She put her shaking hand up to her throat, as if she'd strained her vocal cords. To give her the benefit of the doubt, maybe she didn't yell at people like this every day.

Still, Dusty had had enough.

"You've said all you need to say," he told her quietly, already on his way out the door. "Help yourself to anything in the kitchen. We have cattle to take care of. I need to talk to my head stockman, my grader operator, my boreman and my cook." He mentioned the erratic hot water delivery in the shower. "And dinner's at seven, in the single men's quarters. I'll see you then, and you can tell me what you've arranged."

"If I've—"

He cut her off to drawl, "I'll be on the edge of my seat about it, let me tell you, because I can already feel the spin of the earth slowing down without you there in the center of it all, turning the handle."

"Tell Tom I can't," Shay e-mailed Sonya, feeling sick. "It'll be two days at the earliest."

And that would only happen if she spent around twelve thousand dollars of her own money on helicopter hire, which was more than likely not available given the flood situation, then hit up her expense account at the magazine for a first-class ticket between Brisbane and New York, and flew via Tokyo.

Her head ached and her cheeks burned. So did the spot in her spine that always began to sting when she'd spent too long in front of a computer screen or hunched over a laptop. She'd yelled at a near stranger, and they'd both been pretty damned rude to each other. The fresh memories disturbed her, and she faced the prospect of dealing with him again very soon.

Dealing with him, maybe, for weeks.

She thought about putting a positive spin on the delay, and typed, *I am chasing a great outback human-interest story*. She looked at the words on the screen for about twelve seconds and then deleted them. They sounded lame and deluded.

Tom was testing her. Or maybe it was a power game, something that rode right over everyone else's interests. Either way, she could have found a story that involved a two-year-old saving his mother's life by riding three hundred miles on the back of the family dog and getting rescued by a Hollywood movie star on the way, and Tom wouldn't care.

Okay, no, with the Hollywood movie star he'd care, but if it was just the family dog and the three hundred miles, forget it.

She briefly wished that she worked for the kind of magazine where you just made stuff up, and the more sensational the better. But no, typically, she had somehow saddled herself with standards. How sad.

She actually believed in the value of what she did. She wanted to give the readership of *Today's Woman* an uplifting, well-researched, entertaining, *true* story. She loved the idea that lonely outback farmers might find lasting love because they'd had the courage to put their faces and their stories in a national magazine. Blue-eyed widower Callan, Luke with his award-winning Tasmanian cheeses, goodlooking Brant, shy Dale from Victoria, who rose every morning at four to milk his dairy herd. They'd all put themselves and their hearts on the line.

She wanted to make a difference in people's lives, even if it was only to have them think, *Hey, maybe something like that could happen to me, if I just made a couple of changes.*

Get back to me TODAY if Tom still wants me to come, she finished to her assistant, then hit Send.

Plotting the time difference, she realized that there was no way Sonya would get an answer from Tom today. It was getting on for seven in the evening, which meant nearly five in the morning in New York. Tom was a night owl. He must have been working into the early hours to have summoned her for the alleged crisis meeting three and a half hours ago, but even he wouldn't still be at his desk making dictatorial phone calls at this hour. Neither would Sonya, in Sydney.

She slumped her forehead onto the laptop keyboard, lifting it after several seconds to discover five lines of the letter *U,* keyed in by her right eyebrow. She'd have to call Tom at home, drag him out of sleep and say to him point-blank, "This is what I'd have to do to get to New York—in fact, to get out of here at all. Do you want me to do it?"

Sick to her stomach, she went to the phone in the kitchen that she'd already used to call airline companies. It was Dusty's private landline. There was no cell-phone service out here.

Her boss picked up on the third ring, sounding scratchy and half-asleep. It wasn't a long call. He wanted her in New York, without excuses. She then called every helicopter company she could identify within a radius of several hundred miles and heard all their answering machine messages. All over southwest Queensland, stranded motorists were being rescued, stock were being moved to higher ground, and busy helicopter pilots weren't picking up their phones.

Dusty was right.

She appeared to be stuck.

Leaning against the kitchen wall next to the phone, sipping some tap water, she felt light-headed, drained and empty inside, the whole meaning of her life reduced to two questions. How possible was it for her to get out of here? And as Dusty had so sarcastically suggested, what, exactly, would grind to a halt in the universe if she didn't?

Shay had no idea how to answer either of them.

"Dinner's on," the man himself said from the kitchen doorway.

"I'm not hungry," she told him automatically, wanting

to take as little from him as she possibly could. Truth be told, she was a little embarrassed that she'd lost her cool with him so thoroughly, earlier.

She straightened, tried to give a polite smile, and fought a sensation that the room was spinning. Her head was really burning now. All she'd eaten today were those cookies on the plane, and all she'd drunk was the coffee.

But she was used to that kind of thing.

Her body could take it.

Normally.

A couple of headache pills would help.

"How about if I arrange to have it delivered to your desk on a wheeled trolley with pre-warmed plates and covers on all the dishes?" Dusty suggested.

"Oh, you could—?" she began eagerly, then stopped.

Do that for me?

No.

He was teasing her.

If a dig so pointed and angry could be called a tease.

"I'll come over later, if I need to," she said coolly. "You go ahead." *Because then I won't have to walk across with you.*

He was clever, though, she had to admit. She hadn't seen it at first, but she could now. He didn't merely put her down; he trampled on her entire mind-set with every well-chosen word. She didn't like him, but she could still appreciate his brain.

He had stayed in the doorway, and she realized he was waiting for her, silently refusing to take no for an answer. Possibly because he'd seen that her knees were shaking. Maybe she was hungry, after all.

"I'll be there in a minute," she said, oddly grateful for his silent stubbornness. "I promise," she added.

"No, you'll be there with me. Take a minute if you

want, but I'll wait." He leaned his big shoulder against the doorjamb, to prove it.

"Why are you pushing this?"

"Because you look like you're going to pass out cold. And I'm not calling the flying doctor if you hit your head on the way down."

"I'll cross that strategy off my list, then."

"Yeah, it was pretty transparent."

"My choices are limited in that area."

"Sheesh, we're a crabby pair, aren't we?"

"Well, yes, since you're saying it without smiling."

"And I'm not going to apologize for it, either."

"What's for dinner?"

"I believe it's fillet steak with garlic sauce." He held his thumb and forefinger about an inch and a half apart to indicate the thickness of the steak. The odd feeling in her stomach was definitely a rumble. Her taste buds began to sing. She discovered she was starving. Was that a twinkle in his eye? Could he tell what the words *steak* and *garlic sauce* did to her? "Accompanied by Danish fried potatoes, seasonal vegetables, and peach cobbler and ice cream for dessert."

"I'd like to meet the other people on the station," she said.

"Yeah, they're not as crabby as me."

"But you're honest, I'll give you that."

"Point of pride."

"Honesty is good, but you want to be careful with pride. It's powerful stuff."

"You're right." He frowned, and she thought he was probably thinking about Mandy. Wretched woman.

"If you happened to have a headache pill or two, it might help."

"In the bathroom. Hang on a sec."

He came right back, holding out the two white pills. She'd already poured a glass of the tinny tap water she'd tried a short while ago. He watched her while she downed the pills in several gulps, then asked, "Going to be okay?"

"Hope so."

"That's what happens when you yell. And when you're the unfortunate mug who got saddled with being at the center of the known universe. Raises your blood pressure. Puts extra stress on the blood vessels in your skull."

"Thanks for that insight." There was no point in protesting that she considered herself quite a distance from the center of the universe already, and was desperately afraid that she'd one day end up in outer darkness. "I'll take it on board."

"My pleasure."

Without another word, he ushered her out of the kitchen, standing back to let her go ahead of him through the doorway, across the back veranda and down the steps. At the bottom, she tripped. The clumsiness was a combination of fatigue, poor vision in the sudden darkness, inappropriate shoes and her habitual impatience, and she wished it hadn't happened because he lunged up behind her and grabbed her elbow, throwing himself a little off balance as he did so.

For a moment, they clung together. His breathing went in and out with a slight rustling sound, as if he had his teeth clenched. He smelled as if he'd showered recently, although she hadn't heard him in the bathroom. It was a really good smell. Simple. Clean skin, damp hair, shampoo or some unusually nice kind of shaving cream.

"I'm fine," she insisted, before it was true. The ground seemed to tilt under her feet, even when her eyes said it was straight. "Really, I'm okay now." His grip hurt until she steadied herself further and the ground leveled again.

The air space between their bodies felt too warm. Finally, he let her go.

"Believe it or not, I actually do want you to get out of here alive, even if it's not today," he said.

"I'll look forward to proof of that claim."

"And I would like to continue this insightful conversation, but we're no longer alone."

Shay saw a male silhouette come through one of the motel-style doors in the building she and Dusty were heading toward. The large space at the end of the building was lit up and she could see some other figures moving around.

"What's the setup, can you tell me?" she asked. Her voice sounded wobbly. It was the headache. It had begun to shift into nausea, on top of the pain, and she hoped she'd taken the headache pills in time. She'd been having trouble with stress headaches lately, and if she got to the point where she threw up…she hated that. "You mentioned a cook."

She needed food.

Now.

"The families eat on their own, in their own places. Singles, living in the single staff quarters, get their meals cooked for them. At the moment that includes our pair of stockhands who got married to each other last year, as well as our bore-runner, gardener, governess and a couple of other stockmen. And Prim herself, of course."

"Prim?"

"Primrose McLintock. Our cook."

Two minutes later, Shay concluded that she'd never met a woman less like a Primrose in her life. No wonder everybody called her Prim, although this didn't suit her much better. She was about forty-five years old, round-bodied and red-faced, heavy-footed and hearty, and, if Shay's sense of smell could be trusted, she cooked like a dream.

She was also a voracious reader, it turned out. "Did my

new books show up?" she barked at Dusty. She served the meal cafeteria-style, with people lining up for their helpings then going to find a space at the big table.

"Already delivered," Dusty told her.

Instantly, he seemed different to the way he'd been with Shay in their interactions so far. This probably shouldn't have surprised her, but still it did. He held his body more easily. She was just as aware of its fitness and power, but it seemed more relaxed—a tool for hard work not intimidation. He greeted people with a word or a nod and, even though the atmosphere was casual, you would have known the moment you walked into the room that he was the boss.

"You weren't around," he went on to Prim, "so I shoved them inside the door. Give her a big helping," he added, thumbing in Shay's direction.

The food appeared on the plate, slap, splodge, splash, before Shay could protest and get the portions downsized to fit a sedentary urban lifestyle. Just the smell of it helped her stomach to settle, and if she could only get some of it into her in the next minute, she might just be okay.

Next to her, a wiry man named Andy said, "I finished that fine balance thing you lent me, Prim."

"Oh, you did?" The cook's face lit up. "Wasn't it amazing?" In an aside to Shay, she explained, "*A Fine Balance* by Rohinton Mistry. Fabulous book."

"The most depressing thing I've ever read in my life," Andy said.

"And yet, fabulous. Such a statement about hope." She filled Andy's plate generously.

"You know what, yeah, I could sort of see that. I didn't think I was ever going to get into it, but once I did, yeah, could hardly put it down, and you don't forget it. You should read it, Simone," he said to the young woman next in line.

She snorted. "I'm not a reader." Prim filled her plate.

"Prim'll get you in the end. She'll start you off easy with something light and funny, like those Bridget Jones books they made into movies, and she'll suck you in, and this time next year you'll be dragging your way through four hundred pages of poverty in India and thinking it's amazing."

"So shall we discuss it in reading group?" Prim said.

This time Andy did the snorting. "You are not getting me along to that damn women's group of yours, Prim."

"It's not a women's group. It's a reading group. We read books and we talk about them and gender is not an issue."

"It's a women's group. You and Letty and Jane and Marg and Bronwyn talk about the book for three minutes, then you get into the white wine and dessert, and talk about women's stuff."

"Get that plate a bit closer, Letty," Prim said to the next in line.

"Smaller piece of steak, Prim, thanks."

"Rubbish. You've been teaching all day, and then didn't I see you going for a ride? You need it."

Shay was seated opposite Dusty at the table by this time, holding her head together and her stomach in one place through sheer will. When Letty was satisfied with the size of her serving, she came to join them, with a hello and a smile. From Prim's comment about teaching, Shay guessed she was the governess. She looked to be about Shay's own age, give or take, and she had…oh, interesting detail…an artificial lower half to her left arm. Unselfconscious about it, she put down her plate, picked up her silverware and began to eat.

"Oh gosh, that's good," she said with her mouth full.

She spoke with an English accent, and had English-rose coloring—cornflower-blue eyes, delicate pink-and-white skin, and the shiny remnants of sunscreen slathered across her cheeks and nose. She started talking to Andy about the

book he and Prim had discussed a minute ago, and Shay
realized appreciatively that the governess was subtly drawing the young stockman into exactly the sort of book-
group discussion he'd been so scathing about. She was
probably an excellent teacher.

Shay's first thought about Letty was *Human-interest
story potential*. Her second thought was *Escape ally*. And
her third thought, quickly overtaking the other two and
surprising her so much that she forgot to chew was *Friend*.

Friend?

Aware of Dusty's steady gaze angling in her direction
every now and then, she considered the word and soon
dismissed it.

She had all the friends she needed in New York. Good
friends, and most of them in the same situation as she was.
Busy. Ambitious. Ladders to climb. Glass ceilings to shatter. Career women's health problems to suffer in many
cases, also. Stress-related stomach trouble, migraine headaches, debilitating menstrual cycles. Shay had been diagnosed with endometriosis a few years ago, and when she'd
told Alicia, who traveled constantly as part of her work in
international banking, Alicia had said, "Welcome to the
club."

None of them had enough time for each other, so the
friendship really existed between various cell-phone message
systems, e-mail accounts and answering machines rather
than between actual people. They had sporadic crisis meetings, rather than actually hanging out. Even her best friend,
Sarah, who'd always cared about different things, was hard
to pin down for some quality time now that she was a mom.

But they all moaned about it and laughed about it and
it kept them in the same boat, so they had a lot in common,
and Shay planned to pick up with her friends exactly as
before when she got back to New York a couple of years

from now. There was no reason to look for anything like that here at Roscommon Downs.

"I'm Shay," she said to Letty, and went back to the human-interest story potential. "Tell me what an English rose is doing in a place like this."

The meal lasted for three quarters of an hour and, by the end of it, Shay's headache and nausea had sneaked away without her noticing. Her stomach felt pleasantly full and the salty taste of the garlic sauce still lingered in her mouth. She felt different, and a heck of a lot better.

People had talked cattle business, told exaggerated anecdotes about previous flood experience on other properties, exchanged tips on which volume from Prim's extensive private library to try next. When Andy realized he'd been conned into having a book-group discussion, and that he had even nodded knowledgeably at the word *metaphor,* he scowled at Letty and Prim for a minute, then decided to laugh about it instead.

"You're gonna have me writing flippin' eight-page discussion papers next, Prim!"

Egos had to be both tough and relaxed around here, Shay guessed.

Everyone had reached the tea and coffee stage when she and Dusty left. He'd quietly asked her if she'd like to head back to the main house, and she was ready to go by this time, despite how much—and how unexpectedly—she'd enjoyed the meal.

She'd seen the respect he drew from his employees, and she'd noticed the way her gaze kept getting caught by his. They were too curious about each other and, if anything, the curiosity was heightened rather than lessened by the moments of open hostility between them earlier on. It felt weird.

"We've got coffee and tea in the kitchen," he told her. "Breakfast things, too, in the morning, although Prim does a great hot breakfast, if you want one. It's up to you."

Walking across the damp red earth between the two buildings, Shay took a deep breath and said to him, "Can we start again, do you think?"

"Start again?"

"I need to thank you."

"For dinner?" He glanced at her, and she wished she could see what his eyes were doing. Narrowing because he didn't trust her sincerity, probably. She couldn't blame him for that.

"For putting up with me. I've been incredibly rude today."

"So have I," he answered, blunt and easy.

She liked his voice, she realized—its pitch and its tone and its lazy speed. Her own was just a little softer and it hurt less in her throat when she told him, "But you had better reasons to be."

"Not sure about that. You were right, I should have jumped on Grant and got him to hold the plane five minutes for you. I should have thought straight away that you'd want to head back, once you'd heard the situation. I dropped the ball about that, and now you're stuck. I apologize."

"I'm calling helicopter charters again in the morning," she said, not sure if it was true.

How much was Tom Radcliff just yanking her chain? Did he really need her in New York for a meeting? Or was he only trying to remind her that she belonged to the magazine, and that her future was on the block? If circulation fell like a slicing guillotine, she was the one whose head would roll.

She could see her immediate future dividing into two distinct options, right in front of her. Respond to Tom's pressure and stay stressed and bad-tempered and antsy for as long as it took to make her expensive escape bid from Roscommon Downs? Or accept that she had little chance of getting out of here until the floodwaters receded and use the opportunity to—

Aack!

What was this emotional cliff she'd suddenly come to the edge of?

What was this can of worms sitting in front of her, with the opener already slicing into the lid?

Mentally, she veered away from it, slotting a quick, automatic and familiar pep talk into place.

I am not over stretched. I know what I want. I can do everything I have to do. There will be time later. I like my life. I am a success. The right things will happen. Everyone feels alone sometimes. This is what I have chosen. I am nothing like my parents. I mean, they disapprove of me so much, how could I be? Dr. Chin was presenting a worst-case scenario. I've got time for a child in a few years, if I want one, and I don't even know if I do. I'm fine.

Dusty stayed silent in response to her line about calling charter companies. She could tell he didn't think she'd find anyone to take her. She was glad he'd refrained from making a comment about it.

Grateful, in fact.

To be honest, she must be such an easy target.

They reached the steps up to the house and he stood aside to let her go first. She heard him coming up behind her, his work boots heavy and mellow on the old wood.

"Well, you're welcome here as long as you have to stay," he said, just as she reached the door.

"Yes. Thank you for that."

Because she could tell it was true. She'd seen it over dinner, in the way people talked to her, and in the way Dusty himself sat back and listened to what they all said.

In hindsight, she could even see it in the way he'd been so blunt with her about her chances of getting out of here.

She was a nuisance and she didn't belong, but she was welcome.

She hadn't done a single thing to deserve it, so help her, but she was welcome here all the same.

She didn't understand it at all.

Chapter Three

"You'll have some coffee, or something?" Dusty asked once they were inside the house.

"Herbal tea?" Shay hated the stuff—chamomile, peppermint, whichever kind she tried—but drank it regularly most nights, as a concession to the fact that her stress levels were too high and that she'd been told by more than one medical professional to do something about it.

"Sorry," Dusty said. "I don't have herbal. I only keep the basic kind."

It was preferable to coffee, so she said yes, then watched him casually get out an antique china teapot from the thirties or forties in the most gorgeous blue with a gold trim, warm it with boiling water and make the tea with real tea leaves scooped from an antique tin canister.

He had no idea he was doing anything special.

Suddenly, she wanted to meet his mother.

"Cup or mug?"

She almost asked for a cup, to see if this would be an antique, also, but bone-china cups and saucers were finicky and the idea of wrapping her hands around the hot sides of a big thick mug was too tempting.

They sat in the living room, each on their own puffy, squishy, regency-striped couch, each with their own big thick mug, and she said, "Tell me more about your family." She was a journalist; she was used to asking questions, picking apart what people said and learning who they were, looking for an unexpected story. If she and Dusty were drinking tea together, ahead of her enforced stay on his property, she could at least treat it as research.

"I have a younger brother who's working on a breeding property on the Darling Downs, but he'll probably come back here eventually when he's had more experience, and I have a sister who married a cane farmer."

Something in the way he said this last bit led her to tease him. "Sugarcane? Please! Like that's farming!"

He gave a grin of surprise that did something unexpected to his face. "Nah, it's just that my parents wish she was closer." The grin dropped away and Shay wanted to make it come back because she was still analyzing the unexpectedness.

The whole room seemed to get brighter when he smiled. Something shone right out from the heart of him, as warm as an open fire, as true as a compass pointing north.

But that was ridiculous.

"And your parents?" she asked.

"Think I told you, they're in Longreach." He gulped some tea. "Dad's stubborn, he should probably move somewhere bigger. From Longreach he has to travel too far for some of his medical stuff. But he's spent his whole life in this part of the country and he gets jittery anywhere else."

"And your mother, did she grow up around here, too?"

"Adelaide. Dad was sent there to school, and that's where they met. She's adaptable, my mother. She gets on with people, and she finds the best in them."

"And she loves beautiful things." She kicked off her shoes and curled her feet up on the couch, pivoting around so she could see him at a better angle.

"She does," he agreed. "What about your parents? From New York, like you?"

She nodded.

"What're they like?"

Time to put on her act.

"Oh, my parents are great!" she gushed at once, her voice automatically climbing half an octave to the level she kept for talking about things like family. "Successful, intelligent. They always wanted the best for us—my younger sister and me. We had an idyllic childhood." She drank some tea.

"Lucky," he commented.

"Oh, yes, I have been. Incredibly lucky."

There was a beat of silence. "Do you know something?" Dusty said.

"What?" His tone alarmed her a little.

"I think I like you better when you're being rude than when your voice goes up and gets all sticky like that."

"Sticky?"

"You did it when you first landed, too, talking about... yeah...how thrilled the magazine was about the engagement. I'm sorry, you really put me off with that. Like syrup. *My parents are great! They're ax murderers,*" he mimicked with razor-sharp accuracy. *"They eat small children."* He even got the American accent down right, with the tiny lick of New York that occasionally crept into it, despite the rigorous accent sanitization of her New England schooling.

She swore lightly, before she could stop herself. She fooled most people with the gush, even people she knew quite well. "How did you see that, when you don't know me?" she blurted out.

"I just like honesty better," he said.

"Uh, okay. Noted. And Mandy wasn't honest?"

"No. Sore point."

"Once bitten, twice shy?"

"Something like that."

It resembled her own state of mind. Shay could tell he'd kept something back, but she let it go.

"So tell me what your parents are really like, Shay," he said next.

Honesty.

Nice idea.

A million miles from nowhere, stranded with a difficult man and a hot mug of tea, why not?

"Well, you basically had it with the small children thing," she told him. "Lightly sautéed and served in a white-wine sauce. They're very civilized."

"Yeah?"

She added bluntly, "They're cold. And I never realized some parents were different, until I went home with a friend—my best friend—" Sarah still was her best friend, even though she had to maintain a marriage, her iffy asthmatic health, a new pregnancy and twins, so typically they never saw each other "—and met her family, and discovered…" Warmth and fun and honest yelling. Pizza in front of TV. Toys on the coffee table. Hugs for no reason. How did you summarize all of that? "That it could be different," she finished, unable to put it into better words.

Dusty finished his tea and put his mug down on the coffee table, then leaned back with his arm stretched across the top of the couch. A clock ticked on top of the dark teak sideboard and, from somewhere outside, Shay heard the lowing of cattle. Everything else was so quiet. She guessed the people on Dusty's station went to bed pretty early.

"But they must be proud of your success," he suggested.

"Success? Journalism? Ha! Please! Just maybe, if I was the political correspondent for *The Washington Post*, or something. But women's magazines? And by the way, where's my multimillionaire husband? Where's my fashion sense and charity profile and summer home?"

"So they were brought up to that lifestyle, I'm guessing."

She sighed because it was way more complicated than that. "Do you want to know which famous person I was named after?"

"Uh…" She could see him trying to think of any Hollywood actresses or Nobel Prize winners or ancient queens named Shay. He failed.

So she helped him out. "Che Guevara."

"The— No! The South American communist revolutionary from the sixties?"

"That's the one."

"Is that how it's spelled?"

"No, it's spelled how you'd think." She said it for him. *S-h-a-y.* "They changed it when I was four, just in time for me to get into the right kindergarten."

"Handy."

"Yep." She made the word come out flippant, so he'd understand that the childhood-revelation segment of the evening was over.

It didn't work.

"No, Shay," he said, "you can't stop there." His eyes didn't move from her face. In the soft glow of ceiling lights, they looked like brandy again—a big glass of it that you stared into, contemplating your life. "You have to tell me the whole story."

"Short version?"

"Okay, the short version. Another day, you can stretch it out."

She let that one slide.

"They both come from nice Protestant middle-class educated backgrounds," she told him. "My dad's family was wealthier than my mom's, pretty comfortable. He had a trust fund—he still does. But in their early twenties they went through a hippie phase, and lived in some weird community for quite a while. They had me, then rejected the hippie phase a few years later. Turned their backs on it about as much as humanly possible, in fact."

"And then?"

"They got married, had my sister—whose name is Jacqueline, and it's never, ever shortened to Jackie. Something about the whole alternative-lifestyle episode really scared them in the end. The possibility that they might have been fooled, I think. I actually think they're still scared."

She stopped, knowing she'd said too much.

"Yeah?"

She waved at him. "Just a theory. But, yes, I was named after a communist revolutionary."

"That's amazing."

"Bizarre, you mean."

"No, just interesting. Want to know which famous person I was named after?"

She laughed. "Oh, you were saddled with that, too? Dustin Hoffman, I'm guessing."

"No, Slim Dusty, the Australian country-music singer. Dad's idea. Mum humored him, but did insist that it was officially Dustin, in case I wanted to become prime minister, or something."

Shay laughed again.

"Do you remember the hippie community at all?" he asked her after a moment.

"Not really. Odd details. A meal I hated—something green—and my mother having this tense, grim little verbal tussle with one of the community heavyweights over whether I had to eat it or not. I don't remember who won. It's strange what sticks in kids' heads, isn't it?"

"And your parents didn't retain any good stuff from that time?"

"You mean the free love?" People had asked her this kind of question before.

"I mean…no, not free love. Just love," he said simply. "Hugs and mess and warmth."

The things she'd learned about from Sarah's family.

He'd expressed it in almost the same words.

She shook her head. "No, they didn't. I don't think they were ever very huggy. Maybe that was one of the things that drew them to the hippie lifestyle when they were young and more open. The promise of learning to hug." She flapped her hands. It sounded silly. But Dusty nodded anyway, so she kept going. "But, yeah, it scared them—or other things scared them—and they backed off and ran as fast as they could in the opposite direction."

"Sounds like you've thought about it a lot."

"I come back to it. Sometimes I don't think about my childhood at all."

"Wouldn't want me to think you were obsessed, or anything. Don't worry. I don't. But we get some interesting people out here. Interesting histories. It's one of the things I like about my life. I hear stories more complicated than you'd expect."

"Like Letty's?"

"You saw her arm."

"And there was something different about her left eye, too."

"Yes. It's made of glass. She was in an accident a few years ago, before she left England. I'll let her tell you about it."

The words implied that she'd have plenty of time to learn the full story because she was going to be here for days…because she was stuck with no way out…because he hadn't been on the ball enough to send her back with Grant in the departing plane this afternoon.

"If we're being honest, Dusty," she blurted out, "tell me what happened with you and Mandy and why you couldn't see it coming. It's isolated out here. I would have thought there'd be nowhere for her to hide, emotionally speaking."

He'd seemed perceptive just now. A good listener. Not nearly that blind.

Although maybe she'd been too honest. He was frowning.

She jumped in again. "I'm sorry. That's too personal, isn't it? Just because I chose to spill all that stuff about my parents, it doesn't oblige you to do the same."

"It's okay."

"Doesn't look as if it is."

"Well, I'm angry with myself, and you're reminding me of it."

"I'm a journalist. I'm trained to confront people with searching questions."

"I'll answer if you want. If I can." He frowned. "I usually pride myself on being…straight, you know? Seeing what I want, going for it, getting it right, not taking any bull, not making mistakes. But with women it hasn't worked. Can I get back to you when I've had more time to think about why?"

She groaned. "No, you can't! Stop doing that!"

"Doing what?"

"Saying things like you'll get back to me, that Letty can tell me her own story. Thus reminding me of how long I'm probably going to be here."

"You've seemed a little more relaxed about the fact since dinner. I didn't think it was a banned subject anymore."

"Did you give me tranquilizers instead of headache pills? I'm starting to suspect you did. No, seriously." Her turn to frown this time. "Relaxed, no. Lulled by my sheer powerlessness, maybe? Or in denial?"

She started thinking about it again—helicopter companies, airline schedules, the expense, what Tom might want, the relentless imperative of her career—and discovered that denial was a pretty good place to be.

"I—I think I'd better get to my room." She could start reading those story competition entries, kid herself that she was at least getting work done, and fall asleep over a pile of papers at around midnight the way she usually did. "Thanks for the tea."

"No worries."

She levered herself off the couch. "Why do Australians *say* that? *No worries*, instead of *you're welcome*. It makes no sense! It drives me nuts!"

"We're a nation of philosophers." He stood up, also, and picked up their empty mugs. "We like to remind each other, in daily speech, about our powerlessness to control the universe. I mean, apart from you, of course, because as we discussed earlier, you're turning the handle. But for most Australians, *no worries* is a statement of belief about their relaxed position in the cosmic hierarchy."

"You're making that up."

"Yep."

"And if you're trying to prove that you went to a decent

school and know a few long words, it's okay, I'm convinced." She paused as she reached the corridor that led to her room. "You're quite a bright guy."

"Thanks. I get by."

He dangled their empty mugs by the handles, one in each hand, and for a moment they both stood uncertainly where they were. Shay was glad about the mugs. No awkwardness over whether they should shake hands or do any hippie hugging good-night.

Two single, consenting adults, alone in a house—it could have gotten awkward. Dustin Tanner—*not* named for the movie star—wouldn't be the first man to want to heal his broken heart with a one-night stand.

"Is there a time I should wake you in the morning?" he finally asked.

"Uh, I'll be up, I should think." She never slept in. "Good night, Dusty."

"Good night, Shay. Sleep well."

"Hey, you never know, miracles can happen…." She smiled at him, then went along to her room.

Maybe it was the tea, maybe it was more denial. The miracle did happen, and Shay slept like a log.

When Dusty rapped politely on her door at just after eight, she was still in a doze, and she was shocked to see the time on the bedside clock when she opened one eye. She'd fallen asleep over the sixth of the short-story entries and, even though she'd managed to turn off the light before finding oblivion, the two piles of manuscripts resting on the covers slid to the floor when she sat up.

"Just a minute," she called out.

"No hurry," Dusty called back. "But I've got some news you'll want to hear when you're up and dressed."

Following a statement like this, she was dressed in two minutes, and was practically breathless by the time she'd followed the smell of coffee and arrived in the kitchen.

"Tell me, Dusty!"

"There's a chopper going to pick you up sometime this morning and it'll get you to Longreach by the end of the day. I pulled a couple of strings."

He made it sound like no big deal, didn't go into detail and didn't make any reference to how difficult she'd been on the issue yesterday, but she had an inkling that she really owed him for what he'd done.

"I have to warn you, though, it's not going to be your standard charter flight," he went on. "The guy's mustering on the next property. It's owned by one of the big agribusinesses, and they have their own helicopter division. The pilot's going to fit you in when he can, because the cattle have to take priority, so you might have to experience a bit of mustering on the way, and you might not get to Longreach until dark."

"Thank you! *Thank you!* That is so great! I am so grateful!"

"No worries," he said.

"No worries, Dusty," she echoed, and closed her eyes in sheer relief. "I think I'm starting to get it, now. No worries…"

It sounded good.

Opening her eyes again, she found Dusty grinning at her, and even though she'd by this time decided—When? During her sleep?—that it was one of the best grins she'd ever seen, the thought of saying a permanent goodbye to the grin and Dusty himself didn't weigh her down for a moment.

I have my career back!

I'm not going to end up on Boring Hobbies Monthly.

I can get to New York!

She might even be on a plane across the Pacific today.

If she widened her search for available flights and checked the ones out of Sydney as well…

She ate breakfast over at the single men's quarters, had her bag packed and waiting on the veranda, had Sonya alerted to her imminent escape and was rechecking international flights on the Internet when the air filled with the vibrating sound of chopper blades at twenty after nine.

Dusty had gone somewhere with the grader driver, so she scribbled him a note. *Thanks for everything. Sorry we didn't get a chance to say goodbye. Shay.*

He'd touched her life….Yes, a little, getting her to talk about her parents the way she had, showing her some unexpected facets to his own existence…but he was out of it, now, and she was back on the Shieldpress corporate ladder, where she belonged.

Okay, gathering her thoughts, starting to feel that she was back in control. On the way to Brisbane, she needed to list everything Sonya had to take care of while she was in New York, and she needed to marshal her arguments about the Australian content of the magazine because surely this was what Tom wanted to hear from her. She needed—

"You're the one trying to get to Longreach?" yelled the chopper pilot, coming toward her across the red ground with his blades still slowing down behind him.

"Or Charleville," she yelled back generously. "I'm not fussy."

"I'm not going to Charleville."

"Longreach, then. Longreach is fine."

"Have to find a few cattle first."

"I know. That's fine, too." Everything was fine. She was going to get out of here and that was all that mattered.

Shay felt giddy with relief as they left the ground. A few

minutes later, she felt just plain giddy. Half an hour after that, absolutely bleeping terrified. This was nothing like an airplane ride. The chopper pilot cruised over the flat, flooded terrain, buzzing dark strings of moving cattle as if he were a fighter pilot and the beasts were enemy tanks.

He didn't seem to fly in the same direction or at the same height for more than a few seconds at a stretch, and if Shay had had any idea of which direction Longreach lay in when they'd taken off, she'd lost all sense of it now. The option of walking there seemed easier. Why had she pushed Dusty so hard about getting out of here?

"Can we fly a bit more gently?" she tried to say, but the pilot didn't hear.

He yelled something at her—something helpful and explanatory that she couldn't make out a word of. She hoped it had been, *I'll have you on the ground in five minutes,* because any longer than that and she would die.

Or throw up.

Probably both.

The chopper slid sideways and her stomach rolled. Some of the cattle were being stubborn. Was that the problem? The pilot—she hadn't asked his name—flew lower and slower and she didn't understand what kept them off the ground. It only looked to be a few yards below her. The cattle began to move toward an open gate. The pilot swore and yelled. Something about the rotor RPM.

They were going to crash.

She knew it only seconds before it happened.

The pilot yelled again.

The motor screamed, sputtered and died.

Cattle galloped ahead, splashing in tea-colored water up to their red-brown bony knees.

The chopper slammed crookedly and violently onto a piece of soft ground surrounded by flooding and no bigger than a suburban front yard. The jarring impact was like nothing Shay had ever felt before. Her vision boiled with wild color and then went black, just as her stomach came barging up into her throat.

Chapter Four

Thanks to several terse two-way radio conversations with the people from Williamson International Pastoral Holdings, Dusty knew exactly where to find the downed chopper. He also knew what to bring with him, and that both Shay and Jake the pilot were basically okay. He'd also been able to reach Shay's assistant in Sydney to give her the bare bones about the crash and the consequent delay.

Taking two horses—the only mode of ground transportation that could reach the place through the floodwaters—and filling their saddlebags with equipment, he left the homestead before lunch. By mid-afternoon, he knew he must be getting close because he'd left his own land an hour ago and was now riding a winding route across WIPH's massive and extensively flooded acreage, known as Wilandra Creek.

He'd bargained to secure Shay's evacuation on the WIPH chopper by giving Wilandra Creek's manager permission to open a gate between the two properties and heli-

muster several thousand Wilandra Creek cattle onto the
nearby piece of higher ground that was part of Roscommon Downs, but he hadn't expected his deal-brokering
efforts to end like this.

The head of the pastoral company's helicopter division
was pretty ticked off, too, and the words *pilot error* had
been spoken. The man had made it quite clear that Jake
had to stay with the chopper until the company could send
a mechanic with some equipment, tools and parts to check
out the degree of damage and fix it on site if possible. The
way Dusty understood the situation, Jake might need to
settle in for a wait of a couple of days.

Shay would be luckier.

Dusty had come to her rescue, like a knight on horseback in shining bloody armor, and she'd better damn well
appreciate the fact.

Ahead, he saw something glinting, and realized it was
the sun reflecting off the chopper's bubble-like cabin, par-
tially obscured by a screen of thin vegetation. The two
horses made some final splashes through shallow water,
then came to the patch of higher ground. He saw the two
lonely human figures spring to their feet in a forlorn piece
of shade as they heard his approach, and in another minute
he had almost reached them.

Pelicans, cockatoos and other birdlife filled the air with
bursts of noise as he neared, and the sky was a soaring and
slightly humid-hazed blue—idyllic in a photograph but he
had to admit that Shay and Jake created a desolate image
in the reality of the vast landscape.

Shay stood with her shoulders hunched and shuddering, biting on her knuckle and, for the first time since
Dusty had heard the news, he had time to think about how
terrified she must have been. She looked a mess, and this
was hardly a surprise.

There would have been noise, violent motion, Jake's desperate reaction and the jarring impact, all of it in the middle of nowhere. Both pilot and passenger were lucky not to have been badly hurt, lucky that the radio was still working and lucky that Dusty had been able to reach them relatively easily.

Then had come the hours of waiting, in weather that managed to be hot and unusually humid because of all the water lying around, even though this was the middle of the Australian winter in the cooler regions farther south. Had Shay had any faith that Dusty would show up for her?

He thought about worst-case scenarios and his gut soured suddenly. If the helicopter had crashed even just a few meters higher than it had, or if the pilot's radio had broken on impact, the outcome might have been very different. If she'd been seriously injured he never would have forgiven himself for yesterday's thoughtlessness in not holding back the mail flight.

He didn't usually get caught up in fretting over what might have been. What was wrong with him? He pulled Beau up and shook off the morbid speculation.

Sliding efficiently from the saddle, he walked up to Shay, with Beau's reins and those of Sally, the horse he'd been leading, still looped in his hand. His pulse was jumping strangely and his breathing wasn't quite steady. He really wanted Shay to be okay, but didn't want her to see his level of concern. He couldn't believe he felt this degree of responsibility for her.

"Hello, stranger." Suddenly, he found himself grinning, partly with relief that she seemed to be basically all right and he'd reached her in good time, and partly because, seriously, could you doubt that the universe had a warped sense of humor when something like this happened, after they'd both been so desperate for her to get away?

"Oh, Dusty," she sobbed. "Thank God you're here! Thank you, God! Oh, Dusty." She launched herself toward him, stumbling.

"Hey…What's all this about?" Her vulnerability arrowed right to his heart. "Hey, it's okay…."

"I know. I know, but let me cry anyhow."

Shay had never been so happy to see any human being in her life. She wrapped her jarred, aching arms around Dusty's neck and held him like a long-lost brother, or like her best friend. He smelled of sunscreen, shampoo, eucalyptus-flavored laundry detergent and male skin; his navy-trimmed white polo shirt was soft against her cheek, and he was big and strong and fabulous.

She had not one second's doubt that she was safe now because, if there was one thing to be said for rough physical specimens like this one, they knew how to find their way around a desert in flood, and she couldn't imagine that they ever got lost.

"Oh, Dusty," she sobbed again, and only managed to prise herself out of his deliciously capable embrace when the horse nudging his shoulder reminded her that they weren't alone.

"Are you going to accept it now?" he said.

"Accept what?"

"That the universe has promoted you sideways. Someone else is turning the handle from now on."

"Well, as long as it's you…" she said.

"Me?" He opened his hands in a gesture that said *huh?*

"Doesn't matter. Bad joke. You turning the handle instead, I meant. But it's not important. Just—just get me home safe to your place? Please?"

"No worries, okay? Don't sweat it," he crooned to her, giving her wrenched shoulders a gentle rub. "That's why I'm here."

"Mate…" said Jake, and came forward to shake Dusty's hand.

Shay hadn't really warmed to Jake during the hours of their stranded solitude. He'd been fairly obsessed with his crippled machine, sweating about his future with the company after such an expensive mistake, upset about the prospect of waiting for a mechanic, loudly profane about all of it, and completely uninterested in any of her comparable problems.

"Brought you some emergency supplies," Dusty told him.

"Like what?"

"Food, matches, clean water."

"A tent? A sleeping bag?"

Dusty glanced wryly over his shoulder at the two horses. "Sorry. I had load limitations. You'll have to sleep in the chopper." He looked at the whirlybird, with its runners dug crookedly into the damp earth. "Or maybe under it."

Jake swore again. "They're saying it's my fault."

Dusty didn't enter the debate as to whether this was true—wise of him, Shay considered. "Then this is your penance, I guess," he said. "Listen, I'm going to unpack your gear, and then we'll head back. The water's still rising and there's a crossing that was already getting deep on the way here. We're going to have to take the long way around."

Shay's sense of utter safety in Dusty's presence wobbled and cracked. "The horse you were leading…" she said.

"That's right," he told her cheerfully. "It's for you."

"But—but I don't ride. I've never been on a horse in my life."

There was a moment of painful silence as he absorbed this news, then he drawled,

"Well, I guess today's going to be a great time to start."

"I—I—" She stopped.

There really wasn't a thing she could usefully say.

Dusty unbuckled one of the saddlebags from the horse he'd been riding, and the animal pawed the earth a couple of times, flicking its tail and its ears when flies came too close. The glossy brown creature seemed enormous, powerful and as impossible to understand or control as a tornado…or outback Australia in flood.

Handing the saddlebag to Jake, Dusty told him, "You should be able to find enough dry wood for a fire around here. Pull off the dead branches on the bushes. There are tea bags, a bit of sugar and long-life milk, bread, cans of soup, I can't remember what else. My cook put it together and she doesn't often forget the essentials."

"Beer?" Jake inquired in a pessimistic tone.

Without a word, Dusty flipped open a side pocket in the saddlebag and pulled out two cans, with a blue-tinted ice pack softening between them. He tossed them to Jake like grenades, one at a time, and put the ice pack back in the bag.

"You mean it's even *cold?*" Jake said as his fingers closed around the cans. "In that case, who needs a sleeping bag?"

Dusty turned to Shay. "Ready?" He handed her a wide-brimmed felt hat that looked as if it had been used as a cleaning rag more often than as a shield against the sun. She put it on anyhow. The entire rest of her life was going to be a bad hair day and she didn't even care.

Then she looked at the horses again. "Ready as I'll ever be. Um, Jake? Thanks for…"

"Crashing you?" He made a wry face. "No worries. Anytime."

"Well, for trying to get me to Longreach, even if we fell about three hundred kilometers short."

"Right," said Dusty. "Let's get you onto that horse."

Shay was determined not to complain. Thinking of everything Dusty probably should be doing on the property instead of riding to her rescue like this, she'd already vowed not to earn any more seething reluctance from him than she'd already earned last night.

As a goal, it stretched her from the very beginning, however.

Dusty had brought her some old riding boots. He consigned her grossly inappropriate heels to her overnight bag, which he decreed must be left with the chopper, along with her laptop. "Unless your bag has some survival gear in it that you haven't told me about?"

"There are a couple of things I'd like to grab." Like the underwear she'd fortunately washed by hand last night and hung in her room to dry. "But it's mainly short-story manuscripts," she said.

"There you go, Jake," Dusty said cheerfully. "Something to help start your campfire."

Button your lips, Shay, she coached herself. *Don't let out that moan.* "Do I really have to leave my laptop?" she couldn't help asking.

"Do you want it to work, next time you switch it on? It's going to get jolted around. We'll be wading in some places. It could get wet. And I really don't want any more baggage than necessary. I think it's safer staying with the chopper, Shay."

"Okay." She closed her eyes and gave a short nod, then put on the boots. "I'm ready. I think."

Dusty made his hands into a stirrup shape. "Knee up," he said.

"Sorry?" Thank heavens she was at least wearing yesterday's black trousers, rather than the pleated silk skirt she'd optimistically packed in Sydney for the homeward journey.

OUTBACK BABY

"Put your knee in my hands and I'll boost you up. You're riding Sally. I'm taking Beau, here." He indicated the big, brown, tail-flicking one whom he'd been riding before, and Shay felt some momentary relief. Sally, the black-maned gray, looked friendlier.

Standing beside the pretty mare, she put her knee in Dusty's hands. The impact of the helicopter had jarred every muscle, bone and tendon in her body, however, and the hours of inactivity as she'd scanned the water-logged horizon for signs of his approach had stiffened her even further. Just the simple action of boosting herself up with his powerful assistance burned her shoulders and her back. She gasped as she landed in the saddle.

"She's quiet," Dusty said, clearly thinking that she was afraid. "You'll be fine."

"Yes," Shay managed to say, without complaint. "She seems lovely."

"Okay, now, thirty-second riding lesson. Feet in the stirrups. Heels down. Grip with your knees but don't get tense about it. Reins…Well, you can hold them cowboy style in one hand, or classic dressage style, in two." He demonstrated both options.

"Two," Shay decided out loud because it sounded as if she'd have more control this way.

And a degree of redundancy if one arm suddenly fell off from the pain in her shoulders.

"Everything all right?" he said after he'd shown her.

"You mean that's it? That's how to ride? Don't I have to…um…kick? Or steer?"

"I'll go ahead on Beau. Sally thinks he's her boyfriend. She adores him, so she'll follow. You shouldn't need to give her much guidance."

"And doesn't *he* think he's her boyfriend?" Shay instantly empathized. The rat! Poor Sally! Beau was Adam and Jason and Todd, all over again. Men were the same the world over, even when they were horses.

"Well, he sort of is her boyfriend. He totally agrees with Sally about it. The thing is, he's been gelded, but we don't tell him that. So when I say *boyfriend*, think preschoolers holding hands, not a model, a rock star and black satin sheets."

Shay snorted out a laugh. "That is so cute!"

She was glad about the undignified snort because it disguised the fact that the laugh instantly turned into a groan. The slightest movement made her shoulders ache and her back spasm with pain.

Dusty pulled himself into Beau's saddle with one heave of his thighs and arms. He slid the scuffed toes of his boots into the stirrups, and his legs and butt seemed almost to graft themselves to the horse. He clicked his tongue, nudged the horse's sides with his heels and he and Beau were off. As he'd predicted, Sally immediately took off after them, at the same steady gait.

"You're still in radio contact with your boss, aren't you, Jake?" Dusty said to the pilot as he circled around the stricken chopper.

"When he can be bothered," he confirmed. "It's going to be a bloody boring wait."

"See you later then, mate. Keep smiling."

"Yeah, you, too."

"Will Jake really be okay?" Shay asked after the first fifty yards or so of agonizing movement on the rickety horse. She wasn't convinced that *she* would be okay, but didn't dare to ask how long it would take them to ride to the homestead, in case it sounded like an over-entitled, career-obsessed New Yorker's whiny complaint.

"He should be," Dusty answered. "They're punishing him a little bit, but they'll get to him as soon as they can."

"It seems harsh."

"Life out here is harsh, sometimes."

"I guess it would be."

"There's no point in a station owner or manager having a high tolerance for mistakes, when the land itself has no tolerance at all. That's the way I operate, anyhow."

"According to rules? That rigid?" The questions distracted her from the pain in her back.

"It's not rigid. I don't think it's rigid. I ask a lot from my people, the way WIPH asks a lot from its pilots, but we don't ask for anything that we couldn't or wouldn't give ourselves."

"Okay." She looked at him ahead of her, straight-backed, relaxed, confident, strong in his body and in his convictions.

He was different to most of the men she'd known. Different from Adam, for example. Adam's logic and his ideas seemed so slippery, in hindsight, compared to Dusty's. Had there been any steady sense of right and wrong in Adam's world, or only a shifting landscape of wants and desires?

"Would you rather have stayed with him and taken your chances on an air rescue?" Dusty asked, cutting across her train of thought before she'd reached a conclusion.

"Are you kidding me? I am *never* going in one of those things again!"

"The mustering was pretty scenic, then? You saw the outback from seventeen different angles and altitudes at once?"

"Something like that. I felt so sick to my stomach I thought I was going to die. And then Jake lost control, the rotor speed dropped too low, or something, and I *really* thought I was going to die."

She shuddered, remembering the fear, the pain and the

way she'd been shaking so hard that it had taken her ten minutes to unbend from her seat and climb to the ground after the ugly whine of the chopper's blades and motor had died away.

At which point she'd lost her breakfast.

"It was…" She trailed off. *Don't complain, Shay!* "…Yeah." She brightened her tone. "Great research."

He laughed, but didn't comment.

The knife play in Shay's back and shoulders continued, and her thighs and butt began to burn, also, from the unaccustomed straddle position. The black trousers were comfortable in an executive office, but as riding gear they chafed her skin badly. It was a testament to the degree of pain in her back that the chafing barely seemed to matter.

The landscape around them was incredible, but again her enjoyment of it was filtered through her pain. In the distance—to the west, she thought—she could see what looked like sand dunes the rusty orange color of cayenne pepper. They were dotted with clumps of gray-green grass, as well as dapplings of color from wildflowers in bright yellows and pinks.

Around what she guessed was a major river channel, she saw black swans, pelicans and other birds that she couldn't identify, stalking on stilt-like legs. She caught a brief glimpse of something that looked like a huge eagle, but then it soared higher and she would have had to turn in the saddle to track its powerful trajectory through the sky.

Turning, right now, was not an option. She knew it would hurt too much.

"How far have we come?" she asked brightly, after what felt like an hour.

"A couple of kilometers, probably. Not quite a mile and a half."

No! Not possible!

She pressed her lips together for a moment, then asked, "And how far is it altogether?"

"Longer than my outward journey. There's a detour we'll have to make this time, because the water is still rising and the crossing was already pretty iffy when I came through." He looked at her stiff, ungainly position on Sally's back. "You probably wouldn't be too comfortable with swimming the horses. So it's going to be over twenty miles."

Shay wondered how she'd survive.

The pain got worse. Since Sally just kept walking in Beau's tracks without guidance, as Dusty had promised she would, Shay tried slumping in the saddle, loosening her grip on the reins and letting her feet out of the stirrups. It didn't help. Every rock of the horse's gait made her spine shift, and every shift brought a fresh stab of agony.

They had to have been riding for well over an hour—a real hour, this time, not a mental anguish hour that was actually only twenty minutes—when she admitted defeat and knew she had to say something to Dusty. They'd splashed through stretches of water that came to the horses knees and her trousers were soaked and stained and stuck to her legs, chafing her worse than ever, but this was nothing compared to the pain in her back.

"I don't think I can do this anymore," she gasped out to him.

He twisted in the saddle, frowning. "You're doing fine."

"No. I'm not. My back got jarred in the crash, I think. And my shoulders. I've tried all sorts of positions. I'm sorry. It's getting worse and worse. The shoulders are bearable, but the back…really isn't."

Dusty dammed back a curse word, brought Beau to a halt and took a good look at his traveling companion, expecting to see symptoms of spoiled New Yorker throwing a tantrum about nothing.

The reality was different.

The color had drained from Shay's face, leaving her like a ghost, and her lips were dry. She had pink sunburn flaring on her neck, although her face was protected by the hat he'd given her. He should have asked her about sunscreen, back at the chopper. He should have stopped for a water break before this. There was nothing he could do about the water dripping from her boots and the hems of her trousers, but he knew it couldn't be comfortable because his own boots and jeans were in the same state.

And he should have seen that she was in this level of pain because, now that he'd looked at her properly, he couldn't doubt it. "Why didn't you say something?"

"Because I've given you so much grief already. And because what's our choice?"

Good point.

He considered it.

The sun had dropped toward the horizon. Darkness would soon fall, which meant they'd have needed to stop anyway, within the next half hour. Anticipating a night en route, he'd asked Prim to pack two sleeping bags and a billycan for cooking and heating water over an open fire— the same fire that would dry out the soaking lower half of her trousers and his jeans, he hoped, because wet fabric chafed more than dry.

There were no luxuries, though. No tent. No air mattress. They'd be lying on the bare earth.

He dismounted and went to her, realizing that she would need help in getting to the ground. Seeing how stiffly and carefully she moved as she attempted to ease her sodden leg over the horse's back, he suspected they might be camping out tomorrow night, as well.

"I can't get off," she gasped. "I'm stuck. It hurts too much."

"Take your feet out of the stirrups, lean on the horse's neck. Try kind of rolling off. I'll catch you."

"You'd better."

"I promise."

She yelped and groaned and hissed with pain, although he could tell she was trying as hard as she could, and then she rolled into his arms with a dry sob and he lowered her gently to the ground, feeling her unsuitable silk top slip against his skin. It, too, had been splattered with muddy water, and would probably be useless after this. If she'd had any doubts about leaving her laptop behind, she'd most likely rethought her objections by now.

As if the silk and the laptop mattered. The pain in her back was the critical thing.

"Gee, how high was that chopper when it came down?" he asked her softly, still holding her because she felt as if her legs might give way beneath her if he didn't.

She felt good in his arms—tall and willowy and soft.

Very different from Mandy.

Better.

He shook off the thought and felt her steady herself and take a determined breath. She pushed him gently away, saying, "It seemed like fifty feet. It *wasn't* that high. But it came down so hard, so fast, and I had no idea how to brace, or— And then maybe if I'd, oh, done some stretches or walked around a lot once we were on the ground, but I was so shocked, I just sat and everything stiffened up."

"You're burned, too."

"There wasn't much shade."

"Have you been drinking enough fluids?"

"Jake had water. We'd almost finished it when you arrived, so it's good that you had more for him." She was right to assume that the floodwater that surrounded them would not be particularly safe to drink without boiling. "I'd like some now, if that's okay. I'm thirsty."

He got it out of a saddlebag for her and she drank gratefully, steadier on her feet by this time. "What are we going to do, Dusty?" she asked when she'd finished her drink, and there was an almost childlike note of trust in her voice, as if she had absolute faith in his answers.

He felt comfortable with the responsibility—after all, he knew the country, knew how to survive—and oddly touched at the same time. "Walk a little bit," he answered. "Just take it easy. Help you loosen up. There's a place I'd like to get to about another kilometer ahead. Can you manage that on foot? Half a mile or so? Some of it will be through water."

"I'll have to manage, won't I?"

"If you can't, you have to tell me."

"I'll manage. And then?"

"We'll set up camp."

She nodded. She'd obviously realized that with twenty miles of trackless and flooded ground to cover, they weren't going to make it back to the homestead tonight. "Dare I ask? You had no tent for Jake. Is that because you were saving it for us?"

He shook his head. "But the place I'm hoping to get to has an overhang."

"A cave?"

"Calling it a cave would be a stretch."

He waited for a litany of questions about what the hell she was expected to do with something that didn't even qualify as a cave, and about what he had or didn't have in the crammed saddlebags, but she stayed silent for a good thirty seconds, then simply said, "So we should get walking," and started off. A moment later, she stopped. "Should I lead Sally?"

"Do you want to?"

She flexed a couple of muscles experimentally. "Maybe I'll just walk."

And she did, without a word, through wildflowers and mud and thigh-deep water, until they reached the place he'd had in mind.

Chapter Five

The hour of walking had to qualify as one of the best performances of her life, Shay decided.

She wanted to yell, moan, sink to the ground and sob, pray for death, and beg Dusty, "Ca-a-rry me!" like Sarah's three-year-old twins did. Her wet trousers dragged and chafed, and every time she thought the late sun might dry out the fabric, they came to another place where they had to wade and the trousers got even wetter.

But she kept her mouth shut and just put one foot in front of the other beside Dusty and the horses, over and over again, until she heard him say, "Here we are."

"This is the overhang."

"Yes."

"It's…pretty." There was a line of big river trees not far off, and the dying sun made rich, gorgeous colors in the sky that reflected off the sea of slowly drifting water.

Nonetheless, its scenic attractions would not have featured in a more honest reaction.

She saw the way Dusty tucked in the corner of his
mouth and raised his eyebrows, and added bluntly, "Okay,
it's one of the loneliest places I've ever seen in my life."

Ahh, speaking the truth. It felt almost as good as
stretching her stiff muscles.

He laughed. "It's shelter, and there should be some dry
wood for a fire."

"I'll gather some," she announced bravely.

"It's okay. You should rest now. Prim will have packed
a first-aid kit, so I can give you something for the pain.
Then how about I set up the sleeping bag for you, under
the overhang, and you can take off your wet things, get into
the bag and have a snooze while I get us organized?"

"I'm—"

"You're not fine." His brandy-colored eyes crinkled up
around the edges in a sympathetic smile as he looked her
up and down, and she felt as if he understood her far too
well. "You don't have to say you're fine. It'll be easier for
both of us in the long run if you're honest."

"Really? You're good to me!"

"You've been in a bloody helicopter crash today, and
Jake was obviously playing it down for the sake of his career, because if I'd known you'd gotten this jarred I would
have tried to get hold of a medical evacuation chopper."

To her own astonishment, Shay heard herself say, "That
would have been a waste of resources. There must be people who need evacuation more than I do. I was doing okay
until I got on the horse. But there was something about her
gait…I hope my back has settled down by tomorrow."
This seemed doubtful, when she had to sleep on the
ground. "If I have to walk the whole way back—"

"We'll work something out," he promised her, laying a

sheet of thin green plastic on the dry earth beneath the overhang as he spoke.

He anchored it with stones at the edges, then spread out the sleeping bag. His shoulder stretched, the fabric of his jeans tightened across an impressively firm butt. Shay watched him at work, appreciating his efficiency and confidence on a level of instinct and gut that she couldn't remember ever feeling before. How could he look so fit and supple after such a long day in the saddle?

"Now give me your wet gear and sleep, okay?" he said.

For a blessed hour and a half, she did, lying inside the puffy down-filled sleeping bag beneath the eight-foot high jutting shelf of ocher-colored rock. The effect of the painkillers crept over her and she felt the agony in her back and shoulders miraculously ebb.

It wasn't just a doze, but a heavy, nourishing sleep that had her feeling groggy and disoriented when she first woke. She knew at once where she was—who could forget, even in sleep?—but what was that crackling sound? What was that smell?

She sat up, rediscovering the sunburn on her neck and the general stiffness that the medication couldn't mask. It was fully dark now, but Dusty had lit a beautiful fire within a ring of stones, several yards beyond the overhang. The flames leaped brightly, creating the crackling sounds Shay had heard while still half-asleep.

Her clothes must have dried because they sat neatly folded and within her reach on the sheet of plastic. She sat up and let the sleeping bag slither to her waist. Lifting her silk top, she discovered stains that would never come out, but put it on anyhow, and found it was still faintly warm from the fire's heat. It felt surprisingly good against her skin. The trousers were a different story. The skin on her inner thighs was tender and rough.

Approaching the fire, she discovered that the delectable smell came from slices of onion frying on a blackened sheet of corrugated metal balancing on the stones.

"I'm operating some creative cooking strategies tonight," Dusty said, seeing that she was awake. He squatted, stretched, straightened, leaned. Again, she couldn't help watching him. The man even cooked as if it were some kind of easy evening workout. "Feeling better?" he asked.

"Ask me again when I've had some more water and… um…been for a walk." She hesitated for a moment. "Dusty, if our house is a rock shelf and our cookware is an old piece of roof, can I ask about our bathroom?"

"Your choice of bush, a discreet distance away, but within sight of the fire. You don't want to get lost."

"Lost on the way to the bathroom. A new concept." She drank the water he passed to her, then went off into the darkness for a few minutes. On her way back, she discovered the horses hobbled by some kind of strap on their back legs so that they could graze and drink but couldn't wander too far, and stopped to reach up and stroke Sally on her warm, silky, aristocratic nose.

When she returned to the fire, the onions smelled even better. "And look what Prim packed," Dusty said, holding up a gracefully shaped green bottle.

"What *is* that? Not—"

"Yep." He grinned. "Champagne."

"I love her! Can I drink it direct from the bottle?" *All* of it.

"You'll have to, because she didn't pack any glasses. Or there are two slightly coffee-stained enamel mugs, if you prefer."

"I'll go with the bottle. Strictly medicinal, you realize, don't you?"

"Shay, after the day you've had, I'd authorize strictly

medicinal hundred-percent-proof vodka if we had any. There are also crackers and a can of smoked oysters, by the way, to go with the champagne. We are surviving in style, tonight."

"Have you opened it?"

"Not yet. If you're drinking from the bottle, do you want to stand close by? It's probably been pretty well shaken up this afternoon."

"Not to sound too desperate or anything, but I'll even open my mouth in advance."

It was a crazy moment. They stood together beside the fire. Dusty angled the neck of the bottle away from them, untwisted the wire and pushed on the cork with his work-hardened thumbs. It gave way with a loud pop and jetted out into the desert darkness, while foam began to flood from the bottle's opening and down over his hands.

"Help!" he said. "Even fizzier than I thought."

"Oh no, we're losing it *all!*"

She pressed her mouth to the side of the bottle just as Dusty did the same and they lapped at the cool, sticky foam like animals, with their shoulders nudging each other and their bare arms bumping. They laughed as they lapped. Shay felt the bubbles fizz on her tongue. She felt Dusty's fingers against her lips for a moment, and the slippery glass, and then their sticky wet cheeks brushed together and they laughed some more and the foam subsided, leaving a good half a bottleful still left.

She stepped away, embarrassed. Dusty had foam still fizzing on his jaw and she wanted to brush it away.

Or lick it.

"Don't tell Prim how much we wasted," she said. "Maybe I'll use a mug after all. Oh, my face is all sticky."

"I packed a towel." He gestured, and she saw that he'd hung it on something that passed for a tree—a spindly little thing that leaned gracefully toward the rock shelf.

"Thanks." She grabbed it, wet a corner of it and unstickied her face, standing on the far side of the fire from Dusty because the two of them licking champagne foam from the neck of the same bottle, just now, had felt a little too much like getting their whole relationship onto a deeper level.

When she'd finished, he wanted the towel for himself, and that felt too intimate, also, as she watched him use an adjacent dampened corner, then wipe his face and hands with the same dry section she'd just used. Why had she suddenly become so interested in watching his body in action?

"How are your thighs?" he asked.

"My—?"

"The inner skin. Sore?"

"Uh, yes, a little."

"Because Prim packed some soothing cream if you want to use it. I found it in the first-aid kit when I was looking for the painkillers."

"That would be great."

He got it out for her and then turned discreetly to stir the onions while she stripped her trousers down and rubbed the cream onto her tender skin. It felt almost as intimate as licking the champagne, even though he scrupulously avoided looking. He knew what she was doing, and she knew it wouldn't take much imagination on his part to picture it. She finished as quickly as possible and refastened her trousers, hoping the soothing effect of the cream would last.

"I'm done," she announced, and saw his shoulders relax.

The onions were cooked. Dusty slid them deftly onto slices of bread balanced on smooth rocks, then put the piece of roof back on the fire and started cooking steak.

"Want to prepare our hors d'oeuvres?" he asked. "You don't need an opener for the can. And if you're cold, Prim borrowed something for you from Letty."

Unbelievable.

A few minutes later they were both sitting there, cross-legged on the ground, with enamel mugs of champagne, eating oysters on crackers while steak sizzled and potatoes baked in their blackened jackets in the coals. In her borrowed oilskin cattleman's coat, Shay felt…content.

Strangely so.

Peacefully so.

More than content, really.

Happy, even though she didn't have the slightest idea why.

"Prim believes in serving a balanced meal," Dusty told her. "There's salad and ketchup, too."

"It having been established by the highest authorities that ketchup is a vegetable."

"Exactly."

It tasted so good. Dusty squirted ketchup on top of the onions, put the steak on top of the ketchup and another slice of bread on top of that, so they didn't need plates. They ate the salad directly from the container with two plastic forks, and with the same forks scooped the hot, soft, butter-and-salt-flavored potato out from the middle of the charcoal skins. The fire kept them company, along with the sing of water heating in what Dusty called a *billycan*.

"Do you know what? I hate herbal tea," Shay said when the tea was made and she'd started sipping.

"This isn't herbal, it's just ordinary."

"I know, and it's really good. Which is what's made me realize how much I hate herbal."

"But herbal is what you normally drink?"

She shrugged, feeling foolish. "My doctor said I had to

do something about my stress levels. You know, and on the packet it always has words like *soothing* and *restorative*."

"And you think that combatting the effect of a ninety-hour working week in a hermetically sealed high-rise office with an herbal tea bag or two counts as doing something about your stress?"

"Well," she said indignantly, "yes, something, a little bit."

He laughed long and loud.

"And I did a yoga class once," she said, more indignantly still.

"For how long? A semester?"

"Uh, no, as I said, it was once. A free come-and-try. But then I never had time to actually sign up for the whole class. Even though I did *want* to. But I still try and do some of the breathing."

"You make me laugh."

"I've noticed. It's good to feel useful. Remind me why I'm here, again? Is it because you couldn't manage to tell me I'd be trapped if I didn't get right back on that mail flight?"

"Shay, I could have left you with Jake today, don't forget."

"We were going to stop this, weren't we?"

"Arguing about whose fault it is? I think so."

"I mean, I guess we have to do something to entertain ourselves but this topic is beginning to get old."

"You're right. Do you know what?" He took a mouthful of tea. "It was Mandy's fault. There. I've said it. It's out in the open. It was one hundred percent Mandy's fault and we can leave it at that."

Even though his mention of his recently turned ex-fiancée was pretty light and flippant, it somehow dampened the atmosphere all the same.

Which was probably a good thing.

"I mean, there were some other things that weren't her fault…" Dusty muttered. "That were definitely mine."

He fell silent, took a stick from the ground, stretched forward and poked the fire with it, releasing showers of sparks into the air. Looking up at them, wondering if he wanted a response to what he'd just said, Shay saw the night sky and was astonished at the sheer weight of the stars above her head. She'd had no idea there were that many.

They encrusted the whole inky black bowl of the heavens, and when she really looked closely, she could see subtle differences in their colors. They weren't simply white, but blue-white, or pink-white, or yellow, and in a crooked band across the sky, in the places where she couldn't see individual twinkles, there was a milky, misty quality to the emptiness.

"What *is* that?" she asked Dusty, pointing at it. "That sort of paler, misty trail in the sky."

He looked up. "You don't mean the Milky Way?"

"Ohmigosh," she whispered, after a moment. "I think that is what I mean. You mean, that's our galaxy? The earth's galaxy?"

"It's not mist, you see, it's a billion stars, so many of them and so far away that they just blur together."

"That's why it's called the Milky Way, because it makes the night look milky up there? I never knew that!"

"I guess you've never been somewhere before that had so little interference from lights on the ground. You probably can't see the Milky Way in the city."

"No, you can't." Not that she'd ever thought to look, admittedly. "Wow. Ouch, this is hurting my neck, I think those pills are wearing off, but I can't stop looking. It all looks so close. And so big. Don't laugh at me."

"I'm not."

"You probably are. Secretly. But I don't care."

"I'm really not. I'm not a very secret person. If I was laughing at you, you'd know it."

"So why aren't you laughing? You should be! I'm acting like a five-year-old, here, awed by the stars!"

"That's not something to laugh at. People shouldn't ever lose the ability to act like five-year-olds."

"Yeah? Including the whiny behavior?"

"Well, no, not that."

They stopped looking at the stars, looked at each other instead, and grinned. He'd put on a long-sleeved chambray shirt over the polo shirt. The two collars got in each other's way and she wanted to straighten them so that they sat the way they were supposed to, but she knew she couldn't. What if her fingers brushed against his brown, outdoorsy, sexy neck?

Something—not the sexy idea—made her ask, "Did you bring Mandy camping under the stars?"

"No, for some reason she had a strange reluctance to experience the necessary helicopter crash, first."

"You could have just taken her camping, with an SUV and a tent and camp chairs and a camp shower."

"You think if I'd shown her the stars she might have stayed?" He shifted a little. She didn't look at him, but her whole body knew he was there, back hunched, elbows resting on knees.

"I'm just wondering if she appreciated…" How to put this? "…The things that there are to appreciate out here."

"You've decided there are things to appreciate, since yesterday?"

"Even yesterday I knew there were. Your beautiful house. Letty's courage. Prim's cooking, and her books."

"Mandy didn't really manage to get to know Letty and Prim. She always ate at the house. She had…diet ideas."

"Oh?"

"Shakes. She made a lot of shakes, in the blender."

"What kind of shakes?"

"Brewer's yeast and alfalfa and cooked liver… And, I mean, she had the right to eat what she wanted but, oh jeez, they were disgusting!"

"Did you tell her that?"

"Yeah, I did!"

"But you didn't tell her to come eat with the others, read some of Prim's books and get to know everyone."

"That was her decision, too."

"Yeah?" She looked at him, tilting her head a little. He looked steadily back at her. "Or were you just keeping her to yourself?"

"Are you psychoanalyzing the relationship?" He stirred his stick in the coals of the fire again. It was getting chillier and she was glad she wore Letty's borrowed coat.

"I seem to be, don't I?"

"You do."

"I guess you give the impression that you don't understand what went wrong, and I'm curious about it, too. I'm a journalist, I sometimes ask people interfering personal questions."

"At least you're honest."

"So what was good about Mandy? What was right about her? There must have been some things."

"There were." He thought for a moment, rubbing his jaw against his index finger. "She was a good listener. She had a pretty smile." He thought again. "That sounds shallow, but smiles are important. A pretty smile can be way more important than a pretty face."

"I'd never thought of it like that," Shay murmured, impressed by the observation. A lot of men wouldn't have thought that a woman could have a pretty smile without the face to go with it.

"And she talked about herself in this rambly, psycho-babbly way that didn't make *any* sense, and when I laughed at her about it, she always started laughing, too. I liked that. People shouldn't always take themselves too seriously."

"So what did go wrong?" She remembered how he'd phrased it beside the airstrip. "Why wasn't Roscommon Downs *what she'd been expecting?* Do you wish you'd done more to make it meet her expectations? Could you have, if you'd tried, or were her expectations just too far out of touch with reality?"

He thought about it for a moment, then said, "A bit of both. Her expectations were unrealistic. There's quite a well-known book about one of the big nineteenth-century pioneer pastoral families called *Kings in Grass Castles*. Mandy thought she was going to be the queen, but it's not like that on Roscommon Downs. From my end, I probably stepped back too far, let her have too much of her own space, expected her to make her own way, too much."

"That doesn't sound like such a bad thing. Some women do have a degree of independence, these days."

"I took it too far. There's independence, and then there's lack of support. I trusted her to fill her own needs or ask for what she wanted. But she wasn't straight about that kind of thing. She was one of those women…people…who says, 'I'm fine' about twenty times and then gets angry when you believe she means it. And since she didn't seem interested in getting to know anyone on the station, I didn't push it. I probably should have. I should have pushed her a lot harder to stop the stuff about saying she was fine when she wasn't. If she'd understood, seriously, how much I hate that… But then, with Rebecca—" He stopped.

"Aha! There's Rebecca, too."

"What do you mean, aha?"

"You expected me to assume Mandy was your first girlfriend? I don't think so! You're, what? Around thirty-four?"

"All right. Of course Mandy wasn't my first girlfriend." He reached for his stick to poke the fire again.

"So tell me about Rebecca."

"Rebecca." Another shower of sparks rocketed and spiraled in the air. "Short version. She was another one of our governesses. Really vibrant, a little bit wild, loved horses. We were involved with each other for three years."

"That's a while."

"Yeah, especially since in all that time she never told me she was still married."

"Yikes!"

"Yeah, exactly." He looked at her, then looked away. Shay found herself waiting and hoping for the next time it happened. His eyes in the firelight mesmerized her. "Anyway, we were open and flexible, honest with each other, or so I thought, and I really supported her having a social life and going to local events. Rodeos and track meetings, that kind of thing."

"Well, sure."

"I didn't expect her to go off with one of my racehorse trainer's jockeys."

"Oh."

"But at least then *he* was the one who had to deal with her half-crazy husband when he finally tracked her down."

"That sounds like fun." Shay knew it must have been anything but, and understood all the mess and hurt and anger he'd carefully not talked about.

"I think it explains Mandy a bit more, doesn't it?" he said. Another look—clash, sizzle—and another look away.

"That I went too far the other way with her? That maybe, yeah, I did want to keep her too much to myself."

"You've had about as much luck with women as I've had in getting out of here."

"Which, as we've now agreed, is Mandy's fault. And on that note…we should make an early start tomorrow, so we'd better think about getting to bed."

The word hung in the air after he'd said it. This time he didn't look anywhere near her direction, and all the ease of their conversation by the firelight suddenly disappeared like the sparks flying up into the night.

Chapter Six

"There's only one piece of plastic," Dusty said, stating the obvious.

"But two sleeping bags."

"Yes."

"So we're not going to be idiotic about this, Dusty. We'll share the plastic. It's okay. Unless you think there's a dangerous level of chemistry between us."

A second later, Shay wished she'd left off that final sentence, and especially the last three words. An image flashed into her mind of that crazy moment before dinner when they'd both been sucking foam from the neck of the champagne bottle, laughing.

She'd licked his fingers by accident. Their cheeks had brushed together, wet and sticky and grape-scented. Even without fully touching him, she'd been aware of how strong his body was, next to hers. Their shared laughter suddenly felt as if it had been worth twenty hours of the restaurant dinner conversations, art museum visits and snatched cell-phone exchanges that had built her relationship with Adam. A little kick and twist of female need moved low in her stomach, echoing in her pulse and reflecting all those looks they'd exchanged in the firelight, while they'd been talking.

She closed her eyes and told herself to get a grip.

There was no chemistry!

Really!

They seemed to converse quite comfortably together, when they weren't seething mad at each other, but he wasn't even her type. She valued his practical cattleman's skills *intensely* in a situation like this, valued all that strangely graceful efficiency and masculinity in the way he moved, but they weren't the skills—or the grace—that she needed in the kind of man who fit with her usual existence.

Yeah, fabulous specimens of manhood like Adam and Jason and Todd, said a sneaky little voice inside her.

Opening her eyes abruptly, she waited for Dusty to reply to her line about the chemistry, but apparently he didn't plan to. He'd bent down to straighten the plastic, which had rumpled a little during her earlier nap, despite the anchoring stones. Now he was pulling the second sleeping bag from its tight nylon bag.

"I'm going to sleep by the fire," he said. "I'll keep it fueled during the night so it's still hot in the morning for coffee before we start. I want to get going as early as we can."

"Why are you saying this? Because you think there's not room on the plastic for both of us?"

Shay, you idiot, why push the subject? He's said he values honesty, but not to this extent.

"Because I'll be more comfortable on the ground, that's all," he said.

She stopped pushing.

After ten minutes of largely silent night preparations, they were both in their sleeping bags.

In the night, the ground grew harder and colder beneath her with every painful toss and turn of her stiff, sore body, and the painkillers had definitely worn off. Looking out of the shallow shelter to where the fire still glowed with orange coals inside its ring of stones several yards away, she saw the inert dark shape of Dusty's body lying close to the warmth. He was sound asleep. She could hear the unmistakable rhythm of his breathing.

The desert seemed so quiet and still. Desert? Ridiculous to call it that, when it was flooded on every inch of low-lying ground as far as the eye could see. But the water was a temporary feature, while the isolation and silence would never change.

Silence was a relative term, of course, she decided. As her ears attuned to the night, she could hear frogs fluting and croaking nearby. The birdlife was mostly asleep, but every now and then there came a muffled squawk from high in one of the huge eucalyptus trees that lined a major channel of the river nearby, or a snickering sort of sound from the water itself. She thought she heard a snort from Sally or Beau, too.

But she felt lonely. The physical cold creeping into her from the ground echoed her awareness that Dusty, asleep, and Jake, keeping his lonely vigil with the helicopter, might well be the only other human beings in a radius of ten or fifteen miles. She thought about New York, and could hardly believe the city was real.

There could be ghosts here, of course. She and Jake had flown over an abandoned rammed-earth stockman's hut this morning, and Dusty had told her that there were several early explorers who had perished in the Channel Country long ago.

What must that have been like? Traveling on horseback over those cayenne-pepper sand dunes in the scorching heat of an outback summer, with no understanding of native foods and none of the aboriginal skill at finding secret water sources. A NASA expedition to the moon would have seemed less alien.

She shivered, and told herself sternly to send her thoughts elsewhere.

But thoughts were disobedient entities. The images of ghosts and loneliness stayed.

She struggled out of her sleeping bag and into her borrowed riding boots, freezing like a statue every time her back spasmed and having to slowly shift from the frozen position into her next cautious movement. The process took a while. At least she didn't have to get dressed, since she was sleeping in her clothes. She was so horribly stiff and sore! How would she possibly cover the remaining miles back to the Roscommon Downs homestead tomorrow, whether on horseback or on foot?

It would be a tough, painful day at best.

The realization pushed her spirits lower.

Dusty was still asleep, and she didn't want to disturb him. She crept past him and out into the night, looking for the horses because she needed to make contact with a red-blooded living creature, even if it wasn't human. She found both horses standing close to each other, snoozing in the dark.

"Hi, Sally, hi, Beau," she whispered, and put her arms around Sally's neck.

The horse didn't seem to mind. Her beautifully styled long black mane tickled Shay's cheek—no frizz for this girl—and her breath and body were so warm. But the effect only lasted a short time. Shay gathered her energy and went back to her shelter.

"You all right?" said a voice as she bent awkwardly to straighten her sleeping bag.

"Oh, did I waken you?" She eased herself upright. "I'm sorry."

"It's fine. Are you okay?" he repeated. He propped himself up on his elbow and studied her. She wondered if she would ever get used to the amount of perception that seemed to fill that brandy-brown gaze.

"I was getting cold and pretty uncomfortable," she admitted. "Do you have a couple more of those tablets? Are they mild enough for me to take another dose now?"

"They're fine. Over-the-counter. I think you call it acet-amino-something in America."

"Oh, right."

"They're in the first saddlebag, there, under the over-hang. Do you want me to get them?"

"No, you stay. I can do it." She found the pills, downed two of them with a mug of water, then put them back in the bag. When they got back to Roscommon Downs she was going to thank Prim about a thousand times for pack-ing that first-aid kit.

"You'd better come by the fire," Dusty said. "Noth-ing's going to stop you from being sore tomorrow, but the warmth might help a little."

"I was lonely, too," she blurted out. "And scared."

"Scared? Of wild animals?"

"Of ghosts. It's so isolated. And quiet. And you told me about those dying explorers a hundred and forty years ago, whom even the aboriginal tribespeople couldn't save..."

"Come here. Bring your sleeping bag." He sat up fully, brought a bare arm and shoulder out of his own sleeping bag and beckoned her, and she just didn't have it in her to keep safely away.

She fetched her sleeping bag, while he leaned toward the pile of broken wood he'd kept handy for feeding the fire during the night. He must have taken off most of his clothing, she realized, because his back was bare. He threw on the fuel. It blazed up, and she could feel the welcome heat on her face and front as soon as she got near it again.

"Slide your legs into your bag and sit in front of me," he said.

She wriggled and shifted and winced several times as more jolts of pain ambushed her body, then lowered herself awkwardly to the ground. He circled his arms around her and she leaned against him and that strange, happy feeling flooded into her again.

Her real life and the rest of the world seemed so far away that maybe they didn't really exist anymore, and the only thing that mattered was being safe and warm right at this moment, in close contact with a fellow human being.

"Sleepy?" Dusty asked, after a silence.

"Not yet."

"Me neither."

They sat for a little while. She could feel the rhythm of his breathing in the subtle movement of his body behind her.

"My mother organized a local history of Roscommon Downs several years ago," Dusty said lazily, his voice barely more than a creak. "One of the old-timers remembered a couple who used to travel around in a wagon selling things or doing odd jobs, during the Great Depression. They slept under their wagon on the ground. Sometimes the station people would invite them to use a spare bedroom for the night but they always said no. Said they couldn't sleep indoors. It spooked them and they felt suffocated. I've sometimes thought that would be a good way to be—to need your air and your freedom so much that you couldn't sleep indoors."

"Air and freedom I can relate to," Shay said, "but mattresses are a great invention. I'm still not sleepy, though…"

"We should have brought a few of those short-story manuscripts for entertainment. Were they any good?"

"A couple of them were great. Will Jake really use them to start his fire?"

"Sorry, I shouldn't have put the idea into his head."

"Oh hell, you mean he will?"

"Short stories probably don't feature too strongly on his list of life's essentials. Don't you have copies?"

Relief flooded her. Yes, of course they had copies, back in the office. But since she was half convinced that she'd dropped into some alternate universe where the office didn't exist this week, she hadn't thought of it.

She felt his arms firm around her a little. "Shall I show you the Southern Cross? That's the constellation on the Australian flag."

"I did actually know that."

"Okay, ten points to you. Will you know how to find it, next time you want to look at stars?"

"Um, no."

"Want to?"

"Yes, please." As long as it involves this delicious, undemanding body contact.

"Up there, see those?" He pointed, his arm nudging harder against her shoulder. Despite the long, physical day, he smelled good—a mix of man and soap and the faint aroma of spilled champagne.

She saw the group of four stars. "That's the Southern Cross?"

"No, you see, people get it wrong. That's the false cross.

If you try to use that to find the South Celestial Pole,
you'll be stuffed."

"So what's the South Celestial Pole, and why would I
want to find it?"

"To navigate, or tell time. It's the point in the sky that
all the southern stars appear to rotate around."

"Right. And I need to navigate and tell time this way
because my global positioning system and diver's watch,
waterproof to a depth of three hundred meters, have
been…?"

"Eaten by a crocodile."

"Right," she said again, in a slightly different tone.

"Which we don't have around here, so don't tense up
like that."

She relaxed her shoulders with a sincere effort, and he
laughed, which made her feel funny and fluttery inside. He
could feel and intepret her body language that closely?
Could he tell how good she felt, encircled by his arms and
aware of his strength right behind her?

"Hurry up, Dusty," she said. "Tell me how to find the
South Celestial Pole, because I need to locate true north
now!"

"That's the spirit. You're sounding like an overworked
corporate executive again. Excellent, you must be feeling
better. But it's south, actually."

"Sorry?"

"We're locating south."

He told her the system. Locate the Pointers, also known
as Alpha and Beta Centauri. Locate the true Southern
Cross. Follow the long arm of the cross four lengths, to
reach the South Celestial Pole. Drop your eye to the
horizon. Ta-da!

He also showed her Achemar and Canopus, and the
constellation of Musca—the Fly—and might have shown
her more except that her neck began to ache again. She told

him this and he said, "We should try to get back to sleep, anyhow. We'll learn how to tell time another night."

He put another few pieces of wood on the fire and lay down. Shay saw that he'd used most of his clothing as a pillow, wadding it into his sleeping-bag cover. She hadn't thought of doing that.

"I'm blocking your fire heat," she told him.

"I'm warm. Stay where you are, it's fine."

Very fine.

Too close.

But if she moved she'd either have to shuffle along like a caterpillar in her sleeping bag, or get out of it again and set up a whole new sleeping place. Somehow, she'd grown attached to this particular piece of rough ground, warmed by the fire and Dusty's body.

She lay down, but was still wakeful some minutes later, and wondered how long it was until morning. If she'd learned Dusty's method of telling time by the Southern Cross, she would have known.

She laughed to herself. Who knew that such an arcane skill would have come in handy so soon?

"What's funny?" Dusty said sleepily.

"Nothing."

"Tell me in the morning."

"If I can remember." Although he wasn't quite touching her, she had a strong sense of his body behind her, a buffer against cold and danger and loneliness, somehow vigilant even in sleep, making her feel very safe...

Mmm, and sleepy.

She woke up several hours later, drenched in dew, with Dusty's arm flung around her shoulder.

Dusty knew the moment when Shay first stirred into wakefulness. He felt her body move and stretch, and then go warily still. He'd put his arm around her in his sleep, but when he'd woken ten minutes ago in predawn air that had lost the unusual humidity of the past few days, he hadn't eased away.

Instead he'd lain there trying to work out what he thought about all this. Thirty-six hours ago, he'd sincerely detested her. He'd had no time for her, and had felt the utmost difficulty in following through on the code of hospitality that had been bred in him as a child in an era before satellite communication, the Internet and tourism had lessened the isolation of Roscommon Downs.

He knew he'd let too much of his negativity show, but there'd been something refreshing in acting that way, especially when Shay Russell could clearly give as good as she got and seemed to value the upfront nature of their confrontation as much as he did.

They'd both grown kinder to each other as time went on. Prim's evening meal in the single men's quarters could take a lot of credit for the change—the good food, the friendliness, the lively nature of the conversation, which he knew full well had been pitched at a more elevated intellectual level than Shay had snobbishly expected.

Then they'd had the one-to-one over their mugs of tea. Without that, without its softening effect on both their attitudes, he might not have gone to the trouble of arranging the helicopter deal with WIPH in the morning. He could never have envisaged that it would backfire the way it had…and he certainly wouldn't have envisaged that Shay would be so courageous about it.

Courageous *and* good-humored, which was a further plus, because bravery was pretty hard to handle when it took itself too seriously.

In short, he liked her now.

Which had to count as a change for the better, but it had its downside.

Lying behind her with his arm curved over her body, he felt the chilly fall of the dew and had an instinct to protect her from it by sliding even closer and folding his whole body over hers. The instinct was about a lot more than protection, too. It was achingly, insistently physical.

Male.

Imperative.

It was about the way she smelled and the softness of her skin. It was about his need for release and for renewed proof of his manhood. It was about human connection and closeness, the desire to give and receive the sweet, beautiful blessing of making each other feel good.

Okay, be honest, it was mostly about sex.

Here.

Now.

If not on offer, then at least hanging as an unspoken possibility in the air. He knew Shay would have moved away, even in her sleep, if she'd found him repellent. He knew she'd still be back beneath the overhang if she felt as hostile toward him now as she had been at first.

He also had this—possibly primitive—belief that a healthy heterosexual man and woman could only get to a certain point with friendship and with being honest and relaxed in each other's company if they also, at some level, wanted to rip each other's clothes off.

Yep, it sounded primitive, but he believed it all the same. He thought people were kidding themselves when they said, "He's my best friend," or "She and I are just good mates," but denied any sexual-slash-romantic element to their feelings.

He simply didn't believe that he and Shay would have sat here last night, wrapped in their respective sleeping bags, with her half leaning against him and his arm pressing her shoulder as he pointed upward, looking at the stars, if there hadn't been a very definite vibe.

Whether to act on it, that was the question.

He knew he was in the wrong mental state. If you wanted to get analytical, this would have to be a rebound affair, about proving that Mandy herself was wrong, not that there was something wrong with *him*. To get even more clinical, it was about a man's response to the sudden and unexpected withdrawal of the sex on tap that he'd enjoyed for the past couple of months.

This was the point he'd reached in his thinking when he'd felt Shay's first movement.

"Your hair is soaked," he said quickly, sliding his arm from her shoulder as he spoke. Pointless. Of course she must have realized the arm was there. "It has little beads of dew all over it."

"And let me guess, it looks like an antique doll's hair, right? A million tiny little nineteenth-century corkscrews."

"Yeah." He wanted to touch it, no matter how wet or nineteenth century it was. Then he wanted to kiss her, to see how her mouth felt. The timing was wrong in every possible way, so with a wrenching effort, he let the wanting go.

"It's the moisture," she was saying. "I *hate* my hair when there's damp in the air and I can't get to a salon."

"I like it."

"Oh, you're a man, you have no hair sense."

"You'd rather I did have hair sense and hated it."

"Well, of course!" But she was smiling now. He could tell by her voice, even though he couldn't see her mouth or her eyes.

"The air's much drier today," he told her. "Will it calm down?"

"Not until it's taken its medication."

She sat up stiffly, awkward and cautious with every movement, and he thought of the twenty-five kilometers or more that they still had to travel before reaching the homestead. They didn't have enough water or food for a second night in the open. He could deal with it, their survival wasn't in doubt, but if Shay thought that last night's lifestyle options had been primitive, she would be in for a further shock today.

"Let me take a look at that fire," he said. "And we'll open out the sleeping bags and spread them on bushes to dry."

She held her hand palm up, while he slid out of his makeshift bed. "Won't they get wetter? I think the dew is still falling."

"As soon as the sun gets up, the chill will lift." He stood up and began to unzip the bag.

She looked toward the eastern sky in surprise. "You mean it's not even dawn?" At that moment, the first thin sliver of fire crested the horizon and she gasped. "Oh, wow!"

She sat there watching the changing light while he draped his sleeping bag over a scratchy piece of bush then examined the fire. It had died almost to nothing, but when he dug among the black coals and gray ash, he found a small remnant of glowing heat. Adding eucalyptus leaves one by one so as not to suffocate the coals, he saw first a tiny flame, which soon grew into a crackling blaze as he put on more leaves, then twigs and sticks, and finally pieces of broken branch as thick as his arm.

By this time, the sun had left the horizon and Shay had wriggled out of her sleeping bag and spread it on a bush just like Dusty's. Aware of the need to conserve their clean water, he measured two mugs' worth and poured them into the billy, then nudged a flat rock closer to the center of the blaze. The water in the billy soon began to sing.

Prim had included a juice box each, as well as mini boxes of cereal, UHT milk, bread and peanut butter. When he'd toasted the bread on the end of a stick, and added instant coffee grounds and milk to the billy, Dusty considered that they had a pretty fine outback breakfast.

Shay seemed to agree. "Coffee...!" she breathed, inhaling as he poured it into the mugs.

"Hey! Please! Not coffee. Latte."

"Latte." She laughed. "You are funny."

"Taste it and tell me this is not latte."

She sipped obediently. "Okay, you're right. And I sincerely appreciate the trouble you've gone to in adding preserved milk to instant granules just so a city girl can call her morning coffee by an Italian name. It's...mmm..."

She pressed her lips lightly together, closed her eyes and lifted her face. It was lucky about the closed eyes because he couldn't take his off her pretty mouth. He liked her neck, too, liked the clean, graceful line of her jaw

"...Heaven." She opened her eyes again, and he looked quickly away. "Although, if you want the truth, I would probably have sucked the dry granules off the spoon if I'd had to. Thank you, Dusty."

"Do you think you're going to be able to get on the horse today?" he asked.

She took a doubtful, shuddery breath. "I'll give it a try. And I'll put some more cream on my legs. Otherwise—?"

"Yes. We might get to do some more campfire astronomy tonight."

After they'd finished their breakfast, packing up the simple camp took only a few minutes. Dusty doused the fire with a billycan full of the clear-flowing floodwaters, despite the laughable lack of bushfire risk in current conditions. Their sleeping bags were still slightly damp, but if they did have to camp out again tonight, they could dry them by their campfire before the dew began to fall in the early hours.

The horses had had a peaceful night. Rains earlier in the season had brought good grazing, and they'd been within easy reach of the water despite being hobbled. He unstrapped their legs, took their blankets and saddles from beneath the overhang where he'd stored them, and fastened the girths.

Helping Shay onto Sally's back, he knew after only a few of the mare's paces that it was going to be too painful. Shay winced and hissed, "I'm sorry. There's just something about her gait, or my posture, or something. If there was something to brace against…"

"We'll try it."

"How?" She looked at him, immediately alarmed.

"You'll have to ride Beau, in front of me."

She nodded, and he saw a tiny flash of pink that was her tongue escaping nervously from between her lush lips.

Oh great.

Lush lips, when she'd just agreed to ride with her back against his stomach and her backside against his thighs while big, loose-limbed Beau created a rocking motion beneath them.

Lush nothing.

Lush quantities of mosquitoes, breeding in the floodwaters. Think about that, Dusty. Lush floods of sun on their unprotected skin. Lush, lewd, embarrassing and too-close-to-the-bone suggestions from Prim or Wayne or Andy about how he and Shay might have entertained themselves during the lonely desert night.

He got his equilibrium back and helped her onto the horse. "Do the stirrups help?" he said. "Because I can ride without them, if you want."

"No, you use them," she said. Then she winced and hissed with pain when he hauled himself up behind her.

The saddle didn't give them a lot of space to keep their distance, but then that was the whole point. He reached around and pulled her even closer, using the reins one-handed, keeping his free arm firmly at her waist and still somehow managing to hold Sally's lead rope. The mare would probably stick close to Beau without it, but he didn't want to take the chance that something might spook her and he'd have a runaway horse to further slow their progress home.

"Ready, steady, go?" he said to Shay.

"Ready as I'll ever be."

They managed it. He could tell she must be in a fair degree of pain because she barely spoke. Doing his best to stop her spine from making the slow, rocking, snake-like undulation that seemed to hurt her so badly, he kept his own hold on her firm to the point of cramping every muscle in his arm. It felt incredibly intimate to him— more so because it was about help and support rather than desire.

"Is it okay if I put my head on your shoulder?" he had to ask, because trying to turn it sideways or tilt it back just didn't work. If he ended up with severe neck strain or a pulled muscle on top of her jarring and pain, they could be in real trouble.

"Go ahead," she told him, and they rode cheek to cheek, looking at the route in front of them, the way they'd drunk champagne cheek to cheek last night.

What was the old Sinatra song about dancing that way? Heaven? In heaven?

This wasn't heaven, it was sheer hell. Feeling Shay's soft skin move against his own face with the rhythm of the horse, smelling her shampoo-scented hair and resting his chin on the slippery silk of her tired blouse, he spent the first kilometer in a state of solid semi-arousal, and if it hadn't been for the distracting effect of the cramping in his arm there would have been no *semi* involved.

If Shay could feel it, she didn't let on.

She *had* to feel it, surely, because he could feel her backside right against him, pert and round and spread against the saddle. Unless she was simply in too much pain…

"How far have we gone?" she finally asked.

"About two kilometers."

"Like yesterday. I guess that's my limit. I'm sorry, Dusty. Having you there helps, but it's not enough. Can we walk again?"

"Sure. You should have said before."

"No. I wanted to go as far as I could, so we'd get home today."

But he already suspected they'd lost their last shot at that.

No point in telling her yet.

He dismounted from Beau then helped Shay down and they began to walk.

Chapter Seven

By late afternoon, their route had brought them close beside the river's main channel, on Roscommon Downs' land. Dusty knew the area well, and could estimate with a good degree of accuracy how far they now were from the homestead. By his calculation, they had around nine or ten kilometers to go—roughly six and a half miles.

Shay had done astonishingly well, but she'd needed a long break over lunch and several more smaller ones since. She'd been blunt and up-front about it each time, saying "Dusty, I need to stop," or, "Get going? Not yet. Sorry. I need a bit longer."

He appreciated the honesty and trusted it now. It was good to know that she would tell him what she needed, that she wouldn't complain too soon or keep going too long.

They didn't have a lot of food or clean water left, however. They'd had a lot of flooded terrain to walk through, including a couple of places where they'd had to battle against the current, and over the past half hour she'd slowed her pace considerably, walking with smaller and slower steps. He thought she wasn't aware of it, while he kept revising their time of likely arrival at the homestead later and later.

When it reached the point where the sun had dipped behind the trees that lined the river, and he'd calculated that they'd have at least four hours of traveling in the dark, he accepted that they weren't going to make it home tonight. Their clothing was wet again, and when the air chilled soon after the sun disappeared, they'd get very cold.

"We need to set up camp," he told her.

She nodded. "I was about to say the same thing. Have we come far enough?"

"About six miles to do tomorrow."

"And today we've done twelve or thirteen? Good." She nodded again. Stiffly. "Good. That's bearable."

"Let me try and massage your back tonight, and rig up some kind of heat pack."

On a mental list he checked everything off. Heat pack, water collection system, fishing line, not to mention the usual tasks of wood gathering and dealing with the horses.

He had a lot to do, and seeing the way she looked, he planned to limit Shay's involvement to unpacking the sleeping bags. There was no overhang in this spot to keep the saddles and saddle blankets free of dew. On the other hand, he could see better possibilities for rigging a kind of lean-to with the plastic sheeting. A carpet of grass and wildflowers would give them a more comfortable night on the ground, provided he removed a few bits of prickly desert vegetation first.

The heat pack was easy, too. Shay helped to gather wood and they soon had a fire. Dusty found a smooth rock that didn't look as if it was native to the area. He suspected it had an aboriginal history, and might once have been used as a seed grinder against a flatter rock embedded in the ground. Its tribal significance wasn't important to him now, however.

He heated the stone beside the blaze then wrapped it in his cotton sweater, which he could do without until the evening grew colder. Next, he rigged up the two saddles as a back support and she leaned against them with the hot rock nudging the small of her back.

The water collection system Shay didn't understand at all.

"Why are you putting Prim's plastic storage bags over the ends of those branches?"

"To get us some more water for tomorrow. The leaves will transpire and the water will collect in the bags."

"Won't it taste…leafy?"

"You'll be surprised. It turns out pretty clean. We can boil the river water, as well, but then there'll be a definite flavor of mud and possibly a bug or two."

"Leafy sounds better."

The peanut butter–coated grasshoppers she found a little bizarre, also, but it was the best fish and yabby bait he could think of right now. The good news was that Channel Country waters should be teeming with bream, golden perch and yabbies, if he could find the right underwater habitat, and some kind of pliable, vine-like branch to act as a line.

"You really think you can catch something?" Shay asked.

"I hope so, or dinner's going to be pretty boring."

"What do we have left?"

"Bread, peanut butter, salt and pepper, sugar, ketchup, tea, coffee and milk."

"You're right. That sounds more like a condiments shelf than a meal."

"And I found some desert lime still fruiting."

"Oh, those green berries you picked at lunch?"

"They're not berries, they're a kind of native citrus. A little past their best since they've been on the tree so long, but they'll give the fish a great flavor."

"If you catch anything." She watched with visible doubt as he transformed some fencing-wire barbs into hooks and prepared his makeshift baits. "I should tell you that the one other time in my life I've had anything to do with fishing, on a vacation in Bermuda, I turned out to be a total fish jinx."

"So you think I should walk downstream a couple of hundred meters, to be out of your aura?"

"Could help."

"And you'll stay here with that hot rock against your back?"

"It feels so good, Dusty, thank you."

He left her and combed the riverbank in search of the right mess of fallen branches under the waterline, which would provide quiet spots for fish and yabbies to shelter. Tramping through a patch of gray-green vegetation that reached to his calves, he smelled a strong odor in the air and realized that this was wild onion. If he did get some fish, he could dig up the corms and they'd be eating Thai style tonight, with a lime, onion and peanut-butter sauce.

He got back to the campfire an hour later, with two nice-sized golden perch. At over thirty centimeters in length—twelve inches, Shay would call it—they were a legal catch. He also had at least a dozen yabbies, and the wild onion corms he'd dug up, and he felt like a cross between an aboriginal tribal hunter and a celebrity chef.

Shay had her eyes closed, but she heard his approach. "I'm not asleep," she said. "And I've kept the fire going."

"It looks good. That's the way we want it, a big bed of coals."

"Do we have something to cook on it?"

"Keep your eyes closed and wait for the smell."

She obeyed him, grinning.

He boiled a billy of the cleanest river water he could get, stripped some smooth, soft pieces of bark from a eucalyptus tree and soaked them in the hot water. Then he scaled and gutted the two dark olive and golden yellow fish and spread them with peanut butter, broken pieces of desert lime and rough slices of wild onion corm. He sprinkled the fish with Prim's little paper packets of salt and pepper, wrapped each fish in layers of sodden bark and buried them in a small pit of burning hot ash.

"It was great sitting here while you were gone," Shay said, still with her eyes closed. "I watched Sally and Beau grazing. You're right, they are like preschoolers holding hands, they're adorable. Then a whole flock of kangaroos… *Flock* doesn't sound right…."

"Pod," he suggested.

"A whole pod of kangaroos came lolloping along, eating the grass and drinking from the river. I never realized they use their tails like a third leg when they're moving slowly. And I just sat here and watched them with the hot rock against my back, and I could easily have fallen asleep, only I heard you." She thought for a moment. "What would you have done, Dusty, if I'd said I couldn't stand another night out in the open and wanted to push through to the homestead tonight?"

"I would have told you no."

"And here I thought Australia was a democracy…."

"Australia is, as it should be. Roscommon Downs is a dictatorship, and I'm the boss."

"Ah."

"You have a problem with that?"

"I'm envisaging some sticky scenarios."

"Knowing I'm the boss is what avoids the sticky scenarios. Sometimes you need one man's vision, not a whole lot of competing claims. We had to stop. The horses were at the end of their strength, even if you weren't. If we'd gone on another two miles we would have moved away from the river."

"Where our dinner came from?"

"Exactly. And I'm the one who knows when the trail moves away from the river, and the one who knows how to catch the dinner. So I'm the boss. Are we okay with it now?"

"I was never not okay with it, Dusty. I am deeply grateful that you are the boss, in a situation like this. I was just curious about how you saw it, that's all."

"Well, that's how I see it. And everyone who works for me knows it."

"You're suggesting that I'd better know it, too."

"While you're here."

With her eyes still closed, she listened to his movements for a little longer. She heard the clank of the billycan, the hiss of water, the sound of his boots on the earth, all of it efficient and sure. "Can I smell something now?" she finally asked.

"It's the chef's special."

"Well, it smells good...."

He had a fresh billy of salted water on the fire and was cooking the yabbies, which turned the six-inch-long fresh-water lobsters from green and blue and black to a crab-like pinky red. He flavored them with more of the onion corms, salt and pepper, a sprinkling of sugar and the desert limes.

When the yabbies were done, he broke them open and added the sweet meat to the broth, from which he'd fished out the solid remnants of onion and lime. He added a big dollop of peanut butter and then several slices of crustless bread to thicken the dish into a chunky soup. They'd eat the soup from their enamel mugs and the fish directly from the bark.

Only once it was all laid out did he tell her, "You can open your eyes now."

She did so, and her gaze fell on their feast. "Wow!"

"Tonight your chef is featuring Thai-style yabby and peanut-butter bisque, with ash-baked bark parcels—" By the word *parcels*, she'd started laughing "—of whole golden perch in a peanut, wild onion and desert lime *jus*."

When he got to *jus*, she told him, "Dustin Tanner, you are *such* a show-off! Are you making that up?"

"Nope."

"I guess you're not, because I can smell it, and it smells fabulous. How did you learn to do something like this?"

"It's Prim's fault," he said.

"Yeah?"

"I mean, I learned something about edible bush foods when I was a kid—Mum often used desert lime—but Prim's the kind of person who can teach you things without you even realizing it. You saw her in action with the book discussion."

"I did. She was impressive."

"Letty's begun doing the same thing with her schoolkids. She's pretty bright, too. But Prim has internationalcuisine nights, and guess-the-secret-ingredient contests. She's responsible for the word *jus* in my vocabulary, and trust me it's not something I'm proud of."

Shay laughed. "So tell me more about Prim."

They talked without a break all through the meal and, after Shay had washed out the billycan and the mugs, they reheated her rock and made tea and talked all the way through drinking it.

"How's your back?" he asked eventually.

For some time he'd wanted his sweater back because the temperature was plummeting. The fire wasn't enough to keep the chill at bay when he was dressed only in a polo shirt and some thin chambray. They might even get a frost tonight. But Shay still had the sweater-wrapped rock against her back and every now and then she'd shift it a little. He'd reheated it earlier and knew it would be helping her.

She didn't reply to his question, just reached around, unwrapped the rock, balled up the sweater and threw it toward him. "I'm sorry I kept it so long."

"I didn't ask for it back."

"No, you were a perfect gentleman, but as soon as you asked about my back I could see you were freezing. I should have noticed earlier."

"We should be getting to bed, anyhow." He dived into the sweater as soon as he'd said it, remembering what a loaded announcement it had been last night.

He knew the awareness between them was even more powerful tonight, after twenty-four extra hours in each other's company. He also knew that all the reasons he'd already identified for not giving into it still applied.

Last night, however, he'd deliberately positioned himself by the fire and yet she'd still ended up in his arms. Was he kidding himself, thinking he could stay away from her if she gave him the slightest signal that beckoned him closer?

When he emerged through the neck hole of the sweater, he looked at her—at the way she was staring down, avoiding his gaze, her body wrapped snugly in the oilskin stockman's coat that Prim had borrowed from Letty and packed for her—and wondered just what would be so bad about sleeping with her.

He'd seen his share of American television. If it was

even remotely accurate in its depiction of Shay's demographic as a single New York professional woman, she wouldn't exactly be saving herself for marriage. They could pleasure each other now, and say goodbye the day the airstrip came back into service without a skerrick of regret on either side.

All the same, something held him back.

An inkling of danger?

A misguided and way too traditional concept of respect?

He didn't know. He said quickly, "Hey, I noticed you didn't make yourself a pillow last night."

"I didn't think of it. But I saw yours, and I'm going to make one tonight. I don't have much to stuff it with, though. This coat, but it's pretty stiff."

"Take my sweater."

"Then your pillow will be too thin."

"It won't. My shirt's softer than Letty's oilskin, and there's my jeans and T-shirt. They're bulkier than your silk top and those pants. A better pillow might help your shoulders, if not your back."

She nodded. "Thanks. I'm going to take more of Prim's painkillers, too. We have to get to the homestead by tomorrow afternoon, because by then there'll be none left."

"I'm going to check on the horses."

"My luxury bathroom with the Italian marble and gold-plated fittings is fortunately in the opposite direction."

As they'd done last night, they completed their night preparations largely in silence, but this time they lay down side by side in their respective sleeping bags, beneath the plastic lean-to that would keep the frosty dew at bay.

Hearing Shay shift and snuggle like a cat getting comfortable in a basket of laundry, Dusty knew it would be a difficult night.

* * *

Shay waited for the painkillers to work their magic, hoping that their relaxing effect would lull her into sleep. So far, it wasn't happening. She thought that Dusty was still awake, also. Something about his breathing gave it away, as well as the occasional movements she could hear, just a couple of feet from her.

He'd decided not to maintain the fire overnight. With a less demanding journey to face in the morning, he seemed more relaxed about taking longer over breakfast. The benefit of their early start this morning had been outweighed, in any case, by the number of breaks Shay had needed during the day. She only hoped her back was, if not any better, then at least no worse tomorrow.

She shifted again, and massaged her makeshift pillow, trying to plump it up and get it more comfortable. The nylon sleeping-bag cover felt synthetic and unexpectedly rough against her cheek. She didn't like it. Dusty's cotton sweater had felt a lot softer.

She sat up, very aware of the fact that, since she had used most of her clothing for her pillow, all she wore tonight was a cinnamon-and-cream lace and satin bra with matching briefs—the spare underwear that she'd managed to snaffle from her overnight bag before enacting Dusty's decree that she had to leave it behind with the chopper.

How much light did the fire give off? How much of her would Dusty be able to see if he happened to look? Trying to keep the sleeping bag pulled up high around her chest, she took his sweater out of the bag's cover, along with her own silk top and trousers, and remade the pillow completely.

First she rolled up Letty's oilskin and put it inside the trousers. She made the trousers into a compact package that fit inside her top, and then slid the whole mixed bundle of fabric inside Dusty's sweater, folding it in half and using its own sleeves to make a loose tie.

Much better.

Except for the way the sweater smelled.

Like Dusty himself.

With her cheek pressed against it and one arm tucked beneath, it felt as if she were hugging him, especially when she knew that the reality of a hug lay only a few feet away, breathing steadily in the darkness.

Why did he smell so good?

Why did one man smell *right,* while another just… *didn't*.

Personal choices in aftershave and laundry detergent? Surely it couldn't be as simple as that.

Todd had always smelled right. To be honest, in hindsight, this had been the basis for their whole relationship. He'd smelled right, even though in so many other ways he was all wrong.

Adam hadn't even smelled right, but since the Todd episode had convinced Shay that smell was a poor foundation for lifelong love, she'd ignored the nasal dimension to her feelings. Well, he hadn't actively smelled *bad!* She'd put her mourning for the loss of a warm, delicious male neck to bury her face in into the Life's Not Perfect basket.

Jason… She couldn't remember how Jason had smelled. He was years ago.

"Can't get to sleep?" Dusty said out of the darkness.

"Sorry, am I wriggling around?" There was a particular kind of restlessness to her movements, she knew—a heated, tingling, pulsing kind. Her whole body crawled with need, and every particle of that need funneled into the bundle of perfectly scented fabric she held in her arms.

"A bit," Dusty said. "But I think I'd be awake anyway." He let out a particular kind of restless sigh, and Shay heard his body slide against the soft inner fabric of his sleeping bag. She thought he'd shifted a little closer, but she wasn't sure. "How's the pillow now?"

· "Perfect. At least," she corrected quickly, "it's much better."

It only smelled perfect.

She wriggled and stretched, protecting her back and shoulders with the movement. Bending her legs to bring her body into a curled position, she felt the puffy edge of Dusty's sleeping bag brush against her down-covered knees.

"Do you think of yourself as a typical New Yorker?" he suddenly asked. "A typical New York woman?"

"Is this how you plan to lull me to sleep?"

"Sorry… It's just… I was just wondering."

"That's fine. I'm teasing. I wasn't sleepy yet." They both considered their shared wakefulness in silence for a moment. "But I'm not big on consigning myself to a stereotype, so even if I am typical, you'd have to back me into a very tight corner before I'd admit it."

There was a thick pause.

"That's what I was thinking about doing, you see," Dusty said slowly. "Backing you into a very tight corner." He went silent again, then added in a lower tone, "Of my sleeping bag."

"What?"

"It's okay. Forget it."

She thought.

Of his sleeping bag? Back her into a tight corner of it?

It was quite clear what he meant. Her body crawled and throbbed again. He rolled slightly toward her and their knees pressed harder together.

"Because I'm from New York, and that's what New York women are up for?" She shifted closer without even knowing she was going to do it. If she brought her arm out of the sleeping bag, she'd easily be able to touch him now.

"Yeah, it was clumsy, wasn't it? I was sounding you out, giving you fair warning, or something. But I should have just—" He stopped again, hissed a sigh between his teeth and rolled onto his stomach. The powerful bulk of his upper arm nudged her fingers. As he'd done last night, he'd used his T-shirt as part of his pillow, so his skin was bare.

"Should have just what?"

"Kissed you."

Something slammed into her lower stomach in the thick outback darkness like a kangaroo slamming into a car on a highway at night. How could two words carry that much heat? How could *kissed you* make her so want to be kissed?

"Yeah, that might have been better," she agreed, hearing the way her voice had gone creaky and breathless. She let her fingers press up to his bare, warm flesh, and yet again he shifted closer, making her whole forearm lie against his muscled bicep.

"So is it too late?" he said.

"To—?"

She knew.

But she wanted to hear him say it again.

He did. "To kiss you, of course."

"No," she said softly. "It's not too late."

He eased even closer. Shay could barely breathe. A part of her wanted to meet him halfway, to assert her equality in this most primal form of partnership. A bigger part of her simply waited, in a dizzy and almost painful state of expectation. Her heart beat faster. Her whole body felt hot and ready and aware. She was flooding with desire, melting with it, aching with it, and they hadn't even kissed.

Then she felt his mouth in the darkness—the faintest

whisper of breath and warmth, a rustle of nylon as he moved, followed by taste and pressure and incredible sensation. He smelled perfect, and he kissed...*better.*

He began slowly, exploring her with exquisite patience. His lips felt soft and firm at the same time, angled crookedly against her own mouth. They moved with the same male grace as the rest of his body. There was nothing out of place, nothing clumsy, nothing that jarred. She felt the first hint of moisture and sweetness as his tongue lapped at the sensitive inner skin of her lower lip, and then it disappeared again. The accidental tease made her want so much more.

She had no space in her mind to think it through, but had the hazy understanding that she'd never known a kiss to feel so right, so fast. It was like the meal they'd eaten tonight—unexpected, fabulously fresh, made even better by hunger and by the solitude and the purity of the air.

The whole meaning of her existence narrowed to his exploration of her mouth and her response to him. She heard a little sound escape from her throat—a helpless vocal note that was almost like begging.

More.

Don't stop.

Come closer.

Never, ever stop.

Her lips fell farther apart and this time his tongue washed deep into her mouth. She opened her eyes, and in the glow of the firelight she could just see that his eyes were closed, his lashes lying against his cheeks and his lids smooth and relaxed.

It made her feel as if he'd surrendered to this as completely as she had.

There was no need to watch him. She trusted him. She trusted everything that had happened between them since they'd left Jake with the chopper yesterday, and everything that was going to happen once they reached the homestead sometime tomorrow.

Trusted it, and wanted it, and didn't want to mess it all up with the barrage of self-questioning she could so easily launch into.

What does it mean? *Where will it* go? *What will he* think? *What's the downside and the risk? Where does it fit in my life? How do I know what I really want, here?*

All of that.

She was so sick of doing that.

Suddenly, kissing him wasn't anywhere near enough. She freed her arms from the sleeping bag and reached for him, needing to know how he felt when she held him, needing to feel every ounce of his weight pressed against her and to map every inch of his contoured body with her hands.

He felt so *strong*.

Why hadn't she ever guessed how good it would feel to hold a man this powerfully physical and honed? Why hadn't she understood about the magical contrast between her own softness and his hard muscle mass, beneath the supple covering of healthy skin.

She couldn't get enough of him. When his tongue pushed deeper, she met it with her own, and when he slid down the side zipper of his sleeping bag and rolled his torso half onto her, she cupped her hands over his tight backside and let out a moan of satisfaction.

Then he began to touch her breasts. He brushed his fingertips across her nipple and, seconds later, the ball of his thumb. Sliding his hand inside the lace, he cupped her, then rolled the hardened peak between his fingers, making an electric connection that arrowed right to her soft, swollen groin. He flicked her bra straps down, one by one, making the lacy cups useless, then he slid around to her back and managed to unsnap the fastening in two economical attempts.

They still weren't close enough together. She fumbled for the zipper on her own bag but suddenly her back spasmed, freezing her with the intensity of the unexpected pain. He felt the tensing in her body at once and dragged his mouth away from another endless kiss.

"I'm hurting you." He stroked the hair back from her forehead and kissed the tip of her nose, then her tingling mouth. "I'm sorry."

"No, it was me. I was looking for the zipper."

"Is it okay again now?" His question was tender and totally focused. She appreciated it, knowing that in some men the subtext would have been purely *when can we keep going?*

"My back's okay," she said. "For the moment. It's weird. Sometimes just the slightest bend and twist sets it off. But I can't get the zipper, and I want to. I want to be closer, touching you, Dusty."

He slid a little, so that he was sharing her makeshift pillow. He kissed her shoulder with sweet heat, and kept his hand lightly cupped on her sensitized breast. "Maybe it's best to leave the zipper," he said.

She could hear the reluctance slowing his words and didn't understand. "Leave it? You mean leave it closed?"

"If we get any nearer to each other, you know what will happen."

"Yes. Isn't that the whole point?" She brushed his lips with her fingertips—she loved the shape of his mouth, loved how much better she knew it, now—and he grabbed her wrist and breathed hot kisses into her palm and against the sensitive skin at the base of her fingers.

"Well…yes, it could be the whole point, if you want it to be, I guess."

"I do want it to be. Don't you?" She hadn't expected this hesitation and holding back from him.

"Very much. But what kind of contraception are you using?" he asked softly. "I'm not doing this unless it's safe. Shouldn't you consider that, too?"

The question hit her so suddenly that it jarred her mood almost as much as yesterday's chopper crash had jarred her body. She thought about it for a moment, thought about all the implications, and all the past history she didn't want to have to share with him, then blurted out, "Can't you take it on trust?"

"No, I can't."

"Shoot, Dusty, you can't take it this far and then refuse to go all the way!"

"That's supposed to be my line, isn't it?" She heard the smile in his voice, felt the push of his breathing against her body.

"We're not going to argue over who's saying the wrong thing!"

"Is that what you usually expect, though? For a man to take it on trust?"

"Usually…" she echoed vaguely, then spoke with an edge. "There's no *usually*. That makes it sound as if— I'm not that promiscuous, Dusty. I don't— You know, I've had steady boyfriends. Just a handful of them. I'm not in and out of bed with every man I meet. This is what your typical New York woman question was about. Again. If you want me to analyze why this feels so right… No. Please don't make me do that!"

"My question isn't about your morals, or your past." He swore, as if her misunderstanding was a huge frustration, an affront to his sense of honor. "It's not about analyzing, either. It's about whether this is safe. For both of us. I have no protection. I have nothing unpleasant to pass onto you, either, I'm certain of that."

"Same from me to you!"

His voice dropped low, more tender than anything she'd yet heard from him. "Don't get angry, Shay." He brushed her mouth and she wanted to hunt down the too-brief kiss and get it back. "Isn't it something that needs to be talked about? Isn't it something that protects you even more than it protects me?"

She didn't know how to answer. Her ob-gyn specialist had already told her that unwanted pregnancy was likely to be the least of her problems. The woman was only a few years older than Shay herself and was one of those super-human creatures who juggled motherhood with a Manhattan medical practice.

Dr. Chin had been pretty blunt during a checkup just a few months ago. "If you want kids, Shay, don't put it on the back burner, okay? It's only going to get harder for you with every month that goes by. You're probably already looking at some kind of intervention if you want to conceive. Three or four years from now, you'll be looking for a miracle."

"I'm not even sure if I do want kids," she'd answered, numb with surprise.

"You don't have the luxury of a lot of time to anguish over it, Shay."

"I see. Thanks."

Dr. Chin had gone on to apologize for her honesty. "But I'm not going to have you saying to me, 'Why didn't anyone tell me before it was too late?'"

The whole conversation had stayed with her, word for word, especially what she'd said herself.

I'm not even sure if I do want kids.

Now, halfway around the world from Dr. Chin's exclusive and highly regarded practice, Shay could allay Dusty's concerns about contraception by passing on the message from her doctor in a couple of stark sentences.

She began. "If you're talking about pregnancy, Dusty, you don't have to worry. It's safe."

"Famous last words."

Okay, say it Shay.

My doctor says I'm going to have to work to conceive. The words didn't come. Other words came instead.

"I don't even know if I want to have children," she blurted out. She curled her fingers against his back and had to consciously relax them to keep from digging her nails into his skin. "I mean, it's such a huge commitment. There's so much to consider. I look at my friend Sarah, who's seriously asthmatic, and has twins and a third one due in the fall, and she never has a second to herself. She never goes out. She never sleeps, as far as I can see. She wears sweatpants and running shoes ninety-five percent of the time. People say that the rewards cancel out all that, but I just don't know that I'd make a good mother. My own parents… Well, we talked about that, didn't we? I look at various things about myself and I think, would I pass that on? Would I royally stuff up my child by some huge fault in my parenting? I can see that it would be satisfying once they got older, and you could be proud of their achievements, and have adult conversations with them."

In the darkness, she smiled a little at an imaginary daughter—competent, interesting, intelligent and gorgeous. It was a precious image.

"But then I think about the kinds of conversations I have with my own parents and, let me tell you, they're not by choice and they're definitely not satisfying. It's such a powerful, scary relationship. So if I kill my career and my body and my entire lifestyle by sacrificing everything to this person, or people, who are then going to choose not to want to be with me the moment they're old enough to be any use as equals or friends…" She took a breath, hearing the way her words had sped up. "…Then what's the point? And yet, the idea of little arms reaching up to me, and of me actually *wanting* to make some of those sacrifices, which is a desire that does seem to kick in for most people once they actually have the baby—"

"Shay?" he whispered, pressing his fingers over her lips.

"Yes?" She grabbed his hand and took it away—it was a distraction, with all the stuff she was groping to say.

"Are you writing a book on this?"

"Well, no, I hadn't considered that, but—"

"Because I think you're already up to about chapter five."

"Sorry." She tensed. "I didn't realize you wanted the condensed version."

"But don't you think it's a hell of a lot simpler than what you're suggesting?"

"No. I don't." She'd been fretting about it for months. "I think it is."

"How in the heck can it be simple? It's the most complicated decision I've ever faced! My friends and I—"

"Talk about it for hours. Somehow I guessed."

"Okay." She gritted her teeth. "I overanalyze. I know that."

"But as for how it can be simple… Don't you think some of those big life things just are?"

He lay back and began stroking her body again, as a background to his words. She wanted to grab his hand and say *stop,* and yet there was something good about this. They seemed to be arguing, but it didn't feel angry or unequal or part of an unbridgeable distance.

"Like when you fall in love with someone," he went on, "you don't think, but what if they get hairy in strange places twenty years from now and I can't stand it? What if we run out of things to talk about? What if I lose sleep over them some day because they have to go in for surgery and I'm worried?"

"What are you saying?"

"Don't you think sometimes your heart pulls you so hard, there's no choice and you just have to go where it takes you? You just have to...follow it home?"

Yeah, maybe.

It was a very appealing idea, somehow. Follow her heart home. Could she do that? How did she find out where her heart lived?

"So you want kids?" she asked.

"Yes."

"In one word? Really, Dusty? Just like that. No questions or doubts."

"I can go a little deeper if you want," he drawled. "I can give you the book-length account."

"Please." She ignored his sarcasm. "Tell me why it's easy for you. Tell me why you're so sure, and what you think the benefits are, when to me this is one of the major decisions of my life, and I don't have forever to make it. At all!" Again, there was a tiny moment when she could have told him what Dr. Chin had said. Again, she didn't. Instead, she finished, "And I'm totally unsure about what the decision-making process should even be."

"Well, okay, you want detail? For a start, I'm absolutely bound and determined to have somebody around to do my laundry for me when I'm ninety-five."

"Seriously."

"I am serious. I like the idea that there's hopefully going to be someone who still cares about me that much if I get that old."

"All right, but laundry?"

"Those practical things are a symbol of the way people

should care about each other. Although I do recognize that this is one of the bad reasons for wanting kids—loneliness insurance."

She laughed. "Loneliness insurance. I'll have to add that to the plus column on my pro-and-con list."

"Do me a favor, Shay. Do not ever show me that list."

"So what are the other reasons?"

"*All* the reasons, okay? I want kids for all the reasons. Name a reason for having kids, whether it's good or bad, and it's on my list."

"All the bad reasons are on your list?"

"Well, not the evil bad ones, obviously. Just the normal human bad ones, like hoping I might one day get to be proud of something they did so I could boast about them, and show their photos to total strangers, thus embarrassing the kids and boring the total strangers to tears."

"You are funny. And strange."

"Because I know I want kids?"

"Because it doesn't seem to be *conflicting* you to any extent, when it's such a huge thing."

"Seriously, I think the huge things are sometimes the most obvious. Plus I now understand why contraception is not an issue for you."

The hair on the back of her neck stood up. "Oh?" What had she given away, in that rambling five-chapter piece of self-contemplation? He was absolutely right, she'd gone on way too long, and way too little of it had made any sense.

"Your conflict regarding the childbearing issue is the most effective bloody mood dampener I've ever met. We're never going to get as far as needing contraception in a million years."

"Oh, Dusty…" She buried her head in the pillow.

"Sorry," he said after a moment. "That was too blunt."

"No. I liked it."

"Yeah?"

She thought, then said, "I did. It might be good for me to get slapped in the face by a wet fish more often."

What had she decided just recently about herself and her friends? That they had crisis meetings more often than relaxed, pressure-free get-togethers?

It was true.

She'd dumped that whole rambling piece about whether or not to have kids on Leah and Alicia the last time they'd seen each other, and all three of them had ended up nodding and listening empathetically to each other for hours, tying themselves in emotional knots, no closer to any real insight than they'd been when they'd started.

It had felt good at the time, but now she wondered.

Maybe the whole point about men—the whole reason you might love one and need him in your life on a permanent basis—was that they tackled things differently. They refreshed your outlook. They wouldn't let you get away with certain female weirdness, the way you wouldn't let them get away with being too typically male. You balanced each other out.

Meanwhile, Dusty just wanted to have kids for "all the reasons" and if he occasionally bored total strangers with family photographs, so be it. There was something refreshing about this. Something endearing and healthy and safe.

But then, it was definitely easier for a man.

Which brought her back to where she'd begun.

"Um, if you're still interested, Dusty…"

He shifted and stretched like a lazy lion. "I could be. If you promise to shut up soon."

She laughed. "I promise. And look…you don't have to worry about me getting pregnant, okay? It's—it's—" she stopped and cleared her throat "—just not going to happen. Trust me on it? Can you, please?"

Her voice had gone a little too high. He said nothing, so she borrowed some of his own honesty, got stubborn about not messing this up with too much head stuff, and added very deliberately, "So now you can kiss me again, if you want."

Chapter Eight

"You are making this really hard for me, do you know that?" Dusty growled.

He'd already refused to kiss her about three times, but she wasn't taking no for an answer. He'd drawn his line in the sand and she'd simply reached out with one dainty big toe and rubbed it out, to leave a big mess there instead.

"Here I am," he said, "doing the right thing, and you're punishing me for it."

"I'm not." He could hear the need and impatience and heat in her breathy voice. "*Punishing* is the wrong word."

She shifted her hips and settled more intimately on top of him. Her legs straddled his thighs, and even though there were still two sleeping bags between them from the waist down, there was no such barrier between her silky-skinned stomach and his tensed-up rib cage, or between her breasts and his chest.

He could feel two fabulous, round soft-skinned shapes

pushing against him, and the brush of her peaked nipples, and he knew that every time she made the slightest movement, she did it with total, merciless intent. What had happened to her?

And what had happened to him?

He was on fire.

"In fact, who's punishing who?" she demanded. She cupped his jaw with a feather-light touch and gave him a kiss like a ripe, juicy peach. "Are you still saying no? Really? Seriously?"

"Yes. I have to." He clenched his teeth.

"I really, really don't want you to." Another peach of a kiss, the kind that left your lips glistening and your tongue sweet and dripping.

"Yeah, well, you're making that delightfully obvious," he managed to say.

"I might have to make it even more delightfully obvious if you keep refusing to cooperate."

"Please…do that," he heard himself rasp out.

"So you're mine? I can have my wicked way?"

"You're making it impossible to say no."

He didn't care anymore. He was only human. And he felt so close to her, as if the two of them were the only people who mattered in the entire world. He tried to tell himself that this was just because of their isolation, because of what they'd shared over the past two days, but this didn't make sense or feel like the truth. There was more to it than that.

She was such a maddening woman, and her own worst enemy, asking herself all those complicated, angst-ridden, unnecessary questions about her life because for some reason the simple, necessary questions just scared her too much. He found it a compelling quality. It made him want to laugh at her and rescue her from herself at the same time.

Shay, sweetheart, you don't have to live your life this way.

And it reminded him of someone.

It reminded him of…himself.

Shoot!

But yes, it really did. Not his normal attitude to life, but the way he'd been with Mandy, when he'd tied himself in all those knots of rationalization because the whole relationship had just fallen into his lap thanks to *Today's Woman* magazine. With Mandy herself making all the moves and seeming so sure, he hadn't wanted to let go of something that effortless and easy.

He hadn't asked any of the right questions—hadn't asked the *simple* questions, the ones he'd urged on Shay. He'd dug himself into a trap of his own making.

Next time, he wouldn't make the same mistake. Meanwhile—

Meanwhile…

Ah hell, how was he supposed to do the right thing when Shay so plainly didn't want him to, and when she seemed to know exactly how to get right inside his skin?

"I'm going to forget the jammed zipper on my bag," she whispered. "I'm just going to get inside yours. It might be a challenge. There won't be a lot of room. But that'll make it…interesting…don't you think?"

With a rustle and a slither, she freed herself from her bag.

"It's not going to work," he told her, balanced on the knife edge of surrender. He'd forgotten every reason for saying no.

"Ooh, do you really think you have that much will-power left?"

"That's not what I meant. I meant there really won't be room."

"Mmm, tell me what you're envisaging, in that case. It sounds athletic."

"Oh hell, Shay," he groaned, "what suddenly turned you into such a tease?"

"I'm not teasing. Teasing means promising and taking away. I'm not going to go back on anything I say. My promises are genuine."

"Such a vixen, then."

She gave a throaty laugh. "Vixen? I just know when I have to bring out all my weaponry, that's all."

"Because you're not letting me say no?"

"That's right."

He felt her slide down the zipper on his sleeping bag about two feet, making the top gape. He thought, *I'll just close my eyes and whatever happens will be her doing, not mine.*

"I'm taking this slow," she explained seriously, "because of my back."

Her back? Who was she kidding? Her back was merely a transparent excuse. She slid herself into the bag, her legs slipping silkily past his. One inner thigh brushed right down his body, soft and scented from the soothing cream she'd been using, and he felt the rougher texture of the lace triangle that barely covered the most intimate part of her. He was so ready for this.

"Can you support me a little, please? My shoulders are still pretty sore. When I prop myself on your chest like this, on my elbows, there's a strain."

"A vixen and a tease," he whispered.

Then her back spasmed again and as he held her and waited for the pain to settle, it reminded him of something else he'd learned about her—her vulnerability. What had she said earlier?

You don't have to worry about me getting pregnant, okay? Trust me on it? Can you, please?

Her tone had contained something, an emotion he

hadn't identified at the time and couldn't identify now. It rang alarm bells, though. *Trust me* wasn't another way of saying *I'm on the Pill*. He'd already learned that she was straightforward about certain things. If she were on the Pill, that's surely what she would have said. No, there was something more complicated going on. He'd trusted the women in his life before, and they'd betrayed him and let him down. He didn't intend to let it scar him…but he wasn't a fool, either.

Although every cell in his body clamored its masculinity and told him to forget the issue, he heard himself say, "So while you're lying on me, Shay, before we really get going, here, tell me why I should trust you about the pregnancy thing. What protection have you got in place that makes you so sure?"

As soon as he felt the tension that pulled at her body, he knew they weren't going to make love to each other tonight.

Shay had never slept so tightly cocooned with a man before. The ground felt so much softer beneath her, with her discarded sleeping bag providing a piece of narrow mattress for them both. She braced her back against Dusty and he held her with his whole body curved against hers.

Every nerve ending and every inch of her skin felt as if it were on fire from frustration and wanting, and she couldn't believe that he'd managed to say no to such a primal need. The other kinds of pleasure they'd given each other after they'd finally finished talking might have temporarily eased the aching—enough to allow Dusty himself to sleep—but their effect hadn't lasted in her own body.

Dusty was right.

Everything was so much simpler than she'd ever thought.

It was *incredibly* simple, when it came to the point.

She wanted him inside her.

Nothing else would do.

She couldn't understand quite how she'd ended up telling him so much.

How had he been so persistent and skillful in extracting the story of her medical history and Dr. Chin's warning?

And she absolutely couldn't understand why it wasn't enough for him.

"Probably need medical intervention if you want to conceive?" he'd said. "That's not good enough, Shay. She was scaring you into thinking about your priorities, that's all."

"You think she was *lying?*"

"Lying, no. Presenting a worst-case scenario, yes."

"I mean, that's occurred to me, too, but—"

"I'd probably do it, too, if I were in her position. You said she runs an infertility program."

"Which means she knows what she's talking about."

"She does, and she said *probably.*"

"*Probably,* to give me some hope, Dusty, to soften the reality!"

He ignored her. "And I'd imagine you *probably* don't want to get pregnant tonight, and even if you're *probably* not at the right point in your cycle, I'll *probably* be able to face myself in the mirror sometime tomorrow with a better conscience if I do the right thing."

"Shoot, you have willpower!"

"No, not much, right now, but I definitely have principles!"

Which had brought her to this current state of unbearable physical frustration and nourishing emotional safety at the same time.

She could feel Dusty's arm brushing the undersides of her breasts, reminding her of the way he'd touched them and kissed them so lavishly. When he slid it lower to curve against her hip in his sleep, she wanted to move his touch to a more intimate place, wanted to roll toward him and feel him harden and fill her the way she craved.

There would be other chances.

There had to be.

She might die if there weren't.

And meanwhile she felt strangely happy.... Really... just happy... Ready to sleep, too. Yes...

She only awoke hours later when he eased himself away from her. The whole sky had lightened, even though the sun wasn't yet up. "Stay," she mumbled.

"You stay," he whispered back. "I'm going to get the fire started."

"I'll help."

"You'll have stiffened up again. Let me do it, and I'll heat that rock for you."

"I don't feel stiff."

"Well, I'll take that as a compliment, after all the things we did and didn't do." He gave her his heart-stopping grin. "But stay in the sleeping bag all the same. We still have six miles to go."

Six uneventful miles, as it turned out.

They ate peanut butter on slightly smoky toast for breakfast, and drank the last of the instant coffee. Then Shay doused the fire and rolled the sleeping bags while Dusty saddled the horses. Was this really only their second morning in the wilderness together? She thought about the couple from the 1930s whom Dusty had told her about— the ones who couldn't sleep indoors. She understood them a little better now, she thought.

And then, at around noon, they saw the homestead and outbuildings of Roscommon Downs appear slowly around a bend in the river channel, and Shay cried with relief at the thought of reaching home…even if the home wasn't hers.

"Thank you," she said to Dusty, during their last few moments alone.

"Yeah? Why?"

"Because I can't think of anyone I'd rather be lost in the desert with—even though I really can't believe this is ever a desert, and I know we weren't lost."

He laughed. "You were a pretty satisfactory traveling companion, yourself."

The screen door on the veranda of the single men's quarters flapped and they saw Prim. "You took your time," she called out to them. "We were giving you three more hours then calling for an aerial search."

She thumped down the steps and came toward them, her round and not-very-pretty face lit up in the most brilliant smile. Shay remembered what Dusty had said to her beside the campfire on their first night—that a pretty smile was more important than a pretty face. She wondered if he'd learned this from his station cook.

"Shay hurt her back and couldn't ride," Dusty said to Prim. "So we walked most of the way."

"I could kiss you for putting in the first-aid kit, Prim," Shay came in. "Its stock of painkillers needs replenishing at this point, as well as that fabulous cream."

"You must have run out of food, too."

"Dusty turns out to be a pretty resourceful bush chef. We ate Thai-style seafood."

Prim threw back her head and laughed her deep, throaty laugh. "I am going to have to hear a lot more about this adventure of yours over dinner tonight." The words contained an echo of significance that Prim herself wouldn't understand.

I want to look at Dusty, Shay thought, *but I'm not going to.*

I want to smile at Dusty, like two people with the best secret in the world.

And already everything feels different, now that we're back. We're not alone anymore.

"Boss!" said a man's voice. Someone Shay hadn't met. One of the married men, she guessed, who would have his own cottage in the widespread grouping of homestead buildings.

"Yeah, Dave," Dusty said.

Dave strode up and punched him in the arm, then shook his hand heartily. "Took the long way home, did you?"

"Yes. Had a very scenic detour, thanks to the water over Wilandra Crossing getting visibly deeper while I watched, on the way out. Shay's riding skills aren't quite up to swimming a horse across a flood current, yet."

"Shay's riding skills weren't even up to sitting on straight," she said.

"That was your back," he consoled her easily. "When it's better, I'll teach you to ride. Let's get you inside. I'm sure you want a shower."

He put a hand on Shay's shoulder and nudged her toward the house. She went willingly, feeling a sudden selfish and pretty terrifying need to have the man to herself, the way she had for the past forty-eight hours. The adrenaline and determination that had been coursing through her on and off for days suddenly plummeted and she felt miserable and lost.

"Dave, can you get one of the useless mugs around here to take care of Sally and Beau?" Dusty said, behind Shay. "I'm going to wash and change, these clothes are getting pretty bad." Like Shay's, the legs of his pants were stained to thigh level like a high-tide mark on a waterfront pier.

He was going to come into the house with her, which made her spirits flutter briefly back into life. It was that selfishness, again. She didn't want to lose him to all the demands of the huge cattle station.

But then he added, "I won't be long."

She felt foolish for having thought he might stay with her. What, sipping tea on the veranda? He was a busy man.

"Prim, if there's anything involving peanut butter on the menu for tonight," he called back to his cook, "change it, okay? I like the stuff, but five meals in a row is too much of a good thing."

By the time Shay came out of the shower, wrapped in a towel, Dusty had gone. He'd left a pile of clothing on the bed, and a note.

There's stuff I need to do, so I'll see you later. Make yourself at home. Clothes courtesy of Letty.

She picked up the pile of casual tops, pants, shorts and very practical pairs of clean cotton socks and let them fall untidily back on the bed, wondering when *later* meant.

At dinner? That was hours away.

And so, presumably, was her laptop, still with Jake, wherever he now was.

Seriously, you had to laugh. How much progress had she made since she'd first surveyed this tranquil, pretty spare room almost three days ago? She was no closer to getting to New York or even Sydney. She'd been separated from her laptop and might never see it again.

And in its place she had the much weightier baggage of a new and incredibly inconvenient connection to a man who didn't remotely fit into her life.

She chose a pink tank top, cropped denim jeans and pink socks, and dressed with movements that felt both automatic and still stiff. The shower had soothed her back, but it remained fragile and sore and liable to spasm at any moment.

The thought that she didn't have to push herself to tramp through the wilderness, sleep on the ground, and eat any more peanut butter brought a catlike lift to her bedraggled spirits. There was a lot to be said for creature comforts—for being clean and comfortable, well-fed and permitted to sleep—and she celebrated in style with a ham, mustard and lettuce sandwich, a glass of iced coffee with a large blob of chocolate ice cream on top, and a two-hour nap on top of the clean and fragrant puffy pastel cotton quilt.

When she woke up again, it was almost three-thirty and the house was still quiet. She phoned Sonya in Sydney and told her, "I'm still stuck in the flooding, but at least I'm back at Roscommon Downs."

Sonya wanted more detail. "Because Tom was pretty skeptical about the whole story, I have to tell you."

"You mean he thought I'd *faked* involvement in a helicopter crash as an excuse for not getting to New York? Who is he? Donald Trump?"

"Well, I think you should call him. He says you have to take your vacation days to cover the entire period that you're…wherever you are."

"Southwest Queensland."

"Right. But I think he's pretty much expecting you to keep working, even so. By the way, I have nine feature-article proposals for upcoming issues that need to be okayed, is there an e-mail address I can send them to?"

Shay gave her Dusty's.

"When are you flying out?" Sonya asked.

Good question.

"Two weeks," she said firmly. She had at least that much vacation time owing to her.

"Two *weeks?*"

"If Tom wants to have another editor-in-chief in place at the magazine by then, fine."

Am I bluffing?

Shay honestly didn't know. She wasn't sure that she knew anything about her life, right now.

"Tell her to pack the contents of my desk into boxes," she went on, "and I'll pick them up if I get out of here alive. I've already nearly died trying. Now I'm going to accept that it's not meant to be."

The call to Sonya left her oddly exhilarated and free, but with this feeling came a restlessness she didn't like. What was wrong with her? She drank a glass of cold water and ate an apple, then went out onto the veranda and circled it. It ran all the way around the house, keeping out the harsh sun and adding a tranquil buffer of space that would be a gorgeous place to spend lazy afternoon hours or hot summer evenings.

There was little sign of life. In the distance, she heard the grinding rumble of a heavy engine and the buzz of something lighter—a motorcycle, maybe, or one of the four-wheeler farm bikes she knew they used on properties like this one.

The four-wheeler came into view, and its rider might have been Dusty. She watched, hoping the vehicle and rider would head in this direction, but they didn't. Soon they had disappeared, cut off from her line of sight by the outline of a broad shed. On a low rise farther off, she saw a huge mob of cattle like a red-brown shadow across the land, and guessed that they were being mustered to fresh pasture, or away from the still-rising waters.

She envied Dusty, having work to do.

Back in the house, she discovered his office, which she hadn't seen on her first day here. It contained the usual computer and filing cabinets, as well as bookshelves stacked with farming journals. On the walls, however, there were framed photos of race-winning horses, and these were what grabbed her attention most. The horses were so sleek and perfect.

She didn't know much about horse racing, nor why the photos took pride of place. Her journalist's instincts kicked in and she started reading the printed captions listing the details. Horse's name, race name, distance and type, date, winning jockey, trainer, owners.

Ah, owners.

D. Tanner, B. Smith, C. Woods, R. Middleton.

Or sometimes D. Tanner, B. Smith, C. Woods, P. Morris.

Whatever the combination, Dusty's name always came first.

"Hi," said his voice from the office doorway, and she couldn't help the way her face lit up at the sight of him.

He wore clean jeans and a navy-blue polo shirt, with his sunglasses folded and tucked into the open neck, and he must already have been working hard because jeans, shirt and tanned skin were all streaked with mud. The evidence of his physical lifestyle only made him sexier— which was a new reaction, in her life's experience.

"Hi, yourself." She'd even gone breathless. "You're back."

"To see how you're doing," Dusty explained, even though he knew it had to be obvious.

Her smile almost knocked him over. She hadn't tried to hide her pleasure at seeing him. It was scary how much he just wanted to wrap her in his arms and kiss every bit of skin and silky hair that he could reach.

Yeah, very scary.

He held himself back, feeling that everything was different now, even if their attraction to each other hadn't changed.

"You own racehorses," she said. The tone was a little awkward and almost accusatory, a kind of why-don't-I-already-know-this, as if they should have covered their entire life stories out there in the flooded desert.

He nodded vaguely. He'd looked for her in her room, in the kitchen and living room, on the veranda, a little concerned when the house had seemed so quiet. He'd abandoned her for nearly four hours, and felt bad about it, but too many people had needed his input around the station.

"Part own them," he told her. "With my mates Brant and Callan. Our trainers usually kick in for a ten percent share, too."

Why was he going into this detail? He hadn't thought about the photos in months, hadn't framed any new ones recently. The pleasure he took in the racing syndicate with Callan and Brant was only partly about pride, much more about friendship.

"Brant?" Shay said.

"You interested in racing?"

Was it possible that they'd actually found something they had in common, at last, beyond a shared taste for Thai-style seafood beside an open fire?

"I know nothing about it," she answered.

Okay, no, it wasn't possible. He should have known. And he shouldn't feel this disappointed.

"Well…" she went on. "Last year I flew down to Melbourne, dressed up in a ridiculous hat, four-inch heels and a floaty dress and went to the Melbourne Cup, but that's the sum total of my experience."

"The four-inch heels count for something, I guess," he drawled at her, hoping to get a laugh.

But her thoughts had apparently tracked elsewhere. "Dusty, you just mentioned someone called Brant."

"Yeah, Branton Smith, one of my best mates." He struggled to get this onto a more personal level, to find the right way to talk to her, the way they had when they'd been on their own. "I think it's what the three of us like best about owning the horses—keeps the friendship going. If either of them ever tell me they want to pull out of the whole deal, I'll be gutted. It was my—" He stopped.

So much for spilling his feelings. She wasn't listening.

She'd pressed her fingertips against her temples. "The same Brant Smith I interviewed for the magazine last month? He's a sheep farmer at a place called—"

"Inverlochie," he supplied. Good grief, she'd interviewed Brant for the magazine? Why?

"That's right," she said.

"Brant didn't tell me you interviewed him."

They hadn't spoken to each other for a couple of weeks. Dusty knew that Brant had been stretched lately. Wool prices were down, and his move into the fat lamb market had risks attached. They'd kept the conversation mainly to the subject of racing, with a sidebar on their fellow racing syndicate member Callan's recent engagement to a women he'd met through *Today's Woman* magazine's "Wanted: Outback Wives" campaign.

"…met through the magazine's 'Wanted: Outback Wives' campaign," he heard Shay say. "The story appeared in our June issue. It came out about four weeks ago, and I was really pleased with it."

"I'm sorry?" he said blankly.

"Brant," she clarified with heavy patience, jutting her chin.

He could imagine her speaking to her magazine staff like this—heavy frown, strong jaw, flashing jade eyes, abrupt tone—when they were being slow to grasp an idea. The career woman had been on vacation for the past couple of days, but now she was back. He understood her a little better now. He could see more of the complex woman beneath her facade. He even liked her.

"Yes, but…" he said vaguely, then got a grip. "No, it's my other mate Callan who's engaged to a woman he met through the magazine. And of course I was, too, to Mandy. Seemed like a pretty good strike rate."

"Strike rate?" She frowned again, and the muscles at his temples tightened in frustration.

They weren't communicating very well.

She had a faint red indentation on her cheek and her hair was slightly mussed, although silky clean and a lot less frizzy. He guessed she'd taken a long nap after her shower and was still a little groggy. And maybe he was already too deeply caught up in the responsibility of running Roscommon Downs because the closeness they'd discovered on their trek through the floodwaters had almost gone.

Not that there was any hostility.

They just weren't quite connecting.

"Strike rate," he repeated. "It's a racing term. Percentage of winners to races run. Callan, Brant and I all took part in your Outback Wives thing."

"Callan." Shay frowned. "I remember him. Blue eyes. From South Australia. His wife had died. He was at the cocktail party we held in February. I knew you'd had a couple of friends involved with 'Wanted: Outback Wives,' also, but I couldn't remember who."

"Yes, we all sent in our photos and our details, Callan, Brant and me. It was Brant's sister's idea. Callan lost his wife nearly five years ago to cancer, and…we don't quite know what happened…we think he might have tried to jump into another relationship too soon and he got burned.

Anyhow, he seemed so lost, he didn't know where to start, to get his life back. Nuala thought if we all sent our photos and details in to the magazine, he might at least get some encouraging letters."

"We had a fantastic response," Shay said. "Way better than I'd dared to hope. Sales jumped that month."

She frowned. Maybe the high sales hadn't lasted.

"And Callan did meet someone," Dusty told her. "Jacinda. American, like you. She's a screenwriter, and she was running away from a very bad divorce, needed a place to hide. Callan had her staying with him, with her little daughter, and it went from there. So there was a point where both of us were engaged. Two out of the three of us, a strike rate of sixty-six point six percent."

"But I interviewed Brant, not Callan," Shay insisted, stubborn on the subject.

"Callan and Jacinda didn't want to go public with their story."

"And Brant is engaged to a woman called Michelle. Mish, she called herself. If I had a copy of the magazine, or even my laptop—" She broke off and sighed. "Am I ever going to see my laptop again, Dusty?"

"You can use my computer, if you want." He gestured toward it, feeling stuck—stranded in an awkward impasse more effectively than they'd been stranded by the floodwaters.

She looked just as ill at ease. A little of the stressed-out executive had returned, and he was torn between admiring her single-minded drive and wanting to protect her from herself—her workaholic tendencies—the way he'd have protected a child from snakes and sunburn.

Tonight hovered like a great big question mark in the sky. They'd had a kind of shipwreck romance over the past couple of nights. Such things did happen. Two people thrown together in extraordinary circumstances found an illusory connection that evaporated within hours once their normal lives resumed.

Was this what Shay wanted? A kind of thanks-for-the-memories end to something that had never fully begun? Almost certainly, she did. Her renewed tension suggested it, and it was the only outcome that made any sense.

Or should he check in with Prim this afternoon and find out what supplies she kept in her Aladdin's Cave of a storeroom to equip a love-hungry single stockman planning a night on the town?

"I will e-mail the office, Dusty, I will get them to send an electronic copy of our June issue and I will show you the story!" she said, heated and impatient, as if it mattered. "Your friend is engaged. She speaks with a slight Dutch accent, but—"

"Dutch? That was years ago. Beatrix. That's long gone."

"A Dutch accent, but she's American."

"So Callan, Brant and I have a strike rate of one hundred percent now? That's what you're saying? Two American fiancées and one Aussie ex, all of whom saw our photos in your magazine?"

"She's very pretty. Gorgeous, actually. Brunette with blue eyes. Her hair could use a better stylist, I did think."

"Beatrix was a redhead."

"I'm telling you, it's not Beatrix! It's Michelle. Mish. She seemed really happy on his farm. Even the dogs adored her. I promise you, Dusty."

"He would have told me," Dusty insisted, while wondering why they were arguing about such a weird and unlikely thing. "It's how many weeks ago? That you interviewed him and this Michelle? Six? He would not have kept something like that a secret! This is the craziest conversation I've had in—"

"I'm sorry," she suddenly cut in, and he looked at her to find her eyes narrowed with concern. She stepped closer and her hand hovered at her side as if it wanted to be somewhere else.

"What for?"

"For arguing, and being a pain in the butt." The hand came up, landed on his shoulder. He let it stay.

"I like it when you're a pain in the butt," he said. "I like how you stand your ground. You know, some things change, when your life gets back to normal. But some things don't. Some things are constant, and real." He only thought it through as he said it. "The things I like about you. They're real."

She slowed down at last, enough to say quietly, "The things I like about you, too, Dusty. I'd rather have a healthy argument any day, than have nothing to talk about at all."

And suddenly everything they'd both felt over the past couple of days was back in the air again, superheating it, charging it with electricity, filling it with meaning. He could have kissed her in a heartbeat, but if he did that, he knew he wouldn't want to stop, and he had Dave and Wayne and Steve waiting for him in the machinery shed.

This would have to wait, but at least he could make it a wait that held the right promise.

"Do you want to eat in the house tonight?" he asked. "I can have Prim send something over for us, and we could open a bottle of wine."

She nodded, her eyes wide. "Let's do that. We need to, don't we?"

"Yeah, I think we do," he answered gruffly, knowing he definitely had to find time to see Prim about the inventory in a certain section of her storeroom this afternoon.

Chapter Nine

Shay knocked at the front door of the head stockman's house. Before her knuckles even touched the dark green painted wood, she knew that the reason for her visit was a crazy one, but it was too late to bail out now.

"Hi, Jane," she rehearsed cynically, under her breath. "It's nice to meet you. I'm Shay. And I was wondering if you happened to have any spare contraception hanging around your bathroom that you could pass on to a girl in need."

No.

Even the more delicate way she intended to approach the subject in reality seemed fraught with pitfalls. And judging by the number of kids' voices she could hear inside the house, what were the chances that Jane and her husband had heard of contraception, anyhow?

"Mu-u-u-um? Someone's at the door!" Shay heard.

"Well, answer it then!" said someone else—a boy, she thought.

"I'm making a snack," said the first voice.

"Harry, answer the door!" This was presumably Mum.

"Just a minute."

"Don't let Gemma open it!"

Finally, after a lot of handle rattling, it opened and there stood a little blond angel, of surely no more than two or three years old, with a face covered in some kind of chocolate substance.

"Tum in," said the angel.

"Should I wait for your mom?"

But the chocolate angel had toddled off.

Shay "tame in" as instructed, shut the door behind her and discovered that missy must have had the chocolate substance on her hands as well as her face, because it was all over the inside door handle and now smeared on Shay's own palm.

Hmm.

It wasn't chocolate, she discovered when she cautiously sniffed it. It was Vegemite.

As editor-in-chief of an Australian magazine, Shay had been given a crash course on Australian cultural icons and, bizarrely enough, Vegemite was one of them. Australians loved the stuff. They took jars of it with them when they traveled out of the country, or hunted down international suppliers on the Internet. Providing healthy quantities of B vitamins, it *looked* like chocolate, but it was in fact made of yeast, and was very salty and strongly flavored.

Sonya had shown Shay her own personal version of how best to enjoy Vegemite. She spread it very thinly on slices of crusty French bread along with a generous smear of butter and crunched the whole lot down in big, happy mouthfuls. Shay had conceded that it was edible this way. Tasty, even. But she hadn't gone out and purchased her own jar.

Now she had it all over her hand. What should she do? Lick it off?

"Oh, bliddy hell!" said a cheerful—and pregnant—woman of about thirty-five, appearing in the cool, dim front hall. "Did Gemma let you in?"

"The blond angel with the Vegemite face?"

"I'm sorry. Those are her two current crazes—helping herself to Vegemite straight from the jar and answering the front door. Each one is bad enough on its own, but together they're a disaster!"

"It's fine." Shay instantly liked this woman's open approach.

"You must be Shay. We've heard all about your adventures. I'm so glad you stopped in. I'm Jane. Do you mind washing it off in the kitchen sink?"

Half an hour later, Shay had decided that if there was anyone in the world from whom she *could* ask to borrow contraception without feeling very self-conscious and lamentably disorganized, it would be Jane Portman, but even Jane's casual, cheerful attitude didn't quite get her that far at their first meeting.

Maybe she could work up to it over the next few days… if she and Dusty could wait that long.

No, she decided a moment later, it would be so indiscreet. The news would soon spread. She just wasn't that… brash, or something.

Meanwhile, Gemma turned out to be Shay's favorite kind of angel—into everything and convinced, probably correctly, that "Wanna tiss, Mummy?" would earn her instant forgiveness for any minor mishap such as accidentally dropping a kilogram tub of strawberry yogurt on the kitchen floor and then tracking it everywhere as she "helped" to clean it up. The other four kids, as well as two more who belonged to other families at Roscommon Downs, created similar if slightly less toddler-ish distractions.

Jane attempted to make Shay a cup of tea during all this, and announced eventually, "There! That only took twenty-five minutes!" as she put the two steaming mugs on the kitchen table. "Dinner is scheduled for midnight tonight, I think."

"Why don't you let me help with something?" Shay asked. "I mean it."

Because she'd already offered twice and Jane had said no.

This time the other woman threw out a skeptical glance. "If you keep saying that, I'll take you up on it."

"Do!"

"You said you don't have kids."

"No, but it's obvious I should get in some practice in case one day I do," she said recklessly. *I don't even know if I want kids, Dr. Chin.* "This is full on!"

"Well, not everyone's crazy enough to have five in seven years."

Ooh, window of opportunity on the contraception topic!

Shay couldn't do it.

The magazine that the Australian edition of *Today's Woman* was descended from, a thick periodical called *The Ladies' Weekly Round* had offered some very progressive, cryptically worded pieces of advice on "limiting family size" in the 1930s, in its From Your Family Doctor column. They would have been aimed at just such extravagant examples of motherhood as Jane Portman, even though it was clear that Jane was perfectly happy with her large brood.

But wouldn't it make an interesting article, Shay suddenly thought, to look up some of those old bits of medical and family advice and examine whether any of it still had something to offer women today?

"I've just had an idea," she blurted out to Jane, who had just returned from breaking up an argument between two of the boys. She told her all about it.

"Sounds like great fun," Jane said. "I'd read it. I'd even contribute to it! I have an old Country Women's Association recipe book with some hand-written additions in the back of it, including something called, 'Special Wash for Women.' We think it was my great grandmother who wrote it, but we're not sure."

"You'll have to show me."

But maybe not today. The voices of the two boys were rising in anger again.

Over the top of them, Jane said, "Hey, if you're serious about helping, Gemma would love to have you supervise her bath."

"I'd love it, too."

"You'll get wet. I laugh when they talk about kids' electronic toys being 'interactive.' Gemma's bath will give you the true meaning of the word."

When Shay finally left, with patches of strawberry-scented bathwater decorating Letty's borrowed shirt and jeans, it was after six o'clock. The other kids had gone home and Jane was able to promise Dave, who'd then immediately disappeared to have a shower, "Dinner's in twenty minutes."

Shay hadn't gotten close to the initial incentive for her visit, but she'd come away with something important, anyhow.

If only she could work out what it was.

"Pasta sauce," Prim said to Dusty. "How's that? Too basic?"

"It's fine."

"Because I could think for a minute and come up with something better."

"Really, Prim, Bolognese sauce is fine."

"Some of our fresh fruit and veg is getting a bit low since I can't get into Longreach to stock up, but I could whip you up some mini-quiches with—"

"It's fine, okay?"

"But not very…" She trailed off, making vague loops in the air with her hands. "…Seductive."

"Oh, hell, Prim!" he burst out. "How did you know?"

"I didn't." She grinned, totally unrepentant. "But I do now."

He took a steadying breath. "Actually, on the same subject, I've got a small problem I need help with."

"Yeah?"

"Hoping you might have certain supplies in your storeroom."

She did.

He walked across to the homestead several minutes later, as darkness gathered over Roscommon Downs, still somewhat embarrassed and having sworn Prim to secrecy, but equipped for a very nice evening.

Or, more accurately, twelve nice evenings.

Shay wasn't back. She'd told him she might go and introduce herself to some of the other people on the station this afternoon, so she was probably with Jane Portman or Bronwyn Hemming. Dusty used the opportunity to track down the inexplicable mystery of Brant's supposed engagement to a slightly-but-not-quite-Dutch brunette named Michelle, and called him at Inverlochie.

The engagement story wasn't true.

He knew it couldn't have been.

He and Callan and Brant didn't chat on the phone for hours at a stretch, or call each other to report every little detail of their lives, but they always covered the important stuff. If Brant had got himself engaged, if something that significant had developed in his life, he would have said something about it before this.

And yet…

"I'm flying to Langemark on Sunday," he announced abruptly to Dusty, just when Dusty thought that their conversation was almost over.

"Langemark, the country? In Europe?"

"You mean, as opposed to Langemark, the capital of Mars? Yes, of course Langemark, the country." Brant sounded tense and not particularly happy, suddenly.

Or maybe not suddenly.

In hindsight, he'd been a bit tense throughout the conversation. His initial *Of course I'm not engaged,* Dusty had read as meaning, *Of course I would have told you if I was,* but now he wondered. What else was going on?

"Why?" he asked. "Do they breed good sheep there?" Those places in the north of Europe were really better known for their cattle and horse breeds than for sheep. Friesians, Warmbloods, Hanoverians—

"There's more to my life than sheep, Dusty."

"I know. So tell me why you're going to Langemark."

Because he was in love with Langemark's princess— Artemisia Helena, known to her family and friends as Misha—or, when traveling incognito, as Michelle. Brant's sister, Nuala, was apparently one of those friends, and Misha was Shay's not-quite-Dutch blue-eyed brunette from the magazine interview—only the brunette part was a wig put on as a disguise, the engagement had been a pretense, also—and she was really a blonde.

"You tricked Shay Russell?"

"To get the magazine off my back, and the women who kept making contact. You have no idea, Dusty."

"She's a professional. You know, people give journalists a bad rap, and some of them deserve it, but not all of them. Some of them sincerely try to bring their readers the right stories, and if you're happy to *fake* something for a national magazine—" He stopped, knowing Brant wouldn't understand why he was angry on Shay's behalf, and not having the remotest desire to explain.

Brant was too caught up in his own problems, anyhow, which was probably fair enough. There were two sides to a heck of a lot of life's important stories. He should let this one go.

"She was only here for three and a half weeks," Brant said. "I don't think it was real. It can't have been real. She wanted to stay but I wouldn't let her. I wasn't going to get us both into this stupid, ill-thought situation that both of us would soon regret."

Like my engagement to Mandy, Dusty thought.

He didn't say it out loud.

"I sent her back to deal with her life," Brant went on, sounding anguished about it. "She had to make a formal announcement to the people of Langemark that her wedding was off—she was supposed to marry Gian-Marco Ponti."

"The Formula One driver?"

"As opposed to Gian-Marco Ponti the vacuum-cleaner salesman?"

"Okay, Brant, I get it. Langemark the country, Misha the princess, Ponti the race-car driver. You have to admit—"

Brant wasn't interested in what he had to admit.

"But I can't just let it go," he said. "I've given her three and a half weeks, the same amount of time she was here. If there was any reality to it at all, we should know it when we see each other again. If there wasn't, I'm going to get a twenty-foot-tall medieval castle door studded with bolts and carved royal crests slammed in my face—"

"Or else maybe this long braid of hair rolled up like a rope ladder from a window, while a witch with a wart on her nose chases you, brandishing a broomstick like a lethal weapon."

"Something like that." Even over the phone, Dusty could hear the gritted teeth.

"You have your plane ticket?" he asked.

"Yes, and I'm bloody scared it's not going to work out. She's…pretty incredible."

What did you say to a strangled announcement like that? Dusty had no idea. Brant sounded as if he'd prefer to have all his teeth pulled at once with no anesthesia than to make such statements.

And at that moment, Dusty heard Shay coming into the house. "Listen, mate," he said, "it'll be all right, okay? Whatever happens. It'll work out."

"I don't know if it will."

"I have to go, okay? Talk to you soon? How long are you going for?"

Dumb question, given the uncertain outcome of the trip. Brant didn't answer it.

"Anyhow," Dusty went on quickly, "talk to you when you get back."

"Yeah. And if I go to Melbourne for the spring racing carnival…"

"I might fly down myself. Definitely. That'd be great. Talk to you before then, anyhow."

After a couple more stilted, repetitive phrases, they managed to get off the phone.

"Hi," said Shay, in the same breathless, wide-eyed way she'd said it in his office four hours earlier, when they'd first trespassed into the whole ridiculous question of whether Brant Smith was engaged.

As Dusty had just established, he wasn't. He considered giving her the information…

Considered it for about one quarter of a second and then decided that instead of another tense, pointless argument, he'd prefer to have a great evening. "We're eating spaghetti Bolognese," he said, "and Prim's chocolate mousse for dessert."

"Ooh, not a vitamin in sight!"

"She's getting a bit strapped for fresh food, since the roads are closed. She did offer a side dish of frozen peas and corn. Want me to go over and—?"

"No." She shook her head emphatically, laughing. "I want you to stay right here, close all the curtains and take the phone off the hook."

"Sounds good to me."

Darkness had fallen outside and, with his mother's thick yet summery curtains pulled, the house felt almost as private and peaceful as an outback campfire beneath the stars. Dusty opened a bottle of ruby-red Shiraz and left it to breathe while he and Shay put the sauce into a cooking pot to reheat and water into a bigger pot to boil. They'd be able to eat very soon.

He could almost feel the expectancy in the air between them. Shay kept looking at him when she thought his attention was focused elsewhere. She had color in her cheeks that toned with Letty's pink tank top—and with the socks—and it made her look…not younger, exactly, because thirty-one years old was quite youthful enough for him, thank you very much…but softer, somehow. Happier, too, he thought.

They hadn't touched each other all day.

He wanted to, quite desperately, but even more desperate was the sense that he wanted to get it right, wanted no clumsiness, no rush, no misunderstandings. While he stirred the pasta sauce, she set the dining table, and when he went in there he found music playing and the overhead lighting dimmed.

Shay held two long and elegant red candles in her hands. "Is this too hokey? Candlelight? I just loved the fire so much, while we were camping. I loved talking while we watched the flames."

"There are some crystal candleholders in the drawer right there, I think," was all he said. "I'll bring matches from the kitchen."

She nodded and smiled.

The water was boiling. He added the long strands of spaghetti with unsteady fingers, then went to light the candles. The table looked like a play on the colors of the American flag—white cloth, dark red candles and napkins, wide blue-and-white ceramic bowls. With her back to him, Shay stood surveying her work and this time he didn't second-guess his reaction, he simply stepped close behind her and wrapped his arms around her, lowering his chin to her shoulder and pressing his cheek against hers.

She turned to him and he kissed her long and sweet and deep, and neither of them spoke a word.

They talked later, as they ate.

She told him about her visit to Jane's, and the hectic atmosphere created by so many kids—Gemma and the Vegemite, Gemma in the bath, dinner preparations and even brewing a pot of tea had turned into marathon accomplishments.

"But I like it. And Jane is great."

"She is. You have to be pretty relaxed to have that many kids so close, and another one due in three months. Or if you weren't relaxed before, the kids change you that way."

Her attention sharpened. "You think kids change their parents? Isn't it the other way around?"

"I've heard Jane say that's the way it goes. Babies come into the world with their natures fully formed. Parents are the ones who get shaped by the whole experience, like a piece of wet clay."

"Speaking of wet clay, I did some laundry."

"You're billing Williamson International Pastoral Holdings for the blouse, I hope."

"It's looking that way. Prim gave me some stain soaker, but it may be too strong for silk."

"Oh, you saw Prim?"

Before his own visit to her storeroom?

"Um, yes, just now, on my way back from Jane's," she said, and her cheeks went a darker pink. "As well as the stain soaker, there was a particular item I was hoping she had in stock. A drugstore item."

"And did she?"

He knew what she'd say.

"Someone else had beaten me to it, taken the last twelve-pack, and she had none left…."

They looked at each other, giddy and happy and silly and self-conscious, like a pair of teenage kids. No further words on the subject were needed. Shay hid her smile behind a forkful of pasta and sauce.

"This is good, isn't it?" Dusty said.

"So is the wine."

Even so, neither of them managed to finish a full glass. They had far better things to do.

I'm falling in love with him.

It couldn't be true, Shay decided, because it made too little sense. This strange, fabulous feeling had to have some other name. Or if it really was falling in love, then she should remember having done it…felt it…before, with Adam or Todd, because hadn't she been in love with them?

She tried to remember.

This big pool of warmth inside her.

This giddy happiness.

This sense of trust.

This fascination with every moment they spent together and every word they said, every detail they discovered in common, every intriguing difference between them.

She *must* have felt this way before.

"Hey," Dusty growled at her. "What's happening?"

"Nothing. I'm just…thinking."

"Well, stop!"

He tightened his arms around her and kissed her with such an aura of command that she could barely breathe. She felt the nip and scrape of his teeth teasing out the fullness of her lower lip, and the thrusting caress of his tongue. He tasted of red wine and smelled the way he always did—like himself, and perfect.

She surrendered to the heat of his mouth and the press of his thigh between her legs, and the line of thought she'd been trying to follow drifted away like a jet trail in a blue sky. Nothing else existed but this.

They were still in the dining room. At some point she vaguely thought that they would have to move, get to a bed, some place flat and horizontal, at least, but that would mean stopping, or talking, and both of those things seemed too hard when all she wanted was to follow her body's command.

But then Dusty said with a harsh caress of breath and mouth against her ear, "Oh hell, Shay, I just want to have you right here, right now," and she said, "Yes," and that was the end of it.

He tore off his own shirt, pulled the little pink tank over her head and cupped his hands over her lace-covered breasts, his touch verging on rough in his impatience, but never crossing the line. He tore at her bra, slipping the straps down, wrenching at the fastening, letting the garment slip between them and not caring whether it fell to the floor or what. He just wanted her breasts.

His thumbs found the push of her peaked nipples and traced the line where her soft fullness met her ribs. He bent toward her and used his mouth, sucking her until her nipples were like ice-hot pebbles, grazed and throbbing and wet.

His impatience and hunger pulled at her and made her melt. She gasped and arched her body, and he pressed her against the wall and kissed every inch of skin he could reach while she kneaded her fingers in the muscles of his bare back and pulled him higher or pushed him lower, exactly where she wanted him and where he wanted to be.

It was like opening a floodgate.

They'd wanted this so much last night and had held back. Now they didn't have to. He pulled open his jeans and slid them and his briefs down his tight butt and tighter thighs while she watched shamelessly, loving the sight of his arousal springing free, totally ready for her.

She kicked off Letty's white leather trainers, pink socks and cropped jeans, but when she reached for her own lacy panties, Dusty stopped her. "Let me."

He slid them down, using it as an open excuse to touch her, to run his hands over her bared backside and press his mouth hot against her lower stomach before coming higher to bury his face between her breasts once more.

She ran her hands through his hair and held on to him because she wasn't sure that she'd be able to stand straight without the contact. Her strength was plugged right into his, and she needed him the way she'd never needed anything in her life.

They kissed, their bodies locked together and their hands everywhere.

The phone rang. Dusty had forgotten to take it off the hook. They both ignored it and eventually it stopped. Somewhere, a screen door flapped and a dog barked, and they ignored those things, too. Almost nothing could have stopped this.

She was throbbing and damp and achingly ready for him by the time he whispered, "Now?"

"Yes. Now." Her breathing came in ragged pants and she had to squeeze her own thighs together to slow herself down.

He was as close to the edge as she was, she knew it as clearly as she knew her own name.

In his jeans he had the packets he'd gotten from Prim. It didn't take him long to retrieve one, while Shay held on to him from behind, totally unable to let him go, or to think beyond the moment.

"Wrap your legs around me," he said, turning her in his arms.

They weren't even going to get as far as the floor.

She lifted her body against his, tightened her arms around his neck, let him ease her back against the wall once more. He was so strong. How many men could have done this?

He entered her deep and hard and she shuddered at the sensation of throbbing fullness, the feeling of connection and completion and bliss. They moved together, stretching and rocking, straining to get even closer.

She kissed his neck, tasting his skin and feeling the muscles tighten beneath, with the strain of holding her. "It's too much," she whispered. Too much for his strength.

But it wasn't.

"Oh yes, way too much…" he said. "Way too—" He couldn't even finish.

His breathing began to race and hers raced with it and they clung to each other like shipwreck survivors clinging to a floating log, while need and heat tossed them around like corks in wave upon wave of release that seemed to last for minutes, climbing higher than she'd imagined possible before they slowly settled back to earth.

"Did it hurt your back?" he said, as soon as they were both still.

He hadn't yet lowered her feet to the floor. She was still wrapped around him, holding him tight, closer to him than she'd ever been to anyone. She could feel his chest wall pushing in and out, nudging at her still acutely sensitized breasts.

Her head was spinning.

Or maybe it was the whole earth.

"No, it was fine," she answered. "I don't know why. You'd think it should have hurt. But it was fine."

"It was very fine," he said, drawing out the last two words, his voice as deep and dark as a well. "Shay, it was amazing."

They eased away from each other and he cupped his palms at the tops of her thighs and lowered her slowly and gently from his body. As soon as she was standing he pulled her close again and she felt the way he was shaking. "It was too much for you, Dusty."

"It was perfect. Shh. Stop." He pressed his fingertips against her lips.

She took them away, holding his wrist, then kissed his palm and cradled it against her own cheek. She wanted to speak, wanted to say something big and momentous— something that just might begin to encompass the huge pool of feeling stirring inside her, but nothing would come, so she just kept his hand pressed against her face and stroked it and smiled at him.

He smiled back, and it was so, so goofy. It had to be. She could imagine. If someone had seen them, looking at each other like this, as soppy as Sally and Beau, they would have laughed.

She didn't care.
She wanted more of it.
As much as she could get, for as long as it could last.

Chapter Ten

The grader plowed back and forth across the red-brown dirt of the airstrip, transforming the messy sheet of dry-baked mud into a smooth, hard expanse under the bright morning light.

Shay sat on the hood of Dusty's four-wheel drive, parked at the side of the strip, and watched, while the rumbling sound of the engine spread into the air and drifted away on a breeze. She had her forearms resting on her knees, a broad-brimmed felt farmer's hat pulled low over her forehead and sunglasses shading her eyes, and the camouflage was a good thing because she suspected that at any moment she might start to cry.

The sun had been so bright and strong for the past two weeks, without a drop of rain, either here or farther up-stream in the catchment headwaters. At first it had shimmered and sparkled on acres of floodwater, stretching almost to the horizon, then on narrower channels and shrinking ponds as the waters ebbed, and finally on mud.

Now, even much of the mud had dried.

The river crossings on the roads out of here were expected to be open again within the next couple of days; Prim was itching to get into Longreach to replenish her supplies; and Dusty and his grader driver Steve had walked the length of the airstrip before breakfast this morning and decreed that it could be smoothed out and tested with a couple of heavy vehicles. If all went well, then the mail plane would be summoned this afternoon to take Shay away.

Her stomach churned at the thought, and she couldn't reconcile the way she felt now with the desperation she'd felt about getting out of here just nineteen days earlier. The helicopter crash had changed something at a deep, vital level.

If she'd never gotten into that chopper and tried with such spectacular lack of success to leave this place, she could imagine she might still have considered herself a prisoner. She might never have built the powerful connection with Dusty that had grown during the two days they'd walked through the floodwaters back to Roscommon Downs with only Sally and Beau as companions.

But you couldn't think about those maybes and if onlys.

The chopper crash *had* happened.

And now, two weeks later, the airstrip was dry.

She had to leave this place—the place where Dusty had taught her to ride and shown her his cattle and all the beauty of his vast acreage; the place where she'd talked about books and kids and horses with Prim and Letty and Jane, and about weather and farm machines with Dave and Wayne and Steve; the place where everyone worked hard, but somehow meetings and time management and schedules and deadlines didn't seem so important; the place where she and Dusty had come together with so much perfect, unexpected heat, time after time.

He came up to her. "Looking good."

"Looking great," she agreed.

They smiled uncertainly at each other, with too much to say and no way to say it.

She'd learned a lot about him over the past two weeks. She'd seen the truth in what he'd told her by the campfire on their second night—that he'd never ask his men to do anything he wouldn't do himself, that he was the boss here and this meant doing things his way.

It worked because of the kind of man he was, because he was fair and clear-sighted and capable and honest. So different to Tom in his ivory tower high-rise in Manhattan—Tom who played power games because he could, who made people jump through hoops just to prove his own control, who made decisions then blamed someone else if they turned out wrong.

Caring about a man like Dusty was like knowing your house was founded on solid rock. There was a whole, crucial area of uncertainty and doubt that you never needed to have. Nonetheless, they'd only known each other for two and a half weeks. It would end today, and there was nothing she could do about it because there was no precedent in her life for asking for something different.

Dusty, I don't want this to be goodbye.

How could it possibly work? How could she bare her heart like that with no plan to back it up?

She couldn't.

"Let me run you back to the house so you can pack," he said. "And you probably want to call your office. Are you still going to New York?"

"I—I don't know. I'll fly to Sydney first, and make sure things are running smoothly, find out what Tom really wants. If I still have a job, for example," she joked, then added quickly, "So you definitely think the strip will be firm enough? You were afraid there might be some wash-aways…"

"Only a couple, and they're minor. Steve is filling them in fine with the grader and anyway they're right at one edge of the strip. You'll get out of here today."

She nodded. "Good."

She flicked a glance at him and saw him look quickly away.

"Let me run you back to the house," he repeated, as if he didn't remember saying it before.

He did that thing with his sunglasses that she'd noticed at their very first meeting, pushing them up on the top of his head, then rubbing a frown away with his fingers. She'd never gotten used to the amazing color of his eyes— the warm brandy that she could so easily drown in.

The house was cool and quiet, as usual, after the power-ful force of the sun in this part of the world, even in July, the middle of winter. Dusty called the air charter company that ran the mail flights and Roscommon Downs was added back onto their regular route, with a one-off stop this after-noon to pick up Shay. It was all arranged in a few minutes.

"Longreach?" she heard Dusty say at one point. "That'll be fine." When he got off the phone, he told her, "Your overnight bag is in Longreach. You'll be able to pick it up there, at the airport. And your laptop."

"My laptop? My laptop is there?" Why didn't this feel more like good news?

"Yes, it's being held for you at the main office."

"That's great! Um…going to stay in the house for a bit?" she asked him lightly, trying to hide how much she hoped that he would.

So that they could make love for the last time…the last

perfect time… Or eat together. Or even just sit on the veranda and talk, the way they'd now done so often, sometimes alone, sometimes with people like Letty or Prim or
Jane and Dave.

"Too much to do," he said, his tone clipped. "I'm sorry,
Shay. There's no point in—" He stopped.

"No point in what?"

"We had last night. We've had all those nights…and
days." He dropped his voice lower. "Would it really be any
better, saying to ourselves, *This is for the last time?*"

"No. I guess it wouldn't. Maybe."

"It wouldn't. It would be way worse," he said, sounding
almost angry, and he left the house again a minute later,
after stopping only long enough to grab a glass of cold
water from the fridge in the kitchen.

Shay had a lot to do, also.

She made flight reservations that would get her to Sydney late tonight, provided the mail flight got her to Longreach by five, as well as making a tentative one for New
York for the day after tomorrow, if Tom still wanted her
to go. She wasn't going to get into that issue with him until
she was back in the office with more of a handle on how
things had gone in her absence.

Not that she'd been totally out of touch. From Sonya and
others, she'd received e-mails with lengthy attachments to
them almost every day, and had spent hours working on
Dusty's computer. There was a lot you could achieve via the
Internet from a home office, in the twenty-first century. Still,
it wasn't the same. After a certain point, you needed to be
in the thick of things, or you lost your edge and your over-
view.

She knew that. She wasn't kidding herself that she
could justify staying here so much as one more day.

When she'd made her reservations, she gathered up all

of Letty's borrowed clothes and threw them in the washing machine, wearing a T-shirt of Dusty's over her black trousers, instead of the ruined silk blouse. It hung on her…and it smelled like him. She didn't plan on giving it back.

There was a spiderweb-shaped clothesline behind the house. In the strong sunshine, Letty's things would be dry in time to be ironed and folded ready to return to her well before the mail plane was due.

She was going to miss Letty. And Prim. And Jane.

Everyone.

They were friends now.

And she'd really progressed with learning to ride. After several days of treating her back with respect and doing only some careful stretching exercises, she'd felt confident enough to get back on Sally, under Dusty's instruction, and take some big loops around the homestead buildings. He had even convinced her to try a canter and a trot, and she hadn't wanted him to know how nervous she'd been so she'd tried both and loved both, and could imagine that one day she might actually be good at this.

Riding. This was something she could take with her, something concrete about her that had changed. She mentally added it as an item to a small, sad little list in her mind.

Riding.

Rejecting helicopters as a viable form of transportation.

Appreciating the flavor of golden perch cooked in peanut butter and desert lime.

Understanding just how fabulous an outback cattleman could be.

She packed her few belongings into a canvas sports bag that Dusty had found for her. He'd given her a pocket diary that he didn't need, for when she'd wanted to check dates as she worked, and she flipped through it. She should take it. It had some notes in it that she should follow up on.

Speaking of checking dates…

She looked at today's, and did some woolly-witted cal-culations. Her cycle was normally as regular as clock-work. Relentlessly so. Every fourth Monday signaled the start of heaviness and pain, usually before she even got out of bed in the morning, and always by lunchtime. It seemed to get worse every month, and Dr. Chin had told her this was the effect of the endometriosis.

Today was one of those Mondays, but so far nothing had happened. No doubt it soon would.

She didn't know if Dusty planned to come back to the house for lunch. Probably not, judging by the way he'd acted when he'd told her that there was "no point" in spending any of her last hours here together. She made herself a toasted sandwich and a pot of hot leaf tea, feeling bloated and irritable the way she always did on a fourth Monday. After she'd eaten, she checked the clothes on the line and found them dry. She had just begun to unpeg them, folding them as she went, when Dusty appeared.

Was it time to go already?

Surely not.

Please, not!

Before she could ask, he lunged toward her, took her in his arms and said in a shaky voice, "I've changed my mind."

"About—about the airstrip being ready?"

"About our last time." He swore. "I'm sorry. I can't let you go without…" He lowered his voice and whispered something so hot and graphic into her ear that she flushed and laughed, even while her body began to throb with need.

How could she possibly say no?

He took her hand and she forgot about Letty's clothes. They managed to make it as far as the bedroom, which had been by no means a guaranteed thing on several occasions. Oh Lord, his body felt so familiar now! She knew the way he responded, the sounds he made, and the tiny imperfections of a cattleman's healthy skin—the calluses, the sun damage, a couple of minor scars. She loved all of it.

She loved how hungry and impatient and desperate he seemed today—loved it to the point of tears because it matched the way she felt herself. How could he ever have claimed that they could say goodbye without this?

"My T-shirt's way too big for you," he whispered, as he pulled it over her head.

"It smells like you. Don't try to get me to mail it to you. It's mine, now."

He took her face in his hands and looked into her eyes. "You want to keep it because it smells like me?"

"Can I?"

"Oh hell, Shay, do you have to ask?" He brushed his thumb across her lower lip, then touched his mouth there in its place.

They kissed sweetly and feverishly, while he pulled her hips against his so she knew how much he wanted her. She rocked a little, the slow bump of her body driving him wild, while she exalted in the power they had over each other. She'd given so much of herself to him, and yet she felt safe because she knew he'd given just as much in return.

They were both naked in showing what they wanted from each other today. When it was over, they'd both suffer the same loss.

Did it have to happen?

She knew it did—knew it even while she shimmied out of her clothing, watched him doing the same and waited till she could have his hot body back.

This wasn't one of the romantic stories she'd been chasing to cap her magazine's "Wanted: Outback Wives" campaign. She believed in those stories very much. They happened. They were real. Dusty's friend Callan was happily engaged—although apparently his other friend, Brant, was not. Another once-lonely farmer from one of the wine-growing regions in southern New South Wales had written to the magazine, announcing that thanks to the appearance of his photo in the February issue, he'd married his new city-girl soulmate in June, after a whirlwind romance.

But her own reality with Dusty was harsher.

They'd had less than three weeks together. Surrounded by floodwaters, it really felt like a shipwreck romance— intense but incompatible with their regular lives. Dusty's future lay here at Roscommon Downs. Her own was ultimately not even in this country, but in New York.

Today…now…would be their last time.

"Hold me," she said to him suddenly. "Don't kiss me. Just hold me."

She didn't want this to end too soon. He'd tear himself away as soon as they'd made love, she knew he would, because looking each other in the eye afterward with nothing left that they could safely say would be way too hard.

"Hold you?" he whispered, even though he already had.

"Yes. Just quietly, so I can hear your heart." She pressed her ear against his chest and they both stood there in motionless silence for a long time.

"Shay, if you don't want to do this…" he said at last, his voice creaky as if he hadn't used it in months.

"I do."

"But we've stopped."

"No, we haven't. We haven't!" She cupped his jaw in her palms and kissed him, proving the point. "See?" she whispered, brushing her body with a sinuous, seductive motion against his. "We haven't."

"Good."

"Very good."

"Always." His hands seared against her skin, and neither of them needed to speak another word for minutes more.

At two-fifteen, Dusty drove her out to the airstrip again, to meet the incoming plane. Even when she saw it approaching the ground she hoped it might loop up into the air again at the last minute, hoped the pilot might spot some impediment to the landing. But it came down smoothly and safely, and she knew this was really happening. It was time to say goodbye.

Bizarrely, the clockwork every-fourth-Monday mechanism of her body hadn't gotten going yet. She'd waited for it after that final heartfelt session of lovemaking, expecting it to unleash even more suddenly than usual, but it hadn't. It was now officially six hours late.

Well, two hours, if you wanted to be cautious.

Not significant.

It would be insane to conclude that it was significant. They'd been using contraception, which all along she'd thought unnecessary anyhow.

Nevertheless, thinking back on how long it was since this kind of a delay had happened, she could count over a year of fourth Monday mornings since her arrival in Australia, and not one of them had left her in suspense as long as this.

The tiniest, faintest nuance of a thought that she might be pregnant whispered at the edge of her mind, and she wanted to laugh at herself. Two hours late, and she was pregnant? Two hours late, some heartfelt new questions about whether she wanted children, and suddenly she'd already conceived? Women all over the world, from their teens to their fifties, would live in a perpetual cycle of terror or happy expectancy if two hours late meant pregnancy.

She wanted to laugh at herself, but she couldn't. She felt as if she were hiding something important from Dusty, and wondered how appalled he'd be if she gave him the details.

Two hours late. He'd think she was crazy.

It's all in your head, Shay.

These past two and a half weeks haven't messed with your emotions enough, so now you're inventing extra reasons to feel like your life has been turned upside down?

"I have your e-mail address at the magazine," Dusty said.

"And I have yours, here."

"Let me know how your laptop survived."

"I will."

It was the kind of meaningless small talk that everyone fell into as they waited for the final moment of parting. It was stupid. Why didn't people either say the important stuff, or say nothing at all? It was unbearable.

"Don't wait," she told him.

"I'd better. In case…You know, there could be a mechanical problem, or something. We always wait until the plane goes."

She nodded.

"And he'll have mail for us, anyhow."

"Of course." She'd treasured so much about this period of isolation, she'd almost forgotten that the station people were hanging out for fresh supplies, mail deliveries and the opportunity to go into Longreach or Windorah in a day or two, to see friends or have some entertainment.

The plane had almost reached them now. It was slowing. It had stopped. The propellers were at first invisible, then they became a circular blur, then separate blades. The pilot who'd brought Shay here a million heartbeats ago stepped onto the ground, went around to the cargo hatch and pulled out two big mail sacks. He held them up to Dusty as a kind of greeting, and Dusty thumbed toward the open rear door of the four-wheel drive, as a greeting in return.

"I remember you," the pilot said, when he got closer and saw Shay. Grant was his name, she hazily recalled.

"You should," she drawled. "You flew off before I discovered I didn't need to be here, and the floodwaters came up and I've been stuck. Not that it was a problem, in the end," she added quickly, since she hadn't intended to sound rude.

From the corner of her eye, she saw Dusty glance at her, but didn't know what he was thinking.

"Had a bit of a heli-mustering drama, too, didn't you, trying to get out of here?" the pilot said.

"Word gets around."

"Out here, yes! There've been a few stories to tell, with these floods. Biggest in a while."

"But we'll have no problem getting to Longreach today?"

"It's my next stop."

Dusty took the mailbags from him and loaded them into the four-wheel drive.

"This your stuff?" the pilot asked Shay, taking the borrowed sports bag from her before she replied.

This was the moment. This was when she had to turn to Dusty and say something. The right goodbye. The right thanks for…for…things she couldn't remotely put into words. Oh hell, it was just hopeless. Painful. There was no way in the world to make this moment right.

She gulped down some air and it got stuck in her throat. "Bye," she rasped out.

"Bye."

"And thanks."

"Shay—"

"I know. I know." She flapped her hands, keeping him away. She was wound so tightly that she thought she'd throw up if he touched her. "There's no need to thank you."

Okay, this was it.

She couldn't say anything else.

She just had to go.

Turning from him, she walked to the plane, stopping one final time just before she climbed in, to wave at him. He waved back. When she was seated and strapped, she saw him still standing there almost motionless beside the four-wheel drive, but he was too far away for her to read his face.

Dusty's stomach felt like a rock as he drove back to the homestead, after he'd watched the plane climbing in the sky until it had disappeared.

Shay had gone.

He'd watched it all happen like watching a train crash, powerless to stop it, not fully believing it until all the evidence was spread out in a tangled wreck in front of him. He'd wanted to hold her against his body and say something insane and extravagant like, "Marry me!" but he'd said that to Mandy just a few months ago—she'd made it pretty clear that she wanted him to, had practically put the words into his mouth—and he wasn't going to repeat that mistake.

Mandy had at least made him believe that she wanted to be here, that she would be proud to call herself the boss's wife at Roscommon Downs. He knew Shay couldn't possibly feel the same.

They'd known each other for two and a half weeks.

This would fade.

He wasn't going to act on blind faith and blind need; he was going to act on certainties.

Getting out of the vehicle after he'd parked it in front

of the house, his legs moved mechanically and he'd totally lost track of what he was supposed to do next.

Oh yeah, that's right. Drive out to Four Mile Crossing to see if the track was passable yet, heading into Number Three Paddock, or if Steve would need to regrade it. He'd told Steve that he'd look at a couple of other tracks today, too, and Number Three Paddock itself might be fit for re-stocking as long as the fence line beside the creek had held. He should check it.

But first he needed to talk to Prim. He'd forgotten why, but he was sure he did. When he saw her, it would surely come back to him.

On those same mechanical legs, he stepped up to the veranda of the single men's quarters and met her coming out of the back kitchen door. "Boss," she said.

"Yeah…" he answered vaguely.

"Shay's gone?"

"Yep."

"She was nice. I liked her."

"So did I."

Prim looked at him, waiting for more.

"What else do you want me to say?" he snapped at her.

Prim could never take a hint. "Are you going to keep in contact?"

"She lives in New York."

"Sydney."

"When she's got the Australian edition of the magazine running smoothly, they'll put in a local editor-in-chief and she'll be pulled back to New York for another project."

"You might like New York," Prim said lightly. "For a change of scene."

"Yeah, right!"

"By the way, I thought I should tell you…" She looked uncomfortable, which was pretty rare for Prim.

Rare or not, he wasn't in the mood. "What?"

"Those storeroom supplies you…uh…had me find for you a couple of weeks ago…"

She hesitated again, but this time he just stood there waiting until she spilled the story, whatever it was. He knew what "supplies" she was talking about. Couldn't imagine why she needed to bring the subject up.

"I took a look at the box, just now, when I was tidying up in there, throwing out empty containers and getting ready to reorder. You know, we haven't had anyone calling on their use in a while, so I haven't needed to restock."

"Get to the point, Prim," he growled.

"I checked the date. The pack expired two years ago."

Was that all?

Remembering what Shay had told him about her doctor's warning, he told his station cook, "It won't be a problem," and walked away. Whatever he'd needed to talk to her about could wait because he needed some time on his own.

Chapter Eleven

New York City in the middle of July was its usual hot, steamy self. Locked in meetings for the past two days, Shay had nonetheless managed to squeeze in a hair appointment first thing this morning to deal with her frizz, but she doubted the effect would last.

Through the thickly glazed windows of *Today's Woman* magazine's headquarters, on the thirty-eighth level of a sleek Madison Avenue office building, she could faintly hear the sounds of the traffic below—pumpkin-colored rivers of taxis protesting the slightest delay, the sirens of emergency vehicles on their way to a hospital or police building.

There would be crowds of people streaming along the sidewalks like turbulent rivers, every one of them in a hurry to get somewhere important, there would be power lunches taking place in expensive restaurants, money shifting from one bank account to another in massive amounts.

New York contained the beating heart of fashion and music and art and advertising and so much more.

It was all so familiar, and for so long she'd thrived on it. She'd always felt as if plugging into the city's irrepressible energy was an automatic sign of success, and that negotiating the difficulties of daily life in such a fast-moving, crowded, fascinating place was just what you did to survive.

It strengthened you.

It was necessary.

Today, she'd lost her certainty about all this.

Tom, as expected, had made her jump through all sorts of hoops, and then just as she'd begun to wait for the ax to fall, he'd shown her the Australian edition's latest circulation figures.

Up.

Significantly up.

"You're getting it right," he'd told her. "I wasn't sure that you could pull it off, but you have. Whatever it is you're doing, do more."

Which should have been the point at which she pumped her fist in the air and went, "Yesss!" but instead she'd felt a fresh wave of jet-lagged fatigue and had only nodded at him. "More? Sure. I can do that."

Her period hadn't started yet.

She could point to all sorts of reasons for this. A lot of women had disrupted cycles when they traveled, when they were unusually stressed or when they lost weight. Of those particular boxes, she could check all three. She'd lost several pounds at Roscommon Downs, first during the arduous trek from the stricken helicopter and then because she'd been so absorbed in her shipwreck romance with Dusty that she just hadn't felt like eating three big meals a day.

Even now that the huge cattle station was only a memory, her appetite hadn't returned. She couldn't get Dusty out of her head, and her body remembered his so vividly that if she closed her eyes she could almost feel his mouth on her skin. Two nights ago in Sydney, she'd buried her face in his T-shirt and inhaled his scent.

She honestly didn't believe she could be pregnant, and yet she toyed with the idea in every spare moment—toyed with it and tortured herself with it.

She was seeing Sarah tonight for dinner, and she knew what Sarah would tell her. "Stop letting it mess with your head and just take a test."

But even taking a test…actually going into a drugstore, choosing one, paying good money for it and putting it discreetly into a paper bag…gave the whole thing a reality that she stubbornly didn't want.

The test would be negative and she would have wasted her money.

She would feel like a sad, deluded fool.

She'd have lost her last excuse to think about Dusty, and to rehearse some magical, emotional moment when they might see each other again.

Dear Lord, did she *want* to be having his baby, then? Did she want to be having a baby at all?

They were stark questions, and she was way too confused and emotional to have an easy answer to them.

Her final meeting ended at five-thirty and she took the subway downtown to Tribeca, where Sarah lived with her husband and three-year-old twins in a converted loft. Not for much longer, it turned out. They'd just purchased a craft gallery in Vermont with an old farmhouse attached, and they hoped to be fully settled there before the middle of fall, when Sarah's baby was due.

"Tell me…tell me…how you could make a decision as huge as that," Shay asked as they lingered over Swiss chocolate almond ice cream for dessert, curled up on a squishy couch in front of a blast of air-conditioning. Sarah's husband was out with friends, and the twins were asleep. Her blond hair looked rather limp and damp, but her cheeks and eyes were glowing.

"You mean *explain your craziness?*" she said.

"No! I don't mean that at all. I mean, what was your process? Was it sudden? A lightbulb moment? Did it feel like an act of desperation to save your lives, or—I'm not making sense, I know. Did it come on gradually? Did you argue much about your options? Were you rejecting this lifestyle, or embracing a new one, or—?"

"Hey, slow down. Pregnant people can't follow when you throw up that many questions that fast. They have overheated brains and toxic hormones raging inside them." Sarah's brown eyes widened. "You mean… Are you thinking of not coming back to New York, yourself?"

"No," Shay said quickly. "Not at all. I love New York. I'm just wondering about you."

"Do you know what?" Sarah stretched and rubbed her lower spine. "It was actually pretty simple. We listened to our hearts, and this was what they said, loud and clear, so we made a commitment to working it out."

"That easy?"

"The heart and the commitment was easy. The working it out took longer. We've been talking about it since the twins had their first birthday. It took us a year to find the right place and do a proper business plan, work out the right safety nets."

"You never said a word about leaving the city."

"We don't tell people our baby-name ideas in advance, either."

"There, I'm not seeing the connection."

"Before the baby's born, people will shoot your names

down in flames. Once it's a done deal, no matter what they really think, they'll tell you it's a lovely name, and since it's nobody's business but ours, *lovely* is all I want to hear. Same with Vermont. It's locked in now, so people are thrilled for us. Are you thrilled, Shay?"

She laughed. "On the basis of the argument you've just given me, you'll never truly know, will you? Yes, I'm thrilled. Now tell me your baby names."

"Absolutely not!"

They talked until Sarah began to yawn. Pregnant people got tired early in the evenings, and with her asthma always an impediment, Sarah had to take extra care. Shay tore herself away, feeling that she might have spilled a lot more if they'd just had a little longer to get to the subject. She wished they did have longer, and she was deeply relieved that they didn't.

Which was about as logical as not buying a pregnancy test because she didn't know what she wanted the result to be.

The following day, she flew back to Sydney, skipping Sunday completely when she crossed the international date line. She touched down early on Monday morning.

The fifth Monday morning, not the fourth, and her period still hadn't come.

At the office, to which she took a taxi direct from the airport, everyone congratulated her on the rising circulation figures, including the three women who had a chance of winning her own editor-in-chief position once she relinquished it to return permanently to New York. They saw job security and a possible promotion in the news, and she understood their hunger.

Understood it, but didn't share it.

Maybe she was just too tired.

At three in the afternoon, Sonya told her, "You have a double dose of jet lag. Go home!"

Shay went.

Via the pharmacy two doors down from her high-rise apartment building, with its Darling Harbor views.

She took ages to choose between a surely unnecessary number of test-kit options, felt just as foolish and secretive about the purchase as she'd known she would, and hid the test in her purse.

In the lobby of her building, someone was waiting for her. He stood up like a jack-in-the-box as soon as he saw her, and her legs turned to perished elastic. Her mind flashed to the moment when he'd reached her through the floodwaters, more than three weeks ago, beside the stricken helicopter. She remembered the physical rush of emotion and relief she'd experienced then, as well as her bone-deep appreciation of his strength and competence and heroism.

Remembering the power of those feelings, she wished desperately that she could feel them again now, but she just didn't. She was back in her real life; she was too much of a mess and, considering what she had in her purse, his timing could hardly have been worse.

"Dusty…What are you doing here?"

"Good to see you, too, Shay," he drawled.

"I didn't mean—"

"It's okay," he cut in. "It's a reasonable question. Maybe I should have phoned first. I did call your office to make sure you were in town, and then again from a cab on the way here to discover you'd left for the day. But I didn't want to give you a chance to say no."

"No? Dusty—"

"Because I would have come anyway," he finished simply. "I wanted to see you again."

They looked at each other, while Shay's purse began to emit this deafening radioactive howling sound because of the pregnancy test kit hidden inside it.

Well, no, of course it didn't, but that was how she felt. She wanted to shield the black leather from Dusty's view, as if it had suddenly become transparent. She wanted him here *so much*, for so many reasons, only not right at this moment.

Not until she *knew.*

"Come up," she said.

"Can I kiss you first?"

"No." Romantically, she felt as if she might throw up if he did that. Not a good look for a senior publishing executive in a granite-floored lobby. "Let's—" She didn't know what to suggest. "How long are you here?"

"There's a couple of horses I have to look at. How long do you want me?"

She closed her eyes. "I—I don't know."

Silence.

She opened her eyes again and looked at him, every muscle in her body aching with tension. "Was that the wrong answer?"

"I guess *forever*'s not realistic at this point, is it, for either of us?" His brandy-brown eyes narrowed, as if she were a page of bad handwriting and he was trying to read her.

"No." She pressed the elevator button, then blurted out, "Did you think this through?"

An older woman joined them in their wait for the elevator, and Dusty dropped his voice very low. He bent his head toward Shay and she felt an overwhelming rush of awareness and familiarity that orientated something in her universe once again.

Whatever else was or wasn't happening, this man's body belonged to hers, in this moment, in a way she could never explain and never deny. Standing this close, she could have touched him anywhere she wanted, and even the fabric of his clothing would have felt sensual beneath her touch because of the shape of his body beneath.

"Of course I didn't think it through," he said. "Have either of us been any good at that so far, with each other? I just came. The horses were an excuse. And I thought you might not think it through, either, you might just—" He stopped, and his gaze arrowed to her mouth.

"Kiss you," she said, understanding.

"Don't you want to?" His mouth barely moved.

"Yes, I do."

So much!

He was still leaning close, his hands poised uncertainly in the air as if he wanted to touch and hold her but didn't know how. She could smell the familiar *rightness* of him— another thing that made no sense but was possibly even more powerful because of the very fact that she couldn't understand it. She could see in detail the beautiful, familiar shape of his lips, the tawny fire deep in his eyes, and somehow they brought her home.

"Well, that's something!" he muttered.

The elevator arrived and they stepped into it. The woman stepped in after them, then squeezed herself into the corner by the control panel, as if whatever fatal disease they had contracted was highly contagious. Seeing herself in the mirrored elevator wall, Shay understood the stranger's reaction. She looked horribly pale, with blue half circles beneath her eyes, while the eyes themselves stood out like chips of glittering jade on white velvet.

"Could you press twenty-seven, please?" she asked, and the woman complied with the flicker of a polite smile.

"When do you head to New York?" Dusty asked. He leaned his powerful forearm against the mirrored wall.

"When? I've already been!"

"You mean since you left Roscommon Downs?"

"Yes, I flew out Wednesday, and I got back this morning."

"That's crazy. No wonder you look so tired." He brushed his thumb against the puffy skin beneath her eye, then tucked a strand of hair behind her ear. Her whole body tingled.

"I'm fine."

Dusty raised his eyebrows but didn't reply.

The elevator whooshed up to the twenty-seventh level, leaving Shay's stomach behind. She would be okay once she was safely inside her apartment, she told herself, but then realized this wasn't true. She wouldn't be remotely okay until she'd taken the pregnancy test, and how could she do that with Dusty here?

She'd just have to.

She knew it. No matter how much the task got in the way of everything else thrown up by his unexpected appearance, now that she'd bought the kit, she had to get it over with and know the truth for sure.

Having been forcibly separated from her whole Stressed Out Executive persona for most of the time she'd been at Roscommon Downs, she understood it a little better now that it was back again. There was a certain piece of critical information that she needed before she could move on to formulate her next set of plans, and she needed that information *now*.

The entire universe…in the form of Dustin Tanner…had entered a conspiracy to prevent her from acquiring the information, apparently, but she refused to let the universe win.

"Do you want some tea, Dusty?" she asked him as soon as they were shut inside her apartment.

"Sure," he answered vaguely, looking around as if he weren't convinced this place would even have a kitchen.

It did, but admittedly Shay hadn't often cooked anything in it.

Having gone directly from the airport to her office this morning, she hadn't yet been back here since last week, when she'd sandwiched two unsettled nights in her own bed before heading for New York. The air smelled stale and chemical. She had a cleaner who came in for an hour and a half on Friday mornings, and the faint odor of the products she used still hung around. This didn't help Shay's stomach to behave.

And would the milk she'd bought last Tuesday for her breakfast coffee still be any good?

She filled the electric kettle and switched it on, sniffed at the milk and decided it would just do if Dusty wanted it, checked her supply of horrible chamomile tea bags and discovered she only had two left. Probably a good thing, since she didn't intend to drink chamomile tea-bag tea ever again. As soon as possible, she was going to invest in a china pot, and the kind of black leaf tea they drank at Roscommon Downs.

One concrete plan for her future, at least.

Dusty was waiting in the other room. She peeked out at him. He'd picked up last week's newspaper. He folded it back, read a couple of lines, folded it the other way, dropped it back on the coffee table.

He might be the father of her child.

The kettle began to sing, but she couldn't wait for it, couldn't just calmly make tea beneath the massive question mark that hung over her life. Coming out of the kitchen, she said to Dusty, "Could you excuse me for a moment? I'll finish the tea in a minute."

She grabbed her purse from where she'd flung it on the couch, dived for the sanctuary of the bathroom, and opened the pharmacy bag and the box inside it with shaking hands.

* * *

Left on his own, Dusty considered the fact that so far his visit hadn't gone according to plan.

Well, the plan had been pretty basic.

Check that Shay was actually in Sydney, fly down, tell her he wanted to keep seeing her, have her fall rapturously into his arms…then into her bed…and work out the details later.

He paced through the apartment. It seemed sleek and clean and unlived in, and the granite-and-glass bathroom gave the impression of taking up half the space. He found a framed photo of three people who had to be her parents and her sister, but he suspected it only occupied this space on the teak shelf because that was what people did—they had photos of their family on display. The absence of such a photo would invite more questions Shay didn't want to answer than would the photo itself.

There were two more photos. One showed Shay receiving a journalism award that she'd never mentioned to him, and there was another in which she was almost unrecognizable, grinning into the camera with a pair of identical little girls, aged around two, squishing their plump rosy cheeks against hers on either side.

His heart did something uncomfortable in his chest.

The three faces of Shay.

Ill-adjusted daughter, proud and steely-determined executive, loving human being.

He knew which of the three had traveled up to the apartment with him just now.

The executive.

But why did the executive need to hide in the bathroom?

When she finally came out several minutes later, he remembered that there was a fourth face to Shay—the one he'd seen when he reached her at the helicopter, the one that had first arrowed its way into his heart, the face of a lost child needing rescue.

"What's wrong?" he demanded as soon as he saw her.

She put on a smile. "Nothing. Bit of a stomach upset, that's all. Forty-eight hours of airplane food in one week, what were the odds? Did the kettle boil?"

"Forget the kettle."

"I'd really like a hot cup of tea." She dredged up a laugh that was even less sincere than the smile. "I'm turning into an Australian."

"Let me make it, then," he offered. "Sit down. You look like you wouldn't even get as far as the kitchen."

He put his arm around her shoulder and she tilted her head and, with her eyes closed, pressed her cheek against his hand like a cat. His protective instincts surged, and he decided he wasn't leaving her alone yet, no matter what they ended up saying to each other, even if this meant that all he did was watch over her while she slept.

"Sit," he repeated, and she nodded and dropped to the smoky blue leather couch. "Would you like a pillow and a quilt? Get yourself comfortable, in case you fall asleep."

"I won't," she predicted at once, but he couldn't see what would keep her awake. Himself?

So far, she hadn't given any indication that he held that much power.

Stubbornly, he refused to consider that his showing up here might have been a mistake. He would push through this. He'd left Dave in charge at the station, and had warned him that he might be gone for a week or longer. Dave could reach him by phone if he needed to.

He found the pillow from her bed, and on a chest at the foot of the bed there was a folded white quilt patterned with flowers, so he gathered that up as well. Both items gave off Shay's scent. He had no name for it, and no descriptive words. He just knew it was sweeter and warmer than he would once…a long time ago…have expected for a high-powered publishing executive.

When he reentered the living room, she'd kicked off her shoes, left them lying under the coffee table and gone back to the kitchen to finish pouring the tea.

"Hey, I said I'd do it," he told her, taking the two steaming mugs from her grip. Their fingers touched, and the heel of his hand brushed her wrist.

She smiled thinly. "I couldn't wait that long."

"Not sure how long I can wait, either," he said, dropping his voice low. He could feel the way her body pulled toward his. This wasn't one-sided. Even though she was holding back, a part of her reacted exactly the way he did, wanting him, finding a home in his arms.

She sat back on the couch, silent as she took her first few sips of tea.

"Good?" He wanted more from her. He was accustomed to her honesty, not to this polite, tired shield, and he liked the honesty a lot better.

"Revolting," she said.

"Wha-at?" He let out a relieved laugh. Well, this was honest!

"You've spoiled me. I told you that. I've discovered just how much I really do hate chamomile."

"I could have gone out and got you some other kind, while you were in the bathroom."

He thought he felt her flinch at the word *bathroom*, which didn't make sense. Something was so wrong about this. He'd never seen her with this brittle facade before. It made the ruthless self-absorption of her first few hours at Roscommon Downs seem healthy by comparison.

He'd been able to deal with that.

Easily.

He'd simply attacked back.

Dealing with this was like trying to grab onto handfuls of smoke.

She must be exhausted, he reminded himself, and forced back his instinct to confront her and demand to know what was wrong. It could wait.

In the warm semicircle of Dusty's arm, Shay longed to tell him about the pregnancy test in the bathroom wastebasket, the way she imagined an interrogation subject longed to spill everything under the influence of truth drugs.

Yes, she was exhausted.

And she was pregnant.

The knowledge clanged like a ceaseless bell in her head, drowning out the possibility of hearing what her heart told her, or even thinking about what decisions she would need to make.

She was pregnant.

And she'd had enough discussions with Dusty on the subject of having children to know that he would never be content to act as an accidental sperm donor and then conveniently disappear, to leave her as a single executive mom.

He was a strong, simple, successful, honorable man. He had traditional values. He was accustomed to being his own boss, and to directing others. He would have his own ideas about being involved with this child, and he would expect those ideas to hold sway—ideas about inheritance and influence and day-to-day contact, fitting somewhere in between feudal kingdoms and white picket fences.

Feudal cattle kingdoms.

White picket fences stained red with outback dust.

He'd want his child to grow up at Roscommon Downs.

Welcome back to your life, Shay.

You knew from the first moment that he wasn't your type. Now the knowledge has come back to haunt you in a way you never imagined.

Don't tell him, said a little red cartoon Shay-devil sitting on her left shoulder.

On her other shoulder, there should be a little white Shay-angel with a halo and wings, providing a different answer, but if there was a Shay-angel, she was hiding under Shay's hair and speaking too indistinctly for her to hear.

Don't tell him.

It began to seem like a good idea.

The pregnancy wasn't planned, after all. In fact, they'd tied themselves in knots trying to keep away from each other until they had contraception taken care of—as it turned out, unreliably—and that had been at Dusty's insistence. He'd talked about wanting children, but he'd been quite determined not to father a child with her!

It would be the easiest thing in the world, surely, to ride out his time in Sydney, tell him she didn't want to see him again—skip over a few inconvenient details such as the tender state of her heart, at this point—and send him back to Roscommon Downs in ignorance.

Hurrah.

Problem solved.

The bell in her brain began to clang more softly, and her whirl of thoughts about the pregnancy settled to a deeper level, somehow.

At which point a feathery little Shay-angel tapped her on the shoulder and said, "Excuse me? I got tangled in your hair—you really need an appointment with your stylist—and I'm not sure if you heard me clearly enough just now…"

"Go away," she muttered to the Shay-angel. "Tell me again when I've had some sleep."

Shay, he needs to know...

No.

She couldn't tell him.

Not yet.

Not until she had some idea about what *she* wanted, instead of the dust-stained white picket fence, and some idea about how she was going to get it.

At this deeper level in her thoughts, dark, frightening scenarios began to unfold. She saw personal arguments escalating until they became court battles. She saw lawyers pushing her to demand things from Dusty that she didn't even want, purely as a strategy for achieving what she really needed. It could go on for years. This child of theirs, bred in an uneasy limbo between the city and the outback, the U.S. and Australia, could tangle them in legal wrangling until they had a teenager ready for dating instead of a toddler in diapers.

With all the uncertainties she had about parenthood, one thing Shay knew down to the marrow of her bones was that she didn't ever want to treat a child like a possession or a weapon, exchanged or fired back and forth across the biggest ocean in the world, and yet the seeds of exactly this might already be in place.

It wasn't a far-fetched nightmare. It was a possibility as real as floodwaters in the desert, and the Milky Way overhead.

And she couldn't risk a child's well-being that way.

Which meant, didn't it, that she couldn't tell Dusty about the baby until she was sure the legal wrangling wouldn't happen.

And that might mean she couldn't tell him...ever.

The light began to fade. She put her unfinished tea

down on the coffee table and sank back into Dusty's arms, not sure if he should even still be in her apartment. She should have just asked him to go; she should have told him she didn't want to see him again *before* she'd taken the test....

Which didn't make the remotest sense because if she hadn't been pregnant, if she hadn't had a trans-Pacific, outback-versus-city, possession-slash-weapon of a tiny, precious, defenseless baby growing inside her—oh, wow, it was hard to grasp!—she would want what he seemed to want, a joyful, easy, open-ended continuation.

I wanted to see you again, he'd told her, and she felt the same.

Out of the gathering darkness, and after several tortured minutes of silence, she finally heard his voice. "Listen, I know you're not okay. Maybe it's the jet lag, maybe it's something else."

"I—"

"I'm not asking for an explanation, Shay," he cut in, with his usual authority. "I'm telling you it's okay not to give me one. Just to sit. To fall asleep if you want."

"I'm not going to fall asleep." Even with fatigue overtaking her like paralysis, she couldn't imagine it. The impossible baby, the baby who didn't belong in the outback and couldn't belong in Shay's life, would keep her awake all night long.

"I hope you do," Dusty said.

"Yeah?"

"Yes, because I'd like to sit here holding you while you do. And then tomorrow I'll bring you flowers and take you out to dinner and we can talk."

Talk.

The word scared her.

Talking would be the start of it—of the trans-Pacific,

city and outback, legal battle impossibility of her baby's future.

She knew she'd flinched at the word, the way she'd flinched about the bathroom when he'd mentioned it earlier, and she knew he would have felt the movement. In fact, their bodies were so attuned that she could *feel* him feeling it and then letting it go, putting it into a too-hard basket called *tomorrow,* along with the dinner and the flowers, when she'd had time to rest.

But when she'd had time to rest, she knew, nothing would change.

"Sleep, Shay," he said, pulling her closer.

"Tell me a bedtime story."

He laughed, then took a slow breath and said softly, with his cheek pressed lightly against her hair, "Once upon a time there was a magazine executive from New York who didn't know what was good for her…."

She listened, and his words spooled out like ribbon. He made her laugh, and he made her catch her breath, and very soon she came to a point where she knew she could either keep listening to this and therefore inevitably end up telling him what she'd learned in the bathroom—the thing that might have them hating each other one day— or she could kiss him and get him to stop.

No contest.

No contest at all.

Needing only a tiny movement, she turned her face toward his, brushed her mouth against his lips to drown out the words *firelight* and *under the stars,* and made a powerful bid for his response.

Chapter Twelve

It was the softest, sweetest, laziest kiss Shay had ever had, and it went on forever. Only once they'd wrapped their arms around each other and tasted each other and let their mouths melt together did she realize just how hungry she had been for his touch this past week when she'd flown halfway around the world and back, and hadn't seen him.

"You're too tired for this," he whispered, pulling away a little, but he meant it halfheartedly, and she knew it.

"No," she whispered in reply, and ran the tips of her fingers down his neck and then up into his hair at the back. "It's what I want."

Deliberately, she let her gaze fall to his mouth, with her own lips softened with kissing and just an inch or two away. She saw his tongue lap his lower lip and let her mouth drift closer. She knew it would drive him wild—this close, but not touching. She saw the fan of his lashes against his cheeks as he looked down at her mouth, and then he looked up again and their eyes met and he groaned between gritted teeth.

He gave in, kissing her more hungrily and more deeply until she felt dizzy and breathless and more precious to him than ever. He slid off her clothes, garment by garment. The tailored jacket, the tailored pants, the silk shell blouse, the thread of gold around her neck, and she did the same to him. They laughed a little bit when a button wouldn't push through, and when he couldn't find the hook of her bra. They gasped when they touched each other in places they hadn't touched for a whole long difficult week.

He touched her breasts, covered their tender peaks with his hot mouth, cupped her as if her breasts were made of spun sugar. She realized that she'd already grown fuller there, one of the pregnancy symptoms Sarah had talked about. If he knew her body well enough to notice, he didn't say anything, but he went on touching her and suckling her until her breathing went out of control and she had to grip his shoulders to keep from flying apart.

They came together like two puzzle pieces—warm, soft, living puzzle pieces that had been made to fit. Her brain buzzed and burned with fatigue, but her body didn't care. His hands and mouth brought her back to life, shut out the whole world, made sense of everything. When he filled her, pushing deep as if he could never get deep enough, she had to hold on to him even tighter, for fear she'd lose contact with the earth itself, this felt so powerful and right.

And when their perfect rhythm had settled into stillness, she fell asleep with tears on her cheeks.

She hadn't slept so soundly in a long time. She never felt him stir, never felt the quilt tucking around her, or the pillow puffing closer against her cheek. It was three-fifteen in the morning when she woke up again, according to the clock beside the TV.

No Dusty.

Wide awake, she wrapped herself in the quilt and looked for him, expecting he might have gone to sleep in her bed, since she'd taken the couch. But he wasn't in the apartment at all. She found his note in the kitchen.

I've booked into a hotel. He gave its name and telephone number—a place not far from here, on the opposite side of Darling Harbor. *I'm seeing those horses tomorrow. Pick you up at six for dinner? If I don't hear from you, that's what I'll do. D.*

And if he did hear from her?

She thought about it, working distractedly on her laptop, with first coffee then hot oatmeal at her elbow, until the sun had risen without her noticing and it was time to get out of her robe, shower, dress and head into the office.

If he was "seeing horses," that meant he'd be out for a good part of the day. Sale yards? Racetrack? She had no idea, but could still pick the most likely time. Eleven. She couldn't imagine a man like Dusty hanging around in his hotel room at eleven on a sunny morning, in Sydney's mild winter weather. She could easily leave him a voice-mail message.

She rehearsed it half under her breath, standing beside the phone, wondering if this could really be the Shay Russell she'd known for thirty-one years, running out on her responsibility just because it was scary and tough.

"Last night was a mistake, Dusty, and I don't think dinner's a good idea, either. I've had some time, now, and some sleep, and I don't think we should see each other again. There's no future to this, and I don't see how… *why*," she revised, "…two people would want to maintain a long-distance relationship without a future. I mean, do you? See why? It just doesn't make sense."

She stopped, knowing that if she'd been with her friends

in New York having a crisis meeting over coffee, they could have run with this subject for an hour, talking the whole thing out like squeezing the juice from an orange until there was nothing left but a battered, sticky mess, even without the subject of her pregnancy coming into the picture.

Her whole body suddenly went hot, and she felt as if she'd been wrapped in someone else's skin. It felt wrong on her body. It didn't fit right, and the feeling scared her.

I'm having a baby.

I'm having Dusty's baby.

And that's the way he's going to think about it. He has rights, and he's going to want them to count—in the most honorable and decent and responsible way possible. He'll be the best father in the world, but on his own terms, in his own world, the way he's a great boss at Roscommon Downs but on his own terms and in his own world there, also.

Could those terms ever be hers?

Could she ever belong in that world?

"It's simple. If you're not going to tell him about it, then you shouldn't see him tonight," said the shoulder-dwelling Shay-angel and Shay-devil in unison, although they didn't speak in quite the same voice. One sounded sneaky, the other noble and self-sacrificing.

Frankly, Shay couldn't stand either of them.

She circled away from the phone and slumped onto the couch, knowing she wasn't going to call his hotel to cancel.

She had to tell him about the baby.

She *would* tell him about the baby.

The decision felt right, if not comfortable.

Right, not comfortable, and terrifying.

Still wrapped in a stranger's skin, she took the commuter train to North Sydney for work.

* * *

Shay looked beautiful.

Dusty had never seen her dressed up for an evening out. Her hair was silky and shimmery and soft, curving to frame her cheekbones and jawline in a natural way that left several strands brushing her skin and tempted his fingers into a caress that he was determined to give her tonight. She wore a simple sleeveless dress in a pinky kind of beige, with a wide V neckline tucking between her breasts, and a skirt that floated around her calves.

Her skin-toned high heels lengthened her legs, she had touches of gold jewelry at her ears and throat and she'd done something to her eyes…makeup, which he wasn't an expert on…because they looker softer and grayer today.

Did they?

He got closer, and saw yesterday's glittery green chips beyond the illusion given by shadow and liner. She looked beautiful…and tense…and terrified. For a moment, it disturbed him, the way an animal got disturbed by an approaching storm, but then he remembered that, to be honest, he was terrified, too.

You didn't bother to get terrified in a situation like this unless it was important.

Important was good.

His heart lifted.

He'd come so close to leaving a message with her assistant at *Today's Woman* to say he'd flown back to Queensland. He'd been ninety percent convinced that she would have greeted the news with relief, even though she could easily have called to cancel herself and hadn't, so that had to be a plus, didn't it?

In the end, he hadn't canceled either, he'd instead gone all out to ensure that this would be a night to remember, whatever they ended up saying to each other.

And now here she was, standing in the doorway of her apartment, leaning slightly on the handle as if she wasn't fully confident of her strength and he had to consider that, beyond their shared nerves, her stunning appearance was a kind of gift to him—a gift or an apology.

"You look great," he said, packing enough heartfelt sincerity into the three words to make up for their lack of fluency.

"Thank you." She smiled, took his hand and drew him inside, and he wanted her at once, in the most primal male way possible. "So do you."

Because he'd tried!

Gone were the cattleman's jeans, shirts and boots in which he felt at home. He'd put on his only suit, a dark charcoal one with a pale blue shirt underneath. He'd left the shirt open at the neck because a tie would quite possibly choke him when his throat already felt so tight, but maybe she liked this casual touch, because she reached up and brushed his bare skin there with the backs of her fingers—they shook slightly—and he had to fight to keep his breathing steady.

She smiled in a tentative way. "Let me just pick up my purse. Are we taking a cab?"

"Yes, and you should bring a jacket, too."

She nodded and came back with a beaded purse that matched her shoes and a pale gray spring coat that didn't match anything, but still looked great on her, as far as he was any judge. "Will this do?"

He thought about saying, "Yes, but how about you take it all off for half an hour or so, because what's underneath is even better." In the end, something stopped the words in his throat and he accepted that he'd spend the whole evening in a state of dizzying, hypnotic frustration.

"We have to walk down to the waterfront at Darling Harbor," he managed to say instead. "We're taking a water taxi and eating overlooking the yachts in Rose Bay. And I can't drop that casually into the conversation as if I take water taxis and eat in swish restaurants every day, Shay, because I don't, but…hell…" His fluency deserted him again, suddenly.

I've tried, he wanted to say. *Credit me with that, no matter how this evening ends up.*

She slid her arm through his and squeezed him, but said nothing and he felt the weight of something unspoken hanging between them like summer humidity hanging in the air.

"We're going to have a good evening," she finally said, having held the words back until they left the lobby of her building and reached the street.

"Well, yes, I hope so."

It was already dark, and the night air would be colder on the water. They walked down to Darling Harbor together, with Shay's heels cracking on the pavement and the traffic still noisy and unrelenting on the city streets.

Dusty liked cities. Brisbane, with its wide, winding river, lush gardens and houses set in odd locations in the often steep terrain. Melbourne, which he only ever saw in spring racing season, when the weather could range from windy and wet to scorching hot and still. And this city, Sydney, a frivolous, dramatic, cosmopolitan place where the inhabitants would allegedly sell their souls for a water view.

Could he live in one, though?

He'd never considered before that he might have to. Cities had always meant time out for him—a break and a chance to experience something new. Real life was one and a quarter million of his own acres of richly grassed flood plain and red desert, where the gratification was a lot less instant, the work was harder, but the rewards lasted longer, too.

Would he abandon all that—*could* he, even if it was only

for a few years—to be with Shay? He wasn't at all sure that he could.

"You're quiet," she said.

"So are you."

"How were the horses?"

"Promising. They're up for sale in a couple of weeks. I'm going to report back to Callan and Brant, see what our trainers think. One of them I'd like to bid on."

"How does that work?"

"Well, there's a couple of major avenues for buying thoroughbreds in this country…."

We're remembering how to talk to each other, he thought, after he'd given her more detail and she'd asked her usual alert, interested kind of questions. He liked talking to her, didn't matter what the subject was. He liked the places where their thinking met, and the places where it was different. She seemed interested in exploring the differences, as he was, and that was good.

They reached the waterfront and the taxi was waiting for them. He helped her aboard, then kept her hand in his and they smiled at each other, and he jumped the gun totally and leaned close to whisper in her ear, "I want to see you tomorrow, too, if we can find some time."

She closed her eyes and nodded, and both the pleasure and the terror were clear on her face again, and since pleasure and terror about summed up the contradictory nature of his own feelings, he let it go.

The water taxi zoomed away from the wharf and around under the Harbor Bridge, past the Opera House with its backdrop of city neon and glass and blue-black night sky, past the stretch of lush darkened greenery that was the Botanical Gardens, past the naval dockyards at Garden Island and the distant forest of masts on the yachts moored in Rushcutters Bay.

And with the fresh salt air in his lungs and Shay's warm hand in his, Dusty was so sure that they could do this, that they could make it work for as long as they wanted it to, *somehow,* that he left the taxi man a fifty-dollar tip.

Then, later in the evening, she told him her news….

Over dessert.

She'd say it then.

No, over coffee, Shay revised, because during dessert they happened to be talking about legendary Australian racehorses, and the life story of Makybe Diva, who'd won the Melbourne Cup an unprecedented three years in a row, and it was too interesting and too off-topic…and too much of a good excuse to hold off a little longer.

The coffee made Shay jittery, and she had a buzz of fatigue behind the jitteriness, like the buzz of white noise.

How did you do something like this?

How did you say it?

I know we've only known each other for three and a half weeks. I know this is going to put our relationship under a kind of pressure you never envisaged when you flew down here yesterday. I know I was just as happy to see you as you were to see me, even though I couldn't show it then.

There's a reason I couldn't show it, Dusty.

He watched her fiddling with her coffee spoon, just as he'd watched her struggling with her shrimp and salad and steak.

"Spit it out, Shay," he suddenly said. "What didn't you tell me yesterday?" He thought for a moment, and there was a harder edge in his voice when he added, "Or should it be, what didn't you tell me at Roscommon Downs?"

"Nothing. Not at—"

"Come on…" He pushed his chair back, as if about to get up to leave, and she remembered that he knew how to get angry when he needed to—when there was a result he wanted, when he needed to be the boss, the one with clarity and control. "Is this something I've been through before? With Mandy or Rebecca? Is it suddenly going to turn out that there's baggage or a hidden agenda you never mentioned or even hinted at?"

She grabbed his wrists across the table and said quickly, "I didn't tell you because I didn't know about it at Roscommon Downs. It only happened at Roscommon Downs, and I didn't know about it until yesterday, after you got here." He swore and she thought he must have guessed, so she just blurted it out. "I'm pregnant, and I don't know what I'm going to do about it, yet."

But he hadn't guessed, it turned out.

"*Do* about it?" he echoed, then backtracked, his voice suddenly even tighter and harsher. *"Pregnant?"* She still enclosed his wrists with her grip and now he gripped back, enough to hurt her, although she doubted he knew it.

She could see his reaction, that same feeling she'd had—was still having—of being wrapped in a stranger's skin that didn't fit.

I didn't handle it right, she knew at once.

For either of us.

And yet she didn't know how she could have handled it better for him. Slower? More cryptic? More upbeat?

How to handle it better for herself… Suddenly she couldn't hold back the words. She'd always found it best to be honest with him.

"I'm scared of what you're going to want, Dusty. I—I thought about not telling you at all, so that what you might want wouldn't matter."

She couldn't look at him anymore, his eyes were blazing so much. Instead, she dropped her gaze and watched the monkey grip they were both locked in across the table, his big hands effortlessly cuffed around her forearms.

"I don't want it signed and sealed on the spot that this is going to be an outback baby," she went on, faster. "Your baby, raised on Roscommon Downs, miles from my world. That's…that's more than a lifestyle adjustment, and it's about more than whether we care for each other enough to keep seeing each other. It's a huge thing, and I'm scared," she repeated, looking up again. "This baby is mine more than it's yours—"

"More?" His eyes narrowed, glaring icily from behind his half-closed lids in a way that eyes of such a warm color had no right to glare.

"I know there has to be a compromise. I know you're going to want…" The word that fell out of her mouth was "…Control," which was a mistake, but she couldn't take it back and maybe it was best to have her fears right on the table in their starkest terms.

"Control?"

"Don't just echo my words."

"Your words are making my jaw drop. You think the baby is more yours than mine, but you think I'm the one who is going to want control?"

"Am I wrong, though?"

"I've had two minutes to think about it, for heck's sake!" His voice rose, and someone at a nearby table turned to look.

"I knew in two minutes what you'd want," Shay said, leaning toward him, trying to keep this private. "Tell me I'm wrong. If I say to you, this baby is mine—"

"You just did say that, Shay. You said exactly that."

"—and that I want it raised in my world, not yours, tell me you'd say that's okay, that's fine. I know you wouldn't!"

He didn't answer, just pulled his wrists out of her grip. She could see his hands shaking. With anger?

She waited.

"Tell me how this can have happened," he finally demanded, as if he'd been tricked in some way. He might seriously think he had, she realized. The thought that he didn't yet trust her honesty hurt her. "Your doctor told you you'd have to work to conceive—you said."

"And you told me she was probably presenting a worst-case scenario. You were right. She must have been. The contraceptive failure I'm not so clear on. Is this really what we want to be talking about? Aren't there more—?"

"I have to take it step by step. And I can explain the contraception. Prim looked at the empty carton last week, before she threw it away. The whole batch expired two years ago." He laughed, although nothing was funny. "I told her it wouldn't matter."

"Did you tell her why?"

"No."

"I believed my doctor, Dusty."

Silence. Shay contemplated the people at Roscommon Downs and wondered what they'd think, what Dusty would tell them.

"I don't like your assumptions," he said.

"No, I can see that. And I hadn't intended to…" she spread out her hand "…lay them on the table, just like that. But now that I have, I'm not sorry, because I need to know if it's how you feel. What do you want, Dusty?"

"Shoot, how can I answer that, when you've just pre-empted what I might want by telling me it's unacceptable! How can I tell you, yes, I do want this baby raised on Roscommon Downs, I do want my child to understand its heritage, I do want the chance to be the kind of father I've always imagined I'd be, when you've made all of that sound like a crime on my part. You've sprung this on me…."

"The lapsed expiry date sprang it on me. The pregnancy test sprang it on me *yesterday* in my bathroom, three minutes after we both walked through my front door. I can't soft soap everything I'm scared of, Dusty! It's too important. You have to know I'm terrified of how much we could fight about this."

"Because you think all I want is control."

"Because I'm *scared* all you want is control."

"Which means I can't say, yes, I want a large degree of involvement—Is that control? I don't know—without sounding like a monster. Listen, the whole restaurant is listening to this."

"Then the restaurant owners should give us a cut of their profits for providing their patrons with entertainment."

"Don't you care?"

"You want us to go?"

"I'm going." He rubbed his fingers over his eyes, a gesture she knew. "We both need breathing space. I don't want to think about how much we could fight over this, either. Lawyers on two continents."

He shook his head, sounding scared about it, and his fear gave her a glimmer of hope because at least it was something they shared.

"That's what I'm afraid of, too," she whispered. "Lawyers on two continents."

He didn't answer directly. "I'll get you home, and then I'll head to my hotel."

"I can get myself home."

"Just like you can raise our baby on your own. I'm sure you can. Both things. But I'd like to take you home." He looked around and caught their waiter's attention at once.

He brought the check and Dusty snapped a card into the black folder.

Shay stayed silent, afraid that if she argued about something as trivial as him seeing her home, then they wouldn't have a chance in hell of communicating or coming to an agreement on the vastly more important subject of the baby.

When the waiter returned, he murmured to Dusty, "Shall I bring…?"

"Yes, please."

The man nodded and skimmed off again, returning with flowers. Gorgeous flowers in a riot of color and scent, beautifully wrapped. Shay stood and took them, touching her face to the cool petals as she inhaled their fragrance.

They were fabulous.

And they were so wrong.

Dusty had obviously arranged to have them delivered to the restaurant as a final flourish to the evening, but now… Several people at adjacent tables were still covertly staring, wondering how the flowers fit with the raised voices and hostile looks.

"You're right," Shay murmured to Dusty. "It would be impossible to keep talking about it here."

"Do you want the baby at all?" he asked abruptly.

Tears stung in her eyes. "Yes!" She hadn't said it before, not even to herself, not in such a simple way. "Yes, I want the baby, with all my heart."

He gave a short nod, and she couldn't tell if he'd wanted this answer or something starkly different.

Chapter Thirteen

"We have scores back from three of the five judges on the short-story competition," Sonya told Shay, coming in to her office, "And they've all put 'Misty Blue' in first place."

"Oh, that story was my favorite, too!" Shay said.

She felt a momentary spurt of satisfaction. Her judgment was in line with *some* people's, then. It wasn't in line with Dusty's. They'd shared a taxi as far as her apartment the night before last, and he'd asked the driver to wait while he made the unnecessary gesture of showing her right to her twenty-seventh-level front door.

"But I won't come in tonight," he'd said.

"Not with that meter running."

"Even without a meter running."

"O-kay."

"Because this is all we're going to do tonight, Shay. We're going to snap and fight."

"But if we—"

"And I'm seriously not going to argue about the possibility of us not snapping and fighting if we try hard enough, because it's already getting circular and I think we're trying as hard as we can."

"It bodes well for the future, doesn't it?"

"It bodes bloody nothing! I'll see you, okay? When we've both had a chance to think, and to cool down."

He hadn't been any more specific about when that might be, so here she was in her office a day and a half later, desperately pretending she knew what she was doing, and that she cared about it. And since she was a professional, she was probably managing to fool everyone but herself.

There, she had no place to hide.

She was a mess.

Except during certain odd, unpredictable moments that came several times a day, when the one thing she really understood about her feelings came wafting over her like a rain-scented breeze and made her feel happy, simply happy, in a way she'd never felt before.

She wanted the baby.

She was absolutely over the moon about the baby.

She was over the moon to feel the way her body was already changing, all by itself. Her body knew what to do. It was amazing. She could have hidden her head in the sand over the pregnancy-test issue for weeks longer, ambivalent about it in every waking moment, and still her body would have taken no notice of the foolish head games. It would simply have gone on with its task, the way it was doing now.

Her breasts felt sore. Her taste buds had begun to react strangely. Coffee didn't taste right anymore and toothpaste smelled terrible. Her emotions balanced on a knife edge, and she knew that inside her body, she was making more blood, her ligaments were softening, her hormones were changing.

It was a miracle, and her heart wanted it.

"It's simple," Dusty had said to her out in the flooded desert, when they'd talked about children. "You just follow your heart home."

She hadn't believed him then. How could it be simple? But she believed him now because it had happened.

Had they both somehow intuitively known it would?

Ridiculous.

"We'll wait for the other two judges, and then we'll tee up a story on the winner as soon as we can," she told her assistant. "I so hope she's interesting!"

"Everyone's interesting," Sonya said. "You've taught me that, Shay. Everyone has a story if you ask the right questions. You've really helped me to see that, and I've been wanting to tell you for a while how much I appreciate it."

Shay blinked in surprise. "Oh." She added awkwardly, "Thank you. I forget it myself, sometimes."

Sonya paused in the doorway and tilted her dark head. "Are you okay?"

"Just tired." Shay pasted on a smile.

"A guy phoned for you earlier. He didn't leave a message, or his name. In fact, as soon as I told him you were in a meeting, he seemed to think that was all he needed to know. His voice sounded familiar. I know he's called here before."

"His voice sounded…?"

Like Dusty?

"…Like he knows what he's doing," Sonya said. "If that makes sense."

"It does."

"Should I have pushed him for his contact details?"

"No, it's fine."

Sonya left the office and Shay felt her pulse start to flutter. She knew what would happen. She'd emerge for lunch half an hour from now and he would be waiting. If she didn't emerge, he would talk his way past reception, unglue her from her desk and march her away because it was time for them to deal with each other and they both knew it.

Sure enough, when she'd faked her way through a little more work, she found him seated in the waiting area, flipping through back copies of *Today's Woman* the way he'd have done in a doctor's office. He had the June issue folded back at the spine and she recognized the photo of his friend Branton Smith and the woman Dusty had insisted wasn't Brant's fiancée posed with a sheepdog on a mud-spattered four-wheeler.

What was the dog's name? Suzy? Shep? Sox?

Sox.

Got it.

Like it mattered.

"Hi," he said, patting the magazine a couple of times with the flat of his hand and then putting it down.

"That's your friend."

"Yeah." He looked as if he wanted to say something more.

Well, they both had so much to say, and what they didn't say now, lawyers might one day say for them. Their shared awkwardness—and their fear?—vibrated in the air like a buzz saw, making Shay try to recall irrelevant facts such as the name of a dog she would never see again and causing Dusty to slap a magazine with an orator's hand as if he wanted to make a speech about it.

"Shall we go?" she said.

"How long do you have?" He sounded skeptical, as if

expecting the news that she had five minutes because of another meeting.

"I have as long as we need. Dusty, I do recognize when things are important, other than the magazine."

He gave a short nod. "I could do with some air and some space."

"We could get on a ferry, or something," she suggested.

"Following through on the surrounded-by-water motif from earlier in our relationship?"

She laughed. She forgot, sometimes, that he wasn't always the strong, silent type. He had a way with words, when he wanted to, and she enjoyed it. "It could be appropriate, couldn't it?" she agreed.

Sydney was famous for its harbor, and the commuter ferries were the best way to get out on it, short of hiring a private yacht. They took the train from her North Sydney office to Circular Quay, bought tickets and hopped on the green-and-yellow boat that went to Manly, a half-hour ride.

Shay had begun to feel, sometimes, as if this were *her city*. She loved New York, but didn't have this same sense, there. New York belonged to too many other people, perhaps.

Well, Sydney did, too, so it wasn't logical.

Maybe because, in her snatched hours of weekend spare time, she'd explored Sydney in a different way to how she'd explored New York? She'd ridden a lot of these ferries. She'd walked a lot of waterfront trails and pathways, through the lush, semitropical greenery of the North Shore, or over the windswept sandstone cliffs between Eastern Suburbs beaches such as Coogee and Bronte and Bondi.

"If you want air, we should sit outside," she told Dusty as they boarded, so they sat on an open-air bench midway down the port side of the ferry and the blue-green harbor water slapped past, along with an oil tanker, a couple of smaller ferries and some pleasure boats out for a mid-week sail.

Window dressing, all of it.

They were here to talk.

"Tell me what you want," Dusty said.

His shoulder pressed against her body. It felt like a statement of companionship, but it wasn't enough. She reached down and entwined her fingers through his, and he squeezed her hand. Keeping the contact, they rested their hands where their thighs touched.

Now it was a statement of companionship, and one of hope, which was better.

"The baby," she answered. "I want the baby. I'm happy. I think I…forgot to say it, the other night. Maybe I didn't know it then. I don't think I did. But I'm very happy, Dusty."

"What else do you want?"

"Tell me what you want, first." Because she wasn't sure how to frame her own needs and desires. She didn't want to lose her sense of herself. She did want to slow her life down, make the right space in it for this child. Where was her middle ground?

"No," Dusty said.

She tried to laugh. "So how come you get to go second? Second is the power position."

"That's why," he growled.

"Because you think it's your right."

"Because I've really thought about this. Because I've come up with something…a plan…and I can't see that there's any other fair option." His voice dropped lower as he spoke, until it came from deep in his chest, sounding half like a whisper of passion, half like a tree creaking in the wind. It melted her, totally beyond her control. "So I'm hoping that what you say fits in with that." He looked at her steadily, and she couldn't look away. "And I want to hear it first."

"First," she echoed, indignant. And this time, she really did laugh, untangling her fingers from his grip to brush them against his cheek. "Look at us! This is impossible!"

"Yeah?"

"I'm getting ready to fight with you, and I still want to kiss you."

"Yeah…?" he said again, more softly.

"I always want to kiss you," she admitted.

"You're right, then. It's impossible." His mouth met hers a fraction of a second later.

The kiss was sweeter, Shay thought, because it was so uncertain—because it was the last kiss they might ever have before reaching an impasse that would make any more kisses impossible and unwanted.

She closed her eyes and gave herself to it completely, knowing she'd never forget it. The slow rumble and rock of the ferry, the freshness of the air, the sun on the side of her face, the taste of his mouth, the feel of his skin when she curved her palm softly against his neck, the sensation of giving, of entrusting her senses to his care.

Breaking the contact almost hurt.

"Tell me what you want," he said.

"Oh, are we back to that?" She brushed the frown from his forehead with the ball of her thumb.

"The ferry's halfway to Manly."

"And you get to say what you want on the return journey, is that the system?"

"I thought we'd walk across to the beach and get ice cream, first."

"Ice cream can be good."

"You see? In a whole lot of areas we're in complete agreement."

Suddenly, however, the lightness had gone. "We're putting it off, aren't we?" she said softly. "Kissing each other and— Because it's too hard and we're scared of what's going to happen when we put our cards down on the table."

"Is that what we should do? Put it off longer? Just spend some more time the way we'd be doing if you weren't…"

"Pregnant. It's such a big word."

She touched his cheek again, looked at those eyes and that mouth, imagined what he'd suggested. Imagined just going to Manly on the ferry and eating ice cream as they wandered along the beach-side walkway, enjoying the new sensation of being together in her world instead of his.

"If we don't talk about it now, we'll just be pretending. It won't count for anything, Dusty."

"No, it won't. You're shaking, Shay."

She didn't try to hide her fear. "How much are we going to fight, Dusty?"

"We don't fight when our goals are the same. Have you noticed that? Did we fight, when we were trekking back to the homestead with Sally and Beau? We didn't. Because we wanted the same thing. To get home safe."

"Sounds good. I'm not buying it. Go first." She closed her eyes.

"Listen, if I go first, you don't get to go at all. If there's something you want, then say it now."

Her eyes flashed open again. "I want to stay the person I am, Dusty. That's as far as I've got. And I know we talked about Jane's theory that kids change parents more than parents change kids, but if you somehow enact this feudal dictate that our baby has to be raised at Roscommon Downs…"

She shook her head.

Dusty said nothing, so she went on, "Where am I in that? Where is my part of our baby's heritage in that? Where is my career? Where is my well-being? There's no room for compromise when the distances are so great. Weekend access or shared custody is not going to work between your land and…well, anywhere else in the entire world."

Still without answering, he stood up and went to the ferry boat rail, leaned his forearm on it and watched the harbor. Then he turned back to her.

"You know me, and I know you. I'm thirty-four years old, and you're thirty-one, and neither one of us is stupid. You don't get to our age, you don't make the mistakes we've both made in relationships in the past without learning something. You're right that I want this on my own terms. Isn't it better if we're both clear on that from the beginning? All you have to decide now is whether they're terms you like."

"A take it or leave it proposition?"

"I've thought about this!"

"A take it or leave it proposition," she repeated.

It wasn't a question this time, and he nodded.

"Go ahead. I'm listening," she said.

"My brother will come home and manage the property. He would have done that in a year or two, anyhow, sharing it with me, but now he'll do it sooner, and on his own. I know he'll be okay about it. We'll stay in Sydney for the whole pregnancy, you and I, and for the birth. Until the baby's around two or even three years old. I know you'd have concerns about a baby so far from medical care, and it'll give you a transition period to work out what you want and what's possible with your career." He spoke in clipped sentences. "What you choose to do about working or maternity leave is up to you, and whatever it is, I'll support it. After that, we'll move to Roscommon Downs until our child is old enough to give us some signals about what he or she wants."

"When will that be?"

"At a guess, around eleven or twelve? Maybe later. Toward the end of high school."

"You're talking about fifteen years of my life!"

"Of your life, mine and the baby's, Shay. Your career will have to scale down. That's clear. But there must be ways to work it so that you can freelance. Read manuscripts, like you did with those short stories. Or by then you may have decided you'd like to try something else. Something creative of your own. A new skill you'd like to focus on. There's a lot to do at the station, and you might find it—"

"Stop!"

"What?"

"This is your plan?"

"Yes."

"The thing I'm not allowed to argue against, because you can't see any other option. Take it or leave it."

"That's right." His face muscles barely moved, apart from what was needed to narrow his eyes down to tight slits.

"No! *I* was right!" she burst out. "It's feudal! You've offered a little window dressing, but it's feudal all the same."

"It's reasonable. It keeps you in the city for three or four more years."

"And in purgatory for at least ten." He flinched at her suggestion that Roscommon Downs counted as hell on earth, and she didn't care. All of this was too new.

"It stops us and our lawyers from tearing each other apart, along with our child." His voice had gone quiet. "That's more important, isn't it? I've thought about it," he repeated.

"And now I have to take it or leave it."

"What have you thought of, that achieves those same goals?"

To this, she had no answer. She only knew that something was wrong with everything he'd said, something drastically important was missing from it, and he wasn't going to listen to her when she tried to tell him so.

The ferry shuddered and slowed, the pitch of its engine sounds changed and she realized they'd almost reached the terminal at Manly.

The end of the line…

"Leave it," Shay whispered as the engines slowed. "That's my choice."

"Shay?"

For a long moment, she couldn't speak, but finally she gasped out the words. "You said take it or leave it. I'm leaving it."

Dusty felt as if he'd been punched in the gut. He could see that she was as hurt and angry and at sea as he was, but he didn't know what he could do about it. He had a painful, nagging feeling that he'd missed something, there was something he hadn't said, but he had no idea what it was. Surely the feeling was wrong. He'd been so careful to keep his proposition clear.

Shay blinked back tears and he wanted to take her in his arms, but knew it would be a mistake. He wasn't so very far from the same state, himself. Not tears. More like blocked plumbing—a thick, painful constriction in his throat that made even his breathing hurt.

Hell, he'd tried so hard, just now! He'd tried to be as precise and honest and straightforward as he could. No false promises, no aimless generalizations, no manipulation. They couldn't afford any of that, with a baby in the picture—a baby and so much geographical distance—so he'd been incredibly careful not to fall into it.

Shay had reacted as if he'd suddenly sprouted horns.

"You really mean that?" he said.

"Take it. Leave it. Two choices. Doesn't take long."

"No, I suppose it doesn't," he muttered.

He felt promises and assurances and compromises and flowery words rising inside him and dammed them back, feeling as if the tables had turned on their whole—short—relationship. He was the one who'd told her that the decision to have a child was simple. You just followed your heart home.

Now he was resisting his heart with all his strength because his heart told him, *Promise her whatever she wants. Tell her we can work it out because we want to work it out, and wanting is enough.*

How stupid had he been to tell her it would be simple?

"I'm going back," she said.

"Back?"

"On the next ferry. This one, I guess. It'll make the round-trip."

A crewman slid the gangway into place as she spoke and passengers began to disembark. The two of them didn't have long to keep talking.

Dusty couldn't go back with her. Prolonging their contact would only make the gulf between them even deeper. The gulf deeper, and the connection more painful.

Without the baby, none of this would be happening.

For a moment, he felt a spurt of anger against his unborn child that was so powerful it made him nauseous. *Why are you here? Why are you so damned important, when you didn't exist a month ago? Why do I care about you, and feel responsible for you, and want the best for you, when I don't even know who you are?*

Slowly, slowly, he let the anger go, and was left only with the knowledge that his ultimatum and Shay's choice had already effectively taken his child out of his life. It would be a city baby not an outback baby, now. It couldn't be both.

It would ride the New York subway, not the shaggy little Shetland pony that Roscommon Downs kids sat on almost before they could walk. It would take classes in a heated gym, instead of swimming in a shaded billabong. It would rub shoulders with a thousand strangers every day.

And that wasn't bad. Millions of kids grew up that way. Talents and skills and strengths developed differently in the city, but they developed just as much.

But not for my child...my daughter...my son.

Not for a child who was heir to the heritage of more than a million acres of Channel Country land.

"I'm going to walk along the beach for a while," he told Shay.

"Then you'd better get off the boat." She threaded a wobbly smile across her mouth.

"This isn't the end," he blurted out.

"I guess we'll work something out. Contact. If you want it. Photos of the baby by e-mail." She stopped.

"I don't know if I can do it that way." Because he really thought it might be too hard to acknowledge that he had a child at all, when it was a child he never saw, who had a mother he'd been involved with for only a few weeks.

"Get off the boat, Dusty, please, if you're going."

Or I'll start screaming, said her body language.

He went without saying goodbye, and she watched him—he didn't look directly, but could see her in his peripheral vision, still standing there as he crossed the gangway—and he knew that neither of them intended the no-goodbye thing as a statement of any kind; it had just somehow got lost in the middle of too much emotion.

At his hotel he called Rae Middleton, their horse trainer near Brant, and told her that he and Brant and Callan wouldn't be bidding on either of the fillies at the thorough-bred sale this week, and flew back to Roscommon Downs the next morning.

Chapter Fourteen

Shay hadn't known it was possible to feel this ill without respite.

It felt more like chemotherapy than pregnancy. Nausea ambushed her when she sat at her desk, when she rolled over in bed in her sleep, and the moment she woke up in the mornings, and she was lucky if she made it to the shower before the heaving began.

She learned to have bottled water beside her bed, in the bathroom, on her desk, in her purse, everywhere she went, all the time. Bottled water, tissues, a towel and an empty plastic bowl.

Oh, and chips.

She ate salted potato chips as if they were illegal and she was a long-term user. She lay down on the carpeted floor of her office for a ten-minute nap every two hours because staving off fatigue seemed to relieve a fraction of the nausea. She vainly attempted to take public transportation without breathing, to drink decaf coffee without tasting it, and to watch any TV commercial featuring a kitten, a baby or, for some weird reason, a house-cleaning product, without crying.

At eight weeks from her last period, she had a first pre-natal checkup with an obstetrician whose name she'd been given by the family practice doctor—a general practi-tioner, he was called in Australia—whom she'd seen a couple of times over the past year, and her first question to the man was "Why am I feeling this bad?"

His answer reminded her of what Dusty had once said about why he wanted kids. "For all the reasons."

In the case of her nausea, these reasons ranged from "Some women just do," through to, "And you're on your own, you said. That makes it harder. If you have any un-resolved issues about what's happening, and about your plans for the future—well, any source of stress doesn't help, especially when you're also dealing with a demand-ing career."

"Our magazine did an article a couple of months ago about the superwoman myth," she murmured. One of their staff writers had put it together and Shay had only read it as part of her work. She hadn't let it speak to her. In fact, had she subconsciously closed her ears to everything it had said?

"Exactly," the obstetrician said. "The modern woman can have it all…but sometimes that means she gets the pregnancy symptoms to match."

"Mmm, it's a theory."

"But we'll take a closer look at a few things, anyhow, to make sure there's nothing else going on."

Nothing was.

Various tests showed healthy levels of every pregnancy hormone and bit of body chemistry known to womankind, and a beautiful Thumbelina-sized baby actually—wow!—bouncing around...almost swimming...in its grainy pool of fluid on the ultrasound.

Which left Shay at nine weeks with the same unrelenting nausea and a new and even starker knowledge that her real problem wasn't physical or career-superwoman related or any of that.

It was about Dusty.

His impossible choices.

All the things he hadn't said.

The way his disappearance from her life had left a huge, horrible hole in a part of herself she hadn't even known about before.

She was so angry with him.

And she loved him.

The word tasted strange in her mouth. Overdramatic, wasn't it? But it was the only word that fit with the huge, horrible hole, so...so...

So, oh, against all logic and plans and good sense, she loved him, and no wonder she felt nauseous at least twenty-three hours a day!

At nine and a half weeks of official pregnancy—why did doctors count it that way? Technically, it meant she'd been pregnant before she and Dusty had even met!—and eight weeks since she'd first flown to Roscommon Downs, she made plans to fly there again. Whether this was to tell him she loved him or that she was so angry with him that her stomach had turned permanently inside out, she had no idea.

She didn't tell him in advance that she was coming. The mail plane dropped her off like a big, queasy, potato-chip-and-bottled-water-toting parcel on Thursday afternoon, and there he stood beside a four-wheel drive at the edge of the airstrip, meeting the flight but not knowing that he'd be meeting her.

His strong body was silhouetted against the yawning blue of an outback sky, and even though the airstrip was no longer surrounded by a pretty lake, she could hear and see the pelicans and pink cockatoos in the distance, where one of the river's main channels ran. It was so familiar, and so scary, too.

Dusty would normally have moved toward the plane at this point, to take the two boxes of deliveries. Shay actually saw and recognized the way his body was about to uncoil from its lazy shoulder lean against the vehicle, but as soon as he realized who she was, he froze.

She reached him and just one word broke from his lips.

"Shay…" He flipped his sunglasses up and wiped his fingers across his eyes before dropping the dark lenses back into place.

"I am so angry with you!" she said and burst into tears.

He reached out his arms and she stumbled into them. "Yeah, and I'm pretty angry with both of us." His voice vibrated in his chest, right against her ear.

She heard the thud of Grant's boots on the hard dirt. "Uh, Dusty? You want me to put these beside the vehicle?"

"Thanks," Dusty said, over her head.

"Looks like you're busy, so…" Grant didn't finish.

As the pilot returned to the plane, Dusty added in a low tone, "And I've never been happier to see anyone in my life. Oh hell, Shay…"

She balled her hands into fists and tried to push him away. "Hell is right. I am so ill. I throw up five times a day. It would be ten times a day if I didn't suck constantly on salt and fat and carbs."

"As a very wise woman once said to me, a broken heart is *the* best flavor enhancer."

"No, it's not!" she sobbed. "Nothing enhances any flavor, right now, and my broken heart is killing me."

"You and me, both, sweetheart," he whispered. "What can we do about it? There must be something we can do."

"Tell me you love me! That's all. It's pathetic, isn't it? To come all this way just to beg you to say that?"

"No, dear God, not when it's true, not if it's how you feel, too…"

She hardly heard him. She was crying too hard. "But that's what I want. And you never said it in Sydney, when you told me what you wanted for our child. You never even said, 'I know we can't talk about love so soon, but let's make a commitment to each other for the sake of the baby.' You said nothing!"

"I didn't mean it that way."

"You left me with two impossible choices and no ground for either of them to take root in, and I'm ill about it and I'm angry and I love you anyway. I must, because nothing else makes sense. You gave me your ultimatum, Dusty, so here's mine." She raised her head, not caring what kind of a swollen, red-eyed mess she was in, nor that the tears still streamed down her cheeks while the sobs shook her shoulders. "If you don't love me…if you can't use that word to fill the huge, horrible hole inside you…if you don't have a huge, horrible hole the way I do…then tell me so. If you love me, then say it, because you were right, before. It's simple. It's so simple. And I can't stop crying."

"I love you, Shay." He tightened his arms around her and her fists relaxed back into hands—hands that wanted to hold him hard and never let him go. He kissed her neck in a long, sweet trail, and he smelled, as always, perfect.

"I love you, too, Dusty. I love you. See? Do you see?" She dragged in a shaky breath through her swollen nose.

He found a clean cotton handkerchief in his pocket and whispered, "Here…" and she wiped her eyes. Fifty yards

away, the mail plane's engines began to rev up and its propellers began to whirl.

"It's crazy," she said, "but it fills the hole."

"But is it really simple?" He stroked her hair back from
her forehead, touched her cheek and her neck and her
mouth as if he couldn't yet believe she was real. "That's
where I get stuck, Shay. I always thought it would be. I've
looked for it. With Rebecca. With Mandy. I thought it
would be simple right up until the moment when you told
me about the baby and then—" He stopped.

The plane began to taxi along the strip of red dirt, but
her words defied the noise of the engine. "I'm coming to
live at Roscommon Downs."

"What?" he yelled. "You said—"

"Because if we love each other, it makes sense. That's
where it's simple. That's where you were right, Dusty. If
I follow my heart, it takes me home."

"And home could be here? Not in Sydney or New
York?" He shook his head, as if he didn't believe her.
"You made it sound like a life sentence. You seemed to
hate me for it. You turned around on that ferry. We didn't
even say goodbye. We haven't e-mailed or spoken or—"

She stopped him with her fingers pressed to his lips.
"Yes. Home could be here. Home is here. If we're a family,
not two separate, uncommitted people making a plan to
protect the baby's heritage. If we love each other and stay
true to that. If that's what leads us forward."

"It's what led me, in Sydney."

"But you never said it, you didn't say anything like it."

"Because I didn't know. Not how strong it was. Not until I got back here and there was the huge, horrible void.
And because I was so determined to be clear about the
plan. I didn't want to make vague promises, the kind I've
sometimes heard Jane make to her kids when she's fraz-

zled and tired. 'We'll see…' when really it means, 'The answer's no, but I don't want to fight about it right now.' I thought if were going to fight about Roscommon Downs versus the city it had to be now, and it had to be honest. I had to be honest about how important it was to me that our child should know this life, this place. You had to know that three or four years in the city, and a promise to move back there later on if our child…our children…aren't interested in cattle farming, was the best I could do. It's still the best I can do, Shay."

He looked into her eyes and she understood the value of what he was telling her, and the sacrifice, understood the sacrifices she was prepared to make, too, and suddenly they didn't seem like sacrifices at all.

"It's more than enough," she whispered.

"Are you sure? So fast?"

She told him about her talk with Sarah in New York, and about the doubts she'd begun to acknowledge in her heart even before she'd first come here, and finished, "Besides, throwing up five times a day since you left doesn't tell you I'm sure?"

"Sweetheart, it tells me you're pregnant…." He kissed her, and held her, and then they drove across the red dirt, following their hearts home.

Epilogue

"So that's why I told Rae not to go ahead and bid on the filly," Dusty said. He turned his head to smile at Shay. "Even though the horse looked to have energy and heart and legs, with the breeding to match."

"Sometimes, you have to go with your gut," Callan agreed.

Brant nodded, also. "And sometimes your gut makes up its mind pretty fast."

"I don't know, *gut?*" His fiancée, Misha, also known as Princess Artemisia Helena of Langemark, wrinkled her nose and grinned at him. "Ladies, we can't argue the *pretty fast* part, since we each fell in love with one of these guys within a few weeks of meeting him, you, Shay, and you, Jacinda, thanks to the 'Wanted: Outback Wives' campaign and me in spite of its pernicious influence, but are we in agreement that it's the gut that's involved, here? I don't think so!"

"It's definitely the heart," Shay said. She felt Dusty's hand slip into hers, with a feeling of belonging that felt so familiar and so right. "I don't suppose we'd ever get our men to use the word in mixed company, but they know it's the heart not the gut."

"Hey," Dusty protested. "Who was it who detailed to me exactly how many times a day she was throwing up, largely because things looked like they hadn't worked out for us? That's the gut talking, not the heart."

"That's—" Shay stopped.

That was the baby.

She'd almost reached the end of her first trimester, now. She'd begun to feel a lot better, and hadn't yet started to show. The pregnancy was still a secret between herself and Dusty, however, and they hadn't yet talked about how or when they would share it. If they weren't careful, their friends would soon guess.

The next race was due to run in a few minutes. Was now the moment to spill the news to Callan and Jacinda, and Misha and Brant? She and Dusty looked at each other, smiled at each other, couldn't look away.

"You two…" said Jacinda. "What haven't you told us?"

She was a willowy brunette, who'd been engaged to Callan Woods for almost four months now. They'd left their kids—Callan's two boys and Jacinda's four-year-old daughter—with Callan's mother to make the short hop by air to Birdsville for the annual spring racing carnival. Shay had only met Jac for the first time last night, but already felt as if the two of them would soon be friends.

"Yes, you two, spill!" Misha commanded—because *commanded* was really the only word you could use.

She did that sometimes.

She was a princess and she issued commands.

Shay had trouble getting rid of the mental image of a

glittering tiara on her Scandinavian blond head, and even more trouble equating this woman with the down-to-earth farm girl in the curly brown wig whom she'd interviewed for the magazine back in May.

…*Although that's my fault more than hers*, Shay knew.

She'd spent too long working in magazine journalism to find it easy to treat celebrities of Misha's status as normal human beings. Spoiled prima donnas, yes. Normal human beings, no. Misha didn't seem to be a prima donna, and she was clearly seriously in love with Brant, who'd pursued her all the way to Langemark to make sure of what they each felt, but Shay suspected that the imaginary tiara might stick around for a while, all the same.

"So should we spill?" Dusty said, leaning to say the words softly in her ear, then brushing her mouth with a quick, crooked kiss.

"Let's," she whispered back.

"We're having a baby!" he announced, then added with pride, as if this were a credit to his own personal testosterone levels, "Shay's been sick as a dog."

Since he'd never failed to bring her bottled water, potato chips, tissues, a towel or a bowl when she'd needed them, and had twice during the past two weeks cooked her Prim's bean-and-pasta soup recipe at ten o'clock at night, once in the homestead kitchen at Roscommon Downs and once in her apartment in Sydney, because it was the only thing that seemed as if it might taste right and settle her stomach enough for her to get to sleep without a long and unpleasant side trip to the bathroom…she didn't hit him.

Misha clapped her hands. "A baby? Really? By accident? You know what? I think there's a lot to be said for that! Well…when it's with the right person, which it obviously is for you two, and—" She stopped, and took Shay totally by surprise with a big, warm hug. "It's wonderful! I am so happy for you!"

"Thank you!" Shay hugged her back. "Thank you! We're happy, too!"

Misha pulled back enough to hold her at arm's length. "And you look great, not as if you've been sick as a dog at all."

She was smiling.

Shay smiled back.

Misha looked different, somehow. What had suddenly changed?

Oh.

The imaginary tiara had gone.

"The horses are going into the barrier," Callan reported.

"We have Saltbush Bachelor running in this one, right?" Jacinda said, leaning close against him and stealing his binoculars. He used the opportunity to squeeze her tush.

"It's his fifty-second start," he said. "I'm not sure how much he's got left. But one of the bookies said number three, in the red-and-green silks, is going for auction soon. He's had three wins and a second out of seven starts, good-tempered stallion, lively but easy to handle, and the bookie thought the owner might consider an offer today. We should look at him in the race as much as we look at Salty."

"Salty's not sure about getting into the gate, it looks like," Brant said.

"Pete wasn't sure about entering him," Dusty told the others. "But he decided he was fit. It's really a question of whether the horse wants it."

"Whether he's got the—" Brant stopped.

"The heart, darling?" Misha teased him.

"Well, yeah. You can talk about a horse's heart, as an outback man, it's when you start talking about your own that it gets just that little bit unmasculine." He looked down at her, with a softness in his eyes that said he was pretty capable of unmasculine language where his own personal princess was concerned. It was exactly the same way that Dusty looked at Shay.

The horse finally agreed to go where he was meant to, the barrier light came on, and a moment later the announcer over the loudspeaker system said, "They're racing!" which brought an electric tension to the entire crowd.

Callan stole the binoculars back from Jacinda and glued them to his face. "Come on, Salty," Shay heard him mutter. "Don't get yourself hemmed in at the rail."

Dusty and Brant exchanged a significant, satisfied look, and from what Dusty had told her about Callan, Shay understood what it meant. Callan cared about their horses again, cared about his whole future again, thanks to Jacinda's appearance in his life, and Shay knew it would never have happened without her magazine—the magazine she would be resigning from, she and Dusty had decided, two weeks before the baby was due.

It was still a little scary, and she wondered sometimes if one day she might be ambushed with regret. How did you reach that final state of certainty, she wondered. Not just certainty about love, because this certainty she already had. Certainty about shared lives, for better or for worse, all the decisions and choices and compromises two people had to make together during the course of a marriage.

"Salty, get out a bit wider and make your run," Callan said. To the jockey, he added, "Come on, Garrett, doesn't he have anything left?"

"I don't think he does, Callan," Dusty said. "I think he's looking forward to a cushy future in stud. But look at number three in the red and green."

Even as he spoke, the trouble came. Number three began to make his run just as another horse veered out slightly wider from the rail and there was a misstep and a clash of hooves. For a moment, the jockey in the red-and-green silks looked as if he'd lost control and might also lose his ride. If he fell, there were at least three horses coming right behind him who could trample him into the red outback dust. Shay saw the ambulance start around the outside of the track and her spine began to crawl.

But then the horse got its footing back and you'd have sworn he almost flipped his jockey right back into the saddle. The collective breath of the crowd let out and, even though the ambulance kept moving, it wasn't needed now. The horse had lost ground, but he didn't seem to care. He simply stretched out a little farther, almost flew across the ground and came home by half a length, ahead of a tangle of horsey names that Shay couldn't make out over the indistinct public address system.

"…and Saltbush Bachelor is last of all," the race caller said.

Well, that had been clear enough!

Callan, Dusty and Brant shook their heads ruefully, and stayed silent with disappointment for a while.

"But I tell you what, let's make the owner of number three an offer," Callan finally said. "What's his name? I couldn't hear."

"Rock-a-bye Baby," Brant said. "Which could be an appropriate omen, right?"

"We'll make the offer," Dusty said. "Shay? Do you think? Sweetheart?" He tightened his hold on her and looked into her face, seeking confirmation.

"Yes," she said, and the word tasted good in her mouth. "Yes! I've never been a part of buying a racehorse before. Yes, let's do it!"

"Just like that?" Misha grinned. "Now, what is that? Gut or heart? Or more of a rash, illogical impulse?"

"Definitely a rash, illogical impulse," Dusty said.

The three men looked at each other, reading faces, making decisions, looking at the women they loved. It was a nice moment. Shay felt something settle and cement itself deep inside her—a calm and total certainty about the future, and the decisions she'd made and would go on making with Dusty down the years.

She was having a baby. She and Dusty would get married in some quiet, simple way, and she would become friends with these two women, Jacinda and the princess, and the friendship and her marriage would last the rest of her life.

The little niggle of fear evaporated like water in the desert.

This was right.

All of it.

"So?" she said, grinning, as the certainty spread like heat inside her. "We're making an offer on a horse we've seen in just one race?"

The men knew each other pretty well, and Dusty spoke for all of them…and not just about horses…when he laced Shay's fingers through his, leaned his long, hard body against her and said with a slow, steady smile, "What can I say? Sometimes you just know."

* * * * *

Read on for a sneak preview of Carol Marinelli's
PUTTING ALICE BACK TOGETHER!

Hugh hired bikes!

You know that saying: 'It's like riding a bike, you never forget'?

I'd never learnt in the first place.

I never got past training wheels.

'You've got limited upper-body strength?' He stopped and looked at me.

I had been explaining to him as I wobbled along and tried to stay up that I really had no centre of balance. I mean *really* had no centre of balance. And when we decided, fairly quickly, that a bike ride along the Yarra perhaps, after all, wasn't the best activity (he'd kept insisting I'd be fine once I was on, that you never forget), I threw in too my other disability. I told him about my limited upper-body strength, just in case he took me to an indoor rock-climbing centre next. I'd honestly forgotten he was a doctor, and he seemed worried, like I'd had a mini-stroke in the past or had mild cerebral palsy or something.

'God, Alice, I'm sorry—you should have said. What happened?'

And then I had had to tell him that it was a self-diagnosis. 'Well, I could never get up the ropes at the gym at school.' We were pushing our bikes back. 'I can't blow-dry the back of my hair…' He started laughing.

Not like Lisa who was laughing at me—he was just laughing and so was I. We got a full refund because we'd only been on our bikes ten minutes, but I hadn't failed. If anything, we were getting on better.

And better.

We went to St Kilda to the lovely bitty shops and I found these miniature Russian dolls. They were tiny, made of tin or something, the biggest no bigger than my thumbnail. Every time we opened them, there was another tiny one, and then another, all reds and yellows and greens.

They were divine.

We were facing each other, looking down at the palm of my hand, and our heads touched.

If I put my hand up now, I can feel where our heads touched.

I remember that moment.

I remember it a lot.

Our heads connected for a second and it was alchemic; it was as if our minds kissed hello.

I just have to touch my head, just there at the very spot and I can, whenever I want to, relive that moment.

So many times I do.

'Get them.' Hugh said, and I would have, except that little bit of tin cost more than a hundred dollars and, though that usually wouldn't have stopped me, I wasn't about to have my card declined in front of him.

I put them back.

'Nope.' I gave him a smile. 'Gotta stop the impulse

spending.'

We had lunch.

Out on the pavement and I can't remember what we ate, I just remember being happy. Actually, I can remember: I had Caesar salad because it was the lowest carb thing I could find. We drank water and I *do* remember not giving it a thought.

I was just thirsty.

And happy.

He went to the loo and I chatted to a girl at the next table, just chatted away. Hugh was gone for ages and I was glad I hadn't demanded Dan from the universe, because I would have been worried about how long he was taking.

Do I go on about the universe too much? I don't know, but what I do know is that something *was* looking out for me, helping me to be my best, not to **** this up as I usually do. You see, we walked on the beach, we went for another coffee and by that time it was evening and we went home and he gave me a present.

Those Russian dolls.

I held them in my palm, and it was the nicest thing he could have done for me.

They are absolutely my favourite thing and I've just stopped to look at them now. I've just stopped to take them apart and then put them all back together again and I can still feel the wonder I felt on that day.

He was the only man who had bought something for me, I mean something truly special. Something beautiful, something thoughtful, something just for me.

A sneaky peek at next month...

By Request

RELIVE THE ROMANCE WITH THE BEST OF THE BEST

My wish list for next month's titles...

In stores from 17th February 2012:

❏ His Suitable Bride – Cathy Williams, Abby Green & Kate Walker

❏ Monte Carlo Affairs – Emilie Rose

3 stories in each book - only £5.99!

In stores from 2nd March 2012:

❏ Capturing the Crown – Marie Ferrarella, Karen Whiddon & Linda Winstead Jones

Available at WHSmith, Tesco, Asda, Eason, Amazon and Apple

Just can't wait?

Visit us Online

You can buy our books online a month before they hit the shops! **www.millsandboon.co.uk**

0212/05